Piece of Cake

Derek Robinson grew up in Bristol, read history at Cambridge, was a fighter plotter in the RAF, spent ten years working for ad agencies in London and New York, and then came home via Portugal and the Channel Islands with his American wife Sheila.

Piece of Cake is his fifth novel. What it has in common with the others is a certain debunking of the myths of war. *Goshawk Squadron*, which was shortlisted for the Booker Prize in 1971, is a kind of anti-Biggles. *Rotten with Honour* is a Cold War thriller which suggests that Russian intelligence is at least no stupider than British intelligence. *Kramer's War* describes the delicate balance between co-operation and collaboration during the German occupation of Jersey; it has been sternly boycotted by the island's booksellers. *The Eldorado Network* is based on the case history of a double agent who discovered that inventing what intelligence agencies would like to hear is more profitable than reporting the truth.

Derek Robinson has also written books on rugby and squash, plus a bestselling study of the underground West-country *Patois* called 'Bristle'. He broadcasts a bit. He lives in the Cotswold village of Horton, where nothing happens and long may it continue like that.

Derek Robinson

Piece of Cake

Pan Books London, Sydney and Auckland

First published 1983 by Hamish Hamilton Ltd
This edition published 1984 by Pan Books Ltd,
Cavaye Place. London SW10 9PG
9 8 7 6
© Derek Robinson 1983
ISBN 0 330 28404 5
Scanned and phototypeset by
Datasolve Information, London
Printed and bound in Great Britain by
Richard Clay Ltd, Bungay, Suffolk

For Pam and Wally

Contents

SEPTEMBER
1939

Dawn was beginning to soften the edge of the night as the Buick convertible cruised through the Essex countryside. Its driver was a small man, so short that he had to sit on a cushion and lean forward to see over the Buick's broad bonnet. His right leg was at full stretch; even so, only his toes pressed the accelerator. The rush of air lashed his curly hair forward.

There were three other men in the car, all asleep. Like the driver, they were young and dressed in lounge suits or blazers and grey flannel trousers. One of them, in the back seat, held an enormous stuffed golliwog, half as big as himself.

A pothole made the car lurch. "Sorry," said the driver.

The man beside him slowly woke up. For a while he stared ahead, blinking occasionally at the curving lane in the Buick's headlights, the rushing hedgerows, the branches flickering overhead.

"Sticky," he said. "You're on the right side of the road."

"Of course I am," Sticky said. He flinched slightly as his wheels flattened a dead hedgehog.

His passenger glanced at him uncertainly, and then looked ahead again. He held up his hands and looked at each in turn. "What I mean is," he said, "you're on the wrong side of the road."

Sticky thought about that as he swung the car into and out of an S-bend.

"So I am," he said, and crossed to the left-hand lane.

They drove for another half-mile, through a little village and over a bridge, before the passenger said: "Sticky, how long were you driving like that, for God's sake?"

"How should I know?" Sticky sounded annoyed. "Am I supposed to keep track of everything? Bloody hell, it's hard enough to steer this beast without remembering every bloody little detail. I mean, damn it all."

His passenger sighed, and then belched.

"Anyway," Sticky said, "this is an American car, and over there they drive like that all the time."

"But you're in England."

"Well, so are you."

"Yes, and I like it here, and you could have killed us all, driving –"

"You don't like the way I drive? You don't trust me? Is that it,

Patterson? Fine! Drive the rotten thing yourself." Sticky folded his arms. The car hit a patch of corrugations and drifted across the crown of the road. Patterson grabbed the wheel, over-corrected and had to shove it back. "For Christ's sake, Sticky!" he cried. Sticky deliberately looked out of his side window. The car zig-zagged, jostling the men in the back seat. "Hey, hey, hey," said one. The other simply groaned and clutched his golliwog. "Stop playing the bloody fool, Sticky," Patterson said. The road curved to the left and he made desperate adjustments to keep the car on it.

"What's the matter?" complained one of the men in the back seat.

Sticky tipped his head and arched his body until he was looking backwards over the top of the seat. "My standard of driving does not satisfy young Pip," he said. "I have therefore relished command of this vehicle."

"Get your foot off the gas, damn you!" Patterson shouted. He twitched the wheel and just missed a stone wall.

"Relished?" the man with the golliwog said to Sticky's upside-down face. "What d'you mean, 'relished'?"

"Relinquished," Sticky said, and choked slightly on his own saliva. "I said I relinquished whatever it was."

"He said 'relished,' " the man with the golliwog told the fourth passenger. "Bloody Stickwell's pissed again. Look at him. He can't even stand up straight."

"Where the hell's the ignition?" Patterson demanded, scrabbling for the key with one hand.

"I said relished and I meant relished," Stickwell declared firmly.

"Thank God he's not driving," said the man with the golliwog.

Patterson's free hand thumped Stickwell on the knees until he sat down again. A sharp turn came racing towards them, and Patterson heaved on the wheel just in time. "God damn you, Sticky!" he said hoarsely. The wheel flickered back through his fingers.

"You're driving on the wrong side of the road," Stickwell said. It was true. The lights of an oncoming truck glared. Patterson got the Buick into the left-hand lane and the truck flashed by in a blaze of horns. "For the love of Mike, stop the sodding engine, somebody!" he pleaded.

12

"Think I'll take a little nap," Stickwell said, and closed his eyes. As he did so, the engine started to cough. It picked up for a few seconds, then spluttered and died.

"Now look what you've done," Stickwell said severely. "You've broken it."

Patterson heaved a deep and trembling breath. The Buick drifted along, shedding speed, and he edged it onto the grass verge, where it jolted to a stop. The night was very still. He rested his head and looked at the stars. They shimmered with unnatural intensity, blurring and sharpening and blurring again in a rhythm that matched a slow pounding in his brain. "As I live and breathe," he muttered, "I swear I'll never drop another drink. Drink another drop. Whichever."

"That black velvet did it," said Stickwell. "You shouldn't have had all that black velvet. I didn't, and look at me."

"You look bloody awful," said Cattermole, the man with the golliwog. "You look as if you're about to spew."

Stickwell twisted around to face him. Stickwell had dramatically gloomy features, and in the starlight his eyes were lost in their deep sockets. He studied the golliwog and said nothing.

"I've spewed once tonight already," said the fourth man, Cox. "And it wasn't the black velvet, either. It was all those American martinis before the black velvet."

"I don't remember any martinis," said Cattermole. "Where did we have martinis?"

"In that rotten club. Before the party. *You* remember, Moggy."

"I do not. I certainly had no martinis."

"You had three," Patterson announced. "And then you spewed."

"Our big mistake," said Cox, "was starting off on cider. I said at the time—"

"Were those things martinis?" Cattermole asked. "You mean those funny-tasting things, with the vegetables floating around in them?"

"I think I'm going to spew now," Stickwell said.

"There you are!" said Cattermole triumphantly.

"It has nothing to do with the drink," Stickwell announced. He spoke with some difficulty, as if he had a mouthful of chewing-gum. "It's all this wild careering around. Very sick-making."

"Well, get out, first," Patterson told him.

13

"At this speed? Are you mad, Patterson?"

"Watch out, Pip," Cattermole warned as Stickwell's head began to droop.

Patterson threw open the door and half-fell onto the grass. The sound of harsh retching began. "Shit," said Patterson.

"Highly unlikely," Cattermole remarked. He and Cox got out. There was just enough light leaking into the sky to silhouette hedges and telephone poles.

"Where are we?" Cox asked.

"Sticky ought to know," Patterson said.

"Sticky's got his hands full at the moment."

"Really? That stuff's not worth keeping, Sticky," Cattermole called out. "Chuck it away."

"Why did we stop?" Cox asked.

"Ran out of fuel," Patterson said. "Had to make an emergency landing in pitch darkness. Brilliant bit of piloting."

Cox climbed onto a tree-stump. "Nothing but fields," he reported. "Not much chance of getting the Buick filled up here."

"Sounds like Sticky's doing his best," Cattermole said. The painful noises in the car eventually tailed off into feeble coughs and gasps. Stickwell appeared, grey-faced in the gloom, and stretched out on the grass.

"What time is it? We ought to be getting on," Cox said. "How far to the airfield?"

"Do stop worrying, Mother," said Cattermole. "Have you noticed, Pip . . ." He yawned, and closed his eyes. ". . . noticed that Mother always starts worrying when it's too late to do anything?"

Nobody answered. After a while a bird started to sing in a nearby tree. Stickwell swore at it and it stopped.

"I'm in enough trouble with the Ram as it is, that's all," Cox said. He had a long nose, slightly crooked where he had broken it by running into a gatepost at the age of six, and this made his face look even longer and narrower than it was. "He really hates me. You should have heard him go on about it. He went on and on and on."

"Quite right," said Cattermole. "It wasn't your Hurricane. It belonged to the British taxpayer. You ought to be more careful with other people's property. You behaved abominably."

"I got the lights confused, that's all. I thought green meant up

14

and red meant down. Next thing I knew the prop was chucking out great lumps of grass and the Ram was giving me hell."

Stickwell groaned, and rolled onto his side. "Think yourself lucky," he said. "Chap I knew did what you did, only he cartwheeled the whole bloody kite, arse over tit, right down the runway."

"It's those damn indicator lights," Cox said. "I expect he got confused."

"He certainly looked confused," Stickwell said. "His kneecaps were all mixed up with his shoulder blades."

Cattermole made himself comfortable against the tree-stump. He had a tall, beefy body topped with a surprisingly small and delicate head; he looked like an idealised Grecian prizefighter, which was totally misleading: he was strong but he was lazy. "Anyway, the Ram's in London," he said. "Won't be back till lunch."

Mother Cox prowled around, kicking at dandelion heads which stood white in the darkness. The seedballs shattered and vanished immediately in the still air. "We really ought to start walking, you know," he said.

"Where did you get that damn silly golliwog, Moggy?" asked Stickwell.

"Chap gave it me at the party."

"Jolly decent of him."

"Yes, that's what I thought. Mind you, I had to fight him for it."

"That wasn't very nice."

"Exactly what I told him, Sticky. He wouldn't let go of it. 'Look, old chap,' I said to him, 'this golliwog's no damn use to you any more,' I said, 'one of its arms has come off,' I said. Which it had. Then he said something rather unkind so I punched him in the eye and after that he gave me the whole golliwog, arm and all, without a word."

"Really? Not a word?"

"Not one sodding syllable, Sticky."

"Well, it's the thought that counts, I suppose ... Hullo, here comes a bus."

Mother Cox looked around eagerly. It was not a bus but a tractor, bellowing and backfiring as the driver gunned the engine. It slowed as it neared them and Pip Patterson shouted from the driver's seat: "Jump up! Can't stop! Jump up!" He was towing a farm-wagon. They scrambled aboard it and Patterson accelerated with a suddenness that jolted them off their feet. Stickwell, sprawling in a scattering of straw, saw a light waving in the roadway. Someone was chasing them. In the distance he saw a house, its upper windows lit; as he watched, more lights came on. The man with the flashlight kept chasing until they reached a downward slope and the tractor outpaced him.

Its passengers clung to the sides of the wagon as Patterson, with no headlights to guide him and with the rush of air making him blink and squint, charged down the gradient. The tractor tyres bounced on bumps and spat up a thin spray of gravel. Moggy Cattermole tried lying on his front, but the bouncing hurt too much; so he lay on his back, which hurt even more; so he got to his feet just as the wagon hit a pothole and knocked him down. "Holy hell!" he shouted. Sparks were streaming out of the exhaust.

At the foot of the hill the road funnelled into a narrow bridge over a river. Patterson caught a glimpse of shining water, scarred by the panicking flight of duck. He tightened his grip on the thin wheel and aimed for the centre. As the walls closed in he shut his eyes. The tractor rushed across, its trailer savagely whacking the stone buttresses and leaving a trail of ragged splinters.

When the rumbling ceased, Patterson looked again. They were dashing past a sleeping pub; in the past few minutes the sky had lightened and he read the sign: *The Carpenter's Arms*. A crossroads lay ahead, but he couldn't read the signpost and he had to guess, so he guessed they should turn left and at the last instant changed his mind and turned right, winding the wheel as if the tractor were a boat and feeling it lean all its weight onto one side like a boat. Shouts came from behind, desperate enough to penetrate the din, and he glanced back to see the wagon skidding, its tail drifting wide as the wheels lost their grip. A screech of metallic pain came from the towbar. The wagon strained to escape, failed, got dragged back into line. The shouts were audible as curses. Patterson waved, and settled down to master the controls.

He barrelled across the countryside for a further ten miles while the dawn gradually bleached out the night and at last the sun nudged over the horizon. They might have travelled all the way to the airfield like this if Patterson, getting too cocky, hadn't attempted a flashy gear change while going up a steep hill. He missed the gear and had to come to a halt. He found the gear and tried to restart but released too much power. The tractor leaped forward and snapped the towbar. The wagon rolled downhill for ten yards and gently wedged itself in a hedge.

Patterson switched off the engine, set the brake and climbed down.

"You're a maniac, Pip," said Moggy Cattermole. He sat on the trailer, brushing straw and bits of dried dung from his clothes. His hands were filthy and his forehead was bruised. Mother Cox wore a moustache of dried blood. Sticky Stickwell had rolled in an agricultural chemical of sulphurous yellow. "You're a raving maniac," Cattermole accused. "Why did you have to drive like that?"

"Someone was chasing us. Had to get away. After that I couldn't seem to get the speed down."

"Whose is this stuff, anyway?" Cox asked.

Patterson strolled to the tail of the wagon. "Harold Hawthorn, it says here. Nutmeg Farm, High Dunning. Why?"

"Well, we pinched it from him, didn't we? I mean, *you* pinched it."

"Not necessarily. Maybe the bloke who was chasing us pinched it from Harold Hawthorn."

"Bloody farmers," Stickwell said. "You can't trust them an inch."

"Where the hell did you find it, Pip?" Cattermole asked.

"In a farmyard. Inside a barn, actually."

"There you are, then," Stickwell said. "Obviously a dump for hot tractors. Bloke chasing us was some sort of agricultural fence. No wonder he didn't want us to get away. We know his guilty secret."

"Oh, balls," said Mother Cox.

"How did you start it?" Cattermole asked.

"The key was in the ignition," Patterson said. "I just swung the handle and off she went, first time."

"This must have been their getaway tractor," Stickwell said, brushing yellow powder out of his hair.

"With a great big farm-wagon hitched on behind?" Cox said.

"For the rest of the gang, Mother," Cattermole explained

17

patiently. "We've stumbled on a very big organisation. We shall probably get a medal for this."

"We'll get a colossal bollocking from the Ram if he ever hears about it," said Cox.

"The Ram's in London," Stickwell said. "God's in his heaven and I'm damn hungry. There's nothing like a good healthy spew in the fresh country air to give a chap an appetite."

Patterson climbed back onto the tractor. "Home for breakfast, chaps!" he said. But this time the tractor refused to start. They took turns winding the starting-handle; nothing came out of the engine but soft grunts and feeble puffs of black smoke. "Buggeration," Patterson said.

"Come on, let's walk," Mother Cox urged. He was growing more and more nervous as the sun rose.

They set off. Stickwell and Cattermole began a serious conversation about the significance of becoming twenty-one; the day before had been Pip Patterson's twenty-first birthday. "It's a definite milestone," Stickwell said. "Right to vote, for a start. And you can get married. Take out hire-purchase debts. Go bankrupt. Get a mortgage."

"Who cares about all that junk?" said Moggy Cattermole, who was only twenty. "I'm not interested in any of it. Are you, Pip?"

"Not much." Patterson was beginning to worry about the broken tractor and its battered trailer.

"The big danger, as I see it, is women," said Stickwell. "Once they know you're twenty-one and therefore legally available, they'll do absolutely anything to get your bags off." Patterson looked interested. "Pure and innocent they may appear," Stickwell warned, "but you can't trust 'em in a dark corner on a hot night. That's my experience."

"You don't say?" Patterson was intrigued.

"My father once told me that all women are natural predators," Cattermole remarked. "He said they'd strip you naked and suck your blood and then send you the bill."

"There you are, then," Stickwell said.

"Mind you, he had five sisters and three daughters. And two wives."

"Outnumbered from the bally start, poor devil," Stickwell said.

"What d'you mean, Sticky: they'll do anything to get a chap's bags off?" Patterson asked.

"I think we're going the wrong way," Cox said. Patterson looked at him with dislike. "Well, it's no good us walking *away* from Kingsmere, is it?" Cox demanded. "I think we ought to find someone and ask."

They stopped walking.

"What a bore you are, Mother," Cattermole said. "I certainly shan't invite you to *my* twenty-first party."

Heavy trampling sounds came from the other side of a hedge, and two large horses looked at them. "Hullo!" Stickwell exclaimed. One of the horses blew smoke through its nostrils.

"I think they're trying to tell us something," Patterson said.

Hector Ramsay couldn't wait. He had never had the gift of patience.

When he was a boy his restlessness had been quite endearing, sometimes; at boarding school, or at home in Hampshire, during the school holidays, young Hector had always been the leader of the gang, not interested in explaining or persuading but so brimful of energetic ideas that he usually got his own way by sheer thrustfulness. Or, looking at it another way, obstinacy.

As a young man he went on attacking life with a sledgehammer, as if it were some gigantic clam to be forced open. This was less attractive than his boyish gusto; it showed a relentless determination to succeed that most people found praiseworthy at first, a bit grim after a while, and frankly bloody tedious before long. If it was theoretically admirable for a seventeen-year-old to know so precisely what he wanted – he wanted to be the youngest-ever wing commander in RAF Fighter Command – in practice Hector Ramsay's single-minded ambition was a bore. Even his father (by then retired from the Royal Navy) found him wearing, and his mother had long ago given him up, ever since the time he refused to attend his eldest brother's wedding because it clashed with Open Day at the local RAF station. There had been the most enormous family bust-up over that. In the end Hector had gone with them to the church, slouching and silently contemptuous of the whole silly ritual; but he walked out halfway through the ceremony. He got into one of the hired cars and had himself driven to the airfield, where he spent the rest of the day happily climbing in and out of cockpits. There was an even louder family bust-up when he got home, although his mother admitted to herself that she was wasting her breath.

Hector knew what he wanted, and he couldn't wait to get it. She sometimes wondered why he was so impatient. Because he was the youngest son? Because both his brothers had already done well in the Navy? Was that why Hector chose the RAF? Was he self-centred because he wanted to be a fighter pilot, or did he want to be a fighter pilot because that satisfied his self-centred nature? It depressed her that he was so intensely narrow, and sometimes she even wondered about his brain. His had been a difficult birth, late and awkward and full of pain. Hector hadn't seemed to want to come into the world at all, he'd been dragged into it; and ever since he discovered what it was like, all his energies had been spent on getting far away from it. In a fighter plane. Alone.

So everyone was relieved when Hector Ramsay won a scholarship to the RAF College at Cranwell. He did well, got his commission, got his wings, got his posting to a fighter squadron. The family relaxed and began to treat him like a normal human being. There was even a spell when it almost looked as if Hector might get engaged.

He was flying Gloster Gauntlets – fixed-undercarriage biplanes with twin machine-guns, pure *Dawn Patrol* stuff – from an airfield in Cambridgeshire. She was Australian, a diplomat's daughter, studying at one of the art schools on the fringe of the University. Her name was Kit and she had a freckled candour – together with legs like a dancer's and breasts like grapefruit – that surprised and captivated him. She took him to bed (in her rented cottage at Grantchester) on his third visit, and that experience made him eager to return. What on earth did she see in him? Well, he wasn't bad-looking, he had a kind of unblinking concentration that amused her, and he was in a different class from those flannelled undergraduates, all books and bats and bicycles, who jostled for her attention: at least Hector Ramsay *did* something; sometimes she could even smell the engine-oil on him when he came straight from flying. But what attracted her most was his enormous *need*. Here was a man so isolated that he could not reach out. Kit gave him her love, or so she believed, as an act of lifesaving. He was irresistible. For a few weeks they were like a nut and a bolt: gratifying when together, useless when apart. It wasn't even necessary for them to say very much; they knew what they thought and they knew what they wanted. Once, when they were getting into bed, she paused and sat back on her heels and said, "Presumably you're in love." Hector crouched with his chin on his knees and hugged his bare legs, while he thought about it. "Presumably," he said. They looked at each other. He was thinking: *Am I? How do I know? How can I tell?* She saw the act of thought crease his forehead like wind ruffling water, and she laughed. He raised his eyebrows. "Tell you later," she said. But she never did.

The trouble began when he realised he was becoming addicted to her. If they didn't make love at least every other night, he developed a craving for sex that obsessed him until it was satisfied. Then the craving started all over again. Sex obliterated his interest in food, duty, news, smalltalk, even flying. He could be in the cockpit running-up his engine, getting ready for take-off, and in all the shudder and roar he sat brooding over a vision of Kit seen in the spinning arc of the propeller, naked and ready, while his limbs twitched and went slack and his mouth accumulated saliva. Eventually, reluctantly, he had to straighten up and swallow, forgo his lovely vision, concentrate on getting this throbbing machine up in the air.

It worried him, this addiction. There was the risk that it might affect his health. He noticed a certain lassitude on the mornings after his nights with her. It wasn't weariness or fatigue; it was more like abstraction tinged with irritability, but that sort of thing could easily lead to carelessness. When he was flying, his reactions seemed a little slower, his senses not quite so acute: his eyesight, especially, wasn't as sharp as it ought to be. That was a myth, of course, a tired old joke: too much sex had absolutely no effect on eyesight, none at all; everyone knew that. On the other hand, Hector couldn't focus as quickly or as clearly on distant objects as he used to be able to do. Also there were occasional headaches.

He wanted to discuss it with her but he was afraid to. Talk might destroy everything. He tried to discuss it with the RAF chaplain, failed to find the words, and left that man puzzled and wondering. One night he wrote a painful letter to his father, asking advice, but when he re-read it next morning the facts were so appalling that he tore it up and burned the bits. His hands were trembling; his mouth was twisted sideways in despair and disgust. Before he quite knew what he was doing, his legs were taking him to the adjutant's office. He asked to see the squadron commander, urgently. The adjutant obliged.

"I want to apply for a transfer, sir," Hector said huskily. "Immediately."

"Yes? What's up?"

Hector clenched his teeth and stared at the blurred, upside-down markings on the CO's blotter. "Bad love affair, sir," he said. He felt sick.

The CO propped his chin on his fist and made his pencil spin on the desktop. *Bloody silly reason for a posting*, he thought. *On the other hand it explains why he's been looking like a constipated cow lately* . . . The pencil skittered to a stop. He looked up and delivered his all-purpose, wry smile. "We'll miss you, old boy," he lied fluently.

Hector was lucky. A violent mid-air collision had suddenly created an urgent need for pilots in another Gauntlet squadron which was scheduled to give an important aerobatic display in two weeks' time. This squadron was based outside Aberdeen. Hector was on the train to Scotland that same evening. The last thing he did before he left was send a telegram to Kit. A telegram was much easier to write than a letter, and it had a curtness that suited his state of mind. He never saw her again.

Pilot Officer H. G. Ramsay's file followed him to Aberdeen in due course, with a handwritten note that read *Emotionally immature?* That uncertainty didn't stop him getting promoted to flying officer a year later. Flying was no longer the most important thing in his life. He was hungry for promotion; flying was simply the fastest route to his goal of becoming Fighter Command's youngest-ever wing commander. He went on courses, and passed them. He changed squadrons, changed aircraft, flew Hawker Furies, Gloster Gladiators, Mark Two Gauntlets. His eyesight was no better but it was no worse: things sometimes tended to blur a bit, that was all. It didn't stop him getting promoted to flight lieutenant.

By now the year was 1937 and war was obviously on the way. Hector Ramsay was, naturally, impatient for it. Flying was all very well, promotion was all very well, but what he really yearned for was the chance to lead a squadron in battle, to make a score, pick up a DFC, maybe a DSO. The autumn of 1938 looked very promising. Germany marched into Czechoslovakia and everything pointed to war, what with hundreds of thousands of children being evacuated from the cities of England, trenches dug in parks, gas-masks issued, a balloon barrage over London, all leave cancelled, camouflage paint hastily slapped on the aircraft. To top it all, Hector became a squadron leader.

That was when he got his nickname. He was given a squadron – it was called Hornet squadron, nobody quite knew why – that was equipped with Furies. It was stationed at RAF Kingsmere in Essex – exactly where the German bomber fleets were expected to cross the coast. The Fury was a delightful little biplane with a top speed of 220 mph, whereas Germany's standard bomber, the Heinkel III, could fly at nearly 250 mph. The Dornier 17 was said to be even faster.

At his first meeting with his pilots, Hector Ramsay stood on a table and said: "Gentlemen, prepare to defend your country. Our aeroplanes are too slow. We cannot catch the Hun bombers. Therefore we must ram them."

His announcement caused a thoughtful silence. In the event war did not break out; but from then on, Squadron Leader Ramsay was known as The Ram. Secretly, this pleased him. He acted up to his image – that of a pugnacious, aggressive commander, impatient for conflict, a leader whose men would follow him into the jaws of death if he gave the order – and he worked them hard.

In June 1939 Hornet squadron exchanged its Furies for Hurri-canes. The Ram was immensely pleased. He launched the most impressive training programme anyone could remember. It called for an extremely tough schedule of physical exercises to improve stamina as well as a vast amount of flying and theoretical work on engine maintenance, meteorology, gunmanship and the like. The Ram drove himself as hard as his men, and after five days he went down with a severe attack of shingles. The sores became so painful that he could scarcely move. Bitterly disappointed, he went off to a hospital in Torquay, determined to fight his way back to health in the minimum possible time. The squadron trundled on under a succession of temporary commanders, and this worried him. "Just rest and relax and forget everything for a while," the doctors said. "Let's face it, you're not going anywhere like that, are you?" The Ram smiled and agreed, but inside he was a-twitch with anger and impatience. The shingles got worse before they got better.

He was released in the third week of August and went straight back to Kingsmere. Maddeningly, the squadron was on leave. "The previous CO thought it was a good idea," explained the adjutant, Flight Lieutenant Kellaway. "I mean, what with the balloon likely to go up before very long. A chance to see their families and so on."

"Get them back," the Ram said.

"Now?"

"Instantly."

The telegrams went off. It was three days before the last man turned up. Pilot Officer Cattermole had been salmon-fishing in a remote corner of Ross and Cromarty. He brought a couple of fifteen-pounders, which he donated to the mess. The Ram was not impressed. "I don't like fish," he said stiffly, "and I don't like pilots who take foreign holidays when Hitler's about to go on the rampage."

"Not foreign, sir," Cattermole said. "I went to Scotland."

"Scotland's bloody foreign," the Ram growled. Cattermole widened his eyes. "I've been there," the Ram told him. "I know where it is, and it's not in England, which is the country you're paid to defend, laddy!"

"Britain, actually," said Cattermole, whose mother was Scottish.

"You leave the political geography to me. Now get out of that damned silly fancy-dress." Cattermole was wearing a Norfolk jacket, heather-mixture breeches with knee-length stockings of purple plaid, and hill climber's shoes. "You look like the Hound of the Baskervilles."

Cattermole blinked. "Are you sure you've got that right, sir?" he said.

"I'm the squadron commander," the Ram said, smiling grimly. "I don't *have* to get it right. I just have to say it, and it *is* right. Now I want you flying in half an hour."

Cattermole turned to go, but hesitated. "My Hurricane's having some new bits put into it," he said. "The fitters didn't expect me back so soon."

"Then take somebody else's Hurricane." The Ram waved at a machine that was coming in to land. "Take that one."

"That's a Battle, sir." They shared the airfield with a squadron of Battle bombers: single-engined monoplanes, sadly under-powered. The Ram squinted at it. "Well, what d'you expect me to do?" he demanded. "Turn it into a pumpkin?"

He kept them training all that day, using every available aircraft. They went up in sections of three to practise interceptions on civil airliners heading for Croydon airport. It was at the end of one of these flights that Mother Cox suffered from confusion.

Cox was an average-to-good pilot most of the time. Unlike some, he had a bird-like sense of how and why the aeroplane flew. Where the power came from was a sweet mystery to him: by some magic the twelve cylinders in the Rolls-Royce Merlin engine made the propeller spin at a highly satisfactory speed as long as he followed certain rituals involving magnetos and boost and radiator shutter and various other conjuring tricks in the cockpit; but – despite attending many lectures on the Merlin – he never really knew what made it go. On the other hand he understood instinctively what made a Hurricane fly. As soon as he released the brakes and let it roll for take-off, Mother Cox began to sense the wash of air over and under the wings, the hint of lift in the tailplane, the hurrying stutter of the wheels, and then that vast invisible rush that rewarded the whole machine with the gift of flight.

For Mother Cox it was all as natural as swimming in the sky: he *knew* how his Hurricane felt when he made it bank, or dive, or side-slip; every throb and twitch was a message to his hands and feet and the seat of his pants. The feel of speeding air on his wings was as real to him as the touch of rushing snow to a skier.

All of which made it the more unfortunate that Mother Cox's brain had a design fault. Once in a while it failed to perform some very elementary job, like remembering the difference between left and right, or knowing which way clockwise goes.

On this day he had finished an hour of practice interceptions and he was ready for a spot of tea. He lost height on his approach to Kingsmere aerodrome; turned where he usually turned, just beyond the village church; watched his airspeed drift down from 130 to 120 to 110; and lowered his flaps. The sudden drag checked the Hurricane. Its speed fell away and the great humped nose lifted itself. He could see very little of the airfield ahead but directly below him the rusty tangle of the barbed-wire perimeter fence came into view. He left the wire behind, carefully saving height until the speed was down to 90, and as it slipped into the eighties he let the plane sink and sink, groping for the grass, still holding that last-second balance between lift and gravity until the wheels could meet the ground and run to a safe standstill: another flight, another landing, another scribbled entry in the logbook. The tail-wheel touched and raced. The Hurricane sank onto its belly and hurled Mother Cox against his straps as its gaping air-scoop rammed into the turf and hacked out a brief trench before it got ripped off and flattened, by which time the great two-bladed propeller was digging its own grave with appalling speed and a noise like a thousand circular saws gone berserk, a racket which ceased as the blades thrashed themselves to splintered death and the engine abruptly cut out. Mother Cox had done that. He was frightened and bewildered but he had just enough sense left to do that. The mutilated Hurricane skidded along with its nose in the dirt while Mother Cox wondered what the holy hell had gone wrong. It couldn't be his fault. The undercarriage was locked down. The red lights proved that.

Or should they be green?

Oh Christ.

The Ram was sitting at his desk, leafing through an Air Ministry publication, when Mother Cox reported to his office ten minutes later. He did not look up.

"Hitler has two thousand bombers," the Ram said. He spoke so softly that Cox had to lean forward. "We have fewer than five hundred fighters. Now some of our fighters are biplanes, so they have two wings. Does that make them twice as fast?" He looked up. His stare was intense and unblinking.

"No, sir."

"Half as fast?"

Mother Cox didn't know what to say. He could hear himself breathing; it sounded heavy and deliberate, like a sleeping animal; after a couple of seconds he sniffed sharply, just to break that awful rhythm. "Our biplanes aren't much good, sir," he mumbled. A fear was forming at the back of his mind: the Ram was going to have him transferred to some bloody old Gladiator squadron.

26

"Not much good," the Ram murmured. "Not much good ... That's far too vague, Cox. It really is. War is a precise and calculated business. You shoot to kill. If you miss a Hun, would you say that you are not much good?" Again, the rigid stare. Cox briefly shook his head. "Would you say that you are bloody awful?" the Ram asked. His voice was rising. Cox just looked, his expression as flat as his spirits. "Would you say that you are sickeningly lousy?" the Ram demanded. He threw the Air Ministry publication into a desk drawer and kicked it shut; the bang made Cox jump. "Would you say that you are a sodding disgrace to the Royal Air Force in general and a stinking menace to Fighter Command in particular?" The Ram stood up. "Would you say that you are acting as a collaborator and fifth columnist for the benefit of Nazi Germany," he shouted, "and therefore a traitor, a filthy despicable traitor to your own *country*?" He hit that last word with a passion that made the clerks in the next room stop typing.

"Sir, that's not fair," Cox protested. "Damn it all, I only bust the undercart and –"

"Not fair?" the Ram roared. "Not fair? What if Hitler sends his two thousand bombers against us tomorrow? What if his entire bloody air force is on its way here *now*? How do you plan to shoot them down, Cox? Are you going to run into the wind with your arms flapping and a Colt revolver gripped between your tiny teeth? Because you've made very damn sure that *one* Hurricane won't fly, haven't you? Ploughed up my nice field with its poor suffering belly, didn't you? Bust the prop, gave the engine a hernia, and dragged the aeroplane's guts through the dirt while you sat in the cockpit picking your nose and listening to Ambrose and his Orchestra on your radio, and don't tell me I'm wrong because the control tower kept screaming at you throughout your approach but *you weren't bloody well paying attention!*"

Mother Cox looked at his flying boots.

"This squadron's gone to hell in my absence," the Ram said. His voice had fallen to a rasp. "You treat it like a bunch of playboys in a private flying club. Well, by God I'll see you all in hell first. I'll kick every arse in this squadron until either you make yourselves worthy of it or my right leg gets worn to a bloody stub." He clipped Cox with his shoulder as he strode past him and flung open the door. The faces of the clerks were diplomatically blank. "Get a shovel and fill in that disgusting hole, Cox," he ordered. "You break the shovel and I'll have you court-martialled. Go."

Mother Cox went. It was a very long hole, and darkness had fallen by the time he filled the last of it.

The next day was the last day of August. A sea-fog reached Kingsmere before dawn. By eight-thirty, when the pilots assembled in one of the hangars, it was still blowing across the field in slow drifts of smoky grey, chilling everything it touched.

"I see the war-clouds are gathering again," Patterson said. A couple of heads turned. He was reading a newspaper.

"Are those new war-clouds?" Stickwell asked. "Or are they the same old war-clouds that have been gathering all year?"

Patterson consulted his newspaper. "It doesn't say," he said. "All it says is the war-clouds are gathering and once again Europe is at the crossroads."

"That's a bloody silly place to be," Cattermole remarked. "I mean, what with the war-clouds gathering and so on. A bloke could get jolly wet."

"Our fearless leader has an umbrella," Patterson said. "They've got a photograph here to prove it." He raised his newspaper to show them.

"But have they got a picture of a war-cloud?" Stickwell insisted. "I don't trust these newspaper people. I bet they can't tell the difference between strato-cumulus and cauliflower *au gratin*."

"Can you?" Cox asked.

"Of course I can. Cauliflower *au gratin* is the stuff we chuck at the guests on mess nights."

"And, in your case, probably miss," Cox said.

"Nonsense. Tripe. Utter piffle."

"I thought Strato Cumulus was an Italian film star," Cattermole said.

"Come off it, Sticky," Cox said contemptuously. He was still feeling his blisters from yesterday's shovelling. "How often did you hit the target at that armament practice camp? Never."

"No, but once or twice I nearly got the plane towing it."

Cox sniffed.

"I always used too much deflection, you see," Stickwell explained. "Those training things are far too slow for me. My brain

28

works at lightning speed. One of the drawbacks of genius, suppose."

"That was a remarkably funny joke I made about Strato Cumulus," Cattermole said, looking up into the gloom of the roof, "and not one of you blighters laughed. Not one."

"Joke? You made a joke, Moggy?" Patterson put his paper away. "Sorry I missed it. Affairs of state, you understand. Never mind, I can give you a minute now. Tell it again." He cocked his head attentively.

Cattermole sucked in his stomach, and stared over their heads. "My talent is too fine and rare a thing to be wasted on the wind," he said loftily.

Patterson waited. "That's not very funny," he said. "Sure you haven't left something out?"

Cattermole walked away and began idly kicking the tyres of the nearest Hurricane.

"Actually, it was funnier the first time," Stickwell said. "When Moggy said he thought Cauliflower Au Gratin was a French railway station."

"So it is," Patterson said.

"Test the lights," Flip Moran said to Cattermole. Moran was 'B' flight commander, a stubby Ulsterman with an accent that gave his words a hard cutting-edge. It was his Hurricane that Cattermole was kicking. "Try the horn, why don't you?"

"Somewhere near Bordeaux," said Patterson. "I've passed through it many a time."

"Is it funny?" Stickwell asked.

"Oh, unspeakably hilarious."

"Get in and try her on for size," Moran told Cattermole. "Take a spin around the block. Go on, give her another kick if you feel like it. Give her a real good kick."

"Don't be tiresome, Flip," Cattermole said.

"She's my machine," Moran growled. "Kick your own plane if you must kick something."

"No, I couldn't do that. I'm not at all sentimental about aircraft."

Cattermole's flight commander, Fanny Barton, strolled over. "Stop causing trouble, Moggy," he said, "or I'll beat you up." Barton was a New Zealander, tall and athletic, with hair that was so fair his eyebrows were almost invisible.

"What a good idea!" Cattermole said. "Let's have a scrap, 'B' flight against 'A' flight. Let's have a jolly good scrap. I'm getting cold."

"No," Barton said.

"Game of rugger, then," Cattermole suggested. "We can use Dicky for the ball." He went towards Dicky Starr, the youngest and the smallest member of the squadron. "No fear," Dicky said, backing away. "Just for a couple of minutes," Moggy wheedled. "Come on, be a sport, Dicky. We'll pay for anything we break." He made a grab, and Dicky dodged behind Cox. "Get out of the way, Mother," Cattermole ordered. "I'm too tired," Cox said. "You'll have to go round the outside." Cattermole scowled. "Buck up, Mother," he said. "This is not the proper squadron spirit."

Cox yawned. "Tell the Ram," he said.

A car came sliding through the fog, its headlights making the murk seem more solid, and stopped. The Ram got out, carefully; the scars from his shingles were still sensitive.

"Sorry about all this muck," he announced. "The met people promised me it would lift half an hour ago, and they should know. That being so, I propose to get the whole squadron airborne at once, on the assumption that conditions will have cleared by the time you have to land."

There was a moment of frozen silence while the Ram turned and examined the fog. He turned back and said: "Now that I have your undivided attention, flying is cancelled." They relaxed; some even chuckled. "Instead there will be a cross-country run, twice around the airfield." The chuckling ceased. "Get into gym kit and report to the adjutant at the main gate in fifteen minutes."

The Ram eased himself into his car and drove away.

"At least his eyesight hasn't got any worse," Moran said as they walked back to their quarters.

"What d'you mean?" Barton asked.

"Well, he can see this fog all right. I just wonder if he'll be able to see the enemy as clearly. Before they see us, that is."

"It doesn't really matter all that much. We're faster than they are. They can't get away, can they?"

"Ah, no, of course not." Moran turned up his collar. "Now why didn't I think of that? Dear me, Moran. You're a terrible booby."

30

"Not that it isn't an advantage to be able to see the enemy first," Barton said. "Obviously it's an advantage."

"Maybe we can persuade the Germans to use bigger aeroplanes," Moran said. "There has to be some simple solution."

They assembled at the main gate. "Remember," the adjutant said, "your route is outside the perimeter wire, so you can forget about short cuts. I'll time you. My advice," he went on, as they rubbed their bare arms and hopped from foot to foot, "is take it steady, pace yourself, and don't try to jump the ditches. Run through them. That's what I used to do."

They hooted their derision. Flight Lieutenant Kellaway had flown in the Royal Flying Corps; he was now forty-two; they treated him like an ancient. Stickwell said: "And my advice to you, adj –"

"Yes, yes, I'm sure. Off you go, then. Have a good time. The Ram will be along to see you finish."

Grumbling loudly, they trotted away and joined the road that ran alongside the aerodrome. The talking soon stopped. Kingsmere was a big field, at least three miles around.

After about fifty yards, Stickwell jogged alongside Cattermole. He jerked his head towards the rear. Gradually they dropped back. Stickwell slowed to a walk and let the others disappear into the gloom. "What's up?" Cattermole asked.

"I've had a better idea, Moggy. Let's double back and hang around at the other side of the main gate until those twerps turn up. Then we can just tack on the end again."

"The adj is there. He'll see us go by."

"Not if we cut across the fields. Come on."

They crossed the road and looked for a gap in the hedge. There was none.

"There's bound to be a lane turning off this road somewhere near," Stickwell said.

They walked for a quarter of a mile before they found the lane. It was deeply rutted and very muddy. "I don't fancy that," Cattermole said. "It's knee-deep in dung."

"It's heading in the right direction, though. Come on, Moggy. I expect it links up with a decent road further on."

"Yes, but look at all that manure."

Stickwell looked at it. "All right. What's your suggestion?"

Cattermole frowned. After a moment Stickwell set off up the lane. Cattermole watched him and, without enthusiasm, followed. Trapped between high hedges, the fog seemed, if anything, thicker and colder.

"Shit!" Cattermole said. He stood on one leg and looked at the other foot. "Come *on*, Moggy," Stickwell called, "or we'll be late." Cattermole put his foot down and squelched after him. The lane angled sharply to the left. After fifty yards it was crossed by another and even more primitive lane. Stickwell paused briefly, and then turned right. Cattermole followed. Both his feet were soaking wet, and having wet feet was a condition that Cattermole had disliked intensely, ever since childhood.

"One thing's certain, sir," said the sergeant of police, "it won't be a bit like last time."

"Mmm." Kellaway didn't want to talk about the last time, but he was drinking the guardroom's tea and eating the guardroom's biscuits so he had to be polite. "Ah well," he said.

"I mean, I can't see us going through all that business with trenches and stuff, can you, sir?"

"Hope not, sergeant."

The sergeant broke a biscuit in half, considered dunking it, glanced at the adjutant, and thought better. "You were in the last lot, weren't you, sir?"

"Yes." Kellaway walked to the window. The fog drifted past like wet smoke.

"Still, I don't suppose it was all bad, was it, sir?" The sergeant dunked while he had the chance. "From what I hear there used to be quite a bit of what-you-might-call chivalry when you and Jerry had a scrap."

"Chivalry?" Kellaway gave it some thought. After a while he saw his own reflection in the window and blinked with surprise. He didn't think he looked forty-two. He thought he looked a rather rumpled twenty-one. "Oh, in the beginning I suppose . . . Of course I wasn't there then, but for the first year or two I don't think either side took flying all that seriously. Later on, when it mattered and things got somewhat desperate, I can't honestly remember much in the way of chivalry."

"But it wasn't like being stuck in the mud getting shelled to kingdom-come by someone you couldn't even see, was it, sir?" the sergeant persisted. "I mean, at least you blokes were out in the open. More of a duel, like." The sergeant dropped a duster onto the linoleum and worked it with his foot, removing a couple of faint prints. He should really have left it for the defaulters to do, but he hated looking at smudged linoleum. "I read somewhere that your average RFC pilot lasted three weeks, sir," he said. "Three weeks!" He shook his head.

"Oh, I knew a chap who lasted two years," Kellaway said. The sergeant smiled politely but Kellaway could tell that he was disappointed. "On the other hand the new boys usually got knocked down pretty swiftly," he added. A runner emerged from the fog. Kellaway opened the door and waved. "My goodness, Barton's absolutely covered in mud..." He went out and counted the gasping runners as they finished their first lap and began their second; waited for a while; came in and shut the door. "Two missing," he said. "Maybe they've got cramp."

"I've seen that tree before," said Cattermole.

Stickwell stopped, and looked at the twisted trunk climbing into the fog. "Don't be preposterous, Moggy," he said coldly.

Cattermole went over and touched it. "Definitely the same tree," he called back. "I'd know it anywhere."

"Impossible. We've never been in this field before. You're imagining things."

"Same tree," Cattermole insisted. "You know what that means, don't you?" He walked back to Stickwell.

"I never trusted that bloody silly path in that sodding great wood," Stickwell muttered savagely. "Damn thing went round and round like a drunken corkscrew."

"Talk sense, Sticky. You can't have a drunken corkscrew, for Christ's sake. It's not possible."

Stickwell glared. "All right, then. All right. Since you're the expert, you pick a route. Go on."

Cattermole sighed, and looked unhappily at the wandering grey walls of damp and cold that blotted out all landmarks except the twisted trunk. "There's only one way out of this," he said. "Dead reckoning." He tapped his wristwatch. "Point the hour hand at the sun, bisect the angle between that and twelve o'clock, and you've got true north."

Stickwell wiped moisture from his face. "Where did you learn that?"

"Boy Scouts. I was nearly a patrol leader."

"Nearly? What went wrong?"

"I'd rather not say, if you don't mind."

"Oh, oh, oh."

"Where's the sun?" Cattermole asked, raising his wrist.

The fog had a slightly more luminous quality in one area. "Over there," Stickwell said. He waved his arm through a wide arc.

Cattermole shuffled about until the hour hand was pointing in that general direction. "Bisect the angle . . ." he muttered, and carefully pointed with his right hand over his left shoulder. "If that's north, then the airfield must be . . ." He looked enquiringly.

"South," Stickwell said confidently. "Main gate's on the north side, isn't it?"

"Jesus, I'm cold," Cattermole said.

They strode briskly into the fog. "Whatever happens we must stay on this bearing," Stickwell said. Cattermole, trying to look at his watch and also avoid cowflaps, grunted.

Within a minute the ground underfoot began to be boggy. They plodded on. Stickwell lost a gym-shoe, sucked off by a particularly greedy bit of bog. They came to a ditch, waded through it, and climbed the bank to find a barbed-wire fence on top. Cattermole went over first and got his shorts hooked while straddling the wire. Stickwell tried to free him and dragged the barbs across the inside of his thigh. "Stupid bastard!" Cattermole shouted.

"Don't you talk to me like that," Stickwell said. He was very angry, but he was also on the wrong side of the wire; and he was a lot shorter than Moggy.

Fanny Barton finished the run first. The fog had begun to fade, and Kellaway saw him fifty yards away, running as easily as most people walk. *God, what a splendid-looking chap he is*, the adjutant thought. *I wish I could draw him. I wish I could draw his smile.* As the figure came closer he imagined Fanny Barton's smile, the way it began with the eyes, wide-set above high cheekbones, and then suddenly reached the mouth and stretched the slim lips so that they made deep, bracketing creases outside them; and then just as quickly the smile faded and left Barton's usual expression: alert, watchful, ready.

"Well done, Fanny," Kellaway said, and was rewarded with that flash of smile. "Jolly good show." The others were soon in sight, their wet gym-shoes pattering on the roadway like faint applause. Barton jogged up and down while they came in, everyone mud-streaked and panting dragon-breaths. "Jolly fine, damn good effort," Kellaway called out. "Sterling stuff. Rule Britannia." Billy Starr was the last to finish. They cheered him in, and he ran the last ten yards backwards.

"Truly magnificent," the adjutant said. "Has anyone seen Moggy and Sticky? You should have lapped them."

No answer.

"How odd," he said.

"Those blasted cows are following us," Stickwell said.

"They're not cows, they're heifers," Cattermole told him.

"Thanks very much, Moggy. That's a great help. When the buggers trample me to death I'll feel a lot better for knowing they're not cows. Bloody hell, there's millions of them."

The fog had lifted a little, and the field they were trudging across was indeed full of cattle, many of which were trotting after them.

"They're just curious, Sticky. Ignore them."

"Oh, sure. Ignore a dirty great horn up my rear end. Let's get out of here."

Stickwell began running. The cattle increased speed to a slow gallop. By the time he had covered fifty yards a small herd was cantering after him.

Cattermole plodded on, watching them fade into the fog. Several minutes later, when he caught up, Stickwell was on the other side of a fence and he was throwing lumps of mud at the animals. "Bloody brutes tried to eat me," he complained.

Cattermole climbed the fence. They walked along a farm track and met a man mending a gate. "Which way to Kingsmere aerodrome?" Stickwell asked.

The man looked at them and tossed his hammer from hand to hand. "How do I know you're not German spies?" he asked.

Stickwell glared. "What makes you think German spies go

wandering about Essex in their underwear, covered in shit and chased by wild bloody cows?"

"Heifers," Cattermole said.

The man whacked the gatepost a few times while he thought about that. "Go back the way you came," he said. "Take the second turn on the left, and Kingsmere's three mile straight on."

"*Three* miles?" Cattermole said faintly. "Three *miles*?"

"He's lying," Stickwell said. "He thinks we're spies, he's deliberately sending us the wrong way."

The man contemplated his gatepost and gave it another whack. "Now get off my land afore I set the dogs on you," he said.

"Come on, Sticky," Cattermole said. They trailed back the way they had come.

Shouts of challenge, and unoriginal insults, and howls of pain, and hoots of laughter echoed along the corridor. Fanny Barton lay in a hot bath and listened: that was Moke Miller's laugh, so it must be Fitz Fitzgerald trying to pick a fight with Mother Cox, since Moke and Fitz usually stuck together; and those forthright Lowland curses must be coming from Pip Patterson, who didn't usually put himself out to protect Mother, so he was probably just trying to get past the others without being flicked with a wet towel. The bathroom door shook as bodies crashed against it. Barton breathed deeply and easily. He knew he wouldn't be disturbed. There was a powerful rumour going about that the Ram intended to weed out several pilots, so this would be a very bad moment to annoy a flight commander; what's more, Fanny had always made it clear that he didn't enjoy horseplay. If the others wanted to wrestle and chase and chuck things at each other, that was okay as long as it didn't involve him. He wasn't being stuffy; it just wasn't his style, that's all.

Fanny's real name was Keith. He'd been christened Keith Donald Hugh because his father was intensely keen on cricket; one day, he hoped, his son would play cricket for New Zealand, in which case he would need three good initials to distinguish him from all the other Bartons. The boy was hopeless at cricket. He was good at athletics, but that meant less than nothing to his father: running round in circles, waste of time, where does it get you? After cricket, only two things mattered to Mr Barton: sheep, and the royal family.

His house had very few pictures, but what there were showed either prize Merino rams or King George in his robes. Both subjects had a heavy-lidded, overdressed look, and Keith grew up associating the one with the other. He came to hate life on the farm. It was dreary, exhausting, repetitive work with a lot of greasy, clumsy, bloody-minded animals. The first chance he had, he got out: out of the farm, out of New Zealand, right across the world to Britain, into the Royal Air Force.

That was a very long time ago. Now he was twenty-four and a flight lieutenant. He couldn't even remember how he'd got the nickname Fanny. Everyone had a nickname in the squadron, it was part of Fighter Command's undergraduate quality: an implacably bright, slangy, superficial attitude, the kind of outlook that took nothing seriously except the supreme importance of being in Fighter Command; and that went without saying.

He pressed his feet against the bath, rested his neck on the other end, and slowly tightened his muscles until his body began to emerge from the water. He pushed harder until his buttocks were clear and he was arched, dripping and steaming, in the cool air. After a few seconds the strain made his muscles quiver. Outside, the horseplay had ended; the corridor was quiet. Fanny Barton held his breath and idly wondered what would happen to a well-trained and beautifully co-ordinated body when it received a burst of machine-gun fire at a height of three or four miles. The idea did not disturb him. He had thought about it too often for that; and in any case it would be somebody else's body taking the bullets, not his. He lowered himself, welcoming the warmth, and reached for the soap.

"You're bleeding all over my leg," said Cattermole. He was carrying Stickwell on his back.

"I know," Stickwell said. "Don't worry, it's only my toe. Mind you," he added, "it hurts like hell."

The fog had continued to lift, and now it was only a tawny haze. The lane stretched in front of them, dead straight for at least half a mile.

"You wouldn't have cut your stupid foot if you hadn't lost your stupid shoe," Cattermole grumbled. He stopped, heaved his passenger to a more comfortable position, and plodded on. "I didn't lose my shoe, did I?"

"Think yourself lucky, Moggy. Very, very lucky."

Cattermole thought, and glanced down at the fresh blood streaking his leg. "I hope you haven't got anything, that's all," he said.

"What d'you mean, 'got anything'?"

"I mean I don't want to get infected."

"How the hell can you get infected? *I'm* the one who's hurt, for God's sake. If anyone's going to catch lockjaw it'll be me."

"Lockjaw? Why lockjaw?"

"Oh . . ." Stickwell tried to remember some sixth-form biology. "Blood poisoning. You cut yourself and then tread in cowdung and . . . Anyway, it's not very nice, I can tell you. You go paralysed and die, or something."

"I see," Cattermole said. "And that's the filthy muck you're spreading all over my leg, is it? Thanks very much. Charming, I must say."

Stickwell leaned out and looked down. "You've already got every other kind of filthy muck on your leg, Moggy. Mine won't do you any harm."

"For Christ's sake stop rocking about." They covered another forty or fifty yards in silence. Then Cattermole said: "What time is it? I can't see my watch."

Stickwell twisted to the left. "Looks like ten past ten," he said.

"Ten past ten . . . Say we left about nine . . . Hell, the others must have finished hours ago."

Stickwell grunted.

"The Ram's not going to like this," Cattermole said. "You know how keen he is on physical fitness."

"Potty about it," Stickwell muttered. He was getting pins-and-needles in his legs.

"Kellaway says the Ram keeps talking about chopping chaps who aren't fit enough."

"I'm fit," Stickwell said. "Nothing wrong with me. I just can't walk, that's all."

"Imagine getting chopped and posted to some bloody awful Battle squadron," Cattermole said. "I don't fancy that."

"Do get a move on, Moggy," Stickwell said.

"All because of coming in last in a damn-fool cross-country run. No fear." Cattermole dropped his passenger and began running. Stickwell's legs folded and he sprawled on his back. "Moggy!" he cried. "Moggy, you bastard!"

"I'll tell him you're on your way," Cattermole called back.

"But I can't walk."

"Then hop!" Cattermole shouted. "Hop!" He demonstrated the action, a lanky, filthy, half-naked figure hopping down the middle of the lane. Stickwell sat and watched him go. A breeze was at work on the remains of the fog. He shivered, and got to his feet. "Bollocks," he said to the world at large.

"All right, what's this?" Flip Moran asked. He flashed a card about a foot square and hid it behind his back.

"Messerschmitt 110," said Mother Cox.

"Junkers 88," said Moke Miller.

"Balls. It's a 110," said Pip Patterson.

Moran looked at the other pilots in the lecture room.

"Well, it's not one of ours," said Dicky Starr.

Moran held up the card. "Messerschmitt Bf 110," he said. They stared at the plan-view silhouette of a twin-engined plane. Miller groaned. "So what's the difference?" Moran asked him.

"Twin tail-fins on the 110," said Mother Cox. "*Obviously*."

"Flip had his fingers over the tail," Miller protested.

"Useless fart, Moke," said Patterson.

"The Jerries are very keen on this machine," Moran said. "It seems they're using it in Poland at this very moment."

"It seems they're using everything in Poland at this very moment," said Cox.

"Two Daimler-Benz engines, each as big as a Merlin," Moran said, "so it's not slow. Now then, what's this?" As he flashed another card, Cattermole opened the door and they all turned to look. He was still in gym-kit, and his chest was heaving.

"That's a Fokker," said Fitz Fitzgerald confidently. "Ugly, isn't it?"

Patterson whistled. "But what an undercarriage."

"Hullo, chaps," Cattermole gasped.

"Terrific camouflage job," Fitzgerald said. "Blends perfectly with the sewage works."

"Where's the Ram?" Cattermole asked. "I've looked everywhere."

"He's gone to London with the adj," Barton said.

"What?" Cattermole sagged against the wall. "Why?"

"There's something odd about you, Moggy," Moran said. "Did you omit to shave, or what is it?"

Cattermole sank to a squat, leaving a long wet stain on the wall. "What a swindle," he muttered.

"Is that real blood, Moggy?" asked Starr, pointing.

"Not mine." Cattermole picked feebly at his leg. "Sticky's."

"You ran him down, did you?" said Fitzgerald. "And then you kicked him to death?"

"He had it coming to him, rotten little swine," Miller said. "Bags me his Buick."

"Why've they gone to London?" Cattermole asked again.

"There's a flap on," Barton said. "The Ram's been called to an urgent meeting at the Air Ministry."

"Bloody Poland, I suppose," Cattermole muttered.

"Europe is at the crossroads," Patterson said knowingly. "I told you it was. You watch. Anything might happen."

The telephone rang and Moran answered it. The message was brief.

"Get your woolly socks on," he told them. "That was the controller. Squadron's been put at fifteen-minute readiness."

"It's those damned war-clouds," Patterson said.

When Stickwell hobbled in on blistered feet, everyone else was in flying kit. The squadron remained at readiness for the rest of the day, nervously bored, arguing about the BBC news bulletins (rapid German advances, resolute Polish resistance, intense diplomatic activity) and passing around the various rumours that sifted in from God-knew-where (sector ops room? sergeants' mess? a visiting ferry pilot? the Battle boys across the way?) to the effect that a pair of Spitfires had shot down a reconnaissance Dornier over Kent; the Duke of Windsor had met Mussolini; the Prime Minister had collapsed with a heart attack ("That's the only attack you'll get out of him," Flip Moran remarked); U-boats had torpedoed an American liner in mid-Atlantic; a cloud of poison gas was drifting over the English Channel; and trains loaded with tanks bearing Polish markings had been seen arriving at the Port of London.

It was a long, restless afternoon. At about four o'clock Fanny Barton tried to contact the Ram at Air Ministry, just to know what was really happening. A harassed telephonist connected him to an air commodore called Ramshaw, who seemed to be in a crowded and noisy room; he let Barton say a dozen words, barked "How the hell should I know?", and crashed the phone down. Ten minutes later the adjutant telephoned Barton. "I got some sort of message that you'd got some sort of message," he said. "Not really," Fanny said. "I just wanted to keep in touch with the CO." Kellaway laughed. "So do I, old boy. Haven't seen him for hours."

"What's happening?"

"God knows. This place is pure bedlam. I can't even get a cup of tea."

"We're on standby."

"Are you? Jolly good. Actually I think everyone's on standby, except me. I'm at instant readiness, although for what I really haven't the faintest ... Ah, thanks *immensely* ... Tea at last," he told Fanny.

"They say some Spits got a Dornier over Kent," Fanny said. "Is that right?"

"Spits? I heard it was Defiants from 264 Squadron. Only it wasn't a Dornier, it was a –"

The line went dead.

"Any joy?" Cattermole asked, from an armchair.

"Not much," Barton said.

"Come and play ping-pong, Fanny," Starr called. "I've smashed everybody else. If I beat you I'm world champion."

They were released by the controller at 8 p.m. "So much for your wonderful war-clouds," Cattermole said as they peeled off their flying overalls.

"A little more respect, young man," said Patterson, "or you won't get invited to my twenty-first birthday party."

"When?"

"Today, actually. Not that I've arranged anything ..."

"Don't worry about that, Pip. Sticky, d'you feel like a party? Silly question. Okay, you can drive. Where's Mother Cox? Mother, lend us a couple of quid."

"No fear."

"Well, all right, a fiver then. It's for a good cause. We're going to get blotto."

"I might come with you," Cox said. "I could do with a glass of ale. We won't be late back, will we?"

"Heavens, no!" Cattermole said.

When Squadron Leader Ramsay and his adjutant arrived at Air Ministry, they were told that the meeting had been rescheduled for later in the day; meanwhile a secret briefing had been laid on, so secret that Kellaway was excluded; so secret, indeed, that nobody seemed sure where it was taking place. An elderly warrant officer with a clipboard searched repeatedly through a sheaf of duplicated papers and eventually directed the Ram to a remote anteroom. This turned out to be full of Bomber Command aircrew. One by one they were called out until, after an hour, only the Ram and a Fleet Air Arm liaison officer remained. Nobody knew why they were there. Nobody knew anything about the elderly warrant officer. The Ram cornered a civil servant and for ten minutes there was intensive telephoning around the building. "Group Captain Matthews wants to see you both," the civil servant said at last. "Room 4502."

"Who's he?" the Ram asked.

"I'm not sure. He's either DTA to the AOCFFU, or he's deputising for PQLO on the ADGB. You'll have to ask him, I'm afraid."

They had no opportunity to ask him. As soon as they entered room 4502, Matthews handed each of them a booklet called *Glossary of Anglo-Polish Aeronautical Terms*. "See what you make of that," he said. "Back in ten minutes." He hurried off.

The Ram waited half an hour and then went in search of fresh orders. The corridors were full of urgent figures clutching important documents. He saw a flight lieutenant whom he recognised as the assistant to the staff officer of an air vice-marshal in Fighter Command, and explained his problem. "Crikey, you ought to be in Conference Room G," the flight lieutenant said. "Something to do with anti-aircraft fields of fire, I believe . . ." But when the Ram found Conference Room G it was occupied by a pack of wing commanders arguing about aviation-fuel stocks.

He thought hard for a couple of minutes, and decided to cut his losses and get back to Kingsmere. The adjutant, however, was not where he had left him. He asked at the reception desk. Nobody knew anything about Kellaway but there was an urgent message waiting for Squadron Leader Ramsay: call extension 7171 immediately.

The Ram dialled the number and got a group captain called Blakey. "Ramsey, where the hell have you been?" he asked. "You've missed two crucial meetings already. See me before you go. I'll try and brief you. Oh for Christ's sake *shut up*," he said as another telephone shrilled.

Inevitably, Blakey was no longer in his office when the Ram got there. The day continued like that. By six o'clock, when he was almost too tired to be angry, he came across Group Captain Matthews again. "You can forget about that Anglo-Polish glossary," Matthews said wearily. "It's all been changed. I don't know what the new plan is yet. If I were you I'd get myself a room in a hotel."

"I must find Group Captain Blakey first, sir. He said –"

"Blakey? Blakey's gone to France."

Matthews hurried off. The Ram leaned against a wall and watched the endless tide of Air Ministry staff and RAF personnel flow past. Quite soon, Flight Lieutenant Kellaway flowed with it, chatting to a young WAAF. "Ah, there you are, sir!" he said. "I've been looking all over . . . These are for you." He held out a bundle of dun-coloured files, tied with green ribbon.

"What's that?"

"I wasn't told. The usual bumf, I expect."

"I've seen enough bumf today. Come on, adj, I'm starving. We're going to find a hotel."

They found a hotel and had dinner. During coffee a message came from Air Ministry ordering the Ram to report at 11 p.m. to receive a telephone call from Group Captain Blakey. At 11.15 he was sitting in Blakey's office when the call came through. Blakey was in Paris and the line was bad. The Ram strained to make sense of the cracklings and distortions. The only words he could be sure of came at the very end. "Got all that?" Blakey demanded. "No!" the Ram shouted. Blakey hung up.

The Ram went back to his hotel, went to bed, and awoke at 3

a.m., his brain urgent with anxiety. He considered telephoning Air Ministry for orders. No, no, no: waste of time. He thought of telephoning Kingsmere. But what could they tell him? Or he, them? No, no, no. He walked around the room and saw the bundle of files on the dressing-table. He undid the green ribbon. Reports and records of the squadron's performance at various summer training camps and exercises: air-to-air gunnery, cross-country navigation, tactics of air fighting, formation flying . . .

Ten minutes later he went next door and roused the adjutant. "Get dressed," he said. "We're going back to Kingsmere."

He was waiting behind the wheel when Kellaway hurried out of the hotel, unshaven and sticky-eyed. The Ram had the car moving before the door was shut, and he had it up to sixty before they reached the first corner. Kellaway blinked as the intersection hurtled towards them, and he fumbled for the leather grab-strap as the tyres hammered over some tramlines. "Is there a flap on?" he asked, his voice shaking.

"Not yet," the Ram said. "But there soon will be."

He heaved the bundle of files up from between his feet and dumped it in Kellaway's lap. "My squadron has degenerated into shit condition, adj," he said, and clenched his teeth as the car bucked over a stretch of lumpy road repairs. "The *Luftwaffe* is fighting fit while my lot are fit to drop. They're all cretins."

"Surely not all, sir." Kellaway was struggling to untie the green ribbon.

"No, not all. Some of them are imbeciles, and one or two are mental junkyards. Pilot Officer Cox, for instance. Just look at Cox's score on that elementary navigation test. Just look at it."

"Shocking weather that day," Kellaway said, still picking at a knot. "Wind and rain and –"

"Ah! Goering's promised not to attack unless it's nice upstairs, has he?" The Ram bullied the gearbox into submission as he took a sharp bend. "That's good news for Pilot Officer Cattermole then, because it seems he's utterly incapable of maintaining formation in anything stronger than a mild breeze."

"I seem to remember young Cattermole wasn't terribly well that day, sir," Kellaway said. "Nasty head-cold."

"Yes? And what was Flying Officer Stickwell suffering from when he missed the towed target three days in a row? Scarlet

44

fever? Beri-beri? St Vitus' Dance? Not that Pilot Officer Miller did any better with the fixed target, did he? Somewhere in that bumf you'll find a fascinating account of how Miller and his Hurricane slaughtered several innocent sandbanks but mercifully spared the target. What's Miller's problem, adj? Can't he fly and shoot at the same time? Or was his mother frightened by a bunker?"

Kellaway tried to think of an excuse for Miller and couldn't. "The chaps did do rather well in the aircraft-recognition competition," he said.

"Yes, they did, didn't they? Amazingly well. Came fifth out of nine. By their standards that's bloody brilliant. I expect they all thought they deserved DSO's for that. They only failed to recognise four aircraft in ten. Quite a triumph. Makes you proud to be British."

Kellaway gave up: the knot was unpickable. "It's been rather a difficult summer," he said.

"Don't worry, adj, I've got some solutions lined up. All those jokers will get the boot. You watch me shake the tree, adj. See the rotten apples fall."

Even with the Ram's heavy foot on the accelerator it took them an hour to get clear of London. They made good time up the old Roman road to Colchester and then got stuck behind a succession of milk-trucks and, after them, an army convoy, trundling field-guns at a sedate thirty miles an hour. The sun was high enough to be dazzling when they turned east at Chelmsford. Now the roads were narrower, with fewer passing-places, and the Ram's foot jumped repeatedly from accelerator to brake. Kellaway's arm ached from gripping the grab-strap. His stomach groused loudly about hunger made worse by continuous nervous tension. At last Kingsmere aerodrome came in sight. The RAF policeman saluted and raised the barrier, and the Ram sprayed gravel as he parked outside the officers' mess. It was just six o'clock.

Kellaway got out, and massaged his numbed backside. The sunshine was pleasantly warm and blessedly silent. "Breakfast," he said. It sounded like a one-word history of Western civilisation.

"Bugger breakfast," the Ram said. "You take 'A' flight, I'll take 'B'. I want them on parade in ten minutes, maximum." He strode off.

Kellaway had the easier task: only two members of 'A' flight were in their rooms, Fanny Barton and Dicky Starr. As the pilots assembled, yawning and doing up tunic buttons, he said: "I'm afraid there's no sign of Stickwell, Cattermole, Patterson or Cox, sir."

The Ram stared. His eyes had widened slightly, his nostrils were tight, his whole face seemed stretched. He turned away. "I don't care a damn if you all get killed tomorrow," he said.

That woke them up.

"I do care if this squadron fails to play its full part in the air defence of Great Britain," he said. "I care if these scarce and valuable Hurricane fighters get shot down. I care *very much* if the German bomber fleets not only destroy these Hurricanes but also proceed to destroy their targets, killing God-knows-how-many civilians who at this very moment are gullible enough to put their pathetic faith in your supposed skill and determination when, if they knew what I know, they'd realise you probably couldn't hit a Zeppelin even if you could see one, which is unlikely, because according to these reports, nine out of ten of you can't piss against a wall without filling your left boots to overflowing!"

He paused for breath. The pilots frowned, or gazed at the ground. The adjutant sucked his teeth and thought about bacon.

"This squadron is incompetent," the Ram said. "It cannot fly straight, it cannot navigate efficiently, it does not know its battle tactics, and its aerial gunnery is a waste of good bullets. You are not fighter pilots. You are a cheap, dishonest imitation of fighter pilots. This state of affairs will change, with effect from now. You will do one of two things extremely rapidly: you will get better, or you will get out. That is not a threat . . ."

The adjutant cocked his head. He thought he had heard the sound of horses' hooves.

". . . nor is it a warning. That is a statement of fact. I estimate that within seven days half of you will have been chopped. Always assuming the *Luftwaffe* does not get here first and perform the eliminating for me . . ."

The adjutant strolled to one side and listened. Yes, definitely horses' hooves. Odd.

". . . which I can tell you seems more and more likely with every passing hour. You can also take it from me –"

Two large and shaggy farm-horses cantered around the corner, their broad hooves kicking up pebbles. Cattermole and Stickwell rode one, Patterson and Cox the other. The horses wore rope bridles, with the pilots' neck-ties fastened to them as reins. Cattermole whooped, huskily: he had been whooping a lot; it kept the horse going. Patterson saw the pilots and waved. "You're saved!" he shouted. "The cavalry's here!" Then he saw the Ram. "Oh my Christ," he muttered.

An RAF police corporal came after them on a bicycle, pedalling hard. The horses circled the group of pilots, gradually losing speed. The corporal halted, dismounted, saluted. "Very sorry, sir," he said, breathing fast. "Couldn't stop them, sir. Jumped the barrier, sir. Broke the pole, sir."

The Ram nodded.

"Stop, blast you, stop," Cox said bitterly to his horse. The animals were down to a trot. "Let me off, damn it."

"Cowboys," the Ram said bleakly.

Stickwell slid backwards over his horse's rump and fell to the ground. It was a long way to fall and he was slow to get up. "God, I'm thirsty," he moaned, and realised that it was the wrong thing to say.

"Cowboys," the Ram repeated. "Heading for the last round-up, no doubt."

The horses finally stopped. Patterson and Cox got off. As Cattermole tried to dismount, his horse shook itself and Cattermole went sprawling on his hands and knees. All four men looked bleary, hung-over and stained.

"You seem to have had a busy night," the Ram said. "You seem a trifle fatigued. We can't have that. I know just the thing to buck you up. Squadron battle climb. Take off in twenty minutes." He grinned, briefly, stretching his mouth like someone testing a rubber band, and walked away. Kellaway went with him. 'B' flight waited a moment to let them get ahead and then followed.

Fanny Barton went over to Cattermole, still on his hands and knees, and kicked him. "Get bloody up," he said. "Where the hell have you been?"

"It wasn't my fault, Fanny," Mother Cox told him. "I've been trying to get them home for hours. Honestly."

"Crawler," Patterson said.

Cattermole heaved himself up. "What's going on, Fanny?" he asked. "Has Hitler declared war?"

"No. But the Ram has, and he's looking for pilots to chop, so you four must be top of his list, wouldn't you say? What the blue blazes have you been up to?"

Stickwell scratched his head, and discovered some straw. "Car broke down," he said.

"Want to buy a nice horse?" Cattermole inquired.

Barton kicked him again, but Cattermole was already so bruised by events that he merely blinked. "Corporal, put those horses somewhere safe," Barton ordered. He gave Cattermole an angry push. "Go and soak your heads, all of you," he said.

"I can't possibly fly," Stickwell announced, "not in my condition."

"Then get up there and crash," Barton told him. "And make a bloody good job of it." He shoved Stickwell, who collided with Patterson. "Run!" he shouted. They began a shambling trot, which got faster as Barton threw stones at them.

For fifty yards behind the Hurricanes the grass was flattened by the wash from their propellers.

Hornet squadron, twelve-strong, was drawn up in the arrowhead formation that the Ram favoured for battle climb. Each section of three aircraft formed a V. The Ram, being squadron leader, was at the point of the leading section. Two of the other sections positioned themselves to right and left so as to form a larger V, while the fourth section was tucked in behind. Kingsmere had no runways. Once the squadron was formed-up and heading into the wind it was ready for take-off.

The Ram glanced left and right to make sure everyone was watching him. The control tower had given them clearance. No Battles were wandering in or out of the aerodrome. He checked his watch: nineteen minutes since he gave the order. Not bad. The ground crews had been on duty already, so warming-up the planes had been quite straightforward; nevertheless the pilots must have got themselves kitted out and plugged-in and taxied-out and formed-up in double-quick time. Showed what they could do when they took their fingers out. He released his brakes and eased the throttle open.

Standing on the edge of the field, Kellaway and Dicky Starr watched the squadron start to roll. Dicky was reserve pilot that day; and when the trembling thunder of engines suddenly magnified to an aggressive, ear-battering bellow, he couldn't keep still. He walked and skipped a few paces, his fists clenched in encouragement. The Hurricanes bounced and rocked as they gained speed; stray leaves and bits of paper and old grass cuttings got hurled into the air. When the Hurricanes' tails came up, smoothly and quickly, it was as if large weights had slipped off them. Simultaneously the engine-notes altered, booming bigger and harder now that the wings were cutting the air more cleanly. Dicky Starr watched, and flew with them in his imagination: left hand on the throttle (keep her speed up), right hand on the control column (keep her nose up), feet hooked into the rudder-pedal stirrups (hold her straight), eyes, ears and backside acutely aware of the shape of the formation all around, of the health of the engine in front, of the racing judder of the wheels beneath.

The Ram's Hurricane detached itself from the ground first. As it skimmed the grass the others lifted themselves. Within seconds their wheels were folding inwards and the squadron was climbing hard. The thunder faded to a soft roar, the roar to a growl. The planes diminished to a bundle of dots, which merged into one large speck and was lost to sight.

"Dicky, d'you know anything about rugger?" Kellaway asked.

"Not much." Starr was cautious. "Damn-all, really. They have scrums and things, don't they? And the ball always bounces the wrong way. Why?"

"The Ram's told me to fix up a game against the Battle boys later on this morning. I'm just wondering —"

"Rugger? Us? Against *them*?"

"Why not?"

"Well . . ." For a moment Starr didn't know where to start. "It's Sunday," he said. "Nobody plays rugger on Sunday."

"Evidently the Ram does. He's already had a word with their CO. His chaps are quite enthusiastic."

"I bet they are. Have you seen them? They're gorillas. They'll murder us, adj."

"Nonsense. They're a jolly decent bunch. Anyway, the Ram

reckons you all need a bit of toughening-up. He thinks you've been having it too easy."

"They'll kill us," Starr said gloomily. "They're maniacs. Anyone who flies a Battle must be loopy. That's how they get picked. If you can think, and feel pain, they won't have you." He brightened up. "Anyway, we're bound to get put on readiness again, so rugger's out of the question, isn't it?"

"Wrong, old boy. The controller says we're released to forty-minute availability until twelve-noon. And there's something else, too. The Ram wants slit-trenches dug. Somewhere near dispersal, he says, so you can all dive into them if Jerry suddenly pays a visit. Right here would do, I suppose."

Starr whacked his heel against the turf and failed to make a dent. "Pure concrete," he said. "We'll break our necks."

"I'd better get the digging started." Kellaway went in search of the NCO's.

The purpose of a battle climb was to lift the squadron to combat height in the minimum time. It was hard work for men and machines, the engines slogging away to win a couple of thousand feet every minute, the pilots having to hold tight formation through cloud and air pockets and a change of atmosphere equivalent to climbing the Alps in a quarter of an hour. There was no chance to relax: everything and everyone toiled flat-out. It was the Ram's favourite manoeuvre.

"Jester Leader to Red Three: close up, damn you," he ordered for the third time.

Stickwell was Red Three. His wingtip was ten feet from the Ram's wingtip. He cut the gap to five feet and concentrated grimly on holding position. His stomach kept jumping as if someone were poking it with a pencil, and his mouth tasted stiff and sour; also his skull seemed to be pressing down on his eyeballs. He knew it was only a matter of time before he was sick.

At last the Ram looked away from him. *Just you wait, Flying Officer Stickwell*, the Ram said to himself. *I'll teach you to get blotto. I'll spread your guts all over this sky before I'm through.* He opened his transmission switch. "Jester Leader to Red Two: where the hell d'you think you're going?" he said.

Cattermole was Red Two. He had already been sick: the effect of too much pure oxygen on a system thoroughly abused by alcohol and horse-riding. Oxygen was a well-known hangover cure for fighter pilots but on this occasion, although it had cleared his head, it had also emptied his stomach. He didn't mind being sick but the vomit had splashed onto his gloves and made them slippery. Whenever he tried to wipe them clean, he wandered out of formation. "Sorry, Leader," he said, and drifted back.

You'll be sorry when we get back, all right, the Ram thought. *You won't even stay for lunch, my lad.* He checked on Blue Section. "Tighten up, Blue Leader," he said. "Stop dawdling." Flip Moran brought his section forward by half a length, and the Ram put a mental question-mark beside Blue Two. Miller. Moke Miller. Always larking about. Not a bad pilot but harebrained, no strength of character. It took more than flying ability to be a fighter pilot. In *this* squadron, anyway . . .

At seventeen thousand feet they levelled out and gained speed until they were cruising at about two hundred miles an hour. The last layer of cloud was a mile below them. They seemed to be hanging in a vast blue dome.

"Tighten up, everyone," the Ram said. "Stop wasting space."

The squadron inched together. Pip Patterson, flying as Yellow Three, had to watch his section leader on his right and also keep an eye on Red Two, ahead to his left. Both planes were so close he could count the rivets in the cockpit panels. Fanny Barton was Yellow Leader and he kept a straight enough course, but Moggy Cattermole was forever straying sideways. Patterson's hands were sweating. His ears buzzed and popped; they didn't like battle climbs, and every time they popped, a shower of tiny specks flickered across his eyes. He hated Moggy Cattermole's bad flying. If Moggy drifted out any further, Pip would have to fall back to miss him. Green Section was just behind. Pip had once seen the tailplane of a Hurricane after it had been chewed up by a propeller. It was a mess. The propeller hadn't been much good for anything, either. How the hell did you get down – three miles down – with a smashed rudder? Or a bust prop? Or – if bloody Moggy hit you and knocked you back into Blue Two – with both?

"Sections line astern," the Ram announced. "Flights echelon port. Go!"

He held his position and watched closely for blunders. Green

Section swung away to its left, clearing the air behind him. Red Two dropped into the space behind his tail, Red Three fell in behind Red Two. Yellow Section followed, each aircraft keeping slightly below the one in front in order to miss its wash. Now 'A' flight was in line astern and completely invisible to the Ram. He studied 'B' flight. They were almost in formation, weaving snake-like as an adjustment worked its way through, then settling into a straight line. Not bad, not bad at all. "Shambles," he told them. "Sloppy, scruffy, slow. Wake up! Squadron in vic. Sections astern. Go!" The section wingmen swung out, reformed vics, closed up. He looked across at the twin arrowheads of 'B' flight. "Wake me when you've finished," he said. "And remind me to give you something for your arthritis. Squadron in vic, sections echelon starboard. Go!"

The Ram drilled his squadron intensively for the next half-hour, often changing course as he changed formation, sometimes changing altitude too, and always nagging at them to tighten up, sharpen up, get a move on. It was relentlessly demanding work, but the knowledge that a single misunderstanding could mean a collision completely overcame fatigue; at the end even Cattermole felt clearheaded.

"We can't have a battle climb without a battle," the Ram announced. "Lacking enemy aircraft, we shall make do with cloud formations, which even you should be able to hit." He led the squadron down in a series of plunging power-dives, each culminating in a mock-attack that led to a steep, turning climb and a rapid change of formation to set up the next power-dive. They finished within sight of the airfield. The Ram put them into sections line astern and took them into the circuit.

All the way down he had been thinking about whom to chop. Cattermole, obviously. And Stickwell, of course. Cox? Yes, Cox had asked for it. Miller, too. That made four. Chopping four ought to shake up the rest more than somewhat, he thought.

Halfway around the circuit. Speed: 160 and falling. Undercarriage selector lever to "down". Usual hydraulic whining. Double clunk as the wheels lock. Green light on. All correct.

The big question was: when to chop? Sooner the better, obviously. But with the international situation so tricky the squadron couldn't be left below strength. Not even for a day.

Speed: 135 and falling. Height: seven hundred feet. Slide the hood open and lock it. Nice bit of breeze. Downwind leg. Turn to port. Nice view of the rest of the squadron all strung out, descending. Good plane, the Hurricane. Tough, fast, chunky. And lethal. Blast any bloody Heinkel or Junkers to hell and gone in ten seconds. Five, even. Flaps down. Final approach.

Well, they would all play in this game of rugger, anyway, chopped or not. Do them good. Got to be fit to fight.

Over the barbed wire. Usual crowd waiting to watch the squadron land: groundcrew, fire tender, bloodwagon. And the adjutant, standing over there at the side all on his own. Funny how you could recognise people by the way they stood ...

Maybe four was too many. Three might do. Give Cox another chance. Yes.

Down. Down. Gently down. All power off ... now! Up comes the nose and onward she floats, sinking, sinking, until bump, rumble and squeak, she touches the ground and runs.

Yes, chop three. If not today at least tomorrow. But why not send for replacements now, immediately? Of course, good idea! They might even arrive tonight, with luck. Why not indeed? Yes, definitely. Got to get the old adj cracking on that straight away. Where was the old adj?

The Ram let the Hurricane run off most of its speed, and then used the brakes to swing the nose from side to side until he found him. Kellaway was still standing on his own, near the perimeter fence. The Ram turned towards him and gave the engine a hint of throttle. As long as the massive, uprearing nose of the Hurricane blotted out the adjutant's figure, he knew that he was heading the right way. The Ram taxied briskly across the grass, rehearsing in his mind the orders that would send the adjutant hurrying to the telephone: *Listen, I've decided to chop three of these useless buggers and I want you to –*

With a jolt that made his teeth click, the Hurricane's wheels hit a slit-trench and the plane tripped itself up. The nose dug hard into the turf, its momentum hoisted the fuselage like a heavy flagpole, and the Ram found himself hanging in his straps, looking down the cowling at fragments of propeller sticking out of the grass.

He swore, savagely. He was not hurt, was not even stunned; but he was acutely aware of how foolish he must look. The rest of the squadron was coming in to land. It was imperative that he get out of this humiliating position at once. The last thing he wanted was to be rescued, manhandled to safety by the men he commanded. He could hear people shouting. There was no time to lose.

He disconnected the radio and oxygen leads, released his safety-straps, and got his feet onto the instrument panel. After that it was a matter of swinging his legs over the side and dropping to the ground.

The radio lead was a damn nuisance. It kept knocking him in the face. He flung it away but it bounced back and hit him in the eye.

A patient man would have ignored it, or tied it to something. The Ram grabbed it and hung from it. He had manoeuvred all of his body except an arm and a foot outside the cockpit, when the radio lead popped out of its socket. The Ram's free hand scrabbled uselessly at the Perspex canopy.

It was a drop of only ten feet; but the Ram was a heavy man in full flying-kit plus parachute, and he landed on the back of his head. The impact snapped the third and fourth cervical vertebrae.

Before he fell, groundcrew were running towards him with ladders. Hector Ramsay could never wait. It was the death of him.

The adjutant was on the telephone when Fanny Barton came into his office.

"Well, see if you can give me a couple of minutes with him, would you?" he said. He covered the mouthpiece and whispered: "Air Ministry. Frightfully busy. Flap on." Fanny sat on the edge of the desk. He was still in flying overalls and boots.

"Ah, good morning, sir," Kellaway said. "It's about the CO, Squadron Leader Ramsay . . . I'm afraid he's dead, sir. A flying accident. He fell out of his Hurricane . . ." Kellaway swung his feet onto the desk and listened to the voice from Air Ministry. "Oh no, nothing wrong with his parachute, sir. You needn't . . ." He listened some more, picking his teeth with a matchstick. "Well, to be strictly accurate, sir, he wasn't technically airborne at the time . . ." Kellaway listened, and rolled his eyes at Barton. "Put that way, sir," he said, "you're right, it wasn't a flying accident at all . . . Mmm . . ." Kellaway heaved a sigh. "Damned if I know *what* I'd call it, sir. But call it what you will, it's still a broken neck, isn't it, and . . ."

Barton heard angry words being spoken. Eventually Kellaway replaced the telephone. "He wants to know where we think he's going to find another CO on a Sunday morning. Do we think Air Ministry is some kind of domestic employment agency? Would we like half-a-dozen housemaids and a couple of butlers? Don't we realise the balloon is about to go up?"

"Is it?" Barton asked.

Kellaway looked at his watch. "Come on," he said. "The Prime Minister's going to say something on the wireless in ten minutes. By the way, Fanny: you're senior man, so you're in charge of the squadron for the time being."

They walked from the administrative block to the officers' mess. It was a calm, quiet morning. Swallows and housemartins flashed and flickered between the buildings. The bells of Kingsmere church sounded clear but small. Their miniature clamour ended and a single bell began to toll.

"Poor old Ram," Barton said.

"I cancelled the rugger match, by the way."

"Yes, of course . . . It's so peculiar that he turned off and taxied into that trench. I wonder why?"

The adjutant shrugged. "Peculiar things happen. I remember once a chap was sitting on his tractor mowing the aerodrome when a plane taxied past and the wingtip cut his head off. Sheared it off at the neck, clean as you like. Tractor went on, mowing away, and the pilot took off. Didn't know what he'd done. Wouldn't believe it when he landed, thought we were pulling his leg. We had to show him the head. Chap called Blackmore, Nigger Blackmore. He wasn't a nigger, of course; that was just what we called him." They walked in silence for a while. "No reason why a nigger couldn't fly a plane, I suppose," the adjutant remarked. "Stranger things have happened."

"I've just realised," Barton said. "I shall have to appoint someone acting flight commander."

"Yes. And you'll have to write to the Ram's next-of-kin, too."

Barton hadn't thought of that, and he didn't fancy the idea. "What on earth am I going to say?" he asked.

"Tell them he died while leading his squadron in circumstances of unusual hazard," Kellaway said. "Tell them he exhibited a complete disregard for his own personal safety." They went up the steps of the mess.

Nothing much happened at Kingsmere on the rest of the first day of the Second World War. The squadron – like every other unit of the Royal Air Force – was placed on alert. There were a couple of false alarms, but no attack came. The pilots hung about the mess and grew bored. There was a general feeling of relief that at last the decision to fight had been made, but there was no exultation. This was partly because the Ram's death had left them in the lurch: just when they needed some leadership, their leader was no more. Yet nobody mourned him. Nobody really missed him. It was as if his shingles had recurred and he had gone back to hospital in Torquay, instead of into the station mortuary.

Fanny Barton put Sticky Stickwell in command of 'A' flight and made Pip Patterson Yellow Leader. It was the obvious thing to do: Stickwell had more flying time than the others. All the same, Barton worried about it. He worried about the lack of action, too. Every hour he telephoned Group operations room.

"Still no plots on the table, old boy," Group said.

"Not much of a war, is it? My chaps are bored rigid."

"Give the Hun a chance. It's a long way from Germany, you know. Anyone at your end doing the *Sunday Times* crossword, by any chance?"

"They're all outside, playing cricket."

"Pity. Three down's got me really stumped."

Barton joined Flip Moran, who was leaning out of a window. "Bad news," Barton told him. "Group ops are having trouble with the crossword."

Moran grunted. Together they watched as Fitz Fitzgerald, clumsy in flying-boots, ran up and lobbed a tennisball at Moke Miller, who flailed and missed.

"I keep thinking I ought to be doing something," Barton said.

"You are. You're waiting."

"I mean, as squadron commander."

"You're in charge of the waiting." Moran's Ulster accent was rich and slow, and touched with mockery. "That's a heavy responsibility, Fanny. It's not everyone could make a success of it."

Fitz bowled again. This time Moke slashed at the ball and sliced it straight at Pip Patterson, who was standing drowsing in the warmth. He dropped the catch.

"I wonder what sort of a show we'll put up," Fanny said. "I mean, we're not exactly crack flyers, are we?"

"If you want my opinion," Moran said, "I expect the entire squadron to be shot down and killed within thirty seconds of encountering the enemy. Death will be instantaneous, so there will be no unnecessary suffering. Does that reassure you?"

"Not really." Barton scratched his head on the windowframe. "If we're all killed, who'll write up the squadron log?"

"You're right. I'd better stay behind."

"You wouldn't mind, Flip?"

"Not at all. How d'you spell 'massacre,' by the way?"

"Two q's and a small f."

"Ah. And there was me thinking it had a p in it. What a comfort it is to have an educated commanding officer."

Towards the end of the afternoon an elderly, jovial wing commander arrived. He was making a tour of all Fighter Command bases, lecturing on the German bomber threat. Hitler, he told the pilots, was expected to launch an aerial knock-out blow against England. This meant against London, since the nearest German airfields were three or four hundred miles away and therefore out of range of the rest of England, but in any case London was so exposed and vulnerable that it was the obvious target. The Air Staff reckoned that Germany had at least sixteen hundred long-range bombers available and that this force (if they all got through) could drop about seven hundred tons of bombs on the capital every day for a fortnight. Now that was an awful lot of bombs, the wing commander pointed out, and just to give some idea of what it would mean in human terms, calculations had shown that in the first six months, this scale of bomber attack would kill six hundred thousand people and injure twice that number, not to mention the damage to buildings and things, which would be colossal, of course. "So you see why we're all depending on you chaps," he said, smiling warmly.

Afterwards, he asked if there were any questions.

Moggy Cattermole raised his hand. "Have you any advice, sir," he said, "on the best way to tackle the Hun?" He spoke in a mock-heroic tone of voice, and Fanny Barton flashed him a warning look, but the wing commander was only too willing to answer.

"A leopard doesn't change his spots," he said. "Your typical German was a bully and a brute in the Great War, and he's a bully and a brute now. Like all bullies, he's a coward at heart." Flip Moran shut his eyes. "So take the fight to him," the wing commander urged. "Go in with all guns blazing, that's what we used to do. You'll find the average Hun hasn't much taste for hot lead."

"Thank you, sir," said Moggy. "Hot lead," he whispered loudly, "that's the stuff to give 'em."

The adjutant led their visitor away for a drink, but there was to be no alcohol for the squadron as long as daylight lasted. The Group controller kept them at readiness until dusk, and then released them with a warning to be available again at dawn. It had been a long day. For Cattermole, Stickwell, Patterson and Cox it had been two long days and a long night. "Feel like a beer at the Squirt?" Stickwell asked, yawning. The Squirt was their local pub, The Fountain. Cox shook his head. Patterson thought about it. Cattermole said: "Not if it means walking there and back. D'you know, I think I might get an early night for once."

Nobody else wanted to go to the Squirt; for one thing, it had just started to rain. Cattermole went off to bed. The other three hung about for a while, too tired to make up their minds, and then wandered off to bed as well.

An hour later an airman banged on their doors and announced that the CO wanted them in his office immediately. They were still groggy with sleep when they got there. Barton was sitting at his desk. The adjutant stood behind him. "For God's sake, Fanny," Stickwell grumbled, slumping into a chair. "Can't a chap ever get a decent night's rest?"

"Stand up," Barton ordered sharply.

"Oh, don't be so bloody officious," Stickwell muttered, and did not move.

"Flying Officer Stickwell," Barton said, "I have given you an order."

At once Pip Patterson took his hands out of his pockets. The atmosphere, he noticed, was cold and hard. The adjutant was watching very carefully, and Fanny Barton had a look on his face

58

that said *You tread on my toe and I'll break both your legs*.
"Sticky, you idiot, get up," Pip whispered.

"Bollocks," Stickwell said, with all the force and intelligence of
a three-year-old child. He was still stupid with sleep.

"Come on, Sticky," Mother Cox said irritably. "Do as he says."

"Why should I? I can hear just as well sitting down, in fact I can
hear a damn sight better – Hey!" Stickwell shouted as Cattermole
grabbed him and yanked him upright. The chair fell over.

"Two reasons," Moggy said. "One: he's the CO. Two: you're on
active service."

"All right! let go my hair."

"And three," Pip said righteously, "if we stand, you stand."

"Okay, for Christ's sake!" Stickwell glared at Fanny Barton.
"I'm up. We're all up. What d'you want?"

Barton half-closed one eye and looked at him.

Stickwell straightened his rumpled tunic, rubbed his left elbow,
and smoothed back his hair. Nobody spoke. He eased his collar
and did up a stray button. At last he met Barton's gaze. "What
d'you want, sir?" he asked.

Barton opened the half-closed eye. "I want you to take those
horses back where you found them," he said. "And I want you to
do it now."

Rain pattered against the window.

"We'll never find that field again, sir," Cox said gloomily. "Not
in the middle of the night."

"Oh yes you will. You are commissioned officers in a squadron
of Fighter Command in the Royal Air Force. You are not a bunch
of hooligans living off the land and stealing whatever you fancy.
You'll find the horses loaded on a lorry at the main gate. That's
all."

When they had left, the adjutant said: "Well done, old chap.
Jolly well done."

Fanny Barton was still staring at the door. "Somewhat heavy-
handed," he said.

"Not a bit."

"It felt sort of . . . What did Sticky say? Officious."

"Utter rubbish. You had no choice."

Barton sucked in a deep breath, held it, and let it out in a snort

59

of dissatisfaction. "Why do they have to behave like such bloody lunatics, uncle?"

"Oh well . . . They're all a bit mad, you know. They wouldn't do it unless there was a damn good chance of getting killed, would they? So they can't be completely normal. They're not what you'd call model citizens, any of them. More like vandals, I suppose. They're just itching to be turned loose with an eight-gun Hurricane on some lumbering great bomber. I mean, that's your average fighter pilot's attitude, isn't it? Show him something, anything really, and deep down inside, his first reaction is: What sort of a mess could I make of that with a couple of three-second bursts? Herd of cows, doubledecker bus, garden party – makes no difference what it is, that's the thought in the back of his mind. Not surprising, really. I've often thought it's a damn good job they're in the RAF, otherwise they'd all be out there blowing up banks."

"You really think most fighter pilots are a bit mad?" Fanny Barton asked.

"All the ones I've known." Kellaway laughed as he remembered. "We had a chap once. He used to fly upside-down between the Lines at fifty feet, just to show them what he thought of them."

"Show who?"

"Both sides. Everyone was firing at him, anyway. The French always fired at any plane they saw, as a matter of policy. He used to say it was easier to dodge the stuff when you were upside-down, because you could see it coming up at you."

"What happened to him?"

"Good question. What *did* happen to him? I know they never shot him down, not when he was playing silly-buggers . . ." Kellaway screwed his face up in an effort of memory. "I think one day he just didn't come back, that's all." He strolled over to the window and examined the soaking night. He flinched as a gust flung rain at the glass. "Not an uncommon state of affairs, of course."

"What about you, uncle? Were you a bit mad, too?"

"Ah, well . . ." The adjutant smiled roguishly. "I suppose I must have been. I was bloody lucky, I can tell you that."

"And me? I'm a fighter pilot. How mad am I?"

The question made Kellaway slightly nervous, and he took his time considering it, running a fingernail back and forth along his lower lip. "Let's put it this way, Fanny," he said. "My guess is,

60

when it comes to the push, you'll probably find that you're a good deal madder than you think you are. Anyway, you'll know soon enough, won't you?"

Nothing exciting happened the next day. All morning, the Group controller kept them on fifteen-minute readiness. By lunchtime they were dulled with tedium; they had stopped wearing their flying overalls and boots, because it was too hot; the prospect of the afternoon stretched drearily and endlessly before them, probably even hotter and more tedious. There was a limit to the number of lectures the pilots could be expected to listen to, and Barton had already used up the most interesting ones – emergency landing and ditching procedures; enemy aircraft recognition; how to bale out; ranks and badges of the German Air Force – so he was glad to see a despatch-rider turn up with an urgent package from Air Ministry.

It contained two dozen duplicated documents, each numbered and stamped in red CLASSIFIED SECRET. They were titled *Useful Polish Terms and Phrases for British Aircrew*. With the package came a memorandum, signed by Air Commodore Bletchley, to the effect that each pilot must memorise these terms and phrases within twenty-four hours. It was essential, he said, that not only the contents but also the very existence of this material remain secret.

Fanny distributed them, got each man to sign for his copy, and gave the signed list (with his own countersignature as confirmation) to the despatch-rider, who roared off to London.

For a brief and rare moment, the only sound to be heard in the mess was the whisper of turning pages.

"*Varmvatten*," said Flip Moran, "is Polish for 'hot water.' "

"They should know," Stickwell said. "They're in it."

"*Vad ar det som har hant?* means 'What's going on?' " Mother Cox said.

"And crash-bang-wallop means the *Luftwaffe* has just blown up the railway station," Cattermole remarked. He lay slumped in an armchair, drowsy after too much lunch, his copy lying unopened on his stomach.

"What a cockeyed country," Billy Starr said. "They eat something called *kottbullar med lingon*. Meatballs with cowberries." He made a face. "*Cowberries*."

"I like it," said Moke Miller. "Or as we say in Warsaw: *Jag tycker om det.*"

"You've got until tomorrow to learn that lot," Fanny said. "I suggest you test each other. Okay? Right. I'm going to phone Group." He went out.

Moggy Cattermole took his copy by the corner and dropped it into the waste basket. "Bumf," he said, and shut his eyes.

"Hey, steady on, Moggy," Billy Starr said. "That stuff's secret."

"The Air Ministry knows no secrets," Moggy murmured.

His action produced a few smiles, but only a few; Cattermole was not universally popular. He was bigger and heavier than anyone else, and when he was bored he had a habit of strolling about the mess, snatching newspapers and magazines which he then redistributed arbitrarily, giving the gardening page to someone who had been deep in the football results, and so on. Once, back in the early summer, a member of 'B' flight by the name of Gordon – nicknamed "Flash" because he was so reserved – had seen Moggy coming and had taken a firm grip of his *Daily Express*. A friendly struggle led to a friendly fight, and within a minute Flash Gordon's nose was bent and his *Express* was spattered with blood. It was an accident; but as Flip Moran remarked, so was the *Titanic*. "What you must remember," Flip said, "is that nine-tenths of Cattermole's charm lies beneath the surface." Many agreed.

"Please yourself, Moggy," Billy Starr said. "Just don't come to me for help when we get to Poland."

"Wouldn't dream of it, old boy." Cattermole's breathing had become slow and regular. "The rest of you, please try not to move your lips when you read," he said. "It makes such a din."

He was asleep when Fanny Barton came back with the news that Group had given permission for one section at a time to carry out flying training, as long as the aircraft were fully armed. "Green section goes first," he said. "Then Blue, Yellow, Red." Before he had finished speaking, Green Section's pilots were reaching for their overalls and boots. The others slouched and watched. Fanny looked at this mixture of eagerness and envy and was overtaken by memories of the schoolroom, of inky drudgery, of the lucky few released to play games while the rest remained trapped. "Keep within five minutes of the aerodrome," he said, and that too raised echoes: *Stay in the school grounds* ... Moggy Cattermole's eyes half-opened as Green section hurried out. "Deserters," he said. "Ships leaving the sinking rat. Gun 'em all down."

Now that everyone had something to look forward to, the afternoon passed more quickly. And there was soon something else to talk about: an intelligence officer had been posted to the squadron.

He was a middleaged flying officer with a domed forehead, horn-rim glasses and a face that seemed designed to show off his false teeth – beaky nose, narrow jaws, wide cheekbones. His name was Skelton, and they were impressed to learn that he was a Cambridge don, called up because he was in the RAF Reserve.

"I've never met a don before," Moke Miller said. "What sort of donning do you do?" Skelton frowned. "What Moke means is," Fitz Fitzgerald explained, "what d'you teach?" Skelton pushed his glasses onto his forehead and compressed his features until his eyes were squeezed shut. "I mean, perhaps dons don't teach anything," Fitz suggested.

"In a sense." Skelton's face relaxed to normalcy. "And in the greater sense, perhaps nobody teaches anything. Teaching is a fraudulent word that should be abolished. There is no teaching, there is only learning. One encourages learning. At least, that is the theory." He let out a snort of mirth and replaced his glasses. "History," he told Moke. "Modern history."

"Really?" Pip Patterson was interested. "I've always wanted to know about history. You can tell us all about it."

"I wish I could. I don't know all about it."

"Oh, come on. You must know *some*thing."

"I know something about the later sixteenth century. Not much."

"Sixteenth . . ." Pip worked it out. "That was the Tudors, right? Queen Elizabeth, Spanish Armada, Sir Francis Drake, etcetera?"

Skelton was shaking his head. "I'm afraid my knowledge of them is very sketchy indeed."

Fanny Barton asked: "What *do* you know about?"

Skelton removed his glasses altogether. Without them, his eyes looked worried. "I know something about the development of radical political thought in Elizabethan England," he said. "But I can speak with confidence only about the influence of the Puritan sects in the northern counties."

"Well, that's something," Fanny said.

63

"And with *absolute* confidence, only about those sects in the latter years of Elizabeth."

"I see."

"It's a very rich field, you know, very rich indeed. The source material is extremely dense. One hardly knows where to begin."

"I usually start with A to K," Cattermole said, "and then look in L to Z later on."

"Moggy, behave yourself," Fanny said.

"Might you be interested in the work of the later Elizabethan north-country Puritan sects?" Skelton asked Pip.

Pip weighed politeness against honesty. Honesty won. "No," he said.

"I think you're wise. The more I study them, the less I like them. Thoroughly unattractive people, in the main. It will be refreshing to get away from them."

At some point in the evening, Skelton was nicknamed "Skull". He was rapidly accepted into the squadron, especially when they found he was good at card tricks. As intelligence officer he could tell them nothing new about the war, but then there seemed to be little or nothing worth knowing. The blackout was working. People were busy sticking lengths of tape across their windows to save themselves from being sliced by flying glass. Evacuation continued: the trains were full of mothers and children. Large barrage balloons floated in silvery fleets above the cities. The newspapers were busy with Poland's heroic resistance, with cavalry fighting tanks while Stukas screamed out of the skies and Warsaw burned; but Poland was more than "abroad", it was foreign, distant, remote, not really European at all, more like a part of Russia. A year ago, Hitler had been groping for Czechoslovakia and the Prime Minister had talked of this as "a quarrel in a far-away country between people of whom we know nothing." Czechoslovakia had gone down. Now it was Poland. As far as the pilots were concerned, it was a distinction without a difference.

Not surprisingly – with Fanny Barton absent, attending to paperwork – the pilots soon lost interest in the Air Ministry's secret Anglo-Polish glossary. Flip Moran went around and quietly gathered up the copies and gave them to the barman to keep. The second day of the war ended as boringly as the first, except for one thing. The BBC announced that a passenger ship, the SS *Athenia*, outward bound from Britain, had been torpedoed and sunk in the Atlantic with heavy loss of life, including many children.

That was nasty. That was a damn sight closer to home than Warsaw. The Navy had better get its finger out and do something about those bloody U-boats. Everyone was agreed on that. Group released the squadron at dusk, just in time to get over to the Squirt for a beer.

While he was shaving, Fanny Barton realised that this was now his third day as squadron commander. He wondered why Air Ministry was taking so long to replace the Ram. The thought drifted into his head that maybe they were waiting and watching to see what sort of a job he made of it. If he made a good job, maybe they would let him keep the squadron permanently.

The idea excited and worried him. That face in the mirror looked intelligent and disciplined, but was it old enough? Strong enough? Hard enough? He bared his teeth at himself to see how brave and dashing he looked. Not very. It would certainly be gratifying to be a fullblown squadron leader; thrilling, in fact; on the other hand leading a whole squadron, taking command of a dozen Hurricanes, telling them where to go and what to do, and if he got it wrong then men got blown up, shot down, killed – that was a hell of a responsibility.

Hell of a responsibility.

After breakfast he called a meeting of Flip Moran, Kellaway and Skull.

"I've talked to Group again," he said. "I told them we can't go on sitting around here waiting to be scrambled from dawn to dusk, it's bad for the chaps, they're getting thoroughly browned-off. Well – surprise, surprise, Group agrees. I think they've been given the same treatment by other squadrons. Anyway, this is the new deal: one flight released, the other flight on twenty-minute readiness, starting now."

"What is twenty-minute readiness, exactly?" Skull asked. Flip looked sideways at him. "My dear fellow," Skull said sharply, "if I am to be an effective intelligence officer I need to understand these terms."

"Didn't anybody ever tell you?" Flip said.

"Once, a very long time ago. No doubt the system has been changed since then."

"We're either 'released' or 'available,'" Fanny said. "If we're 'released' we can leave the airfield. 'Available' means we stay here. 'Brought to readiness' means we've got to be ready to take off in whatever time the controller says – thirty minutes, twenty, fifteen, it depends how serious he reckons things are. If he knows he's going to want us off in a hurry he puts us on five-minute standby. If it's a hell of a hurry, two-minute standby."

"I see," said Skull. "Thank you."

"And in an extreme emergency," said Flip, "the ground crews have been trained to catapult the aeroplanes into the sky, using powerful lengths of knicker-elastic."

"How resourceful of them," Skull said. "No doubt it creates a most impressive twang."

"If you two want to practise your backchat, find a better time for it," Fanny said. His curtness surprised them. He surprised himself a little, and he rapped on his desk to confirm his authority. "I'm not satisfied with the squadron spirit," he said. "There's something lacking, I'm not sure what, but . . ." He chewed his lip and looked at them. *That was pretty bloody feeble, Barton*, he thought.

Nobody answered. Skull couldn't be expected to comment, and Flip had gone into his shell. The adjutant was lighting his pipe. "Well?" Fanny said.

Kellaway put his head back. He blew a great plume of smoke at the hanging light and made it rock. "The boys are a bit stale, aren't they? Cooped-up too much, no action. Why not give them a spot of recreation? Fitz has that dinghy of his down at the harbour, and . . ." He stopped to take a shred of tobacco off his tongue.

"I don't think they're stale. On the contrary, they're half-baked." Fanny looked at Flip and thought he saw a tinge of hostility in Flip's expression. Again he surprised himself by welcoming this discovery: the act of command provoked tension, and tension could be enjoyable. Well, well. "Right, this is what we'll do. 'A' flight stays at readiness this morning, 'B' flight takes over this afternoon. That gives 'B' flight all morning to get upstairs and learn a thing or two. Work your flight hard, Flip. I'm sure they'll feel all the better for it."

Flip stood. He seemed to have something in his left eye. He rubbed it unhurriedly. "What do you want us to practise?" he asked at last.

"What do you need to practise?" Fanny gave him five seconds to answer, and said, "It's up to you, chum. Find their weaknesses and get rid of them. Okay?"

On his way out, Flip paused. "You haven't forgotten the Polish phrasebook," he said. All expression was carefully ironed out of his voice.

"No."

"Is there to be an examination?"

"Certainly. I test my lot this morning, you test yours this afternoon."

"Ah." Flip nodded several times, and gently closed the door behind him.

Fanny chewed on a pencil, examined the battered end, looked at the adjutant. "Not exactly jumping for joy, is he?" he said.

Kellaway sat comfortably, legs crossed, arms folded, pipe drawing nicely. "Nose out of joint," he said.

"That's damn silly. He knew I was senior flight commander. What did he expect?"

Kellaway nodded. "Funny chap, young Flip. Too much self-control, maybe. He never allows himself to let rip, does he? Lots of ambition steaming away under the surface, I sometimes think."

Fanny sniffed. "If he has any ambition to remain a flight commander he'd better buck his ideas up, that's all."

"Should I know what all this is about?" Skull enquired.

"Oh . . . nothing serious." Fanny got up and strolled about the room, scuffing the linoleum. "Some of the fellows don't seem to approve of me as boss of this outfit. Sticky wouldn't say a word to me all day yesterday. Moggy won't miss a chance to make trouble, either."

"Nothing new there," Kellaway observed.

"And Mother Cox keeps looking at me as if I might bite his head off."

"Mother's chop-happy," Kellaway said. Skull raised one eyebrow. "Scared of the sack," Kellaway explained.

"Perhaps if you were to reassure everybody on that score," Skull suggested.

"No fear," Fanny said. He jumped, grabbed a roof-beam, and hung easily, arms half-bent. "If someone's no good, I'm going to throw him out." He began doing slow pull-ups. "I'm not here to make the blighters happy," he added.

"I used to be able to do that, once," Kellaway said wistfully.

"Some hundred thousand years ago we could all do it quite expertly," said Skull.

Fanny dropped to the floor and dusted his hands. "Uncle, can you look after this Polish test? Don't ask them everything, just the basic stuff."

"Sorry, old boy. I've got to attend the inquiry." Fanny looked blank. The adjutant said: "You know, about what happened to the Ram. Air Ministry inquiry. Starts at ten in the lecture room."

"Oh." Fanny had completely forgotten. "Of course. Well, you'd better do it then, Skull."

"Actually, Skull ought to be there too," Kellaway said. "I'm attending as a witness, you see, so we need someone to represent the squadron, and obviously you can't go in case of a scramble."

"Blast. No, I suppose you're right. Hell. I'll just have to test them myself, then. What a bind."

"Oblige me with a little information about the Ram," Skull said.

"Fanny's predecessor," the adjutant said. "Fell out of his Hurricane and broke his neck."

"Goodness." This bald statement quite startled Skull. "How tragic."

"These things happen."

"I know, but . . . It must have been a terrible blow."

"Not really." Kellaway tapped out his pipe. "More of a snap than a blow. I doubt if he felt a thing."

"They're not going to like swotting up all that Polish stuff, are they?" Fanny said gloomily. "What am I going to do if they get everything wrong?" There was no answer to that. "Oh well," he said. "Better get on with it."

His first problem was finding the Polish stuff so that they could swot it up. Nobody knew where the Air Ministry papers were. Mother Cox thought that Flip Moran had collected them and put them somewhere. The rest of 'A' flight stood or sat around and tried to look concerned. Fanny heard 'B' flight taking off, and briefly contemplated going over to the control tower, calling up Moran on the R/T, and getting the information from him. He remembered what Moran had looked and sounded like when last seen: unhelpful. Moran would fiddle with his radio to create a lot of howls and crackles and would then report, *Sorry, your transmission garbled*. Fanny turned away and organised a search.

'A' flight hunted enthusiastically in all the most unlikely places: under the carpets, inside the lavatory cisterns, down the backs of the sofas (Pip Patterson found sixpence and half a bar of chocolate), behind the pictures on the walls. Sticky Stickwell accidentally burst a cushion, and got severely blamed by the others: too severely, Fanny decided, after they had worked it up into a kind of contest in condemnation, and he made them shut up. Mother Cox found a mouse in a broom cupboard, and at once they were all in full chase. The mouse escaped, but not before Moggy had broken a lampstand; which prompted another barrage of blame, until again Fanny had to step in and use his authority.

It was galling. He knew they were playing the fool, he knew he was being mocked. He could feel his temper slipping, and yet he didn't know what else to do. For one thing, it was worrying to have lost all those secret papers, for which the Air Ministry had his signature. He stood in the middle of the mess, clenching his fingers around his thumbs, and saw something sticking out behind a row of bottles on the top shelf above the bar.

'A' flight showed loud astonishment and pleasure at the discovery of the papers. "Never mind all that," Fanny snapped. "Who searched the bar?"

"Moggy did," said Sticky.

"Oooh, what a whopper!" Moggy said. "It was you. You know it was you."

"Never. It must have been Dicky, then."

"Me? I'm too small, I can't see up there, I –"

"Who was it got the step-ladder?" Pip asked. "Someone did. Wasn't it you, Mother?"

"That's right, put the blame on me," Mother said huffily. "Every time something goes wrong it's always –"

Fanny hammered a glass ashtray on the bar. "Forget it!" he

69

shouted. "We've found the bloody things. Now let's get to work. Written test at twelve o'clock."

The rest of the morning was silent except for yawns, sighs, the shuffling of feet and the rustling of paper. At noon, Fanny distributed sheets of foolscap and read out his questions, one by one. Half of them called for the translation of Polish phrases into English; the other half, of English into Polish. There were forty questions in all. He was relieved to see that everyone took the test seriously; indeed they looked quite weary by the time it was finished.

As he was collecting their answers, Kellaway and Skull came in with the members of the panel of inquiry. Fanny stuffed the papers inside his tunic and went over to play host.

During lunch the talk was not of the Ram's accident but of Bomber Command's attacks on German warships in their North Sea bases. This, it seemed, was the only form of air offensive approved by the Cabinet, and the bomber crews had been ordered to take the greatest care to avoid injuring German civilians. Twenty-nine Blenheims and Wellingtons had reached their targets; seven had been shot down. Another formation of bombers had dropped leaflets over Hamburg and Bremen by night.

"Leaflets?" Fanny said. "What are we trying to do: bore them to death?"

"Don't you be so sure," said one of the visitors. "When I was on the North-West Frontier we often dropped leaflets. And in Mesopotamia. It was a jolly good way to tell Johnny Arab to behave himself, or else! It worked, too, as often as not. They knew we meant what we said, and they changed their ways."

"Suppose they didn't," Skull said. "What then?"

"Oh, we went back and blew them to bits, of course. But they couldn't say they hadn't been warned, d'you see? That was the point. It's very important to follow correct form with these people."

"Did our bombers sink any *German* ships?" Kellaway enquired.

"I expect we knocked a few of them about a bit," said the visitor. "The really interesting thing is what happens now. I can't see Jerry letting us have a go at him without him coming over here and having a go at us, can you? Frankly I hope he does, and the sooner the better. Then the Government will have to think again. The gloves'll be off, and we can really hit Jerry where it hurts."

"So you expect a counter-attack pretty soon?" Fanny said.

"Don't you?" The visitor steered his last potato into the middle of his plate and forked it with a deadly stab. "I think you should."

The warning increased Fanny's nervousness about leaving Flip Moran in charge while he took 'A' flight up. He went to his office and telephoned Group operations room. They had no news. Nothing had changed. The only plots on the table were friendly.

"The weather's begun to close in a bit," Fanny said. "We've got three-tenths cloud at about five thousand feet here."

"That will probably thicken. The met men expect six- or seven-tenths by the end of the afternoon. Still fairly high, though. Nothing to worry about."

Fanny thought: *The sooner I'm up, the sooner I'm down.* "We'll go now," he said.

"Good for you. I shall watch your perambulations with interest."

Fanny called the officers' mess, asked for Pip Patterson, and told him to get 'A' flight off their backsides and moving because take-off was in twenty minutes. He also told him to ask Flight Lieutenant Moran to report to the CO's office at once. Then he telephoned the flight sergeant in charge of the ground crews and gave orders for 'A' flight's aircraft to be warmed up. He sat back and listened to the silence and realised he had done it all wrong: he should have left the ground crews to Pip, and he should have told Flip to meet him in the locker room, or better yet at his plane. Now he was stuck here, waiting. Blast. Why didn't he *think* first?

Five minutes passed. Fanny was twitching with angry impatience; he could feel his heart thumping as if it were trying to get out. He allowed one more minute, watching the second hand stroll around the face of his watch, and then he set off. He met Flip Moran coming along the corridor: not slowly, but not rapidly, either. "For Christ's sake, Flip," Fanny said. "Where the hell have you been?"

"I've been in the lavatory, moving my bowels," Flip said. "That's something we mere humans have to do occasionally." His voice was dead level.

"Well, you chose a bright bloody time to do it."

"Is that so?" Flip allowed his eyebrows the smallest flicker. "Had I known you were interested in my bowel movements I would have recorded the size, weight and specific –"

"Don't be so bloody silly. Anyway, I haven't got time to argue about it now."

"I'm not arguing," Flip said.

Fanny looked at his watch. Thirteen minutes to take-off, and the locker room was miles away. He forced himself to be calm. "Listen," he said. "Two things. First: if there's any kind of flap while we're up, *any* kind, I want to know about it straight away, which means you get on the R/T and tell me. Understood?"

"Even a thick Irishman can understand what that means."

Fanny felt the sting of sarcasm. "Good. Secondly, I want to know what you were up to with those Polish-language papers. Why the hell did you hide them behind the bar?"

"Hide? I hid nothing. The stuff was left lying all over the mess, so I gathered it up for safe keeping."

"Too damn safe. We couldn't find it."

"I don't know why that should be. Everyone saw me give it to the barman."

Fanny opened his mouth to say *Then why* . . . But he knew the answer, and looking at Moran he knew that *he* knew it too. Which meant that everyone knew. 'A' flight had made an ass of him. He was their squadron commander and they were treating him like some doddering old school-teacher. Jesus Christ Almighty, there was a war on! Did they want to start another?

He turned and walked out of the building, fast. An airman was cycling by. He ordered him off the bicycle, took it and pedalled hard, past the admin block, past the mess, past the stores and the sickbay and the camp cinema, to the huts where the pilots had their locker room. Hurricanes were roaring in the dispersal bays; some were beginning to taxi out. He dropped the bicycle and ran inside. The room was empty. He unbuttoned his tunic with one hand while he rummaged in his locker for a long white sweater. His tunic opened and a bundle of papers splashed to the floor: the Polish test answers. Fanny swore, scrambled them together and was stuffing them into the locker when he noticed something odd about the top sheet. He pulled it out. Every question had been answered with the same short phrase: BALLS TO YOU. Nothing else. BALLS TO YOU, forty times over. He looked for the name at the top. Mickey Mouse.

Fanny pulled out the next sheet. Another Mickey Mouse had written UP YOUR KILT! forty times. He checked the next. Mickey Mouse again: ARSENAL 3, BLACKPOOL 1, was the

72

answer to everything. Another sheet, same name. *I must not pick my nose in class*, it said, over and over. Only Mother Cox had signed his name and made an attempt to do the test, and most of his answers were blank.

Fanny's hands trembled as he shoved the papers into his locker. There was a heavy stiffness deep in his gut, as if he had swallowed a stone. He knew that this sort of thing could not go on. There had to be a showdown, and soon. One part of him demanded it. Another part dreaded it.

The light at twelve thousand feet was like watered whisky. 'A' flight had climbed through layer after layer of cloud spreading in from the North Sea: ragged, mucky-looking stuff, torn with holes. The last lot lay spread below them now, like all the world's dirty laundry, and the next layer hung gloomily a couple of hundred feet above. Fanny Barton studied it, calculated that the sunlight was too far away to be worth reaching, and decided to stay here, in this cramped and cheerless stretch of air. Training would be more difficult here, and that suited his frame of mind very well.

He put the flight into sections astern, increased speed to just over 250, and warmed them up with a sort of giant slalom, diving and climbing in a snaking series of S-bends. For five minutes he threw the flight about as severely and as unpredictably as he could, seeking to shake the wingmen loose. The formation stretched under the strain but it never broke. Finally, when his legs were beginning to ache and his lungs to gasp, he called for a loop. It carried the flight, inverted, up in to the belly of the top cloud; and as they curved down out of it he saw, with a sideways flicker of his eyes, that Red Two and Three were still more or less where they should be. They might be idiots but they could fly. It made him angrier than ever.

So much for the warm-up. Now for serious training.

At that moment his radio crackled and the Sector controller spoke.

"Jester Red Leader, this is Cowslip. Are you receiving me?"

Barton acknowledged. Cowslip requested his position. Barton thought fast and said they were approximately over Foulness Point. He was guessing but a guess was better than nothing.

For ten seconds the radio was silent. 'A' flight cruised along its dank corridor, going from nowhere to nowhere. Then another crackle.

"Jester Red Leader, this is Cowslip. Ten-plus bandits approaching Thames Estuary. Steer one-five-zero. Make angels five, over."

Barton was so startled that for a moment he did nothing. The prospect of actual imminent combat with enemy aircraft briefly took his wits away. The radio crackled and he woke up, acknowledged, and led his flight in a steep, diving turn to the south-east, plunging them into the shabby mass of cloud like a blade into a mattress.

As they flashed into clear air again, Cowslip gave him a new course to steer: one-three-zero, and told him of a second hostile force, strength five-plus, following the first. By the time 'A' flight was down to seven thousand feet a third raid had been reported, strength fifteen-plus; less than a minute later they were told that a fourth had been detected, this one the biggest of all: over twenty aircraft. Every plot was heading for the Thames Estuary. It was a massive German attack, and it was aimed at London.

The atmosphere at five thousand feet was murky, a moving junkyard of grubby cloud which made even the gaps look somehow stained and dark. To Fanny Barton it was the perfect setting for a fight: already in his imagination he could see Hun bombers blazing in this gloom; and he drove his flight along at a tearing speed, desperately afraid that other squadrons might get there first. The sky was a shifting jumble, some of it stacked high, some of it dumped like rubble, and he searched the gaps in a kind of suppressed frenzy so that when at last he glimpsed the enemy he blinked, and at once they were gone again, lost. But others in the flight had seen them too. "Bandits ahead one mile, Red Leader. Crossing port to starboard, gone into cloud."

"Okay, I saw them. Jester aircraft, turning starboard, go." Barton banked steeply and set a course that might – if the bombers flew straight – bring about an interception. The air was more turbulent at this lower level, and the Hurricanes were bucketing about like a fairground ride. Barton had to keep both hands on the control column, which suddenly reminded him (with a lurch of panic) that his gun-button was on "safety". He thumbed the catch off, took a deep breath to steady his voice, and said: "Jester aircraft:

arm your guns." He was just in time. As he spoke the bombers slid into view, ahead and above, perfectly silhouetted: three Junkers 88's. They appeared so beautifully, so cleanly, that his lungs expanded for sheer joy. "Attack, attack!" he called. He hauled back on the stick and tasted jubilation as the leader swam steadily bigger and blacker in his sights. Every muscle was tensed to hold the Hurricane steady when he pressed the button, but even so the blaze of fire that raced from his wings made him flinch. His eight guns shaped a long cone of golden destruction. It passed in front of the bomber's nose at first, and then seemed to wash down its fuselage, the tracer sparkling and beading like a magic show, until it slid off the tail and Barton half-rolled away, eager to clear the space so that Yellow Leader coming up behind him could have a crack too. He overdid the manoeuvre, turned too hard. His vision went foggy. Centrifugal force had sucked blood from his brain, and he wasted long seconds in recovery. When he could see clearly again, far away to his left a bomber was dropping in a long spiral of smoke, a spiral that grew tighter and faster as the smoke grew denser. Well, that was one less Junkers 88 to worry about.

No other plane was in sight. He flew straight and level for a moment, searching. He couldn't believe they had all gone, and yet the sky was vacant. A stuttering crackle caught his attention. It was like a row of toy balloons bring burst. Yellow lights streamed past his cockpit. He was being shot at. He shoved all the controls into a corner and flung the plane onto a wingtip. A blurred shape whizzed past and soared away. His Hurricane clawed its way around the turn and he caught a glimpse of his attacker, a tail-end profile: Messerschmitt 109. Cheeky bugger! Barton gave his plane full bore and chased hard, but the closest he could get was six hundred yards. He shot off the remainder of his ammunition and saw the German vanish into cloud.

He went home.

"Thus your total claim," Skull said, "is two Junkers 88 bombers definitely destroyed, one severely damaged and probably destroyed, and three Messerschmitt 109 fighters damaged, of which one was possibly destroyed."

'A' flight had all landed safely, they were in the locker room, and they were thoroughly pleased with themselves.

"Damn good show," said Stickwell. "Extremely damn good show. Highly extremely very wizard damn good show all round. What?"

The others laughed. Even Fanny Barton smiled, sharing in the general relief and excitement and pride, although he kept his hands in his pockets to hide their shaking. He tried to stop thinking of his kill but his memory would not abandon those three or four lethal seconds; it kept returning again and again, fascinated by the focus of those splendid streams of fire ripping their way down the belly of the bomber. That was the most wonderful thing he had ever done. It had all been so quick, so good, so *right*. His mind was gloating over it, but why not? It was sheer perfection. And the rest of 'A' flight had seen him do it. Marvellous. Superb. Exactly what was wanted.

"If only we could have had a crack at the bombers too," Patterson said. "We'd have polished off Moggy's 'probable.' "

"He didn't look terribly well after I'd peed all over him," Cattermole said. "Lots of smoke coming out of the port engine, and so on. Then he vanished into this large black cloud. For all I know he's still there. You could always go back and have a look, Pip."

"Don't be daft, Moggy. How on earth can I find him if he's inside a cloud?"

"Yes, of course, I never thought of that. He's probably got his eyes closed too. That makes them very hard to see, you know. Devilish cunning, these Huns."

"It's all right for you jokers," Dicky Starr said. "You got a bunch of 88's handed to you on a plate, while us mugs in Yellow Section got jumped on. I had to scram so hard I nearly blew up the engine."

"That's nothing," Mother Cox said. "When those 109's got behind me I turned so fast I bent my Hurricane's wings."

"Really?" said Patterson. "Show me."

"You can't see it now. I turned the other way even faster and bent them back again."

Loud derisive laughter. Skull, making notes, crossed out his last entry.

Fanny Barton cleared his throat. "Nevertheless, the important thing is that you did shake off the 109's, you did get into position to fire at them, and you did damage them."

The three members of Yellow Section nodded.

"Okay. See you all in the mess." As they went out he added: "Well done."

Skull sat at the trestle table, putting his combat reports in order. One was dog-eared, and he carefully smoothed the corner.

"What's the matter?" Barton asked. Skull looked up. "You're not exactly sprinting to the phone, are you?" Barton said.

"Ah." Skull pursed his lips. He was pressing his knees together like a spinster in a short skirt. "I believe the German Messerschmitt 109 fighter has a range of slightly over four hundred miles, thus giving it an operational radius of some two hundred miles." He tugged his glasses halfway down his nose. "I read it in a book," he explained.

"I believe you."

"And I understand that the nearest German airfield is at least four hundred miles away."

Barton walked over to a window and looked across the aerodrome. The grass was tinged silver by the wind and in the very far distance trees were slowly shaking their heads. "I suppose they must have carried extra long-range tanks, then," he said. "You know: the disposable kind."

"Nobody reported seeing anything like that."

"Well, they wouldn't, would they? The Jerry pilots dropped them before they attacked."

"Yes, of course." Skull rolled up the combat reports and scratched his head with them. "It's still a very long way back to Germany, into a strong headwind."

"Perhaps they came from Holland."

"Holland is neutral."

"Well, maybe they took off from an aircraft carrier, then."

"To the best of my knowledge the German Navy has no aircraft carriers."

"Oh." Barton turned from the window. "In that case it looks as if some bright spark has invented a new long-range fighter, doesn't it?"

"Mmm." Skull unrolled the reports and frowned at them.

"Which means that you were *not* in fact attacked by Messerschmitt 109's —"

"Come with me, Skull," Barton said. They went out and walked across the grass to Dicky Starr's Hurricane. Barton ducked under the starboard wing and pointed to a slanting row of bulletholes. "That's not dry rot," he said.

"Indisputable," Skull said. "I'll go and telephone Group."

Barton went into the anteroom of the mess with a sheaf of papers in his hand and a clear intention in his head. He was going to hammer 'A' flight for their intolerable insolence and shoddy irresponsibility and generally insubordinate behaviour in connection with the Anglo-Polish test. That sort of thing went beyond a joke. It was a challenge, a defiance of authority, an act of mutiny.

Well, maybe not quite an act of mutiny, but definitely an instance of serious indiscipline, and a fighter squadron had to have discipline. Above all came discipline.

But when he went through the door Barton was taken aback by the feeling of fierce exhilaration he met. The whole squadron was in fizzing high spirits. The talk everywhere buzzed with enthusiasm and sparkled with laughter. Moke Miller played the piano, badly but cheerfully. Pip Patterson's hands swooped and curved as he re-created part of the air battle. Dicky Starr stood beside him and grinned and nodded vigorously.

Barton paused. He coughed. Nobody paid any attention. He whacked the sheaf of papers against his palm, and called: " 'A' flight!"

It took them several seconds to stop talking. In the silence Moke Miller hit a splayed chord. Several pilots laughed. Barton, looking grimly dutiful, had a moment of fright: he didn't know what to say next. He raised the test papers. The gesture felt theatrical, wrong. "You all know what these are," he said. That didn't sound right either.

"Citations, sir?" Moggy Cattermole suggested brightly. "We've all won medals, and quite right too! After all we did shoot down a vast number of very nasty Huns. I myself got three —"

Cheers and happy insults drowned his voice.

"I got five," said Stickwell.

"I got seven," Mother Cox said, "but I gave a couple to young Dicky because I felt sorry for him."

"Bilge!" Dicky Starr cried. "Who d'you think lined up three Messerschmitts and put one burst through them all?"

"Me," Pip said. "I'm so glad someone was watching."

Starr attacked him with a cushion. Barton stuffed the papers into his pocket: how could anyone criticise them, let alone lambast them, in their moment of victory? As he turned away he thought he saw Stickwell give him a glance of amused contempt, but when he looked again Stickwell's back was turned. A hectic free-for-all was going on, with chairs overturned, cushions flying, and mess servants nimbly removing cups and saucers and glasses.

Barton walked away and sat in a corner. He felt slightly sick; everything was happening too fast; he wasn't sure whether he was leading the squadron or following it. The adjutant dropped into the next chair and put his feet up. "Congratulations, sir," he said. "Damn fine show."

"Thank you, uncle."

"First scrap, no losses, and two Huns. I should think you're very pleased."

"Of course."

The adjutant examined the shine on his shoes. "If I might make a suggestion, sir."

"Yes?"

"Let the chaps see how pleased you are. Slap them on the back, ask them what they thought about the scrap, make a bit of a fuss of them." Kellaway gave a wry smile, which took the edge off his suggestion. "Funny thing about war," he said, "it's all done by kindness."

"Why should they need a slap on the back?" Barton asked. "They seem pretty pleased with themselves as it is. Anyway they only did what they're paid to do. I see no reason to make a fuss about it."

"As you like, old boy. You know best."

"It'll be soon enough to celebrate when the day's over. Group thinks Jerry might come again. We're all back on fifteen-minute readiness, you know."

"So I hear."

Barton saw Flip Moran. He beckoned him over. "I'm surprised 'B' flight didn't get scrambled," he said.

Moran simply stood, looked and waited.

"I suppose Ops decided we were closer," Barton said.

Moran found a bit of dead skin on the end of his little finger and chewed it off.

"Has 'B' flight done its Polish test?" Barton asked.

Moran, still chewing, nodded.

"How did they get on?"

"They passed."

"I'd like to see the papers."

"I thought you might. They're in your office." Moran strolled away.

"Something wrong?" Kellaway said.

"Nothing that a good boot up the arse won't cure." Barton stood up. "Funny thing about war," he said, "it's not all done by kindness."

As he walked to his office he met Skull, who was making for the mess. "Group are not at all happy about those long-range German fighters," he said. "They've asked for a thoroughly detailed description. It seems that our side suffered some losses in the engagement too."

"How many?"

"Well, one pilot got shot down and killed and several others –"

"Only one killed?" Barton scoffed. "That's nothing to get upset about, is it? What does Group expect, against a great mob of Jerry bombers?" He looked up as a section of Battles passed overhead, engines labouring to gain height, wings rocked by the wind. "How much damage did they do?"

Skull squinted at the vanishing Battles. "Damage? I've no idea. Aren't those ours? Have they been somewhere?"

Barton gave him a disgusted look. "Use your brains, Skull, for Christ's sake," he said.

"My dear fellow," Skull said stiffly, "I made it quite clear when I was allocated to Intelligence that I hold no pretensions to intellectual potency."

Barton walked away. "Keep me informed," he said over his shoulder.

'B' flight's Polish test papers were in his in-tray. Moran had set them only ten questions, all of which they had answered correctly. Nobody scored less than full marks.

Barton covered his face with his hands and let his whole body go limp. He felt physically tired and mentally weary. That patrol had taken a lot out of him. His body wanted a hot bath but part of his mind refused to relax. How could everyone in 'B' flight have got a perfect score? It wasn't possible, it wasn't credible, it was all a cheat and a swindle. Flip Moran had made a travesty of the test, and he had made that obvious. Another challenge. That meant another showdown. Damn. Damn, damn, damn.

The telephone rang. It was Skull. "Group Intelligence need more information about the bomber formation you encountered. In particular they have asked for details of any distinguishing features."

Barton found himself clenching his jaws until they hurt. "What the hell's the matter with them?" he demanded. "Can't they look it up in their files? The planes were Junkers 88's. Hell's bells, Group should know more about that type than we do."

"Quite. But as they pointed out, you led the attack and therefore you were in the best position to notice anything unusual."

"Such as what?"

"For instance, did you observe any return fire from the German gunners?"

"No."

"But you made your attack from below?"

"Yes. So what?"

"Can you remember if the aircraft had visible tail-wheels?"

Barton searched his memory. "No. I mean, I don't know. They were silhouetted, you couldn't possibly make out that sort of detail."

"I see." Skull's pen scratched, and stopped. "Thank you." He hung up.

Barton sat at his desk for a few minutes, growing more and more annoyed with Skull, with Group, with Moran, with everyone, until he couldn't sit still any longer. He gathered up all the test papers and all the Air Ministry secret glossaries and went off to find the adjutant.

Kellaway's door was shut. His clerk looked nervous, and there were angry voices inside. Barton went straight in and banged the door hard against an elbow. It belonged to a middle-aged man with a face like a ripe apple. The man swore, but another man, younger and taller, dressed in whipcord breeches and a windcheater, ignored him.

He was too busy shaking a long and calloused finger in the adjutant's face. "Bloody larceny, that's what it is!" he shouted. "Bloody housebreaking! Bloody highway robbery! Bugger me, we don't need no little old 'itler comin' 'ere to rob us blind when we got the bloody Raff doin' it already! If you don't –"

Barton slammed the door as loudly as possible. A china ornament fell off a shelf and shattered. "Who are these people?" he said.

"You in charge here?" the younger man demanded.

"Shut up," Barton said.

"By Christ, you talk to me like that, after what's been done, I'll shut *you* up, matey, see if I don't." The whites of his eyes showed big and clear, and there was spittle at the corners of his mouth. Kellaway came forward quickly and got between them. He said: "This is Mr Parker –"

"Barker."

"Sorry, sorry. This is Mr Barker, and that gentleman is Mr Hawthorn. He's from High Dunning," Kellaway added pointedly.

"Stupid young bastard," Hawthorn growled. "Nearly broke me arm."

"These gentlemen are local farmers," Kellaway said, "and it seems they feel they have cause for complaint because –"

"You the commandin' officer?" Barker interrupted.

"No," Barton said.

"Where is he, then?"

"Flying. He won't be back for hours."

Barker took a folded document from his hip pocket and glanced at it. "Where's Flying Officer Stickwell, then?"

"He's flying too. There's a war on, remember?"

"Just as well, p'raps. If I met 'im I'd just as likely break 'is bloody neck for 'im, seein' the condition 'im an' 'is pals left my 'orses in. You give 'im this." He thrust the paper at Barton. "That's a summons to answer criminal charges, that is."

"And I want damages, too," Hawthorn said. "Eight pound fifteen and six that trailer cost to put right, not to mention the petrol."

It took twenty minutes to get rid of them. When they went, Barton was left holding thick letters of complaint from each man, a letter from the chairman of the Essex branch of the National Farmers Union, and a carbon copy of their joint letter to the Secretary of State for Air, which had also been copied to the local MP; all of which Barton had promised to hand over to the CO for his urgent attention as soon as he landed.

"Moggy Cattermole told me they put everything back where they found it," he said to Kellaway. "He said it was raining buckets and nobody saw them. What makes these yokels so damn sure of themselves?"

"Sticky's Buick. He left it outside Hawthorn's farm."

"I think I'll kill him," Barton said. "I think I'll ram this bumf down his stupid throat and kill him dead. I think I'll do it now."

As he turned to the door the telephone rang. Kellaway answered it. "I see," he said. "Dear me, that is a problem. He's here now. Why don't you come over straight away?" He hung up. "Engineering officer," he explained. "Some sort of trouble over spares, he needs your help."

Barton dumped his load of paper on the adjutant's desk and sat down. "I can't believe the Ram had to put up with all this," he said.

"Ah, that reminds me: the inquiry. They decided to reconvene in a week's time so that we can furnish them with a bit more evidence." Kellaway gave him a piece of paper. "Rather a lot more evidence, actually."

Barton propped his elbows on his knees and scanned the sheet without enthusiasm. "'Describe airfield security arrangements,'" he said. "'Report any and all recent instances of sabotage or fifth-column activity...' Sabotage?" he said. "What on earth has sabotage got to do with it?" The paper buckled in his fingers.

"They're a bit twitchy at Air Ministry now," Kellaway said.

The engineer officer arrived. He was a thirty-year-old flying officer called Marriott, with sandy hair, chewed fingernails, and defeated eyes. "It's really quite simple, in a complicated sort of way," he said. "But the upshot is you've only got nine operational Hurricanes."

"What about the reserve aircraft?" Barton asked.

"Either in use or waiting for spares. There was Cox's wheels-up landing, and the Ram's accident, and after today's action four of 'A' flight's planes need repairing but we haven't got the parts and we can't get them because we haven't got the proper forms which we must have in order to indent for parts. D'you want to know where the proper forms are?"

"Yes."

"They're lost. I'm pretty sure they got sent by mistake to RAF Kings*mead*, which is up in Lancashire. They're always getting stuff that's meant for RAF Kingsmere."

"Well then, get some more forms, for God's sake."

"We can't," Marriott said. "The form that has to be used to apply for *more* forms is also in the parcel that went to RAF Kingsmead. We haven't got any more of those forms here."

"You need a form to get a form," explained the adjutant.

"But that's bloody silly," Barton said. The others nodded. "Have you explained all this to the people at the spares depot? What do they say?"

"No form, no spare," Marriott said. He handed him a long typewritten list. "They won't budge."

While Barton was reading the list, Skull came in. "Whatever it is, I don't want to know," Barton muttered.

"That, I'm afraid, is all too likely," said Skull. There was a gravity in his voice that made them all look. "I shall tell you what Group Intelligence has told me. No bombs have been dropped on London, or indeed anywhere. No German aircraft has been seen to fall in the area of the Thames Estuary, although a very careful watch is kept. The watchers – members of the Observer Corps – did however see a Bristol Blenheim crash in flames. And a squadron stationed in Kent, equipped with Blenheims, has reported that one of its patrols was attacked and an aircraft is missing."

For a moment the room was touched with horror. Barton looked from Skull to the adjutant, but Kellaway had turned away and was staring out of the window. "That was nothing to do with us," Barton said, and his voice had a rising inflexion. "We didn't see any Blenheims. We saw Ju-88's, the controller steered us right onto them, I mean he gave us the height and position and everything, spot-on. It was a damn good interception. It really was."

Nobody wanted to follow that. Barton folded Marriott's list in half and then in half again, and rubbed the creases. "It wasn't anything to do with us, that's all," he said. "I'm positive of that. Absolutely positive." He unfolded the list, flattened the paper, and placed it on top of his little stack. "Damn it all, I should know, I was there."

Kellaway took out his pipe and squinted into the bowl. "What filthy luck," he grunted.

"It does look very much as if something rather awful has happened," said Skull.

"Well, it was nothing whatever to do with *us*," Barton said defiantly. "Now can we please get on with this spare-parts problem? I want –"

"The fact is, there have been no German aircraft at all over England today," Skull said.

Barton could stand it no longer. He jumped to his feet. "How the hell do you know?" he cried. "What about all those hostile plots they picked up – five plus, ten plus, *twenty* plus? Where did they come from, if not from bloody Germany?"

"I can't tell you that," Skull said. "What I can tell you is that according to Group our tracking stations saw no trace of any of those plots returning across the North Sea towards Germany. Not one. And, as I have said, no German aircraft has been seen to fall. None."

"They just flew round and round in circles and disappeared up their own tail-pipes, did they?"

"Mistakes do happen," Kellaway said. "I remember –"

"Save it," Barton snapped. "I haven't got time." But he had nothing further to say, either. There was a painful silence while he stood and glowered at the adjutant's empty chair, and listened to the creak of the windowframes in the wind, and the distant pecking of a typewriter, and the coming and going of footsteps in the corridor. One set of footsteps came all the way to the office. The door opened and a man in civilian clothes looked in. He was about thirty, and he was wearing a soft brown hat, tweed hacking-jacket, tattersall waistcoat and dark grey slacks. Barton's immediate reaction was: *National Farmers Union, get rid of the bastard.* "Hornet squadron?" the man said. He had a brisk, cheerful voice and a confident expression. Kellaway nodded. "Good," the man said. "I'm Squadron Leader Rex, and I'm your new commanding officer."

Kellaway made the introductions. Rex shook hands. "Thank you for holding the fort till I got here," he said to Barton. "I expect it's all been plain sailing, has it?"

"No, sir. For one thing, we've got a serious spare-parts problem." He found Marriott's list and gave it to Rex. "Only nine aircraft are operational."

"Oh-oh! That won't do. Okay. Thanks. Anything else?"

"Well, we're still stuck with the inquiry into the previous CO's death. They've asked us for a whole load of information, I mean stuff that's going to take a hell of a lot of digging out ... It's all down here, you see."

Rex took the sheet of paper and dropped it into a waste bin. "We can forget that. Anything else?"

Barton looked from the bin to Rex and back again. "Forget it," he said. "I see. All right. Well ... There's also been a bit of a dust-up with some local farmers. We've had a summons, formal letters of complaint and so on."

Rex accepted these too and dropped them in the bin. "Not important. Any more?"

Barton took a deep breath. "Yes, sir. These Anglo-Polish things. Glossaries. They came by despatch-rider yesterday from Air Ministry. We had orders to memorise them within twenty-four hours, but I'm sorry to say the rest of the squadron simply hasn't co-operated. In fact it's worse than that, far worse. I mean, just look at these test papers ..."

Rex took the entire bundle, weighed it thoughtfully in his hands, glanced at Barton, and let it fall into the bin, which was now so full that some of the glossaries spilled out. "I wouldn't worry about it if I were you," he said.

"But sir, I've signed for those," Barton protested. "I mean, damn it all, they're *secret*."

"I'm sure they are. Almost everything is, these days. Especially when it comes out of Air Ministry. Even their toilet paper is covered by the Official Secrets Act. That's in case someone discovers that half the Air Staff has the runs. Which as a matter of fact they do, right now."

Barton was bewildered. "You mean to say all that stuff is ... is useless?"

"It's just not important."

"It's also not Polish," Skull remarked. He had picked up one of the glossaries and was leafing through it. "As far as I can tell, these foreign phrases are Swedish. *Tack-tack*, thank you. I'm sure that's Swedish. *God morgon*, good morning. Yes, it's Swedish. Well, well."

"Someone at Air Ministry got confused, I expect," Rex said. "Poland, Sweden, Ruritania, Patagonia, it's all the same to them. Talking of confusion, I take it you've heard about the poor old Blenheim?"

The four men waited for each other to answer. Then Barton, not looking at him, said: "That rather depends, sir. What have you heard?"

"It was a technical fault." Rex took out his car keys and spun them on his finger. "Part of our tracking system went on the blink and began seeing double. It was supposed to be plotting aircraft out to sea, but this afternoon for some reason it began picking up stuff that was actually flying behind it, inland. The echoes got reflected or something; anyway, stuff that was over land showed up on the screen as if it was over the North Sea. I assume you understand the basic principles of all this black magic?"

Nobody spoke.

"Neither do I," he said. "Anyway, the upshot was, Group saw an unidentified plot on the table, heading this way from Germany, so they scrambled a section of Blenheims to intercept it. Unfortunately this boss-eyed tracking station kept seeing double and so those Blenheims showed up on its screen as *another* raid coming in from the sea. Consequently, Group scrambled more fighters. Consequently, up popped another raid, so there had to be yet another scramble, and thus it went on until in due course somebody bumped into somebody else and, alas, it all ended in tears."

"The eye sees what it expects," Skull said. "A not-infrequent phenomenon."

"And the weather didn't help," Rex said. "Low cloud, bad visibility. Also the Blenheim does look remarkably like a Junkers 88, especially –"

"Wait a minute, wait a minute," Barton said. "We got shot-up too, you know, and we weren't flying Blenheims."

"No, but you were attacking them. No doubt someone else saw

87

you do it and jumped to the conclusion that you were a bunch of Me-109's."

"The Hurricane," said Skull, "does look remarkably like the Messerschmitt 109, from some angles."

"You're bloody knowledgeable all of a sudden," Barton growled.

"I base my observations on your own experience," Skull said evenly. "After all, you pursued a Hurricane and sought to destroy it."

"This is all just airy-fairy theory," Barton insisted. "Nobody has any real evidence to back it up. For all you know, there *were* three Junkers 88's swanning around up there this afternoon. All right, so nobody on the ground saw them. So what? They probably crashed miles out to sea! Who knows? You've said yourself the tracking station was on the blink, so why –"

"Because," Rex interrupted firmly. "Because I've talked on the phone to the CO of the Blenheim squadron. His chaps wrote down the identification letters they saw on the fighters that attacked them. I've got the letters here." He handed Barton a scrap of paper. "I'm sorry," he said. "It's nobody's fault."

Barton glanced at the paper and crushed it in his fist. No matter how tightly he squeezed, he could not stop the trembling. "It's all very well for you," he said. He was swallowing repeatedly.

"Don't destroy that bit of paper," Rex said sharply. "There's a name on the back. It's the CO of the Blenheim squadron. They're based at Manston. Take a plane and nip over there now and apologise." He put his arm around Barton's shoulder and steered him to the door. "Get back here as soon as you can," he said. "I'm going to need you. We're off to France tomorrow."

Rex watched Barton go, closed the door, and leaned against it. "Well, now," he said.

"France." Kellaway prodded the overflowing waste bin with his foot. "So that's why none of this stuff matters any more."

"I have a feeling I've forgotten something," Rex said.

"Spare parts," Marriott prompted.

"Of course! Stupid of me. What's the problem?" Marriott described the problem. "Bloody forms," Rex said. "There's the real enemy. How far is it to this unhelpful dump, anyway?"

"About thirty miles, sir."

"Right. Adj: I need two large trucks and a dozen men with rifles, please. It's a funny thing," he said to Marriott. "About this time of day I always feel like killing someone."

The trucks came back two hours later, heavy with booty. Marriott had them unloaded immediately, and the ground crews got to work on their aircraft.

"Did you have to shoot anyone, sir?" Kellaway asked Rex.

"No, it was very dull. Nobody was prepared to fight except the duty officer, and he wore glasses, so we locked him in the lavatory."

"There's bound to be hell to pay, though, isn't there? Eventually?"

"Well . . . they've got to catch us first. I told them I was CO of a Sunderland flyingboat squadron, based on the Isle of Skye. And we'll be in frog-land tomorrow. What happens the day after that is neither here nor there. Come and have a drink, adj."

The morning was magnificent: an English September day at its best. It looked, felt and tasted like the start of a new and glorious age. The sky was hugely blue, the clean, cool blue of tropical water, with a thin drift of herringbone clouds sketched in to give it a greater sense of depth. It was nine o'clock; the air was still chill in the shadows but pleasantly warm in the sunshine. The turf had a crisp bounce underfoot; birds flew and sang as if they had never heard of Poland. It was a day when nothing seemed impossible.

Squadron Leader Rex walked quickly across the airfield towards his pilots. Rex always walked quickly. One of the first things Kellaway had noticed about him was that he had only two speeds: fast, and stopped. Now Rex's dog was trotting briskly at his heels and even Kellaway and Skull had to skip occasionally to keep up with him.

"Good morning!" Rex called. "I hope nobody had beans for breakfast, we don't need a tailwind today." He dumped his parachute on the wing of the nearest plane. "You are all trained and expert pilots, officers and gentlemen, so there's nothing I can tell you about flying the Hurricane except that if you crash it and kill yourself, your next-of-kin will be sold into slavery to defray the cost of replacement. However, there are three things you should know about France. One is that the French are a nation of appalling alcoholics. If anyone offers you a drink, take it; you'll be doing him a favour. The second is that French women are staggeringly beautiful. When they ask you into bed, take your boots off first. If you enjoy it, take your hat off afterwards. It's important to observe correct form. You are ambassadors for your country, remember. The third thing to know is the French suffer from the strange delusion that they invented flying. Some of them think they're Napoleon too: They're all a bit loopy, in fact. Very few speak English, so obviously the rest can't be making much of an effort to be normal. That's their loss. But we can set them an example. We can show them who really invented flying, who makes the finest fighter aircraft in the world, and who flies them the best. This, by the way, is Reilly, the squadron mascot." He clipped a leash to the dog's collar and handed it to the adjutant. "Reilly's mother was a labrador but, as you can see, he's got a streak of collie in him. Let that be a lesson to you. Always keep a sharp look-out, or you might receive an unexpected poke, with regrettable consequences. Right. Everyone ready? Off we go."

They dispersed, and Fitzgerald found himself walking near Moran. "Bright spark, isn't he?" he said.

"Indeed, the man is positively incandescent." Moran made it sound like a medical condition. "I just wonder how long before he burns out his filament."

"Oh, come on. Give the chap his due. He got Micky Marriott his spares, didn't he?"

"Certainly. That's why we're leaving so early, in order to stay one jump ahead of the law."

Fitzgerald laughed. "You're a great comfort, Flip. Until I began talking to you I thought the sun was shining, but now I see it's actually pissing down."

Moran grunted. "I'll say this for him. He's a big improvement on the fellah before him. But then he would have to be, wouldn't he?"

"Fanny did his best."

"That was exactly the trouble," Moran said, and headed for his Hurricane.

Fanny Barton was the only pilot not flying that morning. He had come back from Manston the night before suffering from headache and earache. By the time he found Rex he was also developing a sore throat. He couldn't hear clearly or speak easily, so his report was very brief. He went early to bed. The symptoms

90

were still as bad in the morning and when the squadron took off he was stretched out in the sickbay with all the curtains drawn and a pillow pressed against each ear to try to seal out the raucous racket. The windowframes stopped rattling, the glass stopped buzzing, the din faded to nothing. Barton relaxed and gazed at the dim, grey-white ceiling.

He was haunted by the memory of the CO of the Blenheim squadron. The man had been so utterly, hopelessly perplexed. Not angry, not bitter, not grief-stricken; just baffled by Barton's attempt to explain. He had stood with his shoulders hunched and his hands jammed into his pockets, staring into Barton's face, searching for more than Barton had to give. The man heard, he understood, but it just wasn't enough; the explanation didn't match the tragedy. In the end Barton had to give up. He said goodbye and flew home, but the image travelled with him, trapped in his aching head.

Skull and the adjutant stood on the edge of the field and watched the squadron gradually assume formation as it began a wide circuit.

"How do we get to France?" Skull asked.

"A couple of troop-carriers are coming to take us. Bombays, probably."

"Yes?" Skull bent down and picked a daisy. "Bombays . . . Are they . . . I mean, can they . . . The thing is, I've never flown before."

"Don't do that, Reilly!" Kellaway said, tugging at the leash. "Why must dogs always sniff one's crotch?"

"How safe is it?" Skull asked.

"Oh, it's not dangerous unless they bite, but that's –"

"No, no. Flying. How safe is flying?"

"Oh, that." Kellaway scratched the dog's head. "Well, it's perfectly safe, isn't it, Reilly? As long as nothing goes wrong."

"But how often does something go wrong?"

"I've never bothered to keep score. It doesn't really matter, does it? Once is enough, if it happens to you. I mean to say, the accidents that happen to other people don't count."

"They count to them, surely."

The adjutant took out his pipe and rapped it against his heel. "That's their silly look-out, isn't it?"

Skull gave him a baffled glance. Kellaway turned away to watch the squadron, now in sections astern – four arrowheads, snugly arranged behind each other – swooping in a fast, shallow dive over the airfield, the leader waggling his wings in farewell. The two men waved. The formation angled up and climbed away, leaving a pulse of thunder and a trail of smoke. "They make it look so damnably easy," Skull said.

In the sickbay, Barton lay face-down, his head throbbing like an ancient refrigerator, and willed the noise to go away and leave him alone.

The doors of the dining-room of the Hotel Lafayette swung open and Squadron Leader Rex strolled in at the head of Hornet squadron. They moved with all the ease and self-assurance of young men who are proud of their uniform, sure of each other, and well primed with drinks bought by someone else.

The diners stopped talking and turned to look. Several applauded. When a girl wearing a creamy rose in her black hair threw a kiss, Moggy Cattermole caught it like a cricketer, one arm flung high, and she laughed. By now some of the diners were standing to applaud. Rex made a little detour to shake hands with one of them, and the applause redoubled. The head waiter came forward. Rex shook hands with him too, and they chatted while the pilots took their seats at a large oval table. "Fighting fit, *merci bien, Georges*," Rex said. "*Et vous?* Still *fort et brillant*, like good champagne? I always tell my friends, *plus ça change, plus c'est le même Georges . . .*"

Dinner began. The Lafayette was one of the three best hotels in Le Touquet and in 1939 its food was the best of all. After the first two courses had been served and eaten and his glass refilled, Moke Miller turned to Flip Moran and said: "Before I enjoy myself too much, Flip, tell me whether or not I can afford all this."

Moran gave him a grim smile. "What if I said you can't?"

"Just have to get plastered and forget it, I suppose."

"Put your mind at rest, then."

"Really? Marvellous! I'll get plastered on that."

"Your new boss arranged this shindig," Moran said. "Therefore it shouldn't appear on anybody's mess bill. It bloody well better not appear on mine, that I can tell you."

"Got a hilariously funny story to tell you, Flip," Sticky Stickwell announced over the talk. "This'll test your sense of humour, which some of us think you haven't got much of, not that it's really your fault because after all you can't help being a thick Irish bog-trotter, can you?"

"Stickwell's pissed already," Moran said. "You can tell by the way he keeps poking the celery into his ear."

"Manners, Sticky!" Patterson said sharply. "Remember where you are, for God's sake. The correct form with celery is to stuff it up your nose. Isn't that right, sir?"

"Quite right," Rex said. "And for an encore you stuff it up your neighbour's nose."

"Ah, but," Stickwell said. "I have these very small, aristocratic nostrils. See? So that lets me out."

"What's this funny joke, then?" Miller asked.

"In any case, radishes are what you stick in your ear, not celery," Patterson said. "And sometimes rhubarb for afters."

"Correct. The important thing," Rex told them, "is to remember to keep your head on one side, otherwise the custard goes down your neck."

"Hilarious funny story," Stickwell declared, looking at Moran. "Pay attention, Flip. It's all about a man who had a wooden leg, called Kelly. Now the question is, what was his other leg called?"

"Bollocks," Moran said.

"Oh." Stickwell looked hugely disappointed. "You've heard it before. What a swindle."

"Did you know there's supposed to be a chap in the *Luftwaffe* with a wooden leg?" Mother Cox said. "Pilot, I mean."

"Dash it all, that's not very sporting," Cattermole complained. "Can't shoot a chap with a wooden leg."

"Certainly not, it hasn't got the range," Rex said. When the laughter died down, he added: "But whether he's got a wooden leg or two glass eyes or a pregnant grandmother with the DT's, the first Jerry we come across gets a bellyful of our Brownings at the earliest possible opportunity." There was a happy growl of "Hear! Hear!" all around the table. "More wine!" Rex called. "We'll drink to that." They drank to that.

It had been a good day for Hornet squadron. They had crossed the Channel at a height that gave them an immense view: from the isles of Holland in the east to the Normandy peninsula in the west, while behind them the coast of England curved away, Sussex blending into Hampshire, until it became a blur that was Southampton. The sea lay like costly blue-green wrapping-paper, caught by the sun in a glittering ribbon of light. It was a view that teased and tantalised: there was always more to be seen, always more than the eyes could take in. Pip Patterson, flying as Yellow Two, looked down and could not believe that a world as sunny and splendid as this was at war. He tried to imagine a German plane up here, invading this same piece of sky, coming in to the attack. He could picture it as clearly as a scene in the cinema, but it was no more menacing than that. The enemy guns fired but they could not harm him. They could not even make him blink.

The squadron reached the French coast at Cap Gris Nez, turned south and crossed Boulogne. After a few minutes Le Touquet lay below. They went down in a slow, broad spiral that was calculated to advertise their presence to the inhabitants. At five hundred feet Rex led them over the sea, turned, and paraded unhurriedly past the town, the aircraft flying half-banked to let the watchers get a good look at them. At the edge of town they straightened up and climbed, swinging inland. "Squadron in vic, squadron in vic, go," Rex said. The sections fanned out from their line-astern formation and moved up to create the familiar blunt arrowhead, with Green Section at the rear. "Jester squadron, listen to me," Rex said. "We shall carry out a power dive to the harbour and come out in a Prince of Wales feathers by sections, except for Green Section which will carry out a separate Prince of Wales by aircraft. Is that clear?" The section leaders acknowledged. "Right. Keep it fast and tight."

The Hurricanes nosed down, and all over Le Touquet faces looked up. The mounting roar of the twelve Merlin engines ripped open the peace of the morning with a disciplined savagery. Now the watchers on the ground could see the upper surfaces of the aircraft and the glitter of their cockpits, almost in plan-view. Rex held the angle for a few seconds more, feeling the controls stiffen in the plunging rush, then hauled back on the stick and held it to his stomach. As the squadron reached the harbour it was going flat and flat-out; a second or two later it was flinging itself into the sky, with Red Section climbing straight up, Yellow Section soaring off to the right, Blue Section off to the left: an aerial picture of the plumes of the Prince of Wales' feathers. Behind them, Green Section duplicated the manoeuvre in miniature.

The squadron re-formed, did a few more tricks, and landed at Le Touquet civil airport, feeling cock-a-hoop. That afternoon the Bombays arrived with the ground crews and the admin section. Rex had a phone call from the Air Officer Commanding in the Pas-de-Calais. Evidently Hornet squadron's arrival had impressed the French enormously; the AOC thought it might be a good idea to put on a similar show over Dieppe. Hornet squadron flew down to Dieppe, stopped all work in the place for fifteen minutes, and flew back. Rex announced that they were all bloody useless and that he'd arranged a celebratory dinner at the Hotel Lafayette, eight-thirty for nine. "I rather like this war," Moke Miller said brightly. "Can we have another when it's finished?"

Skull, Kellaway and Marriott were not invited to the dinner. They ate more modestly in a small restaurant and then strolled about the town. Out of curiosity, they went into the Lafayette. Robust singing could be heard coming from the dining-room. "Isn't that a hymn?" Skull asked. They paused and listened. "It's *The Church's One Foundation*," he said. "What a dreadful dirge."

"That's a slightly different version," Marriott told him. "That's one of the squadron songs."

"Really? How does it go?"

" 'Our name is Hornet squadron,' " Kellaway recited flatly, " 'no good are we. We cannot shoot, we cannot fight, nor march like infantry. Yet when it comes to pay parade, we shout with all our might, Per Ardua Ad Astra: Fuck You, Jack, I'm All Right.' "

"I see," Skull said. "Not the most fervent of sentiments."

"What d'you expect?" Marriott asked. "Land of Hope and Glory?"

"At least it has the merit of optimism, whereas –"

"No, no, no," Kellaway interrupted. "They don't go in for that sort of patriotic tosh. You mustn't expect them to wave the flag, Skull. It's not their style."

"Evidently." Skull was not feeling tolerant; the flight across had been very bumpy and he had twice been sick. He indulged himself in mild sarcasm. "I must remember to avoid using subversive terms like valour and courage and self-sacrifice," he said. "One doesn't want to upset the chaps, does one?"

"That's the ticket," Kellaway said, pleased at this easy understanding. "No politics."

They went upstairs to the bar and met an American, who bought them drinks. "I saw your fancy flying this morning," he said. "That's a sharp little airplane you got there."

"Finest fighter in the world," Marriott said.

"Well, I'm glad to see it." He was a Republican state senator from Minneapolis, on holiday in Europe. His grandparents, he said, had emigrated from Poland. "It's about time somebody stood up to those Nazi bastards."

"We'll do our best," Kellaway said.

"I always had a lot of respect for your Royal Air Force. You know why? Discipline. Not like the French. They think all it takes to win is a lot of dash and daring. That's bunk."

"Everything's very scientific nowadays," Marriott said.

"Sure. You got to have a better machine," the American said. "I looked at your outfit this morning, everyone disciplined, all flying as one, and I said to myself, now that's a real war-machine. It's tough, it's hard, it's ruthless, it's –" He stopped. The sound of singing was advancing up the stairs and everyone in the bar had turned to look.

The song was the Dwarfs' March from the film *Snow White*, but it was oddly jerky. When Rex came in view he was walking on his knees, with his arms folded across his chest. The rest of the squadron followed in line, all on their knees, arms folded, shoulders swaying. "Hi-ho! Hi-ho!" they sang. "It's off to work we go!" The line shuffled hard, in and out of the drinkers. "We work all day and get no pay hi-ho! Hi-ho hi-ho hi-ho! Hi-ho! It's off to work we go!" They lapped the room and Rex led them out, still on their knees, still chanting.

"Mad buggers," Marriott said.

"Is that how your fighter pilots normally behave?" the senator asked.

"Yes, sometimes."

"It's pretty sophomoric."

Marriott looked at Skull. "Callow," Skull said. "Immature."

"Some of them are a bit young, of course," Marriott said.

"I can't see Hitler's *Luftwaffe* pilots romping around on their knees," the American said. "They take their work too damn seriously for that, unfortunately."

"Must relax occasionally," the adjutant said. "Anyway, I thought our chaps looked jolly good. At least they were all in step."

"Except Moggy," Marriott said.

"Well, Moggy's left-handed, you've got to make allowances for –"

"And Miller and Cox," said Skull.

"They were probably following Moggy. Anyway, drill isn't so terribly important for pilots."

"You people still have a pretty good Navy, don't you?" the American asked.

There was a tumbling crash in the stairwell and the march of the dwarfs came to a sudden stop.

"I thought that might happen," Kellaway said. "It's not so easy to go downstairs as it is to come up. Your feet get in the way," he explained. The American looked at him, unblinking. "Actually, it's a very good exercise for toughening people up," Kellaway went on. "Sharpens their reflexes. Excellent training for ... well, all sorts of things."

"Parachute-jumping," Marriott suggested.

"Yes. Exactly."

"I see." The American finished his drink. "You boys plan to do a lot of that, do you?"

"Oh, no, no, certainly not. But –"

"May I get you another?" Skull asked. "I'd be most interested to hear about political conditions in Minnesota. I myself have an aunt in Wisconsin and two cousins in Oklahoma. I understand the winters are quite severe."

"Scotch," said the American.

For two days, Hornet squadron did nothing but put on flying shows. They gave demonstrations above Rouen, Le Havre, Beauvais, Amiens, Arras, Calais and Boulogne. Whatever effect this had on French morale, it did the squadron a power of good. They were entertained to lunch at French Air Force bases and to dinner by Le Touquet Chamber of Commerce. They were fed, flattered, and pointed out in the streets. The flying was enormous fun. Then the rains came.

It rained for most of a week, a driving downpour that fell out of a cloudbase that seemed to hang as low as a basement ceiling.

Rex gave everyone local leave but it was too wet to go anywhere. The airport restaurant had been requisitioned for the officers' mess; they hung about, sprawling on its leather banquettes, writing letters at its round marble-topped tables, complaining about the peculiar drinks available from its neon-lit bar, and making loud yearnings for decent pints of beer, real pork sausage, and the latest *Daily Mirror*. France, they agreed, was the dullest place they had ever seen. Not to fly was always boring, but not to fly in France was worse, far worse. There was nothing to do. You could go to the pictures, but who wanted to sit in the dark, watching a lot of frogs jabbering at each other? Might as well stand on any street-corner. *And* get soaked through by this filthy frog weather. If this was the best the French could do they ought to be bloody well ashamed of themselves. Kingsmere used to get a bit foggy but at least you didn't need thigh-waders to cross the road. What a rotten aero-drome. What a rotten country. What a rotten war. It wasn't a war at all: nothing was happening.

Something happened. Late one morning, Air Commodore Bletchley turned up.

"I'm not going to make a long speech," he told the assembled pilots. "I just want to keep you fully briefed about the war situation. We at Air Ministry take the view that it's not fair to expect a chap to put his heart and soul into something unless he knows what good it's going to do. So you ask: what's this war all about? And why have you been sent to this lovely sunny country?"

Polite chuckles. Rex's dog, Reilly, yawned.

"There's a saying, 'An Englishman's word is his bond,' " Bletchley went on. "Well, we gave our word to Poland. So did France. And when Hitler launched his treacherous attack on the gallant Polish nation – a nation that rose from the ashes of the last war, remember – how could we stand idly by and watch those brave and freedom-loving allies of ours trampled beneath the Nazi jackboot? Of course we couldn't. The time had come for all right-thinking men to stand up and be counted. When Poland, reeling under the blow of a wicked and cowardly invasion, appealed to us for help, her call did not fall on deaf ears. That is why we have entered the battle on the side of this brilliant and patriotic country which has made such an outstanding contribution to twentieth-century civilisation. By siding with Poland against the Hun, we are standing up for freedom. We are standing up for democracy. We are standing up for the right to live in peace and justice. We are taking the path of honour, and with such as you to guard it, I am sure that it will also be the path of glory and eventual triumph."

Bletchley stepped back. The squadron coughed and shuffled its feet, uncertain whether or not to applaud.

"Air Commodore Bletchley has kindly said that he will answer any questions," Rex announced.

Nobody spoke. They had been taken aback by the nobility of their mission. Reilly yawned again.

"With your usual admirable skill you seem to have covered everything, sir," Rex said.

"Who's going to win the Grand National, sir?" Moke Miller asked.

"Not Hitler," Bletchley said.

That was a good ending; they all enjoyed that; and they trooped in to lunch in a high good humour. Rex placed Skull on one side of their guest and Kellaway on the other, while he sat opposite. "I'm afraid you've caught us ill-prepared, sir," he said. "Just *soupe à l'oignon* followed by *sole meunière*. There's a very reasonable white Bordeaux, though, and the Camembert's not bad."

"Good heavens. When I think of the stuff we used to eat in France. Stew three times a day."

"Next time you come, sir, we'll give you a decent lunch. I've got my spies out looking for some top-class cooks. Really top-class."

"Well, good luck," Bletchley said.

The soup was served.

"You were over here for the last show, sir?" the adjutant asked.

"Yes. Flanders, mainly. We were flying Sopwith Pups, lovely little bus. Great for potting Huns. Unfortunately I had to retire hurt before I could win the war single-handed."

They chuckled sympathetically.

"Fascinating country, Poland," Skull said.

Bletchley took a moment to change direction. "Oh, very," he said. "Quite unique, really."

"Tell me . . ." Skull polished his spectacles with his napkin. "When Germany is defeated, is it the Allies' intention to restore Poland?"

"I should damn well hope so."

"And all the Polish boundaries? Will they be restored too?"

Kellaway chuckled. "It wouldn't be much of a country without boundaries, would it?"

"Did your boy get into Oxford all right, sir?" Rex asked.

"I merely wondered," Skull said, replacing his spectacles, "because it was only a year ago that Polish troops occupied the Teschen area of Czechoslovakia. Will they be allowed to keep that?"

"Oh, Czechoslovakia! Don't talk to me about Czechoslovakia." Bletchley dismembered a bread roll. "Not really a nation at all, was it? Just a mixed salad. Frankly, I blame the politicians for trying to cobble it together. I mean, who in his right mind would have given Czechoslovakia three and a half million Germans? I ask you."

"So Hitler was right to march in."

"It was inevitable. I mean, I don't like the little blighter, and given half a chance I'd blow his ugly head off, but I can't honestly blame him for what he did in Czechoslovakia. Basically he took back what belonged to him."

"If only he'd stopped there," the adjutant said, "things might have been all right."

Rex signalled for the wine. "Wonderful musicians, the Poles," he said. "I could listen to Chopin all night."

"That's very interesting," Skull said. "You don't mind my asking you to clarify these political matters?"

"Not at all," Bletchley said.

"I'm supposed to be intelligence officer here, you see."

"Absolutely."

"Ivor Novello for me," Kellaway said. "I say: hasn't he got a new show in London? Or am I thinking of the other bloke?"

"Of course, there are also several million Germans living in Poland," said Skull. The sole and the wine arrived together.

"I rather think you'll like this, sir," Rex said confidently.

"I'm sure I shall. What d'you mean?"

Skull said: "The Peace Settlement gave Poland all of West Prussia and a good deal besides. In fact twenty years ago rather a lot of Germany ended up inside Poland."

"Your very good health, sir," Rex said. They drank. "It's got *authority*, if you know what I mean," he said, "and yet it's *piquant*."

"Very true." Bletchley worked his lips. "Yes. A good *piquant* wine, that. Damned *piquant*."

"Noël Coward," Kellaway said happily. They looked at him. "Just remembered," he explained. "The other bloke."

"Look, I don't know about all these peculiar Prussians who're supposed to have been shanghaied to Poland in 1919," Bletchley said. "Statistics prove nothing, anyway. What I *do* know is an awful lot of Jerry stormtroopers are chucking their weight about in Poland right now, and it's got to stop."

"D'you know what I dislike most about the fascists, sir?" Rex asked. "It's their awfully poor taste. I mean, one look at their uniforms tells you they're not gentlemen."

"And it's not true that they make the trains run on time, either," Kellaway said. "I met a chap in a pub who told me he was always missing his connection in Rome. Propaganda, that's all it is."

"Anyway, I hope I've put your mind at rest," Bletchley said.

Skull gave a twisted smile. "A consummation devoutly not to be wished," he said.

"You mustn't mind old Skull, sir," Kellaway said. "We got him from a university. They were having a sale."

"The Poles also invaded Soviet Russia in 1920," Skull said, "as a result of which their eastern border was extended to take in twenty-seven million people who are certainly not Polish and who have not the slightest wish to become Polish. The same applies to a quantity of Lithuanians. My restless mind wonders whether or not we are fighting for their independence, too."

Bletchley grunted.

"How's your sole, sir?" Rex asked.

"Let's get one thing straight," Bletchley said. "This is not a war about boundaries."

"Good Lord, no," Rex said.

"I mean it's not *completely* about boundaries."

"Far from it."

"This is a war about decency, about . . . about . . ."

"Spot more wine, sir?"

"Yes. Thanks. Decency, that's what we're fighting for. Thanks.

101

Just keep that idea clear in your mind," Bletchley said to Skull. "That's what really matters. Nothing else matters."

"Not Poland?"

"Yes, Poland, for heaven's sake! The Poles are a very decent people. They don't go around beating up Jews."

"Oh yes they do," Skull said firmly. "The Poles beat up Jews regularly, vigorously and with every sign of keen enjoyment."

"Rubbish."

The adjutant caught a warning flicker of the eyes from his CO. "Skull, old chap," he said, "change the record, would you? It's getting a bit worn."

Bletchley drank some wine and forced himself to smile. "Let's face it, talk never won a war," he said. "What you chaps need is some decent action. Then you'll really have something to talk about."

"It's like playing cricket, isn't it?" Rex said. "Waiting to bat is always the hardest ... Your boy's a pretty fair cricketer, isn't he, sir? D'you think he'll get a Blue?"

Air Commodore Bletchley visited the hangars and walked past the Hurricanes, slapping them on the engine-cowling as if they were horses lined up in stables. "Jolly good," he said. "Now remember, Rex: keep your squadron on its toes. And if you ever need anything, call me at Headquarters. Goodbye." He got into his car.

Rex went back to the mess, found Kellaway and Skull, and took them into a quiet corner. "What d'you make of all that?" he asked.

"Poland's had it," Kellaway said. "As soon as I heard him use that word 'gallant,' I said to myself 'Old boy, Poland's been scratched.' It's all over for them."

"Skull?"

"Poland has been carved up by its neighbours for centuries," Skull said. "I see no reason why it should not be carved up once again."

"Right, we're agreed. Forget Poland. So now the question is: What the dickens are we doing sitting here?"

"We're waiting for Jerry to invade France, aren't we?" the adjutant said.

"Are we? I'm not so sure. If you look at the map, we've got Belgium next door."

"That's the way he came last time."

"Yes. *And* he got thoroughly bogged down." Rex nodded at the drenched, drowned view of the airport. "What price Flanders fields in this weather? Frightfully muddy. Besides, it's getting late in the year. No, I think we're in the wrong spot, gentlemen. Nothing's going to happen here."

"And the right spot is where?" Skull asked.

Reilly wandered over and licked Rex's hand. After a while Rex lay back in his chair, one hand propping his head, his faithful hound at his feet, and allowed a smile to play over his face. "The right spot," he said, "is where danger lurks and honour beckons."

Kellaway sighed. "I say, Skull," he said. "Was all that stuff true, about Poland?"

"Was it *true*?" Skull was quite offended. "My dear fellow . . ."

"Sorry, sorry." Kellaway sighed again. "Oh, well. I'll go and see about a spot of tea, I think."

Three days later, Hornet squadron was airborne again, flying southeast.

Below them, saturated fields gleamed and glistened in pale sunlight. The sky had a cold, scrubbed look, with leftover scraps of cloud swept along by a gusting, thirty-mile-an-hour wind. The squadron flew in a very loose vic at only four thousand feet. This was because Rex had Reilly in his cockpit, curled between his legs, and he didn't want to distress the dog with extreme altitude.

They landed at Rheims, refuelled, lunched, and flew on, this time more east than south.

The sun gained a little strength and picked out more clearly the wandering scars of old warfare. The pilots looked down on the marks left by mile after mile of trench-system. It was as if an endless furrow had been ploughed out by some dreamy giant who had turned this way and that as he walked, opening the earth as easily as a finger splits a rotten seam; and had then forgotten it, abandoned it, left it to mend itself or not. Alongside it ran the remains of a smaller ditch: half an inch away from the air, two hundred yards on the ground; and running parallel with that was an even softer marking. These were the second and third lines of trenches. On the German side the same pattern repeated itself, one-two-three, like breakers picking up strength as they advanced.

And everywhere the scab and pox of shell-holes. They spattered no-man's-land with the frozen impact of rain-drops hitting water. They left a million craters on either side, and the afternoon sun caught them and counted them all. Twenty years of grass and weeds had begun to coat the damage, but it was a feeble answer to four years of high explosive.

Châlons was left behind them; then Sainte-Menehould; Clermont; Verdun with its fortress, its huge cemeteries, its ugly memorial tower. After that the land fell sharply to a wide plain and they reached Metz. To the north lay neutral Luxembourg. Forty-odd miles to the east they could see the haze of factory smoke that must be Saarbrücken: Germany.

They flew halfway to Saarbrücken and then turned south. Ten minutes later they landed at a small, all-grass airfield on the edge of somewhere called Lunéville.

The pilots went for a walk through the town. It did not take long. "What a hole," Dicky Starr said.

"Someone has blundered," Rex said. He looked very grave. "This won't possibly do."

It had to do, at least for a while. The convoy of trucks bringing the groundcrews, cooks, batmen and administrative staff arrived late that night, led by Kellaway and Skull in Stickwell's Buick convertible, which had been smuggled over (contrary to all regulations) by an army-officer friend returning from leave.

They were all billeted in a brand-new block of flats with no heating and erratic plumbing. For the next week, Flip Moran commanded the squadron while Rex drove around the countryside in Sticky's Buick, with the adjutant to navigate. At length he found what he wanted: an adequate airfield within striking distance of Metz and Nancy, a requisitionable château less than a mile away, some shooting in the surrounding hills, and good riding in the grounds of the estate. It was called Château St Pierre. "Given a decent winter," he told Kellaway as they stood on the terrace, "we might even get a spot of skiing in the Vosges."

"Where on earth are we going to get skis, sir?" the adjutant asked.

"Wake up, uncle," Rex said patiently. "This is war, when all things are possible. Remember?"

OCTOBER
1939

Fanny Barton rejoined Hornet squadron and found it a happy unit.

"This is a smashing place," Flash Gordon said as he showed Barton over the house. "Lovely big bedrooms, a socking great library where we play ping-pong, jolly nice anteroom with a log fire and a bar . . ." He opened a door. "Look, this is the billiard room." Barton glanced inside: two full-size tables, with deep leather armchairs all around. "Colossal, isn't it? And there's a swimming-pool in the grounds, and a tennis-court, and a thing for clay-pigeon shooting. We've even got a squash court! Must be the only one for hundreds of miles. Soon as we get some rackets, Pip Patterson's teaching me how to play."

Barton had never heard him talk so much. Flash Gordon was the man who listened, who laughed at the joke (slightly later than everyone else), who was on the edge of the photograph, half-obscured by the man in front. He always looked neat and squared-off, his hair cleanly parted and his features regularly distributed, as if his face were ready for kit-inspection. When people thought of him (which was not often) they thought of a uniform rather than a personality.

"Who owns this place?" Barton asked.

"Some Paris banker, I think."

They went onto a balcony. "Not bad countryside, is it? The aerodrome's on the other side of those trees. It's just an emergency field, really, but Lord Rex is having it extended."

"*Lord* Rex?"

"Yes. Didn't you know? That's what we call him now. It suits him, don't you think? Some head waiter in Metz kept sucking up to him and saying 'Yes milord' and '*Tout de suite*, milord,' so we just kept it going. The CO doesn't mind. In fact I think he rather likes it. He's a marvellous chap."

Barton looked down at the wide, flatstoned terrace from which a flight of shallow steps led to a domino pattern of lily ponds. "Done much flying?" he asked.

"Bags. We haven't shot down any Jerries yet, but that's their fault. We never see them. Well, the odd Dornier stooges over at twenty thou but he always beats it before we can get near. We're not allowed to chase them into Germany, you see. D'you speak French?"

"Not much."

"The frogs around here all gabble away like mad ... Still, they seem to know what we want. And some of the French popsies are really smashing. *Très formidable*."

Barton glanced at him. "Where are you from, Flash? I forget."

"North London. Hendon."

"Oh, yes." London: biggest village in the world. Barton realised what had happened: Gordon had finally left home. All his RAF training and service had been spent no more than a train-ride away from his parents in Hendon; now he was released, liberated, let off the leash in this wonderfully foreign country where everyone drove on the wrong side and drank wine night and day, and where sex was more than a technical possibility, it was a definite probability because it was a well-known fact that the French had virtually invented passion and they had definitely invented the brassiere, which meant that they knew how to get the bloody thing off, a problem that was often discussed in the mess, some saying that you could do it one-handed after a bit of practice and others claiming that they had encountered a species of safety-catch which obstinately defied all efforts, even using both hands and a pair of pliers. Flash Gordon listened to these discussions very carefully.

"Well," Barton said, "I suppose popsies are much the same wherever you go."

"Not these," Gordon insisted. "These popsies are hot stuff. Just you —"

"Hullo, Fanny." Flip Moran stepped onto the balcony. "Did you get your ears repaired, then?"

"Yes, thanks." Barton had rather dreaded meeting Moran again. "The doctors gave me some stuff for them."

"Very clever people, doctors." Moran leaned on the balustrade. It was impossible to tell if he was being sardonic; his Northern Irish accent put a heavy slant on every word he spoke. "You were away such a terribly long time," he said, "we thought for sure the Air Ministry had given you a squadron of Spitfires all to yourself."

"What? That'll be the day." Barton was damned if he was going to apologise; on the other hand they all had to live together and he wasn't proud of his performance as acting squadron commander. "I don't think I'm cut out for that sort of job. No, they made me stick around over there for the inquiry."

"What inquiry?" Gordon asked.

"Into the Battle of Southend Sands," Moran said. "Isn't that what they're calling it?"

"Yes." Barton didn't want to talk about it but Gordon still looked puzzled. "Where the Blenheim went down," he said.

"I understand the man's name was MacArthur," Moran said.

"MacArthy." Barton turned and looked away. There was absolutely no need for Moran to go into this sort of detail.

"Is that right? MacArthy, was it? He might have been Irish, you see."

"I've no idea."

"Well, whatever he was, I'm sure they gave him a proper send-off, poor fellah."

"He got a military funeral."

"Of course he did. After all, he died on active service, defending his country."

Barton clenched his teeth. He felt resentment boiling up inside him but he knew that he simply could not afford to have a row with Moran. It was going to be difficult enough to be accepted back into the squadron as things were. "The inquiry completely cleared everyone in this squadron," he said. "It was not our fault."

"Of course it did," Moran said. "Of course it wasn't. MacArthy, MacArthy . . . I used to know a MacArthy, we trained together, he had this flaming red hair, an awful funny fellow he was, kept us in fits of laughter all the time . . . David McArthy."

Barton stared at him. Moran's broad black moustache hid any expression but Barton was sure Moran was lying. "Was he a small chap with big feet?" he asked.

"That's right. That's him." Moran nodded vigorously. Flash Gordon smiled, just to make it unanimous.

"Couldn't have been the same man," Barton said. "This MacArthy was a big chap with small feet."

"Ah. Is that right? Well, now."

"And his name wasn't David," Barton said. "It was Henry."

"Fancy that," Moran said. "Well, we all make mistakes, I suppose, even the best of us."

Rex was only a squadron leader but he knew his way around the Royal Air Force. He was a product of the RAF College at Cranwell. During the peacetime years, as he served in different squadrons on various bases, and as he went about the country to attend courses here and there on this subject and that (eventually even giving an occasional lecture himself), and as he flew in Fighter Command's annual exercise, and took part in war games and ceremonial fly-pasts and official visits to aircraft factories – as he did his job, Rex kept in touch with his Cranwell contemporaries and his old instructors. He knew who was on the way up, who was on the way out, and who was too clever for his own good. He knew who could be flattered, who could be ignored, and who could be baffled with bullshit. It did him no harm that his father had been a Conservative MP who had served for a spell as PPS to the Secretary of State for Air; the old man still had a lot of contacts at the Air Ministry. "Some people say, usually somewhat bitterly," he told his son, "that it's not what you know in this world, it's *who* you know. They're absolutely right, of course. Knowledge is useless without friends. It's an arrangement that's worked damn well for me. Apply yourself, and I see no earthly reason why it shouldn't work for you too." Young Rex applied himself. By the time he took Hornet squadron to France he could manipulate the system more successfully than any other man of his age and rank.

In one respect he was lucky. He looked right. He looked just like a man who ought to command a squadron of fighters: taller than average, alert-looking, well-built, with a natural curl to his chestnut hair and a questing gleam to his eye. His mouth was wide and strong and ready to smile; his jaw had a tiny cleft; his nose was straight; his eyes were grey, and they expressed an unblinking self-confidence. Rex had worked hard and mastered everything the RAF could teach him about being a fighter pilot. He had the self-assurance that comes when you know there is no question you cannot answer. Rex knew his strength. When he arrived at RAF Kingsmere and dumped all Fanny Barton's paperwork in the waste bin – the farmers' complaints, the accident inquiry's questionnaire, and so on – he knew that he could get away with it. The raid on the spares depot was rather more of a calculated risk, but not much: in time of war a fighter leader was expected to show powers of initiative when carrying out orders. Rex had got his squadron airborne and over to France, as ordered. That was the only justification he needed.

And he was popular. "Everyone's been very chipper since he

took over," the adjutant told Barton. "Even Mother Cox has stopped biting his nails. The thing is, he's such a tremendous wangler! He wangled our transfer down here when Pas-de-Calais got boring, and then he wangled a move to this drome, and he wangled the requisition of this lovely great house. He's even wangled us some decent cooks, would you believe. All the old sweats are being posted back to Blighty and we're getting some top-line civilian chefs instead, chaps who've just been called up. God knows how he wangled that, but he did."

"That's nice," Barton said.

"Well, it makes a pleasant change after the Ram, you must agree."

"And after me," Barton said.

"Oh, don't talk tosh, Fanny. I thought you coped magnificently under really very difficult circ —".

"Yes, yes, sure." Barton, having picked at his scabs, regretted it already. He said: "The only thing the CO can't wangle, it seems, is a scrap with the foe."

"True. Just before we came here, there was a spot of action, I believe, and half-a-dozen French bombers went to pot. Then some of our Battles trundled over to drop a few bombs and bumped into some Jerry fighters and had rather an unpleasant time. But now that Poland's down the drain, everyone's put up the shutters. Jerry doesn't bother us and we don't bother him."

"Not much of a war."

Kellaway laughed. "Fanny, you remind me *exactly* of a young chap who joined our outfit in 1917, during a bit of a lull. 'This is a feeble sort of fight,' he used to say. 'Call this a war? It's a swindle. I want my money back.' Then all of a sudden the balloon went up again and he had all the war he wanted, and a bit more besides. *That* changed his tune in a hurry." Kellaway stooped and tugged a frayed thread from the cuff of his trousers. "He was so keen! Keen as mustard. Trouble was, he didn't have the faintest idea what he was getting into, and by the time he found out, it was too late."

"What happened to him?"

Kellaway spread his hands. "Who knows?"

Barton found Rex in the squash court, playing Cattermole. They were using tennis rackets and a red rubber ball as big as an apple.

It was too bouncy: the rallies went on and on and on, until the players collided, or tripped and fell. Sprawled on his back, Rex saw Barton watching from the gallery. "Welcome back!" he called, panting. "You've got 'A' flight again, Fanny."

"Right-ho, sir."

"You saw this bastard trip me then, didn't you?"

"Afraid not, sir."

"Treachery. I'm surrounded by treachery." Rex got to his feet and found the ball. "My point," he said.

Cattermole was squatting against a wall, wiping sweat from his eyes. "Balls," he said. "You hit me on the leg."

"Rubbish! You were trying to kick the ball." Rex whacked it so that it ricocheted all around the court. "You're not fit, Moggy, that's your trouble."

"I was quite fit until you smashed my ribs with that bloody great club you're holding."

"What's the score?" Barton asked.

"Four-nil," Rex said.

"Five-eight," Cattermole said.

Barton left them to their game and went to the bar for a drink. Stickwell was there, playing liar dice with Patterson and Cox. "Hullo," he said. "I didn't expect to see you again. I thought they were going to cut your head off in the Tower of London."

"Not a funny joke." Barton pulled up a bar-stool.

"Certainly not. Treason is no laughing matter. Can't have chaps going around shooting down the king's Blenheims. I give you ... oh ... two pairs," he said to Patterson.

"The inquiry cleared me," Barton said. He was getting fed-up with telling people that.

"Did it? Good show," Patterson said. "Two pairs, eh? All right." He kept two dice and rolled three. "Let's face it, the Blenheim's a bloody awful fighter ... I give you three queens." He passed the leather cup to Cox.

"It's a bloody awful bomber, too," Stickwell said.

"Not as bad as the Hampden," Patterson said. Cox sat crouched over the dice, worrying. "At least the Blenheim looks like a plane. The Hampden looks like a frying-pan with wings on."

"Bloody awful kite," Stickwell agreed. "Not as useless as the Battle, but still bloody awful. Get your finger out, Mother."

"They sent a dozen Hampdens to bomb some Jerry ships last week," Barton said. "Shambles. Half of them bought it."

"Flak or fighters?" Patterson asked.

"Fighters."

Cox threw the dice. "Oh Christ," he muttered.

"109's or 110's?" Patterson asked.

"Dunno."

"Bet you they were 110's," Stickwell said. "Stands to reason, doesn't it? Two engines are better than one. They make it go damn quick, and the nose is free to carry lots of dirty great guns. Trust the krauts to come up with a brute like that."

"I bet they're turning out 110's by the score," Patterson said. "By the hundred, probably."

"Speak to me, Mother," Stickwell said.

Cox agonised for a moment, and then passed the dice. "Four queens," he said quickly, and chewed his lip.

Stickwell took them and rang the bell on the bar. "Want a beer? Four queens . . ." He looked under the cup. "By God, you're a dreadful rogue, Mother." Cox smiled nervously.

"Thanks," Barton said. They had been in no hurry to buy him a drink.

"Four queens is actually a very modest claim," Stickwell said. "I myself can see five of the ladies, with one eye shut . . ." He rolled three dice. "My goodness: three more. Where *do* they come from? Beers all round, please," he said to the steward. "Pip: I give you a full house, jacks on queens."

"Very sexy," Patterson said, and squinted under the cup. "They've started breeding," he announced. "Prolific little buggers, the royals . . ." He threw the dice.

"I suppose this means you'll take over 'A' flight again," Stickwell said. Barton nodded. "Oh, well," Stickwell said.

Barton waited. "What's that supposed to mean?"

"Would you believe it?" Patterson said. "What astonishing good luck."

Stickwell yawned, and Barton felt his temper begin to slip. "Listen," he said, "don't jump to the conclusion that it was my Blenheim that got shot down. It could easily have been yours."

"Full house, kings on queens," Patterson said to Cox.

"Not a hope," Stickwell said to Barton. The steward gave them four beers. "Kings on queens?" said Cox, not touching the cup. "I don't know about that."

"Sticky couldn't hit a Blenheim," Patterson said. "He's a rotten shot. Can't get his key in the door, sometimes."

"Not a hope," Stickwell said.

"I don't know about kings on queens," Cox said slowly. He peeked under the cup and winced.

Barton said: "For all you know, maybe you missed your Blenheim and hit mine by mistake."

"Not a hope."

"I'll roll two," Cox decided. "No, make it three ... Oh, damn it all, roll four."

"Well, you certainly sounded confident enough when we landed," Barton said. "You were a crack shot that day."

"Not a hope."

"At last!" Cox said. "I knew my luck would change. I give you aces on queens, Sticky."

"Not a hope, old boy. Put this round on Mr Cox's account," Stickwell told the steward. "Cheers, everyone."

They drank. "I'm going to take up bloody knitting," Cox muttered. He uncovered the dice: a pair of tens; the rest was junk.

"Hey," Barton said. "This is good beer. Is it French?"

"It's Whitbread's," Patterson told him. "Lord Rex has a barrel flown in from London twice a week."

"My God."

"Best CO we ever had," Patterson said.

"I like it here," Stickwell said. "Or, if you prefer, *Jag tycker om det.*"

"No, I don't prefer," Barton said. "But I'll buy another round, if you like."

"Fanny is not as stupid as he appears," Stickwell said to the others; and by that use of his nickname, Barton knew that he was accepted again. Not exactly welcomed, but accepted.

That evening after dinner, Rex called a meeting of the pilots in the library. He stood by the crackling fire, with a huge oil painting of a dying stag behind him and the dog Reilly sprawled at his feet.

"Right, settle down everybody," he said. There was a pewter tankard in his left hand, and the firelight flickered on his jaw. "I

114

want to talk about the war, such as it is." He scanned the faces of the squadron, testing their attention.

Moggy Cattermole softly broke wind. "Sorry," he said at once. "Not a comment. Too much cheese."

"If only we could connect your tubes to the Merlin, Moggy," Rex said, "the Hurri would do another ten knots."

"But the Huns wouldn't come anywhere near us," Fitzgerald said.

"And there," Rex said, "you have put your finger on it."

"That's a trick worth seeing," Flip Moran said, and there was laughter. Fanny Barton watched, and was impressed. This was a very different Hornet squadron: much more relaxed, more together. "If anyone can think of a way to bring the Hun to battle," Rex said, smiling, "I'll stand him a night at the Folies Bergère." He took a sip of his beer, to cover their silence. "It's a problem, isn't it? The men in grey won't come out and play. Obviously the weather's not going to get any better from now on. If you want my candid opinion, we shan't get any sport, any *real* sport, until next spring."

Billy Starr said: "You mean . . . Hitler's just going to sort of hibernate?"

Rex shrugged. "It makes sense. France isn't Poland, is it? The French army is the biggest in Europe. They've got their Maginot Line, and they've had a month to mobilise."

Miller raised his hand. "Please sir, can I go on leave, sir?" he said. More laughter.

"Actually, leave is a very definite possibility," Rex said, which pleased them, "but before that, there's work to be done in the air. We've had a lot of fun putting on shows for the French. Very impressive performance. That's to say, it impressed the French. It won't impress the Germans."

He ran his foot along Reilly's back. The dog rolled over and displayed its stomach.

"What everyone's got to understand," Rex said, "is that this war isn't going to be like the last show. Not a bit like it. Everything's changed. Last time, your typical fighter pilot was a solo act. Now he's part of a team, and that's how he's got to think and fly and fight: as one of a team. Right, uncle?"

"No question, sir," the adjutant said, taking his pipe from his mouth. "Teamwork pays. 'Squadron spirit,' we used to call it. All for one, one for all."

Rex nodded, a little impatiently. "That was on the ground, of course, but when you took off, you were on your own, weren't you? No radio, for instance. It was a matter of picking out your Jerry and having a crack at him and hoping you were better than he was."

Kellaway blew down his pipe-stem.

"Which you were," Rex said generously. "A damned sight better."

The adjutant scratched his ear, and gave a wry smile. "I don't know about that," he said. "A lot of luck came into it. You were as good as your plane, and so was he."

"That hasn't changed," Moran said.

"Well, we know our machines are superior," Rex began, but the adjutant hadn't finished.

"You say it was a matter of picking out your Jerry and having a crack at him," Kellaway said. "What most of us tried to do was sneak up on the Hun while he wasn't looking, shoot him in the back fast, and bugger off home before his pals turned up."

There was a gust of laughter.

"Well, it worked," Kellaway said.

"Times have changed," Rex said. "When the enemy comes at us he's going to come in quantity. You won't be attacking individuals, you'll be attacking formations. There's only one way to hit a formation, and that's with another formation."

Kellaway nodded. "We found that," he murmured.

"So Hollywood's idea of the ace fighter pilot is out of the window," Rex went on. "The brilliant individual who dogfights like a demon is a thing of the past. With closing speeds of over six hundred miles an hour there simply isn't time for that sort of fun and games. The effective fighting unit nowadays is all of you. It's the squadron . . . Skull," he said, apparently suddenly unsure of himself, "what are eight twelves?"

"Eight twelves are eighty-six," Skull said without hesitation.

"Nonsense," Cox said. Skull widened his eyes. "Ninety-four," he said. Cox groaned. "Well, it's somewhere in that region," Skull retorted. "Ninety-six," Cox declared. "Possibly, possibly," Skull murmured.

116

"Ninety-six machine-guns," Rex said. "That means this squadron can deliver twice as much fire-power as an infantry battalion – provided we're in the right place at the right time, in the right numbers. And *that* means manoeuvring the squadron around the sky with parade-ground efficiency, all twelve machines moving as one, so that when we strike, we strike as a team! Frankly, chaps, I'd like to see the German bomber formation that can stand being blasted by ninety-six Brownings. What?"

They chuckled at the prospect. Reilly got up and wandered away.

Cox said: "What about their fighters, sir?"

"Our first and foremost priority is the bombers," Rex said firmly. "We knock them out first. That's paramount. The fighters will have to take their turn afterwards."

Kellaway took his pipe from his mouth as if to speak, then changed his mind and put it back, slowly.

"It seems to me, sir," Barton said, "that what you've been saying adds up to using the Fighting Area Attacks. Well, we've been practising those for years."

"Of course you have." Rex took a little book from his pocket and flourished it. "All the answers are here, in the Manual of Air Tactics. You know, they're not complete fools on the Air Staff. They worked out a long time ago what's the best way to tackle the German Air Force. Each one of the six Fighting Area Attacks is tailormade for a different bomber formation. And the key to success with these attacks is *tight, close, precise, formation flying.*" Rex whacked the manual against his open palm to emphasise each word. "That's why formation flying is the mainstay of Fighter Command training. You take your squadron . . ." He held up his free hand, fingers widely splayed. ". . . and combine it . . ." The fingers clenched. ". . . and bring all its guns to bear . . ." He crashed his fist against the manual. ". . . and you've got a knock-out punch that'll deck your enemy good and proper."

"Serve him right, too," Fitzgerald said.

"When do we start?" Dicky Starr asked.

"You start tomorrow," Rex said, "learning how to fly in formation. At the moment you're fart-assing all over the sky like a lot of pregnant ducks. Thank God Hitler's taking a rest. It gives us a chance to get this squadron on top-line before the balloon goes up. Right now you don't know what close-formation flying means."

There was a startled silence.

"What does it mean, exactly?" Cattermole asked.

"It means being able to scratch the next plane in the armpit with your wingtip," Rex said.

Flash Gordon stumbled sideways and knocked over a small table. Everyone turned to look. "For Pete's sake!" he said heavily. He sighed and moved away. "It's Reilly," he said. "He's gone and done a . . . you know. Done his business. On the carpet."

There were groans and cheers, but Rex cut them short. "That's your fault," he snapped. "Someone's been giving him snacks. Reilly gets fed once a day, nothing more. Start messing his system about and this is what happens. I won't tolerate it."

Eventually a mess servant came and cleaned up the carpet, but the atmosphere was not the same. Rex took Reilly for a walk. The pilots drifted off to the bar.

"So if you want to make a good impression tomorrow," Stickwell suggested, "remember to shave your armpits."

"Slimy ponce," Cattermole said.

Under the Ram, close-formation meant wingtips five feet apart. Rex had different standards.

The squadron still flew in the traditional vics of three but day by day these arrowheads became tighter. The five-foot gaps shrank until one wingtip was directly behind another. After a week, the wingmen had acquired the skill and confidence to tuck themselves into the airspace between their leader's wing and tailplane. Seen from above, the squadron appeared to be interlocked like a jigsaw puzzle.

It was from above that Rex liked to inspect them. After forty minutes' drill he would order Fanny Barton or Flip Moran to take over his position at the point, while he climbed five or six hundred feet. As he viewed the whole tightly-knit arrangement he transmitted corrections by radio, telling Blue Two to ease back a fraction or Yellow Three to come up a shade. When the pattern was precise he would order a change of course or formation. His favourite formation was sections-close-astern. With the wingmen snugly tucked in, and the sections neatly slotted behind each other, the squadron had the thrustful look of a giant spearhead. It created an impression of perfect discipline, absolute unanimity. Sometimes Rex watched them fly like that for a minute or more, just for the pleasure of it.

Nobody else took much pleasure in the training. It was grindingly hard, and tough on the nerves. There were several little knocks and scrapes, mere touches that had a terrifyingly violent effect. One moment the squadron was cruising along, the aircraft occasionally easing up and down like boats in a soft swell, and then for no particular reason Pip Patterson and Dicky Starr brushed wingtips, no more than a tickle but *Christ!* the tickle was a sting. The two planes jerked apart, wings flickering like windmills, and the spasm panicked the entire formation. Outside planes dived for empty air; the men in the middle tried to look six ways at once; the squadron scattered. Only Rex flew straight on. When, eventually, they reassembled, their hearts were thudding and their skin was sweating, and a few hands and feet had a constant tremble, which did not make close-formation flying any easier or safer. Rex was uncompromising. "Close up, Jester aircraft," he ordered. "Now you know what happens when you daydream at 250 mph. Get organised, get together." The training went on.

By the time they landed and gathered to look at the buckled wingtips it was all a great joke. "Pretty shoddy stuff, this," Fitzgerald said, ripping bits of fabric off Patterson's wingtip. "We've got better canvas on our deckchairs at home."

"Good gracious," Patterson said. "Somebody's made a nasty hole in my aeroplane."

"Dicky had something to tell you," Flash Gordon said. "He came over and gave you a little nudge."

Starr said: "No, no, far from it. *You* were trying to tell *me* something, Pip."

"Hullo, hullo." Marriott, the engineer officer, strolled up. "Been attacked by golden eagles, have you?"

"It's your rotten canvas," Fitzgerald said. "It falls to bits as soon as someone looks at it."

Cox joined them, and poked his finger into the damage. "You ought to get that mended," he said.

"It was all right until you touched it," Patterson said accusingly.

119

"Don't muck about with other people's aeroplanes, Mother," Starr said.

"Personally," Cox said, "I think they ought to make special cast-iron kites for chaps like you."

"As a matter of fact Hawkers are making all-metal wings for the Hurricane right now," Marriott said. "We might even get some one day."

"No thanks," Starr said. "I'll stick to my good old canvas wings. Much easier to flap, you know."

"Dicky flaps rather a lot," Fitzgerald explained.

"Are you people going to do much more of this?" Marriott asked, pointing to the wingtip.

"Only when we're flying," Patterson said. "After that your troops can have a go. They're much better at it than we are."

Marriott looked at him sideways. "All complaints in writing to the management," he said.

"Please sir," Flash Gordon put up his hand. "That big fan in front keeps making a rotten draught, sir."

"Jackass!" Marriott chased him, tripped him, and pretended to jump on him.

"Hullo," said Moggy Cattermole, trudging past. "What's going on?"

"Rain dance," said Fitzgerald.

"Keep it up," Cattermole told Marriott. "I could do with a break."

Nobody disagreed. The weather was on Rex's side, and there was no end in sight to his close-formation training. They found it physically tiring and mentally exhausting. "I don't know why I'm so whacked," Miller complained to Flip Moran. "All I have to do is fly straight and watch you."

Moran twitched his nose, which was about as demonstrative as Moran ever got. "Doing the right thing is never tiring," he said. "What takes it out of you is making sure you don't do the wrong bloody thing."

Miller thought about that. "It's not as if the Hurricane's a bitch to fly," he said. "She keeps station beautifully. But now that we're all on top of each other you can't relax for an instant. It's such bloody hard work, Flip."

"Perhaps that's the idea."

"Perhaps." Miller looked at his fingernails, and quickly shoved his hand in his pocket. "Oh well . . . Come and have a drink."

Most of the pilots were drinking more; not a lot more, but enough for the adjutant to notice. He also noticed that some – Stickwell and Miller, particularly – seemed not to be sleeping well. Others – Gordon, Starr, Cox – were going to bed earlier than usual. This was not altogether surprising. On top of Rex's formation training, Headquarters at Rheims kept the squadron fairly busy with patrols at section strength in the hope of catching a careless intruder; so far, few had been seen and none had been caught. All in all, life was becoming a grind. But when Kellaway suggested as much to the flight commanders they quickly put him straight. "I have no complaints, uncle," Moran said. "None at all. Nor does any man in my flight."

"Of course not, Flip. Far be it from me to interfere. I thought one or two of the chaps were looking somewhat shattered, that's all."

"They're not shattered," Barton said. "They're just not used to hard work. Did you hear about this morning? Last thing we did was squadron in vic – the ace-of-diamonds pattern – only *inverted*."

"What you used to call upside-down," Moran said.

"In close formation?" Kellaway was amused and amazed. "Gosh."

"Not particularly close," Moran said.

"But close enough for some," Barton added.

"My stars . . . Well, as long as everyone's happy."

"They're not paid to be happy," Moran said. "They're paid to fly."

"True, true. But upside-down . . ." The adjutant chuckled.

"It keeps the sun out of their eyes."

"Next week we're going to start flying backwards," Barton said, "to keep the dust out of our eyes."

Kellaway said: "Talking of flying backwards, did I ever tell you –"

"Yes," Moran said firmly. "Several times."

"Oh."

"Tail-Slide Thompson," Barton said.

"That's the chap. Mad as a –"

"He climbed into the wind and if the wind was stronger than he was, the plane slid backwards," Barton said. "We know."

"People say it's impossible, but I saw him do it. I even saw him *land* backwards, once, on Salisbury Plain." The adjutant used his hands to mime landing backwards. "Tommy was in a Farman Shorthorn. You could land those things at twenty miles an hour. Well, maybe not twenty. Ridiculously slow, anyway. Call it twenty. And if the breeze was doing, say, twenty-one miles an hour –"

"He was bound to end up going backwards," Barton said.

"That's right. In fact –"

"He stuck his tail-skid in the grass and snapped it off," Moran said. "You told us, uncle."

"Did I?" Kellaway dropped his hands. "Lots of people won't believe it. You'd be surprised."

"Listen, adj," Moran said, "if you want to do something for us, for God's sake have a word with the CO about his bloody dog."

"Reilly? What's Reilly been up to?"

"He keeps pissing on people," Moran said. Kellaway laughed, but the other two did not. "You wait till he soaks your bags too, uncle," Barton said. "You won't find it so funny. He got me yesterday. I was standing on the terrace after breakfast, and damn me if Reilly didn't wander up and squirt all over my left leg."

"Your left leg! You don't say." The adjutant was intrigued. "Does Reilly really make a habit of this . . . this habit?"

"See what you can do, adj," Moran said. "Otherwise someone's going to boot the beast into the middle of next week."

"Dear me, we can't have that," Kellaway said. "It's bad luck to kick the squadron mascot. Awful things might happen."

"I can imagine," Moran said.

Kellaway and Skull stood on the roof of the Hôtel de Ville in the centre of Nancy, and looked out across the Place Stanislas. It was early afternoon and the light was perfect, filtered through high, flat cloud that held a soft luminosity. It suited the grace and spaciousness of this elegant square, with its tall, big-windowed buildings, topped with balustrades. The city reminded the adjutant of Bath but he decided against mentioning this; Skull was bound to have something perceptive and difficult to say in reply, and Kellaway wasn't all that interested in architecture anyway. He sniffed the air and breathed deeply. "I like autumn," he said. "Don't you? Sweeping up the leaves and making bonfires. Apples. Chestnuts. Logs. Football. That sort of thing." He stared thoughtfully across the rooftops. "Squirrels," he added after a moment. "Bright little animals. I've always had a soft spot for squirrels."

"Indeed you have," Skull said. "We all have. It's called skin."

"Skin?"

"They bite. Squirrels have sharp teeth and evil tempers. You should think of them as tree-rats. They can be rabid, you know."

"Squirrels? Surely not."

"There was a tree outside the library in my college at Cambridge that was infested with squirrels. They used to beg for titbits, and then bite people. Mainly the dons, of course. Undergraduates rarely used the library."

"Good Lord." Kellaway reviewed this news from all angles, and came up with an explanation. "They couldn't have been normal squirrels," he said.

"The Master ordered them destroyed," Skull said. "A man came and put poison in the holes in the tree."

Kellaway sighed. "Why can't people be a bit more tolerant?" he asked.

"Greedy little brutes," Skull said. "Not worth saving."

"Oh, rubbish! Squirrels aren't greedy. And besides —"

"I was referring to the dons," Skull said. "They constantly took food into the college library. One kept finding their crusts in the Britannica. The sound of gnawing and belching was quite deafening at times. It's not as if they were clever men; they were very stupid. That's probably why they ate so much: to compensate for their lack of intelligence. I suggested to the Bursar that the squirrels be infected with bubonic plague in order to raise the intellectual standing of the college, but he had no imagination. A dull man."

The adjutant took a short walk to the corner of the parapet. He didn't know whether he believed Skull's story or not, but he knew that he liked squirrels and he liked autumn and he felt that somehow he was being cheated out of his simple pleasures. "It seems a dirty trick to kill a bunch of squirrels just for behaving like squirrels," he said.

"Oh, the squirrels didn't die. They simply moved to another tree."

"Ah." Kellaway felt better. "Sensible creatures."

"Yes. The tree died, of course. Poisoned."

"Here they come." Kellaway's ears had picked up the faint groan of aircraft engines, and the two men turned to face the noise.

Hornet squadron appeared from the south-west, flying at five hundred feet in their basic ace-of-diamonds formation. They crossed the city at no great speed, turned and came back. By this time the roar had brought people into the streets and the Place Stanislas was thickly dotted with watchers. Rex waggled his wings, and the squadron changed shape to sections-close-astern; the stretched arrowhead. They held that for ten seconds. He signalled again. The Hurricanes casually, swiftly, expertly relocated themselves in a diagonal line to his right. Another signal: the line divided and formed two single files, in parallel. The leaders banked outwards and peeled back, the next machine following and so on until the formation was again in two straight lines, retracing its course. Now the leaders simultaneously performed a slow roll. The second planes copied them, and so the manoeuvre corkscrewed its way down the flights, until the tail-end Hurricanes were rolling and levelling out together. "Oh, good show!" Kellaway cried. He was taking photographs as fast as he could wind on the film. In the square, people could be heard clapping and whistling and shouting.

The display went on for another five minutes. It ended with the squadron climbing to three thousand feet, turning and swooping fast over Nancy in the shape of a giant letter N, soaring away to regroup, and then diving back in a formation that depicted the Cross of Lorraine. "Brilliant!" Kellaway shouted. They flashed past, and the bellow of engines flooded the square. At the edge of town Rex's Hurricane suddenly angled up and led the squadron into the sky. The emblem was outlined sharply like a great sword. They climbed hard, and soon they were lost to sight.

Going downstairs, Kellaway had a new bounce to his stride. "Weren't they magnificent?" he said. "I mean, what teamwork!"

"Very entertaining," Skull said.

"It was all so artistic, and yet there was such ... such ..." Kellaway clenched his fist, striving to capture the right word. "Such *power*. Immense power. D'you know what I mean?"

"Thoroughly enjoyable," Skull said. "Very pleasing to the eye."

"I bet you we've done the frogs' morale a power of good. The boys looked really *marvellous*. It makes you feel proud, doesn't it?"

"Not particularly."

"Oh, come off it, Skull. Where's your patriotism?"

"My dear Kellaway, you can be childishly simpleminded at times. You speak of that flying display as a work of art. I ask you: what is the function of the Hurricane fighter? It is to carry machine-guns which will fire bullets which will kill German airmen. The thing is simply a machine for killing people. Just like the tank, the battleship, and the rifle with bayonet. Of course you can dress up those instruments of death, you can put flags on them, you can give the men fine uniforms, you can play exhilarating march-music and you can stage all sorts of elaborate parades in which they perform complicated mass manoeuvres, like a gymnastic display or a chorus-line, all of which may be more or less gratifying to the eye and ear. But the dressing-up is merely a cosmetic act designed to prettify and disguise the prime function, which is to kill."

They entered the foyer, a wide, marble-floored area. The adjutant was silent. "Correct me if I am wrong," Skull said. "The tank exists to blow up enemy tanks. The battleship exists to drown enemy sailors. The bayonet exists so that the soldier can stab his opponent to death. The whole purpose of the armed forces can be summed up in one word: killing. Now, I don't find that goal – in your words – marvellous, or magnificent, and try as I might I cannot bring myself to feel proud of it. Grateful, perhaps, as one is selfishly grateful for the existence of men who keep the sewage system working. But proud? No."

They emerged into the street. Some people passing by saw their uniforms, waved and shouted happily, and pointed upwards. Kellaway grinned and waved back. "All I can say is, if that's the way you feel, you'd better keep it to yourself, old man." They got into the back of a staff car, and while the driver was still hurrying around to the front, Kellaway said: "Frankly, Skull, I'm surprised you joined the Reserve. With your opinions, the RAF seems completely the wrong place."

"Not at all. You forget that I am a historian. What's happening now is history."

The car moved off. Kellaway looked out of the window. "Pretty sordid stuff, according to you," he said.

Skull shrugged. "One tries to be open-minded," he said. "If anyone can show me the glamour in a man's head getting blown off, I shall do my best to see it."

Hornet squadron had long since landed at Montornet when Kellaway and Skull arrived. Montornet was a big, modern aerodrome of the *Armée de l'Air*, with all-weather runways and tall hangars, occupied by two squadrons of French bombers, Potez 637's The visit was the *commandant*'s idea: he thought the pilots might discuss concepts of attack and defence. Three bombers were drawn up on the concrete apron by the control tower, and everyone was clustered around them.

The adjutant found Flip Moran squatting under the belly of one plane. A Frenchman stood beside him. Moran rapped the belly with his knuckles.

"Big bombs?" Moran asked. "*Beaucoup de* bombs?"

"*Cent kilogrammes.*"

Moran stood up and looked at Kellaway.

"Two hundred and fifty pounds," Kellaway said.

"Blind O'Reilly . . . Not much of a bang, is it?" He gave the Frenchman a wave of thanks. "*Bonne chance.*" They strolled away.

"He's going to need it," Moran said.

"Yes? Why?"

Moran wrinkled his nose. "It's just a sort of naughty girl's Blenheim. No knickers, very vulnerable."

Rex came hurrying over. "Flip, old chap . . . Pop upstairs and swan about a bit with one of their kites, would you? It's rigged up with cine-guns and they're mad keen to show how good their gunners are. Do a few mock-attacks, that sort of thing."

Moran nodded. "Pretend to shoot it up."

"That's right."

"Should I also try to shoot it down?"

Rex took off his cap, ran his fingers through his hair, and replaced his cap. The angle was just short of jaunty.

"Better not," he said. "They're giving us dinner later on."

"Ah." Moran's habitually sombre expression brightened a fraction. "We mustn't spoil their appetites, then." He went away.

"Congratulations on the Nancy show," the adjutant said. "All the inmates were full of admiration."

"So it seems. The mayor sent me a telegram." Rex found the paper and unfolded it. "*Félicitations . . . beau spectacle . . . avions formidables . . . toute confiance . . . victoire . . .*" He tucked it away again. "The *commandant* gave it to me when we landed. Quick work, eh?"

Kellaway nodded, and thought: *Damn quick.* It was only ten minutes' flying time from Nancy to Montornet. "It got top priority, I suppose."

"Better than that. The mayor sent it yesterday. Look at the date."

"Yesterday? He hadn't seen the show yesterday. How could –"

"Oh, he knew what to expect. Besides, if he hadn't sent it yesterday we probably wouldn't have got it today, would we?"

"True, true."

"Very logical, the French."

"Yes."

"Courteous, too. Pity their communications are so bloody awful."

There was a reception at three, preceding dinner at four: an early meal so that the visitors could fly home before darkness. Flip Moran came in at three-thirty, the outline of his goggles still showing, and got himself a drink. Moggy Cattermole turned and saw him. "Ah, the flying film star! Come and meet my friend, Captain . . . uh . . . Michelin."

"Lieutenant Martineau," the Frenchman said. He was slim and pale and serious-looking.

"This chap here is Errol Flynn," Cattermole told Martineau. "He's not much of a pilot but he's a lousy actor."

"The name's Moran." They shook hands. "That's a terrible thing, that Potez. You want to get rid of that fast."

"I have just talked with the pilot," said Martineau. "He says he has you destroyed five, six times."

"I had him destroyed before he ever saw me."

Martineau hunched his shoulders and pursed his lips. "The *ciné* will show," he said. "You are dead by us."

"No you're thinking of Rudolph Valentino," Cattermole said. "He couldn't fly, either."

"Moggy, piss off."

"See? Very temperamental," Cattermole said to Martineau. "Ask nicely and you'll get his autograph. Spencer Tracy, Cary

Grant, Maurice Chevalier." Cattermole wandered away. "Greta Garbo," he called. "Rin-Tin-Tin. Fu Manchu."

"Forget the *ciné*," Moran said. "You've got blind spots everywhere and damn-all armour."

"We cover each other," Martineau said. His English was neat and smooth. He held up both hands. "This machine covers that machine. *Oui*? When you attack, we shoot you in the ... uh ... *Qu'est-ce-que-c'est* ... ?" He knocked his hands together.

"Crossfire."

"*Oui*, crossfire." Martineau smiled gratefully.

"But I'm not *in* the sodding crossfire," Moran said.

"Yes, that is where we catch you."

"I tell you I'm not bloody there."

"We practise it often," Martineau said.

Moran gave up. Cattermole came back and raised his glass. "Buster Keaton!" he said. "Groucho Marx!"

"Donald Duck!" said a one-armed Frenchman. He too raised his glass.

Cattermole joined that group. The one-armed man was a captain, elegantly uniformed, with a black eyepatch that made him even more dashing. He carried an ebony walking-stick hooked over his surviving arm. "You look like something out of *Treasure Island*," Cattermole said. "Only smarter."

The captain merely looked back.

"Jacques does not speak English," another of the group explained.

"Just as well," Cattermole said. "I got him mixed up with Lord Nelson. Not a popular hero in France, I believe. Better start again ... Groucho Marx!" he said to the captain.

"Donald Duck."

They clinked glasses and drank. "What happened to the rest of him?" Cattermole asked the others.

"A bridge," one of them said. He had to stop and think of the words. "A bridge of a river. Jacques has had a problem. It is a little bridge, and he is in a big plane. You understand?"

"He flew under the bridge."

"*Pas complètement*. Not ..." He snapped his fingers, hunting the word. "Not altogether. Yes?" He beamed happily.

"Definitely not altogether. Harpo Marx!"

"Popeye!" said the one-armed captain. They toasted each other.

"Where is this bridge?" Cattermole asked.

"Oh, it is on the Moselle," said the other officer. "At Thionville. But since Jacques, nobody must do it. *Trop dangereux*."

"*Toujours l'audace*," Cattermole said.

That silenced them for a moment. He realised that he had said the wrong thing.

"Your spectacle at Nancy was very exciting, I believe," the officer said. "People say you fly very close."

Cattermole made a wry face. "*Au contraire*," he said. "Very far apart. Very boring. I went to sleep several times."

The officer translated. The others laughed, and made comments. "They do not believe it is so easy," he said.

"Piece of cake, old boy," Cattermole said.

"*Morceau de gâteau*," the officer told them, and they laughed again.

"Betty Grable!" Cattermole said. "Marlene Dietrich!" said the one-armed captain. They drank to each other. "Thionville," said Cattermole. "That's the other side of Metz, isn't it?"

At dinner, Dicky Starr found himself sitting next to a tall, thin colonel who was slightly morose with drink. "Jolly good kite, that Potez," Starr said brightly. "*Bon* . . . um . . . *avion* . . . um . . . *avec* . . . um . . ."

"Do not fatigue yourself," the colonel said. "Yes, you are right, the Potez is an excellent machine, of course."

"Fast."

"Extremely rapid. Today that is more important than ever. It is why we have the Potez constructed very light. The more light, the more fast."

"I bet the pilots like that."

"Of course. They wish more armour and more guns but that makes heavy, so . . ."

"You can't have everything," Starr said.

"However one hundred kilos of bomb is not much, I think," the colonel said, examining his fingernails.

"It is if you drop it in the right place," Starr assured him. "And I bet your chaps –"

"Do we need really three men?" The colonel turned down the

corners of his mouth. "Why not a crew of two? One must ask these questions."

"Two would certainly be lighter. *And* faster."

The colonel studied Starr's face. He nodded thoughtfully. "It is a question of getting the most out of the machine. Suppose now we remove one man . . ."

"Make faster," Starr said. "Yes."

"And we add one bomb."

"Ah! Well, now . . ."

"Bigger hit," the colonel pointed out. "More explosion."

"True. But more heavy, more slow." Starr was beginning to wave his arms about.

"*Not* more slow. *Not* more heavy." The colonel wagged his forefinger. "One man out, one bomb in."

"I see what you mean," Starr conceded. "Swings and roundabouts. Not make slower. I mean, make not slower. Make not faster either, come to that." The words were beginning to sound jumbled. He took a swig of wine to clear his head. "It's as broad as it's long, isn't it?"

The colonel was silent for a while. "No," he said. "It is two metres more broad."

"Anyway, it's a jolly good plane," Starr said, "and I bet you're glad you've got it."

"Of course. The Potez is simply the best machine we have, an excellent machine, superb, incomparable. You have no machine like it, I believe."

"Heavens, no!" Starr said.

The colonel nodded glumly. He picked up a spoon and looked at his upside-down reflection. "Anyway, it is not for long," he said. "Soon we get the new Bloch 174 which is a greatly more excellent machine."

"Really? Even better than the Potez?"

The colonel shook his head: a tiny, unambitious gesture. "Better in every conceivable way," he said sadly.

The dinner was long and lavish. As it approached the dessert stage, the adjutant leaned across to Rex and murmured: "One of them is bound to make a speech, you know." Rex nodded. "The trouble is," Kellaway said, "half their lot don't speak English, and

130

hardly any of our lot speak French." Rex nodded. "Oh well," Kellaway said.

In the event the hosts made three speeches. The first, by an old general, all in French, all very stirring, was incomprehensible to Hornet squadron. Then the *commandant* made a safe, orthodox speech in French. Then he made it all over again in English. He sat down to polite applause.

Everyone looked at Rex. Some of the looks were rather weary. Four speeches on a full stomach was asking a lot.

Rex stood. He held a bundle of notes. "*Mon président, messieurs*," he began confidently. "*Mes amis, les enfants du paradis, mademoiselle d'Armentières, Athos, Porthos et d'Armagnac*."

A ripple of laughter. He glanced at his notes, thumbed through them, tore them in half and tossed the bits over his shoulder. "My *français* is pretty bloody *terrible*," he said, "and some of your *anglais* is a *crime passionnel*. Nevertheless, *grâce à Dieu*, I'm sure that *entre nous* we have enough *savoir faire* to make our *bonhomie* and *camaraderie* continue long *après* this *tête-à-tête*."

General appaluse.

"What, you may ask, is the *raison d'être de* Hornet squadron? Well, *nous sommes ici* to help you *donner le coup de grâce* to that *sale boche* Adolf Hitler."

Rumble of approval.

"*Pour nous*, this is both an *affaire d'honneur* and an *affaire d'amour*," Rex said. That went down well. "*Ensemble* we shall give Hermann Goering and his *Luftwaffe* a very *mauvais quart d'houre!* It will be a *tour de force* that will leave him *hors de combat*! France and Britain will turn the *boche* into *pomme de terre purée!*" Hearty cheering. "They talk about *donner* and *blitzen!*" Rex cried. "We say to them: *rien ne va plus!*" Tumult.

When the noise died down, he said: "*Tout le monde* in England is *au fait* with the glorious French *Armée de l'Air*. The *crème de la crème*. You are *chevaliers* of the sky, *sans peur et sans reproche*." The Hornet pilots thumped the table; the Frenchmen smiled modestly. "We say to you, *merci bien* for this . . ." Rex gestured widely. ". . . this *pièce de résistance*." More table-thumping. Rex fingered an empty wine-bottle. "Enough. *Après moi*," he said, glancing in the direction of the lavatories, "*le déluge*." That was

131

hilarious; they literally fell about laughing. "*Enfin* I say to you," he declared, "*Bonne chance, au revoir* and . . . *vive la France*!"

The applause was intense; Rex had to stand again and acknowledge it. Then the French sang their squadron songs, and in reply Hornet squadron performed their Seven Dwarfs Special. Fifteen minutes later, knees aching, they took off and flew home.

Kellaway and Skull discussed Rex's speech as they drove back to Château St Pierre.

"It was all balls, of course," Kellaway said, "but it certainly rang the bell, didn't it?"

"He has the right touch. It's something nobody can learn: either you have it or you don't."

"He knows he's good, you see," Kellaway said, "and that gives him confidence. He's a bit arrogant, in fact. The chaps like that. They trust him, they respect him."

"And sometimes he frightens them."

"Does he?" The adjutant thought it over. "Maybe he does. But then, they like being scared, don't they? Otherwise they wouldn't be where they are."

The bomber slid out of a bank of cloud like a heavy trout leaving a stretch of weed.

"Got him," said Rex. "Three o'clock low." His voice was lightened by altitude and radio-transmission. "Right, let's make a clean kill," he said.

Hornet squadron was heading north; the bomber was a thousand feet below, flying eastward. The morning was fine and clear. There were occasional patches of dazzling white cloud; between these patches, the hills of the Vosges could be seen a long way below, dark green with pinewoods, light green with pastureland: all as casual and comfortable as a rumpled bedspread. The rivers were ribbons, the roads were threads; the castles on the peaks were tassels. Nothing moved down there. It was a picture, not a country.

The squadron was echeloned to starboard. "Sections close astern, flights echelon starboard," Rex ordered. "Go."

He watched the bomber. It was still boring steadily towards Germany, same speed, same course. When he looked up, Green Section was tucked behind Blue. He knew that Yellow Section must be following Red.

"Aircraft, line astern, go," he said.

He studied the bomber again, gauging its speed: 140 or 150 mph.

Two lengths to his right, 'B' flight was nose-to-tail. Slipstream turbulence jostled them slightly.

"Here we go, then. Number three attack, Number three attack. Turning starboard – go."

Rex banked right. The bomber disappeared under the Hurricane's nose. He straightened up, glanced back to make sure everyone had done the same, and said: "Aircraft, form vic, go."

The sections obediently rearranged themselves in arrowheads. The bomber was about a mile ahead. In the vastness of the sky it looked as small as a bird.

"Good. Now, Blue and Green Sections orbit here. Blue and Green only, turning starboard, go." 'B' flight banked and swung away. "Going down," Rex said. Red section nosed into a gentle dive. Yellow Section throttled back slightly and followed a few hundred yards behind.

"Red Section, fire, go," said Rex.

The target expanded steadily until its lumbering bulk filled his reflector sight. Rex braced himself. "*Tatta-tatta-tat*," he said under his breath, and immediately ordered: "Red Section, break starboard, go."

Moggy Cattermole, flying as Red Three, broke starboard and yawned. They had been doing these practice interceptions for nearly forty minutes, each attack as precise and well-drilled as classical ballet, each theoretically ending in success, each bloody boring. He stretched his neck and worked his shoulder-muscles, and watched the bomber trudge along. Yellow Section broke off its mock-attack, and 'B' flight descended. The bomber was French, a Bloch 200, thick and hulking, with slabby wings and a fuselage as boxy as a cattletruck. The front gunner sat in a turret like a glass dustbin stuck on the nose. Cattermole could see him clearly. The man was reading a book.

'B' flight closed, and swung away. The squadron re-formed. The Bloch turned north. Rex would let it escape and then he would find it again. Boring. Bloody boring.

Cattermole checked the bank of dials in front of him, searching for trouble. Airspeed indicator, artificial horizon, rate-of-climb indicator, all normal. Engine RPM, boost gauge, fuel pressure, oil pressure, oil temperature, radiator temperature. Nothing wrong there. Fuel gauges. Magnetic compass. Turn-and-bank indicator. Everything working perfectly.

"Bloody awful British workmanship," he muttered. He leaned forward and rapped the oil-temperature gauge. The Hurricane wobbled slightly but the needle on the gauge remained steady. "Shoddy," he said. He sat back and turned the transmission switch on his oxygen mask. "Red Leader from Red Three," he said. "I've got a hot engine."

"Check oil temperature, Red Three."

Cattermole counted silently to three and said: "Boiling oil, Leader."

He saw Rex looking at him, searching for evidence of failure. "Okay, Red Three, buzz off home," Rex said.

Immediately Cattermole let his left wing drop to the vertical and he fell away in a long and luxurious plunge. The squadron was high above him, and his airspeed had built to a howling three hundred and fifty miles an hour before he started hauling back on the stick. The controls were stiff against the rush of air, air that resisted them like floodwater, but soon the nose came up and up, and up still more as he held the stick against his stomach, investing all that momentum in a loop. It wasn't the kind of thing you did with an overheating engine, but nobody was likely to notice: Hurricane pilots could see very little directly below them.

Upside-down in the top of the loop, Cattermole saw the gloomy forests of Germany floating in the far distance like dark green clouds. Faintly he heard Rex say: "Aircraft, line astern, go." Then his plane fell out of the loop. He half-rolled and flattened out, and headed north-west. The radio in his Hurricane was tunable. He lost Rex and found some dance music: *Anything Goes*. He joined in, not knowing the words but pom-pom-ing happily.

The bridge over the Moselle at Thionville turned out to be a nasty piece of work. It was modern and concrete, broad enough to carry four lanes of traffic, and not very high. Cattermole circled the town at a thousand feet and studied the central span. It was by far the widest but the curve of the arch was low: the gap seemed as flat as a fried egg. Also there was traffic on the river: barges and things. Straight away Cattermole decided it was impossible.

Damn-fool frogs! No wonder they got their bloody arms chopped off. Serve 'em right.

All the same, having come this far ... Might as well stooge down and beat up the place, just to show the frogs who was boss.

Cattermole flew upstream for about a mile and turned. At this angle the bridge looked more like a dam, with no light visible through its spans. He nudged the throttle and eased the stick forward. The Merlin's growl jumped to a roar. He felt a firm shove in the back, and the world below began to rise up and race by, full of living detail: trees that waved, trucks and cars buzzing along the road by the river, smoke blowing from chimneys, swans on the river. The river was ridged with ripples that never moved; it looked as hard as marble. He levelled out at twenty feet and flashed under some power cables almost before he saw them. With four hundred yards to go, the bridge looked very different: light now showed clearly beneath it and the centre span reached wide. Without consciously deciding, Cattermole made his decision; damn it all, that's what bridges were for, wasn't it? Especially big ones. With astonishing suddenness the bridge rushed at him, its grey-white bulk turning black against the sky, and it swallowed him. The plane was off-centre. He corrected with rudder and stick; but too late: as the bridge spat him out from its racketing gloom his starboard wingtip missed the concrete arch by inches. He rocketed into daylight with his mouth wide open, his eyes staring, a surge of sweat all over his body. A motorised barge was heading straight at him. Both hands snatched the stick into his stomach. The Hurricane seemed to bounce on air and vault over the vessel's masts with a jolt that left his guts seeking his stomach. Cattermole rammed the throttle forward and climbed for safety and sanity and peace, and kept climbing until his mouth had stopped gasping. When he looked down, the barge was still there, angled to the current. It seemed to have collided with the bridge. "That was a remarkably stupid thing to do," he told it. "People like you shouldn't be allowed out."

Fifteen minutes later he was making a circuit of the field at Château St Pierre. He closed the Hurricane's radiator before his final approach and by the time he touched down the engine-temperature gauge was climbing nicely. A few healthy bursts of power while he was taxiing pushed it up several more degrees. He opened the radiator before his groundcrew reached him and kept the engine running so that they could see the gauge too. It was hot as hell.

The rest of the squadron hadn't returned yet. Cattermole went off to the mess for a beer. He felt he'd earned it.

The mess servants were drawing the heavy velvet curtains in the billiard room, and Rex was chalking his cue. Patterson sprawled on one of the buttoned-leather couches; Stickwell stood in front of the log fire, hands in pockets, toasting his backside. They were all watching Cattermole.

"Blue in the centre," Cattermole said. He stooped and lined up the shot, blinking as he changed focus. There was a neat click of ivory; the blue departed like a faithful messenger and fell obediently into the pocket. "Brilliant," Cattermole said. He raised his eyes. Micky Marriott, the engineer officer, had come in and was watching. "Tradesmen around the back," Cattermole said.

"There's nothing wrong with your engine," Marriott said.

Cattermole walked around the table, extracted the blue and placed it on its spot.

"Your fitter checked it, and the flight sergeant checked it, and then I checked it," Marriott said. "There's no overheating."

Cattermole leaned far over the table and casually potted a long red. "Must be a faulty gauge, then," he said.

"The gauge works perfectly," Marriott said.

"I think . . . the pink," Cattermole decided. But the pink refused to go down. "Thank you very much indeed," he said to Marriott, not looking at him. "I couldn't have missed it without you."

Rex came forward and examined the set-up on the table. "Is this something urgent, Micky?" he asked.

"It's not the first time it's happened, sir, that's all. And I take exception to having my lads waste the whole afternoon checking out faults that don't exist.".

Rex selected the red he fancied and sank it with a quick, clean blow. "Funny creatures, aeroplanes," he said. "They'll do one thing on the ground and another thing altogether in the sky."

"Just like women," Stickwell said. "Princess in the parlour, baggage in the bedroom." He rattled his small change in his pocket. "True," he said.

"Have you tested my machine at twelve thousand feet?" Cattermole asked Marriott.

"You know damn well I haven't."

"Ah, well then." Cattermole leaned his cue against Stickwell, strolled away, and sat on the couch, thus sitting on Patterson, who let out a yelp of pain. "That's where it was overheating, you see, at twelve thousand. I never said it was overheating in your tatty hangar, did I? Frankly, old boy, what you and your grimy assistants get up to at ground level is neither here nor there. It's what happens in the wide blue yonder that concerns me." He put a cushion on Patterson's face to stifle the groans.

There was a pause while Rex potted the black.

"Nothing's been changed in your engine," Marriott said. "It's exactly as it was when you reported it duff. I'll bet you a week's pay it doesn't overheat when you take it up tomorrow."

"No, you won't," Rex said. "I'm not having the maintenance of the aircraft turned into a private gamble."

Marriot chewed at a thumbnail. "In that case, let somebody else fly Cattermole's plane tomorrow," he said. "Then we'll see."

Rex took a long time to play an ambitious and complicated three-cushion shot that just failed. "Perhaps," he said.

Marriott turned and went out. Stickwell strolled over to the table.

"Damned mechanics," Cattermole said. "Just because they know how to change the oil and top-up the battery, they want to rule the world."

Rex walked to the fireplace and took his tankard of beer from the mantelpiece. "I'm not concerned about his political ambitions," he said. "I just wish he'd do something about those appalling fingernails of his. They quite put me off my food."

Stickwell laughed so much he missed the cue-ball. Patterson, however, did not laugh; and it wasn't only because Cattermole was sitting on him. Come to that, Cattermole was no joke either.

Next morning the trees that fringed the airfield were hidden by the rain. The sky dumped its load so heavily that the spray on the terrace bounced knee-high. The tennis-court was flooded, the driveway became a shallow stream, water trickled under the french windows and soaked the edge of the carpets. The wind boomed in the chimneys, and the air was much colder.

Marriott came back from the field after breakfast, his gas-cape shining with water. "Go back to bed for a week," he said. "There's a lake over there you could swim in. I've had double covers put on the Hurricanes: those hangars leak like buggery. It's blowing like a bastard, too." Rainwater kept dribbling out of his hair and making him blink.

They were all standing in the conservatory, watching the weather wash everything a uniform, blurred grey-green.

"What a shame," Fitzgerald said. "Just when Moggy was itching to go up and test his engine."

"No need," Cattermole said. "Air temperature's down. Can't overheat now. Perfectly safe."

"I think I'll have a toilet-roll fitted in your cockpit," Marriott said.

"If you like, old chap. Make it something soft, won't you? We Cattermoles bruise easily."

"I'll make it sandpaper."

"I say, Marriott, old boy," said Stickwell. "What d'you think of that?" He held up his little finger.

Marriott stared, suspiciously. "Looks all right. Why?"

"Nothing. It's just that while you were looking at it, Reilly was pissing over your left foot."

Marriott glanced down to see the dog uncocking its leg. He stepped back hastily, but Reilly had struck. The conservatory echoed with laughter. Marriott glared at Rex. "For Christ's sake, sir!" he said.

"If you will go around dressed like a lamppost," Rex said suavely, "you must expect the consequences."

Cattermole squatted on his haunches and rubbed Reilly behind the ears. He was feeling very satisfied. Nobody had complained about a Hurricane flying under the bridge at Thionville. It looked as if he'd got away with it.

By midmorning the wind had worked itself up to a gale. Rex telephoned Area HQ at Rheims and then summoned the adjutant. "Even the ducks are grounded," he said. "Who's in line for leave?"

Kellaway found the list. "Sticky Stickwell and Flip Moran."

"Okay, send them home. And we can start making a dent in these invitations." He fished about in a tray marked FROG BUMF and pulled out a letter. "The local school, village of Pont-St Pierre. They want a couple of chaps to go down and address the kids."

"How about Flash Gordon?"

"Flash? He's awfully young, isn't he? He looks like a schoolboy."

"Well, he *was* a schoolboy not so long ago. Anyway, he's become very keen lately. He does body-building exercises and takes cold baths and practises with his revolver on the range. He's determined to be the first to shoot down a Hun."

"All right. Let's send Flash and Fitz."

Kellaway hesitated. "I don't think Fitz speaks any French."

"Who cares? He's got a pretty face. All he has to do is smile a lot and guard his honour."

It wasn't a bad description. As a child Jeremy Fitzgerald had been full of impish charm, but adolescence had strengthened his looks: the mouth became wider, the cheekbones firmer, the eyes steadier. He was slim and lithe, an agile and unquenchable games-player as long as size didn't matter; not brilliant but not stupid; popular because cheerful and cheerful because popular.

His mother adored him; there were photographs all over the house. His father – something of a tycoon in the wholesale electrical supplies business – wasn't so sure; he'd sent the boy to public school in order to get all that narcissistic nonsense knocked out of him. Girls, his father noticed gloomily, weren't very keen on young Fitz. The good-looking ones felt upstaged and the plain ones felt humiliated. Fitz himself couldn't understand this: he'd never considered his face to be anything special; it was so familiar that it was ordinary. Later, when he left school and began to understand, he felt cursed by his looks. One day he was flipping through a magazine when he saw a photograph of an RAF pilot. His head was completely covered by helmet, goggles and oxygen mask. Fitz's mother was horrified, but he knew what he wanted and his father did nothing to stop him. By the time he got his wings Fitz had lost all self-consciousness. Everyone was equal in Fighter Command. He was just another golden boy.

Pont-St Pierre wasn't much of a village: a grocery store, a bar, a blacksmith's, a church, and a hump-backed bridge over a red, rushing stream. The school was the biggest building.

"God, what a dungeon," Fitz said.

Flash Gordon parked Sticky's Buick by the front door and switched off the engine. Rain drummed gloomily on the roof. "Dungeons are underground," he said. "This looks more like a morgue."

"Well, whatever it is, let's do our duty and get back to the mess fast."

As they ran to the door it was opened by a woman in her late twenties. "*Bonjour*," she said. "Sorry, I mean hullo. Do come in. I'm Mary Blandin. Isn't this weather frightful?"

She was small, a good six inches shorter than Fitz, with black hair cut in a pageboy bob that just covered her ears, and she wore a blue woollen dress with a red sash that measured the slimness of her waist.

They introduced themselves. "You're not French, I take it," Fitz said.

"Yes and no. It's all rather confusing. Look, why don't we hang up your wet things and you can meet Mademoiselle Ligier."

They took off their coats and tramped along a corridor painted chocolate-brown. Mademoiselle Ligier was teaching a class of eight-year-olds. They were utterly silenced by the arrival of the two officers.

"*Bonjour*," said Flash. "*Enchanté de faire votre connaissance.*"

"How do you do. This is a great pleasure. Shall we speak in French? Your accent is excellent."

Flash felt himself begin to blush. He tugged his nose. "Can't remember any more," he said.

They smiled. "Let's use English, then," Mademoiselle Ligier said. "But you must tell me when I go wrong."

"Oh, I don't know about that." Flash looked to Fitz for help, but Fitz merely raised an eyebrow. "Well . . . Do my best," Flash mumbled. He felt clumsy and exposed. He was making a mess of this. He wished it was over.

"The children are always talking about you," she said. She was younger than Mary Blandin, with glossy chestnut hair tied in a pigtail, large brown eyes that had a certain wariness about them, and a surprisingly wide mouth: surprising because her chin was

140

long and pointed. Not beautiful; not even pretty, but remarkable, all the same. "They talk about your aeroplanes, I mean," she said.

"Hurricanes," Fitz said. The children heard him; they wriggled and whispered. "Can you say 'Hurricane'?" he asked them. "Say 'Hurricane.'"

For a moment they were paralysed with shyness. Then a few brave boys called out: "*Orry-ken . . . Orry-ken.*"

"Not bad," Fitz said.

"Damn good," Flash said, and immediately regretted it. Swearing in front of the children: bad form.

"Would you like to meet the other class?" Mary Blandin asked Fitz, and took him away. "You'll stay for lunch, won't you?"

In the event they stayed to the end of the afternoon. Flash was always slightly nervous of Mademoiselle Ligier – he was not accustomed to being on close terms with schoolteachers, especially attractive ones – but he enjoyed himself with the children. He drew an enormous Hurricane on the blackboard, with arrows pointing to the various parts: fuel tanks, radio, guns, and so on, and he helped them colour it in. Meanwhile he could hear Fitz teaching the other class to sing *London Bridge Is Falling Down*. Later, they played on opposite sides in a game of football in a covered yard. Fitz was very good at allowing small boys to rob him of the ball and then showing astonishment at their skill. They found that very funny, and sometimes they ended up stumbling over their own feet. Flash could head the ball repeatedly like a seal in a circus. They thought that was very clever.

After school, Mary Blandin boiled a kettle on a gas-ring in the staff room and made some tea. "You were a big hit," she said.

"Nice kids," Fitz said.

Total agreement there. Outside, rain was hurrying the day to an end. Sooty drops occasionally fell down the chimney.

"Jolly lucky for us you both speak English," Flash remarked.

"Not at all," Mademoiselle Ligier said. "It was why we invited you here. We like to speak English. I studied English at university. I would like to teach it, but these children are too young."

"Well, you can talk English to me any hour of the day you like," Flash said, suddenly full of confidence.

She sipped her tea and gave him a calm, contented look, curiously

141

cat-like. "Thank you," she said. "I also studied anatomy and biology."

"Ah, that's different. Not much I can tell you about them, I imagine."

She sipped her tea again. "One never knows."

Mary got up to draw the blackout curtains, and Fitz went to help her. "What took you away from England?" he asked.

"Mr Blandin did. My mother was French so I grew up bilingual, and I married a Frenchman, a doctor. We lived in Metz for five years and then he died." Fitz tugged the curtain straight and glanced at her, expecting more. "That's all," she said. "He just died. It happens sometimes. Even to doctors." She moved to the next window and stood on tiptoe to get a good grip. Fitz looked at her legs. "You didn't go home?"

"I couldn't face being a widow in Harrogate, always scratching my chilblains and dreaming of being seduced by insurance salesmen. It's different in France. The French treat widowhood more cheerfully."

"They've had more experience."

"True."

Blobs of sleet were beginning to dot the windscreen of the Buick as Flash drove back to the château. He had the heat full on. "Funny pair," he said.

"Yes. Smart, though."

"Oh, absolutely. Very smart. Too smart for a scruffy little village school."

"I suppose so." Fitz stared at the saturated beams of the headlights. Flash had taken off the blackout masks; no enemy pilot could see anything in this weather, even if he were crazy enough to fly. "They must like it here."

"No, Nicole's bored. She wanted to teach in the city, in Paris or somewhere, but the year she got her university degree her father died, and now her mother's an invalid who won't leave the village. Rough luck, eh?"

"Rough." Fitz was thinking of Mary Blandin's superb neck. He had first noticed her neck as he followed her along the corridor when they arrived. It showed white and strong below her pageboy haircut, curving cleanly under the blue dress. His imagination rested his hand on the firm curve . . . he sniffed suddenly and sat up straight.

"Too hot for you?" Flash asked, and pushed down the lever on the dashboard.

Winter came quickly and early. The leaves were soon stripped from the trees and blown into soggy heaps. The landscape of eastern France became flat and cold. The tall grasses and weeds of summer died back, the fields lay black with rain, and cattle took shelter behind walls and hedges. Often, the only sign of life came from the crows and rooks that whirled aimlessly in the wild gusts, black confetti tossed at the racing sky.

Rolls of steel mesh were delivered to the airfield at Château St Pierre. Squads of airmen unrolled them across the grass, splashing from puddle to pool. When Micky Marriott drove a 15-hundred-weight truck along the track, mud squirted up through the holes and the mesh sank from sight. Rex decided not to trust a Hurricane to it. Flying was postponed indefinitely. Once or twice there came a break in the weather and a German aircraft flew over, very high. Evidently the *Luftwaffe* had concrete runways. Few members of Hornet squadron noticed the intruders. The pilots were either on leave, or shopping in Metz, or playing squash, or re-visiting the village school at Pont-St Pierre.

One day, Air Commodore Bletchley paid the squadron a visit. Rex took him to the library and gave him sherry.

"It's only a run-of-the-mill amontillado, I'm afraid," he said, "but I think you'll find it not lacking in palate."

Bletchley took a mouthful and rolled it around his mouth as if he were rinsing his teeth. "Bags of palate," he said. "More palate than you could shake a stick at."

Rex topped up his glass. They lowered themselves into armchairs, to the gentle hiss of leather cushions. Reilly watched them for a moment, sombrely reckoning the odds against getting a snack. He stretched in front of the fire, and heaved a sigh. A couple of burning logs collapsed.

Rex said: "What's the gen, sir?"

"The gen, old boy, is wet. Like everything else at the moment. I can tell you with absolute certainty that the French Army is wet, the British Army is wet, and the German Army is, with any luck, soaked to the skin. This entire bloody war is at present covered with a thick layer of mildew."

"Surely something must be happening, sir."

"I believe General Ironside is being treated for rust."

"Dear me." Rex stretched a leg and rubbed Reilly's back. "What about the Navy? They like this sort of weather, don't they?"

"You heard about the *Royal Oak*?"

"Yes, but that was just German propaganda, wasn't it? They're always –"

"Not this time. They sank her. Some crafty U-boat got inside Scapa Flow and let fly. Exit one battleship."

"Good Lord, that's bad." Rex glanced at his watch. "You'll stay for lunch, sir, won't you? Splendid. The Admiralty's a bit cross, I suppose."

"Thoroughly fed-up, I'm told. It's not so much the dreadnought as the indignity and the fact that there's precious little they can do in return. I mean, Hitler's sitting pretty, isn't he?" Bletchley heaved himself up and wandered over to a window overlooking the flooded tennis-courts. "Frankly, old boy, I'm very disappointed in this war. It's not done what I expected, not in the least. I sometimes wonder why we went into it in the first place."

Rex drank his sherry.

"If you want my opinion," Bletchley said, "I think the whole thing will fizzle out by Christmas and you'll be back at Kingsmere by New Year's Day. Talking of Kingsmere . . ." He came back and stood by the fire. Reilly sniffed his trouser-leg. Rex refilled his glass. "Thanks. I've had a running battle with some twerp at Air Ministry who claims there were all sorts of horrible irregularities and suchlike going on when your lot were stationed there. Fights with local farmers, trouble with accident inquiries, God knows what else. I don't suppose you personally had time to notice anything?"

"Not a thing, sir."

"That's what I keep telling them."

"I was in and out like a flash."

"Of course you were."

"Mind you, from what I hear, Squadron Leader Ramsay . . . I never met him, of course, but . . ."

"Bit of an odd bird, Ramsay. I keep telling them that. If anything went wrong it must have been Ramsay's fault."

"The chap was under terrible strain."

"Oh, frightful. No wonder he went off the rails."

"Could have happened to anyone."

"Right."

"Right."

Bletchley finished his sherry. Rex reached for the decanter but the air commodore shook his head. "You said something about lunch, I believe."

"You've caught us on a very ordinary day, sir. It's partridge again. But I've had a very drinkable Côte du Rhône breathing overnight."

As they walked to the dining-room, Bletchley said: "The one thing I can't get them to believe is that Ramsay rose from the dead and pinched a whole load of Hurricane spares one fine night."

Rex said nothing.

"Trouble is, the silly ass of a flight lieutenant who was in charge of the depot has taken it personally. He's gone all round the Hurricane squadrons, swearing vengeance. Now he's applied for a posting to France."

"A persistent blighter."

"Protheroe. Flight Lieutenant J. D. Protheroe . . . Did you say partridge?" Bletchley sniffed appreciatively.

"I got hold of a chap who used to be at the Savoy Grill," Rex said. "He's an absolute magician with kidneys, too." They entered the dining-room. The tables had fresh flowers from the château's hothouse. "Tell me, sir: how's your boy getting on at Oxford?" Rex asked.

The horses laboured up the stony track, placing their feet carefully between the twisted roots of pinetrees. The sky was Mediterranean-blue, and where the pines sheltered some oaks their leaves were a radiant red-gold like reflected firelight. But the air was damn cold. A northeasterly wind whipped all the warmth out of the sunlight and rattled the oakleaves. It made the riders hunch up and hide their ears in the tall collars of their fleecelined jackets. It helped freeze their backsides, which were already bounced and bumped into numbness by the unfamiliar saddles.

Rex led them onto the ridge and stopped in a small clearing. "Time for a stirrup-cup, chaps," he said.

They dismounted and took off the rifles slung about their shoulders. They stamped up and down, beating their arms and flexing their legs to relieve the stiffness. Rex passed around his silver hip-flask.

"Funny-tasting whisky, this, sir," Moke Miller said. "Smells of . . . iodine."

"That's Jeyes' Fluid, you fool," Cattermole said. He poured himself a tot and downed it. "Best quality Jeyes' Fluid, too."

"Just the thing for a sink like you, then," Mother Cox said. Cattermole reached out and seized Cox's nose and twisted, hard. Cox howled, escaped, and kicked him on the shins but Cattermole was wearing flying-boots and did not flinch. He reached out again and clipped Cox on the ear. Cox kicked again, aiming for the crotch. Cattermole caught his ankle one-handed and Cox, to save himself, grabbed the nearest body: Patterson. They both tumbled down.

"Please sir," Dicky Starr said, "Moggy keeps mucking about, sir. Sir, it's not fair, sir."

Rex ignored him. "That's pure malt whisky," he told Miller. "From the Isle of Islay. My family has a share in a small distillery to the north of Bruichladdich, you know."

Cattermole was unbuttoning his fly. Patterson and Cox hastily scrambled out of the way. Reilly trotted over and watched, ears erect.

"Pure malt, eh?" Miller said. "Fancy that."

"The peat-stain in the burns creates the flavour," Rex explained. "South of Bruichladdich the malts taste completely different."

Cattermole walked around the clearing, pissing hard, in pursuit of Patterson. The others dodged his spray. Reilly followed, yapping excitely. "Piss off, Moggy!" Patterson shouted.

"People will tell you a malt is a malt," Rex said. "Never believe it." He spun the top back on the hip-flask. "Always look north from Bruichladdich, laddy," he said. "You won't regret it."

Cattermole was still trailing Patterson.

"I owe you an apology, Moggy," Dicky Starr said from a safe distance. "I always thought you were full of shit."

"For Christ's sake, Fanny," Cox complained, as Cattermole at

146

last exhausted his bladder, "can't you keep this idiot under control? He's a bloody menace." Cox rubbed his ear. "A joke's a joke, but . . ."

"I don't know what you're talking about," Barton said evenly. "Everything seems all right to me. Or, to coin a phrase: *Jag tycker om det*."

He left Cox scowling and strolled over to the adjutant, who was sitting against a tree, out of the wind.

"Fine view," Kellaway said. The hills trailed away below in a great horseshoe, with the château near its mouth. Streaks of standing water glistened on the airfield like fresh snail-tracks.

Barton shielded his eyes and stared hard. "What's going on down there?" he asked. The wind made his eyes water and he turned away, blinking. "Someone's working on the field."

"Good God!" Kellaway was envious. "Can you really see that far? I expect it's Micky Marriott. He's got his troops out digging ditches to try and drain off the floods." Kellaway squinted in the wrong direction. "I'm not sure I can even see the bally 'drome from here," he muttered.

Barton squatted. He picked up a couple of pine-cones and knocked them together. "Moggy chucks his weight about far too much," he said. "The man's a pain. Why doesn't Rex tear him off a strip?"

"Not his style. Anyway, you're Moggy's flight commander, Fanny. You sit on him if you want to."

Barton kept knocking the cones together until bits began to break off.

"No, they don't deserve it," he said. "They fart-assed about when I was acting CO. I'm not going to do them any favours now."

"Ah," Kellaway said.

"They didn't scratch my back. Why should I scratch theirs?"

"I can't fault your logic, old boy. Of course it won't make you any more popular."

"I didn't join the Royal Air Force to be popular, adj." He threw the battered cones at a tree, and missed.

"I've often wondered: why did you join?"

Barton laughed, briefly. The honest answer was that he joined to get away from New Zealand and the stupidity of sheep; but he couldn't reveal that. "To serve the king!" he declared. "Also the queen, jack and ten. Why did you join?"

"Because I wanted to be a hero," Kellaway said without hesitation. "And when I think of the real heroes I knew in the last war, marvellous men, who are all as dead as mutton, and I'm still here, it makes me wonder." He turned his head and looked Barton full in the face. The cold wind had stiffened Kellaway's face and tightened the skin around his eyes. "It makes me wonder, Fanny," he said again.

Barton was startled but he was saved from responding. Rex cried: "To horse!" They got to their feet. "Marvellous chaps, Fanny," Kellaway said. "The most wonderful men you could wish to know, all snuffed out. But not me. Not me. Why not me?"

Barton felt puzzled and slightly embarrassed. "I'm afraid I don't understand, adj," he said.

"No, it doesn't make much sense, does it?" Now Kellaway seemed to regret his own remarks. "The arthritis must have got into my brain. Dunno about you but I'm getting more than slightly peckish. Roll on grub-time, say I."

They rode for another hour, Rex map-reading, and halted in the lee of the slope where a hollow gave extra shelter. They lit a fire, and cooked and ate pork sausages (from Harrods of Knightsbridge) with French bread and bottles of very cold Whitbread's Pale Ale, after which there was fruit cake and chocolate biscuits. They sat or lay around, drowsy with fresh air and food, looking past the shimmer of their fire. The hillside was studded with giant chestnut trees whose branches occupied the air so completely that the ground was bare and the trunks stood like columns in a cathedral. Behind, at the top of the ridge, the wind boomed and howled. It was wonderfully restful. "Bring your weapons, gentlemen," Rex said. "We're going for a little walk."

He set off at his usual brisk pace, walking parallel to the ridge.

"Why the artillery?" Moke Miller enquired. "Isn't it safe?"

"Wild boar. We might get a shot. Deer too, so they tell me."

He led them for a mile over increasingly broken terrain, the chestnuts giving way to spruce and silver birch, and then stopped. Between a pair of young trees stood a small cairn. Carved on a large flat stone set in the middle were the words *Un Aviateur Allemand Inconnu*. Moss blurred the letters. "Thought you'd like to take a squint," Rex said. "Last resting place of some poor Teutonic knight of the air."

"Humble yet tasteful," Fitzgerald said.

"More than you can say of the krauts," said Cox.

"One of your scalps, d'you think, uncle?" Starr asked.

The adjutant smiled, and shook his head. "Hope not," he said, with some feeling. Starr said: "Come off it, uncle. He'd have done it to you if he'd had half a chance, wouldn't he?" The adjutant nodded. "Well, then," Starr said.

A leaf came slowly spinning past. The adjutant caught it, crushed it, and let the fragments blow out of his hand. "I don't feel at all guilty about the Germans I had to kill," he said. "On the other hand, it says this fellow was *inconnu*, which means they couldn't identify him, so he almost certainly got burned to bits."

There was a gloomy pause while they considered that.

"Look," Rex said, "you can see where he hit the trees." There was indeed a short downward channel where trunks had been snapped off and branches torn away. The scars were very weathered.

"How did you know about this place?" Barton asked.

"One of the frogs at that bomber base told me. I expect there are dozens just like it."

"Hundreds," Kellaway said.

"Bloody lonely spot to die," Miller said.

"Show me somewhere that isn't," Cox said, which made Kellaway look at him with interest.

"Everybody keep still," Cattermole ordered. "I've just seen a fox."

Immediately they all turned their heads. It was a young dog-fox, fifty or sixty yards up the slope, loping along a trail that angled away from them. The animal had a perfectly balanced, wonderfully easy action: he seemed to tick along, his legs no more than clipping the ground. His tail streamed out, big and red. He looked clean and fit and utterly at home in these woods. "What a beauty," Dicky Starr breathed.

"Vermin," Cattermole said. He worked the bolt-action.

"Hey!" Starr said. Moke Miller loaded and raised his rifle too. "Come off it, for Pete's sake," Starr said.

Now Patterson and Cox raised their rifles. At last the fox noticed them. He stopped and watched, head cocked, ears alert. He seemed interested and unafraid. "What's the point?" Starr demanded, but Rex and Barton were also taking aim. "After three," Cattermole said. "One, two –"

"Run!" Starr shouted. The rifles crashed out an untidy volley, brutally deafening, and the fox was kicked sideways so that it rolled uphill in a spinning flurry until it whacked into a tree and bounced out and stopped.

"Tally-ho!" Cattermole cried, and led the charge. Reilly raced alongside, barking joyfully.

Starr turned his back on them and glared at the adjutant. Kellaway was finding a comfortable spot to sit on the cairn. "Stupid bastards," Starr said. "Childish bloody thugs. Feckless cretins."

Kellaway took out his pipe and began the soothing ritual of filling it.

"I feel bloody sick," Starr said.

"Breathe deeply," Kellaway advised. "You don't want to lose your lunch up here, old boy. It's a long way back to the mess and we've eaten all the grub."

Only two bullets had struck the fox, but the rifles were military .303 Lee-Enfields and the damage was great. One shot had smashed through the ribs and torn a great wet scarlet hole in the guts. The other had hit the head below the eyes and ripped away much of the jaw. Nevertheless the fox was not dead. Its lungs were pumping and it was making a series of thin, choking barks. Rex reloaded, put his rifle against its ear, and blew half its skull off.

"For Christ's sake," Starr muttered miserably. "They couldn't even kill the bloody thing properly."

While Cattermole cut off the tail as a souvenir, the others examined the spot where the fox had been standing. Some of the bullet strikes were several yards off-target. One had stripped bark from a branch ten feet above ground. "Not too brilliant," Barton remarked.

"Hell of a kick, this gun has," Cox said.

"That's the beauty of the Hurricane, isn't it?" Rex said. "When you've got eight Brownings, each squirting twenty-odd bullets per second, you can afford to spray 'em about. It's actually the most efficient way to attack."

"Really?" Cox was feeling somewhat jumpy: the fox was a bloodier mess than he had expected. "Spraying's more efficient?"

"Oh yes. You get target-saturation, you see. Tests have proved it, Mother. Quite conclusively."

"Did you spray that German Blenheim, Fanny?" Miller asked. "Or did you drill it through the middle?"

"You get yourself up in a Blenheim," Barton said, "and I'll show you."

"Fanny's still a bit touchy on that subject," Patterson said to the others, out of the side of his mouth.

"He honestly didn't realise it was a Blenheim," Cox said.

"He thought it was a four-engined Sunderland flyingboat," Miller said. "From certain angles they both –"

"You'll get my boot up your backside from no uncertain angle if you don't shut up." Barton's face was stony.

"See?" Patterson whispered loudly. "Touchy."

Rex finished wiping bits of blood and brain off the muzzle of his rifle. "Come on, chaps, let's go," he said. "Reilly! Heel, sir! Leave that alone, damn you."

Unwillingly the dog followed them, licking its chops. Kellaway too set off. Dicky Starr let them get ahead before he climbed the slope and piled the biggest stones he could lift on top of the dead fox. He ran and caught up as the others reached the horses. He was first man into the saddle, first to set off.

The sun was now low, and the light under the trees was washed with purple and shot with gold. Mother Cox found himself riding alongside the adjutant. "That cairn," he said. "Nice of the French to go to so much trouble."

"Oh well. Once a chap's dead you might as well treat him decently."

Cox ducked his chin into the high sheepskin collar and nibbled on the edge. "Can't say I go a bundle on that *inconnu* business, though."

"Fortunes of war, old boy."

"Yes, I know, but ... You see, I don't mind taking my chances with Jerry upstairs but it does seem a bit rough to do your stuff and maybe run out of luck – well, that's all right, I'm not complaining about that, but supposing I come to grief somewhere, not that I'm planning to, but just suppose the elastic band snaps or a wing falls off or something, and I find myself at twenty

151

thousand feet with no visible means of support, well, all I'm saying is, I don't want to end up listed as 'missing,' thanks very much."

"Mmm. Point taken, old boy." Kellaway was beginning to imagine the glow of whisky, both in the glass and in the throat.

"I mean, it's such a piddling word, isn't it? *Missing*. Makes you sound as if you lost your way, or got locked in the lavatory. Damn silly."

"Yes. Mind you, it happened to lots of chaps. In the last show, I mean. French especially, French infantry, good God yes, whole regiments went missing, whole brigades, all just blown to smithereens. Ever heard of the Ossuary?"

"No."

"Up at Verdun. Ossuary, it means bone-pile or something like that. You don't know what missing means until you've clapped eyes on that place, Mother. Two whacking great tombs full of all the bones they brought out of Verdun. Three hundred thousand men, all *inconnu*. Three hundred thousand, Mother!"

"Well, I don't care. The frogs can do what they like. I don't want it to happen to me."

"Of course not, but –"

"I mean, you couldn't ask for an easier name, could you? Cox, C-O-X, that's all I want. It's not much to ask."

"True." Kellaway exercised his right shoulder: the cold was seeping into it. "Funny word, smithereens. When I was small I used to think it was a place. I thought people got blown to smithereens the same way they got driven to market. I wonder what smithereens really are?"

Cox found a handkerchief and blew his nose. "I mean, it's like having dirty plugs," he said.

Kellaway thought it over. "Don't quite follow, old boy," he said.

"You know, adj: dirty plugs. Engine's not firing properly. It's *missing*."

"Oh." Kellaway nodded. "Missing. Yes."

"I honestly don't care where I end up," Cox said, "as long as it's *definite*. I hate being kept in the dark."

Kellaway tucked his chin onto his chest. Cox's statement suggested several remarks but the more he thought about them, the less helpful they seemed. He raised his eyes and saw Patterson, riding several lengths ahead of them. Patterson stood in his stirrups, pointed his knees outward, and waggled his behind. Evidently his crotch was feeling squashed. "Good heavens!" Kellaway said. "Baggy Bletchley!"

Cox looked where Kellaway was staring and saw Patterson re-settle himself. "Come again, adj?" he said.

"I've just remembered, after all these years. Baggy Bletchley. I *knew* there was something familiar ... My stars, what a turn-up for the book. I must tell Rex ..."

But as he checked his horse, Moggy Cattermole came cantering up, whooping and waving the fox's brush. "Stand by to be blooded!" he shouted. "Get your gore here, while it's fresh!"

"Keep that filthy thing away from me," Cox said.

"Look out, Moggy, I want to see Rex," Kellaway said.

"Got to join the club first, uncle." Cattermole swung his horse around to block the trail. "Everyone gets blooded! Old English custom! Rules of the hunt!"

"Rubbish," Cox said.

"*And* it's a new squadron tradition." Cattermole moved closer. "Lord Rex says so."

Cox stared suspiciously. Cattermole flourished the brush, and smiled. "For God's sake keep that muck off my uniform, that's all," Cox said.

Cattermole grabbed him by the shoulder and thrust the brush down his neck. Cox wrenched himself away. Cattermole gave Kellaway a dab on the nose, and charged off in pursuit of Patterson, hallooing loudly.

"Hulking great oaf," Cox said crossly. He tried to look at his shirt collar but his chin got in the way.

Kellaway stopped and waited for Rex to arrive. He said: "I've just remembered something rather unusual about Air Commodore Bletchley. You might —"

"Who's that?" Rex pointed ahead. "Isn't it little Dicky? This should be worth watching."

The trail climbed in a great left-handed curve, cutting across a slope that grew steadily steeper. Cattermole, having blooded Patterson and Miller, had ridden on and reached Starr.

"Piss off and play with your sadistic friends," Starr said to him.

"Now, now. No excuses, young Richard. CO's orders, everyone gets blooded."

"You sicken me, you lot."

"For shame! It's a grand old English tradition, Dicky! Where's your patriotism? Besides, this stuff's good for the complexion."

Cattermole hustled his horse alongside the other. The path wasn't wide enough for two and Starr's mount began slipping on the outer edge. Starr said: "I won't –"

"You will, you little runt." Cattermole jabbed the brush at his face. Starr ducked under it and slammed his elbow into Cattermole's ribs. Cattermole gasped with pain, lost balance and almost fell backwards. His left boot kicked up and smacked Starr's horse in the mouth.

Rex and Kellaway saw the horse rear and stagger. Its hind legs struggled to keep to the path, and failed. The animal stumbled, twisted in mid-air and plunged down the slope with a violence that hurled Starr onto its neck. It bolted for the bottom, missing trees by inches, kicking up a wake of dead leaves, and releasing a screaming whinny of fear and pain. Finally, unable to stop, it smashed into a patch of scrub and briar and was lost to sight.

"My God, that doesn't look too good," said Kellaway.

"He should have fallen off immediately," Rex said. "Pointless staying on a horse that's out of control."

"Blind instinct, I suppose."

"No wonder the beast panicked, the way he wrapped his arms around its neck. Thoroughly bad form." Rex cupped his hands and shouted. "Moggy! Go and bring him back, quick as you can. Everyone else, wait here."

They assembled and waited in silence. It was getting dark, they were tired, the wind was merciless.

"What were you saying about Air Commodore Bletchley?" Rex asked suddenly.

"Oh . . . Nothing important." The adjutant tucked his hands into his armpits. "I just remembered him from the old RFC days, that's all. We used to call him Baggy Bletchley then. He was just a lieutenant, of course."

They waited. "Why Baggy?" Miller asked.

"Well, you know . . . Everyone had a nickname."

"Did he look baggy?"

"Oh no. He was quite smart, as I remember."

Miller sniffed. "Too complicated for me."

154

One of the horses stamped and snorted. They were getting cold, too. "If you want to know, it was because of his balls," Kellaway said. That revived their interest. "Bletchley had very big balls. They hung unusually low. I suppose they had to, because of their size. Anyway, there was a story that he went to be measured for a new uniform, and the tailor took his inside-leg measurement, and then he asked him . . ." Kellaway cleared his throat. "He said to him: 'And do you dress left or right, sir?' And Bletchley is supposed to have replied: 'Just make the knees extra baggy.' "

Their laughter was cut short by the distant crack of a rifle. "So that's why he was called Baggy," Kellaway said. "I wonder what that was?"

"Moggy's shot an elephant," said Patterson.

"Or Dicky's shot Moggy," said Barton.

"Maybe Moggy's shot himself," said Cox.

"Maybe the elephant shot both of them," Miller suggested. "In which case we can all go home."

"Actually, elephants are supposed to be quite harmless," Barton said. "Unless they get angry."

"Knowing Moggy," Cox said, "he probably shot the wrong elephant in the wrong place for the wrong reason, and now the beast's hopping mad."

Soon Starr came trudging up the slope. Cattermole followed, leading his own horse.

"Dicky's nag broke a leg," Cattermole said. He showed them a rip in his sleeve. "Brute tried to savage me when I went near it. No appreciation at all. I had to shoot it."

"Damn!" Rex said. "That's most unfortunate. We shall have to pay for it now, I suppose."

"How much is a horse these days?" Patterson asked.

"Twenty or thirty quid. Three or four thousand francs."

"Less the meat value," Cox pointed out. "Big horsemeat eaters, the frogs."

"You all right, Dicky?" Kellaway asked. Starr nodded. Blood was congealing from a cut over his right eye. "Better jump up behind me."

Starr said not a word on the way back, and the adjutant knew better than to try to get him to talk. They returned the horses to the stables and drove to the château.

After dinner, Fanny Barton found Rex in a corner of the anteroom, brushing mud and burrs out of Reilly's coat.

"In my opinion, sir, Cattermole's getting rather too big for his boots," Barton said. "He's having a bad effect on the other boys. I really think he needs to be cut down to size."

"I see." Rex found some seeds stuck to a hind leg, and teased them out. He looked up, reacting to Barton's silence. "So cut him down to size, then," he said briskly. "He's in your flight, isn't he?"

"I thought a few words from you might have more effect, sir."

"Of course they'd have more effect. They'd reduce your authority. A flight commander's job is to command his flight, Fanny. I'm not going to do it for you. I've got enough work on my hands keeping this hound presentable. Ah, thank you." A mess waiter brought a pint of beer. Rex put it on the floor and Reilly started drinking, his tail going like a pump-handle. "It puts gloss on his coat," Rex said, "and lead in his pencil. By the way: if you want to see Cattermole, he's just come in."

"I'll think it over," Barton said.

"What a good boy." Rex stroked Reilly, who had finished the beer and was looking around the room. "He's picking his target, bless him," Rex said fondly.

Micky Marriott's drainage ditches began to work. The aerodrome improved from a swamp to a bog. The air was still bitterly cold, and snow fell in the Vosges, but at least there was some prospect of flying again. When the wind was in the right direction the front windows of the Château St Pierre trembled gently to the heavy roar of Merlin engines being run-up and tuned. Two or three times a day condensation trails could be seen overhead, but they were thin and high and shortlived and nobody paid them much attention. To the east, the French and German artillery were silent.

Flash Gordon and Fitz Fitzgerald had volunteered to stay on duty while the others went riding. Now they got permission to leave the camp. "Back to school again?" Rex said. "I never knew such a thirst for education."

"It's very encouraging, sir," Fitz said. "The kids can't get enough of us, it seems."

Flash said: "We help them with their handwriting, sir."

Rex rolled his eyes. "Be sure you don't dip your nib in the wrong ink-pot, that's all."

It was a slow morning for the rest of the pilots. They wrote letters, played Ludo, tried to find some jazz on the radio, looked at old copies of the *Daily Mail* or *Daily Mirror*. At eleven-thirty a group captain arrived from Area HQ to give a lecture on the importance of not flying over neutral Luxembourg, Belgium or Holland. It was a mercifully short lecture: he had really come to sample Hornet squadron's famous food. By noon everyone was gathered at the bar.

"Any news from England, sir?" Rex asked the visitor.

"Nothing special. The war's hit the rugger clubs rather badly but racing's not affected, thank goodness. All enemy aliens have been arrested, of course, and shipped off to some remote corner of Cumberland, which seems a bit rough on Cumberland. Still, it means we're spared the endless letters those people used to write to *The Times* about the Jewish problem. I can't tell you how bored I got with the Jewish problem. They really are the most depressing people, can't seem to get along with anyone. All that fuss about foreskins and ham sandwiches; I mean why can't they unbend a bit and behave normally, like the rest of us? Not that –"

"It's a matter of religion, sir," Cox said.

The group captain had not been expecting an answer. "A matter of religion," he said. "Ah. You ... You sound as if you might know something about it."

"I'm half-Jewish. My mother." The other pilots glanced at him curiously. *Old Mother Cox, half-Jewish; fancy that. Come to think of it he has got rather a long nose. Not that it makes any difference, of course ...*

The group captain switched his expression to one of interest. "Tell me," he said. "What do you think of the overall so-to-speak situation, Mr ..."

"Cox," said Rex.

"How appropriate," the group captain murmured.

"Well, I'm not an expert, sir," Cox said. "I mean, I don't want to live in Palestine, I'm not a Zionist, my parents don't keep a shop in the East End of London and they haven't been beaten up by Oswald Mosley's fascist thugs. But what I've often wondered is how Hitler's Nazi party thinks that killing off some of the greatest brains in Europe is going to help them win the war."

Skull asked: "What would you do, if you were Hitler?"

"I'd recruit every Jewish genius in sight," Cox said promptly. "Even if I had to wear fourteen skullcaps and eat *gefilte* fish three times a day."

The group captain chuckled and sipped his beer.

Behind his hand, Miller muttered: "What the hell's *gefilte* fish?" Starr shrugged: "Never heard of it."

"I'm glad you think wars are won by brains," the group captain said to Cox. "I'm sure our lords and masters would agree."

Rex led the laughter.

"Mind you, sir," Cox said, "the other thing I can't understand is why all those people who escaped from Germany to avoid getting put in Nazi concentration camps have now been arrested and put in British concentration camps instead."

"Steady on, old chap," Cattermole protested. "I mean, play the game." He held his beer against his chest, fingers grasping the tankard, handle pointing outwards: it was the squadron style. "British concentration camps? That's a bit steep, Mother."

"You are rather off-course, old chap," Rex said. "We simply don't go in for that sort of thing."

"I rather suspect you'll find it's more a sort of protective custody," the group captain said. "Not an actual concentration camp *as such*."

"Call it what you like," Cox said, "it's still barbed wire, isn't it?"

"As a matter of fact," Skull said, "the British invented the concentration camp. Against the Boers."

"And the South Africans are now our allies and a splendid bunch of chaps they are," Rex said rapidly, "so they obviously didn't hold it against us. As you can tell, sir, Hornet is rather a special squadron. We don't go in for stuffy conventional ideas here. We encourage originality and initiative and so on."

"Sounds jolly democratic," the group captain said.

"Well, that's what we're fighting for, after all."

"Is it?" Skull fumbled for a pen. "Are we? I ought to make a note of that. I thought it was something to do with Poland."

"Correct," the group captain said.

"Ah." Skull held up the pen and frowned at the nib. "In that case, when shall we declare war on Russia?"

"Pay no attention to him, sir," Fitzgerald said. "Old Skull's got an IQ of seven hundred and forty-three, so he overheats easily. We have to change his oil twice a week."

"No, it's a simple question," Skull said.

"What a fierce fellow you are, Skull," Rex sighed. "One war isn't enough."

"Well, Russia has invaded Poland, just as Germany did. Russia has annexed even more of Poland than Germany did. To be consistent, therefore, we should –"

"We should go in to lunch," Rex said. "Nothing very grand; I'm afraid, sir: just Strasbourg *pâté*, a local fish, and some cheese, but I'll be interested to hear what you think of our Pinot Blanc. I reckon it's one of the most *symmetrical* wines available, but you know far more about these things than I do . . ."

They trooped off.

Mary Blandin walked over to where Fitz Fitzgerald was pushing a little girl on a swing. "Stay to supper," she said.

"That's awfully nice of you." Fitz stopped pushing. The little girl squealed and waved her feet. "The problem is, you see, Flash and I came here in the same car, so . . ."

"Don't worry. Flash will be looked after."

"Really?" Fitz looked across the playground. Nicole Ligier was talking to a red-headed boy who was sitting on Flash Gordon's shoulders, gripping his hair in both fists. "Well, in that case," Fitz said, "it would be churlish of me to refuse, wouldn't it?" The little girl squealed louder. "All right, you noisy monster!" he cried, and began pushing. "Will there be rolypoly pudding?" he asked Mary. "I'm a pushover for rolypoly pudding."

She narrowed her eyes and looked mysterious. "We shall see," she said.

Dicky Starr's handwriting was neat and simple. The important words were underlined in red ink, and there were green-ink lines drawn between the different sections. "Knowledge is power," his father had once told him; and Starr had kept careful notes of everything the instructors told him at every stage of his flying training. These notes filled ten thick exercise books. The page now open before him had his thumbprint in the top right-hand corner (leaky fountain-pen). He had framed it in red and green.

Dicky Starr kept these notes because he believed that everything in the world could be explained and understood. Disorder worried him. He felt bewildered by the pointlessness of the killings during yesterday's horseback outing and he was angered by the fact that nobody else seemed to care. Everyone agreed Moggy Cattermole was a chump, but nobody did anything. Not even Fanny Barton. Dicky Starr was very conscious of his own size – he was as short as Sticky Stickwell and a good bit lighter – and he hated having to get other people to fight his battles. So he said nothing. After lunch he went off to study his notes in a corner of the library where there was a turret-like room screened by a red velvet curtain.

The page with the framed thumbprint was all about cloud formations.

Very high cloud (above 20,000 ft). Cirrus: this means "curly", e.g. cloud looks like lambs' tails. Stratus means "a layer" and resembles faint chalk-marks all going the same way. Cirro-cumulus is made of small blobs of cloud perhaps forming a pattern such as ...

Enraged. That was the word. He hadn't been angry when they shot that fox; he'd been enraged. He'd been overtaken by a rushing fury that seemed to grab him by the guts. At that moment he'd wanted to kill them. Snatch up his gun and blast someone's head off. If the adj hadn't been standing there he might have done it, might have run wild, the taste had been in his throat, the raging hunger.

It was a new vision of himself and it shocked him: the Dicky Starr who made lots of model aeroplanes and brushed his teeth after meals and passed all his exams had somehow turned into a potential killer. Of course as soon as they'd let him go up in an eight-gun Hurricane he'd known that he was in that seat for the purpose of destroying enemy aircraft, but it was a technical task, knocking down planes. Now there was a part of him that wanted to kill, that actually relished the prospect of blowing someone to bits. That wasn't nice. People had always said what a nice chap Dicky Starr was, and he had believed them. Now it turned out

160

that he wasn't at all nice. He stared at his framed thumbprint and worried.

The curtain swished. "So there you are, little man," Cattermole said. "Skulking in your tent. That won't help you. I want four hundred and thirty-seven francs and fifty centimes, and I want it now." He strolled around the little room, sniffed at the view, ran his finger along a shelf of books. "Come on, come on," he said.

"I'm not talking to you," Starr muttered.

"I don't care a tiny toss whether you fiddle, fart or sing the old school song. Just pay up."

Starr began reading his notes. Cattermole plucked the exercise book from his fingers and put it on a high shelf. Starr folded his arms and gripped his biceps until his thumbs hurt. "What a very clever thing to do," he said. "That must have taken every brain in your body."

"Cough up, little pygmy." Cattermole clicked his fingers. "Get your purse out of your knickers."

"I'd sooner be a little pygmy than a giant shit."

"Don't bore me with your dreams, shrimp. Cash, cash, cash. Give."

"There's only one thing I'd like to give you, and that's a red-hot bullet up the backside."

Cattermole shook his head. "Pleasure later. Business first."

"What's this, a lovers' tiff?" Patterson wandered in, bouncing a ping-pong ball.

"Ah, Pip. You're another. You owe me four hundred and thirty-seven francs and a bit," Cattermole told him. "The stables charged us three-and-a-half thousand francs for that wretched horse, the one Starr went joyriding on. Eights into three-and-a-half thou go four thirty-seven point five, so that's your share of the damage."

"For God's sake!" Patterson said. "That's nearly three pounds. I'm not paying that."

"Lord Rex says you are."

"It was all your fault," Starr told Cattermole. "You made it happen, you ought to pay for everything."

Cattermole perched on the windowsill and examined him. "You're in a proper little tizz because I shot your pet fox, aren't you?" he said.

"If you mean I was disgusted, yes I was. It was barbaric, just the sort of behaviour you expect the Gestapo to –"

"Pip shot the animal too. Why not blame him?"

"I only shot it because everyone else was having a go," Patterson said. "I mean, if it was going to be dead, I might as well make sure it was good and dead."

"You nearly all missed," Starr said.

'There you are then, it's just as well I shot straight, otherwise . . ." Patterson stopped as he realised where that argument led. "Anyway, it was only a fox," he said. Starr clenched his teeth. "Damn good fox, of course," Patterson added.

"I'll tell you your trouble, Dicky Dwarf," Cattermole said. "You're squeamish. That's why you'll never be any good as a fighter pilot. You're completely covered with squeam, my lad. Squeam all over you. You ought to see a doctor about it. Tell him –"

"Oh, shut up, Moggy!" Patterson cried. "Dicky's a bloody good pilot, as good as anyone in this squadron. Christ, you're never happy unless you're kicking someone in the balls, are you?"

"I do it for their own good," Cattermole said blandly. "It hurts me, I assure you. I suffer agonies."

"Oh yes? What about Micky Marriott?" Starr demanded. "You treated him pretty badly, didn't you? That day when you came back early because your engine was overheating. You treated him like dirt."

"Did I? Possibly. Ages ago. I scarcely remember."

"I remember all right," Patterson said. "You were bloody rude."

Cattermole poked his little finger in his ear and studied the findings. "One must keep the peasants in their place," he murmured.

Starr got up and looked out of the window. "I was duty officer that day," he said. "I was in the tower when the CO told you to break off and go home. I heard it on the R/T. I logged the time. And I logged your landing. You were at least fifteen minutes late."

"Hullo, hullo!" Patterson said.

Cattermole yawned. "What a nosey little boy you are."

"Fifteen minutes?" Patterson said. "You stooged around for a quarter of an hour with a red-hot engine?"

"Certainly not. I investigated a certain bridge over the Moselle at Thionville. I examined it from all sides, including underneath."

"Thionville," Patterson said. "Thionville. Where did I see something about that?"

"Memo from Area HQ," Starr said. "Dangerous flying. They blamed it on a French Morane."

"Purblind fools," Cattermole said.

"I remember. They didn't like it, did they?" Patterson said.

"Area HQ disapproves of flying," Cattermole said. "It wears out the aeroplane."

"Did you really go under that bridge, Moggy?" Patterson asked.

"Of course. That's what it's there for."

"If you did," Starr said thickly, "all I can say is it must be childsplay."

"Well, there's one way to find out, sonny-boy." Cattermole glanced at him, waited, and got off the windowsill. "As I thought," he murmured.

"Listen, I could do it," Starr said. "I just don't see the point, that's all."

"Very well, I'll bet you. Double or quits. If you do it, I pay shares in the horse for both of us. If you don't do it you owe me double. That's . . . what . . . eight hundred and seventy-five francs."

"Done," Starr said, without thinking.

Cattermole looked at Patterson. "Feeling brave today?" he asked.

"Same stakes?" Patterson knew he was playing for time. Cattermole nodded. Time ran out. "Money for old rope," Patterson said.

Cattermole ruffled Starr's hair in passing. "Thionville," he said. "Dreary little dump." He sauntered off. Starr smoothed his hair and watched him go. He felt tricked and trapped. He looked at Patterson, but Pip was bouncing his ping-pong ball. No help there.

Flash Gordon got halfway through unbuttoning his shirt when he remembered the widow Ligier, sitting beside the fire. He had been in the big farmhouse kitchen for so long – three hours, almost – and the meal and the wine and the conversation had been so pleasant, that he had forgotten Nicole's mother; she never spoke, never moved from her chair; just rested and smiled in the general direction of the two young people. "Are you sure this is okay?" he muttered.

"She cannot hear us," Nicole said. "Even if she could, she cannot understand. And she can see very little. To her eyes you are just a shadow."

"Goodness. How sad." He blinked doubtfully at the old lady as Nicole's fingers undid the last buttons and tugged the shirt over his head. He was wearing a singlet; that came off too. "Now raise your arms," she said.

"I feel like a prisoner-of-war."

"Do you? That's interesting." She slipped her hands across his ribcage, and he inhaled sharply. "Your body is made to be a piece of armour, you see. It expects attack and it guards against that."

"Jolly clever."

"Your ribs protect your heart and lungs, for example." She ran a finger along the bottom edge of his ribcage. His chest was very white and almost completely hairless. "Human biology is the most interesting subject in the world," she said. "At university it fascinated me."

"Yes? I've never thought about it very much." She moved behind him and traced the muscles of his back. "You were saying something about arteries," he said.

"Arteries are wonderful. They take your blood everywhere but they hide themselves behind your bones for safety."

"I say, that's brilliant."

"But sometimes they must approach the surface. These are places where the body is very vulnerable." She searched with her fingertips until she found the throb of artery in his neck. "Here," she said. Her fingers moved to the inside of his elbow, his upper arm, his armpit, the hollow of his collarbone. "There . . . and there . . . Up there . . . Down there . . ."

"Fancy that," he said huskily.

"Next time," she said, lightly probing his abdominal muscles, "I shall explain the liver and the kidneys. Also the spleen."

"Holy smoke." The firelight played on his torso. Madame Ligier blinked and smiled. Flash Gordon wasn't sure what the hell was happening to him, but he was more than happy to let it continue.

A quarter of a mile away, Fitz Fitzgerald knelt by the fire and

164

arranged chestnuts along the top of the grate. Mary Blandin came and sat beside him. "Brandy," she said.

"I say, that's jolly decent of you."

"Is it?" She gave him one of the glasses. "I'm not sure I want to be jolly decent. It sounds like going country dancing with three pairs of knickers on."

Fitz knocked a chestnut into the fire. "Sorry," he said. "Hotter than I thought."

"Poor Fitz." She tickled his stockinged feet and made him squirm. "Tell you what: I'll be jolly decent if you will too."

"Ah." He sucked his finger. "I'm not sure about that. You see, I've never worn three pairs of knickers."

"There was a time," she said thoughtfully, "when I refused to wear any knickers at all. Happy days, they were."

Fitz sipped his brandy and studied her profile. It was golden in the firelight. "Tell me more. Tell me all, in fact."

"I was aged five. After that I got sent to school, thoroughly knickered all year round. They were amazing things, those school knickers. Like twin carrier-bags. Girls used to keep all sorts of things tucked inside them. Pencils, money, apples, handkerchiefs, love letters. Boxes of matches. I used to keep my diary there."

"Hot stuff, was it?"

"Oh, no. Soggy. Moist with tears. Amazing, really, when I think of the days and weeks and months I used to sob and weep my little heart out . . ."

"Well, it's no fun being unhappy." Fitz almost took her hand. He felt strong and protective.

"I wasn't unhappy, I was conceited," she said. "I thought I was a tragic figure."

"You did? Why?"

"No special reason." Fitz looked puzzled, so she said: "I was a remarkably stupid child, you see. Now you, I'm sure, had a happy childhood."

Fitz shrugged and drank more brandy. His childhood had in fact been very cheerful, but that was an ordinary sort of fact and one he didn't feel like revealing; not yet, anyway. "Who's he?" He pointed at a photograph. "Don't tell me. A cousin. No, it's your brother."

"What makes you say that?"

165

"Same eyes."

She tugged at her lower lip while she studied the picture: a waist-upwards shot of a young man glancing at the camera as he opened a bottle of wine. "He certainly had nice eyes," she said. Fitz suddenly felt lost: he'd taken a wrong turning somewhere. "That's Paul," she said. "My poor dead husband."

The words were spoken so blankly that Fitz wasn't sure whether she was being candid or facetious. "Ah," he said. "Yes . . . Good picture, isn't it? Did you take it?"

"No, he did. He had a special gadget on the camera. Paul was mad keen on photography. He took thousands of snaps of me."

Discussing the late Paul Blandin made Fitz uncomfortable and he sought an escape. "Still got them?" he asked.

"Oh, yes. Lots."

"Show me."

She fetched a leatherbound album. "You're taking an awful risk, you know," she said. "You might be bored to tears."

Fitz smiled. He balanced the album on his thighs and opened it at random. Three shots of Mary swimming in an outdoor pool. Something lurched softly in the pit of his stomach. "Nice," he said. He would have liked to look more closely, but instead he turned the page, and his eyes widened. Mary standing at the poolside, drying herself. No costume. Mary stretched out on the towel, face down. Naked. Mary bouncing on a divingboard, caught by the camera in mid-air, arms upflung and knees slightly bent, skin shining with water; totally and magnificently nude. "Yes, I see what you mean," he said. "The work of an expert." He shut the album and handed it back to her. He cleared his throat, and studied the chestnuts.

"Are you shocked?" She was leaning back with the album held against her chest and her pleated skirt spread like a seashell.

"No, of course not." He glanced sideways, chin up to meet the challenge. They were both being so serious that spontaneously they laughed. "Well, maybe I was a bit shocked at first. Somewhat. Not unpleasantly. Far from it."

"You see . . . I get very fed-up with men who keep looking at me and wondering what I'm like with no clothes on. It's . . ." She wrinkled her nose. "Waste of time," she said.

"Point taken." Fitz nodded several times. "So now I know, then."

"It's simple curiosity, after all, isn't it?"

"Aren't you curious, too?" Fitz took a good grip of his ankles and hung on tight. "Don't you want to know what I look like?"

"I'm sure you're beautiful. Meanwhile I'll take all your sexual machinery on trust."

"Very kind of you."

They sat and listened to the hiss of the fire.

"Or perhaps I'm too trusting," Mary said. "I mean, how do I know you're all there?" He recoiled slightly. "Well, let's face it, Fitz, you gave me this back in a bit of a hurry, didn't you? Two pages were enough for you." He straightened up and squared his shoulders; his mouth was half-opened. "You didn't even see the best pictures," she said, rubbing her chin on the top of the album. "They're in colour, too. I had a lovely tan in those days, and –"

"*Give me that damn book!*" Fitz shouted. He lunged for it, lost his balance and fell against her. She kissed him, easily and sweetly, on the lips. Behind them the chestnuts were beginning to smoke.

"Enjoy yourself?" Flash Gordon asked.

"Quiet. Very quiet. Family album by the fire, that sort of thing." Fitz yawned. "You know."

Flash changed gear and put on speed.

"How about you?" Fitz asked. "Good time?"

"Nicole's mother was there."

"Ah. Tough luck."

"We talked about biology. Nicole's an expert. I learned a lot. If you took all your veins and arteries and things and tied them together, how far d'you think they'd stretch?"

"Haven't the faintest."

"Twelve thousand miles."

"My goodness."

"Yes," Flash said. "Makes you think, doesn't it?"

A sheen of frost gave the airfield a fine, furry coating. Every blade of grass was cased in crystals. The wheels of the speeding Hurricane crushed the frost, creating narrow tracks of black-green. Its tail-wheel made a thinner line, just a pencil-stroke across the whiteness, and this line was the first to cease as the nose came down and Pip Patterson saw the horizon.

That was better; he felt happier when he could see where he was going. The field went past in a silvery rush. His cockpit hood was open and he could smell burnt oil coming off the engine. The smell was sharp in this freezing air, and it reminded him of something. What was it? The rumbling bounce of the Hurricane turned to a racing tremble, and the plane took to the air. Patterson eased back the stick, raised the wheels, corrected a dip in the starboard wing, slid the hood shut, and remembered that smell: it was the reek of the fairground, especially the stink coming off the engine that drove the merry-go-round. Hot oil. Greatest thrill in a young lad's life, riding the galloping horses with that exciting stink in his nostrils. Nothing compared, after that. Not even driving a Hurricane at 300 mph. After all, what was a Hurricane? A bus. The kite was as big as a bus, half as comfortable, ten times as noisy, nowhere to put your luggage, bloody cold in this weather. So what did that make the pilot? A bus driver. Only difference, the scenery was a lot more interesting on the average bus route. The trouble with sky was it went on long after it ran out of anything to say. Especially on a day like today. Nothing but a lot of remote, blank greyness. You might as well go around with your head in a paper bag.

Patterson turned and flew back over the airfield, waggled his wings, and climbed away. Looking back, he could see the rest of the squadron standing beside Rex outside the pilots' hut. A couple of them waved; he waggled again in response.

"Good enough," Rex said. Evidently Micky Marriott's drainage ditches had done their job: the ground was firm. "The rest of 'B' flight – air-testing this morning, thirty-minute readiness this afternoon. 'A' flight at readiness this morning, air-testing after lunch. Let's have all machines fully operational by tomorrow. Check everything! You'd be surprised how much can go wrong with a Hurricane when it's been left standing in a draughty hangar all week. Bronchitis and swollen ankles and God knows what. Right, adj, we'll stroll back, shall we? Where's Reilly?"

They walked towards the château, Reilly crisscrossing behind them, hunting scents.

"Beautiful air," Kellaway said, inhaling vigorously. "I've always liked winter, ever since the last show. You can't beat a good hard freeze. It solves the mud problem, it kills the bugs and –"

"Gordon's a queer fish, isn't he?" Rex asked.

168

"Who? Young Flash?"

"Yes. Not quite . . ." Rex wrinkled his nose. "I don't know. Not quite up to snuff. What's his background?"

"Just . . . ordinary."

"Yes . . ." Rex nodded in time with his pace. "Very ordinary. He picks his nose."

Kellaway puffed out his cheeks. "Don't we all?"

"Not in public. And he gets unpleasant spots on the back of his neck."

"That's scarcely his fault, sir. He's only twenty."

"Nasty habits, adj, nasty habits. And while we're on the subject, what's the matter with Starr?"

"Oh, Dicky's a bit moody, that's all. I expect –"

"He looks thoroughly constipated. That's no good. I want all my pilots to be good squadron men. Starr looks like a constipated dwarf. He's letting the side down, adj." Rex took a flying kick at a frozen thistle. "Why doesn't he grow up? Why don't they both grow up? I don't mind telling you, I'm getting a bit fed-up with some of these chaps. I want a squadron I can be proud of, not a lot of spotty pygmies."

They passed the guardroom at the main gate. The sentry presented arms; they returned the salute. Reilly came cantering up and made a detour to sniff the sentry's legs. The man rapidly shouldered arms but Reilly jetted a sprinkle on his snowy gaiters and got away a second before the rifle hurtled down and its butt crashed to earth. The dog caught up with its master and licked his gloved hand.

"Time to bring in some new blood, uncle," Rex said. "Breeding counts, you know."

Pip Patterson sat hunched in his cockpit, checked the trim and let the Hurricane fly itself.

He felt tired and bored. He had done nothing much since he took off, just chucked the kite about to make sure everything worked. One of the rudder-pedals felt a bit sloppy; that was all. The Merlin was in good voice, the controls were responsive; he could go anywhere, do anything. He sat with his limbs slack and watched the grey sky drift by.

It was a familiar feeling. Patterson was often bored with his own

169

company. He needed other people to stimulate him. He wasn't stupid; in some subjects – navigation, Morse, radio – he was brighter than average. His trouble was that he *cared* about nothing very much; not even about himself.

Patterson's family owned several coal mines in Midlothian. Pip was the fourth child, third son, and he had been brought up comfortably, even generously. He'd gone to the school of his choice – Loretto College, near Edinburgh; his brothers were there already, so he didn't get bullied much. He was sixteen when he heard about a new international college in Geneva where boys and girls mixed and wine-drinking was encouraged. He spent a year there, learned how to meet girls, how to get drunk, how to ski, how to play cards. He was good on skis and bad with cards. He envied his friends' zest for poker, but there was no gambling instinct in him, no appetite feeding on risk, no sense of the theatre of the game. If he made himself gamble he played bluntly and obviously, which was no fun for anyone.

He was more successful with girls because he was a good listener. One or two fell in love with him, or at least with his freshfaced Scottish looks, the dark lashes over the grey eyes and the straight, clean-lipped mouth. Nothing lasted, neither the poker schools nor the girls nor the snow. Pip came home a month early, bored.

His father gave him a blue BSA motorcycle, and later a red MG car with a leather strap across the bonnet. Nobody had anything special for him to do. He went off and took flying lessons. Flying came easily – it was a cross between skiing and driving the MG – and when someone suggested joining the RAF he couldn't think of a reason not to do it.

That was how he came to be sitting in this Hurricane, twelve thousand feet over eastern France. The land below looked as flat and dead as a sepia photograph. Nothing was happening outside the aeroplane. Or inside it.

Patterson tilted his head to his left and watched the blue-green flicker of flames in the exhaust-stubs. They looked like soft feathers, you could almost reach out and stroke them. A wandering gleam drifted into the corner of his eye: a feeble sunbeam, glinting on his canopy. The gleam got stronger. The sun wasn't on that side. He straightened his head with slow curiosity, and abruptly jerked it to the right. The gleam was a fighter coming at him, small at first but magnifying with astounding speed so that even as his muscles tensed to respond it was too late, the plane was on him, huge as a house, filling the sky, and he gave a shout of terror, flung up an arm. With a brief blast of sound the fighter hopped over his Hurricane like a child playing leapfrog, and vanished. *"Bastard!"* Patterson screamed. His hands and feet were jumping with fright, his heart was banging, the Hurricane was trying to fly sideways. He shoved all the controls into a corner and sent the machine down in a slanting dive, away from danger. Too slow: another fighter whizzed from behind and boomed over him, so close that the wash rocked his wings. It banked to the right so he turned hard left, ramming the throttle. The Merlin couldn't be roused that fast and the Hurricane wallowed. Another fighter came from nowhere, zipped under him and rocketed away, screwing itself into the sky. Patterson's head was like a punchball flung all ways as he tried to dodge and search at once. Then the engine gave him its power and he stuffed the nose hard down and ran for his life.

Five thousand feet below, he levelled out and made damn sure there was nobody within a mile of him.

The fighters had disappeared. He'd never know who they were: Hurricanes from another squadron, perhaps, or French Moranes. Practical jokers, anyway. Full of high spirits. Skylarking. Happy to find a dreamer and scare the shits out of him. What fun.

Patterson turned for home. He felt angry with himself, disgusted. He'd been made to look a fool. Well, he was a fool. He certainly wasn't anything brilliant. *Silly sod*, he said to himself. *Why don't you get your finger out your arse for once?* He looked down and saw the town of Metz a couple of miles to his right. *Don't just look at it*, he told himself.

Five minutes later he was circling Thionville.

Patterson had never flown under a bridge. He drifted down in a wide spiral, looking at the river, at the bridge, at the bends and cliffs below the bridge. He'd flown under power cables once, but that was in a Tiger Moth and the cables had been strung high across a wide valley. Nothing to it.

He gave himself plenty of height, about fifteen hundred feet, and flew a dummy run above the river. The bridge slid under his wings. He turned and flew back. It was a busy morning down there: lots of traffic, quite a few small boats. A mile above the town he turned again and made another run, this time at six or seven hundred feet. There was a lot of water coming down. In several places it had flooded over the banks and he could see a frill of ice around the pools. The concrete spans of the bridge were a flat, featureless white. Waterlogged branches were trapped against its supports, catching nests of rubbish. As he crossed over, dozens of faces looked up, all as blank as little saucers.

Patterson turned again and went back to the start.

From a hundred feet the river looked as smooth and black as tarmac. A hundred feet was too high, of course. At fifty feet, ripples showed in the tarmac. Trees flicked past, regularly, like markers ticking off the distance. Power cables came and went overhead. Fifty was still too high. He squeezed the controls, sank to twenty, came up to thirty, felt sweat on his palms, sensed the roar of the engine beating back from the surface. The gap under the bridge looked wide and flat, like a slice of watermelon. He touched the rudder to centre the aeroplane. His thighs and calves ached with stiffness. The river seemed to shrink to nothing as the bridge rushed at him, big and hard, and suddenly the Hurricane felt huge, too huge, its wings stretching, and Patterson hauled back on the stick with all his strength. The plane bucked over the top as if kicked in its guts, missed a streetlamp by inches, and Patterson gave it all the throttle he dared while pressing the stick to his stomach. "No thank you," he said aloud. "No thanks, no thanks." The words came out flatly and harshly. "Thanks a lot, but no thanks. No thanks. No thanks."

Micky Marriott was waiting beside the groundcrew when Patterson landed. "Any problems, Pip?" he asked.

"Rudder-pedals are a bit spongy. Otherwise she's fine. No problems at all."

He trudged over to the locker room. He was wiping the inside of his leather helmet when Dicky Starr came in.

"Have a good time?" Starr said.

"Joy ride."

Starr watched him hang up the helmet and fold the towel.

"What about the bridge?" he asked. "Did you get there?"

Patterson nodded. He stretched, enormously.

"Well?"

Patterson gave him a tired but happy smile. "Piece of cake," he said.

Starr nodded, and went out. Patterson sat down and looked at his left hand. One of the fingernails was ragged. *Must do something about that*, he thought. The fingers trembled like a drunk's.

All morning Starr sat in a corner of the pilots' hut, re-reading his notebooks. The rest of 'A' flight dozed, played cards, argued, stared out of the window. One or two of them made remarks to him but he only grunted so they left him alone.

At midday they were released. They walked the half-mile to the mess for lunch, Starr keeping himself apart from the others.

The house was warm and full of noise. 'B' flight was back too; the gramophone was going, Moke Miller was at the piano. Starr went upstairs to wash his hands and face. Soap got in his eyes and he couldn't find a towel. "Fucking useless dump!" he cried, kicking a waste basket.

He left its contents scattered over the floor and walked back to the staircase. A small crowd had gathered in the hall at the bottom: Rex, Kellaway, Skull, some pilots, all greeting Air Commodore Bletchley and a pair of army officers, who were getting out of their coats. As he watched, Moggy Cattermole and one of the officers left the group and started to come upstairs. Cattermole was talking, describing the château. He kept one hand in his pocket and gestured elegantly with the other.

It was a double staircase, and the other side was empty. Starr moved towards it. Cattermole saw him. "There goes our resident deaf-mute mentally retarded dwarf," he said in a high, clear voice. "Ignore the uniform. Starr is actually a non-combatant. His testicles have not yet descended, I'm afraid. We take it in turns to give him a good shake every morning, but so far no good."

Starr turned. His anger had been simmering for two days; now it boiled over. There was a sudden thumping of blood in his temples and he felt a prickling at the back of his neck. His hands wanted to throw something. There was nothing in reach except a massive circular brass tray on which letters were left for posting. Starr seized it, spilling envelopes, knew at once he couldn't throw it far enough to hit Cattermole, and in despair and disgust flung it down. It bounced once, clanging grimly, and landed at the top of the

173

stairs. A brilliant idea grabbed him. He ran, he jumped, and his backside hit the tray with a crash that thrust it over the edge and sent it tobogganing down the stairs.

"Tally-ho!" he bawled. His feet were tucked under him, his arms outstretched, his fists clenched. The staircase curved and the tray whacked into the side, scarred the paintwork, bounced out. Part of Starr's mind tried to tell him he was doing something appallingly stupid. Another part said he was about to break his neck.

The tray racketed on. Everything was a vibrant blur: the stair-posts flickering, his head bouncing. He glimpsed the army officer vaulting over the banisters but Cattermole seemed trapped, paralysed. "*Hornet!*" Starr howled at him for no reason, and ducked.

At the last instant Cattermole tried to jump. One foot was off the ground when Starr's shoulders smashed against his knees. Cattermole cartwheeled like a circus act, his legs high, his small change showering from his pockets. Starr careered onward with his eyes tightly shut. "*Hornet!*" he shouted again. Then the tray hit the bottom and he was hurled head-first onto a large white rug. He skidded across the floor, his mouth full of wool. When he opened his eyes, blood was soaking into the white rug and he could see a lot of blue and khaki trouser-legs around him. "Jesus," he whispered.

"We used to do that on mess nights," Bletchley said. "Jolly good fun."

"You can work up quite a turn of speed, can't you?" said an artillery major. "I wonder how fast he was travelling?"

"Would you like to have a go?" Rex offered courteously.

"Not before lunch, thanks."

The adjutant said: "Don't bleed all over that rug, Dicky, there's a good fellow."

Starr got to his feet. "What rug d'you want me to bleed over, for Christ's sake?" he asked angrily. To his astonishment they all laughed. Miller slapped him on the back. Mother Cox gave him a clean handkerchief. "Bloody good prang, that," Flash Gordon told him.

The other officer, an infantry captain, came over. "Awfully sorry," he said. "I'm afraid I landed on one of your servants and I've rather broken him."

"Put it on Mr Cattermole's mess bill, adjutant," Rex said.

"Hey!" Cattermole shouted. He was sitting on the stairs, fingering his teeth. "That's not fair, sir."

"Nonsense. You should know better than to take our guests upstairs when Starr is coming down." Rex picked up the tray. "Get some more of these, uncle, would you? We'll need them when that frog bomber squadron comes to visit." He struck the tray with his fist and made it boom. "Races!"

Starr took the handkerchief from his nose. "Cresta Run," he said. Everyone laughed again. It was remarkable. He began feeling much better.

They went off and had drinks and then lunch, and soon he felt even better. A sense of daring still gripped him; he could be outrageous and get away with it. "Why don't you chaps attack?" he asked the army officers.

"Same reason Jerry won't attack us: too much rain," said the captain. "Half his forward positions were flooded out. The Moselle's very high, you know. Beyond Luxembourg all the German trenches on the right bank are awash and –"

"All right," Starr said. "Attack somebody else, then."

"Such as?"

"Italy. Mussolini's very pally with Hitler, isn't he?"

"Yes, but –"

"Is it raining in Italy?"

"Actually, most of the Italian forces are in North Africa," the major remarked.

"Even better. Less chance of rain."

"Small technical problem," the captain said. "Italy's neutral."

"That wouldn't last long once you attacked them, though, would it?" Starr argued. "Get your guns out, loose off a few shells, and Bob's your uncle. No more bloody silly neutrality."

"You make it sound so easy, Dicky," said Cox.

"Well, it *is* easy. Nothing difficult about going to war. Just pot a few wops and you're in business. Isn't that right, Skull?"

"It's always worked in the past," Skull said.

"Ah, but this war is different," Bletchley told them. "Look at Poland."

"Air power," Rex said, nodding. "Crucial."

"All right," Starr said, "if you don't fancy attacking Italy, let's invade Russia."

175

"Why?" asked the major.

"Teach them a lesson. I mean to say, Hitler wouldn't have been so bolshy without Stalin's help."

"I see," the major said. "And after Russia, what then?"

"Home for Christmas."

"Nothing to it," Miller said.

"Easy as falling downstairs," Starr said. That made them laugh. "Isn't that right, sir?"

Bletchley gave him a fond, paternal smile. "You're the expert, Starr. If you fall upon the Hun the way you fell upon Cattermole, I shall have no complaints."

Patterson had been very quiet during lunch. He was aware that Cattermole kept glancing in his direction but they were at opposite ends of the table and he pretended to be interested in the conversation around him.

It wasn't until they were back at the airfield that Cattermole found him on his own. "Squadron practice tomorrow," Cattermole said. "Close-formation stuff, all day."

"Who says?"

"Lord Rex. I heard him talking to Baggy Bletchley. There's going to be a socking great display somewhere on Armistice Day and we're down to do our flying ballet."

Patterson shrugged. "So what?"

"You owe me eight hundred and seventy-five francs, my son. Lord Rex is going to be drilling us from sparrow-fart to sunset, isn't he? You've missed your trick." Cattermole snapped his fingers in front of Patterson's face; with his other hand he poked at Patterson's tunic pockets, searching for money.

Patterson said nothing.

"Come on, pay up. I need the cash."

Still Patterson was silent. He re-buttoned his tunic pockets, glanced quickly at Cattermole, and looked away. There was a very slight twist to his lips.

Cattermole let his hands drop. He rocked back on his heels and studied Patterson's face. "Do you mean to tell me," he began, and waited for an answer.

"Piece of cake, Moggy."

"You actually flew under that bridge?"

"Well, that's what it's for, isn't it?"

Cattermole kept staring at him. Patterson watched a groundcrew start a Hurricane. Oily smoke laced with orange flame jetted from the exhausts. The engine crackled like a bushfire and slowly settled down to a dull roar.

"What was the river like?" Cattermole asked.

Patterson cocked his head to watch a rigger test the Hurricane's rudder. "Pretty wet," he said.

"Hmm." Cattermole walked away, stopped, looked back. "There's been a hell of a lot of rain since I did it," he said.

There was a pause while he watched Patterson and Patterson watched the throbbing aeroplane.

"I thought it might have made a difference," Cattermole said.

Fanny Barton came out of the pilots' room with Dicky Starr. They were wearing flying kit and carrying parachutes. "Sure you're all right, Dicky?" Barton said. "Nose okay? You don't want a nosebleed while you're on oxygen and –"

"I'm fine. Stop worrying."

They tramped across the grass, slightly bow-legged in their flying-boots.

"You've seemed a bit off-colour lately, that's all. I thought –"

"Nothing serious, Fanny. Touch of indijaggers. I took a dose of salts this morning. Right as rain now."

"You certainly came down those stairs like a dose of salts."

"I did, didn't I?" Starr allowed himself a quick grin. "That's the fastest bloody old Moggy ever got airborne, I bet."

They parted, each heading for his plane.

"Still, if you didn't have any trouble," Cattermole said.

"Piece of cake," Patterson said. They watched Starr's Hurricane taxi away and turn into the wind.

"Tell me, sir: are all fighter squadrons like this?" the infantry captain asked.

"I suppose Hornet's rather special," Bletchley said. "Chartreuse, if you've got it," he told the waiter.

"Bring the air commodore a *framboise*," Rex ordered. "A rare liqueur of Alsace, sir. Very subtle, very discreet. I know you appreciate an understated flavour."

"See what I mean?" Bletchley said to the others. He raised his arms in a gesture of pampered surrender.

"Tradition has a lot to do with it," Kellaway said. He blew a cloud of pipe-smoke and squinted at the changing, dissolving shapes. "Pride. Gallantry. Pluck." He was not drunk but he was not completely sober, either. "It all adds up."

"I mean no criticism, you understand," the artillery major said, "but in my regiment a subaltern would never have dared to speak in the mess in the way your young pilot spoke. It's just not done."

"Fighter pilots are rare birds," Rex said. "You can't keep them on a tight rein or they go off the boil. They're rather like . . . how shall I put it . . . cavalry of the sky."

"Knights of the air," Kellaway murmured.

"You encourage your chaps to be outspoken, then," the infantry captain said.

"Enterprise and initiative matter as much to me as discipline and dedication," Rex said. He cocked his head as Bletchley tasted his *framboise*. "You see what I mean about the understatement, sir?"

"My goodness, yes." Bletchley sucked his lips. "It hits you in the eyes straight away, doesn't it?"

Dicky Starr stood the Hurricane on its tail and let it carry him vertically through a thin skein of cloud.

It was like coming up from a deep dive in a swimming-pool, seeing the surface approach, bursting through. The big difference was that he kept going, kept climbing high above the cloud, until the fighter had spent its momentum. For an instant it hung, slowly turning like the sails of a windmill. Then gravity won, and the plane fell sideways. As it regained speed it naturally and willingly straightened out, and Starr got ready for another fullblooded powerdive. A pleasant tremble built up in the controls, a sense of colossal energy harnessed to his feet and hands. Just for the fun of it he performed a slow roll. Three miles beneath him, the blurred landscape rotated.

He came out of the dive at ten thousand feet, held the stick back and soared into a huge and happy loop.

He was simply air-testing the Hurricane but for the first time in his life he was really chucking it about the sky, stamping on the pedals, hauling on the stick, flying the damn thing to its limits, and discovering that the Hurricane's limits went a bloody sight further than most people reckoned. It was vastly encouraging, wonderfully exhilarating; he felt as if he were a jockey on the finest, fastest thoroughbred in the world. He inhaled gratefully, enjoying the Hurricane's special atmosphere: a blend of oil and dope, leather and webbing, dust thrown up by aerobatics, and the pure, metallic taste of oxygen. It was the smell of the office. That was what fighter pilots called the cockpit, the place where they did their job, where they were boss.

Dicky Starr looked out at his wings. Forty feet from tip to tip. He looked forward at the powerful curve of his engine cowling, tipped with its shimmering disc, flanked by its red-hot exhausts. So what if he was only five foot six? This was his Hurricane, *his*; and nothing was impossible.

He dipped a wing, searched around, and saw Metz. He flew north, found Thionville, and went down like a plunging hawk.

'B' flight was in the pilots' hut, playing brag. Pip Patterson kept winning.

"This is a pathetic game," Miller said. "Childish. Why can't we play real poker?"

"Because the queen of hearts and the jack of clubs are missing," Fitzgerald said. "Also the ace of spades. Shut up and deal."

"I don't see what difference that makes," Miller said. He dealt three cards each. "Strewth, what a junkyard." Patterson, on his left, had not touched his cards. "Broken your arm?" Miller said.

"I'm playing this hand blind." Patterson bet five francs. "Blind brag. Now it's double to stay in."

The others grumbled and bet. One by one they dropped out as Patterson raised the stakes, until only Miller remained. Miller's tongue polished his upper lip while he studied his cards. "No fear," he said, and threw them in.

Patterson took his winnings. He scraped the cards together. "Aren't you going to see what you had?" Gordon asked.

Patterson shrugged, and shuffled the pack.

"Don't you care?" Fitzgerald said.

Patterson cut and dealt. "What difference would it make?" he said.

"You might shit yourself with shock," Miller said. "Then at least we'd get some value for our money."

Starr's shadow raced him for the bridge. After a day of clouded skies the sun had broken through and its angled rays flooded the countryside with light. The sunlight came from behind his left shoulder. It was perfect for low flying: every detail in the landscape was picked out with utter clarity, the colours were vivid, there was no glare; he could judge depth and distance perfectly.

The Hurricane was behaving beautifully. It was strolling along at two hundred and ten, leaning in and out of the bends of the Moselle, sinking gradually from fifty to forty to thirty feet as Thionville came nearer. Power cables passed overhead, a long way up, no danger there. Starr kept his racing shadow in the corner of his eye as a guide to height while he studied the advancing bridge. It looked quite low: big and strong but surprisingly flat: not much space beneath, not even under the centre span. If Moggy and Pip hadn't done it he'd have said there wasn't room. Optical illusion, obviously.

The illusion persisted. He dropped to ten feet to make more space. The river blurred, the white concrete mass reared up, and the skin on the back of his neck crawled. It couldn't be done.

His shadow hit the bridge an instant before he rushed into the gap, still desperate for space. The Hurricane dipped again. Starr's hand trembled. The prop thrashed the surface and the radiator-scoop under the belly rammed into the river like a bucket. Starr yelled and snatched the column back but the scoop dragged the nose hard down and the propeller made an explosion of foam. Starr was hurled onto his straps. His head smashed against the instrument panel. The Hurricane fought its way into the sunlight, nose-down, half-covered in spray, and soon exhausted itself. People on the bridge saw its tail rise slowly and slide out of sight, hurried on by the current. The river smoothed its surface. The echoes died. More people ran over to look, but there was nothing to see.

Sticky Stickwell tried to step from the bookshelf to the mantelpiece but his legs were too short. "It's not fair," he complained. A cushion just missed his head. He climbed higher up the bookshelf,

180

jumped, and landed, wobbling hard, on the mantelpiece. A cushion struck him and he fell off. "Knickers!" he cried.

"Your turn, Mother," Cattermole said. Patterson collected the cushions.

'A' flight had finished testing its aircraft and 'B' flight had been released early. They had returned to the mess to find Stickwell and Flip Moran back from leave. Now they were all in the anteroom, playing the squadron's new game. It was simple and dangerous, just right for fighter pilots. One man tried to circle the walls of the room without touching the floor while the others bombarded him with cushions.

Mother Cox began on the mantelpiece. He stretched his legs to the bookshelves, and shuffled along them to the window, ignoring a shower of cushions. He made quick time along a windowsill, a radiator, and another windowsill, and reached the door.

"Now he's in trouble," Fitzgerald said, but Cox had planned his route. He reached down and opened the door a couple of inches. As cushions thudded against him, he carefully stood on the door-knob and gripped the top of the frame. A gentle push would now swing the door wide and put him within easy reach of a sideboard.

Fanny Barton thrust open the door and Mother Cox went flying. The rest of the squadron stumbled about, doubled-up with laughter.

Barton closed the door and leaned against it. He didn't feel angry or impatient; he didn't feel anything, really, except a dull wish that they would shut up.

Eventually they did stop laughing. "You can't stay there, Fanny," Miller said. "You're blocking the course."

Barton raised his hand, palm outwards. "Can you all be quiet for a minute?" he asked.

"If it's in a bad cause," Cattermole said.

"Well, Dicky Starr's bought it," Barton said. "Is that bad enough?"

They moved to the bar. Pip Patterson bought a round of drinks. "Don't go mad," Flip Moran told him. "Keep half-a-crown for the wreath." Patterson, not looking at him, said: "It's only brag winnings."

The drinks were handed around and everyone waited for Fanny Barton. "Cheers," Barton said, making the word curt and unemotional. They drank. Barton saw Flip Moran's glance; it held a hint of approval. The correct tone had been set.

There was nothing to be said: Barton had already told them all he knew. Starr had been overdue, no flap, probably forced-landed somewhere. Kellaway began phoning the nearby airfields. Then Area HQ rang up. Thionville police had reported a Hurricane in their bit of the Moselle. On the bottom. Identification letters noted by eye-witnesses. End of story.

Moke Miller took a handful of peanuts from a dish on the bar. "Hungry?" Cox said.

Miller ate. "Life goes on," he mumbled.

"Funny you should say that," Flash Gordon remarked. "I bet none of you knows how long the average human hair lives."

They waited. "This had better be hilarious, Flash," said Stickwell.

"Three years," Gordon told them. Still they waited. "I mean each hair on your body has a lifespan of between two and four years," he said. Miller munched his peanuts. "Not many people know that," Gordon added.

"And what happens to it after that?" Fitzgerald asked.

"Oh, it dies and falls out. Then another hair grows."

"Pardon me while I sit down," Moran said. He perched on a bar-stool. "This is all too frenzied for my poor brain."

"Ah, but the really interesting thing is that each hair is a different age to the hair next to it." Gordon smiled in harmless triumph. "That way, they don't all fall out at once."

"With a roar like thunder," Cattermole said. "Awakening the baby and frightening the horses in the street."

"Where did you get all this drivel, Flash?" Miller demanded.

"It's not drivel, it's true. My girl friend Nicole told me. She's got a university degree in biology."

"Ah, but that's *French* biology," Stickwell said. "Frogs aren't made like you and me. Their kidneys are covered in mustard. I should know; I just had some on the train."

"Don't talk tripe," Gordon muttered, annoyed.

"And their tripe is stuffed with prunes. Most uncomfortable, don't you think?"

"Time for my bath," Cattermole said. He went out.

"Anyway, I bet you haven't got the faintest idea how fast your

182

toenails grow," Gordon declared. "And where would you be without toenails? Ever stopped to think about that?" Nobody answered.

Patterson finished his beer and went upstairs. He went to his room, stretched out on his bed, but got up after a few seconds. He brushed his hair and examined his fingernails. One nail was ragged; he filed it smooth. A coin lay on the bed; it had slipped from his pocket. He picked it up and took out the rest of his change and counted it. It was French money, light and silvery, unlike the heavy British coinage, and when he'd counted it he still didn't feel it was worth anything. The house was very quiet. He held his breath and listened. Nothing.

He decided to have a bath. He took his towel and walked along the corridor, past Cattermole's room. It was empty. So were the bathrooms. He saw light coming from a doorway at the end of the corridor: Starr's room.

Cattermole was in there, searching the wardrobe.

"What's the game?" Patterson asked.

"It's no game, laddy. It's business. Little Dicky owed me eight hundred and seventy-five francs. Remember?" Cattermole shut the wardrobe and began rummaging in a chest of drawers.

"You can't possibly collect that bet."

"No? Watch and see. I won, and the stuff's no good to him any more, is it?" Cattermole dumped handkerchiefs and socks on the top. "I hope the twerp didn't take his wallet up with him," he grumbled. "That's strictly against orders, that is . . . Ah!" He found it under some shirts.

"My God . . ." Patterson tasted bile, and had to swallow. "You rotten sod, Moggy."

"Four, five, six hundred francs. Damn. Oh, and fifty. Six-fifty. Not enough. Hang on, what's this? A fiver! A genuine English fiver . . . What's that worth?"

"I don't know and I don't care."

"Say . . . eight hundred francs. Pip, have you got change of a hundred francs? No? Too bad. I'll just have to owe him a couple of bob." Cattermole pushed the notes into his pocket, tossed the wallet into the drawer, swept the clothing on top of it and banged the drawer shut with a swing of his hips. He flicked the light off and walked away, leaving Patterson in the dark. "Piece of cake, Pip!" he called in a high, mocking voice.

Patterson sank until he was squatting on his haunches. *If you had any guts*, he told himself, *you'd go after that bastard and smash his face in.* To his surprise he found that he was crying.

The night spat rain, and the drops made long black streaks in the glare of the floodlights. The drops pecked at the oily, hurrying surface of the river but the marks were instantly healed. By contrast the steel ropes that vanished into the water cut a perpetual, livid scar.

These ropes descended from the top of a British Army mobile crane. Its driver was accustomed to recovering overturned tanks; he knew his stuff. The engine roared, the crane bucked and clanked, the ropes strained and slackened and tightened again, vibrating like fiddle-strings. Gradually, foot by foot, the load came up.

Barton, Kellaway and Skull stood on the embankment, downstream of the crane, and watched it work. If they raised their heads they could see the bridge, lined with hundreds of spectators. This was the best free show in Thionville since the Tour de France came through in 1933.

Skull shaded his eyes against the dazzle and peered again at the black hole under the bridge. "It still seems to me," he said, "a most extraordinary thing to try to do."

"Yes, well, you're not a pilot," Barton muttered. He was tired and hungry, and they had already talked the matter to death.

The steel ropes strained, the crane laboured. Its driver rested the engine, swung the arm a few feet, and tried again. A cluster of bubbles as big as footballs hit the surface and burst.

"I don't think I ever flew under a bridge," the adjutant said. He hunched his head deeper inside the turned-up collar of his greatcoat. His gaze was fixed on the river, where turbulence was developing. "I flew through a railway station once. It didn't have much roof left, of course."

A buckled wingtip broke the surface. The crane driver stopped hauling for a moment so that the current could straighten the load. The wingtip swung through a quarter-circle and checked. The bridge was busy with pointing arms. The rudder appeared, streaming ribbons of fabric, and then the whole of the upper part of the Hurricane emerged in a rush of pouring water.

Five minutes later the plane lay on the embankment, shining, crumpled, its ribs exposed, its propeller snapped. The crane driver climbed down and untied the ropes. An RAF ambulance started its engine. Fanny Barton walked forward. Skull took a pace after him but Kellaway held his arm.

Barton climbed onto the port wing and tried to slide back the hood. It was stuck, probably locked shut on the inside. The crane driver gave him a crowbar. He smashed the Perspex, released the lock, slid the hood.

Dicky Starr lolled in his straps like an exhausted child in its push-chair. His nose was split but the river had washed away all the blood. His flying-boots paddled in six inches of dirty water.

Barton took Starr's smooth, pointed chin in his hand and tipped his head up. The eyes were slightly open. They looked at him as if they were hiding some clever, subtle, private joke. "Idiot," Barton said.

He got down and signalled the ambulance. Already the crowd on the bridge was thinning. The show was over.

NOVEMBER
1939

The funeral went badly.

The adjutant had arranged for Starr to be buried in the church-yard at Pont-St Pierre. Fanny Barton should have been in charge of the ceremony but he developed a persistent earache. Rex gave the job to Cattermole.

Green Section had to remain on duty at the airfield; the rest of the squadron (including the mascot, Reilly) drove to the village at midday. Rain had fallen for most of the night and half the morning; now everything dripped. The sky had a tired and grubby look. The trees behind the church were full of crows; every few minutes they took off and circled, silently, and when they landed on the branches again they were nearly invisible: black on black. The silence was oddly disturbing. It was as if the birds were too despondent to comment.

An RAF chaplain was there, talking to the bandmaster of a regimental band that Area HQ had borrowed from the Army. Cattermole went over to discuss the proceedings. In his service greatcoat, with a sword and scabbard, he looked enormously tall.

The coffin lay in an open lorry near the gates. On one side of the lorry the bandsmen were grouped in a circle, all facing inwards, discreetly passing cigarette-butts, professionally at ease. On the other side the pilots gathered. They tried not to look at the freshly dug grave halfway up the sloping churchyard.

Rex alone was willing and able to talk.

"That band will want feeding afterwards, uncle," he said. "Can our cooks cope?" The adjutant nodded. "It's good to see a few natives here," Rex said. A dozen villagers stood watching; some wore black armbands. The adjutant smiled. "Jolly good show," he said. "Mind you, so they should," Rex said. "We're here to defend them, after all." The adjutant smiled. "Jolly good show," he murmured. Rex glanced sharply. "Buck up, uncle," he said.

"Sorry." The adjutant hid a yawn. "Don't know what's the matter with me. I keep thinking about lunch. It's kidneys today."

"Yes? So what?"

"Nothing. I rather like kidneys, that's all."

The intelligence officer joined them. "Had he been drinking?" he asked. "That would explain a lot."

"Who?" said Rex.

"The deceased. I heard you mention kidneys. If the autopsy showed –"

"Not his kidneys," Rex said. "Not Starr's kidneys, for God's sake."

"Whose, then?"

"Forget it, Skull," Kellaway said. "Not important."

"Oh." Skull was offended by the rebuff. "If you say so."

"How much longer do we hang around here?" Rex grumbled. Reilly recognised the impatient tone and trotted over. Dog and master exchanged sympathetic looks.

"Kidneys unimportant," Skull said. "Must remember that."

"Jolly good show," the adjutant said.

"It's not just your kidneys, you know, Skull," Flash Gordon said, joining the conversation. "You don't need your gall bladder or your spleen. In fact you don't need half your stomach! Take the average chap's intestines –"

"Not now, old boy," Kellaway said.

"Moggy!" Rex called. "Finger out, if you please!"

Cattermole stopped gesturing in the direction of the grave and said something to a sergeant, who nodded, saluted, and moved away.

"It's true, though," Gordon said. "I read it in a book."

"Oh, jolly good show," Skull said bleakly.

"Spot of hush, please," Kellaway said. "The big picture's starting."

Four airmen lifted the coffin from the lorry and placed it on their shoulders. It was draped with the Union Jack. The flag was new; its colours looked too bright for the drab surroundings. "Poor old Dicky," Stickwell murmured. "He's been gift-wrapped." Patterson suddenly turned away and stood with his shoulders hunched, his chin pressed down, his jaws locked tight. "You all right, Pip?" Stickwell asked. Patterson nodded. His legs kept wanting to fold the wrong way and there was something foul lurking at the bottom of his throat. He was horribly hung-over, but it wasn't just that. His fingers clutched his thumbs, squeezed them against his palms, and he concentrated on not falling down. "You look bloody awful," Stickwell said. "You look like a used French letter. Have a swig." He offered his flask, but Patterson shook his head. "I'll have a drop, Sticky," Miller said. The flask circulated.

Meanwhile the band had begun to play *Abide with Me*. Cattermole marched after the pallbearers; there was a space; and the rest of the squadron followed. Patterson came last, constantly afraid that his legs would fail him.

A firing squad of airmen had already taken up position on one side of the grave. The coffin was placed on wooden slats that spanned the hole. Cattermole stood opposite the firing squad. The pilots shuffled into a loose half-circle and everyone waited while the band blew the last, sad notes. For a second the churchyard was utterly silent, and Fitz Fitzgerald suddenly realised what they were about to do. They were all there to put Dicky Starr in that deep black hole and bury him for ever and ever. No more ping-pong, no more towel-fights, no more sliding downstairs on a brass tray. Dicky was dead. Drowned. Dead and gone and never more to be one of the boys. For a long moment Fitzgerald felt numbed, helpless, defeated.

Then the chaplain began to speak, and almost at once Fitzgerald's mind wandered from the words of the burial service. He found himself reading the brass plate on the coffin. *Richard Finlay Starr. Royal Air Force.* Finlay. It made Dicky sound old and mature. And what a huge grave they'd dug for him! Far too big. He'd be lost in a hole that size. Wonder where Moggy got his sword? Damn silly, pilots wearing swords. They used to wear spurs, according to old uncle . . .

A sergeant barked orders. The firing squad aimed at the sky and a broken volley banged like a string of firecrackers. The pallbearers came forward and took the weight of the coffin on canvas slings. The wooden slats were removed. Cattermole drew his sword and saluted. They lowered the coffin into the grave until little of the slings was left to pay out. The coffin, however, was still hanging a couple of feet from the bottom. The pallbearers glanced at the sergeant. He signalled to keep lowering. They stooped and leaned forward but the earth at the edge was wet. One of them slipped and let go his end of the sling. The head of the coffin fell with a muddy thud; the other end slid free and crashed to earth. The pallbearers stumbled; one nearly lost his balance altogether. "Sweet Mother of God," said Flip Moran quietly.

The pallbearers scrambled back, sweating and ashamed. Cattermole sheathed his sword. He picked up a handful of earth and threw it into the grave. The sergeant barked an order and an airman stepped forward with a bugle. He was halfway through the Last Post and making a good job of it when Reilly trotted towards him. Fitzgerald saw, and refused to believe. Surely someone would call the dog back? But Rex was staring at the sky, Kellaway was inspecting the grave, Skull was polishing his glasses, Flip's eyes were shut. Reilly took a sniff and quickly pissed on the bugler's leg. The Last Post wavered, cracked, blared and fell apart. Everyone looked, but by then Reilly had moved away.

Twenty minutes later the pilots were gathered beside their transport, ready to leave as soon as Rex had finished telling Cattermole, Kellaway and the sergeant what an appalling shambles they'd made of everything.

"Can't understand it, sir," the sergeant said. "I checked them coffin-slings myself. Standard size."

"Act of God," suggested Kellaway.

"Anyway, my bit went all right, sir," Cattermole said.

"In all my years –" Rex began again, when Skull arrived with an angry Frenchman wearing muddy overalls and carrying a shovel.

"I may be wrong," Skull said, "but I think this gentleman has a valid complaint. According to him, Starr is in the wrong grave. That particular hole was especially prepared to receive an unusually large farmer, with space reserved for his wife to follow in the fullness of time. Our grave is elsewhere. It's smaller and not so deep."

"You buffoon," Rex said to Cattermole.

"Sir, be fair. How was I to know? I simply went where the firing squad was."

"Ah, but that's where you sent us, sir," the sergeant said. "Remember? I said to you –"

"Get him shifted," Rex ordered grimly. "Get him out of the wrong damned hole and into the right damned hole. Do it now. Where was this peasant when we needed him?" he asked Skull.

"At home, eating his lunch," Skull said. "He takes rather a dim view of people being buried at lunchtime. Bad form, apparently."

"Doubledecker, see," the sergeant said. "Extra deep. Nothing wrong with the slings."

"I don't want to know," Rex said. "I don't want to hear any more. All of you stay here and get it sorted out." He strode away, calling for his driver.

They trailed over to the open grave and looked down.

"Dicky Starr flies again," the adjutant said.

Immediately after lunch the squadron assembled in the library, where Rex had a few hard, cold words to say.

First, about Starr's death.

There was absolutely no room in Hornet squadron for tearaways, daredevils or stuntmen. Anyone who was desperate to fly beneath bridges or through tunnels or down coalmines should leave his name at the adjutant's office, and steps would be taken to find war-work more suited to his talents, such as testing minefields by walking through them with his fingers in his ears.

Investigations had revealed that other aircraft besides the one flown by Starr had recently been showing an unhealthy interest in the bridge at Thionville.

If this was prompted by idle curiosity into the underwater performance of the Mk I Hurricane, it was to be hoped that no further experiments would be attempted.

Apart from the extravagance and waste inflicted upon the British Exchequer, there was the reaction of the French authorities to be considered.

In future, any aeroplane approaching Thionville would be shot down by French anti-aircraft guns.

The frogs were being very snotty, and there was nothing worse than a snotty frog.

Second, about the Armistice Day Fly-Past.

The loss of Starr had disrupted training. A replacement pilot was on his way. He would have less than a week in which to learn the drill, slot into the formations, become one of the team. This squadron had a reputation to keep. It was the finest tight-formation outfit in Fighter Command. Bar none.

What's more, they would be performing in the presence of a Very Special Personage at the Armistice Day ceremony.

If anyone made a cock-up he'd find himself towing targets over the North of Scotland for the rest of the war.

Third, about the funeral.

It had been an absolute shambles, an insult to the dead, a disgrace to the Service, and a very large black in the annals of the squadron.

It wouldn't happen again. Each officer to practise funeral drill with a burial party, including firing squad, bugler and NCO. A dummy coffin would be interred in a simulated grave, repeatedly, until the ceremony was performed perfectly. Skull would coach officers in this duty.

That was all.

The pilots scrambled to their feet as Rex and Kellaway walked out. The door shut.

"All right, who pinched Lord Rex's teddybear?" Stickwell asked.

"What d'you mean?" said Cox.

"Well, he's got the guts-ache about something, hasn't he? It's not just poor old Dicky. I mean, that sort of prang happens. Why blame us?"

"Maybe someone tore a strip off him," Gordon suggested. "Maybe he got a bollocking from Baggy Bletchley or someone."

"Or maybe you simply got what was coming to you," Barton said. "The CO's only doing his job."

Moran nodded soberly; too soberly. "I go along with Fanny," he said. "After all, he was like that once."

Barton fiddled with the cotton wool plugs in his ears, and winced.

"If you ask me, I think he's got his little chopper out," Miller said. "He's looking for somebody to chop."

"I don't see why," Cox said.

"He's fed up because we haven't got a score," Cattermole said. "Every other squadron in France has bagged a Jerry, but not us. He wants blood. Personally I don't blame him. It's no fun being CO unless you can wallow in gore occasionally, is it? If we don't get a Jerry soon, I bet you a fiver that Lord Rex chops somebody." He closed his eyes and smiled.

"But that's not fair," Fitzgerald said.

"The question is: who?" Cattermole said.

"Whom," Cox muttered.

"I think," Cattermole said, his eyes still closed, "it'll be Pip."

They all looked at Patterson, who was picking at a tiny wart that had developed on his left thumb. He stared back, guiltily. "What?" he said.

"Why?" Moran asked Cattermole.

"Because he bleeds so easily," Cattermole said. "Pip is an easy bleeder, aren't you Pip? Ideal for chopping."

"Oh, shut up." Patterson sucked his thumb and wished, as he'd been wishing all day, that his head would stop throbbing. "If I get chopped," he said sourly, "I'll damn well take you with me." He knew that didn't make sense, but he didn't care. He'd made his wart bleed. He didn't care about that either.

An hour later, Rex signed something, gave it back to the adjutant, and stood up with relief. At last his desk was bare. "Bumf, bumf, bumf," he said. "This isn't a war, it's a paperchase. I bet the German Air Force hasn't got to wade through endless bumf." He strolled to the window and looked down. A mock grave had been dug at the edge of the lawn. Skull, Mother Cox, a sergeant and twenty airmen were down there, getting ready for burial practice. "Always assuming there is a German Air Force," he said.

"True, sir." Kellaway was not really listening. He was still checking through the correspondence, reports, forms, memos, returns, summaries. "Have you written to Starr's parents?"

"Yes and no. I've done a draft." Rex took a sheet of paper from a desk drawer and re-read it. Outside, there came the distant bark of orders followed by the unhurried crunch of boots slow-marching on gravel. "This won't do," Rex said firmly. "It won't do at all." He handed the draft to Kellaway. "I can't possibly tell them the truth, but that simply sounds mysterious."

"Yes. The bit about 'exceptionally harzardous circumstances.' And yet no mention of the enemy."

"Makes him sound like a spy."

There was a long silence while they reviewed the problem.

"His parents are what, again?" Rex asked.

"Minister. The Rev and Mrs Starr, somewhere in Dorset."

"Ah. Yes."

A volley of blanks was fired, only slightly raggedly.

"Tell you what we used to do in the last show," Kellaway said. "If a chap played silly-buggers and wrote himself off, his CO used to inform the parents that he'd given his life in the manner his comrades had learned to expect of him."

"Hmm." Rex scribbled that down and looked at it.

"If you like, you can always chuck in the old line about 'conduct above and beyond the call of duty,' " Kellaway suggested. "I mean, that's true enough."

Rex nodded and wrote. Sweetly and cleanly, the notes of the Last Post arced across the afternoon like a beautiful, effortless bird, swooping and climbing.

"And it wouldn't be wrong to say he'll be sorely missed," Kellaway added. "Especially as he hadn't paid his last month's mess bill."

Rex took the bill and glanced at the bottom figure. "You should have told me," he said. "I don't like officers getting into debt. It's untidy."

"Dicky didn't have much choice, I'm afraid. I found his bank statements when I cleared out his room. Overdrawn, poor little blighter. Stiff letter from the bank manager."

"How much?"

"Twenty-seven pounds four shillings and ninepence."

Rex sat down, took a chequebook from his desk, wrote two cheques, and gave them to the adjutant.

"That's not absolutely necessary, you know," Kellaway said. "There's the RAF Benevolent Fund and various other –"

"It's a squadron affair," Rex said crisply. "Let's keep it in the squadron."

Flip Moran found Pip Patterson in one of the bathrooms, having a shower. He was standing quite still, propped against the tile wall, his legs braced, his head and shoulders pounded by the spray.

"You're on duty," Moran said. "Blue Section's at available."

"Okay." Patterson didn't move.

Moran spread a towel on a radiator and sat on it. "What was all that about, in the library? If I didn't know you were a hardened, ruthless fighting-man I'd have said you were a bit upset about something."

Patterson let the streaming water erase all expression from his face.

Moran shifted: the radiator was getting uncomfortable. "That was an awful waste, what happened to Dicky Starr," he remarked.

Patterson curled his toes.

"Sometimes it's a terrible burden, being a thick Irishman," said Moran. "The world makes no sense at all. D'you ever find that?"

196

Patterson held his face to the spray, and flinched as the tiny jets battered him.

Moran got up and turned off the shower. He tossed the warm towel to Patterson. "Come away from there before you're drowned entirely," he said, and went out.

"Apple," said Flash Gordon, chewing.

He was sitting in the Ligiers' kitchen, blindfolded with one of Nicole's silk scarves. Grandmother Ligier was dozing by the fire.

"You are sure?" Nicole asked.

"Absolutely." He swallowed. "I know an apple when I eat one."

"No you don't," she said. She pulled off his blindfold and showed him an apple, intact, and a pear with a piece cut from it. "You ate a piece of pear. See?"

"Well I'm damned." He took the apple and smiled in wonderment. "How the dickens did you do that?"

"Oh, it is simple. Smell is sometimes stronger than taste. I put the apple under your nose and then I put a bit of pear in your mouth. Old trick."

"That's absolutely amazing." Gordon stretched his legs and propped his elbow on the table while he sniffed the apple. "D'you know any more like that?"

"No." She wound the scarf in and out of her fingers. "Now I think I have told you everything I know about the human body."

"What a pity." He polished the apple on his sleeve and made it shine a deep, waxy red. "I suppose I ought to be more careful when it comes to lovely ladies and apples," he said lazily. This was their sixth meeting and he was fairly relaxed. "Didn't some chap get into trouble that way a long time ago?"

She watched him and said nothing. He had such a smooth face it was hard to imagine him shaving. His nose was snub and his lower lip was very full and strong. When he noticed her silence he glanced at her, and he cocked one eyebrow in a curiously individual way, half-challenging, half-uncertain, that she found touching. What he saw when he glanced made him keep on looking. Her eyes were bright and there was something in her expression he had never seen before. Curiosity? Mischief? Impatience? He put down the apple and straightened his tie. "He probably ate a different kind of apple," he said. "All a fairy-tale, anyway. Personally I could never understand why –"

"Come with me." She stood up.

"Where are we going?"

"To the summerhouse in the garden."

"Oh." He got his coat. "Won't it be jolly chilly?"

"Yes." She opened a chest and took out four blankets and a towel. She gave him the blankets. "But not for long." She picked up a flashlight and a half-full bottle of red wine and went out by the back door.

Flash Gordon hesitated, looking from the open door to the blankets to the apple to the fire alongside which the old lady snoozed. Its flames jumped in the draught. "Crikey," he said thoughtfully, and went out, shutting the door behind him.

"Well, that was a first-class grade-A disaster," Fitz Fitzgerald said. He wanted to sound nonchalant or indifferent but he could hear the bitterness grating in his voice.

"No, it wasn't," Mary Blandin said. "You mustn't exaggerate, my love." She began poking the fire to make it blaze.

"I seem to have exaggerated *my* love. Or something." He was slumped in a chair by the dinnertable, which had not yet been cleared. "Bloody stinking hell," he muttered. He reached for the wine-bottle and filled his glass to the brim.

"Don't be broody." She sat opposite him and cut herself a slice of cheese. "And don't swig that wine. It's a very good Traminer and not cheap. If you want to get drunk, go and buy a couple of litres of *ordinaire*."

"Thanks for your sympathy," he mumbled. But he put down his glass.

"Oh, sympathy, sympathy! What good's sympathy?" There was no annoyance in her voice: just a touch of brisk, good-humoured impatience. "All it does is feed your self-pity, and since there's no earthly reason for you to feel sorry for yourself I'm not going to encourage anything of that sort. Besides, it doesn't suit you."

"All right." Fitz hunched his shoulders and stuck his jaw out. "What d'you want me to do? Tell jokes?"

"Yes, please. If they're really funny."

She drank a little of his wine while he glowered at the cheese. "Don't know any," he said.

"Fitz, you're a fraud. You're a failure and a phoney."

"Wait a minute. Just remembered." He chewed on a knuckle for a moment. "About the bloke who won an elephant in a raffle."

"Get on with it, then."

"Well, his friend offered to train it." Fitz spoke flatly, almost curtly. "He said he could teach it to sit down. This chap said okay, so his friend went over and gave the elephant the most almighty kick in the balls, and sure enough it sat down."

"Education is a wonderful thing."

"Yes. Well, the chap didn't think so. He asked his friend if he couldn't teach it something without being cruel. His friend said yes, he could teach it to shake its head. So he went over to the elephant and whispered in its ear: 'D'you want another kick in the balls?' And the elephant shook its head." Fitz swung his head slowly, ponderously and gloomily.

Mary laughed. "That's a rotten joke, Fitz."

"All right, you tell one."

"Ladies don't tell jokes."

"Who said you're a lady?" He watched her top up their glass. "Come to that, who said I'm a man?"

She came around the table, stood behind him and put her arms around his neck. "You're not the first, you know," she said. "It often happens. Just don't worry about it. Nature knows best. It's not automatic. It's not like putting your penny in a slot machine and always getting a bar of chocolate." Her hands slipped inside his unbuttoned shirt.

"I once lost a penny in a slot machine on Victoria station," Fitz said, staring into space.

"There you are, then."

"Perfectly good penny. No chocolate. Bloody swindle."

She kissed his ear.

"Fruit-and-nut," he said. "Platform three."

"Goodness me," she whispered. "It must have made a very deep impression." Fitz stood up, shoved the chair aside, and embraced her. A couple of rogue tears leaked from his eyes; he was glad she could not see them. "Talking of making deep impressions," she said after a moment, and gently rocked her hips.

"I know." Fitz sighed. "God moves in a mysterious way."

"True. I can feel him moving."

Fitz wiped away his tears and glanced at the door leading to the stairs. "Perhaps . . ." he began. From the street came the familiar sound of a car horn, jaunty and insistent. "Oh, bugger!" he said crossly.

The two men were halfway home before either of them said anything.

"Enjoy yourself tonight?" Flash asked routinely.

"Not bad. You?"

"No complaints." Flash changed gear, unnecessarily. "Nicole showed me some more experiments."

"Uh-huh."

Flash drove in the wrong gear for a time and then changed back to the right one. "She's really hot on biology and anatomy and all that stuff," he said.

"I'm glad somebody understands it," Fitz said.

Flash chuckled as if Fitz had made a witty remark. "Amazing creatures, women," he said. "Full of surprises."

There was no answer to that. They drove the rest of the way in silence.

Rex had Hornet squadron airborne soon after breakfast next morning. There was a fine, clear sky and he wanted to practise something new for the Armistice Day display, even if the replacement pilot hadn't arrived yet.

"Nothing flashy about this manoeuvre," he told the pilots gathered in the crewroom. "It's to be part of a very solemn ceremony, so I want it done in perfect unison, like Trooping the Colour. You'll each find a coloured smoke canister fixed to your fuselage, with a switch in your cockpit. Right?" He looked at Micky Marriott, who nodded. "Good. Now, we're going to paint the cross of St George in the sky. 'B' flight crosses behind 'A' flight. Height one thousand. Speed one-fifty. Release smoke for six hundred yards. Must have perfect timing and absolute uniformity. Clean start, clean stop, straight lines, square angles. St George for England all over the sky. Symbol of victory. Also loyalty. Remember who's going to be down there watching."

"Who, sir?" Stickwell asked.

"Any other questions?" Rex said.

"A royal personage, you ignorant fart," Cattermole told Stickwell. "If you ask him nicely he might cure your pox."

"It's not mine," Stickwell said. "I'm just looking after it for a friend."

"Let's go," Rex said.

He took them up to eight thousand. For the first half-hour they practised familiar routines: flights in line astern, changing to sections in close vic, then squadron in vic – his favourite ace-of-diamonds pattern – followed by the compact spearhead formation. Finally, on his word of command, the flights detached, peeled off to left and right, and fell steeply.

He saw the horizon swing to the vertical, felt his straps hugging his ribs, glanced at his wingmen, plunging sideways, knifing the sky with their wingtips. The growing rush of air worked on the Hurricane's shape and straightened it easily into a normal nose-dive. The horizon wheeled level again. The fields and woods of France lay spread in a thousand dull shades of brown and grey and green. The land looked dead and empty, but as Rex eased back the stick, wintry sunlight flashed and flickered on a ragged network of streams and ditches. For a second the reflections ran like spilled mercury. Then the angle was lost. Rex flattened out and turned towards the airfield.

Kellaway and Skull were standing on the balcony of the control tower – a two-storey wooden hut – when Marriott joined them.

"Perfect conditions, Micky," the adjutant said. "No wind to speak of."

"That's rather a shame," Skull said. "A nice westerly breeze would have blown everything over the German lines. Just imagine –"

"I hope the bloody things go off when they press the switch," Marriott said. "I've never worked with smoke flares before. It's not even RAF gear, Lord Rex scrounged it from some Army Co-operation unit, the stuff's probably as duff as hell."

"Haven't you tested any of them?" Kellaway asked.

"Not at a hundred and fifty miles an hour, I haven't."

"Here they come," Skull said.

'A' flight came out of the north, five Hurricanes immaculately in line abreast. As they crossed the airfield perimeter, plumes of smoke burst from them: snowy white from the flanking aircraft, crimson from the three inside. Immediately the bands of colour spread to meet and make a wide, bold stripe. As 'A' flight went past, 'B' flight crossed behind it, completing the emblem.

"Jolly clever," Kellaway exclaimed. He wound his camera and aimed it. "Damned impressive, I say."

"Congratulations, Micky," Skull said, and suddenly sneezed. "Sunshine," he explained.

"At least the stuff works," Marriott said.

The deep drone of aero-engines altered subtly. The flights had banked away from their smoke-laying runs. They would circle the airfield and make a low, slow pass down the middle in salute of the royal personage. "Sod it," Marriott grunted. "Oh dear," Skull said. Kellaway sighed. The smoke had not ceased when the flights turned. The streams of colour angled through ninety degrees and continued to flare across the sky. Marriott said: "It's easier to light those damn things than put them out."

"What a shame," Skull said. Kellaway took another picture.

Rex cut short the rehearsal and landed. "Not quite what I had in mind," he said.

"Very good up to a point, sir," Kellaway observed.

"And rubbish thereafter. Sloppy. Scruffy."

"It's easier to light those damn things than put them out," Marriott said.

"Well, there's got to be a solution. I want to see the cross of St George up there, not an endless stream of bloody bandages trailing all over the sky." They began discussing technicalities. Meanwhile, the rest of the squadron was landing and taxiing to the dispersal points. The pilots walked across the field with a slouch-shouldered, heavy-booted trudge that seemed to come instinctively to them, as if to express their contempt for any kind of movement except flying. Moke Miller found a football in the grass; a casual kick-about developed.

"Trouble is, sir, they're not *made* to go out," Marriott said gloomily. "They're made to burn to the end."

"I wish –" Rex began.

"Sir!" The duty NCO leaned out of the control tower, holding a telephone. "Ops officer at Area HQ. One hostile aircraft over Plombières. Can we intercept?"

"No. Tell him we're refuelling." The NCO vanished. Rex looked at the adjutant and gave a snort of disgust. "Pointless sending anyone to Plombières with half a tank."

"Absolutely, sir."

"Just our luck. No trade for weeks, and when Jerry shows up we're refuelling."

"Luck of the draw."

"That's curious," Skull said. He had moved apart from the others and was staring at the sky. The smoke trails had drifted eastward, giving the pattern a new perspective. "It doesn't look a bit like the cross of St George now," he said.

They looked at it.

"What it rather resembles," Skull said, "is a well-known Nazi symbol."

Rex turned away. Skull was right. Only two arms of the cross were bent but that was enough. The sign in the sky looked like a huge, radiant, incomplete swastika.

For a moment, dismay silenced him. A swastika. Even *half* a bloody swastika. Plastered all over the sky. By him. "What a mess," he said weakly.

"When I was a child," Skull said, "if I made a mistake in a painting, nanny told me to turn it into a cloud." Kellaway and Marriott looked at him, uncertainly. "Or perhaps a tree," he told them.

Rex looked at the sky. If only it would snow, or rain, or blow a gale.

A distant telephone rang its toy bell. The duty NCO was at the window again. "Area HQ, sir," he called. "It seems they've had reports –"

"Yes, yes, I know." Rex waved the man away. The action revived him. Already he was reconciled to the disaster; now it was time to fight back. "Get upstairs and talk to HQ, uncle," he said. "Butter them up, baffle them with bullshit, you know how to do it." Kellaway hurried away. "Micky, I want new smoke fitted on a couple of planes. Make it three. Any colour. Fast as you can." Marriott turned and ran. "Take-off in five minutes!" Rex shouted after him. A couple of pilots heard and paused on their way to the crewroom. "You two," Rex shouted. "Go with Marriott. We haven't finished yet."

"Goodness," Skull said. "Nanny will be pleased."

"Give her a big kiss for me," Rex said, pulling on his gloves. He felt better now that he was doing something.

"You wouldn't say that if you saw her moustache," Skull said. "By the way: did you have an appointment with a priest? One seems to be heading this way."

It was indeed a Catholic priest, striding across the grass with a brisk heel-and-toe action, his cassock billowing, his iron-grey head erect. "Take care of him, Skull," Rex said, and set off for his Hurricane; but the priest waved, called, and altered course to intercept him.

"*Monsieur le commandant? Bonjour. Père Alexandre, curé de Pont-St Pierre.*" He was an inch taller than Rex. "*Je désire une explication, m'sieur.*" His manner was stiff, his voice harsh. "*Votre pilote, le jeune homme Starr. Il n'est pas membre de l'église catholique.*"

"How the hell did he get in here?" Rex asked Skull.

"No idea, sir."

"This is supposed to be a fighter drome. Some frog dogcollar just wanders in and —"

"*C'est une affaire très sérieuse, m'sieur!*" He shook a warning finger at Rex. "*Je vous le dis, il faut faire quelquechose! Tout de suite!*"

Rex sighed. "What's he ranting about?" he asked.

"Something to do with poor Starr," Skull said. "It seems he wasn't a member of something."

"Christ Almighty," Rex muttered. The priest glared. Rex turned and saw Marriott leaving his Hurricane. Marriott gave a thumbs-up. Rex cupped his hands and shouted to his fitter: "Start up!" The man was on a wing-root, peering into the engine. He waved acknowledgment. "Take care of this loony," Rex told Skull. "I'm off." But when he moved, the Frenchman seized his arm. "*C'est presq'un crime!*" he rasped. "*C'est une désécration!*"

Rex wrenched himself free and took a couple of steps back, but the priest followed. "Look, you silly sod," Rex said. "I don't talk your wog bloody lingo, so just keep your sticky hands off me. Compree?"

"*En anglais?*" the priest said challengingly. "You want we speak English? Good! *M'sieur* Starr — not Catholic. Yes?" Rex's

204

Hurricane burst into life, and the priest had to shout. "My church – Catholic. People – Catholic. Ground – Catholic. Starr – out! Compree?"

Rex pointed to his plane, which was blasting black smoke from its exhausts. Then he pointed to the sky, and tapped himself on the chest. "*C'est la guerre*," he bawled. The priest frowned suspiciously, but made no move to stop Rex when he walked away.

His fitter climbed out of the cockpit. The engine cowling was still unbuttoned, and he crouched on the wing, adjusting something. His cap got swept off by the prop-wash. Abruptly the roar mounted in pitch and strength. The Hurricane shuddered. Its left wheel climbed over the wooden chock. The plane lurched and slewed, the other chock lost its grip, and before Rex could start running, his aircraft was careering away from him, out of control. It hit a bump and rocked wildly. The fitter fell off the wing, rolling fast to dodge the tail-wheel.

Rex stood and watched it go. He felt the same sick helplessness he experienced in a bad dream: this could not be real, awful things like this didn't happen to him, huge failures, public humiliations, runaway disasters. The Hurricane was picking up speed all the time but it was not running straight, it was always curving to the right. Groundcrew and pilots scrambled clear. Somebody fired off a red Very light: the flare soared beautifully and uselessly. A fire tender appeared, bell clanging, and raced across the grass as if to sideswipe the plane; but at the last moment it swerved away. "Gutless runt!" Rex shouted. The Hurricane was doing a steady thirty miles an hour and veering more and more to the right. There was still hope: if it kept tightening its turn it might go round in a circle and then keep on circling until it ran out of fuel or someone got into the cockpit. There was still hope; but not for long. With the fire tender hard behind it, Rex's plane came roaring back, right wheelstrut telescoped by the strain, right wingtip brushing the grass, and it rammed a parked Hurricane fair and square, hitting it with a wallop that bowled it over and left it totally bent. The runaway fighter sprawled over it in a collapsed and crumpled mess. The impact had stopped the engine dead. Various coloured fluids sprayed or squirted or drained from the wreck. Something inside it exploded like a popped balloon.

Rex released his breath. He turned his back on the scene and tramped wearily to the control tower. He clambered up the steps. Kellaway met him. "I don't believe it, adj," Rex said. "It's a conspiracy. I mean, what happens next? Bubonic plague?"

"Not our lucky day so far, sir. There's a cup of tea going, if you'd like one."

Marriott appeared. "I've called the Amiens depot, sir. Replacement aircraft on the way."

The adjutant said: "Ah, that reminds me –"

"What about HQ?" Rex asked.

"Yes. Well, they heard about this peculiar sign in the sky. *Gendarmerie*, French Army, God knows who all. Big flap – fifth columnists signalling to the enemy. You know how the frogs panic." Kellaway began scraping out his pipe. "I played the innocent. Suggested harmless explanations. Freak cloud formations, old contrails, migrating birds. Smoky bonfires."

"*What?*" Rex said.

"Well, not bonfires. I just made that up."

Rex grunted. "D'you think they believed you?"

"No." Kellaway blew sadly through his pipe-stem. "No, I suspect they didn't."

"Damnation," Rex said. "That means an inquiry."

Kellaway nodded. "Two inquiries." He pointed at the wrecked Hurricanes.

Rex turned on Marriott. "How the blazes did that happen?"

"She jumped the chocks, sir. Simple as that."

"No, it's not. What was the fitter doing, revving the engine so hard? No wonder –"

"It wasn't the fitter's fault, sir. He had to get out of the cockpit, and he –"

"Whose fault was it, then? The stupid chocks, I suppose?"

"Yes, sir." Marriott was stiff-faced but sure of himself. "The chocks were at fault. They're too small for the Hurricane's wheels. Always have been."

"That's marvellous. Two machines written off, so we blame the chocks. The board of inquiry's going to love that."

"Maybe they'll recommend bigger chocks, sir," said Marriott. "I hope so. Those things were designed for biplanes, half the size of a Hurricane. I've made that clear in more than one memo to the area equipment officer." Marriott paused, and added: "With copies to you, sir."

Rex threw his gloves, one after the other, into a chair. He threw his flying-helmet after them. "To hell with memos," he said. "You make your own chocks. That's an order."

Marriott scratched the back of his head, tilting his cap over his eyes. "It might be better if you put that in writing, sir," he said. "If I start using non-standard equipment and anything goes wrong —"

"Do it!" Rex snapped. There was an uncomfortable silence. He flicked a finger at the adjutant. "And get something typed up for me to sign." Kellaway nodded.

Skull came in. "Well, young Starr's got to be moved again," he said.

"What?" Kellaway was startled. "But we've paid for that grave."

"You arranged it with the sexton, I believe."

"Yes."

"But not with the priest."

"No. He was away at some religious bunfight."

"Well, he's back, and he wants the body shifted now, today, before it contaminates someone." Skull grinned maliciously, and accepted a mug of tea from the duty NCO. "He doesn't want any vile, decaying Methodists mixed up with his good, putrefying Catholics. Here's to sanctity."

The adjutant screwed his face up into an expression of puzzled concern. "How on earth did the fellow find out that Dicky Starr was a Methodist?" he asked.

"He didn't say, but my theory is —"

"I don't care," Rex said harshly. "I don't want to know. I just want that bloody body permanently disposed of, understand? I want it put away for good. Get me? Laid to rest. And that means *rest*. Not bloody well hopping up and down like some damned dervish. I mean, what the bloody hell's going on, for Christ's sake?"

They were briefly silenced by his anger, tinged with desperation. Then Skull said: "Do dervishes really hop? I know they whirl, but ... One is so ignorant of Arabic religious ritual. It's quite appalling."

"I'll have Starr shifted, sir," Kellaway said gruffly.

"Today," Rex told him. "Let's get *some*thing right on this station."

The adjutant gave a grunt of pleasure and waved his pipe to attract their attention. "I knew I had a bit of good news, sir. We've got a replacement pilot." He fished a sheet of paper from his pocket and smoothed it. "Pilot Officer Christopher Hart Ill. He's —"

"What? What was that? His name is Ill?"

"So it seems, sir."

Rex sat on his gloves and helmet. He passed a hand over his face as if wiping something away. "His name is Ill," he repeated. "Pilot Officer Ill."

Kellaway shook the paper, and half-laughed. "Sorry! Of course it's not. You clod, Kellaway! He's not Ill, he's *three*. Roman numeral for three. The chap's American, it says so further down, US citizen, he obviously calls himself Christopher Hart the Third and —"

"They've *what*?" Rex came out of his chair as if stung. The chair toppled and crashed before the duty NCO could reach it. "They've sent me an *American*?" His voice was faint with fury.

"Yes, sir."

"A bloody Yank? They expect me to enrol a foreigner into my squadron? We've run out of Englishmen, is that it?"

"Well, I don't —"

"We obviously have, haven't we? And why not? We can't do anything right, so who cares? When we fly, we fuck everything up! When we're on the ground we smash the sodding kites together! Jesus Christ, we can't even bury our dead without at least two shots at the wrong bloody hole! No wonder they send us the odds and sods, they probably think he'll fit right in, another clown for the circus!"

"I'm sure not, sir," the adjutant said gently.

"Are you? I'm not! I'm not sure not, sir! They're sending us a bastard Yank and you know what that means. A cowboy! Don't shake your grey head at me, uncle, I've met Yankee so-called aviators before and I tell you I *know*. They chew gum and they smoke cigars before breakfast and they wear crêpe-soled brothelcreepers in the mess *and I tell you their flying is not worth a twopenny shit!*"

"Not all, surely," murmured Skull.

Rex ignored him. "What the blazes do they think I've got here? The Foreign Legion? A dump for every stray wog, dago or aborigine that wanders into Fighter Command? Why don't they send me a few halfcastes or a brace of Untouchables while they're at it?"

"I know where I can get you a couple of stunted African pygmies, cheap." The voice came from the balcony.

"Who the hell is that?" Rex demanded.

"Pilot Officer Hart," said the adjutant. "He arrived twenty minutes ago."

To his credit, Rex had the sense and the self-control to leave the control tower immediately and drive back to the château. The adjutant took charge of Pilot Officer Hart.

"You mustn't be offended by the CO's remarks, old chap," Kellaway said. "The thing is, he's had rather a bad morning."

"Yes, I saw it all." Hart's accent was unobtrusive: very little twang, just a broadening of the vowels. He had a strong mouth, a short wedge-shaped nose and eyes that were curiously wide-set. At first sight, Kellaway guessed his age at twenty-one, twenty-two maybe; but he was fooled by the boyish jawline and the slight hollows in the cheeks: when he looked more closely he saw that Hart's brow was fine-etched with lines, and there was a certain distance in his eyes, a self-confidence that came only with time and experience. "I saw it all and I heard it all," Hart said evenly. "Squadron Leader Rex doesn't like Americans. I understand that. There are plenty of Americans I could do without myself. If he doesn't want me, he doesn't have to have me. It wasn't my idea to be posted here in the first place."

"Well, let's not rush our fences."

Skull asked: "Where are you from?"

"Hornchurch, 74 squadron. Spitfires."

"And what made you join the Royal Air Force?"

"I was wanted for murder in three Midwestern states," Hart said, "and Fort Zinderneuf was closed for renovation."

"My goodness."

"I expect you could do with a spot of lunch," Kellaway said. "And perhaps a beer first?"

"I suppose everybody asks that question," Skull said.

"Everybody," Hart agreed. "And they're never satisfied with the truth, so I've stopped telling it."

"What is the truth?" Kellaway asked.

"I'm dying of a rare and incurable disease," Hart told him. "And me with my whole life ahead of me. Ain't it a shame?"

"Point taken," Kellaway said.

They reached the château just as a staff car delivered Air Commodore Bletchley. The adjutant left the others and hurried over to greet him. "Morning, Kellaway!" Bletchley said. "Such a glorious day, I couldn't stand being cooped up at Rheims so I decided to toddle down and poach some lunch. I expect we can get this other thing straightened out while I'm here?"

"I'm sure we can, sir." The adjutant thought fast. Couldn't be Starr's burial; might be the Hurricane chocks; more likely the smoke-trail nonsense. He played safe. "It's all in the day's work, so to speak."

"I'm not so sure. Anything involving newspapers, it pays to box careful."

"Yes, of course. They always get everything wrong."

Bletchley snorted cheerfully. "I hope not. We need them."

Kellaway pushed open the big double-doors and stood aside. "Very true, sir," he said, thinking: *Newspapers? Newspapers? What was Baggy on about? Better box careful, as the man said.* "Heard about the squadron's latest stunt, sir?" he asked as they went upstairs. "Coloured smoke flares. Patterns in the sky. Very dramatic."

"Sounds fun," Bletchley said. Kellaway gave up.

Rex was surprised and disturbed to see someone from Area HQ so soon after the blunders of the morning, but he put on a good face, bustled about, seated him in a comfortable chair, and called in Kellaway and Skull for moral support.

"Now, then." Bletchley crossed his left ankle over his right knee, exposing an inch or two of sock-suspender, which he snapped against his milk-white calf. "I expect you've been wondering about this journalist you've been saddled with. Actually, it's not as bad as it seems."

"Journalist, sir? Nobody's told us about a journalist."

"Damn. You should have had a signal." Bletchley looked at Kellaway, who shook his head. "Bloody Air Ministry . . . Never mind, I can brief you. The thing is, the War Cabinet want to do something to counter all this attention the *Luftwaffe*'s been getting. Ever since Poland, Goering's been bragging that he's got the biggest, fastest, toughest air force in the world. All lies, of course. Still, it's time our side of the story got told, especially to the neutrals, so we've arranged with one of the big American newspaper chains to send a war correspondent to live with a fighter squadron. That's you."

"An American newspaperman? Living in the mess?" Rex made a sour face. "He'll make a damned nuisance of himself. You know what they're like, sir: iced water and coffee and peculiar cocktails with bits of fruit in them at all hours of the day and night, I mean it's not fair on the servants."

Bletchley chuckled, and shook his head. "I doubt it."

"Besides, what's there for him to write about? He can't fly and nothing interesting happens on the ground. He'll be bored to death in a week. Send him to a bomber drome, they're always up to something."

"Too late, my boy. It's got to be you, and for one very simple reason. You're getting an American pilot posted here soon."

"He's arrived," Kellaway said. "Came this morning."

"And he leaves this afternoon," Rex declared.

"Oh?" Bletchley cocked his head.

"I will not tolerate furtive, underhand behaviour," Rex said. "I cannot stand people who skulk about and lurk in corners to see what they can overhear. It disgusts me."

"Hart wasn't lurking. Quite the opposite," Skull said. "He went onto the balcony because he thought you would wish some privacy in which to make your remarks about ... well, about this and that."

"He shouldn't have been in the control tower in the first place. No idea of the proper form. Typical crude and arrogant –"

"I told him to report to the tower," Kellaway said.

"I don't care," Rex said stiffly. "My commission is from the King. It says nothing about taking charge of any casual destitute barnstormer who turns up on the doorstep. I've no room for Yankee mercenaries, sir. I don't like them, I don't trust them, I don't need them."

"Too bad," Bletchley said. "This one stays."

"Sir, be reasonable –"

"See here, Rex. The pilot's the bait for the journalist. That's the whole deal! No pilot, no journalist. Which would be a severe disappointment not only to me but also to the C-in-C Fighter Command."

That took Rex aback. "Stuffy Dowding's behind this?"

"He's taken an interest, yes." Rex was silent. "If this young American is here already," Bletchley said, "I really ought to meet him, shouldn't I?"

Rex could think of no reason why not. "He'd better be a red-hot pilot, that's all," he muttered.

"My dear Rex, I can't tell you how pleased I am to see a little bloody-minded bigotry in you," Bletchley said. "I was beginning to think you were downright decent and fair-minded, and that would never do in a fighter leader, would it, uncle?"

"Never, sir," the adjutant said cheerfully. "We proved that last time."

Chris Hart stayed. Air Commodore Bletchley bought him a beer, took him aside, and said: "Hornet is a damn good squadron, you know. Maybe the Hurri isn't as quick as the Spits you've been flying but it's still a hell of a good bus, and you're better off here in many other ways. Nearer the action, for a start. If you want to bag a few Huns, this is the place to be. And just look around you! Finest mess in Fighter Command. They live better here than we do at Area HQ. Terrific bunch of chaps, all the flying you want, excellent chance of blowing the odd Jerry into little bits, and then home to a game of squash, a hot bath, and a five-star dinner! I mean, what more could you want?"

Hart eased his collar, and Bletchley caught a glimpse of shiny, dark-red scar-tissue at the side of his neck. "Have you talked to the CO, sir?" he said.

"Storm in a teacup." Bletchley gestured with his gin-and-tonic as if to erase the incident from memory. "All a misunderstanding."

Hart smiled, and looked away. He seemed completely at ease. "I understood it perfectly," he said.

"Yes, but . . ." Bletchley had to stop and think. He had never before met a pilot officer who treated him so much as an equal. "That's water under the bridge now, isn't it? Mustn't harbour grudges, old boy. Time to link arms and face the common foe. After all, what's a few hard words between friends? It was all done in the heat of the moment, wasn't it?"

Hart sipped his beer, and nodded.

"There you are, then," Bletchley said.

"They're sending us a bastard Yank," Hart said evenly. "A cowboy. I've met Yankee so-called aviators. They chew gum. They smoke cigars before breakfast. They wear crêpe-soled brothel-creepers in the mess. Their flying is not worth a twopenny shit."

Bletchley grunted. For a moment they stood and looked at the crowd around the bar.

"All right," Bletchley said. "Stay here."

After a minute he returned with Rex.

"Welcome to Hornet squadron!" Rex said. There was a curious, half-triumphant lift in his voice, as if to say *I bet you never expected that*.

"Okay," Hart said.

Neither of them offered to shake hands. Rex examined Hart for a moment, until he realised that Hart was examining him in return. He turned away. "You're in 'A' flight," he said. "Excuse me." He walked away.

"I'm glad that's settled," Bletchley said. "I'm sure you'll like it here. This is a very proud squadron, you know."

"Show me a fighter pilot who's full of pride," Hart said, "and I'll show you a fighter pilot who's full of shīt one minute and full of holes the next."

Bletchley chuckled. "Now you're just being provocative."

"You reckon? I'll tell you what, sir. Let's meet again in six months and see who's still alive and flying, out of this bunch. Not more than half, I bet. And not Squadron Leader Rex."

Bletchley was intrigued by Hart's calm confidence. "How can you be so sure?"

"Because I've met men like him before," Hart said, "and they're all dead."

"What a morbid chap you are ... Come on, let's get some lunch before the vultures descend." As they crossed the anteroom, Bletchley said: "Where did you meet these men?"

"In Spain. Very proud people, the Spanish, but given a five-second burst from a Messerschmitt 109 dead astern, their pride went all to pieces."

"Yes, I suppose it would." Bletchley paused at the dining-room door and made sure nobody was within earshot. "You fought in the Spanish Civil War?" Hart nodded. Bletchley said: "I'm guessing, of course, but I'd say you were on the Republican side." Again, Hart nodded. "In the circumstances," Bletchley said, "you'd be well-advised to keep that under your hat."

Hart leaned against the doorframe. "Sir, are you trying to tell me something about the CO's politics?"

"Heavens, no. Squadron Leader Rex is a thoroughgoing Tory, of course. There's not much room for the brotherhood of man in a cockpit, is there? But politics have nothing to do with it. Franco's lot won. Your lot lost. In these circles, there's no prize for coming in second, so my advice is forget about the whole sad affair."

"I'll never forget Spain," Hart said.

"Then at least remember it quietly," Bletchley said.

They went in to lunch.

A signal came, advising the imminent arrival of an American war correspondent; but the correspondent did not arrive. "Jake Bellamy," the adjutant said to Skull. "I don't think the CO will take to that name, somehow." He filed the signal and said nothing; Rex, he thought, needed a little more time to recover his poise.

In fact the cock-ups and confusion of the past few days were being steadily put straight. Dicky Starr was dug up and reinterred in an unimpeachably Protestant cemetery in Metz, after which the adjutant called on the village priest to apologise. They exchanged statements, each in his own language, neither understanding the other. The adjutant was cheery, the priest increasingly stiff and stuffy. Kellaway soon lost patience. "If you ask me it's all bosh, tosh and drivel," he said as he got up to go. "In the last show we just bunged the body in the nearest boneyard. Nobody asked to see the chap's membership card. He'd snuffed it, that was good enough. Well, you've got a buckshee hole now, haven't you? Lucky feller. What are you going to do with it? Hide it in the crypt, or raffle it for Christmas?" The priest slammed the door.

There was no inquiry into the giant half-swastika: Baggy Bletchley was told about it and when he returned to Rheims he took care of the complaints and queries. There was an inquiry into the loss of the two Hurricanes, but it was brief and its findings blamed nobody: other Hurricane squadrons had reported similar accidents, and bigger chocks were being issued.

Replacement aircraft were quickly ferried in. The weather was patchy, with snow showers in the hills, but the squadron trained every day. Micky Marriott solved the problem of switching off the smoke flares and the locals got used to the sight of giant stripes decorating the sky.

Hart replaced Starr as Fanny Barton's wingman in Yellow Section. It took him a day to adjust to the Hurricane; after that he quickly mastered the formation manoeuvres, flew skilfully, kept position tightly. Rex had no cause for complaint. On the ground, he ignored Hart as much as possible. This was easy, because Hart was rapidly accepted by the rest of the squadron. His was a fresh face, a pleasant voice and an unconventional mind. "Moggy," Kellaway said in the mess on the day he arrived, "I'd like you to meet Christopher Hart the Third, from America."

"How do you do?" Cattermole shook his hand. "The third, eh? I myself am loosely related to Edward the Seventh of England."

"Who isn't, these days?" Hart said.

"King Edward," Cattermole said. "Not just a good potato but a damn fine cigar."

"When you put it like that," Hart said, "I begin to see the resemblance."

"What are those two talking about?" Miller asked.

"Moggy's potty," Fitzgerald said. "Ever since Dicky knocked him over coming downstairs and he landed on his head. Potty."

Gordon said brightly: "The average adult human brain weighs three pounds."

"Three pounds," Moran said. "Would that be before or after cooking?"

"Flip, I'd like you to meet Christopher Hart the Third," the adjutant said. "From America."

"My uncle Fergus had a boat called the Kate McGrath the Fourth," Moran said, shaking hands, "but it sank."

"That's nothing," Patterson said. "My father had a prize bull called Maxwell Bugleboy the Seventh, but the beast died."

"And what happened to the bull?" Moran asked.

"Funny thing about names," Stickwell said. "I used to drink in a pub called the Henry the Eighth."

"That's not very funny," Patterson said.

"Ah, but I was sick in the carpark."

"Make a note of that," Cattermole told Hart. "Being sick in a carpark represents Sticky's finest piece of marksmanship so far."

"It wasn't in the middle of the carpark," Stickwell said.

"Never mind. Nobody's perfect."

"As a matter of fact, most of it went over the fence and into somebody's back garden. I made rather a mess of his dwarf geraniums."

Hart said: "You've got to be pretty accurate to hit dwarf geraniums. It's not as if they were petunias or begonias."

"There was a stiff breeze, too," Stickwell said. "I had to aim-off for wind."

"Frankly, old boy, I think you deserved a gong for that," Kellaway said.

"Perhaps a small gong," Stickwell agreed.

"A dwarf gong," said Hart.

"Christopher Hart the Third is extremely intelligent," Stickwell said, "for an American."

"I say: why did you join the Royal Air Force?" Mother Cox inquired.

"Because of the polo," Hart said.

"But we don't play polo."

"Right."

Moran said: "What we do instead is we slide downstairs on brass trays at breakneck speed."

"That's almost polo," Hart said. "Nobody's going to notice the difference."

Later they introduced him to the Cresta Run. More trays had been acquired, so now 'A' and 'B' flights could race each other down the double staircase. Hart did well: he beat Moke Miller by several feet. At some point during the races he got his nickname. The novelty of Christopher Hart the Third had worn off. Someone shortened it to CH3, and CH3 he remained.

"I wish I could teach you something," Flash Gordon said.

They lay in each other's arms, snug in a cocoon of blankets.

Above them the roof of the summerhouse was lost in shadow. The smoky glow from the hurricane lamp reached no higher than the windows. Occasionally it showed up a snowflake, caught on the glass for a few seconds and then blown away.

"*Tu m'apprends l'anglais,*" Nicole murmured.

"Rubbish."

"*C'est vrai. Tu m'apprends l'argot anglais et . . . et des blagues.*"

"*Blagues*? I never taught you any *blagues*. What are *blagues*?"

"Jokes." She curled her legs around his.

"Oh, well! . . . I suppose so. It's not much, compared to what you've taught me about the human body and so on. Like what happens when you blink, the way the fluid over your eye gets wiped off and runs down a little hole into your nose. I'd never have worked that out for myself. Not in a million years."

Nicole nodded without opening her eyes.

"Clever little arrangement, that," Flash said. "I suppose it's the reason why your nose is underneath your eyes." He squinted at his own nose, as if to test the theory. "Anyway, I haven't told you anything half as useful as that." He was feeling very grateful to her. He wanted her to know how deeply appreciative he was. "Have I?"

"*Alors . . .*" She made her head more comfortable. "Tell me something, if you like. Some good English."

"I wish I could. I don't know any . . . Hang on. There's a bit of Shakespeare they made us learn at school." Nicole smiled. Flash cleared his throat. "Now all the youth of England are on fire, and silken dalliance in the wardrobe lies: now thrive the armourers, and something something something in the breast of every man: they sell the pasture now to buy the horse; something the something of all something . . . Damn." He shrugged. "I never could remember it all."

She linked her hands behind him. "It sounds nice," she said. "What does it mean?"

"It means the balloon's gone up. Everyone's off to war. It's from Henry the Fifth, where he decides to go and wallop the frogs at Agincourt, and –"

"That butcher!" Nicole thrust herself away from him and sat up. "Invader! Bloody killer!"

"Look out, Nicole, you're making a terrible draught."

217

"Your Henry was a brute, a *cochon, un tyran, un barbare!*"

"Who says?" Flash was enjoying the view of her splendid breasts. "I think you're just a bad loser. After all we beat you fair and square. The fact is —"

"The fact is you English invaded France. What right had Henry and his greedy army to walk all over France?"

"Dunno." Flash took his eyes off her breasts and was surprised by the anger on her face. "I expect we —"

"You were as bad as the *boche*, you English. If I had lived then, I should have defended France *contre la tyrannie de l'Angleterre. Moi, une femme!*"

"Just like Joan of Arc," Flash said, and knew at once it was the wrong thing.

"*Oui! Comme Jeanne d'Arc!* Who was born near here!" Nicole flung off the blanket and stood up. "Killed by you English, *n'est-ce-pas?* Killed by the fire! *Une martyre pour la France!*" She seized her clothes and strode out, leaving the door wide open. The hurricane lamp flickered. Flash shivered. *Bloody women*, he thought. *Just when you're ready for second helpings, they go off the deep end.* There was a box of apples nearby. He took one and munched it.

At the other end of the village, Fitz had just stepped out of a hot bath and was drying himself. The hot bath was something of a gamble: he knew it had an effect on your performance because someone had told him so, but he couldn't remember which way it was supposed to work. Surely the important thing was to feel completely relaxed. He stopped towelling and examined his state of being. Was he relaxed? It was hard to tell. He examined himself again, more rigorously, searching for causes of anxiety, signs of tension. There was nothing to worry about; nothing. So why where his toes curling?

Some sorts of food were supposed to do the trick. Oysters, especially. Not easy to get oysters in Lorraine in November. On the other hand, other types of food were supposed to take the starch out of you. Cheese: which side was cheese on? He'd had rather a lot of cheese at lunch. What if cheese made you sluggish? Like thick engine-oil making it hard to start the Merlin in cold weather?

Perhaps the weather made a difference.

Or the moon.

He wished there was a book that told you all about this. You'd think someone would write a book. If only there was something you could sort of rub on yourself, just to get the equipment warmed-up and generally pointed in the right direction ... He opened Mary's bathroom cabinet and sniffed the contents of various jars and bottles. One liquid had a pleasant scent of lemons. Hadn't he read somewhere once that lemons put lead in your pencil?

He twitched his nose and glanced down at the equipment. Jesus, it certainly looked as if it needed encouragement. It looked as if it was trying to hide behind itself. Lemons. Or was it melons?

He put the bottle back in the cabinet. Relax completely: that was the main thing. Well, he *was* relaxed: totally, utterly, absolutely relaxed. He wiped the mist off the mirror, smiled confidently at himself, and went out, curling his toes against the carpet.

Flash picked him up, as usual, a couple of hours later. "Have a good time?" he asked as they drove away.

"Oh, the usual," Fitz said. There was a long pause before he asked: "How about you? Learn anything new?"

Flash laughed, but not much. "I learned you can't win 'em all," he said.

Fitz grunted, and looked out of his side-window. "I could have told you that," he said.

Fanny Barton saw it first: a bird, wheeling between two clumps of trees about a mile away, to the west of the aerodrome. A big bird, a heron or perhaps a buzzard. The squadron had just landed after a final rehearsal for the Armistice Day display and the pilots were straggling across the field. It had been a good rehearsal; everyone was pleased; even Rex was laughing at something Sticky was saying. Fanny couldn't make out the words. His ears were still buzzing. He looked at the clouds, trying to guess tomorrow's weather. There seemed to be a bit of everything up there. He took a deep breath, and his ears popped. Noise came at him as if he had thrown open a window: shouts, the clump of boots, an engine's growl. He looked for the bird. It was still there but bigger and thicker and flying more boldly than any bird. Fanny stopped. "Hey, look at that," he said. Nobody heard him. The silhouette swelled, the growl deepened. "Hey!" he shouted. "Aircraft!" Everyone stopped. The machine seemed to get very much faster as it got nearer: within seconds it was streaking towards them, dipping to twenty feet, its propeller disc shimmering, the growl becoming a huge, hoarse shout: a Messerschmitt 109, pearl-grey underneath, green on top, and going a damn sight faster than any Hurricane could travel. Everyone ducked as the fighter seemed to vault over them, smashing them with a storm of noise. Then it was gone. By the time they had straightened up and turned, the German was halfway to the perimeter, climbing like a rocket.

"Bloody cheek!" said Rex.

Cattermole took out his revolver, aimed carefully, and fired. The Messerschmitt, once again no bigger than a bird, flew steadily eastward. "I think I winged him," Cattermole said.

"He dropped something," Fitzgerald shouted.

They gathered around the object. "Better not touch it," Mother Cox advised.

"Don't be bloody silly," Stickwell said. "It's an old jerry, that's all." He turned it over with his foot. It was indeed an enamel chamber-pot, much dented and scarred. "Made in England," he said.

"Well I'm damned!" Flash Gordon's voice had gone up several tones. "Why on earth did he do that?"

"It's an insult," Patterson said. "This means war."

"It means they're as bored as we are," Rex said. "Personally, I think this is a very encouraging sign. Now they're starting to come out to play. You watch: we'll get some real sport soon."

They kicked the jerry across the field, playing football, and then hung it on the wall of the crewroom. Flip Moran and CH3 were the last to leave. "What do you make of it?" Flip asked him.

"That 109 could have killed us all if he'd had a mind to," CH3 said.

Flip combed his hair. "I noticed you were the only one to hit the deck." He put his cap on. "Very smartly," he said.

"I reckon it pays to make yourself small when someone points a gun." They went out into the fading light of the afternoon. "Where were the lookouts?" CH3 asked. "Why wasn't the alarm sounded? What happened to the airfield defences?"

"They're all organised," Flip said. "They're just not manned every minute of the day. We've got . . ." He shrugged. "I was about to say we've got better things for the men to do, but that doesn't sound very clever."

"The CO thinks Jerry's coming out to play," CH3 said.

"Figure of speech."

"Ah."

"It's the English, you see. A great sporting nation, the English."

"Sure. More sporting than the Germans?"

"By far."

"God help us."

"Well ... God isn't much of a sport either. Mind you," Flip added, "from what I hear, the devil's a very bad loser too. It gets so a fellah doesn't know which way to turn."

Rex went straight to his office, whizzed through the paperwork on his desk, picked out the urgent stuff, dictated half-a-dozen letters or memos, and then grabbed the first pilot he saw – Fanny Barton – for some squash. They played flat-out, split a ball and smashed a racket, and came off in a lather of sweat. Rex took a shower, went by his office to sign the letters and memos, and whistled for Reilly. They took a walk in the grounds. He delivered the dog to the kitchens for its dinner, and went back through the grounds, relishing the sharp evening air, unhurriedly returning the crisp salutes of passing airmen, feeling marvellously fit and knowing that an excellent dinner would soon be served to him. His mouth watered at the thought. More airmen; more salutes. It was like owning a country estate: servants, sport, entertainment, all the rewards of a smooth-running and spacious establishment, provided by a grateful and generous government. He took the front steps two at a time. It was a good world, until he went inside.

Five or six pilots were bunched together at the bar, making more noise than usual. The adjutant stood amongst them, looking jovial. He saw Rex approaching and made room for him. "Sir: may I introduce you to Jake Bellamy," he said. "Miss Bellamy, I'd like you to meet our commanding officer, Squadron Leader Rex."

"Hullo," she said. They shook hands. Rex was startled but he behaved impeccably: smiled, made the beginnings of a bow, held her hand a fraction longer than was strictly necessary. "How do you do, Miss Bellamy," he said.

She was small and slim, and she looked good in a war-correspondent's uniform of khaki gabardine slacks and tunic. She wore a grey silk shirt with a knitted brown tie, and her hair was a glossy black, cut just short of her collar. Her face was not beautiful but it was interesting and pleasant to look at. The pilots were obviously fascinated by her. She accepted their attention easily. She seemed the calmest person in the room.

"Well, this is a surprise," Rex said.

"I'm sorry about the confusion over the name," she said. "There *was* a correspondent called Jake Bellamy and because people can't believe in a woman doing this job they think I must be him. Same initials, you see. I'm Jacky."

"Jacky's going to write stories about us, sir," Stickwell said. "She's going to tell everyone what terrific fighter pilots we are. Especially me."

"Is that right?" Rex said, trying to look pleased.

"No," she said. They all laughed, Rex last. "I just cover the war. Whatever happens, I report it. I guess I'm over here to help keep score."

"And which newspaper do you work for?"

"A chain. My stuff gets syndicated."

"You know, Jacky," Fitzgerald said boldly, "you're not terribly American, are you? I mean . . ." But he ran out of confidence.

"Plenty of Americans are not terribly American," she said. "Are you terribly English?"

"Yes, of course I am."

"No, you're not," Patterson said. "You wear suede shoes and you don't like kippers. You're a phoney."

"Pay no attention," Fitzgerald told her. "Pip's Scotch, so he doesn't count."

"May I get you a drink, Miss Bellamy?" Rex asked. She smiled, and pointed to the bar: she already had a glass of orange juice. Rex accepted a tankard of beer, and drank deeply. "I'm flattered by your presence, of course," he said, "but is there really enough for you to write about here?"

"No. I aim to spend a lot of time out in the field, but if I can use this as a base I'd appreciate it."

"Personally I think it's a brilliant idea," Miller said. "Have you got any friends?"

"Colleagues? Sure. Dozens of them."

"Not *men*," Miller said. "More like you, I meant."

"A word in your ear, uncle," Rex said. He took the adjutant aside. "This must be a mistake," he said. "She can't possibly be meant to stay here. The whole idea's totally unacceptable."

The adjutant looked troubled. "The thing is," he said, "we had a room reserved for her – for Bellamy, that is – and now she's moved into it. I don't see how we can . . ."

"But this is an operational unit, for God's sake. Not a damned charm school."

"The room's no problem. We've got umpteen rooms to spare. And I honestly don't think she'll get in the way. She looks young but she's quite well clued-up, you know. Been a war-correspondent in China and in South America, Uruguay or Paraguay or . . ." A burst of laughter made them glance. "Besides, she gets on jolly well with the chaps, doesn't she?"

Rex sniffed. Kellaway knew at once he had said the wrong thing. "I don't want distraction," Rex said. "I want concentration. This is *my* province. That woman must go."

"I forgot to tell you," Kellaway said. "She's reporting the Armistice Day display."

"I don't care if she's reporting the Second Coming." But Rex remembered Baggy Bletchley's remarks. This woman was here at the suggestion of the office of the C-in-C Fighter Command, Air Chief Marshal Sir Hugh Dowding, who had no jurisdiction in France but had a lot of influence. "Damn," he said. "Damn."

While they were talking, CH3 came in and was introduced to Jacky Bellamy. They shook hands and said hullo, and she studied his face for a couple of seconds. "We've met before. You wouldn't remember. Colorado, 1936. The two-man bobsled event." There was a suppressed eagerness in her voice. "You broke some kind of record, didn't you?"

"That was on the second run. Third run, I broke my leg."

She clicked her fingers. "So you did."

"Were you competing?"

"I was working. Newspapers."

There was the briefest of pauses while he took in her uniform. "Ah," he said, and with it the distance between them suddenly became enormous. "I see."

"You've changed a lot in four years." She had forgotten the

other men existed. "If I hadn't been told you were here I don't think I'd have recognised you." His face was empty of expression. He simply nodded, and looked at the space beyond her shoulder. "That was the first time I ever got a byline," she said. "I'll never forget it."

"Excuse me. There's someone I have to talk to." He walked away.

"What's a byline?" Miller asked. She didn't hear, and he had to repeat his question.

CH3 had a brief conversation with Rex. "Is she here because of me?" he asked. "Yes," Rex said. "Look, sir, I know how newspapers work," CH3 said. "They'll print a lot of trash, a lot of lies."

For a moment, Rex almost liked him. "Too late now, old man," he said. "I'm afraid we're stuck with the lady." He went back to the bar.

On Armistice Day the cloudbase was above ten thousand feet, the air was bright and clear, the breeze was steady at ten miles an hour. On the airfield at Area HQ, Rheims, the flags of the colour-parties flared beautifully.

Hornet squadron's display came after all the marching and playing and singing and praying and standing in silence; it was planned as the climax of the occasion.

Rex led his Hurricanes through a demonstration of close-formation flying that, for speed and precision, excelled anything the audience had ever seen. He saved the best for last. When his flights created the cross of St George five hundred feet above the royal reviewing stand, the streams of colour appeared suddenly and cleanly and vividly; a vast, bold banner discovered in the sky in a matter of seconds. The squadron re-formed; climbed until it was only a blur, a mutter; turned and dived at full throttle; levelled out over the stand with a blast of noise that seemed to flatten the grass; and soared superbly in Prince of Wales feathers, each section streaming smoke, bright red and blue plumes curling away from the central white: a great royal emblem, sketched with godlike speed and skill against the empty air.

The squadron landed in close formation – aircraft in vic, sections astern – and Rex was presented to the royal visitor. This was only an obscure duke, pressed into war-work; genial, chatty and clueless;

steered everywhere by staff officers; his brow constantly creasing under the unfamiliar weight of an Air Marshal's cap. But he asked Rex a lot of questions, and while they talked the flashbulbs flared like flattery on all sides. When at last Rex saluted and marched away, he saw Jacky Bellamy at the front of the crowd, taking notes. *All trash*; *all lies*. He was tempted to seek her out and suggest that he might check her story for accuracy. After all, Hornet was his squadron, not hers, but people would believe what she wrote: her story would become the reality.

No. To do that would be to play the game her way. Which meant conceding that the game mattered. He put her out of his mind, found his men, led them off to lunch.

She turned up there, too, but she sat among the junior pilots. Rex heard little of their conversation, except for one exchange. "How about the German fliers?" she said. "D'you really want to kill them?"

"Got to," Moggy Cattermole said. "They don't make good pets."

She looked for other answers.

"It depends," Fitz Fitzgerald said. "If we meet Jerry upstairs, he's fair game. Meet him down here, on the ground – different story."

"Suppose he bailed out, for instance," Flash Gordon said. "Well, the scrap's over, isn't it? No hard feelings. Buy him a drink, probably."

Moke Miller said: "It's just his bad luck he's on the wrong side. No point in getting all bloodthirsty about it. Leave that to the pongoes." She raised an eyebrow. "Brown jobs," he explained, "Army." Rex stopped listening: they were giving her all the right answers.

Air Commodore Bletchley had sent a Percival Gull down to Château St Pierre to bring Jacky Bellamy to Rheims. It was a nice afternoon, and the Gull was a sporty little plane; he decided to pilot her back himself. If anything, the cloud was now even higher and thinner: it looked as pure as porcelain.

They were halfway home when Hornet squadron passed them, a thousand feet higher and impeccably assembled by flights, echeloned to port. Bletchley climbed to give her a better view of the formation. As he did so, it suddenly changed direction until it was heading south. Bletchley pointed, and after some blinking and squinting she saw another aircraft, high, just beneath the cloudbase. It was flying eastward. "Looks like a French bomber," Bletchley said. "Rex may do a practice interception."

"Isn't that sort of risky?"

"Why should it be?"

"The bomber might shoot back."

Bletchley smiled. She felt foolish, and concentrated on making notes. The squadron was climbing hard. It changed formation, changed direction, changed formation again. Rex was working his way up to and behind the bomber, which was still crawling across the white cloudbase like a fly on a ceiling. Another change of course, and the squadron neatly divided itself into two flights.

Bletchley nudged her. "Some dozy frog pilot is about to get a nasty shock," he said happily.

The first flight was moving ahead of the second, gaining on the target as if the bomber were winching it in. The aircraft were in line astern, and now they stretched their line, easing apart. The leading Hurricane suddenly grew antennae of fire, long red-and-yellow whiskers that tickled the bomber's tail-unit. "Christ!" Bletchley said. The Hurricane swerved away and the second fighter flung its brilliantly speckled lines at the bomber. This time Jacky Bellamy could see the coloured fire sparking and bouncing as it hit the fuselage and wings. The third fighter carried on the attack. A thin black scarf of smoke trailed from the bomber's port engine, and as the fourth Hurricane opened fire the bomber slipped sideways, gently and slowly, like a tired bird dropping to earth after a long flight. "It's a bloody silly Dornier!" said Bletchley.

The rest of 'A' flight sprayed the bomber, and then 'B' flight strolled up to it and took turns at gunnery practice. Both engines were pouring smoke and hits were falling off the wings and body, yet the aircraft refused to burn or explode. It fell more steeply, and as it fell it slowly turned until it had reversed its course. It was actually diving towards the Gull. "If that blighter blows up," Bletchley said, "I don't want to be in the neighbourhood." The Dornier was curling to its left: he took the Gull the other way. Jacky Bellamy pressed her face against the side-window. The bomber went past in a rush, making smoke like a locomotive. She saw hundreds of glittering bullet-streaks, deep rips in the wings, a radio aerial lashing itself to death, half the undercarriage dangling, the Perspex canopy and nose-dome shattered.

Bletchley flew steeply banked circles so that they could watch it go in. It gained speed all the way down. It must have been doing five hundred miles an hour when it hit a small brown field. The impact had a predictable ferocity that made her wince, but still there was no fire, no explosion. "Probably out of fuel," Bletchley said. "Silly man! Well done, Rex. Big party tonight, I expect."

The French bomber crews drove over from Montornet at Rex's invitation to help Hornet squadron celebrate.

After a large and liquid meal, the cultural exchange began. They played Cresta Run, racing each other down the double staircase on brass trays. The winners each drank a pint of beer; the losers drank two pints. Hornet pilots won easily. Montornet challenged them to a rugby match in the smoking-room. They used an inflated Mae West for a ball. Montornet won but lost its CO with concussion. Again the penalty for the losers was to drink two pints to the winners' one. They adjourned to the ballroom, Montornet carrying their commandant on a door which had accidentally come off its hinges when he hit it with his head, and there was a short pause while Stickwell was spectacularly sick into a potted plant. The Frenchmen sang a short patriotic song. Rex then explained the next game, called Tank Corps. An obstacle course of pianos, lamp standards, ornamental urns, potted plants and so on, had been set up so that it circled the room. At opposite ends were two motorbikes. The aim was to catch and hit the bike in front. Pursuit was complicated by a rule that said the pillion passenger had to hold his hands over the driver's eyes and shout instructions in his ear, while everyone else stood in the middle of the room and pelted their opponents' motorbike with tennis balls. That game went particularly well – Moke Miller dislocated a finger, Flip Moran got a black eye, and a Frenchman flattened his nose on the handlebars: much blood – but it ended in a draw when the French bike hit a piano and overturned, losing all its petrol. There being no outright winner, both sides drank two pints of beer. The Frenchmen were singing a brisk hunting song when the adjutant came in with the news that it was snowing heavily. They all went out and threw snowballs. The puddles had frozen, and an orgy of

227

ice-breaking developed, everyone smashing thin sheets of ice over everyone else's head, the ice shattering loudly and brilliantly in a welter of witless destruction.

Kellaway, Skull and Bletchley watched from the terrace. "Nice to see the boys enjoying themselves," Bletchley said.

"Is this the standard celebration?" Skull asked.

"It's more or less routine. Why?"

"I just wondered. The German Air Force is supposed to have some fifteen hundred bombers. At this rate, total victory is going to place an enormous strain on the kidneys."

The ice-smashing had ended and the fliers had formed a tight circle, the squadrons intermixed. They were singing *Yes! We Have No Bananas*, bawling the ridiculous words into the tumbling snow.

"Nothing is impossible at that age," Kellaway said.

"Oh?" Skull turned up his collar. "Would be it tactless of me to mention the name of Dicky Starr?" he asked.

"They've forgotten all about him, Skull," the adjutant said. "In fact I doubt if he ever existed."

"That's sheer mental laziness."

"Not a bit of it," Bletchley said. "You don't understand fighter pilots, old boy. The thing is, a good fighter pilot never dies. If Starr died, he obviously wasn't a good fighter pilot. Furthermore, a *bad* fighter pilot is a contradiction in terms, so he couldn't have been a fighter pilot at all. Simple, really."

"Let's go and have a nightcap," Kellaway said. Skull was a decent fellow, and jolly good at crossword puzzles, but he would keep complicating things.

Shooting down the Dornier had a settling effect upon Hornet squadron. They had lost their collective virginity, and that was comforting: every other fighter squadron in France had scored a kill long ago: now Hornet had proved itself. Rex was happier. The interception had been immaculate, absolutely classic. It had justified all his training. What's more it had been watched by an air commodore and a war correspondent. What could be better?

At first there had been some discussion of the Dornier's strange behaviour. Why had it trundled across the sky and allowed them to attack it so easily? Why hadn't it jinked and dodged, or dived for home, or fired back? Various theories were touted – fuel shortage, or jammed controls, or the kite was on a photo-recce run, or maybe the rear-gunner was too sick to look out, or it could be that the German skipper was lost and therefore so busy with his maps that he didn't notice a dozen Hurricanes on his tail. Whatever the answer, it now lay thirty feet below a small French field, broken into a million pieces. Soon the pilots stopped wondering. All they remembered was the kill itself: the big black marauding Nazi intruder they had chased and caught and destroyed. The kill glowed in the collective memory of the squadron like a triumphant first night in the memory of a cast of actors. Nothing could spoil it. Nothing else mattered, in comparison.

The November days became shorter and greyer. Rex relaxed his training to give the groundcrews more time for maintenance and modifications. For a few weeks the château looked more than ever like a country house full of young men who were old friends: they motored about the countryside, played games, read bits of detective stories, went riding, played Jack Teagarden and The Inkspots and Edith Piaf on the gramophone, took snaps of each other doing silly-ass things, ate too much, occasionally got blotto, played more games. They absorbed CH3 during this period, without discovering much about him. Nobody liked to ask. It was very peculiar having an American, evidently a rich American, in the squadron. If you had somebody with a mild eccentricity – an Honourable, say, or someone who had played rugger for England – you could ask him about it, find out more about the chap. But CH3 was a fullblown Yank. Nobody had ever been to Yankeeland; not even the adj. What sort of question could you ask CH3 that wouldn't make you look a damn-fool? In any case CH3 himself didn't seem to want to talk about it. He was affable and amusing, and if he made no close friends he made no enemies either – apart from Rex, and everyone knew that was just the old man being a bit snooty.

After their first meeting the two Americans saw very little of each other. This was only partly because Jacky Bellamy was often away, driving around Alsace-Lorraine in search of stories. It was mainly because whenever she was in the mess, he was either over at the airfield or in the squash court, thrashing the daylights out of anyone who wanted a game. He was an astonishingly good player, with a drive like a whiplash and a drop-shot as soft as a silk duster. He seemed to drift about the court instead of running, until mysteriously everything was in his favour and he struck: no luck, no near-miss: a quick, complete kill. It was beautiful and merciless. Yet people liked to play CH3. He put so much of his own talent into the game that some of it rubbed off on them: he made them better players.

Every pilot had his own groundcrew: a fitter for the engine and a rigger for the airframe. CH3 made a point of meeting his ground-crew every day. They got to know him – he always scrutinised the propeller, searching for splinters or cracks in the wooden blade; he liked his cockpit canopy to be spotlessly clean and highly polished; he wore his straps more tightly than most pilots – and he got to know them. Corporal King, his fitter, was balding and moonfaced, a good listener who had nothing to say about anything if it did not involve the Rolls-Royce Merlin aero-engine. His rigger, LAC Todd, was younger, a twenty-five-year-old who looked eighteen: curly red hair, big grin, an afterthought of a nose, narrow shoulders and a neck like celery. Even the smallest overalls looked baggy on him.

The glamour of serving an American pilot excited Todd: it was like working for royalty. When CH3 bicycled into the hangar one afternoon wearing crisp white shorts, a white monogrammed sweater and a royal-blue muffler, Todd was even more impressed: *sporting* royalty. Together they looked over the aeroplane.

"Seems okay," CH3 said.

"Yes, sir."

He squatted and looked at the undersides of the wings. "Who had her painted like this?" One wing was white, the other black.

"Dunno, sir. The kites have always been painted like that. Since before we left England, sir."

CH3 grunted and got up. "Black and white," he said. He got on his bicycle. "Just like the whisky. Very distinctive." He hooked a pedal up.

"Been playing tennis, sir?" Todd asked.

"Squash."

"Ah." Todd nodded. "Good fun, is it, sir?"

"Don't you know what squash is like?"

"Never seen it, sir."

"Oh." CH3 made the pedal spin. "Well, you play inside a closed court. With a racket. You hit the ball against the wall. Sometimes against two or three walls."

"Sounds complicated."

"No, it's very easy. You seem pretty fit, you ought to have a go." They looked at each other: the American calmly assessing, the Englishman frankly admiring. "Would you like a game of squash?"

"Me, I'll try anything, sir. Only I haven't got any proper kit."

"Borrow mine. Four o'clock tomorrow?" CH3 rode away. "I'll square it with the flight sergeant," he called.

Todd stood up and watched him disappear into the dusk. He realised that he was breathing more deeply, his chest was out, he felt inches taller. There was nothing left to do but sweep his section of the hangar. He got a broom and swept it as it had never been swept before.

The sky was like a bad water-colour, with fuzzy blues leaking into dirty whites that blurred into wet greys. And the colours were always running. Squadron Leader Rex led 'A' flight through a sky that was shapeless to start with, and that kept on changing.

In thirty minutes he had seen nothing but this swirling mess. He expected to see nothing. The Area ops officer had spoken of a strong likelihood of enemy intruders entering this sector. It was difficult to understand why Jerry would take the risk. There was damn-all to see.

"Yellow Section, close up," he said, without having to think about it.

Yellow Section crept forward and edged inwards. The flight hit some turbulence, and all six aircraft bounced and wallowed and came together again.

"Nice and tight, please," Rex said. "Don't dawdle."

They reached the limit of their patrol, turned, and came back.

Moggy Cattermole, flying at Red Three, got the frame of his cockpit canopy lined up precisely with Red Leader's propeller disc. Now, if he kept his head quite still, he could hold formation perfectly.

Stickwell, at Red Two, also had his eyes on Rex, but he was thinking about lunch. Steak-and-kidney pie with flaky pastry. Crisp on top and juicily absorbent beneath. Yum.

Yellow Leader was Cox. His head scarcely moved; his eyes flickered from left to right, endlessly checking that Patterson and CH3 were tucked in properly, while he made sure that he himself remained squarely behind Rex's tail. Cox was worrying, in a casual way, about his heart. All the men in Cox's family died of heart attacks before they were sixty. His uncle Bertie had gone like that, only two weeks ago. Cox often worried about the grim, unfair inevitability of this. Sometimes he worried so much that he made his heart thump and race.

Patterson was trying not to think of Dicky Starr, but it was difficult. Sometimes he had a brief fantasy of Starr joining the flight, just turning up from nowhere with a wave and a grin and tacking on. This annoyed Patterson. He was not accustomed to being bothered by his imagination. He wished he could think of something else.

CH3 was searching the sky like a man in a strange city, hunting for street signs.

Rex, as flight commander, saw everything and saw nothing worth seeing: a wandering rubbishtip of dirty cloud. Not surprising: Operations were off their trolley to expect enemy action on a day like this. A silvery Heinkel 111 floated out of one cloud and into another. "Jester aircraft, turning to port, turning to port, go!" Rex said.

They trailed him obediently, a cluster of little fish in a murky stream, while he pursued his estimated interception course. His eyes were opened wide: there was great danger of collision in these conditions. The silvery Heinkel appeared again, in the wrong place, half a mile to his right, flying in the wrong direction along a ragged tunnel of clear air. "Jester aircraft, turning to starboard, turning to starboard, go!" Rex ordered.

He reefed the formation round as hard as he dared, but a vic of three Hurricanes measured about a hundred and twenty feet across. By the time it had wheeled about, the Heinkel was gone. "Damn!" Rex said. Smoke fled his exhausts as he rammed his throttle open.

For sixty seconds they hunted the bomber, speed building as time passed until it was obvious that they were chasing nothing, very rapidly. They burst into a stretch of open sky: empty except for wisps of mist. "Balls," Rex said crossly. "Okay: back on

232

course." He eased the flight into a long half-circle. Halfway through the turn, something glistened. Weak sunlight had found a cockpit canopy. Rex glimpsed, far off, a bulbous-nosed twin-engined plane with a stick-like fuselage. *Dornier 17! Christ Almighty! What is this? International Air Day?*

His orders were crisp, brisk, lucid. The flight checked its turn, reversed its bank, and ducked into a dive. The other aircraft was also diving, falling towards cloud cover. Rex braced his feet, flicked off the safety-switch of his gun-button, and enjoyed the pouncing, vibrant howl of the Merlin as it ate up space. "Yellow Three to Leader," said a voice in his ear. "Four aircraft in the sun. Look like fighters."

Rex kept his eyes on his target for three, four, five seconds. It had been the American's voice. He jerked his head around, squinted into a hazy dazzle that made his eyes water, found nothing. He turned back and searched for the target but now clusters of melting purple-red blemishes spoiled his vision. He blinked hard. "Anyone see where that Jerry went?" No reply. "Anyone else see those fighters?" More silence. Then he heard the American voice: "Yellow Three to Leader. Four aircraft still in the sun."

Rex swore to himself. He tried to stare through the fading blemishes and failed. "Levelling out," he announced. The flight curled out of its dive. Everyone snatched a look into the damp glare of the sun. Nobody spoke.

"What have you got to say for yourself, Yellow Three?" Rex asked.

"Yellow Three to Leader. Aircraft now gone into cloud, heading east."

"Fancy that." Rex paused for a long moment. "Yes, fancy that." Another pause. "Let's go home."

Skull unscrewed the cap from his fountain-pen. "What fortune?" he asked.

Rex tossed his helmet into his locker and elbowed the door shut. "Found three, lost three. Two Heinkels and a Dornier. Area: Faulquemont-Morhange-Dieuze."

"Area what?"

"Make it 'Metz,' " Rex said.

233

"Shocking weather up there," Stickwell said. "Like swimming in vegetable soup."

"Looked like mulligatawny to me," Cattermole said.

"Skull can't spell mulligatawny," Stickwell said.

"Anything else happen?" Skull asked.

Several pilots looked at CH3. He was wiping the inside of his flying-helmet and oxygen mask.

Skull screwed the cap back on his fountain-pen. "The third aircraft," CH3 said, "was a Hampden."

Skull unscrewed the cap again. In the silence it made a curiously scratchy sound.

"I saw a Dornier 17," Rex said. "The range was too great for markings but the silhouette was unmistakeable."

"Did anybody else get a good look at it?" Skull asked. Nobody had. "I suppose the two types are not dissimilar," he said. "It wouldn't be the first time –"

"It looked like a Dornier and it acted like a Dornier," Rex said. "It buzzed off the moment it saw us."

"You seemed very positive," Skull said to CH3.

"The crew-section on the Hampden is twice as deep as on the Dornier," CH3 said. "It stretches as far as the trailing edge. The Dornier's got a short, stumpy crew-section which stops level with the engines. This was a Hampden."

"Rubbish," Rex said. He put his cap on.

"Anyway, you couldn't make out that sort of detail," Cox said to CH3. "The thing was miles away. Just a blur."

"Not to me. I saw a Hampden. And," CH3 said to Skull, "four fighters in orbit above us."

"Identifiable?"

"No. They were in the sun. Probably Messerschmitts."

"The funny thing was," Rex said, "when we went to look for them they'd gone away. So had the Dornier, of course."

"Did I tell you, Skull?" Cattermole said. "I personally saw a dozen Italian seaplanes, three striped Zeppelins and a large golden eagle, all flying in ever-diminishing circles."

"Lunch," Rex said, and led the way.

Lunch was a slightly spiky affair.

Jacky Bellamy had come back from a tour of the Maginot Line. "Half the French Army don't shave," she said. "Discipline's poor."

"No self-respect, you see," Kellaway said. "Same last time."

"And their flak batteries seem to fire at anything with wings. I saw —"

"No shop in the mess, please," said Rex.

"Oh." She looked at the others, but they were all busy with their soup. "Sorry. I didn't know." She felt herself go slightly red in the face. With those few words, Rex had cut her down to size.

For a long moment nobody spoke.

"Flip," Rex said, "you have a discriminating palate. Baby lamb chops. We have available a sound if undistinguished St Emilion, or would you live dangerously and open some new *rosé* from Provence, breeding unknown?"

Moran finished crunching a *croûton*. "For myself, sir," he declared stolidly, "being a buccaneering sort of a rake, the last of the Ulster playboys, 'twould be the *rosé* and devil take the hindmost."

"The *rosé* it is, then," Rex said.

"But with the fate of my comrades entrusted to me," Moran went on, his voice sinking to a rasping gloom, "all thought of self departs. Their stomachs are in my hands, d'ye see."

"Gruesome thought," Moke Miller said.

"Better than the other way around," Fitzgerald said.

"Fetch the St Emilion," Rex told a waiter.

Kellaway had been thinking. "You know, if I couldn't shave every morning," he said, "I think I'd die."

"At least you'd get a decent funeral, uncle," Fanny Barton said. "You should have seen the job we did on the crew of that Dornier. Very smart, very classy. Just like the Brigade of Guards, we were."

"Good God, don't say that," Patterson exclaimed. "I've got a cousin in the Coldstream. They're all screaming pansies."

"Tell me, Yellow Three," Rex said, "do you have screaming pansies in America?"

"No, sir," CH3 said. "The climate doesn't suit them."

"That's odd," Rex said. "I could have sworn I'd been screamed at by an American pansy."

CH3 put down his spoon. Skull said quickly: "A friend of mine used to grow very loud begonias. Quite deafening, they were."

235

Jacky Bellamy almost said something, then looked at Rex and kept quiet. CH3 picked up his spoon.

"A buttercup once belched at me," Stickwell said, "but that was in Wales, so it probably doesn't count."

Mother Cox had not been listening to this chatter. He was still worrying about the funeral. "Without going into the gory details, Fanny," he said. "I'm surprised you found anything to bury. I mean, they went in awfully fast."

"Yes. I think there were a few hands and things. Not a lot."

"Amazing things, hands," Flash Gordon said. "I bet you don't know how many bones there are in the human hand."

"I do, but I'm not telling," Miller said.

Rex leaned back as the baby lamb chops arrived. "Tell me, Yellow Three," he said, "how do you cope with all the corpses in your country?"

"Sandbags in the coffin," Kellaway told Barton. "That's what we did in my day."

"I don't understand your question, sir," CH3 said.

"It's more than you think," Gordon told them all.

Rex smiled upon the *mange-tout* peas being heaped on his plate, and then smiled at CH3. "You know: corpses. All those people shot by gangsters."

"They miss more than they hit," Jacky Bellamy said. "Everyone knows, but the papers are too scared to speak out. It's a national scandal."

"We don't have gangsters where I come from," CH3 said. .

"You don't?" Rex tasted the wine, and smiled again. "How curious. So all Americans don't go around looking nervously over their shoulder for fear a machinegun might open up on them?"

Skull began to speak, but Rex raised a hand and stopped him.

There was no sound apart from the irregular clatter of serving-spoons and forks. Jacky Bellamy, seated midway between Rex and CH3, took a professional interest in their appearances. Rex had thrust his head forward, slightly turned as if to favour a good ear. CH3 was sitting back, fingers resting on the edge of the table like a concert pianist waiting for his entry. His face was expressionless but his eyes had an interesting glitter.

"You want me to answer that question, sir?" he said. "Very

well. The answer is, Yes, I saw fighters above us in the sun, and Yes, I'm afraid of being shot up with machineguns."

"Thank you, Yellow Three," Rex murmured. He turned to Jacky Bellamy. "I take it you know why he's called Yellow Three."

"Why?"

"Because there isn't a Yellow Four."

It was a CO's joke, so they all laughed. Even CH3 smiled. Watching him, Jacky Bellamy noticed how rarely he blinked. His face was always alert yet always completely under control. She had to force herself to look away.

Kellaway signed the despatch-rider's receipt book and took the envelope into the CO's office. "Addressed to you personally," he said. "From Air Ministry via Rheims."

Rex slit the envelope and shook the contents onto his blotter. Kellaway strolled over to the window and glanced at the sun: a soft yellow disc, soft as butter behind the drifting clouds. He knew he'd never fly a fighter again, yet he couldn't lose this automatic habit of checking the sun. And whenever there was no glare, no dazzle, like today, he always felt better. Safer. More alive. "You know, it's funny," he began.

"This is good," Rex said.

Kellaway turned. Rex was reading a page of a newspaper.

"This is very good," he said. "I tell you, uncle, this isn't bad at all." Gently and carefully he flattened a crease, and read some more. "*Aerial chess, played for the highest stakes* ... I rather like that ..." He was quite overtaken by delight; Kellaway had never seen him so pleased. "Listen to this: *They stalked, they pounced, they struck as one man.* My goodness, this is priceless. Excellent."

Kellaway came and looked over his shoulder. It was a photocopy of a page from a New York newspaper. The headline ran: *RAF Fighters Sweep Skies Over France: German Bomber Knocked Down "With A Flick Of The Wrist": Eyewitness Report*

"She's no fool, that woman," Rex said.

"They don't identify the squadron," Kellaway said. "They couldn't, of course."

"Who cares?" Rex said. "Everyone knows it's us."

Rain began pattering on the skylights of the squash court as LAC Todd arrived.

CH3 was all in white. Todd wore black RAF-issue gym-shoes, black socks, blue football shorts and a proper squash shirt that CH3 had lent him. The gym-shoes were old and squeaky; the shorts were baggy. Todd was much thinner than he looked in his rigger's overalls: his knees and elbows were bony, and his neck still had the sharpness of adolescence. He grinned too much, kept his shoulders hunched, hid his arms behind his back. CH3 knew that the best solution to all this selfconsciousness was a brisk and enjoyable game. He gave Todd a racket and they began whacking the ball about.

For a raw beginner, Todd wasn't bad. He'd obviously played a bit of tennis: he had ball-sense, he judged the bounce well, he enjoyed hammering a volley. CH3 explained the rules and they played a game, with CH3 feeding him shots to give him confidence. Todd was desperately keen to learn, to justify the invitation. He copied everything he saw, and he was touchingly grateful for tips. "Thank you, sir," he said each time, until the American said, "Listen, on court just forget the sir, will you? It makes me feel old and feeble." Todd was startled but pleased. "Your first name's David, isn't it?" CH3 asked. Todd nodded.

The second game was better. Todd was more relaxed, his shots had a more confident flourish. CH3 stopped feeding him and began testing him. The rallies grew longer and harder. Both men were enjoying themselves, but Todd was having the time of his life.

"Look, David," CH3 said between points. "You can save yourself a lot of energy if you . . ." For the first time, Todd was not listening. He was glancing nervously at the gallery overlooking the court. Cattermole, Stickwell and Patterson were looking down on them.

"Hello, David," said Cattermole in a sing-song voice. He sounded like an elderly vicar greeting a favourite choirboy. "Say hello to David, you chaps." Stickwell and Patterson said hello. Stickwell waved his handkerchief.

"Okay, your service," CH3 said, but Todd had come to attention in the presence of these officers.

"Who's your thin friend, Yellow Three?" Stickwell called out.

"I do like those shorts," Patterson said. "Smashing colour. Green, isn't it?"

"I wonder if he'll grow into them?" Cattermole said. "I'll ask him, shall I? David: do you intend to grow into those shorts?"

"Or are you going to share them with a friend?" Stickwell inquired.

"This is LAC Todd," CH3 said. "He's my rigger. If you want to watch, shut up. If you don't want to watch, buzz off."

"Carry on, Yellow Three," Cattermole said with a baronial gesture. "See what you've done?" he told the others, "you've gone and upset him, him and David both, you ought to be ashamed of yourselves. Now behave nicely and watch the clever men hit the silly ball."

Todd served, stiff with tension, and sent the ball flying into the gallery. "Bugger!" he said miserably.

The three officers applauded. "Damn good shot!" Patterson cried. "Hole in one!" Stickwell said. "Game, set and match, isn't it?"

"The ball, please," CH3 called.

"Did the boy David say he'd scored a bugger?" Cattermole asked him. "What is that exactly? Is it like a birdie?"

"It's more like a hole-in-one," Stickwell said.

"Oh, *very* good, Sticky!" Cattermole said. "Did you hear that, Pip? I asked . . ." He began repeating it all.

"I think p'raps I'd better be getting back, sir," Todd muttered. His face was a dull red; his shoulders were hunched again.

"Garbage!" CH3 said. "We haven't finished the game. You might win."

There was more commotion up in the gallery. Miller and Fitzgerald had arrived, both wearing squash kit. " 'B' flight's stood down," Miller said. "Christ, I'm cold!" He leaned over the railing. "Get on with it, you two!" he shouted.

"Stay there. I'll get another ball," CH3 said.

"Honestly, sir, I'd rather not," Todd pleaded.

"Who's that?" Fitzgerald asked Patterson.

"Some rigger, apparently."

"Rigger?" Miller lowered his voice, but not much. "I thought this court was for officers."

"Why aren't they playing?" Fitzgerald asked.

"They haven't got a ball," Stickwell said. "It's all very sad."

CH3 stood staring up at the gallery, spinning the racket in his left hand. The five officers gazed down at him. Abruptly, he turned and put his hand out. "Thanks very much," he said; but Todd was so rattled that he misinterpreted the action and gave back the borrowed racket. CH3 took it and held out his hand again. Todd didn't see it. He was halfway to the door.

"You're absolutely right, Sticky," Cattermole said in a nasal drawl. "It really is very, very sad."

Todd got in and out of the changing room as fast as he could. He bundled his uniform together and headed for the airmen's quarters. CH3 walked with him. "You have a natural ability for that game," he said. "You ought to develop it."

Todd said nothing.

"I mean, with your skill, I bet you'd soon beat any of those clowns back there. They're not so hot."

Todd ducked his head against the flickering rain. He went around a corner and almost collided with his commanding officer.

"Hullo, hullo!" said Rex. "What's the rush?"

Todd stood stiffly, hugging his uniform to his chest.

Rex was wearing a trench-coat and carrying an open umbrella. His other hand twirled a leather leash. He took a pace back and examined Todd. "Been playing football?" he asked cheerfully. "Who won?"

"Squash, sir," CH3 said. "I invited LAC Todd to play squash."

Rex turned his head and peered, as if he had not seen the American before. "Did you, by God?" he said. "Did you really?" He looked at Todd again. "What a frightfully friendly thing to do. And did you find the leading aircraftsman a satisfactory play-mate?" The dog Reilly came galloping across the grass and began busily sniffing ankles.

"It was a good game, sir," CH3 said.

"Oh, I'm sure it was a splendid match." Reilly pissed on Todd's right foot. "No quarrels, no bad temper, just the two of you, alone, grappling with each other, like the athletes on some Greek vase."

"Is that all, sir?" CH3 said. "Because in case you hadn't noticed, it's raining, and your dog has just urinated on this airman."

Rex laughed. "Reilly? No, not possible. Reilly wouldn't do a thing like that, would you, Reilly? Reilly didn't really disgrace himself, did he, Todd?"

LAC Todd stared wretchedly past Rex's left ear.

"Jolly good," Rex said. "Keep up the football. Got to stay fit to beat the Hun, eh? Carry on, Todd." As the airman disappeared into the darkness, Rex said: "I'd like a little chat later on, Yellow Three. Come, Reilly! Off we go."

"Hullo," Corporal King said. "Been swimming?"

Todd dumped his uniform on his bed and found a towel.

"I thought you were playing squish at the Ritz," King said.

"Fucking stupid fucking cunt," Todd said.

"Sorry I spoke."

"Not you. That fucking Yank."

"I told you it wouldn't work," King said. "You wouldn't listen."

"I'd like to kick his fucking stupid head in," Todd said. "He doesn't know his fucking arse from his armpit."

"Just as long as you do," King said, "and just as long as you keep away from both of them. Right?"

When the pilots assembled for drinks before dinner they discovered that the bar was free. By that time everyone had seen Jacky Bellamy's newspaper story; what they didn't know, until the adjutant told them, was that Baggy Bletchley had just telephoned from Headquarters to say that Rex had got the DFC for leading the attack on the Dornier. Tonight, drinks were on the CO.

After dinner CH3 was playing backgammon with Skull when Jacky came over and sat beside them. Without looking up, CH3 said, "No comment and that's final."

"I just want to watch."

"No, you want a story. You people always want a story." He rolled his dice and made a move.

"Unless you're playing for the Crown Jewels there's no story here, is there? Who's winning, anyway?"

"Don't tell her," CH3 warned Skull. "You'll end up in the sports section of the Cleveland *Plain Dealer* with your name mis-spelled."

"I'm surprised at you," she said. "I really am. What happened to the First Amendment? Aren't you fighting for things like the freedom of speech?"

"Not me. I'm in this for the money."

"Eleven shillings a day?" Skull said.

"You don't mean to tell me it's gone up *again*?" CH3 rolled his eyes.

"I can't believe that you want to see newspapers abolished," she said. "So, if they're desirable, why not help to make them better?"

"I don't want to see sewers abolished either, but . . . Look here," he said to Skull, "are you sure you want to do that?" Skull nodded. "Then I re-double you," CH3 said.

"I accept."

"There's a difference, surely," she said, but CH3 refused to be drawn. He played fast, slapping the counters around the board. "Okay," she said, "I don't defend everything that appears in every paper, but I think it's unreasonable for someone as newsworthy as you to expect *not* to be news."

"I don't play in your backyard," CH3 said. "Why should you play in mine?"

Skull said: "What exactly did you do? If it's not an impertinent question, which I realise from what you say it must be, so I withdraw it."

"I made my garden grow."

Skull looked at Jacky Bellamy. "When I knew he was going to be here I checked the record," she said. "Youngest American male to win a gold in the Winter Olympics. Bobsled. Also climbed a couple of mountains that nobody had climbed before. Won a few ocean races. That sort of thing."

"Goodness," Skull said to him. "You *were* busy."

"I was, and it was all my own business. Nothing I ever did made a damn bit of difference to anyone but me."

"Look, you really can't be the judge of that," she said.

He ignored her. "Which is why I never talked to people from newspapers. They were going to get it all wrong anyway. They always do. They sell their papers by telling people what they want to hear, and believe me that's a long way from the truth."

She sat up. Her voice was still calm but her eyes were wide. "You mean for example reports about this war? About cities getting bombed, civilians getting killed?"

"I mean like the sort of junk you just wrote about us."

"How can it be junk? I wrote what I saw."

The game had stopped.

"Sure," he said. "You saw the Dornier get hit and crash and they're all dead. That's fact. What you wrote about the way it happened, that's junk."

242

"The *way* it happened?" She was puzzled. "It was a perfect interception, that's all there was to –"

"Wrong. That Dornier should have got away. Our tactics were terrible. We took half a year to get into position – all that wheeling and shifting and re-arranging formation, it was like Aunt Phoebe's dancing class."

"It worked."

"What did you call it? Aerial chess? Hooey. It wasn't even aerial hopscotch. We didn't stalk that thing. We clumped around the sky like a herd of cows. We didn't use the sun, we didn't use height, we came in dead astern one after another as if we were taking it in turns to go to the lavatory."

"But it *worked*."

"They must have been asleep." Skull was listening carefully. So were two or three nearby pilots. "Those black-and-white wings of ours make this squadron stand out like a chequerboard. Any normal bomber crew would have spotted us first time we banked and gone like hell for home, but they just chugged along. Something was wrong, mechanical failure, oxygen, food poisoning, I don't know what, but that wasn't a normal Dornier 17. It was half-dead when we hit it. An angry canary could have brought it down."

That was too much for the listening pilots, and there were muttered protests. Jacky Bellamy sat back in her chair and looked at him seriously. CH3 said: "Now aren't you sorry you asked?"

She shook her head. "Asking is what the job is all about." She got up and walked away.

"Whose throw is it?" CH3 asked. Skull looked at the dice and frowned. CH3 sighed and scraped the counters into a heap. "Bloody woman," he said.

Fifteen minutes later they had built another game to a beautifully balanced struggle when a mess servant told CH3 the CO would like to see him in his office.

The adjutant and Jacky Bellamy were there too, comfortably seated. ". . . and that was the end of him!" Rex was saying as CH3 came in. They chuckled. "Well now, Mr Hart." Rex took a pipe from a little rack on his desk and squinted into the bowl as if something might be hiding there. "My spies tell me you have been spreading alarm and despondency, contrary to section tiddly-pom of the Defence of the Realm Act."

CH3 said nothing.

Rex began shredding tobacco and filling his pipe. "You have been trying to persuade Miss Bellamy that our successful destruction of an enemy bomber, without loss to ourselves, was a piece of monumental incompetence and an act of folly without parallel in the annals of the Royal Air Force." He stuck the pipe in his mouth.

"No, sir."

"Ah. You mean there is a parallel? Tell me about it."

"No, sir, that's not what I mean, and you know it's not what I mean."

"Oh. Do I?" Rex switched the pipe from one corner of his mouth to the other. "Well, since you seem to understand me better than I understand you, perhaps you'd care to explain yourself."

"All right. Her report made the interception look like a triumph of military aviation. She suggests we won because we outflew the enemy. I don't agree. I think our tactics were lousy and we won because we were lucky."

Rex lit his pipe and studied the American through the smoke. "I see. Now tell me, Mr Hart. Would you say that the Air Staff, who saw fit to commission you and equip you with a Hurricane, are experienced and intelligent men?"

"I guess they do their best."

Kellaway uttered a little high-pitched snort: whether of surprise or amusement it was hard to say.

"But their best is not good enough for you. The Air Staff created the system of Fighting Area Attacks to destroy enemy bombers. I used one such Attack. We destroyed one such bomber. You, however, feel that we should have acted otherwise."

"Yes."

"You think that the combined and unanimous opinion of the Air Fighting School, the Air Staff, and the Commander-in-Chief Fighter Command, Sir Hugh Dowding, is wrong?"

"Yes."

"You think that a pilot officer with less than a month's experience in France is qualified to rewrite the Manual of Air Tactics?"

CH3 breathed in deeply through his nose. "*Yes,*" he said. He heard the ice-cubes tinkle in the adjutant's glass.

"Why?" Rex was getting impatient. He tossed his pipe into a huge glass ashtray. "What makes you so amazingly qualified?"

"Spain."

"Not good enough. Spain was a scruffy little civil war. An insurrection. No proper front, and lots of garlicky peasants getting their heads blown off because the anarcho-syndicalists wouldn't take orders from the Marxist-Trotskyites. Typical dago shambles, in fact."

"The Germans learned a lot from it."

"Your side lost, I believe."

"That's not the point. We should take advantage of the German experience and –"

"My dear Hart, I'm here to smash the Hun, not to imitate him. Now, if you have any specific tactical proposal to make, I'm prepared to listen."

CH3 thought for a moment, and shook his head. "Let's not waste each other's time, sir. If you're convinced the official tactics are right, you won't budge whatever I say."

Rex stared at him for several seconds. "A piece of advice, Hart," he said. "While you are in my squadron, if you cannot speak courteously, then better to remain silent. That's all."

Skull had gone to bed, but Fanny Barton, Flip Moran and Moke Miller were still at the bar. "I take it you have been suitably chastised, young man," Moran said. "Have a drink."

"More than chastised," CH3 said. "I have been converted. I'll take a beer, thanks."

"Converted to what?" Barton asked.

"The new air tactics. Haven't you heard? From now on we're to attack the enemy in alphabetical order. I tell you, it's revolutionary."

"But we won't know the Jerry pilots' names," Miller objected. "Or am I being dense?"

"Don't worry, that's only on Tuesdays and Fridays. Mondays and Thursdays we take off in order of height, shortest first and tallest last, and we attack in order of age, starting with the youngest. Shouldn't you be taking notes?"

"The pencil's broken," Moran said.

"Also there's a relationship between altitude and inside-leg measurement, but I've forgotten what exactly. I'm afraid Rex became a little incoherent after he chewed my head off and swallowed it."

"Don't expect any sympathy from me," Barton said. "You asked for trouble and you got it."

CH3 sipped his beer.

"Let's face it, old boy, you were talking a lot of balls," Miller said.

CH3 grunted. "I suppose the whole thing is a grim warning never to speak to the press."

"You can't blame Jacky," Moran said quickly. "If you say her story's all wrong, she's got to do something. She has to go to the CO. You gave her no choice."

"You don't particularly like newspaper people, do you?" Miller asked.

"That's got nothing to do –"

"All right, let's forget it," Barton said. "You've just put up a small black, CH3, that's all. It's not wildly important. Let's all forget it."

Moran nudged the American. "You know what they say in England," he told him in his heavy Ulsterman's voice. "If you can't say anything nice, then for the love of Christ don't say anything at all." He nodded sternly. "Begorrah," he added. "Whatever that means."

Next morning Area Operations sent the squadron to patrol a section of the Maginot Line south of Strasbourg. The weather was a strange mixture of gusty rainstorms and bright, warm sunshine. When they flew through rain the clouds towered and overhung them, leaking blackness as if soaked in ink. When they reached sunlight the clouds became sparkling white terraces, hugely spaced. They were only at five thousand feet but the air was sharply cold.

Rex allowed the formation to loosen when they met turbulence but as soon as they entered smooth air he called them together again. Only one aircraft gave him trouble. Yellow Three was frequently out of position, sometimes by as much as a length. Each time he looked around, it seemed, the American's Hurricane was drifting away like a feckless child. There were no enemy aircraft about, indeed no aircraft of any kind to be seen except for one very highflying machine that Rex spotted when it was too far inside Germany to be pursued; but there was always the possibility of flak, and there was navigation to be done, there were landmarks to be looked for, weather to be watched. "Close *up*, Yellow Three," he said yet again.

"Closing up, Leader."

They hit the fringe of a heavy shower. Rain-drops smeared the cockpit canopy, coated it, got blasted away by the rush of dry air. Rex glanced to left and right. "For God's sake close up," he said.

Pause. "Closing up, Leader."

"Look: what's the matter with you?"

No answer.

"Jester Leader to Yellow Three, is your aircraft faulty?"

"Not faulty, Leader."

"Are you unwell?"

"Not unwell, Leader."

"Then for God's sake hold formation. I've got better things to do than watch you all the time."

Long pause. Then: "Yes."

"What the hell's that supposed to mean?" Rex looked across at CH3. The man wasn't even paying attention: he was gazing up at the clouds.

"Message understood, Leader." Already, Yellow Three was ten feet out of position. Far away on the other side of the squadron, a burst of French flak soiled the sky. Rex ignored it. "Hopeless," he muttered.

When the squadron landed, Rex strode across the turf towards Fanny Barton. Barton saw him coming and raised a hand to forestall him. "I know," he said.

"You're his flight commander, Fanny. Sort him out. Right?"

"Right, sir."

"Good." Rex turned away. "Now, where's the only intelligent member of this squadron?"

Rex's rigger slipped the leash, and Reilly came bounding across the airfield. Rex ran lumberingly towards him, arms spread in greeting.

Fanny followed CH3 into the flight commander's office and kicked a chair as an invitation to sit. "I'm supposed to give you a bollocking," Fanny said. "Frankly, I think it's too damn childish for that. You do realise you're behaving very childishly? You can formate as well as any of us, when you want to. Last night the CO put you in your place, quite rightly in my opinion, and today you do all you can to ruin the formation. I call that childish." Fanny stopped speaking. He realised that the other man wasn't listening. CH3 had put his feet on the table. His head was tipped back and he was blowing steadily at the ceiling, where a balsa-wood model of an Me-109 hung from a thread. His breath made the fighter sway.

"Lovely little plane," he said, almost to himself. "You know, Fanny, this is my third war. I should have learned how to lose gracefully by now, shouldn't I? I can't seem to get the knack."

Fanny thought about that for a moment. The most he had accomplished so far was the confirmed destruction of one Blenheim. He abandoned the idea of a bollocking, and sat down. "*Three* wars?" he said.

"Yes. When we didn't win in Spain I went to China and you know what? We didn't win there, either. So I came back and joined the RAF. Nobody seemed to mind my depressing record."

"You know what the British are like. They admire a good loser."

"Mmm. Trouble is, I'm a *bad* loser. I remember we had one outstandingly good loser in Spain. We called him Harry because he was a Pole and his real name sounded like broken bottles. Harry was a great believer in showing the enemy who was boss. No dodging about: that was sissy. Fly straight and low and treat them with the contempt they deserve. I'll say this for Harry: he knew which side the angels were on."

Fanny waited. "What happened to him?"

"Oh . . ." CH3 stretched, and laughed at the memory. "Well, one day Harry told three of us we were going to demoralise the daylights out of some enemy unit or other. So off we went. In Polikarpovs. Ever seen one? Tubby little Russian biplane, not bad for combat, no good if you plan to fly through a hail of death. Not that I'd ever actually been through a hail of death, but when we reached the target we discovered it had a great number of German flak batteries around it. Let me tell you, Fanny: German flak is very good. Harry didn't give a damn. Harry led us in at two hundred feet, straight and level, spreading a thick layer of contempt as we went. Not me. I took one look at that flak and I turned and I beat it. Harry and the others lasted four, maybe five seconds. Then the flak blew them away. Simply blew all three of them away: *poof-poof-poof*, just like that. It was really very funny, the way it happened. Like a Disney cartoon. I know I laughed all the way home."

Fanny did not smile. "No joke for Harry and his wingmen, though."

"Harry was a joke to start with."

"A very expensive joke." Fanny stood up; he did not approve of making fun of war. "Now then: what's to be done?"

"Nothing." CH3 swung his feet to the floor. "I'm not going to keep tight formation when we're on patrol. It's stupid. Eleven men watching each others' wingtips and tails, while the leader looks at the sky? No thanks. I'll make myself some space so I can stop worrying about a collision and use my eyes to see Jerry before Jerry sees me."

"If we all behaved like that," Fanny said stiffly, "the entire squadron would be scattered all over the sky."

"Sure. That's how Jerry learned to fly in Spain. They call it the finger-four." CH3 spread his fingers like a fan. "Two pairs, wide apart. No sweat, and very useful."

"But no damn good for Fighting Area Attacks. They *depend* on tight formation flying."

"Yes. Another reason to scrap them."

Fanny stared. He felt both angry and baffled. "You're bloody determined to go your own sweet way, aren't you? Squadron discipline and loyalty and . . . and . . ." He couldn't think of another word. "They mean nothing to you?"

"Not a damn thing. I told you: I'm a bad loser. There's only one thing I care about, and that's not getting jumped by a Messerschmitt." CH3 was relaxed and smiling; the fingers of his left hand beat out a happy little rhythm on the edge of the desk. "There were Messerschmitts around this morning, I'm sure of it. All that sun and cloud? Right up their alley. I could smell 'em!"

"Pity you couldn't see them."

CH3 looked at his watch. "How about some lunch?"

Fanny did not move. He made his voice as flat and empty as he could. "You'll get kicked out if you go on like this."

"So what? I didn't ask to be posted here. I was very happy flying Spits at Hornchurch, you know."

"You might get sacked from that, too."

"Come on, Fanny. I'm hungry."

249

"You won't co-operate?"

CH3 walked to the door. "I don't mind dying for freedom or democracy or King George the Sixth or whatever the hell it is we're fighting for," he said, "but I'm damned if I'll die to satisfy Rex's neat and tidy mind."

They went to lunch.

As Rex came bustling downstairs with Reilly, heading for a teatime walk, he heard someone hammering in the anteroom.

It turned out to be Moggy Cattermole. He was standing on a chair by the wall opposite the bar. "Hullo, hullo," Rex said. "What's all this?"

"Squadron trophies, sir." Moggy climbed down to give him a clear view of three wooden plaques, which he had hung on the wall. Mounted on the left-hand plaque was a fox's brush. "You remember what a battle we had with that brute, up in the mountains? Worth recording, I thought."

Rex pointed to the middle plaque, on which was mounted a much longer tail. "Where the devil did that come from?"

"Blunt end of a horse, sir. The one I shot after it went mad and tried to eat me. Very savage beast."

"Oh." Rex flicked the tail with his gloves. "Horse, eh?"

"Well, we had to pay for it, so I thought –"

"And what's this?" Rex craned his neck. "Looks like a boot."

"It is a boot, sir. The remains of one, anyway." The sole had sprung loose, the uppers were scarred and stained, and the top had been very roughly chopped off above the ankle. "It came out of the Dornier. This was about the only thing we could find that was big enough to have mounted."

Rex sniffed. "Is it ... um ... empty?"

"Oh, yes, sir." Cattermole spun the hammer in the air and snatched at it. "I gave it a jolly good shake," he said as he stooped for the hammer.

"And you've got one more, I see."

"Yes, sir." He picked up the fourth plaque. It carried the broken spade-grip from the top of a control column. "Memento of the squadron's first kill. Slightly before your time, of course."

"You don't mean the Battle of Southend Sands?"

"Yes, I couldn't get a bit of the actual Blenheim Fanny potted, but one joystick looks much like another, and –"

"Definitely not, Moggy."

"Oh. Really, sir?"

"It's simply not on, old boy."

Cattermole sighed. "If you say so, sir."

"A question of form, you see."

"Oh well. Bang goes fifty francs."

"It wouldn't be the proper form. I mean, just suppose it got into the papers. To tell the truth, I'm not altogether happy about that boot . . . Still, leave it up for the present. We've got to be so damned careful nowadays . . ." Rex summoned Reilly and went out.

Cattermole watched him go. He smoothed the horse's tail, straightened the plaque with the boot on, and looked at the broken spade-grip. "They don't make them like they used to," he said.

He went upstairs and knocked on CH3's door. The American was lying on his bed, reading a letter.

"Got a minute?" said Cattermole.

"Depends what you want to do with it."

"I want to roll it up, set fire to it, and stuff it up your backside," Cattermole said amiably.

"See my agent." CH3 turned a page. "He takes care of that sort of thing."

"I don't expect you to understand this, because you're an American, but the fact is you're not playing the game, Hart."

CH3 put down his letter.

"I mean to say: all that piffle you were talking with the Bellamy woman last night. And your boorish behaviour this morning." Cattermole wandered over to the dressing-table and began using the hairbrush. "It's not fair on the CO, that's all. I mean, you don't take advantage of a fellow when he's just won the DFC. It's simply not on."

"I haven't been taking advantage of him. I just don't agree with him."

"Fine. Splendid. Excellent." Cattermole put down the hairbrush and inspected the shadows under his eyes. "All we ask is that you shut up and do as you're told."

"If you're looking for the mascara, it's under my handkerchiefs."

Cattermole turned away from the mirror. "He works damned

hard, you know. It's no joke leading a fighter squadron, and you're making his job considerably harder."

"Don't worry about it, Moggy. You know what? You're looking a little peaky yourself."

"I said you wouldn't understand. It's a question of knowing the proper form, I suppose. Well . . ." Cattermole shrugged his shoulders. "If you won't play the game for the CO's sake, you might spare a thought for the other chaps. *They* know when they're well-off, even if you don't. I don't suppose you've noticed it, but . . ." He stroked his nose. "We're a very lucky squadron."

CH3 got off the bed. "I don't suppose you notice it, Moggy," he said, "but whenever you go all sincere, you have a heavy fall of dandruff." He brushed Cattermole's shoulders with his hands.

"Listen, Hart: who d'you think pays our mess bills? How do we manage to afford all this terrific grub? And wine? And English beer? And stuff like new squash rackets and gramophone records and the latest magazines all the time? Eh? Ever thought about that?"

"You're snowing again, Moggy."

"I'll tell you who pays: Squadron Leader Rex. Of course we each give our little cheque to the adj, but that doesn't cover half the cost. Hornet squadron is the luckiest squadron in Fighter Command, and it's all thanks to Rex, who happens to be the best CO any of us has ever known."

"So you say."

"And it's about time you realised it."

"You mean if I don't start behaving nicely, Rex will cancel the *Tatler* and we'll all live on cheese sandwiches?"

"I mean there is such a thing as self-control and consideration for others. What we call 'good manners.' "

"Oh, oh." CH3 put on his shoes. "Any time the British mention manners, watch out for a kick in the gut."

Cattermole twitched his nostrils. "Very glib, very transatlantic. It's what I should have expected. After all, with your money, you can afford to be selfish."

CH3 doubled up, clutching his stomach and moaning.

Cattermole watched with distaste. "Look here, Hart," he said. For the first time there was real anger in his voice. "If you can't

252

develop some real squadron spirit, why don't you just buzz off?" He strode out, leaving the door wide open.

When CH3 went downstairs he met the adjutant. "A word in your ear, old chap," Kellaway said. They went into the library. "Far be it from me to curb a chap's style," he said.

"That's good," CH3 said, "because everyone else keeps trying to."

"Do they? Can't say I'm surprised. You do sometimes rock the boat a bit, you know, and that makes things uncomfortable for everyone."

"For instance."

"Well, take last night, that little shenanigan over Jacky Bellamy's report. There was absolutely no need to ridicule the squadron the way you did. That just upset everybody."

"Tactics. I criticised the tactics."

"Maybe that's what you *meant* to do. But you lashed out so violently that you did more damage than you thought. Squadron spirit . . ." Kellaway straightened a book. "It's a very precious thing, you know."

"But I was right, adj."

"That's another point. There are ways of making suggestions, changing things, putting your ideas across, and I don't mind telling you: your way won't work. Too much loud pedal. People resent it."

"You mean the CO resents it."

Kellaway thought before answering. He strolled across the room, examined a couple of titles, strolled back. "I've been in this Service for over twenty years," he said. "Some of the men I flew with are air marshals now. Perhaps I'm old-fashioned, but when a pilot officer tells a squadron leader that the C-in-C Fighter Command has got his tactics all wrong, I don't find it particularly funny."

"What did you expect me to say to him? It's true. The system of Fighting Area Attacks stinks "

"There you go again."

"All right, let's say it's unreal, it's clumsy, it –"

"You've never seen it work, old chap. You can't condemn it."

CH3 waved an arm in exasperation and hit a lampshade. Light and shadow chased each other over the room. "Sorry . . . You forget the Dornier, adj, that poor pathetic –"

"No, I don't. But Fighting Area Attacks are designed to destroy bomber *formations*, whole squadrons or even wings of enemy bombers, all flying in a mass."

"It makes no difference, for Pete's sake! In Spain we –"

"In Spain you weren't part of a Hurricane squadron."

CH3 took a deep breath, held it in his lungs, let it out slowly. "I know I'm right," he said.

Kellaway looked at him for a moment. "You weren't right yesterday afternoon, though, were you?" he said.

CH3 cocked his head. "Wasn't I?"

"Your game of squash with LAC Todd. That court is for officers only."

"So I've been told. Simple snobbery. One of the less attractive features of the Royal Air Force."

"And you decided to change it."

"Sure. You can have your class system, but don't expect me to adopt it. Todd's a human being, the equal of any of us, and I'll treat him as such."

"Yes? Even if the result of your treatment is that Todd is thoroughly embarrassed and humiliated?"

"That wasn't my fault."

"Todd thinks it was. He's asked to be moved. Transferred to 'B' flight."

For once CH3 had nothing to say.

"It's worse than that." There was nothing friendly about Kellaway now. "Todd is on a charge. He got into a fight. It seems that another airman had been provoking him, making unpleasant suggestions about his sporting relationship with an officer, so Todd hit him."

CH3 groaned.

"Unfortunately, Todd got rather badly knocked about. He's not really built for brawling."

"When does his charge come up? I can give evidence –"

"No fear. You're the last person Todd wants helping him in any way. He's made that very clear."

CH3 threw up his hands. "None of it makes sense."

"On the contrary, it makes very good sense. We have a system, and by and large it works, provided people like you don't mess it about. You were wrong about Todd, weren't you? It's not

254

inconceivable that you might be wrong about some other things, too."

"No, there's a difference. Anyway, who cares? I'm never going to agree with Rex, and very soon Rex is going to get fed up with that and kick me out. So I've got nothing to lose, have I?"

Kellaway rubbed his eyes. "Come on," he said wearily. "The sight of all these books makes me dry. I'll buy you a drink."

November went out in a prolonged storm of wind and rain, turning to sleet. Very little flying was possible: just occasionally the wind dropped enough to let an individual Hurricane go up for height-testing or to check some modification. One of these flights went violently wrong.

The pilot involved was Mother Cox. He took off and entered the cloudbase at three thousand feet. He could scarcely see his wingtips; moisture raced over his canopy; the aircraft lurched and bumped like a farmcart. To his surprise, he found that he was enjoying himself. The fighter felt strong. He trusted his instruments and he had faith in his own ability. For a moment he suffered a flicker of anxiety: such confidence was worrying. Then he took an enormous chance and decided not to worry about anything, not even about his peace of mind. He tried it, and it worked. Nothing fell off the aeroplane. Mother Cox burst out of cloud and climbed into sunlight that filled the vastness of the sky like a shout of freedom.

At ten thousand feet he levelled off and took a good long look at his domain. He was the sole and undisputed tenant of heaven. One mile below, a colossal quilt of snowy cloud had the decency to hide the gloomy Earth from him. When he looked up, the blue was so endlessly perfect that his eye began searching for a scratch or a speck; but the only distraction was a smear on the Perspex. From time to time, the cockpit buzzed or trembled to the throaty power of the Merlin.

Mother Cox let the nose drop a few inches and celebrated his good fortune with a long, slow barrel-roll. It went so well – hand and foot and eye smoothly co-ordinating to sling the Hurricane around the inside of a great invisible cylinder – that he did it again. Halfway through, when he was upside-down, there was a bang like a whack from a sledgehammer. The plane buckled and things whizzed past the cockpit. At once the engine began to scream and race; everything vibrated furiously: Cox was shaken in his straps until his teeth rattled. The Hurricane skewed drunkenly, as if trying to fly belly-first. The instruments were a blur. But the scream of the engine was the worst: the Merlin sounded agonised. Cox fumbled, found the throttle, dragged it back.

The noise sank to a moan and the vibration faded to nothing. He found the horizon and worked the plane back to more or less its normal flying attitude, except that it was badly nose-down. Then he saw that he had no propeller. He switched off the engine. The hub stopped spinning. All that was left was a couple of splintered stubs.

By the time he had told the tower, he was very near the cloud, gliding in a steep spiral. It was not until he entered the cloud and experienced almost total silence, as well as gloom and wetness, that he began to be afraid. Everything felt wrong: his senses told him he was going uphill and must stall. He forced himself to believe the instruments. When he dropped out of the cloudbase he couldn't see the aerodrome and panic squeezed his guts. But the tower saw him, and a voice in his ear told him which way to steer.

The Hurricane was eager to get down. It was always trying to fall forward. He kept tugging the nose up, watching the airspeed, feeling the start of a wallow, pushing the nose down, searching for the field, willing it nearer, hearing the whirr of air get louder, tugging the nose up again.

The ground was all trees and barns and lakes. There was one decent-looking meadow but by the time he saw it, it was under him. If he turned, he might fall out of the sky. He went on.

Crash drill. What was the crash drill? A running fight was going on between his imagination and his intelligence. He felt like a helpless spectator. *Tighten your straps!* The instruction seemed to drift sideways into his mind. He contemplated it for a few seconds, decided it was a good idea, and did it. *Open your hood!* Yes, that was right, too. But he had to loosen his straps to do it. Something wrong there. He heaved the hood back, and was amazed to hear the whinny of a horse. Other noises reached him: crows calling, the buzz of a motorcycle.

What else? He tightened his straps again. Undercarriage? *Use your hand pump!* He hand-pumped the wheels down and immediately felt the drag slow the aircraft. *Oh Christ, Cox, now you've done it, you bloody fool, now you've killed yourself* . . . The ground ahead was all bumps and holes. Landing there, wheels down, meant a cartwheel for certain. With nearly full tanks, too. He slid between the tops of two trees and startled a woodpigeon: it clattered away, climbing steadily. "Lucky sod," Cox said miserably. A long gust of wind bent the treetops and helped to hold the Hurricane up. He crossed the perimeter fence with inches to spare. His wheels were so near the wire that he instinctively hoisted his feet.

The jolt and tremble of his tyres on the grass was a glorious sensation. Inside his gloves his hands were slippery with sweat. He let the plane run to a halt, and he was still slumped in the cockpit when the first truck reached him. Fanny Barton leaped up. "What happened?" he asked. Cox tried to speak but failed. He was trembling like a patient in fever. They had to help him out, and then help him walk.

Jacky Bellamy was away, in Metz, when all this happened. It was evening by the time she returned. Fitz and Flash passed her on their way out. "Hullo, Jacky!" Flash shouted. "Heard about poor old Mother?"

"No?"

"Nearly died of fright, silly blighter. Can't stop, we're late."

She looked into the anteroom, the library, the billiard room. All empty. The entire squadron seemed to have gone out. As she was walking from an empty reading-room to an empty coffee-room, faint music reached her. She followed the sounds to the ballroom. CH3 was sitting at a grand piano, trying to improvise a blues and making rather a mess of it.

She leaned on the piano and watched his fingers stumble and trip and go back and stumble again, until he finished the sequence and looked up. She was trying not to laugh. "I got *Stardust*," she said, "and a bit of *Stormy Weather*, but what was *The Ride of the Valkyries* doing in there?"

"Just making up the numbers." He ran a finger up the keyboard and reached for his glass.

She sensed that, for the first time, he wanted to talk; and immediately she distrusted the feeling: it was too close to her own strong wishes. Yet the sense of his loneliness persisted. That glance, when he first looked up, had stayed on her for a second or two longer than was strictly necessary. "It's quiet tonight," she said.

"I guess they've all gone out." She reached into the piano and plucked a string. "What's all this about Mother Cox?"

"Nothing." He began working on some chords. "Nothing to interest you."

"I'm interested already."

"Your readers wouldn't understand."

"I'll explain. That's my job."

"If you explained properly they wouldn't read it."

"Why not?"

He gave her a look of wide-eyed amusement. "Because they don't want to know what flying fighters is really like. They prefer the comic-strip version, it suits their Mickey-Mouse minds. So that's what you've got to serve up, isn't it? Lots of fearless gung-ho action." He abandoned the chords and started on a ragged melody. "Mother's little accident wouldn't please them at all."

He added an uncertain left hand to the ragged melody. After a little while she turned and went out.

Ten minutes later she was back. "I found Micky Marriott and he told me the whole story. Well, not quite all. He couldn't explain why Mother was in such a state of collapse."

"Mother thought he was going to die, obviously." CH3 turned his back on the piano and rested his elbows on the keyboard: two bundles of notes clashed. He let the noise fade. "But you can't write that. It's unattractive."

"I still don't understand. It was an emergency, I realise that, but Mother's a trained pilot. Why go all to pieces once he'd –"

"A Hurricane weighs three tons. Without a propeller it flies like this Bechstein." He banged the bass keys with his elbow. "People don't enjoy the prospect of sudden death. It upsets them."

"Micky says he's asleep. Exhausted."

"Well, I've seen tough, grown-up fighter pilots land without the strength left to blow their nose. Don't tell your editor, he wouldn't approve." He shrugged. "Naturally you've missed the real story, but don't worry: he wouldn't like that either."

"What real story?"

"Why the Hurricane still has a wooden prop when the Me-109 has a metal job, and with variable pitch too."

"Micky says you're getting metal props."

"That's progress. Now all we need to do is throw away the rest of the plane and fix a Spitfire to the prop."

"You really rate the Hurricane that badly?"

"I might, if I gave it much thought." He exercised his neck; it was a habit he had. "As it is I don't expect to be here long enough to care."

She walked to where she could look him in the face. "Why won't you let yourself like me?" she asked. "I'm not asking for a mad passionate love-affair, just . . ."

"Aren't you?" He made his fists into binoculars and studied her.

"All right, then: I *am* asking for a mad passionate love-affair, but I know darn well I'm not going to get one so I'll settle for some old-fashioned friendship. I mean, that wouldn't break your bank, would it?" Her voice was level and quiet. "We're here, so why not enjoy it? Why make the worst of it?"

He lowered his hands. "I didn't join Fighter Command to enjoy myself."

"Yes, you are. You're just not prepared to admit it."

He was looking away, staring at a knot in the floorboards, covering and uncovering it with his foot.

She sighed. "Oh well," she said lightly. "You've won again, I suppose. It must get very boring for you, always making fools of fools like me. Goodnight."

"I bet you don't use those stories," he said. As she went out, he was playing again: the same old stumbling, clumsy, splayed-note blues.

DECEMBER
1939

Winter stopped toying with storms of rain and sleet, and got down to serious business.

For three days and nights the sky dumped snow. It fell thickly, with a stiff westerly wind always bringing up fresh supplies. It fell so fast that one man with a shovel could not keep fifty yards of pathway open. By the second day, the drifts were chest-high, the airfield was cut off, and the mess was obliged to use tinned milk. By the third day the electricity and telephone lines were down and the mess was candle-lit. Snow coated the windows on the exposed side of the house, darkening the interior even more. Periodically, masses of snow lost their grip on the roof and tumbled thunderously to the ground. Log fires blazed night and day. There was nowhere to go, nothing to do. Boredom became acute. On the third afternoon Moke Miller came into the anteroom and announced that Sticky Stickwell was reading a book. This was not believed. Miller led the rest of the squadron to the library. "See!" he said.

"Is this wise, Sticky?" asked Cattermole. "You know what the doctors said."

"What?"

"Too much reading turns your eyeballs hairy."

"That's not funny. You'd think I'd never read a book before."

"Have you?" asked Fitz.

"Of course I have. It was very interesting. It had a green cover, just like this one. This one is very interesting, too."

"In your experience, as a reader of green-covered books," said Flip Moran, "would you say they tend to be on the interesting side?"

"Piss off," Stickwell said.

"He's non-committal," Mother Cox told Moran. "I've seen it happen before in cases like this."

"Stupid sods," Stickwell muttered.

"Did you hear that? Alliteration!" Moran exclaimed. "The poor devil's alliterating already."

"Well, he'll just have to clean it up afterwards," Cattermole said. They trooped back to the anteroom. "What's alliteration?" Miller asked Fitz. "Dunno," Fitz said, "but you get it from books."

The fourth day was windless and dazzlingly bright. Rex had every man in the unit shovelling snow, and by mid-afternoon the driveway leading to the road was open. The pilots retired to the bar and compared their blisters. There was much talk of visiting Rheims or even Paris as soon as the snowploughs cleared the road. By nightfall it was snowing hard again. Skull and Kellaway went out onto the terrace before dinner. The air was like a pillowfight. "Funny stuff, French snow," said Kellaway. "Not a bit like English snow."

"Hmm." Skull made no comment. Kellaway was a good chap, and remarkably adept at persuading drunks to go to bed, but he would sentimentalise so.

"Just look at it! Typical. Never knows when to stop."

"I expect it's the same in Germany," Skull said.

"Worse. Much worse. They haven't got the Gulf Stream, you see."

"Neither have we."

"Yes we have. It comes up past the Scilly Isles. Daffodils, early potatoes. I know, I went there for holidays."

"This is France, uncle."

"You're telling me! Just look at it. God knows the weather was bad enough in '14–'18 . . . What a country! They've simply got no idea."

"I thought you rather liked the French."

"Wouldn't give you tuppence for the lot of them. Come on in, I'm freezing."

In fact it was getting much colder. After a week of sporadic snowstorms the temperature stayed below freezing and the sky had the chill grey of hammered lead. Micky Marriott improvised a snowplough on the front of a three-ton truck and bashed a path to the airfield, by which time the truck's clutch was burnt out. He kept a few groundcrew in the hangars around the clock, warming up the engines every few hours to keep the oil fluid. But there was no chance of any flying.

Rex made the best of it: he sent two men on leave – Patterson and Miller – and he took a week's leave himself. "Try and keep them occupied," he said to Barton and Moran as he got into his car. "I don't want the squadron putting up any blacks while I'm away, especially with the frogs."

The flight commanders went inside. "The old man's away for a week," Barton announced.

"Whoopee!" Cattermole said. "Now we can get down to some

steady raping and looting, with a spot of arson to keep the cold out."

Barton turned on him. "Listen, you," he said, aiming a forefinger like a gun. "Any playing silly-buggers and you won't know what's hit you."

Cattermole stared. "It was a joke, Fanny," he said.

The rest of the squadron watched, hoping for an exciting bust-up to enliven the grey morning.

"Bloody silly joke," Barton said. "Just keep your peculiar sense of humour to yourself for the next seven days."

As the flight commanders went out, Cattermole slumped in his armchair until he slid off the seat and collapsed on the floor. "Crushed and humiliated," he said.

"Well, what did you expect, you great oaf?" Mother Cox asked.

"Fanny hasn't forgotten those carthorses," Stickwell said. "Also the secret Polish phrase-book."

"*Jag tycker om det!*" cried Flash Gordon. It was always good for a laugh.

"I've forgotten what that means," Stickwell said.

"Old Cherokee proverb," CH3 told him. "It means: a prune is a plum that thinks too much."

"Look here, you squalid crew." Cattermole stood up and scowled. "I want you to be on your best behaviour while Rex is away." He kicked Fitzgerald on the leg. "D'you hear me?" He threw a small leather pouffe at Cox. "No mucking about! Fanny and Flip expect us to behave nicely, so . . ." He tipped CH3 out of his chair. ". . . so we mustn't disappoint them. Got that?"

"What d'you mean, a prune is a plum that thinks too much?" Sticky asked the American, who lay where he fell, quite relaxed. "That doesn't make any sense."

"It does if you're a prune," Flash Gordon said.

"Think about it," CH3 said lazily.

"No fear," Sticky said. "I don't want to end up all wrinkled."

"Remember!" Cattermole said. "I've warned you."

The flight commanders went to see the adjutant. "Well, they can't get into much trouble here, can they?" Kellaway said.

"What about when they're not here?" Fanny said. "We can't keep them confined to camp all week."

"I don't suppose you could send them on a tour of inspection of the Maginot Line?" Flip suggested. "A walking tour."

"Tell you what I can do." Kellaway fumbled through a heap of papers, and found a letter. "Invitation from a local vineyards. Trip round the works, lunch with the boss, sampling in the cellars."

"They'd like that, the swine."

Fanny nodded. "Knowing them, they won't be able to crawl for two days afterwards. Got anything else, adj?"

"Leave it with me. I'll see what I can drum up."

The tour of the vineyards was a great success. Next day the pilots were suitably subdued when they visited an anti-aircraft regiment near Châlons; they were even quieter after the soldiers had demonstrated the quick-firing capability of their batteries. Sticky Stickwell, who had been slow to move away, was still slightly deaf the following day, when they went down a coalmine for no particular reason except that it was a large mine and would take a lot of walking through. After that came a snowstorm, which filled a day, and then there was an official visit to Strasbourg.

The city was deserted. It faced the German frontier, and at the outbreak of war the entire population of two hundred thousand had been moved out. As they drove through it, the Hornet pilots saw an occasional gendarme or military policeman patrolling the bare streets; otherwise nothing: even the pigeons seemed to have gone.

They went to a French army strongpoint on the Rhine; and a hundred yards away, on the opposite bank, they saw their first German soldiers. They were kicking a football about. One of them headed the ball and knocked his helmet off. Laughter came gently but clearly across the hustling black waters.

"This is all very chummy," Kellaway said to the French officer who was their guide.

"It is absurd. Ridiculous. Last month they put up a big banner: *C'est à votre attaque seul que nous riposterons!*"

"Come again?" said Flash Gordon.

Skull said: "We won't fight if you won't."

"What did you do?" asked Kellaway.

"We used that." The Frenchman nodded at a black van with the huge horn of a loudspeaker on top. "Selections from *Mein Kampf*. How Hitler planned to annihilate France."

"Ah-ha! Jolly clever. I bet that shut them up."

"No, it was a mistake. Now they have their own loudspeaker. You will hear."

"Haven't they painted something on that wall?" Mother Cox pointed across the river.

"It says: *La France aux Français*," the officer told him.

"Funny thing for a Hun to say."

"They're trying to foment distrust," Skull explained. "Implying that we British are meddling in French affairs."

"We have made our response," the French officer said. He showed them a wall on which was painted *La Pologne aux Polonais!*

"I thought that was a sort of a dance," Fitzgerald said.

"It is," CH3 said. "France for the French, Poland for the foxtrot. Get it?"

"Ah." Fitzgerald nodded doubtfully. "Yes."

"Very French. Very sardonic."

"I suppose so." Fitz forced a brief, suspicious smile.

"*Jag tycker om det*," Flash Gordon said brightly, but nobody laughed.

"Here they come," said the French officer gloomily. "Punctual as usual."

A company of German troops marched out and faced the French bank. At a signal, they waved. Another signal: they stopped. "Ten seconds of friendship," the Frenchman said. "Now they sing." At once the soldiers sang, their voices enormously amplified by a loudspeaker van twice as big as the French one.

"I can't stomach that," Kellaway complained. "Let's see about lunch, eh?"

They went back to the cars. Before they got in, Barton counted heads. One man was missing: Stickwell. "Go and find him, Moggy," Moran said.

"No fear. He's nothing to do with me."

"We can't go without him."

"Yes, we can. Wonderful opportunity."

"Sticky!" Fitzgerald shouted. "Where are you, Sticky?"

No answer.

"I expect he's gone to the pictures," Cattermole said. "He's very keen on the pictures. Come on, I'm hungry."

A voice suddenly boomed at them like an angry god. "*This is the BBC Home Service. Here are the latest cricket scores. Middlesex, 418 for 3; Surrey, 26 all out. Not much of an innings from Surrey but what the hell can you expect from the dump where Moggy lives? Bugger-all. Next: Somerset, 418 for 9 ..."*

"I'll break his bloody neck," Fanny Barton said. "Come on."

The voice went on, harsh and thunderous and ceaseless. It competed with the German choir and won.

"... who is wanted by the police for indecent exposure. Uncle Kellaway is eighty-three years old and wears a red wig. Now for some gardening news. This is the time to prune your peas, or pee on your prunes, please yourself, I don't give a damn ..."

They tracked down the French loudspeaker van. It was parked behind a timberyard.

"Stickwell! Shut up!" Barton shouted as he advanced.

"... No news from Africa, where things look black, but the weather forecast shows a deep depression surrounding Fanny Barton, who's just coming into the straight and making a late burst, yes, it's Fanny Barton out in front and as they come to the post it's Fanny Barton ..." The van jumped forward and accelerated away. *"... it's Fanny Barton finishing second!"* the loudspeaker bellowed triumphantly, *"and the rest are nowhere!"* The van disappeared around the corner, still shouting.

When they got back to the cars, Stickwell was sitting in a back seat, pretending to read a French newspaper. The van was not to be seen. "Where on earth have you been?" he said. "I've been looking all over for you."

Moran laughed, and even Barton had to yield a sour smile. In fact everyone found it funny, except Cattermole. "Very juvenile," he said stonily. "Rather like writing on lavatory walls."

"What's that, Moggy?" Stickwell asked blandly.

"You're a mental runt. You've no guts. That's why you're such a pygmy. Guts all fell out."

Stickwell clutched his stomach with such sudden anxiety that the others all laughed again.

Cattermole was unusually silent throughout lunch. Moran watched him and turned to Barton. "Moggy's sulking," he murmured. "He doesn't like playing second fiddle, especially to Sticky."

To everyone's surprise, Rex was quite amused by the incident. "I bet the frogs were livid," he said.

"They kicked up a bit of a stink," the adjutant said. "They claim that Sticky bust their loudspeaker."

"Typical. Snotty lot, the French."

"Unfortunately they don't seem willing to let it rest."

"Hmm." Rex walked to the window. A light snow was falling, gently blotting out the footprints and the tyre-tracks. "I'm not having them in here, breathing garlic into people's faces . . . What's the airfield like? How's Micky Marriott getting on?"

"It's still unfit for flying, sir," Barton said. "He needs to plough out a strip at least sixty feet wide and he hasn't got half that."

"So we can't fly for what, five days? A week?"

"Unless it thaws, sir."

"It won't thaw," the adjutant said confidently.

"Hmm." Rex breathed on the window and waited to see a patch of frost melt outside. "I'm very pleased to find the squadron so full of enterprise and initiative. That's the sort of thing I like to encourage. I think I'll send the flights on a survival test. Into the Vosges. For a week." He breathed again, a long and thoughtful exhalation. "Yes . . . That should stymie the frogs. And give the chaps something to occupy them, too." He turned, smiling. "You can go along with them if you like, adj."

"No fear," said Kellaway comfortably.

"It'll be awfully quiet without you," Rex said to his flight commanders. "I must get Skull to find me a good book. The exercise starts tonight."

The pilots assembled in the library for briefing. Because Moke Miller had not yet returned from leave, CH3 was switched to 'B' flight to make the numbers equal. Rex's instructions were simple. They would be taken by lorry to the Vosges and dropped, separately, in remote spots, each with only a hundred francs and enough rations for twenty-four hours. No map, no compass. Their task was to survive for one week on their own resources. Only one restriction: no criminal behaviour. Any questions?

Glum silence.

"Oh, one other detail," Rex said. "There may be a few companies of French mountain troops out looking for you. With dogs. I understand they're inclined to be rather ill-mannered, so don't stand any nonsense from them."

He went out.

"This is all your fault," Cox said to Stickwell.

"What? Me?" Stickwell spread his arms and put on a look of amazed innocence. "Honest, sir, I never done nuffink, sir." He was like a depravéd schoolboy.

"No. You're too stupid," said Cattermole. "You're also too gutless."

"Hey, hey! Steady on," Flip Moran said. "There's no need for that, now."

Cattermole stood with his hands thrust deep into his pockets, scowling at the carpet. "I can't stand fakers, that's all."

"What the hell difference does it make, anyway?" Flash Gordon said. There was a heap of winter clothing on the table. He tossed a balaclava at Stickwell. "Try that for size."

It was still gently snowing that night when they left.

The halt in flying also checked the quarrel between CH3 and Rex. Nothing more was said about close-formation flying or combat tactics, but it was obvious to everyone that the argument wasn't over. Soon they would be flying again, and what then? A showdown, presumably. There was a general expectation that Rex would cut CH3 down to size. CH3 was usually friendly enough, although a bit inclined to spike people with deadpan remarks, but on the subject of flying he was a pain in the arse. He knew everything; he'd done it all; he wouldn't stand for any difference of opinion. He didn't discuss: he stated. And that got up everyone's nose.

"As you know, sir, it wasn't my idea to have him here in the first place," Rex said. He was walking in the grounds with Air Commodore Bletchley; Reilly zigzagged in front. "What makes it worse is that he really doesn't care whether he stays or goes."

"He's told you this?"

"Not me personally. But he's made it clear to others that he expects to go. So he should, of course. Anyone else would have *gone*, long ago."

"I see." They passed a dozen airmen with shovels, widening the path. Bletchley said: "What doesn't he like?"

"Everything. He doesn't like the way we fly. He doesn't like our battle tactics. He doesn't even like the colour of the aeroplanes, would you believe. Come to that, he doesn't think much of the Hurricane itself."

"Doesn't he, by God? He's off his rocker there."

"He wants to change the guns. In fact he wants to change a lot of things. Fortunately he hasn't been able to influence my pilots. He's become such a crashing bore that they simply change the subject."

"I gather he didn't make himself too popular by going all sniffy with Jacky Bellamy about your Dornier."

"Ludicrous. It's one thing to bitch and bind after things go wrong, but this chap was pooh-poohing the squadron's first success! I mean, really . . ."

"He reckoned it was a fluke, or something."

"What concerned me slightly was whether she might listen to him. You know: two Americans. I had a little chat."

"So she told me. You convinced her."

"Good."

"Yes, we need that woman. Seen her latest piece?"

"No?"

"Oh, it's first-rate. She wrote up the military funeral you gave the Jerry crew. Brotherhood of the sky, generous victors, clean-cut English youth pay tribute to a gallant foe, that sort of thing. We came out of it steeped in Christian decency. Went down a treat in Washington, I'm told. I'll send you a copy."

They watched Reilly flounder in the snow, trying to chase a squirrel. "Daft dog," Rex said fondly. They climbed the steps to the terrace and went inside.

Sherry.

"Cheers. Well, Rex, what's to be done?"

"Since he's determined to be chopped, sir – cheers – I shall have to chop him, shan't I?"

"If you do, will he be discreet about it?"

"No. Probably not."

"No. In any case that sort of thing always gets out and people always get it wrong. Stuffy English squadron cold-shoulders unorthodox Yank, that sort of thing. Could do great harm."

"But that's absurd. We all know –"

"It doesn't matter what we know, Rex. We need American help to fight this war, or so I'm told, although why that should be I can't understand, they certainly weren't much use last time, not until it was too late anyway . . ." Bletchley took a mouthful of sherry, worked it around his teeth, and swallowed. "Hart stays. Look at it this way: he's the price you pay for Jacky Bellamy's articles. What you must do is make sure he shoots down a Jerry as soon as possible. Then she'll really have something to write about."

Rex nodded sombrely. "Frankly, sir, what gets on my tit is his rotten formation-flying. It's quite deliberate. I honestly don't see how I can tolerate that. It's not fair on the rest of the squadron."

"There's a simple answer. Don't take him with you."

Rex raised an eyebrow.

"Let him fly on his own. I'll get you a new pilot to replace him, plus an extra Hurricane. Then Hart can fly his own patrols. I can send you a bit of bumf to cover it, if you'd like."

Rex examined the idea from all sides.

"It might look better," he said, "if it had a name."

"All right. Let's call him your Reconnaissance Liaison Unit."

Rex nodded. "That'll do nicely. Thank you, sir. He's not a bad pilot, you know. He just doesn't fit in. Reconnaissance Liaison. Good. Perfect."

Not much snow fell during the week of the survival exercise but the air was cold and it grew steadily colder, with a wind that came hunting out of the north-east as if it had an old score to settle. The adjutant could not remember such a cold winter. He went for a stroll one evening and felt the bodywarmth being sucked from his face and hands and neck. Ten minutes of that was enough. He went in and stood with his back to the fire and wondered how they were getting on.

Stickwell was the first to give up.

He arrived in a taxi on the Wednesday afternoon, sneezing hard and slightly burnt about the right foot, which had been too near his campfire when he dozed off. There were also some fingers that looked frostbitten.

Kellaway had to pay the driver. It came to nearly two thousand francs. "Where on earth have you come from, Sticky?" he asked. "Christ knows, uncle," Stickwell said hoarsely. "It might have been Bulgaria. Or maybe Belgium. It began with a B, anyway.

272

They weren't very nice." He sneezed. "Kept telling me to bugger off. So I did." As he hobbled inside, clutching the adjutant's arm, Reilly snarled at him. "They all do that," he said. "Just 'cus I pinched one of their bones, they all gang up on me. Rotten stinking lousy greedy filthy brutes."

Rex came down the stairs. "You didn't last the course," he said. "That means you're dead."

"Yes, sir." Stickwell wiped his dripping nose on his stained sleeve. "I thought being dead would be more fun." He sneezed again.

"Poor show."

Next day a French army ambulance brought in Cattermole. He said he had cholera; they said he had food poisoning. On Friday, Mother Cox was delivered by the *gendarmerie*: a charge of arson was being considered. "They've got it all wrong, adj," Cox said earnestly. "It wasn't really a barn, it was a sort of a hen-house, and it wasn't any use to anyone, you could tell . . ." He was followed by Pip Patterson, also in a taxi; he was crippled with chilblains. Fanny Barton was the only member of 'A' flight to walk home. He limped up the driveway on Saturday morning, intact but exhausted and twelve pounds lighter.

"No sign of anyone from 'B' flight," Kellaway said to Skull. "That's funny."

"Perhaps they all got captured by French mountain troops."

"No, Rex invented them. I expect Flip's trudging around in circles somewhere. He was always hopeless at navigation."

Sunday passed. Skull telephoned several hospitals and *préfectures* in and around the Vosges. Nothing. Rex began to look worried. "We can't afford to be caught at half-strength," he said. "What if the snow goes? 'A' flight's in no shape to fly."

On Monday morning, the extra pilot promised by Bletchley arrived. His name was Dutton; David Dutton: tall, heavy-shouldered, with a bushy ginger moustache. Kellaway took him into the mess and introduced him. The pilots did not move from the armchairs in which they lay sprawled.

"Hullo," Dutton said.

"Don't be so sure," Cattermole said, not looking up.

"I beg your pardon?"

"If you're a replacement," Stickwell began. He paused to cough wheezily. "Who are you replacing?"

"Whom," Cox muttered.

"No idea," Dutton said.

"I'm dead," Patterson said feebly. "Replace me." His eyes closed.

Fanny Barton was slowly waking up. "Hullo," he mumbled.

"This is Dutton," Kellaway told him.

Barton blinked, and drifted off again. Silence, apart from slow breathing.

"They've had rather a rough week," Kellaway explained.

"Yes?"

More silence. Cox settled deeper in his chair. "Whom," he whispered to himself.

"Well," Dutton said, "Perhaps I'd better . . ." A prolonged blast on a two-tone car horn interrupted him. He followed the adjutant to the window. On the forecourt was a green Bentley Continental tourer, with the top down. " 'B' flight's back!" Kellaway announced. Nobody answered.

A minute later, Flip Moran crashed into the room, followed by Fitzgerald and Gordon, each fighting to beat the other through the door. Then came CH3, playing a small accordion. "Scramble, scramble!" Moran shouted. "Everyone outside for lifeboat drill! There's a war on, you know!" Fitzgerald and Gordon rushed around, tipping armchairs. Cattermole swore grimly. Moran blew shrill blasts on a whistle. They all looked tanned, fit and smartly uniformed. "Where on earth have you been?" Kellaway asked. CH3 sounded a confused but happy chord. As the accordion wheezed shut, a flap on the top sprang open and a little cuckoo popped out. "Switzerland," CH3 said. "You missed a treat, adj."

"Switzerland," Rex said heavily.

'B' flight was in his office, together with Kellaway and Skull. The skies had cleared and the room was awash with sunlight.

"Explain," he said to Moran.

"There's not a lot to tell, sir. As soon as we met up we —"

"Wait. You all met up? How? You were dropped at least ten miles apart."

274

"Smoke signals. CH3 lit a fire and made smoke signals. We all headed for them."

Rex sniffed, and looked sideways at CH3. "Red Indian lore, no doubt."

"I saw it in the movies, sir."

"Then we found a village," Moran said. "We pooled our cash and took a taxi to the nearest town. Épinal. Then we caught a train to Geneva."

"Money?"

"CH3 telephoned his bank in New York. They cabled some dollars to a bank in Épinal. That took a few hours, of course."

"We went to the pictures," Flash Gordon said. "Greta Garbo. Very nice."

"Arrived Geneva on Tuesday," Moran went on. "Then we –"

"How? How did you get into Switzerland without passports?"

"I had my US passport," CH3 said. "My uncle happens to be at the American embassy in Berne, and he fixed things for the others."

"His uncle happens to be the ambassador," Fitzgerald told Skull. Skull nodded wisely. Rex had turned away.

"We bought the Bentley in Geneva and drove to Chamonix and skied for the rest of the week," Moran said. "Then we came back."

"Jolly good hotel," Fitz said. "Lots of popsies, damn good band, bar never closed. Super."

"All paid for in dollars, I take it," Rex said.

"The skiing's probably better at Gstaad," CH3 said, "but we couldn't get through: the pass was closed."

"What appalling luck," Rex said. "My heart aches for you."

"Still, we had a smashing time in Chamonix," Gordon said. The Swiss are –"

"That wasn't the object of the exercise though, was it?" Rex demanded. "I sent you on a survival scheme in the Vosges, not a popsy-party in Switzerland."

"You didn't tell us *not* to go to Switzerland, sir," Moran said.

"You knew very well what was intended."

"I know what the orders were, sir. You said our task was to survive for one week. How or where we did it was left to us."

"Rubbish. You didn't solve the problem, you ran away from it."

"If I may say so, they exercised a certain strategic *nous*," Skull

275

remarked. "Supposing the Vosges to be full of nominally hostile troops, the best course was to move into a safer area. Why, after all, face the enemy on his terms?"

"Because the real thing doesn't work like that!" Rex barked. "You've got to take war as it comes, not as you'd prefer it! You can't dodge risk because it's . . . it's . . . it's *inconvenient*."

"Then the terms of the exercise should have said so," Moran declared stolidly.

"They did. The spirit of the test was perfectly obvious. You were to survive *on your own resources*."

"I used my resources," CH3 said.

"And they helped you spend them." Rex waved dismissively at the others.

"I take it we were meant to co-operate," Moran said.

"Besides, it wasn't all plain sailing," Fitzgerald added. "I had to haggle like mad with the bloke who owned the Bentley."

"Oh, get out."

'B' flight went away.

"The trouble with the rich," said Rex, "is they think they can buy their way out of everything."

"You should know," Skull said.

Rex was taken aback. He slapped some files together and banged them into a tray. "What's that supposed to mean?" he asked.

"Well, by any normal standard your family is extremely rich, isn't it? All those factories. Corsets and so on," Skull told Kellaway.

"Foundation garments," Rex said. "And I'd rather it wasn't generally known, if you don't mind."

"Don't blame you," Kellaway said.

"It's not a question of snobbery. I don't give a damn whether the factories make knickers or nutcrackers. I just don't want people thinking I'm a soft touch, that's all."

"Then why do you pay half of everyone's mess bill?" Skull asked.

"Because I choose to. Hornet squadron means a lot to me. I like to think that we set the standard in Fighter Command. I like to think we're something special, in the air *and* on the ground."

"We are," Kellaway said loyally.

On the way downstairs, Rex said: "What's he going to do when he meets a flock of Messerschmitt 110's? Cable his bankers in New York?"

"You're taking it personally," Skull said. "You should concede that they exhibited considerable initiative, and accept that fact."

"They *dodged*," Rex said. "Well, they won't dodge again, I can assure you of that."

The windows in the summerhouse were made of stained glass. At night the colours died, but the hurricane lamp hanging from a beam was just strong enough to pick out the reds, the blues and the greens. There was an oil-heater beside the door. Hot air trembled above it and lifted specks of dust in a helpless rush towards the roof. The place smelled of paraffin and old apples and hay. The hay was underneath a sheet of canvas, and the canvas was underneath Nicole and Flash.

He felt hot. He put his arms outside the blankets and stretched. His left hand touched a pile of apples, so he took one and ate it, quietly. He was still hot. He opened the blankets and let the air get at his body. Nicole groaned when she felt the draught, so he re-arranged the blankets. She snuggled into them like an animal making its nest, and gave a little grunt of contentment.

After a moment she opened her eyes.

"Flash . . ." Her voice was still croaky with sleep. "Why haven't you tell me . . . told me . . . that you go away . . . for a week?"

"I didn't have a chance, Nicole. It all happened very suddenly, you see. Would you like an apple?"

"You could have send me . . . sent to me . . . a letter."

"No time, my love. All very urgent, you see. Action stations, emergency, all hands to the pumps." He took a last bite. "Besides, I'm not much good at letters."

"Where did you go?"

"Can't tell you, I'm afraid." He looked for somewhere to put the core, and finally stood it on top of an empty wine-bottle. "Top secret."

Nicole pressed her face into the blankets. "You disappear during a week," she said, muffled. "I think you never, never see me again."

"Yes, well, that's war for you, isn't it?" The top of her back was exposed and he ran a fingernail down her spine. She shivered. "England expects, and so into the valley of the shadow of death ride the six hundred ..." He rubbed his arms, which were developing goosepimples; and that jogged his memory. "Hey! Just remembered. I bought you something."

He jumped up and fetched a book from his greatcoat pocket. "*The Miracle of Human Biology*, by a bloke called Braine. It's in English, I got it in Geneva. It says –"

"*Genève? En Suisse?*"

"Yes. Only you're not supposed to know that, sweety. Better forget it. All fearfully hush-hush, you see." Flash squatted on the blankets, his feet tucked under him. The hurricane lamp picked out the ripple of his ribcage. It gilded his narrow shoulders and his slim flanks but left his front in darkness. Nicole, watching him, thought he could be any age from fifteen upwards: he was so completely unmarked, so light and free. *He seems more natural with his clothes off*, she thought, and then told herself: *Well naturally, of course he does, you idiot* ... "There's a very interesting bit about why people blush," Flash said, flipping the pages. "Do you blush, Nicky? I used to blush all the time. He says –"

She reached out and plucked the book from his hands. "I don't care what he says. *Ce n'est pas important.*"

"Oh." He linked his hands on the top of his head and rocked on his heels. "Well, *qu'est-ce que c'est* ... um ... *important?*"

"*Nous sommes importants.*" She wriggled out of the blankets, and something in the pit of his stomach lurched. He stopped rocking. *Steady on, Gordon*, he told himself. *You'll do yourself a damage if you go on like this* ...

"Listen, Flash," she said. "Perhaps you go away again next week, yes?"

"No. Well, it's possible. I mean, the way I see it –"

"I don't like to be left alone. It makes me very unhappy."

"Oh, me too." He gripped his left big toe with his right, and made them wrestle. "I agree, it's a shocking bind. But that's war for you, isn't it? Not much anyone can do."

"There is one thing we can do."

"What's that?"

"The same as lots of other people do."

"We've already done that. I can probably manage another helping, if that's what –"

"Flash listen. It's different for you. You have your squadron,

your friends, your flying. But I am alone. When you go away
... You could be transferred tomorrow and then ... Don't you
understand? I'm no good alone. I'm afraid."

"Get yourself a dog. Nice labrador."

She hit him with the book.

"You've gone and broken it," he said, rubbing his arm.

"*Good! Good!* I break all your arms! I break your legs! I break
your head, your stupid English head!"

"Not me, you idiot. You've broken the book."

She hit him with it again. Torn pages fluttered.

"For God's sake! What the hell's the matter with you?"

Now she was crying. Within seconds the tears were running
down her cheeks and splashing on her breasts. Flash had never
seen anyone cry so much, so fast. He was alarmed but he was also
intrigued, and made a mental note: female tear-ducts. "What's
wrong with labradors?" he said. "Very chummy dogs."

"You, you're a stupid! You don't think, you don't feel, you have
no heart ..." She went off into a stream of tear-stained, hiccuping,
incomprehensible French.

"Well, I'm sorry I'm a stupid," he said. He put his arms around
her and to his surprise she came willingly, eagerly. "It's not my
fault. I happen to come from a very long line of stupids. You may
not believe this, but my family is descended from an original
Norman stupid. His name was Sir Gordon de Stupid. If you want
pure stupid breeding, you couldn't do better than us."

"I want. I want very much."

"Ah." Suddenly he understood, and the shock of discovery
startled him. "You actually want ... I mean the idea is that you
and I ... Are you sure? It's a jolly big step, you know."

She said something incoherent to his chest, but it sounded happy
and affirmative.

"Yes. I see. Well, why didn't you say so, in the first place? You
could've saved all this fuss." They lay down, still in each other's
arms. Flash found a part of the book under his ear, and fished it
out. "Here it is!" he said. "Braine on blushing. Lie still while I
read it to you."

"I know all that stuff."

"Ah, but this is about *English* blushing. It's in a class of its own.
Listen ..."

The important thing, Fitz told himself as he walked to the front door, *the only thing that matters, the thing that matters more than anything else, is not to worry about it.*

He swung the knocker. His stomach was as tight as a washboard.

Relax completely and forget it. Otherwise you make yourself your own worst enemy. Just let nature take its course.

Mary Blandin opened the door and gave him such a happy smile that he swayed slightly. They kissed, briefly, and he went in.

You have nothing to fear but fear itself, Fitz thought sternly. Where had he read that? In one of the sex manuals he bought in Switzerland? No . . .

"I missed you a lot," she said.

"Me too. I kept wishing I had a photograph."

"So did I. We ought to take some."

"With or without clothes?"

"I don't mind. Which would you prefer?"

"I think I'll compromise. I'd like you in Wellington boots and white gloves."

"All right, and I'll have you in spats and a black mask."

The thought of it made him anxious. "I brought you these," he said. They were gramophone records, from Geneva.

"How marvellous! Paul Whiteman, Count Basie, Henry Hall . . . You *are* kind."

He told her about the survival exercise, while she cooked apple pancakes. CH3 interested her. "I'd like to meet him, one day," she said.

"Why not? Mind you, he's a funny chap. Very charming and clever and all that, but a bit ruthless. Not much give-and-take."

"You value a bit of give-and-take, do you?"

For a moment he thought she was teasing him, and the pulse in his head hammered a little. "I don't know," he said. "We all fly together, so we ought to trust each other. The trouble with CH3 is he's got his own way of doing everything. That's no good, is it? If you join a squadron, you join it."

"Perhaps it's because he's always had too much money."

"Maybe. Maybe he thinks he's entitled to everything."

They ate, and argued cheerfully about the rights and wrongs of inherited wealth. Fitz drank quite a lot of wine, which Mary noticed, and he noticed that she noticed it. *That's nothing to worry about*, he told himself.

Later, they pushed the table into a corner and danced to the new records. Fitz was a good dancer. They slow-foxtrotted with his strong right arm guiding her, and he began to enjoy himself. She was lithe, and light on her feet, and she responded willingly. He was in command!

While he was re-winding the gramophone she turned off the lights, leaving only the glow of the fire, and went to her bedroom. She came back wearing a sleeveless silk dress that gleamed like ivory in the firelight. They danced again: *Blue Skies, Tea for Two, You'd Be So Nice to Come Home To*. She put both arms around his neck. "Mary," he murmured. "You're not wearing anything under that dress, are you?"

"It took you an awful long time to find out, Fitz."

"Well, the light's not very good."

He took the silk in his fingertips and raised it to her shoulders. Now her skin gleamed like ivory. She curled her head out of the dress. He let it fall, and they walked to the bedroom. He was trembling, his heartbeat seemed to have an irregular wallop in it, he lost two buttons getting his shirt off; but as soon as he slid between the sheets and his hand touched her side, he knew it was no good. They hugged eagerly and kissed greedily, but there was a part of him that wasn't having any.

"Poor Fitz," she said after a while.

"I'm not poor, I'm penniless."

"Never mind. One day we'll both be rich."

"Not a hope. I think my assets have been frozen."

"Never mind, dear. I expect it's like riding a bicycle. One day, all of a sudden, it'll come naturally."

"Are you sure?"

"Positive."

"That's terrible news. It took me four whole years to learn how to ride a bike."

"You couldn't have been really trying."

"I kept falling off."

"No danger of that here. I'll keep a tight grip on you."

Eventually he got dressed, and they played the rest of the gramophone records until Flash Gordon bipped his horn outside.

It was only when he was going out that Fitz saw the broken window in the front door. It had been roughly patched with plywood. "What happened here?" he asked.

"Oh . . . Nothing important. We've got some unpleasant characters in the village. They don't approve of the British." She pointed to a yellow crayon scribble on the door: *Merde anglaise.*

"Good God! That's awful."

"I agree, dear. The colours don't match." Flash was revving his engine. "Go on, it's freezing."

Fitz was dreading the routine enquiry he got from Flash about what sort of evening he'd had, but tonight he was spared it. Flash had big news. "Guess what!" he said, rear wheels spinning on the packed snow.

"What?"

"Nicole wants to have a baby."

"Really? What on earth for?"

"Dunno. Why not? Perfectly natural thing for a woman to want, I'd have thought."

"Yes, but . . . Are you sure? I mean, doesn't she want to get married first?"

Flash was about to say: *No, she didn't say anything about that,* when he got an urgent warning signal from a remote corner of his brain; and he remained silent while he rapidly reviewed recent events. Marriage? Was that what she'd been driving at? Marriage. Ah. Not just babies. Marriage too. "Yes, I expect so," he said casually, but his mind was still being bombarded with violent images of vicars and organs and confetti and bloody bridesmaids and blurred photographs in the local paper. Christ Almighty! Marriage!

"Well, that's nice," Fitz said. "Congratulations, Flash. I hope you'll both be very happy."

"Piece of cake," Flash said; and saw it in his mind's eye, a colossal great slice of wedding cake, the size of a barn door, all covered in icing; and him eating it, for ever and ever and ever. Shit. Too late now. He'd said yes.

The long-range weather forecast indicated little change. Rex sent Cox and Fitzgerald on leave.

For a couple of seconds, Fitz considered not going. He was

worried about Mary's safety: the smashed window, the scribbled obscenity. She lived alone. Perhaps he had brought this hatred upon her, by visiting her so often. There was anti-British feeling in the area; others had noticed it. Rex saw him hesitate. "It might be now or never, Fitz," he said.

"I'll go." There was his family to think of, too.

"Truck leaves in ten minutes," the adjutant told him. "There's a plane from Rheims with some spare space. Catch that and you'll be in London tonight."

Fitzgerald packed fast and ran downstairs with his bag. He met Cattermole returning from squash, very content after beating the new man, Dutton. "Moggy," Fitzgerald said. "Do me a favour? I'm off on leave. Would you keep an eye on Mary? Pop in occasionally, make sure she's okay? I'm a bit worried. She's on her own, you see."

"Of course I will!" Cattermole said heartily. "You go off and enjoy yourself and think no more about it. I'll see she's all right."

"You're a gent," said Fitzgerald gratefully, and ran for the truck.

Fanny Barton discussed with Kellaway and Skull the matter of Cattermole's hostility towards Stickwell. What made it puzzling, he said, was the fact that they used to be the best of friends. Now, all of a sudden, Moggy seemed to hate and despise him. He really was quite vindictive. Kellaway said it was just boredom. That was Kellaway's standard explanation for anything peculiar or pointless that pilots did. "No action, you see," he said. "No Huns to hunt, no Boche to bag. You can't expect them to keep it bottled up." Barton pointed out that they weren't all being bloody; just Moggy, and only to Sticky.

Skull put it down to post-adolescent instability. "Say again?" said the adjutant. It was a familiar experience at university, Skull explained. Young men often developed friendships of a certain intensity, and sometimes there was a reaction, equally strong, in the opposite direction which ... "This is Fighter Command," Kellaway interrupted. "Not a lot of pansies with silk hankies stuffed up their sleeves." Skull was not discouraged. Fighter pilots, he pointed out, were young men with a strong romantic streak, highly competitive, obliged to lead a largely monastic life, and therefore ... "Drivel!" barked the adjutant. "Bosh, tosh and poppycock!" Skull smiled, and said no more. Barton wondered what was the best thing to do. "Get 'em back into action, old boy," Kellaway said briskly. "It works like a dose of salts. I've seen it time and time again." Barton nodded. Micky Marriott had three snowploughs whacking away at the drifts that rolled across the airfield like ocean swells; but it would be a few days yet. And meanwhile Moggy never missed a chance to needle his former friend. "God knows what pleasure he gets out of it," Barton muttered. "The pleasure of destructiveness," Skull suggested. "That is, after all, Cattermole's *raison d'être*, isn't it?" Kellaway scoffed: "Raisin pudding!" Barton went away, little the wiser.

CH3 had a very short meeting with his commanding officer.

"Reconnaissance Liaison Unit," he said. "Does that mean I liaise with reconnaissance or vice versa?"

"Please yourself."

"And have I your permission to modify my Hurricane?"

"No."

"One last question, sir. What the hell is going on?"

"It's called the phoney war," said Rex. "If you don't understand it, I can't explain it to you."

Cattermole borrowed a motorcycle and went to visit Mary Blandin. He took a small present with him: a book of Irish poetry that he had found on Flip Moran's bedside table. She was surprised to see him, and amused by Fitz's concern for her, and touched by the gift. She made coffee, and they talked about Fitz. "He's very conscientious, isn't he?" Cattermole said. "In some ways older than his years, in some ways younger ... D'you find that?"

She thought, and nodded. "He does get awfully anxious at times."

Cattermole smiled enquiringly.

"Nothing special," she said. "Just little things. But he takes them so seriously."

"It's a good fault, Mrs Blandin."

"Oh, please! Call me Mary."

"May I? Thank you. And you must call me Lance. Everyone else does ... No, he's a very hardworking chap, is young Fitz. It

284

was one of the things that first impressed me when he joined my flight."

"He's in your flight?"

"I'm his flight commander, yes."

"My goodness. I'm honoured."

"On the contrary, Mary, I'm privileged. You've no idea what a pleasure it is to escape the responsibilities of command and enjoy the company of a beautiful woman."

That brought the colour to her cheeks. "I'm afraid I live a very sort of unexciting life, compared with yours, Lance."

"You underrate yourself," he murmured, "enormously."

Cattermole stayed for only half an hour. On the way out he saw the broken pane and the scribble. "It's some kind of greasy crayon," Mary said. "It won't wash off."

"Wait here." He went to the motorbike and dipped his handkerchief in the petrol tank. The crayon dissolved and vanished in a couple of wipes.

"You're brilliant. I would never have thought of that." A combination of frosty air and gratitude made her eyes sparkle. "Now you've ruined your handkerchief. Give it here, I'll wash it out." She took it before he could argue.

"You're very kind. You also make uncommonly good coffee, and in all respects you are a truly delightful person. Goodnight." He stooped and kissed her on the cheek.

The machine started at the first thrust of his leg. She watched him speed away, changing gear briskly, until the tail-light vanished.

He came back the following night to collect his handkerchief. There was a fresh obscenity scribbled on the door. This time she gave him a rag to dip in the petrol tank.

"Mary, who is treating you in this frightful way?" he asked gently, when they were inside.

"Someone in the village. You can't be a schoolteacher without offending parents, I'm afraid."

She made coffee and they talked about the village children, about her own childhood, about parts of England that they both knew. Cattermole could be a very good listener when he chose, and Mary found herself remembering incidents and anecdotes from long ago, all of which he found vastly interesting and entertaining.

His attention was so flattering that she began to feel guilty. "I wonder what Fitz is up to at this very moment?" she said suddenly.

"Oh, heaven knows." Then he chuckled in a way that made her look. "One thing's certain: he won't be writing long letters every day."

"Does he usually?"

"Not usually, Mary: infallibly. I've often wondered what the deuce he finds to say to ..." Cattermole shrugged. "... whoever-it-is."

She smiled, briefly. "It can't be easy."

"I've no doubt young Fitz is on the spree, painting the town pink, drinking the bars dry, and reminding society that nobody's daughter is safe when a fighter pilot's loose. At least, that's what he'll tell us when he comes back."

"He's a very good dancer." It was the only safe thing she could think to say.

"Is he really? D'you like dancing? You should. You have the figure for it."

Mary found the records from Geneva while Cattermole wound up the gramophone. As they danced he tested his observations, and found that he was right. She had a very good figure indeed.

Next night there was yet another abusive scribble for him to clean off the front door. "Persistent blighters, aren't they?" he said.

"Yes. I'm at school all day, so it's easy for them."

"Have you told the police?"

"The French police? I don't need to. The village bobby is very anti-British. If the spelling weren't so good, I might think he was doing this."

"You're very brave about it, Mary."

"Oh, well. I haven't much choice. Anyway, dirty words can't hurt me." But she was very glad to see Cattermole. All day she had been wondering if she would come home to more filth on her front door, and when she had seen it she had been afraid, and had slammed the door behind her and given herself a big drink, fast. Cattermole was tall and strong and very reassuring. She felt able to relax and to seem as brave as he thought she was.

They were roasting chestnuts at the open fire when it happened. He had brought some wine, a Sylvaner, and they were trying to find words to describe its taste and colour. "No, Mary, you're quite wrong," he said. "*Not* winter sunshine. And certainly not fields of golden buttercups."

"I wasn't serious about the buttercups."

"That's a relief. For a moment I feared you were turning into the Fairy Queen."

"Oh. Would that be so bad?"

"Catastrophic, my sweet. I have it on the evidence of my governess, who was the third biggest liar north of the Tweed, that fairy queens slide down moonbeams."

"Sounds like fun."

"Depends what you mean by fun." He rescued a smoking chestnut. "That's how pixies are born, you know."

"What? By sliding down moonbeams?"

He nodded. "Harley Street is quite unanimous."

"Well, they're all wrong. Everyone knows that pixies are made by rubbing two rainbows together."

Cattermole made a little show of spilling his wine. "That," he said, "is by far the most erotic statement I have heard all week."

She smiled with cheerful pleasure; it was a long time since she had so amused and impressed a man. "Anyway, I still think it's like winter sunshine," she said.

"No. I'll tell you what it is." He topped up his glass and looked at her through the wine. "It's you, in that absolutely stunning dress."

She was wearing the sleeveless silk dress, the colour of old ivory. For a long moment she simply sat and enjoyed his admiration. Something banged like a big firework and the room seemed to explode inwards with a crash of glass and shattered wood. The curtains billowed violently and on the opposite wall a picture was suddenly ripped across; it jumped and hung slewed. Mary was knocked flat by Cattermole's diving body. "Keep still!" he shouted; but she had no choice: he was lying on top of her. He was holding the bottle of Sylvaner, and she could feel the wine soaking through her dress. The last fragment of glass tinkled. He rolled off her and ran across the room. The lights went out. He was back, helping her up. "Keep your head down," he said. They scuttled into the bedroom and sprawled on the floor. "Better," he said. "Nice stone walls. I think that was a shotgun. You're not hurt? Good. Stay there."

"For God's sake don't go!" She forbade herself to cry. It was only shock. Be sensible: control yourself. She found herself crying, sobbing for breath, all control gone. There was a muffled thud as Cattermole dragged everything off the bed, mattress and all. Then he was back, lifting her onto the heap. "Keep below window-level," he said. Her arms were around him, and they lay together until she had exhausted her tears.

"You're soaking wet."

"Wine."

"That's no good. Better take it off."

"Yes."

But she did nothing, so he unbuttoned the dress and peeled it away. *Surprise, surprise*, he thought. He sat on the edge of the mattress and untied his shoes, carefully, so as not to get the laces knotted. Half a minute later he was in bed, and she was curling her arms around him. "Don't go, don't go," she whispered. "Wouldn't dream of it," he said. "Quite the reverse."

Stickwell raised the revolver, aimed, fired. The explosion ripped out the calm of the day, and the recoil flung his hand upwards. He brought it down and fired again, teeth clenched and eyes squeezed half-shut.

His fourth shot hit an ear.

"That's better, Sticky," Flip Moran said.

"Really? I didn't see anything."

"Yes. You got an ear."

They walked over to the targets, a row of statues set up in a corner of the kitchen garden behind the château. Moran pointed to the missing ear. "See?"

"Damn. I wasn't aiming at that chap. I was after the next-but-one."

"You don't say?" Moran's thick black moustache twitched. "My stars, Sticky, you're an awful dangerous man with a gun, and that's a fact."

"It's not funny, Flip. I told you, I can't shoot to save my life. Well, that doesn't worry me, I don't care what Moggy says, I'm not afraid of getting killed, I can face that. But I ought to be able

288

to do something before I snuff it, oughtn't I?" He spun the revolver on his finger.

Moran took it from him and applied the safety-catch. "This proves nothing, this thing," he said.

"What about the Dornier? I missed the Dornier completely."

"That didn't matter."

"It mattered to me, Flip. The trouble is my eyes seem to go funny when I try to shoot someone down. They keep blinking. That's no good, is it? It happened at the Battle of Southend Sands. I couldn't even hit a bloody Blenheim!"

"Just as well."

"Not the point, though, is it?" Stickwell picked up a chunk of the ear and tried to replace it on the statue's head, but it fell off. "I sometimes think Moggy's right," he said. "I'm not cut out to be a fighter pilot. All my family have funny eyes, you know."

"Moggy knows nothing. The man's a bag of wind."

"Uncle George is totally blind. Can't see a damn thing."

"Ah, just wait, Sticky. One of these days you'll stuff a Jerry all on your own, and after that you'll wonder what the fuss was all about."

"I hope you're right," Stickwell said gloomily. "I've got to do something about it, anyway." He took back the revolver, and began practising quick draws from his canvas holster. "He keeps *on* about it, I don't know why . . ." On his third attempt he dropped the gun. "We used to be quite good pals, but now he can't stand the sight of me. I don't understand it."

A heavy growl had been chewing at the tranquillity of the day: engines getting tested. Now the growl, like an animal baring its teeth, became a roar, and the roar fed on itself and grew fiercer. "Hullo, hullo," Moran said. They turned to face the sound, and before long a Hurricane sprang into view and thundered directly over the château. "Micky's got the field open," Stickwell said. "Terrific. Now we can go out to play." The Hurricane came back and flew all around the grounds of the château in a near-vertical turn. "That's Flash," Moran said. "He's full of old buck now he's got himself engaged, isn't he?"

Cox and Fitzgerald came back from leave to find the squadron in a state of keen excitement. On two consecutive days, enemy aircraft had been found and attacked. In all, three Dornier 17's and six Heinkel 111's had been involved, including one glorious occasion when the entire squadron had come across a formation of three Heinkels and chased it twenty miles, starting at eighteen thousand feet and ending at ground level with the German aircraft jinking furiously as they raced over the frontier.

"Krautland's still out-of-bounds," Moke Miller told Cox and Fitzgerald, "so we had to let them go. Pity, really. Another mile and –"

"My kite got slightly stitched-up by one of their gunners," Pip Patterson said. "Dumbo got a packet of flak through a wing."

"Dumbo?" Cox said.

"Dutton. And Sticky came back with half a mile of telephone wire wrapped around his tail-wheel."

"Cracking good fun," Miller said. "Have a good leave?"

"Ate too much," said Fitzgerald.

"Got taken to the opera," said Cox.

"You poor buggers. Anyway, there should be plenty more sport tomorrow. The Hun seems to be up to something."

That night, Fitzgerald went to see Mary Blandin. He went alone; he didn't tell Flash that he was going; he slipped away quietly after dinner. On the way there, he wondered about this secrecy. What was he ashamed of? Nothing. But he was afraid of something, he had to admit that. The dread of failure followed him like a bad shadow. If nobody else knew, did that make the failure any the less? Rubbish! Thus, despising himself already, Fitz went up to Mary's cottage and banged on the door of a dark and empty house.

He knew it was empty as soon as he swung the knocker. No crack of light around the blackout curtains. No smoke from the chimney. The windows shuttered, in fact.

He stood in the starry night and listened to his breath making smoke-plumes in the freezing air. After the first sense of shock there was a certain relief. At least he was spared having to make yet another limp excuse.

There was an *estaminet* down the road. He went off and bought himself a drink, thinking: *She might have sent me a note. No consideration.*

The year ended with a fine flurry of action. 'A' flight got sent to investigate an unidentified aircraft reported between Bar-le-Duc and Toul, climbed to 25,000 feet and found a Dornier 17. They chased it for thirty miles and shot it down in flames near Lunéville. 'B' flight when on patrol came across a Heinkel circling St Mihiel, apparently lost. They put one engine out of action and killed the upper gunner, at which point the German pilot put the plane into a vertical dive. He pulled out, very skilfully, at low level and tried to land on a small civilian airfield, but the bomber's remaining engine kept dragging it sideways and he flew into a wood. There was a large explosion and many trees caught fire. When Moran landed, his windscreen was smeared with blood: the blood of the Heinkel's upper gunner.

Jacky Bellamy happened to be in the control tower when 'A' flight got the Dornier. She was able to follow the entire sequence of events, from the sighting to the kill, by listening to Rex's comments and commands given over the R/T. She wrote it all down. It was a good story for her: the quiet calm on the ground contrasting with the crisp, crackling aggression five miles in the sky; the long chase; the total victory. She saw CH3 in the mess that evening and mentioned it.

"I'm pleased you're pleased," he said.

"I take it that means you're not wildly impressed."

"Should I be? The odds were six to one. Why did they have to chase it so far before they destroyed it?"

"I don't know. Why?"

"The tactics were wrong. They obviously didn't achieve any surprise."

"Tactics again." She wrinkled her nose, and that offended him and he began to turn away, so she said quickly: "Anyway, you can't always guarantee surprise, can you?"

"All right, forget tactics. Just think about six fighters attacking one bomber continuously over a thirty-mile stretch. Something's got to be wrong with the gunnery."

"You mean the guns jammed, or something?"

"No. I mean most of the shots missed. For a start, the guns are harmonised wrongly. They're aimed so as to make the bullet-streams converge at a point four hundred yards ahead of the aircraft. That's no good."

"Why?"

"It's too far. Four hundred yards is nearly a quarter of a mile. D'you know what sort of target a Dornier 17 presents at a range of a quarter of a mile? It looks like a matchstick."

"Yes, but surely that's only the beginning of the attack. You keep firing, you get closer, the thing gets bigger, so –"

"So now the bullet-streams are converging way *beyond* the target. You've lost your lethal density. You're spraying shots all around the area, instead of focussing your fire on one vital spot."

"I see." She thought about it. "So why do they harmonise at four hundred, then?"

"Because they reckon the average RAF fighter pilot's such a lousy shot that if he had to come in close and fire a short burst, he'd miss. This way, he can stand off and fire a long burst and miss."

"They didn't all miss today."

"Look," he said patiently. "You asked me and I told you. If it's not what your readers want, I can't help that."

She went to see Rex.

"Well, of course, he wasn't there, was he?" Rex said. "I suppose if you're not there, thirty miles sounds a lot, but believe me when you're covering five or six miles a minute, it goes by in a flash ... Did he mention the Dornier's speed? No, I thought not. Racy customer, the Dornier, especially going downhill, which this one was, since he had a vast amount of height to spare. That meant we had a flat-out tail-chase. What did he tell you about the guns?"

"Wrongly harmonised."

"No, the Dornier's guns."

"Oh. Nothing."

"Really." Rex tugged gently at an eyebrow. "Well, nothing is not an adequate description, I'm afraid. Four machineguns, two of them rear-facing – one dorsal, one ventral, so the field-of-fire is very well calculated. Unlike us, these gunners don't have to fly their crates. They can concentrate exclusively on destroying us. Hence I was not too anxious to offer them an easy target, which takes me to the question of gun-harmonisation. What was his complaint, again?"

"The harmonised range is too great."

"This squadron, like every squadron in Fighter Command, uses the Dowding Spread. You've met Air Chief Marshal Dowding?"

"No, but I know he's C-in-C Fighter Command."

"A fine officer and a true gentleman. I had the honour to attend a meeting where he analysed the thinking behind the Dowding Spread. He made three crucial points. One: an enemy bomber is a relatively big target. Two: the bullet pattern created by the Dowding Spread is big enough to compensate for pilot error. Some error is inevitable in air fighting, and by using a heavy spray rather than a jet, one is more likely to splash the enemy. Third: a range of four hundred yards places the fighter *outside* the effective defensive fire of the bomber."

"Makes sense."

"We think so. And there are several German crews who would agree, if they could speak."

She went back to the mess. "I checked it out with Squadron Leader Rex," she said to CH3. "He explained everything, he answered all your objections, and I have to say his version makes a lot more sense than yours."

He cocked his head. "I'm surprised at you. I thought the first thing they taught you at journalism school was never to believe anything official."

"It's not that easy. Sometimes it's just as stupid to *dis*believe everything simply because it's official. I reckon this is one of those times."

"Reckon away. Go ahead and write it. I should care."

Mother Cox looked up from an *Illustrated London News*. "For goodness sake!" he said. "What's he been binding about now? Doesn't he like the way we part our hair?"

Moke Miller immediately took out a comb and parted his hair in the middle. It made him look foolish, and for a few days everyone else copied him. As a result the squadron resembled a bunch of 1920's danceband musicians. "You will tell us if we've got it wrong, won't you?" Miller asked. CH3 smiled and said nothing.

Fitzgerald visited the cottage twice more, and then asked Cattermole if he knew where Mary was.

"Not the foggiest. Gone away for Christmas, I expect."

"Was she all right when you saw her?"

"Couldn't have been better, Fitz. First-class."

"Nothing worrying her, then."

"When I left her," Cattermole said, "she seemed very contented."

"Good. Thanks for looking after her, Moggy."

"What else are friends for?"

Dumbo Dutton was a burly, amiable young man whose only claim to fame was that he owned a copy of *Lady Chatterley's Lover*, bought in Paris on his way to join the squadron. He was reading it in the anteroom after lunch, and making occasional gasps and soft whistles for the benefit of the others, when Rex tapped him on the shoulder and said they were going flying. A couple of aspects of his close-formation drill needed a bit of polishing.

They went above the weather, exchanging a dead snowscape for a fresh, bright world of sunshine. The air was astonishingly clear: Dutton saw mountain peaks to the south, and realised they must be Swiss Alps. The sky was a soft, pale blue at the horizon, deepening as he looked up until it became indigo overhead. As he kept turning his head it faded to turquoise and then, beyond the sun, to a shining buttermilk. He had seen nothing like it outside the cinema.

They flew for nearly an hour. Rex was pleased, and said so, which made Dutton happy.

They dropped down through the clouds and circled the airfield. It all looked smudged and grubby: the sun was nearly down; the light was flat and listless. Rex landed first. Dutton made a wide circuit to give Rex plenty of time to clear the runway, and then made his approach. Now undercarriage down. He tugged the selector lever and it wouldn't move. Damn. He heaved hard but it seemed locked. "Wake up, Dumbo!" he said aloud, remembered the thumbcatch, squeezed and pulled. Down went the undercarriage, thud-thud, two green lights, but as he lowered the flaps he realised he'd drifted away from the runway while he had his little panic, and now the ploughed-out strip was off to his left.

He sideslipped and suddenly realised, as he glanced down at the blank stretches of snow, that he was quite low. It was hard to judge height in this grey, gutless light, but really this was too low, in fact far too low! He gave the engine a bucketful of throttle and hauled back the stick to go round again. The Hurricane see-sawed, stalled and, its propeller thrashing furiously at the end of the bellowing Merlin, spun awkwardly.

Rex was taxiing when he saw the Hurricane land on its tail just inside the perimeter fence. It bounced like a pogo-stick and went a clear forty feet in the air. He saw its wings in silhouette like the arms of a gymnast attempting a cartwheel. Then it whacked its nose into the runway with a bang that penetrated his own engine-roar, and everything either folded up or flew off or bounced away.

By then Rex had his machine turned around and he was racing it back up the strip. Sparks were sizzling around Dutton's cockpit from fractured electrical leads when he reached the crash, and the air stank so much of petrol that he was coughing and choking as he wrestled and struggled with the hood. All around, chunks of hot metal sizzled in the snow. He kicked out a Perspex panel, got both hands around a torn metal frame, and heaved. The hood fell off. The instrument panel was half-buried in Dutton's crumpled body and coloured cables were smoking and sparking everywhere. Rex got Dutton under the arms. He bent at the knees and straightened so powerfully that both the pilot and the dashboard came free. He ran with them, away from the stench of fuel. It was only when he laid them down that he saw that Dutton had no legs. At that moment a wing-tank went up with a whoosh of flame, and the fire-truck and bloodwagon arrived.

Later, the adjutant took Skull to Dutton's room. "You might as well learn how to do this," he said. They went through the belongings. "Read all his letters. Anything unpleasant, chuck it on the fire." They packed his clothes in his suitcase and found a packet of contraceptive sheaths under his socks. "That goes out, straight away," Kellaway grunted.·

Flash Gordon appeared in the doorway. "Dumbo said I could have it when he was finished," he said. Skull stared.

"On the dressing-table," Kellaway said.

"Thanks." Flash took *Lady Chatterley* and left.

JANUARY
1940

The school holidays came to an end but Mary Blandin did not return. Fitzgerald visited the cottage several times. He asked Flash if Nicole knew anything; she did not. "I shouldn't worry if I were you," Flash said. "You know what women are like. Brains like grasshoppers. She probably wrote to you and forgot to stick a stamp on."

"All the same, it's a bit peculiar."

"Women are peculiar, Fitz. Nicole is very peculiar sometimes. The other day I happened to mention that we won the battle of Waterloo and she went off the deep end for hours and hours. I had to put a stop to it finally."

Fitz gave up worrying about Mary for a moment. "How did you manage that?" he asked.

"Oh ... you know," Flash said. "Ways and means."

The trenches of the British Expeditionary Force had been flooded by the storms of November; now they were thick with ice and often blocked with snow. More than one sentry, drugged by the cold, drifted into sleep and never woke up again. Tanks and Bren-gun carriers froze to the mud as if welded. Aircraft refused to start, guns failed to fire. A Morane pilot broke both legs in a forced landing on a hillside, crawled out of the wreckage and was dead from exposure when the search party found him an hour later.

In the face of a perpetual struggle to keep warm, the formal war lost much of its meaning. Hornet squadron still went up looking for trouble but by now everyone knew that finding the odd Dornier or Heinkel doing a recce flight was largely a matter of luck, a bit like going out with a gun to get a pheasant: if the birds didn't appear, then that was that. The real fight was inside the squadron, where Cattermole was still gunning for Stickwell. The original cause (whatever that may have been) no longer mattered: Stickwell was simply a target, and Cattermole lost no opportunity of sniping at him, belittling him, snubbing him. It was all very adolescent. Rex knew it was going on but he considered it a purely personal matter (which in a sense it was) and did not interfere.

Meanwhile Stickwell did his best to ignore Cattermole. Whenever he could, he avoided him. On a gloomy afternoon, when flying had finished, Cattermole came into a room by one door and

Stickwell went out by another. CH3 saw the smile on Cattermole's face and got up.

He found Stickwell sitting on a staircase, looking at an oil painting of a horse. "Ugly brute, isn't it?" Stickwell said.

CH3 sat beside him. "Why don't you do something?"

"What, for instance?"

"You can't just let him push you around. You can't keep dodging him."

"Thanks very much. Now I know what I can't do."

"Okay, stand up to him. Give as good as you get."

"You mean go and pick a fight with him? That's bloody silly. That makes me as stupid as him." Stickwell stood up. "I don't hate him, you know. I don't hate anyone."

"Perhaps it's time to start."

"No." He turned and climbed the stairs. "I tried hating people, once. Soon learned better."

Simon James Stickwell had never been much of a success until he astonished everyone by becoming a fighter pilot.

For a start, he was an orphan. His parents died of fever in the Gold Coast, where they were missionaries. He was then one year old, and it would have been much less inconvenient for everyone if he had gone with them. Instead he had to be shipped to England. He was taken into the home of an aunt and uncle. When he was three, the uncle died; when he was six, the aunt followed. Young Simon got dumped on an obscure relation, a woman in her early thirties who was childless. Her husband treated the boy's arrival as a deliberate insult and left her. She took care of Simon until he was ten, then sent him to a boarding school and emigrated to Australia.

All his early memories were of people disappearing.

School could have been worse. He got bullied a bit but he learned how to cope: if he couldn't run away he gave in and let them do whatever they wanted. Usually they got bored and stopped. He paid a price for this passivity: he was considered weak and soft, a bad sport, a poor loser, a general waste of time. None of the staff bothered much with him, for which he was glad. He didn't mind getting rotten results in everything; what he dreaded was having some keen young master try to buck him up, give him special

300

tuition, prove he could do better if he really tried. Young Stickwell knew there was no chance of that. For as long as he could remember, people had always looked at him with a certain resignation. He knew what that look meant. He knew his place.

The money for his school fees ran out when he was sixteen. Some relatives in Kent accepted him without enthusiasm, and that was where he got into trouble.

They had a daughter, also sixteen but taller than he was, beautiful, talented and assured. Simon fell in love and inevitably it was abject love, the kind that was bound to fail even if she had found him the slightest bit attractive. He was undersized and apologetic. She was fluent in French and German, understood calculus, and had a tennis serve that left scorchmarks on the grass. The more he adored her the more she despised him, but she had been brought up to have good manners and he was thoroughly sick with unrequited love by the time she lost patience and snubbed him, good and hard.

It was a sentence of death. Simon knew he couldn't live without her; now she had made it clear he couldn't live with her.

That evening he was missing when the family sat down to dinner. A search began next morning. The police found him two days later, deep in the airless gloom of a plantation of fir trees.

They took him home on a stretcher, but there was no question of his staying there. The girl's father drove him rather a long way to a nursing home that was run by a man the father had known at university, and left him. It turned out to be a discreetly camouflaged asylum for kleptomaniacs and dipsomaniacs and miscellaneous misfits who were not yet eccentric enough to be certified.

When he realised that he had been rescued only to be abandoned, Simon entered a state of resolute, self-destructive rage. He ate nothing and he threw all his food at the walls. He tore down the curtains and smashed the chairs and fouled his bed. The nursing staff let him live in the wreckage for a couple of days, but when he kept on throwing his food they began knocking him about. Simon did not resent this. He knew he deserved it. Indeed he wanted to be punished. If they rubbed his face in his filthy sheets he fought them because that was what they understood. If they held him and shoved food down his throat he did not fight them because he knew that he could make himself throw up when they had gone. He was wretched but he was not altogether unhappy. After sixteen years at the lower edge of mediocrity, it was curiously reassuring to hit bottom, even if hitting bottom was painful.

After about a month of this, he woke up one morning feeling extremely tired. Breakfast was on a tray just inside the door, as usual. He lay and thought about chucking it at the walls. He looked at the walls and could not find a clean spot anywhere. He fell asleep again.

He awoke at midday when they brought his lunch.

Sausages. They smelled good. He looked at the stains on the ceiling and found them ugly. After a while he got up and ate a sausage. The walls were ugly, too. In fact the whole room was ugly. He took another sausage and looked out of the barred window at the sunshine and the waving trees while he ate.

Next day they left the door open when they came to collect his lunch tray. He stood in the doorway and inspected the corridor. It was very long and very cool. Occasionally someone walked by and he watched them approach, pass, depart. An hour of this was enough to tire him out. He went to bed and slept until evening.

At the end of a week he had reached the end of the corridor. A middleaged man had his office there. Simon watched him at work: writing notes, reading letters, making telephone calls, going away, coming back.

It seemed silly to stand in the corridor, in his pyjamas, so Simon sat on a chair just inside the office. The man didn't seem to mind.

On his third day inside the office the man offered him a small piece of chocolate. After that he got a small piece of chocolate every day, although not always at the same time. It became the most important moment of his day.

Then, after a week, the man inexplicably failed to give him a piece. The day came to an end, he closed his notebooks, locked his desk, put away his fountain-pen, and stood up. Simon stood up too. His heart was racing. "Chocolate!" he said.

The man shook his head. "Not today," he said: not angry but not friendly. "Not while you smell so awful."

"All right," Simon said defiantly. "I'll have a bath."

"All right."

When he came back, clean and in clean pyjamas, the man was listening to some music on a gramophone. They ate a little chocolate

302

and listened together. The record ended, and they listened to the silence. Simon felt it coming, like a fast train approaching; he knew it was unstoppable; he dreaded it, but before he could get up and leave, it happened. He was in tears. He cried until his chest ached and his eyes throbbed, while the man held him. At the end, when there were no more tears to be cried, the man gave him a towel. Then he gave him a small glass of brandy and put him to bed.

After that Simon talked to him every day. He asked for cleaning materials and he scrubbed out his room. He asked for paint and brushes and he redecorated it. The work was very tiring: he would paint a bit, take a nap, walk down the corridor for a chat, paint a bit more. He liked their chats because they were never serious. They usually just talked about his childhood.

When the room was finished he asked for more work and the man found him some gardening to do. He felt stronger, he didn't tire so quickly. Things began to go wrong again. He was sawing some logs one day, and making a very good job of it, when he saw the man talking to another patient. That startled and annoyed him. He finished the logs, getting angrier all the time, and didn't even bother to stack them. He went inside, mud on his gumboots, barged into the office, and sat down, glowering. "Now I know," he said. "You're just like all the rest."

"What do you mean?" He went on writing a letter.

"You've chucked me, haven't you? I've had the push. Goodbye, Simon, you're on your own again. Isn't that right?"

"There are certainly other people here who need to be looked after, if that's what you mean."

"And I can go to hell for all you care!" There were more tears, more chest-aching, lung-bursting sobs; but this time the man did not hold him. At the end he gave him a fresh towel, and waited until he was calm. "What do you think that was about?" he asked.

Simon sat and thought, his face half-buried in the towel. "Dunno," he mumbled. After a while he found a handkerchief and blew his nose. "I just felt so ... so ... so *fed up*." There were bits of mud on the carpet. He collected them and dropped them in the waste basket. "Everything's so rotten," he said.

"How is it rotten?"

Simon slumped in his chair and linked his hands on the top of his head. They looked at each other for quite a long moment.

Suddenly Simon gave a little snort of laughter. "It's no good," he said. "I mean, it's obvious, isn't it? I was jealous."

"You were jealous."

"You knew it all the time. Why didn't you tell me?"

"What good would that have done?"

"It might have saved a lot of . . ." Simon stopped and looked away. "No, I don't suppose I'd've believed you. God Almighty . . . I'm not a very nice person, am I?"

"Aren't you?"

"Jealous. Lazy. Greedy. Phoney. Stupid."

"There's nothing stupid about discovering what sort of person you really are."

"What if I don't like being that sort of person?" He got up. "Don't answer that," he said as he went out. "Idiotic question."

That night the nightmares began.

He tried to describe them but it was hopeless. "Everything goes wrong," he said. "It's all upside-down and it keeps getting worse. I know something horrible's going to happen *because of me*, and I can't stop it, or . . . Damn, that's not right . . . I mean it's partly right but . . . Oh, Christ. It's just . . . *evil*."

The evil visited him every night; sometimes twice a night. He awoke rigid and terrified, one pace from catastrophe. In the morning he felt bruised and exhausted. This went on for three weeks. "I dread going to sleep," he said. "The bastards are waiting for me, they're trying to destroy me."

"Why do they want to destroy you?"

"God knows." Simon felt intolerably wearied by the question. The bloody nightmares were bad enough; why did this bastard have to keep poking and prodding at them? He needed help, comfort, something to take the pain away, not this endless bloody questioning, why, why, why . . . "It's all right for you," he said heavily, "you just sit there, don't you? Nothing ever hurts you, does it?" An urgent thudding in his head boomed into a frantic pounding and a great surge of hate raged across his senses. He covered his face with his hands. "Oh Christ," he moaned. "This is what it's like, I'm having one now."

After a few seconds the waking nightmare passed, and the room returned to normal.

"I wanted to kill you," Simon said.

"Yes."

Even then it took him a long time to understand fully what he had said; and even when he understood, he was reluctant to admit it.

"That's what they've been about, haven't they? Nobody was . . . Nothing was trying to destroy me. The nightmares were just trying to kill you."

"Yes."

"God in heaven . . . But *why*? It doesn't make sense. I mean . . . I like you."

"Perhaps . . ." He shrugged, and gave the most cautious of smiles. "Perhaps you had to kill me because I knew too much."

Simon laughed, but only briefly.

"I think," the man said, "we both deserve a brandy."

Simon left the nursing home two months later. They had found him a job at a nearby civilian airfield, as office-boy in the flying club. The manager, who was also the instructor and barman, asked Simon if he'd like a couple of lessons in a Tiger Moth. "Great fun," he told him. "Mind you, it helps if you're a bit mad." Simon accepted. The manager said he was the best pupil he'd ever had. A year later he was in the RAF.

When CH3 left him, Stickwell wandered about the upper floors of the château until he came across the adjutant's office. The door was open. "Hullo, uncle," he said.

Kellaway grunted. He had a pencil between his teeth and he was searching through a thick bundle of dog-eared carbon copies. His desk was littered with files; more files were stacked on the floor. Micky Marriott sat opposite him, searching through another bundle of papers. "Do something for you?" Kellaway said around the pencil.

"Is this where I join the Foreign Legion?" Stickwell asked.

Marriott muttered: "It must be here somewhere."

Kellaway, still searching, shook his head and sighed.

"All right then, how about the merchant navy?" Stickwell asked.

"Hey, look at this." Marriott pulled out a blank sheet of paper.

"Or the cowboys?" Stickwell leaned against the doorframe. "Or the Texas Rangers, or the Salvation Army, or *anything*?"

305

Kellaway and Marriott stared at the blank sheet. "I bet some twerp put the carbon paper in backwards," Marriott said.

"Anybody need a good street-sweeper?" Stickwell asked.

"Stop playing silly-buggers, Sticky," the adjutant said stiffly. He took the blank sheet. "You mean *this* is the copy? Or what ought to be the copy? Hell's bells . . ."

Stickwell left them peering at nothing, and wandered on. Rex's office was just around the corner. He tapped on the door and went in. There was nobody there. He walked over to the desk and saluted the empty chair. "Just came to tell you, sir," he said. "I'm off to win the war."

Rex was, at that moment, showing Dumbo Dutton's replacement, Pilot Officer Lloyd, around the château. "Gun room," he said, rapping on the door as they walked by. "D'you shoot?"

"Just woodpigeons, sir." Lloyd had a melodic Welsh accent. "On the farm, you know."

"Yes. Well, there's deer around here somewhere. I'd like to get in a spot of stalking once these have come off." He raised his right hand, still bandaged: a relic of Dutton's crash. "Billiard room over there. Library. Ballroom up at the end. Not a bad little billet, is it?"

"Very good, sir."

"I pinched it off some frog plutocrat . . . Have you met our unspeakable Yank?" he asked as CH3 came in sight. "Lloyd, Hart. Hart, Lloyd." They shook hands.

"Hart is so unspeakable that everyone refers to him by some sort of chemical code which I don't pretend to understand: CO_2 or V8 or 4711 or something."

"Have you been pissed on yet?" CH3 asked. "Rex has a dog called Reilly who pisses on people."

"Reilly's not very discriminating, I'm afraid," Rex said. "He'll splash anything lower than a squadron leader."

"I didn't know there *was* anything lower than a squadron leader," CH3 said.

"Actually, you and Reilly have a lot in common," Rex said to him. "Since neither of you can catch a damn thing. How are your reconnaissance liaison flights going, by the way? WC2 is our

Reconnaissance Liaison expert," he told Lloyd. "He's quite invaluable. Wherever he goes, Jerry is never there."

"Good heavens," Lloyd said.

"So we always know that Jerry *must* be somewhere else." Rex smiled proudly at CH3. "It's not a vast amount of information, I agree, but it's utterly reliable."

"This is a truly wonderful squadron," CH3 told Lloyd, "provided you like being pissed on."

Rex was already walking away. "Billiard room," he said. "Library. Squash court around the back . . ." Lloyd hurried after him.

"Don't forget to tip the guide," CH3 called out. "Sixpence is enough."

Five minutes after take-off, Stickwell's Hurricane jumped a wood, left a line of treetops swaying in its wake, dropped to ten feet over a meadow, and went through the French flak belt before they could catch it. He noticed guncrews running, a flicker of fire from a machine-gun, and out of the corner of his eye he saw tracer, like a string of party lights, drifting behind him. Then he was easing the fighter up and over the Maginot Line – someone in a pillbox had a shot at him – and a sprint across no-man's-land took him into the German flak, which was wicked and got rapidly wickeder.

The Maginot was a thin line: a concrete tunnel made bombproof with earth. The Siegfried Line was three miles deep, laced with wire, spattered with pillboxes, striped with concrete barriers. The ground swelled and dipped and every hilltop held a battery. Stickwell saw the gun-muzzles flash and then the sudden blots of flak appeared, ahead and above and around, dirty-brown and feeble-looking until one of them burst nearby and exposed its ferocious little red-and-yellow heart with an angry grunt that cut through the roar of the Merlin.

He was too high. He ducked down to the valley floor and zigzagged strenuously. His stumpy legs ran out of strength to work the rudder-pedals just as the valley ended. He blinked at the wrong time, nearly hit the hillside, yanked the stick back and bounced like a sports car hitting a hump-backed bridge. "Watch it, dopey!" he shouted, and then, more quietly: "Oh, no!"

It was like flying into a lavish New Year's binge where the air

307

was thick with coloured streamers. The next valley was alight with tracer: curling lines of red, of green, of orange, climbing, slanting, crossing. The first guns had warned them he was coming. Too tired to zigzag, he tried to dodge by leapfrogging but that felt stupid so he heaved the stick into his stomach, shut his eyes, and climbed. Something hit the machine and made it shudder. "Go away!" he shouted, and kept his eyes shut. He was small and he made himself smaller. He pictured the Hurricane shrinking to a dot. When he was sure he was at three thousand feet he looked. The altimeter was creeping up to two thousand and there were more flak-bursts than he could count. A hole the size of a plate showed in the starboard wing near the red-and-blue roundel. There was cloud as thick as fleece only a few hundred feet above. "Come on, come on, come on," he said, over and over, until he barged into its clammy sanctuary and gave everything a rest: body, mind and aeroplane.

Bad start.

When he took off it had seemed like a bright idea to stay at zero feet, catch everyone by surprise, whiz into krautland, find a fighter field, do the dirty deed, whiz back home.

Not healthy at zero feet. Better think again.

Guessing he was clear of the flak belt, Stickwell eased down until he broke cloud. He dropped one wing, studied the ground, saw nothing but forest and field and hopped back into the cloud, not too disappointed.

He repeated this three times. The next time, he saw more forest and field plus a twin-engined plane, quite low, flying north.

He turned and followed it, still ducking in and out of cloud. Within two minutes it led him to a large *Luftwaffe* airfield: three concrete runways, a dozen hangars, plenty of aircraft dotted about. He looked it over for three seconds and then ran away and hid.

"Congratulations, Simon," he said aloud. "You have located the enemy and you have him at your mercy. Now jump on the buggers and win the war. Piece of cake."

From beside his seat he pulled out the battered metal chamberpot that had been dropped by the Me-109, and placed it between his knees. He slid open the cockpit hood and locked it. "Piece of cake," he said again, and before he could give himself a chance to think, he shoved everything into a corner: stick, rudder, throttle; and hurtled into clear air.

The triangle of runways spread across his windscreen, tilted almost vertical. Aircraft were perched on them like flies on a wall. Some of the flies were moving. Stickwell felt a tremor begin to build as the speed increased. He straightened his legs to get more force on the rudder-pedals and wrapped both hands around the spade-grip of the control column. A red flare burst above the airfield tower and fell sideways. The howl of the Merlin grew and intensified, like a power saw screaming at a hardwood log, and he rolled the Hurricane straight, swinging the airfield back to the horizontal. Suddenly everything down there seemed to be moving. Men who had been walking were running, vehicles were vanishing behind hangars, the very hangars were changing as their huge doors slid shut. The activity gave Stickwell a surge of confidence: he was making them jump! Then the flak opened up and everywhere the sky was dotted and blotted with bursts of brown and puffs of white.

He levelled out at fifty feet and aimed for the control tower half a mile away. It was like flying through a tunnel: everything in front was abnormally clear and sharply detailed, everything to the sides was a streak, a blur. The flak ceased. "Thank you!" Stickwell shouted, and then saw why: a plane had just taken off, was heading for him. Twin engines, long thrusting snout, lean and hungry look: Messerschmitt 110. The pilot hauled its nose up and four points of fire blazed from the top of the snout. "Hey!" Stickwell shouted. The streams of bullets seemed to strain upwards and chase him, but the Messerschmitt was always ten feet too low. It flashed beneath him. "You bastard!" screamed Stickwell. The fright left him furiously angry. He skidded away from the tower, chucked the Hurricane onto the other wingtip and whipped back in a full circle, hunting for the 110.

It was gone. Nowhere. "Bugger it!" he bawled. The flak returned, chasing him with its dirty snowballs, and he was overtaken by rage. Everyone ganged up on Sticky! He kept turning, looking for blood, and into his tunnel vision swam a line of parked aircraft.

The blast of his eight Brownings made him flinch, and their recoil checked the Hurricane like a headwind. He kept his thumb on the button and gloried in those rods of golden fury converging to thrash and smash one German plane after another, until he had swept past the line and there was only a petrol bowser in view so

309

he gave it a massive burst and felt it blow up beneath him and help the Hurricane on its way like a wave heaving a boat.

It was a good time to go. A dozen ropes of tracer in lots of jolly colours were snaking about, seeking to snag him. Planes were getting airborne all around, mainly little 109's. Something walloped the Hurricane's tail and made the plane skitter. Bullet-strikes pounded the engine-cowling, stripping paint, flinging ricochets past the cockpit, some bouncing off the reinforced windscreen. Stickwell prayed nothing was bust and hared over the perimeter.

Jinking and swerving between a house and a haystack, he felt something loose banging about in the cockpit. He was over a hill and crossing a lake before he felt safe enough to look down. It was the old metal jerry. He'd forgotten to drop it.

A glimmer of wintry sunshine leaked through the clouds as he banked, turned, and aimed for the hill. It tinged the lake with silver, leaving the rest of the water twice as black, twice as cold. He was amazed at what he was doing: he muttered, admiringly: "This isn't like you, Sticky." Racing over the hilltop he passed an Me-109, going flat-out in the opposite direction: gone before he could even wave. A mile or so ahead, thick black smoke climbed high, billowing like deep velvet.

The Hurricane smashed through the smoke and reappeared in the middle of the airfield like the demon king in a pantomime. He swung towards the tower, tossed the jerry out of the cockpit, immediately slammed the plane into an opposite bank, and flew straight into a burst from a heavy machinegun.

The instrument panel seemed to blow itself to bits. For a second, Stickwell couldn't see through the chaos of splintered glass and wood. Automatically he levelled out and climbed. That gave the flak batteries a better view. There was a hell of a bang under the port wing and the poor bloody Hurricane was hurled on its side. When he got it straight the cockpit had cleared and there was a great rip in the port wing with petrol gushing from it. Automatically, he dived. "Make up your sodding mind!" he shouted at himself. The barrier of smoke loomed up and he rushed at it thankfully.

The hill led back to the lake, the lake to a river. Nobody chased him, nobody caught him. He followed the river through a forest, staying always at tree-level, counting every mile he put between himself and that frightful place, until eventually the truth was inescapable. He had got away with it. Amazing!

Well, perhaps not so amazing. The light was getting bad: that glimmer of sunshine had marked the end of the afternoon. Now gloom blotted out the horizon. Stickwell felt safe enough to climb to a thousand feet and try to get his bearings.

From a thousand feet the world looked equally bleak in all directions. His compass, of course, was a ruin. Bearings would not be easy to get. His left wing had stopped leaking petrol, which meant that one tank was empty. The Merlin sounded happy enough. But how long, oh Lord, how long?

The answer to that was twenty-seven minutes.

Stickwell guessed which way France lay and tried to keep a straight course in that direction while searching for landmarks. The cockpit stank of some disgusting chemical from the smashed-up panel, and his face was stinging: he touched it and shards of glass came away on his gloves; but as long as the Merlin was happy, he was happy. He was happier than he had ever been. He had proved himself. He belonged!

After twenty-seven minutes the Merlin coughed once, and then died. The nose dropped. Stickwell poked his head out and tried to see something helpful through the windmilling propeller. It was gloomy down there. Nothing but fields. Oh well, one field was as good as another. He watched and waited while the Hurricane whooshed softly downwards. He could hear the fluting of air in the gun-ports. A lovely sound. He noticed a hedge drifting past, and then everything seemed hidden by the wings so he guessed it was time to haul the stick back. He guessed too soon. Slightly less than three tons of fighter fell out of the sky like a truckload of bricks. Stickwell's body jack-knifed inside his straps and his head cracked against the gunsight. The plane bounced twice and went skating across a muddy pasture, but he knew nothing of that.

"Overdue?" said Rex. "Who gave him permission to be overdue?"

"More to the point, sir," Moran said, "who gave him permission to fly?"

Rex looked wistfully at the billiard table and handed his cue to Mother Cox. "If you don't win now," he told him, "I'll have you grilled in parsley butter with an apple in your mouth." He took Moran outside. "You didn't know he'd gone?"

"He didn't even get clearance from the tower. Just climbed aboard and skedaddled."

"So he might be anywhere." Rex ran his knuckles along the top of a radiator. "And anywhere is a big place. Especially at night."

"I talked to his fitter," Moran said. "He says Sticky took that old tin jerry with him, the one the Messerschmitt dropped."

"Curiouser and curiouser."

Rex went upstairs and told the adjutant.

"Sounds as if he was pissed," Kellaway said. "He wandered in here a couple of hours ago, talking a lot of cock."

"What, for instance? It might give us a clue."

Kellaway scratched his head with the eraser-end of a pencil. "He said he wanted to join the cowboys."

Rex sighed, and walked over to a typewriter. Using one finger, he hit a few keys at random. "Anything else?"

"Or the merchant navy, he said. Frankly, I didn't pay much attention. You know what they're like. They all talk a load of cock half the time."

Rex nodded. "You'd better tell Headquarters he's missing."

Hornet squadron was sitting down to dinner when Skull hurried in. "Rheims just called," he said. "The French army have a report of an aeroplane apparently making a forced landing near the Belgian border. They seem to think it might be a Hurricane."

"Seem to think?" Rex said. "Might be? What's the matter? Can't they go and look?"

"No, they can't. It's inside Belgium." Skull spread out a map. "There. Between Bouillon and Florenville," he said. "Near Sedan."

"About sixty miles from here," Moran said. "I bet that's him."

"If so, the Belgians will, of course, have interned him," Skull said confidently. "They guard their neutrality very jealously, so I'm told."

"Damn their neutrality!" Rex cried. His fist came down on the map with a crash that made the candelabras flicker. "I want my pilot! Who's with me?"

At ground level the night was so black that the pilots crossed the field with arms outstretched. A local thaw had melted all the snow.

Only the squelch of the gumboots of the man in front guided them; and when the French officer stopped, the line behind him bumped into each other and stumbled and cursed beneath their breath.

The Frenchman steered Rex to an oak tree and showed him a ladder that was lashed to the trunk. It proved to be the first of three. Rex guessed they were fifty feet up when they stopped climbing. The darkness was fractionally less: after a lot of staring between the branches he thought he could see the blurred beginnings of more fields.

The officer took Rex's arm and pointed it. *"Par là,"* he whispered. *"Peut-être cent mètres, pas plus. Au milieu d'un champ."*

Rex stared beyond his arm, but it might as well have been pointing into a coalsack. *"Vous pouvez le voir?"* he asked.

"Non. Mais nous avons illuminé la terre avec une fusée éclairante. Vous comprenez? Lumière brillante."

"A flare. You sent up a flare?"

"Oui, oui."

"Didn't it attract the Belgians? *Faire venir les Belges?*"

"Non."

They climbed down.

"Gather round," Rex said softly. "Stickwell's Hurricane is apparently in the middle of a field, about a hundred yards ahead. Now the French have, at my request, already cut the barbed wire to let us through. They've also stationed a very large tractor by the hole. We're going to take some wire rope and tow the plane back over the border. We're also going to collect Stickwell, of course, if he's there. Who's got Reilly? I'll take him now. Right, off we go. If anyone gets lost, find the rope. That'll lead you home."

The French officer guided them to the wire. A hulking caterpillar-tractor made a heavier blackness in the night. Someone sitting on it cleared his throat as they passed. Another man gave Rex the looped end of the wire rope. He stepped through the gap and leaned forward to make the rope pay out. The drum squeaked as it turned, in time with his steps. Others took hold of the rope and the resistance vanished. Rex tramped forward with Reilly at his side. The drum-squeak faded to nothing.

He took short paces to avoid splashing through puddles, and counted his paces. At a hundred and twenty he stopped and looked around, still blind in the blackness. He could smell the Hurricane, an unmistakeable reek of oil and petrol and coolant. Reilly smelled it too and strained against his collar.

The wreckage lay thirty yards to the right. One wing had snapped in half; the other had buckled and was pointing upwards, like an extra rudder. The tail-unit was nearly torn off and the fuselage looked thoroughly dislocated. All this he saw by the shielded glow of a flashlight.

The cockpit was empty.

Rex found Moran. "If the Belgians took him," he whispered, "they'd have left a guard, wouldn't they?"

"Maybe he bailed out."

"This looks more like a belly-landing to me."

Moran fingered the edge of the cockpit. "The hood's been locked open. Maybe he got thrown out and broke his neck."

"Maybe. Look: you get the rope fixed. I'll scout around."

He walked slowly along the track ploughed out by the Hurricane, feeling the broken turf under his feet. Reilly was not interested. Reilly wanted to go a different way. Eventually Rex gave in and allowed himself to be towed behind the dog. Reilly got more excited, thrusting this way and that as the scent twisted and turned, until he suddenly stopped and began scratching at something. Rex took out the flashlight and flicked it on and off. They were standing beside a fox's earth. He dragged Reilly away. "This is serious," he told him.

The rope was hooked around the Hurricane when he got back. Rex sent the new man, Lloyd, to tell the tractor driver to start hauling. The rest stood with their hands in their pockets and shivered. They had left the mess without having had dinner, and it was starting to rain.

Reilly howled.

"Shut up!" Rex hissed, and jerked the leash. Reilly howled more loudly, a long and passionate delivery. Rex stooped and groped for him. Reilly felt the leash slacken and he leaped forward, breaking Rex's grip, and charged into the night. "Heel!" Rex commanded, uselessly.

"Bloody foxes," he explained. "Oh well."

For another minute they stood listening to the feeble patter of the drizzle.

The tractor rumbled distantly. The rumble rose to a roar and,

314

as if this had been a drumroll in a circus, a searchlight split the night. It came from the Belgian end of the field and it shone almost horizontally, boring a dazzling hole through which the rain drifted like smoke.

"Everybody down!" Rex shouted. They flattened themselves on the boggy grass. The searchlight scanned fast and found the Hurricane, which by now was bouncing and bucking as the rope began to wind in. Caught in the narrow glare, the wreck seemed to be making its own way over the field, and the searchlight followed it as if fascinated.

For five seconds they pressed their faces in the mud. A loudhailer spoke, harshly and incomprehensibly. Rex raised his head. "Keep well away from the plane!" he called. "Get back to the wire! Run!"

They heaved themselves up and ran, splashing and skidding. The Belgians noticed something: the searchlight wandered suspiciously. Just as it was about to start nibbling on the first runner, it changed its mind and swung back to the other side of the field. There it hunted around until it found Stickwell, lurching across the grass while Reilly repeatedly jumped up and scrabbled at him.

Everyone stopped. They could hear Stickwell snarling at the dog: "Gerroff! Gerroff! Bloody animal . . ." The loudhailer manufactured another string of urgent noises. Stickwell seemed suddenly to become aware of the light. He turned and squinted at it through his fingers. More loudhailer. He dropped his hands and walked on. A rifle cracked. Stickwell halted. Reilly sat and scratched himself behind the ear. "What's up?" Stickwell asked vaguely.

"Forget him!" Rex told the others. "Leave him! Keep running!"

Rex stood, sucking in dank air as the squelch of gumboots receded. He switched on his flashlight and waved it, signalling to the Belgians; then he threw it, with a careful underarm lob, away from Stickwell. The beam flickered through the night, bounced, and stayed on.

Rex fell flat. The searchlight raced over him and started searching. At once he was up and running, calling Stickwell's name. Reilly heard, and came to meet him. They blundered about, splashing through shallow pools. "What's the game?" Stickwell asked, complaining. Rex ran at the voice and they collided. Rex grabbed an arm and headed for the barbed wire. "Here, what's

315

the rotten game?" Stickwell demanded. "Come *on*!" Rex urged. Stickwell fell down and took Rex with him.

The searchlight was coming back. It had another look at the Hurricane, now being hustled along at a steady pace, and then rediscovered Stickwell and Reilly, with Rex as a bonus.

The loudhailer barked. It was obviously an order.

"Come on!" Rex said. "Run, you silly bugger!"

Stickwell got up. The light was merciless. It bleached him, flattened him, rubbed out all colour. "Wossa game?" he muttered. His legs folded. Rex caught him and heaved him onto a shoulder and set off at a slithering trot.

The fizz of the bullet overhead reached his ears before the bang. He tried to zigzag and dodge the searchlight but it tracked him with appalling ease. Mud doubled the weight of his boots. All the time, the loudhailer kept barking, the tractor roaring, the battered Hurricane squealing and screeching. The next fizz-bang sounded closer, much closer, an angry insect looking for trouble. *Two warnings*, he thought. *Third time unlucky*.

Obviously they wouldn't miss. Aiming along this beam was like dropping stones down a well. Stickwell grew heavier with every stride, but the wire seemed to get no closer.

The next bang was different: less crack, more wallop. *Missed!* he thought. Three more bangs chased each other, and the searchlight died. Rex pounded on, aiming for the tractor's roar. He reached the wire before he fully understood. That had been revolver fire back there.

He scrambled through the gap, dumped Stickwell and staggered a few more paces, his lungs labouring, his heart hammering. Reilly frolicked, delighted at this unexpected fun. Everyone was safe, it seemed. So who shot the light? No, everyone was not safe. Someone was still being chased over the field. Bobbing flashlights showed the pursuit.

Cattermole charged home with ten yards to spare. That left the Hurricane, which was still being winched in. The Belgian frontier guards seized hold of it and tried to drag it back, but all they got was the tail-unit, which snapped off. The rest of the wreck scraped through the hole in the wire.

The tractor abruptly ceased its roaring.

The Belgians gathered, waved their rifles, and shouted a lot of bad language.

The Hornet pilots faced them and sang the squadron song.

Rex found Cattermole. "Did you pot that light?" he asked.

"It seemed the best thing to do."

"Damn good show."

Rex found Stickwell. "What happened to you?"

"Not sure. Lots of things. Got a shocking headache. Went to sleep in a bramble bush. Woke up when Reilly peed on me. Not very nice, that. Got a shocking headache."

By now everyone was listening.

"Well, I'm pretty sure what happened, even if you're not," Rex said. "And I'm even more sure what's going to happen next. You're chopped, Stickwell. Understand? Chopped."

Stickwell did not understand. A French army doctor asked him what day it was and which country he was in; examined the lumps on his head; and diagnosed severe concussion.

They found a British field hospital outside Sedan which accepted him, and they drove home. Behind came the broken Hurricane, piled onto a truck like booty.

In a grey and empty month, when the war that began with *blitzkrieg* had already been rechristened *sitzkrieg*, news of Hornet squadron's daring rescue delighted the other RAF units in France, especially those who had been shot at by Belgian anti-aircraft batteries. Rex took a stream of congratulatory telephone calls from other CO's. "If you want to know the truth, old boy," he told them, "I never could stand the taste of Brussels sprouts ever since my nanny forced me to eat the bloody things by the bucketful. If we ever capture a Belgian pilot I shall stuff him with boiled cabbage, just to square the account."

Air Commodore Bletchley drove down from Rheims. "Officially, the Belgians will get an apology and you will get a reprimand," he told Rex. "Unofficially, you did the right thing. In any case the Belgians need a dig in the ribs to help them make up their minds which side they're on."

The doctors let Stickwell get up on the second day. He had a black eye and a split lip, and the bruises on his forehead were turning

317

the colour of over-ripe plums. He was restless yet tired. He had a good appetite, but sometimes he felt oddly distressed in a way he could not describe. They wrote *Delayed Shock* on his file and gave him a large jigsaw puzzle to assemble.

His first visitor was Cattermole.

"God, you look awful," he said as he came in.

"Do I, Moggy? Do I really?" It was the nicest thing Cattermole had said to him in weeks, and he felt deeply touched. He said: "It's your fault, you great oaf. I only did it to shut you up, after all."

"What did you do?" Cattermole stretched out on the bed.

"Well, it's funny but I can't remember."

"Nothing? Not even the old tin jerry?"

"That rings a bell." Stickwell leaned on the bedrail. "Did I take it with me?"

"The general opinion in the mess is you went off and bombed Luxembourg with it."

Stickwell laughed and hurt his lip, but it was worth it.

"Not Luxembourg," he said. "I went somewhere else. Lots of coloured lights. Awfully pretty."

"Zurich, probably. Anyway, the chaps told me to tell you to hurry up and get better. You're needed at Flash Gordon's wedding."

"Good old Flash."

Cattermole lifted a bottle of medicine from the bedside table and sniffed its contents. "I didn't know whether you wanted to contribute to his wedding present, Sticky, but anyway I chipped in a couple of hundred francs for you ... What's this stuff?"

"Oh, just some magic mixture. Of course I want to ..." Stickwell searched through his pockets and gave Cattermole three hundred francs. "Is that enough?"

"What on earth does it do?" Cattermole took a sip.

"Dunno. Bucks you up, I suppose."

"One teaspoonful three times a day ..." He took a long swig, and rolled his eyes. "Christ! You shouldn't be taking this, Sticky. It's got a kick like an elephant-gun."

Stickwell found that enormously amusing. He laughed so much that he had to sit down. "Funny you should say that, Moggy. I've just remembered something." He felt blood dribble down his chin, and he sucked his lip. "I know this happened. It's as clear as day, honestly. There was this row of German planes, all lined up, and

318

I went along the row and hit them all. Blasted the lot. All blown up. I did it. I really did."

"Good show." Cattermole drank more medicine.

"I was tremendously angry, you see. You've never seen me when I'm really angry, have you, Moggy?"

"I nearly forgot: I had the Buick serviced for you. Here's the bill. Those brakes were in a very bad way, you know. You could have killed yourself."

Stickwell took the bill without looking at it. "I just realised, Moggy. That makes me an ace, doesn't it? You only need five, and I must have knocked out six or seven. So I'm an ace now."

"Oh, absolutely." Cattermole finished off the medicine. "You're a royal flush, Sticky. I've always said so. You want to stay off this stuff, old boy, it's pure poison. Now then." He got off the bed and lobbed the bottle at a waste bin, but missed. "Anything I can do for you? Grapes? Knitting? Lascivious ladies?"

"I wouldn't mind some decent beer."

"You shall have a crate of it. Cheerio, Sticky. Make sure you come back to say goodbye. The squadron won't be the same without you."

When he had gone, Stickwell tried to work out what he had meant by that, and came to the conclusion that Cattermole must have been posted. *What rotten luck*, he thought.

CH3 flew every day that the weather allowed, which in this appalling month meant no more than three or four times a week. He wore every piece of clothing he could get on: long underwear, three pairs of socks, three shirts, two sweaters, his fleece-lined jacket, a silk scarf, a woollen muffler. At ground level the air was so crisp that it stung the nostrils and the throat. At ten thousand feet the cold struck like a deathwish. At fifteen thousand he shivered so violently that his boots kept jumping on the rudder-pedals. Despite three sets of gloves – silk, wool, leather – his fingers were achingly cold. If he went up to twenty thousand the cold became more than painful: it drained the strength he needed in order to concentrate. Half an hour's patrolling at twenty thousand feet left him drowsy with fatigue, grudging the effort it cost to move his head an inch either way. Nevertheless he always made the effort, turned his heavy head more than an inch, searched the treacherous

319

sky. There was never anything to see except the white blaze of the sun.

One day, when he landed, Rex was waiting at dispersal.

"I'm about to do something very unwise, CH3," Rex said as they walked towards the crewroom. "I'm about to place myself at your mercy, up to a point."

"Yes?" CH3 heaved his parachute onto the other shoulder. "You mean, you want to do a deal."

Rex smiled. "You're not very trusting."

"No. Trusting others has proved unhealthy. The ones I trusted are all dead."

"In that case you understand the limitations of power. I, of course, have very little actual power. You know, CH3, leadership is a confidence trick. You have to persuade men that you can do absolutely anything, otherwise they lose confidence in you and instead of following eagerly into the jaws of death they begin wondering whether perhaps they should go to the lavatory instead."

"You want my advice? Always go to the lavatory. Then if you can't avoid the jaws of death, at least you're comfortable."

"I'm sure you're right. You see, the point I'm making is that I can't do just what I want, so I certainly can't do just what *you* want. On the other hand, if the chaps start believing that all I can do is say no, then the squadron spirit suffers."

"So say yes more often."

"In other words, do what you want."

"Yes."

"Change the formation, change the tactics, change the gunnery, change the kites, change everything."

"Yes."

"You might as well say change the commanding officer."

"Why? You do a good enough job in other respects. They like you, they respect you."

"Nice of you to say so. But that's the point, isn't it? They respect me precisely because I take command. How much respect d'you think I'd get if I followed every bit of tuppeny-hapenny advice I got from every pilot officer on the station?"

"Especially an American."

"That certainly doesn't help, I agree. The fact is, CH3, you're being damned unfair. You're exploiting your peculiar status here, taking advantage of the fact that you have special privileges, and doing your best to make my position thoroughly awkward."

"That's not my intention."

"Oh, bosh! You know perfectly well that we started off on the wrong foot, and ever since then you've been taking potshots at me."

"And you at me."

"AH right! For God's sake, if it makes you any happier I'll apologise." They had reached the cluster of hangars and huts, but instead of going inside, Rex stopped. "Look: I'm human enough to like being liked. How about a truce? Nobody wins but nobody loses, and we all start afresh. For the good of the squadron." He offered his hand.

"That's a cute speech," CH3 said, "but a lousy deal."

Rex dropped his hand. "Oh well. I didn't really expect you to agree so easily . . . Come on, I've something to show you."

He took CH3 into a hangar.

"You don't imagine that I think wooden propellers and canvas wings are the last word in aviation, do you?" he said. "It's taken me three months' hard wangling to get this crate."

It was a new Hurricane. It had metal wings and a three-bladed metal propeller.

CH3 walked around it, slowly. He let his hand drift over the immaculately smooth skin. He swung up onto the wingroot, glanced into the cockpit, jumped down, ducked between the wheels and examined the airscrew. "Are we all going to get these?" he asked.

"Eventually. This one's yours."

CH3 gave a snort of surprise. He turned to look at the Hurricane again, and prodded a tyre with his toe.

"All new tyres," Rex said. "I'll even throw in a free tank of petrol."

"Why me? I thought the best plane always went to the CO."

"Call it a gesture of goodwill. You see, I've been around long enough to know that nobody ever gets everything he wants. I don't, you don't. It's important to recognise that fact. I often think one of the differences between your country and mine is in our attitude to compromise. I honestly and sincerely believe that compromise can be an honourable solution. In this case, for the good of the squadron, I'm fully prepared to compromise."

CH3 stood facing him, with his head resting against the leading edge of the wing. "And you want me to accept the honourable solution too."

"I want to stop all this bickering and get on with the job, which is far bigger than both of us."

"Or, putting it another way: I can have this new Hurricane provided I keep my mouth shut."

Rex put his hands in his pockets and hunched his shoulders. The hangar was bleak, chilling, deserted. "I don't make deals, CH3," he said gently. "I simply do my best, and hope that other people will do the same. The Hurricane is yours."

"Fine. Let me tell you where I stand. My idea of an honourable solution is winning. I want every possible advantage I can get — fair, unfair or downright deplorable. I've never yet met an enemy pilot who was willing to compromise, and neither am I."

Rex went to the door and looked at the sky. "And loyalty?" he said. "Decency, fair play, unselfishness? All the things we're fighting for?"

"Fighting *for*, yes," CH3 said. "Fighting *with*, no."

Rex walked away. He found his car and drove back to the château.

The adjutant met him on the stairs, and said: "Any luck?"

"I tried to make him feel like a cad," Rex said, going up. "I don't think he knows the meaning of the word."

CH3 got hold of his groundcrew and had the Hurricane rolled out and started up. The engine snarled happily to itself, like a dog guarding a new bone. When he released the brakes, the fighter bustled eagerly around the perimeter. The propeller blades were set at fine pitch, which meant that they cut the air more easily, and during take-off he could be generous with the throttle. At something over half the normal distance the plane came unstuck from the ground. Even flying cautiously, he was at fifty feet when he would usually have been at ten.

He did a climbing circuit to test the controls, and then changed the pitch to coarse. The effect was remarkable. It was like changing gear in a car. As the blades bit more deeply into the air, the whole performance of the Hurricane improved without any greater effort by the engine. It flew faster, it climbed more easily, it manoeuvred

322

more readily. CH3 took it up to twelve thousand and threw it about the sky. The wings felt splendidly sturdy. They did everything he asked of them, so he asked more and still more, until he was flinging the Hurricane into violent banks and turns that would have brought creaks and tremors of complaint from his fabric-covered machine. This new plane seemed to enjoy that sort of treatment. It still wasn't a Spitfire, but it had something even the Spitfire lacked: an enormous sense of solidity; a reassuring reservoir of strength. He had the feeling that you could treat this Hurricane very badly indeed and it would always forgive you.

He came down in a long, lazy spiral and shifted the propeller to fine pitch. The Hurricane ghosted over the barbed wire, picked its spot, leaned backward and flared its wings, and settled sweetly on all three points.

"To tell the truth, Fitz, I still don't remember an awful lot about it," Stickwell said. "All I know for sure is I popped over to Hunland and got mixed up in a terrific scrap."

"Well, you're looking much better."

They were sitting on his bed in the hospital, eating dates that Fitzgerald had brought.

"Yes, I feel tremendously better. I'm a different man now, Fitz."

"That black eye's almost gone."

"It was like going solo. Nobody can do it for you, can they? And afterwards . . . Everything's altered, hasn't it?"

"Jolly good." Fitz spat out a date-stone and lobbed it onto the top of the wardrobe.

"The way I look at it, a chap's got to make the most of any experience, because that's what experience is for. Damn good dates."

"I know what you mean, Sticky. I had an amazing experience quite recently. With a girl."

"Whoopee."

"A woman, really. And it's changed me completely. I mean, while it lasted it was . . . I don't know . . . very exciting. Very vivid."

"So was mine, old boy. Coloured lights everywhere."

"It's funny, isn't it? You're really walking on air for a while."

"Dancing on air, more like it."

"Yes. And then . . . All of a sudden it's over. Finished. Just like that. Pooph!"

"Pooph indeed. Also bang-crash."

"I mean, the whole business was such an eye-opener. Not while it was going on, of course. I thought I knew what mattered at the time, but now I know better. See what I mean?"

"Absolutely," Stickwell said. "You've put your finger on it."

Fitzgerald ate the last date. "Nearly forgot," he said. "I'm collecting for Flash's present. Want to chip in?"

"Yes." Stickwell blinked. "No, wait a minute. I thought I already did, didn't I?"

"Not so far."

"I was sure I did."

"Well, I ought to know, didn't I?"

"What was that I gave Moggy, then?"

"Dunno. When?"

Stickwell concentrated hard. "Damned if I can remember. The old memory's been acting a bit peculiar lately."

"You're probably getting mixed up with the wreath we got for Dumbo Dutton."

"Dumbo who?"

"There you are, you see." Fitzgerald got up. "Anything I can get you? Toothpaste, books?"

"I could do with some decent beer." Stickwell frowned and looked out of the window. "Decent beer," he said again, thoughtful.

Suddenly Fitzgerald felt very sorry for him. "It must be rotten, getting chopped," he said.

"Bloody appalling," Stickwell agreed. They shook hands. When Fitzgerald had gone, Stickwell began to worry about him. Perhaps he'd got that girl into trouble and Rex was being old-fashioned about it. That seemed unlikely, though. Or maybe Fitz had given the girl the push. Or perhaps *she'd* dropped *him*.

It was all too difficult. He forgot it.

Flash Gordon's wedding took place at a small Protestant church in the nearby town of Mirecourt; Nicole had wanted to get away from her village and its angry priest. Fitzgerald was best man. The minister was an old family friend of Nicole's, and he made the service mercifully brief. Gordon managed the responses adequately;

Nicole was completely at ease; the squadron sang a hymn with gusto, and then hurried out to form an archway of dress-swords. As he followed the happy couple down the aisle, Fitzgerald noticed someone standing in a corner, by a pillar. It was Mary.

They met outside. "Hullo, you," he said.

"Hullo yourself." She was wearing a hat with a half-veil, and seemed glad of its protection. "I'm surprised you even want to speak to me."

"Don't talk such twaddle." He tried to look cheerful but the grin came out thin and crooked.

"You want to know what happened."

"Well . . ."

"Of course you do, Fitz. It must have seemed very strange. Not even a letter."

"Yes. Strange." They began walking slowly on the crisp gravel, going nowhere, not looking at each other.

"I had to go away," Mary said. "I can't explain. It wasn't anything . . . It wasn't your fault. I mean it wasn't because of anything you'd done. It was just . . ."

Fitzgerald nodded. He understood. It was because of what he had *failed* to do. Mary had gone away to spare him any further shame, and to spare them both any more embarrassment. She had done what *he* should have done. "Quite right," he said.

"I didn't go far. Neufchâteau. Some friends run a business there. They were very kind."

"Good."

"No, it turned out to be not much good, in fact. All my fault, really. Nobody to blame but myself, and it gets very dreary, sitting around blaming yourself all day, so when I heard that Nicole was getting married I thought I ought to . . ." She ran out of words.

"I'm glad. Look, Mary: we're having a sort of a reception-thing for Flash and Nicole back at the mess. Why not come and join us?"

She reached up and touched the line of his jaw. "Lovely," she said.

The reception-thing turned out to be a major celebration. There was a large contingent from a nearby Battle squadron and a party of vivacious nurses. A trio played cheerful jazz. Everywhere, champagne popped and foamed. This was champagne country. At eight bottles for a pound, why drink anything else?

Mary seemed to enjoy the party. Fitz could see that she impressed his friends. Moggy Cattermole was especially charming to her. "You know, Fitz," he said, as he stopped a waiter and handed around glasses of champagne, "this is what we're all fighting for." They laughed, as much at his style as at his words. As they drank, Fitz wondered briefly whether Cattermole had meant they were fighting for Mary or for champagne; but it didn't matter, it was just Moggy playing the silly-ass. They moved on. Stickwell came over, wobbling slightly, a bottle in each hand, and topped up their glasses. "Mary, this is Sticky," Fitz said.

"I've been chopped. Still, it's not the end of the world, is it?"

"Of course not."

"That's where you're wrong, young Fitz. It *is* the end of the world. I don't care. It's a rotten world, isn't it?"

"There are plenty of other squadrons, Sticky."

"I like good old Hornet. My advice," he said to Mary, "never be an ace. Aces get chopped." He wobbled away.

"Concussion," Fitz said. "He's not well."

She gave him her glass, still full, and folded her arms, hugging herself. The party swirled and laughed and talked around them. Fitz felt that she had suddenly gone away from him. He was not surprised when she said: "This is silly, but I've had enough. I can't stand all these people. God, that sounds conceited . . . Can we go, Fitz? Look, you needn't leave. Just get someone to drive me home. It's not your fault."

"I seem to have heard that before. You've really got to stop saying it, it's quite unnecessary." He finished his champagne and hers, and went to borrow a car.

The cottage was as cold as a cave and just as dark. She opened the shutters while he lit a fire. The kindling was brittle: it blazed high and bright. They stood side by side and watched the flames. "Dust everywhere," she said. "I daren't think what that bed's like. Damp and cold, obviously."

"Can't have that," he said. He fetched the mattress and the bedding and spread them in front of the fire. By now the logs were radiating heat, driving back the chill. She found an unlabelled bottle, half-full of some dark red liqueur. They sat on the mattress and sipped the stuff.

"I don't know why you put up with me, Fitz," she said.

"It must be because I love you, I suppose." He had never said it before, and now he was slightly shocked at the ease with which the words came out.

She kissed him, and that was another surprise. They undressed, and pulled the sheets and blankets on top of themselves. She was shivering so much that he had to hold her tightly for several minutes. After a while he realised that her trembling had changed subtly: it was starting to bring pressure to bear, and this was increasingly enjoyable. In the end he discovered the simple truth, which was that all he had to do was follow his inclination. It was so easy, it was irresistible. For the second time that day he was slightly shocked to find how easy it was.

"There you are," she said. "Piece of cake, wasn't it?"

He laughed at her slang. "Does that make me an ace?"

"Aces get chopped. Remember?"

"You know too much gen. You'll have to sign the Official Secrets Act."

Fitzgerald was pleased yet uneasy. It had been too damned quick: he suspected that he had taken more than he had given, but he was afraid to talk about it. Indeed, neither of them felt completely at ease.

He left, saying that he had to return the car, and she lay in bed and watched the fire collapse as the day ended. It was a maudlin scene, and she knew it, but nevertheless she found herself in tears, and she cried herself to sleep.

Stickwell said his goodbyes to Kellaway and Skull, and went to see his commanding officer for the last time.

"Nothing personal about this, you understand," Rex said. "It's simply and purely a matter of discipline. You beetled off and had a crack at Jerry on his home turf, which you knew was totally against orders. If I let that sort of thing pass, everyone's going to start popping over for a bit of sport to brighten up a dull afternoon, aren't they? War isn't all fun, you know. Well, best of luck."

There was a car to take him to the station for the long train-

327

ride across France. "Don't come out," he said repeatedly, as he went around the mess shaking hands, "it's horribly cold, you'll freeze." They were all very sympathetic; they promised to write, to keep in touch, to look him up whenever they ... In the end he stopped listening and got his coat and cap and his gloves and just went. The driver was waiting. At the last minute, Cattermole came running out with a piece of paper.

"Nearly forgot! Rex asked me to give you this, Sticky," he said. "I think it's just a few odds and ends he'd like sent out from England."

Stickwell glanced at the list. "Bloody hell, Moggy," he said. "This is going to cost a packet."

"Don't worry about that. Send me the bill, I'll make him pay for everything. Rex is rich enough, after all. I say: aren't you taking the Buick?"

"Bloody doctors reckon I'm not fit to drive yet."

"Oh, that's intolerable. Listen, I know a chap who's going on leave next week. Would you like him to ferry it back for you?"

"Marvellous. Can you really do that?"

"Piece of cake. Don't give it another thought."

The car sped away and Cattermole hurried inside.

"What was all that about?" Miller asked.

"Sticky gave me his Buick," Cattermole said. "Sort of a going-away present."

"Lucky devil," Miller said.

FEBRUARY–
APRIL
1940

The heron stood motionless in the shallows beside the island, legs like stilts balanced on their own reflections, and waited for food to swim by. It was a big lake, a mile long and half a mile wide, with this conversation-piece of an island planted in the middle. There was no breeze to ruffle the surface. The hills were still white with snow, and that made the lake look blacker than ever. Far away, a dog barked twice: two scratches in the silence. Then the silence healed over and there was nothing but the lake and the island and the heron, utterly motionless.

The bird turned its head as it heard a sound: a faint, dull groaning. The groan grew to a growl and the heron took off. Its huge wide legs unfolded and one flap heaved it into the air. By now it could see the danger: an aircraft flying low, just crossing the lake-shore, aiming for the island. The heron cranked its wings, straining to make height so that it could find safety, but the plane was fast and within seconds its guns erupted. Eight streams of fire converged in a cone of destruction four hundred yards ahead. The heron climbed sturdily into this whirlwind of bullets and was battered sideways, ripped and slashed and broken, a feathery lump of blood and guts that splashed into the lake as the Hurricane zoomed overhead and climbed away.

Eleven more Hurricanes followed, one after the other, each firing a prolonged blast. A plywood target stood on the edge of the island. Most pilots managed to clip it. One hit it in the middle.

"Jolly good show," said Air Commodore Bletchley.

"Most impressive," agreed a visiting air vice-marshal.

"Thank you, sir," said Rex.

They were standing beside their car at the head of the lake, watching the display through binoculars.

"Did you see that bloody bird?" the air vice-marshal asked. "Total write-off! I've never seen anything like it."

"I have, sir," Rex said mildly. "I saw a Dornier just like it."

"And so did I," Bletchley said. "That was a real eye-opener, that was. Fantastic firepower in these Hurricanes. One good long burst on target and it's goodbye target."

"Here they come," Rex said.

The squadron had re-formed in tight formation. It swooped in a gentle curve over the lake and flew past the watchers. The pattern was as precise as if it had been stencilled on the sky. "I say!" the air vice-marshal murmured. The wingtip navigation lights winked on and off in a simultaneous salute, and the air vice-marshal touched his gloved hand to his cap. "Very fine," he said.

"Come on, Reilly!" Rex said. They got into the car, the dog beside the driver. "I hope you like venison, sir," Rex said.

"A thought occurs," said the air vice-marshal. "Aren't you taking something of a risk, leaving your aerodrome without any cover?"

"I've got a chap up on patrol, sir," Rex said. "He'll take care of any stray Jerry . . . Home, driver."

CH3 was five miles high and freezing. An enemy aircraft was cruising over eastern France, with no apparent purpose. It was only just in sight. He had been following it for an hour, ever since it crossed the frontier just south of Strasbourg, and so far he had never got close enough to identify the type. It was just a dot that kept moving away. It knew he was there. If he opened the throttle to close the gap, it simply climbed some more. The higher they went, the more the Hurricane wallowed. And the intense cold was like a sickness that struck continuously.

So CH3 seemed to be losing, but he persisted because he knew that the German was not winning, either. Swanning around the top of the sky accomplished nothing. The aeroplane was either on a hit-and-run bombing raid or on a photo-reconnaissance mission. Far below, at twelve thousand feet, there was a screen of cloud that stretched to the horizon. It looked like the desert floor, it was so far down. To find his target, the German would have to go beneath it.

On the other hand he probably had more fuel, so he could wait. He also had a navigator, so he knew where he was.

CH3 decided to take a chance. He made a conspicuous exit, dropping a wingtip and falling vertically so that his star-shape caught the weak sunlight. It was a long way down, and the controls were growing stiff by the time the Hurricane slashed through the cloud and he saw France again. Within thirty seconds he had found a landmark. In three minutes he was back where he started, near Strasbourg.

He was gambling that the German had originally planned to fly the shortest course to his target. If he visited that target now, the direct route home would follow the same course in reverse.

The cloudbase was ragged and CH3 wandered through the tatters, skulking like a poacher, searching endlessly. The ground was snowcovered; anything flying across it ought to show up. The Merlin coughed and he switched fuel tanks without having to look.

Seven minutes passed. Nothing changed: the same scruffy cloud up here, the same frozen terrain down there, and in between an ocean of emptiness. His neck ached. His eyes were tired. The German had outguessed him and gone home another way. The cold and the endless searching were hurting his eyes: they began watering, creating little specks and blurs. He blinked. The specks vanished, all but one, far away to his left. It grew to a tiny brown blot, as if someone had poked a rusty nib at the sky.

French flak.

CH3 banked hard and straightened out in time to see a line of brown blots appear, reaching westward. He extended the line and found a plane a thousand feet below it, a Dornier-17, leaving a twin trail of thin black smoke in its hurry to get home.

Geometry was against it. As soon as the German pilot saw the Hurricane he knew that they were flying an interception course, and he swung violently away and began climbing for cloud. CH3 watched the Dornier sacrifice speed for height and reckoned that it would fail by about a hundred feet. In the event his Hurricane performed better than he expected. The Dornier was at least two hundred feet from sanctuary when CH3 eased up behind it, saw its wingspan grow to fill his reflector sight, and pressed the gun-button while he counted *one, two, three*. Converging streams of fire raged into the bomber. Its rear-gunners had been taking hopeful squirts at him even before he came within range; now they stopped. The Hurricane fell back a little, jolted by the recoil. The Dornier swerved sideways and fell from view. When he found it again it was diving like a gannet.

CH3 caught it and dipped below its slipstream to miss the turbulence. Someone was manning the belly-gun again but the German pilot started dodging and swerving and the shots flew wide. CH3 fired a burst that missed but it scared the pilot into a panicky skid, and while the Dornier was off-balance he fed another blast of bullets into it and an engine caught fire. From then on the German pilot was a passenger, and soon he was a dead passenger. CH3 swung wide and curved back to spray bullets into the bulbous cockpit. Shards of glass made a glinting trail that got swallowed in smoke. He climbed away and noticed flak all around. They were over the German lines. He dodged about to fool the gunners and watched the Dornier go sailing into a hillside like a drunk walking into a wall.

"I'm afraid the criteria are quite specific," Skull said. "I can't credit you with a kill without corroboration. Sorry."

"Someone must have seen it go down."

"Perhaps. Give me a map reference and I'll ask around."

"South of Strasbourg. I don't know precisely where."

"That makes it rather difficult."

"Tell you what, Skull. Let's forget about it."

"No wreckage, no eye-witnesses . . . It's awfully difficult."

"No, it's worse than that. It's embarrassing."

"On the other hand if you're sure –"

"No, no. Far from it. It may have been a trick of the light. Or perhaps a large bird. An angry crow or the like."

Skull fingered the combat report. "I ought to put down something," he said.

"Write: *enemy aircraft driven off in easterly direction*," CH3 told him. "They can't get you for that."

At this stage of the war, most encounters ended with the enemy being driven off in an easterly direction. German aircraft came over singly, at great height, to probe the Allied defences, and at the first sight of trouble they turned and raced home. Jacky Bellamy had to work hard to make a story out of that, but she was a hard worker and by adding some pen-portraits of the pilots she created a neat little two-part series. Part one told how the timid German pilots scuttled for safety rather than prove themselves in combat. (*British fighter pilots have christened the enemy "the bashful Boche." Said one young RAF flight lieutenant: "All we ever see is their tail units. If that's the way the Germans want to fight, they ought to design a plane that flies backwards."*) Part two put forward a reason for the German failure of nerve: the clear superiority of the Hurricane squadrons. It was no secret that the Hurricane carried eight guns, and Jacky Bellamy made the most of this. *The ferocity of their fire-power has to be seen to be believed*

334

... German bombers have been hacked in half by a storm of bullets before they even saw their attacker ... a speedy retreat is the only hope ... only fools and martyrs take on the Hurricane; the Nazis are not complete fools and they seem to have exhausted their stock of martyrs ...

It was these reports that led to something of a showdown with CH3.

They met by chance in the village *estaminet*. She had stopped off for a glass of wine. He was playing backgammon with a Frenchman. She came over and watched.

"Been out collecting more junk?" he asked, not looking up.

"If I wanted to write junk I wouldn't drive all over eastern France. I'd stay home and make it up."

"Same result."

"Yes? Tell me one thing I've got wrong."

"That stuff you wrote about the German Air Force. The feeble, timid *Luftwaffe* put to flight by the magnificent eight-gun Hurricane. That junk." He threw a double-six and galloped his pieces around the board. His opponent sniffed ruefully.

"It's not junk. It's what's happening."

"It's dangerous guff. So the Germans aren't attacking. That doesn't make them weak, or scared. So the Hurricane knocks down one or two. That doesn't make it a worldbeater. Those gallant aviators back there in the mess: they're beginning to believe your fairy-tales, you realise that?"

"Eight guns is twice as many as any German fighter carries. That's no fairy-tale."

"Look: doubling the fire-power doesn't double the hits." The game rattled on at a brisk pace as they talked. "All it means is the bad shots miss twice as much. Gunnery in Fighter Command is lousy. The harmonisation –"

"We've been through all that, remember? I checked out your theories. I talked to Rex, I talked to Bletchley, I even talked to some experts from Air Ministry. I'm sorry, but your argument doesn't stand up. It really doesn't."

He hunched his shoulders and concentrated on the game.

"Look, I don't say that because I enjoy hearing it," she said. "Believe me, I'd sooner make friends than make war."

He shook his head. "I'll tell you what you'd sooner. You'd

335

sooner I fitted your stereotype and acted like a Hollywood ace, swashbuckling about in the blue. Your readers would buy that."

"They buy the truth."

"No. They buy lies." The game ended. CH3 handed over some coins. They shook hands and the Frenchman went away. "You'll never understand," he told her. "All you can see is sexy aeroplanes and dashing pilots and you report it as if you're covering the Olympics. You'll never understand that there's no more glory in pumping tracer bullets into a rear-gunner's stomach or setting a Messerschmitt on fire and burning the pilot to death than there is in smashing an enemy soldier's face with a rifle butt or sticking a bayonet through his chest. But you can't afford to understand that, so you write junk and your newspaper prints lies. I don't care. It doesn't stop the truth happening, it just makes it dirtier and more painful."

"For someone who doesn't care," she said, "you get mighty agitated."

CH3 stretched his legs and closed his eyes. After a moment Fitz Fitzgerald came into the bar, looking cold and dispirited. "Hullo," he said. "Guess what? My girl's just given me the push."

"Mary?" Jacky Bellamy said. "Why? What on earth have you done?"

"Not enough," Fitzgerald said flatly. "That's the whole damn trouble."

She had looked tired when he arrived at the cottage. Her eyelids seemed heavy, and her hair had lost some of its gloss. "Hard day at school?" he asked. She nodded, with a sad little smile, and when he kissed her she turned her cheek to his lips and rested her head on his shoulder. "You ought to be in bed," he said. As the words came out he realised what a very good idea that was; but she shook her head and said she'd be all right in a little while. Fitz opened the bottle he'd brought. They had a couple of drinks and she brightened up a bit. Night is young, Fitz told himself. Bags of time yet.

He was wrong.

They had something to eat: nothing special, just cold meat and pickles. They began talking about her pupils, which led to memories

336

of their own childhoods and the general awfulness of growing-up. "Crushes were the worst," Mary said. "Do boys have crushes?"

"Well, I remember a certain amount of hero-worship."

"No, no. Worse than that. I mean we had crushes on just about everything: older girls, younger girls, teachers. Even horses."

"Good lord. Very busy."

"It must have been a terrible bore for the grown-ups."

"I don't regret having left all that behind, do you? I mean, childhood is supposed to be all sunny and innocent, but . . ."

"After the age of four, you do nothing but fret."

"Right. And make horrible gaffes. Like . . ." Fitz twitched his nose. "On second thoughts I'd better not say."

"Yours couldn't have been any worse than mine."

"Want to bet? If you'd met me ten years ago – five years ago – you'd've paid me to go away."

"I don't believe it."

"True. I was vain, greedy and selfish, and the reason you can't believe that, Mary, is because you are fundamentally honest and decent and generous, which in my opinion is completely unfair but jolly nice for thugs like me."

Her face gradually crumpled and she began to cry. Fitz was astonished. "My dear Mary!" he said, and put his arms around her. He was more astonished when she pushed him away.

"It's not your fault, Fitz," she said. "I just can't go on."

"Why not? What's wrong?" He had been brought down so abruptly that he felt helpless.

"We've got to stop. It's no good." Her face was shining with tears. He pushed a handkerchief into her hand. "Not your fault," she said. "I shouldn't . . . Please, please . . ." A jerky sobbing was fighting the words. "Let's . . . stop. We're no . . . good together . . ." A wave of sobs overwhelmed her voice. They broke with a violence that was painful.

"Oh Christ Almighty," Fitz said. He sat on the arm of a chair and knotted his fingers. "Don't say things like that. I always knew I wasn't exactly a world champion, I just hoped . . . Hell's bells! I did my best, you know . . . Oh, what a bloody silly thing to say. *Bugger it!*" Mary's shoulders were still heaving. "To hell with sex!" he shouted. "To hell with everything! It's not bloody worth

337

the candle!" He grabbed his greatcoat and ran. He could still hear her as he went down the front path.

"Not at all," Rex said. "Only too glad to help."

"Thanks. It's kind of a technical question. I guess I'm just gathering background material."

"Go ahead."

"Battle tactics. As I understand it, the recommended technique in Fighter Command is to open fire from long range and keep firing a long burst as you close in."

"Actually, you're not supposed to know that, but ... Yes, in general that's correct."

"Suppose I play devil's advocate. Suppose I say it's better to close to *short* range and fire *short* bursts, because after all even if you miss you haven't wasted much, and you can always go round and try again."

"Counsel of despair, Miss Bellamy. We don't encourage pilots to think in terms of failure. The short-range-short-burst school of thought is superficially attractive, but on closer scrutiny it turns out to be a hangover from the last war."

"When they didn't fly so fast."

"That's certainly one factor. Another was the general unreliability of guns in those days. You couldn't be sure of getting in a long burst even if you wanted to."

"I hadn't thought of that." She made a quick note. "And I suppose those machines were a sight more fragile, too. A quick burst in the right place was probably enough to knock a plane to bits."

Rex nodded. "Your modern bomber is a very different story. It has to be struck firmly and repeatedly for there to be any hope of a successful interception. I can assure you that these battle tactics are resolved at the very highest level of Fighter Command. I happen to know that Air Chief Marshal Dowding himself put his finger on the crucial element in favour of the long-burst-long-range approach." Rex took a model of a Hurricane from his desk. "Each time you open fire, the recoil depresses the nose of the aeroplane." The model twitched. "Just a fraction, but enough to take your sight off the target. Fire short bursts, and you repeatedly lose your target. Fire a long continuous burst and you get a chance to correct, to adjust, to destroy." He put the model away, and smiled. "Simple as that."

"Seems pretty conclusive." She put the cap on her pen. "I keep hearing about Spain," she added. "What d'you make of Spain?"

"It was a crude and rustic war," Rex said, "and the hobbledehoys lost. I don't think there's anything to be learnt from it. I really don't."

Cattermole bumped the door open with his shoulder and came into the mess sideways.

"Birthday?" Boy Lloyd enquired.

"Moggy wasn't born," Moran said from behind a week-old *Daily Mirror*. "He couldn't get his big feet through the hole."

"How did he get here, then?" Cox asked.

"I was carried shoulder-high in triumph," Cattermole said, "with cringing wogs and frogs scattering garlands in my path. Move your legs." He sidled past Lloyd and dumped two parcels on a table.

"Lillywhites," Lloyd read from the label. "Isn't that the posh sports shop? My god, it is." Cattermole had snipped the string, ripped the cardboard, and was taking out squash rackets.

"D'you always buy them by the dozen?" Lloyd asked.

"Certainly not. I never deal with tradesmen. These are the gift of an admirer. Have one. You've already pawed it with your greasy Celtic fingers so you might as well keep it." Cattermole opened the second package. It contained a pair of silver-backed hairbrushes, a Hardy's trout-reel, and some silk pyjamas.

"What d'you want those for?" Cox asked.

"My skin is very sensitive."

"Gifts from another admirer?" Moran asked. Cattermole ignored him. He found the invoices, threw them on the fire, and settled down to play with his new trout-reel.

Rex had given Flash Gordon permission to live out, on the understanding that he would have to move back in a hurry if the war flared up. Nicole had found a neighbour to look after her mother, and the couple settled down in the cottage. She was determined to have a baby. Flash did his duty nobly and frequently to that end. It was, for him, a complete and happy life. After Nicole there was

339

flying; after flying there was Nicole. He always had something to look forward to.

For her it was different. They were in bed one evening, and he was telling her the latest squadron gossip, when she said:

"How long do you remain pilot officer, Flash?"

"God knows. Why?"

She tucked her head against his shoulder and was silent for a while. Her hair tickled his nose. He snorted softly, blowing it away. "Because when you are promoted," she said, "we can find somewhere better than this to live."

"Ah. Yes. Of course." He had never thought of moving. "That would be nice. Are you sure it's worth it, though?"

"Why not?"

"Well, with the war and everything. You know what the RAF's like. Always posting chaps."

She was silent for a moment. "Flight Lieutenant Gordon," she said.

"Not half. Flight Lieutenant Gordon, DFC and bar."

Nicole pressed her face against his chest and made grumbling noises. Flash relaxed. He knew that sound. Everything was all right.

More of the new Hurricanes were delivered. Rex took one and gave others to the flight commanders and senior pilots. The weather improved. The snow gradually melted, until all that was left were diehard streaks of white, underscoring the contours of the countryside. At night black ice glazed the roads and fog lay in ambush. Military drivers – never the most patient of men – sent their vehicles waltzing and bouncing over hedges and ditches, or somersaulting down hillsides, or careering into buildings, or colliding head-on with other traffic to make a wreck that formed an extra hazard for the next military vehicle to come barrelling cheerfully through the icy murk.

That was how Hornet squadron lost four vehicles in a week. Two men died, seven were injured. Rex discussed the problem with Skull and the adjutant. "Only one solution," Kellaway said. "Put governors on all the gearboxes. Then they can't go fast."

Rex said: "What about the fog, though?"

Kellaway found a dead matchstick and poked about in his pipe.

"Fog's fog, isn't it?" he said. "If the silly buggers insist on racing around with their eyes shut you can't stop 'em."

"But it's playing hell with our operational efficiency, uncle. I don't mind losing the idiot drivers; we can always get more drivers. It's the chaps they take with them that bother me. Two perfectly good fitters and an armourer – *my* armourer, I might add – all in hospital. Not to mention an absolutely irreplaceable pastry-cook with a compound fracture of the right arm."

"Yes. I shall miss that steak-and-kidney pie," Kellaway murmured.

"Any ideas, Skull?" Rex asked.

"In my opinion the weather is a minor contributory factor," Skull said. "I suspect that these men are bored. You promised them a war. After six months they have experienced no adventure, no excitement. So they go out and make their own."

"That's absurd," Rex said.

"So is war."

"How d'you know?" Kellaway said sharply. "You've never seen one."

"No, but I read the book," Skull said, which made them stare.

Warm westerlies blew away the ice and fog and dried the airfield. Daffodils and narcissi bloomed in great yellow and white stands all over the grounds of the château, and flocks of birds came and went. At sunset, when they circled the tall trees, they were so closely packed that it was impossible to regard them as individual creatures: they moved as one, a community in flight. Mother Cox was showing Stickwell's replacement, a flying officer named Trevelyan, around the grounds, when he pointed to a mass of birds wheeling overhead. "Bloody clever animals," he said. "One of them's obviously leading, but which one? How do they know?" As they watched, the birds swerved simultaneously and the texture of the flock was transformed. "How do they signal?" Cox asked. "How do they miss each other? It's a mystery. *Bloody* clever animals."

"Rex is pretty hot on close-formation stuff, I hear," Trevelyan said.

"Rather. He likes to be close enough to count people's teeth."

"Does he really?" They strolled on. "Not, I trust, when they have become scattered across the landscape."

"Oh, nobody's pranged yet. All you need to do is keep an eye on your leader. Easy."

Trevelyan was an Old Etonian, which pleased Rex, but he was also very tall, which was a disadvantage. His head touched the cockpit canopy and the rudder bar could not be adjusted to fit his legs comfortably. As the latest arrival, he inherited the worst Hurricane: a much-patched veteran with an engine past middle age and a tendency to sidle that demanded a bootful of rudder. Trevelyan's formation-flying was not good. Rex put him in Green Section, back at the tail of the squadron where there was nobody behind him to back into.

CH3 remained the odd man out. He sat in silence at the squadron briefings. Apart from routine reports to Skull, he had nothing to say about his solitary patrols, and the others soon stopped asking him. Cox explained the situation to Trevelyan. "It's not exactly a feud," he said. "The CO's done his best to bring him round, but the Yank won't budge. I mean he wants everything *his* way. So we've rather left him to his own devices. He hasn't been sent to Coventry or anything like that. It's just that he's quite convinced he could make a better job of CO than Rex, and as it happens we rather like having Rex as boss, so there's not a great deal left to talk about."

"He sounds a bit of a bore," Trevelyan said.

"He was, for a while. But then we shut him up, and now he just sort of hangs about. Even Jacky Bellamy's given up on him ... Have you met Jacky? She's a great girl. We've got all her newspaper stories in an album in the mess. Buy her a drink and she'll make you a hero. Not really. But she's a terrific writer, all the same."

The Hurricanes, scattered about the edge of the aerodrome, were already bellowing like a cattlemarket when the pilots left their hut. It was a breezy morning after a showery night and the sky held more cloud than clear air: mainly big fat stuff, wallowing from west to east at about three thousand feet; but through gaps could be seen a much higher layer, while down at five or six hundred feet, thin streamers were blowing like smoke. It was the sort of day when a pilot would be able to see five miles one moment and five yards the next.

Rex had briefed them for a routine patrol west of the Maginot Line. CH3 was planning to go further north, to the Luxembourg border. He was halfway to his Hurricane when he heard someone shouting his name. It was Rex. He was in his flying kit, parachute slung over one shoulder, and he was playing with Reilly, dangling the leash so that the dog kept jumping and snapping. He waved. CH3 tramped back.

"You're not very happy about my close-formation flying," Rex said.

"That's right."

"You consider you have a better alternative."

"Yes."

"Well, now's your chance to prove it." Rex rolled the leash into a ball and hurled it. Reilly bounded away. "I get the squadron together at a couple of thousand feet and then you take my place. I clear off and watch. Fair enough?"

"I don't know." CH3 was taken aback. "Where are we going? I need to tell them how it works and . . ." Reilly came frolicking back, offering him a mouthful of soggy leash. "I mean, what's the plan?"

"You were at the briefing. Nothing's changed."

"Yes, but —"

"Look: you can explain everything when you take over. It's not frightfully complicated, I hope?"

"No, but —"

"Fine. See you upstairs, then."

The squadron took off by sections. CH3 sat in his cockpit, engine ticking over, and watched them go. Each section of three Hurricanes waddled into line, paused, and pitched forward, exhaust stubs gushing black fumes that faded when the tails rose, as if the rush of air had blown the engines clean. He could identify the pilots by the way they left the ground. Fanny Barton eased up gradually, building speed before he climbed. Moran came unstuck and made a quick thirty feet: if he wasn't on the ground he wanted to be right off it. Cattermole retracted his undercarriage as soon as he was airborne: wheels spoiled the look of the thing. Cox left his wheels down for several seconds, just in case. Fitzgerald wobbled a bit: his feet twitched on take-off. Patterson was always higher than the rest of his section. Gordon always waved to his groundcrew. Lloyd was a bit slow. Trevelyan was even slower.

At the end of a wide circuit the squadron had formed up, sections astern, twelve machines snugly interlocked. CH3 was airborne, trailing them by half a mile. They climbed another thousand feet, passing through the heavy shadows of billowing clouds, and levelled out. Headphones crackled, and Rex said: "Jester Leader to Jester aircraft. Change, change. Pilot Officer Hart takes command, Hart is now Jester Leader, out." Rex opened his throttle and pulled away, climbing hard.

"Okay, Jester aircraft, now get this." CH3 had closed the gap; he was fifty feet behind and above them, and he saw the flicker of faces as they glanced around. "Squadron will re-form into three, repeat three, sections of four aircraft. Green Section ceases to exist. Green Leader joins Blue Section as Blue Four. Green Two becomes Red Four. Green Three becomes Yellow Four." He repeated the orders and got confirmation from each member of Green Section. "Okay, when I say go, Green Section splits up and all sections echelon port. Is that clear?" Nobody spoke. "Okay. Sections echelon port, go."

This was old familiar stuff. Red Section – still lacking a leader – flew on; Yellow and Blue Sections slid to the left.

"Ease out," CH3 ordered. "Make room for your number fours." He watched while this happened, and then surged forward and settled into his place as Red Leader.

Rex was high above, watching.

"Right, this is the deal," CH3 announced. "We're going to spread right out. I want Blue Section half a mile to my left. I want Yellow Section a quarter-mile to my left. Understood? Okay. Blue Section, go." He watched the four Hurricanes bank and turn, shrinking rapidly. "Yellow Section, go."

He gave them half a minute to get settled, and said: "Good. Now, Jester aircraft: I want each section to re-form in line abreast and spread out. One hundred yards between aircraft. Got that?" Again, silence. "Let's do it, then. Jester aircraft, go."

They scattered. Now all twelve Hurricanes were strung out in a line nearly a mile long.

Trevelyan, flying as Blue Four, was on the extreme left. He felt strangely isolated. Blue Three, a hundred yards to his right, was unidentifiable, too far away even for hand signals. Trevelyan searched down the line and eventually found the furthest plane, Red Two, looking as big as a broken matchstick. This strung-out, thinned-out formation made Trevelyan uneasy. There was too much sky, too little company. He found himself drifting inwards, towards Blue Three. He drifted out again.

"Everybody makes a continual search," CH3 announced. "Twelve pairs of eyes looking for the enemy. We see him before he sees us."

The squadron droned eastward. There was nothing to see but the awkward-looking hills of cloud a thousand feet above, leaning and toppling as the wind drove them. The line of aircraft stretched and concertinaed: it was difficult not to wander when you were turning and twisting to squint into every corner of the sky.

After five minutes, necks were starting to ache.

"Hard work, right?" CH3 said. "So make it easier. Share the search with your wingman. He covers you and you cover him."

"Don't understand," someone said curtly.

"Okay, I'll explain. My wingman is Red Two. I watch his tail, he watches my tail. Understand?"

"Shit, that's flak!" someone shouted. A patch of shaggy blobs sprouted directly ahead of Yellow Section. Almost immediately they were flying through the smoke and bouncing on the turbulence.

"Climbing, climbing, go!" CH3 ordered. The squadron angled upwards and passed over a second cluster of bursts.

"Fucking frogs! Can't they see?" a voice complained.

"Let's go down and strafe the bastards," another said. Several voices agreed and gave encouragement.

"Shut it up!" CH3 shouted. "Stay off the air!" But then a different, deeper voice cut in. "Jester Leader, this is Blackjack, state your position, over."

Blackjack was the operational controller. CH3 did four seconds' hard work on the map strapped to his knee. "Jester Leader to Blackjack. My position five miles east of Rambervillers, over."

"Jester Leader, this is Blackjack . . ." Long pause. The cloudbase was getting close. He could hear the controller's breathing. It was impossible to transmit while Blackjack was on the channel. He levelled out just below the cloud and hoped everyone else would

345

do the same. "I have a bogey for you," Blackjack said, sounding calm and stately. "Steer zero-six-zero, over."

"Zero-six-zero, okay."

"Jester Leader this is Blackjack, what is your present height?"

"Blackjack, this is Jester, my height three thousand." CH3 hunted desperately to left and right. He could see only five Hurricanes, very widely scattered. Where the hell were the rest? Blackjack cleared his throat and said: "Jester Leader, this is Blackjack, do you mean feet or metres?"

"Jester to Blackjack, feet, feet, over."

"Blackjack to Jester, your bogey is at eight thousand feet, over."

"Eight thou, got it. Jester aircraft, steer zero-six-zero. Jester Blue Leader and Yellow Leader, acknowledge that, over."

But Blackjack had more to say. "Jester Leader, this is Blackjack. Bogey flying south-west to north-east. You have a stern chase, Jester, over."

"I know. Come in, Yellow Leader, Blue Leader."

"Blue Leader to Jester Leader, where are you? Over."

"Speed of bogey," declared Blackjack, "estimated two-fifty."

"Jester Leader to Blackjack, for Christ's sake *shut up!*"

"Yellow Leader to Jester Leader, I'm in orbit above cloud with Yellow Two, over."

"Jester Leader to Blue Leader, find Yellow Leader in orbit above cloud and regroup. All Jester aircraft who can see me, waggle your wings."

CH3 was checking the response when Blackjack returned, sounding puzzled. "Your last transmission somewhat garbled, Jester Leader. Please repeat, over."

"Okay, Jester aircraft, I see you too," CH3 said. "Power climb to eight thousand, go." But as he advanced the throttle, something flickered in the corner of his eye and made him check. He turned his head and saw, tumbling behind him, a broken Hurricane. Instinctively he brought his plane round in a tight, skidding turn, all the time watching this broken Hurricane flopping and fluttering like an injured moth. Then, as if it were a piece of trick photography, the cloudbase released a fully-opened parachute, and he watched that instead, a curiously perfect, flower-like creation, round and white, drifting serenely. Then another Hurricane appeared. It came sliding out of the cloud, curling away from the parachutist and

346

putting its nose down as if it had an urgent appointment. The urgency was deceptive: the Hurricane had no propeller.

"Right-ho, Mr Hart," Rex said over the radio. "I think that's enough, don't you? Find some friends, if you can, and go after that Hun. I don't imagine you'll find him. I'll tidy up this mess. Have a nice time."

CH3 saw the broken Hurricane flutter down, crash and burn. He turned and steered zero-six-zero and buried himself in cloud. He didn't find any friends, and he didn't find the intruder. By the time he landed at St Pierre, the others were down. He asked his fitter who was missing. Flash Gordon, he said. And the new man, Trevelyan.

The adjutant paused outside the library to adjust his collar. It was a detachable white collar from a civilian shirt, worn back to front, and the stud was sticking into his neck. He went into the library and stood with his head bent, peering studiously over the top of his glasses. "Flight Lieutenant Protheroe?" he said.

"That's me." Protheroe got up from an armchair. He was a burly young man, prematurely bald, with a belligerent thrust to his jaw.

Kellaway tipped his head far back so as to examine him through his glasses. "Ah, there you are," he said. "I'm the chaplain."

Protheroe came over and shook hands. "Pleased to meet you, padre." Kellaway was wearing a black eyepatch, and a strip of sticking plaster covered his upper lip. "Been in the wars?" Protheroe asked.

"Fighting the good fight, like all of us here. Come and meet my little flock."

They walked through the château to the foot of the grand staircase. Kellaway picked up a bible and read in a loud voice: "'Assemble yourselves, and come, all ye heathen, and gather yourselves together round about.' Joel, chapter three, verse eleven."

"Amen!" shouted Moke Miller from the top of the stairs. He came tobogganing down on a huge brass tray, banging and booming, and made Protheroe dodge as he skated across the hall floor. Already the next man was on his way down. Kellaway helped Miller to his feet. Miller was wearing an eyepatch, a white collar back-to-front, and a strip of sticking plaster on his upper lip.

"My assistant chaplain," Kellaway said. Miller shook hands with Protheroe as Patterson skidded across the floor and fell off his tray. He too wore an eyepatch, sticking plaster and a reversed collar. "My deputy chaplain," Kellaway said. Patterson shook Protheroe's hand. Kellaway was helping Cattermole to get up. "My second assistant deputy chaplain," Kellaway said. Lloyd arrived and fell off his tray.

One after another the entire squadron, including Rex and Marriott, came careering down the staircase, each wearing an eyepatch, a dogcollar, and a sticking-plaster moustache. Kellaway introduced them all as junior chaplains.

"Good show," Protheroe said, smiling grimly. He was determined not to lose face.

There was a short pause while they stood in a circle and looked at him.

"Isn't this a fighter squadron?" Protheroe asked.

Kellaway took up his bible again. " 'Awake, ye drunkards, and weep; and howl, all ye drinkers of wine, because of the new wine; for it is cut off from your mouth.' Joel, one, five." He shut the book firmly.

"I think that answers your question," Rex said.

"I'd like to meet the commanding officer," Protheroe said.

"He's dead, poor bugger," Miller told him.

"Really? That must have been sudden." Protheroe was fighting back. "What was his name?"

"Poor-Bugger," Fanny Barton said confidently. "Air Vice-Marshal the Reverend Sir Stanley Poor-Bugger."

"Yes," Protheroe said. "Of course. It would be."

"He always spoke most warmly of you," Kellaway said. "Shall we have some lunch? Perhaps you'd say grace. We're all hopeless at it."

Lunch was noisy. Much wine was drunk. CH3 came in halfway through, followed fifteen minutes later by Flash Gordon, limping and scratched about the face. Last to arrive was Trevelyan, who had a bandage around his head. Each man was introduced to Protheroe as a chaplain. Protheroe kept a poker face, ate his meal, and took no part in the conversation, which was stiff with profanity. He was thinking.

Protheroe had been in the RAF for fifteen years; he expected to give it all his working life. He was hardworking, obedient, ambitious and determined. He shaved each day in cold water and his uniform was pressed each night: the creases were as crisp as notepaper. Rex's raid had damaged Protheroe's career-prospects. Nobody blamed Protheroe but he had been made to look foolish. Well, now he had located the men responsible; now the record would be put straight: formally and officially. When lunch was over he would drive back to his base, submit his report identifying the guilty parties, and allow the force of law to take effect.

Half a roll hit Protheroe in the face. He showed no emotion. He brushed the crumbs off his cheek and said to Cattermole, who had thrown it: "You people are too stupid to realise how stupid you are."

"Sorry," Cattermole said. "Don't quite follow. I'm a bit stupid, you see."

That was marvellously funny. They pounded the table.

"Don't waste your stupidity on me," Protheroe said. "Save it for the courtmartial. I'm sure they'll find your actions most amusing."

That was when Cattermole got up and went out.

"Would you like to see the chapel?" Kellaway asked. "I can play Chopsticks on the organ."

"You fighter boys make me sick," Protheroe said.

When he left, they shambled out with their drinks to see him off. There was one more surprise. Someone had painted a large white cross on the roof of his car. "More hooliganism," he said evenly. "Another charge." The roar of an aero-engine surged beyond the trees. "What's that?" he asked. "The wrath of God?" He drove away.

"Bloody tradesman," Rex said. "Bloody troublemaker."

"Can he really get you courtmartialled?" Cox asked.

"Well, at least we pulled his pisser for him," Miller said.

Kellaway yawned enormously. "Christ, I'm tight," he said.

"Why were you late for lunch?" Rex asked Gordon.

"I had to bale out. Trevelyan flew into me."

"No I didn't," Trevelyan said. "You flew into me. Knocked my prop off."

"Well, you both missed some damn good partridge," Rex said.

"Was that partridge?" Moran asked. "Mine tasted like pork."

"I think I might go and have a little lie-down," Kellaway said.

They straggled inside. CH3, standing by the door, raised a hand as Rex approached and began: "I want to –"

"Later." Rex went past him. "You've wreaked enough havoc for one day."

The broken cloud of the morning had been replaced by a thick, low layer the colour of dirty snow. Dusk would come early. When Cattermole took off he found the light at five hundred feet little better than at ground level; all the same, he had no difficulty in spotting Protheroe's car. As it worked its way along the lanes to the village, he flew leisurely figures-of-eight behind it.

Beyond the village the roads improved. Protheroe got onto a stretch of military highway, straight and wide, built during the Great War. Traffic was light. He put his foot down. The cobbled surface made a brisk drumming that blended pleasantly with the throb of the motor. He was planning his report, testing phrases in his mind, searching for the right style. It had been a crime, he thought. Treat it as a crime. Let the facts do the work. Spell out the flagrant illegality, of course, but . . .

Out of nowhere came a mild growl. Protheroe cocked his head. It was like a whining dog, but harsh and resonant. The growl suddenly magnified itself to a stupendous blast of sound that made him instinctively duck. The car fishtailed and he had a second fright before he got it under control. The Hurricane streaked away in front, skimming the road, so low that he could see the tops of its wings, and then soared and was lost to sight.

Protheroe had been badly frightened. He stopped the car. As his heartbeat slowed, he told himself that this was simply further proof of guilt. The only point of this idiocy was to scare him. It wouldn't work. He despised them for thinking that it would.

He drove on, and gradually in place of fear came anger. He put on speed, aiming the car down the long, wide highway, thinking of what had just happened and what was going to happen. He did not see the Hurricane coming back towards him until the plane was a mile away, flying head-high down the middle of the road, very fast. Protheroe didn't slow: he was damned if he was going to be scared twice. But the Hurricane kept coming. It filled the road. It got closer and bigger with an appalling rush. The thing was hellbent on ramming him. His wits were scattered. He screamed and flung the wheel over.

Cattermole tucked the stick back and hurdled the skidding car like a hunter taking an easy fence. When he turned and flew back to look, the car was upside-down at the bottom of an embankment, steaming gently. In a nearby field a young horse kept galloping in circles.

Kellaway went upstairs and had his little lie-down. CH3 got his car, drove to Nancy and saw a film. The rest of the squadron continued the party, since there was no apparent reason to stop it and everyone was agreed that it was a damn good thrash, especially as Rex was bound to pick up the tab for most of the booze; he always did. The party had ignited spontaneously when they gathered in the mess after the morning's disastrous patrol. Nobody had been killed, which was something to celebrate, and CH3 had made a monumental cock-up, which was also worth recording, and then this prize pratt Protheroe had turned up, which put the tin hat on everything. There was plenty to drink about.

Next morning, breakfast was a sombre meal.

"Pass the butter," CH3 said.

"Please don't shout," Moran said. "There are people here trying to die."

"Not me," Cox said. "I died an hour ago. I can still taste the embalming fluid. Ghastly."

Skull came in and sat down. "Several large fried eggs," he told the waiter, "and a pile of greasy bacon, please, with a couple of smelly kippers and a bowl of bubbling gruel." Groans and moans sounded around the table. "How nice to hear from you all," he said. "The CO is currently having a bath. Kindly meet him in the library in half an hour."

The meeting was brisk. "I have to attend a conference in Rheims," Rex said. "That leaves me just five minutes to sort out yesterday's nonsense. Flash, what happened to you?"

Gordon had told the story so often that he was bored with it. "Climbing through cloud as per orders, sir. Hell of a bang at the rear end, kite goes haywire, controls up the spout, yours truly bales out."

"Hugo?"

351

"Much the same, sir," Trevelyan said. "I was trudging up through that wodge of cloud. Next thing I knew, my prop was chewing away at somebody's tail. Goodbye prop. I managed to put her down in a field."

"Good show."

"Had to go through a fence first."

"She's somewhat bent, then."

"So am I, sir. My skull is now hexagonal."

Rex looked at CH3. "Your comment?"

"That extended formation is meant for clean-air conditions. It lets everyone see –"

"But you sent these chaps through cloud like that."

"Only because Blackjack came on and fouled things up. If Blackjack hadn't –"

"Oh, but Blackjack did. And Blackjack had every right to, because that's why we were on patrol, wasn't it? To intercept intruders? As directed by Blackjack?"

"Yes, but his controlling was lousy, he was slow and longwinded and verbose and –"

"You don't like his style, is that it? Well, I'm not always enchanted by your style, either, but I hope I don't write off a brace of Hurricanes every time it happens. Now then: what's the point of this emaciated-looking formation?"

"It frees every pilot to use his eyes. Nobody gets jumped."

Rex glanced at his watch. "And you consider it worth losing the united punch of the squadron just so that everyone can develop a stiff neck?"

"That's a false comparison. You can't begin to fight the enemy until you see him."

Fitzgerald said: "Come off it, CH3. Anyone can spot a gaggle of Heinkels. Even Moggy, and look at his eyes."

"You look," Cattermole said. "All I can see is a red mist."

Fanny Barton raised a hand. "I must say I don't see the point of having *every*body looking *every*where *all* the time," he said.

"You would, if . . ." CH3 stopped.

"If what?"

"Well . . ." CH3 scratched his jaw. "I was going to say, if you'd flown against the Condor Legion, but . . ."

"Oh, Christ," Miller grumbled. "Not bloody Spain again."

There was a discreet knock at the door. "My driver," Rex said. "Carry on the discussion, if you wish." He went out.

The silence was bored and slightly hostile. Eventually Flash Gordon stood up. "Look," he said, "I had plenty of time to think while I was hanging underneath that brolly yesterday. I mean, it makes you think when something like that happens. It was my life," he told CH3. "It was your clever idea, but it was my life, and I kept thinking, What would Nicole say if she could see this? She'd say ... Well, she'd say something very rude in French." There were a few quiet chuckles. "So this is what I think," Flash went on. "I think Rex is a bloody good CO. I mean, look at the way he rescued old Sticky from the bloody Belgians. Look at what he did when Dumbo Dutton pranged. This squadron means everything to him. Of course he's tough on us, of course he won't tolerate sloppy flying, and personally I'm damn glad of it. Rex is a hell of a good leader, the best I've ever known, and I'll follow him anywhere. But I'm damned if I'll follow *you*."

"Because I'm not a hell of a good leader," CH3 said.

"You couldn't lead a church parade."

Gordon sat down, looking flushed and angry. It was the longest speech he had ever made.

The adjutant came in. "Guess what," he said. "That prick Protheroe. He bought it on the way home. Car smash."

"Driving too fast, I expect," Cattermole said. "Young men are so impetuous nowadays." He sprawled in his armchair and closed his eyes. "Rush, rush, rush. It's the curse of the age. Where it will all end I shudder to think."

The air grew warmer. Fields changed from brown to green; trees softened their shape; it was possible to walk in the woods without wearing gumboots. The french windows were re-opened and the pilots sat on the terrace in the sunshine. Life was pleasant again; in fact when spring got into its stride, and the orchards displayed their extravagant froth of blossom, life began to be quite cheerful; which made Fitzgerald's despondency all the more apparent.

He stared into space a good deal, went for solitary walks, played squash as if he wanted to lose, got tight very easily, and lost five or six pounds in weight. One day he wandered into the adjutant's office, sat down and said he wanted a transfer.

"What's up, Fitz?" Kellaway asked. His left knee hurt. It had never been the same after he'd crashed his SE5a in a shell-hole near Sedan. He pounded it with his fist, which did no good. Nothing did any good. Bloody stupid knee. He gave it another thump for good luck. "Don't you love us any more? Is it something we said?"

"I'm letting the squadron down, uncle. I'm not up to scratch any more."

"Balls." Kellaway pulled up his trouser-leg and examined his knee. "Your flight commander hasn't complained. Rex hasn't said anything. What's wrong? Whatever it is, I'll swap you my knee for it."

"Oh, it's just ... *everything*." Fitzgerald put his head in his hands and stared at the floor. "I mean, what the hell's the point of anything? It's all a waste. It's a joke. That's all I am, anyway. A piss-poor joke."

The adjutant wasn't listening to the words. He knew that tone of voice, that wretched growl of self-pity and bitter, unfocused resentment. What Fitzgerald needed now was sympathy, understanding and encouragement. On the other hand Kellaway's left knee was on fire. "It's that bloody silly woman, isn't it?" he said, and Fitzgerald nodded. "What's wrong?" he asked. Fitzgerald shrugged. "Widow, isn't she?" Kellaway said. "Well, get over there and give her a good poke. Everything looks different in bed."

"That's just the trouble," Fitzgerald mumbled. "I can't seem to ... you know ... bring it off."

"Bollocks," Kellaway snapped.

"It's true. Mary told me, she said it wasn't any good, she couldn't go on, and she burst into tears." Fitzgerald sniffed hard. "She was really upset, uncle. I could tell."

"Bloody silly women," the adjutant said crossly.

He got his cap and gloves, took a car and drove to the village.

The midday break had just begun. He met Nicole in the school playground. The children clustered around to stare at the old man in the funny uniform. "Hullo," Nicole said. "If you want to see Mary, she is inside."

"Good." He set off, and then came back, trailing children. "What's the matter with her?" he demanded.

Nicole deflected a sticky hand reaching for his shiny tunic

buttons. "Mary is . . ." She blinked, searching for the English word. "Pregnant," she said.

"Ah." Kellaway paused. He ruffled a couple of heads. "That's better. I don't think I'll bother to see her after all. *Merci, madame.*"

All the children waved as he drove away. He waved back. "Dirty little horrors," he said. He really disliked children.

"Flying a fighter is a dangerous business," Rex said. "Anyone who cannot accept that fact would be better off doing something else."

"I don't want to do anything else," CH3 said.

They were in Rex's office. The adjutant stood looking out of the window.

"Flying fighters is also a team business," Rex said. "And it seems you don't want to join the team."

"Not when it's playing to lose, no."

Rex lost patience. "If I had my way, Hart, I'd boot you out of that uniform in no seconds flat. Ever since you joined this squadron your whole attitude has been carping, negative, presumptuous, insolent and generally crass in the extreme. You've done nothing, and yet you think you know everything. You're a self-righteous, self-opinionated prig."

"And you're a playboy," CH3 said. "This isn't a fighter squadron, it's Rex's private flying club."

"Hey, steady on, lad," Kellaway said, turning.

"You're proud of these trophies, aren't you?" CH3 picked a silver tankard from Rex's desk. "*Champion Flight, Formation Aerobatics, Hendon Air Pageant, 1938.* Very pretty."

"Pretty to watch," Rex said. He was making an effort to control his temper. "Tough to perform, and a supreme test of skill, courage and co-ordination, but you wouldn't know about that."

"Don't kid yourself. I know what goes on. You're keen on close-formation stuff because it flatters your vanity. Everyone has to watch *you*. You manipulate the squadron. You put them through their tricks. They're like trained dogs."

Rex sniffed. "Your trouble, Hart, is you're incapable of thinking unselfishly. Certainly I take pride in leading a well-trained squadron. Contrary to your peculiar notions, there is no room for vanity in discipline. There's no room for cold feet in a cockpit, either. I understand you've had armour plating installed behind your seat."

Kellaway snorted. "Oh, for God's sake . . . Have you really?" CH3 was silent. "Fancy putting a whacking great hunk of iron smack off-centre," Kellaway said. "You'll ruin the balance of the whole machine."

"Flying a fighter is of course a dangerous business," Rex said. "But you don't destroy the enemy by wrapping yourself in sheets of steel."

CH3 had nothing further to say.

"Perhaps that explains your pathetic record," Rex said. "Go away, Hart. You make me tired."

When he had left the room, Rex and Kellaway looked at each other.

"He's obsessed with safety," Kellaway said. "Armour plating! I ask you."

Fitzgerald was sitting on the front step when Mary came home from school. She sat beside him. The afternoon sun was full on their faces.

"Oh well," she said. "I suppose everyone knows now."

"Just Kellaway and me. Nobody else."

"It doesn't matter. I can't keep it a secret for ever, can I?"

Fitzgerald examined the backs of his hands, checking the pattern of freckles. "How do you feel about it?" he asked, very cautiously.

"Mixed."

"Oh." He turned his hands over and examined the palms. "Well, I suppose that's understandable."

"Fitz, for God's sake stop being so damned reasonable." She was not angry; just forthright. "It's not a reasonable state of affairs, is it? I mean, I haven't behaved reasonably. Neither has nature. It's all most unreasonable, if you ask me."

He scrutinised his thumbs while he thought about that, but he could make no sense of it. He put his thumbs away and tried a different tack. "The point is," he said, "it seems that I got a rather false impression of . . . um . . . things."

She leaned against the door and closed her eyes.

"You see," he said, "I thought –"

"I know. I know what you thought."

"I mean, when you said that –"

"Yes, yes, yes. I know what I said."

"Stop bloody interrupting." That made her open her eyes. "We've had enough confusion and misunderstandings, Mary. It's time we got everything straight. I went away because I thought you thought I couldn't ... you know ... ring the bell. Sexually speaking. Such, it appears, was not the case. So what was wrong?"

"Nothing. I was upset, I didn't know what to do for the best, it was all my fault and I didn't see why you should suffer for it."

"Suffer? Who's suffering?" He took her hand. "Look, I know I'm supposed to get down on my knees for this, but my left leg's gone to sleep."

"You don't want to marry me, Fitz."

"Mary, stop making my decisions for me. I know what I want. Now then: what do you want?"

The corners of her mouth turned down in a smile of defeat. "You're so manly when you're masterful," she said.

"I take it that means yes," Fitz said. "And about bloody time, too."

Horsedrawn ploughs turned the earth, leaving strips as fresh as corduroy for the birds to feed on. The other war between Russia and Finland went on. Mary Muir Blandin married Jeremy Stanhope Fitzgerald in the Protestant church at Mirecourt and afterwards Flash Gordon gave him a lot of boring advice. France and Britain wanted to send troops through Norway and Sweden in order, so they said, to help Finland; Norway and Sweden refused permission. Rex had the grass tennis-courts mown and marked out, and Barton organised a tournament. The Russo-Finnish war ended, in Russia's favour. 'B' flight bagged a Heinkel. Britain and France sent an invasion fleet to neutral Norway but Hitler's forces landed there the day before it arrived. Germany overran Denmark too. Cattermole received a parcel containing six silk scarves and a bill, which he threw away. The weather suddenly became warm enough for swimming, and the pilots found a perfect pool in the stream that ran through the grounds. 'A' flight saw, for the first time, a formation of Messerschmitt 109 fighters, but they were only testing the Allied defences and no contact was made. Himmler ordered a concentration camp built at Auschwitz in Poland. Swallows and housemartins streaked up and down the stream, hurdling the swimmers and gorging on insects. Both flights saw the Luftwaffe's

357

new twin-engined fighter-bomber, the Me-110, but only at a distance. Mussolini told the US ambassador in Rome that Germany could not be defeated. Cattermole received an anxious letter from Stickwell, asking him to make Rex pay his bills. Belgium announced yet again that it was neutral. The weather was so fine that Micky Marriott had the grass on the aerodrome cut twice a week. It was going to be a hot summer.

MAY
1940

For Hornet squadron the war really began on the tenth of May 1940 at two minutes past noon. At the time, however, none of them realised this. Eleven of the twelve Hornet pilots knew nothing about it because they were all looking the wrong way. The twelfth, Hugo Trevelyan, was dead.

Even before he died Trevelyan was feeling weary. They all were; nobody had slept terribly well. The fortress guns on the Maginot and Siegfried Lines had rumbled and thundered all night, and the pilots had been pulled out of bed at three-thirty. It was light when they gathered at the airfield, with nothing for breakfast but mugs of tea. Before they could finish drinking it, they were ordered off. According to the ops officer enemy aircraft were all over the place, but a thick haze blotted out everything up to five thousand feet, and above that the sky was a light blue blank. An hour and a quarter later they landed, got the first news of the invasion of Belgium, ate a real breakfast, and flew another patrol. By now fires on the ground were scorching holes in the haze and pushing bundles of smoke up through it. Rex saw several clusters of aircraft at a great distance, looking as tiny as pinheads, and failed to get near any. A second breakfast was eaten at ten-thirty. The ops officer had them airborne again at eleven-fifteen, patrolling a line Metz-Luxembourg. That ended any lingering doubts. If the fighting had entered Luxembourg, the big bust-up was on.

By twelve noon they were at eighteen thousand feet, and breathing oxygen. Rex had the flights close-echeloned to starboard. The Hurricanes were snugly interlocked, wings well overlapped, and Rex was content; but automatically he said: "Keep it close, chaps. Nice and tight." Over the town of Luxembourg they turned, sprawling slightly, and tightened up again as they flew south. "Bandits at eleven o'clock," Rex said. "Prepare for a number two attack."

After such a long and empty morning, the shock of seeing twenty German bombers affected everyone: the entire squadron twitched and rippled as the pilots leaned forward to look. They were Heinkel 111's, rank upon rank parading towards France. Behind them came an escort of Messerschmitt 110's, a couple of dozen in groups of four, stepped up as if to give everyone a good view ahead. At first glance they looked frighteningly many and powerful. At second glance they were a bloody marvellous target.

Rex manoeuvred the squadron, changing speed and course to bring about the correct angle of interception. Each wingman watched his leader, each leader watched Rex; and when they could they glanced at the glittering enemy, a thousand feet below. Hugo Trevelyan was Green Two, the last man on the right. He was paying special attention to Green Leader, not wanting to lose him if the formation suddenly turned. He neither saw nor heard the Messerschmitt 109 that dropped out of the sky behind him. It fell below and used its momentum to arc upwards so that the Hurricane flew into its sights. It opened fire at two hundred yards. The twin machine-guns mounted on top of the engine released a total of one hundred and twenty bullets in two and a half seconds; the two cannon in the wings each fired fifteen rounds. The cannon shells went wide but more than half the bullets ripped through the cockpit floor, through the seat, and through Trevelyan.

His left thigh was hit first. The blow was so immense, shattering his thigh-bone, that he threw up his arms and arched his back. The parachute protected his buttocks but the bullets hacked and smashed his lower spine, chopping the great veins and arteries it guarded, perforating the flesh, battering the pelvis, almost breaking the body in half. The last few rounds flicked up through his abdomen, missing the kidneys, hitting the stomach, breaking a few ribs. But by then he was dead.

The 109 flipped and climbed and lost itself in the dazzling sky. Trevelyan hung in his straps, his right foot nudging the rudder-pedal. Nobody noticed his Hurricane drift away and tip sideways. "Squadron in aircraft close line astern," Rex said, "flights echelon starboard. Go!"

The Hurricanes formed two lines, each nose to tail. Still nobody missed Green Two. Nobody looked for him. "Keep close, keep close," Rex said. "We'll take the bombers first. Good hunting."

He led them down in a curling dive. The Heinkels paraded immaculately but the 110's were hurrying forward. Fanny Barton, following Rex, felt a great sense of unreality: it was all too well-ordered, too formal, too like an air display. Not even the bright beads of tracer pulsing out of the Heinkels persuaded him that this was battle, that these machines could destroy and be destroyed. Then he was choosing his target, and bracing himself, and firing, and with the crash and shudder of guns all unreality vanished. The

362

parade fell apart, the sky was full of dodging, skidding, twisting planes. Barton hauled his Hurricane into a half-turn, glimpsed blurred shapes go charging by, and flew straight through a flight of 110's. Everyone fired, nobody scored. He was bewildered: there was no shape or sense to this battle, just a lot of rushing about, taking potshots. A Heinkel slid into his vision. He grabbed the chance, thumb hard on the firing button, and saw all his shots pass far behind its tail. As he took his thumb off, a Hurricane slid across the space he'd been shooting at. Barton shouted with horror and relief. His hands were wet with sweat inside his gloves and his heart was hammering as if he had run up a mountain. Something rattled and thumped like a runaway donkey-engine: bullet-streams raced above his head, flickering past the propeller disc. Barton shoved everything into a corner and dragged the Hurricane through a turn that made the rivets creak. His eyeballs were straining to see behind him.

Nothing. Empty sky. He reversed the turn, searching everywhere. Nothing. His attacker had vanished. He climbed, circling and searching. They had all gone. It was startling. He was quite alone.

Two long trails of smoke led his eye downwards. The aircraft on fire were a mile or more below: tumbling specks. As he watched, a third plane hit the ground and exploded with a tiny spurt of flame. "Goodbye, whoever you were," he said aloud. It had, in fact, been Trevelyan.

They were full of excitement when they landed. The ground crews had seen the black streaks behind the gun ports in the wings and they were eager to hear about the action. There was much shouting and laughter and re-staging of attacks with twisting, aiming hands. Everyone except Barton and Boy Lloyd claimed to have damaged the enemy. Rex, Moran and Patterson claimed probables. Cox and Miller claimed definite kills. Nobody had seen Trevelyan go down. Rex considered it likely that he had simply stopped a bullet in the engine and made a forced-landing somewhere.

The cooks had sent up some lunch: chilled cucumber soup, poached salmon with salad, and strawberries. There was also Alsace beer on ice. It was a hot, still day. The conversation slackened as they ate, and half an hour later most of them were asleep.

At ten to three the telephone rang. Another patrol: Metz. They lumbered, stiff and sticky with sweat, to their aircraft, feeling stupid with sleep and heat. A quick whiff of oxygen cleared the head, and the blast of air into the cockpit as the planes charged over the grass got them fully awake.

They circled Metz for half an hour, looking for raiders that never came. All around the horizon, columns of smoke signalled the results of bombing, and while they orbited the city they saw fresh smoke gushing up, fifteen or twenty miles to the south. The haze had returned, and the bombers, if they were still present, were hidden.

Rex kept asking the controller for business. The controller told him that when reliable information became available he would pass it on; he sounded harassed. They circled Metz again. A French Potez came out of the east, limping badly. As it passed they could see holes in its wings. One of the tail fins was thrashing about, and the port engine was spilling coolant fluid. Suddenly that propeller ceased turning and the machine veered to its left. The squadron began another circuit, and the last they saw of the Potez it was dropping fast.

The controller ordered them back to base. As they made their circuit before landing they saw a double row of bomb craters in the next field. Dead sheep lay like patches of late snow.

Kellaway was waiting to tell Rex what had happened: a raid by aircraft so high that they were scarcely visible. "Not the slightest warning," he said. "Damn good bombing from that height, wasn't it? Too damn good. Pity you weren't here. Never mind; they're bound to come back. Want some tea?"

"Any word from Trevelyan?" Rex asked. The adjutant shook his head. "Better call Rheims," Rex said. "Tell them to send a replacement."

"I already have," Kellaway said. "I asked for two." Wearily, Rex massaged the goggle-marks around his eyes. "Two," he said. "You never know," Kellaway said. "Someone else might catch cold."

Miller, Patterson and Lloyd went to look at the bomb craters. Fumes from the high explosive hung in the air and made them cough. "What an appalling pong," Miller said. "Reminds me of my young days in the chemistry lab. I used to make stinks just like that."

"Pity you didn't blow yourself up," Lloyd said.

"Oh, I was only farting," Miller said.

"I feel sorry for the poor bloody sheep," Patterson said moodily.

"I never farted in front of a sheep," Miller said. "What sort of cad d'you think I am?"

"Listen," Lloyd said. The others looked at the sky. High-flying aircraft could just be seen: splinters of metal proceeding silently and inscrutably. "So what?" Miller said. "Nothing to worry about, is there?" But Lloyd was not looking upwards. "That one over there isn't dead," he said.

The sheep had been split open and disembowelled. Its guts were black with flies, which rose with a resentful buzzing and re-settled at once. Its head and shoulders were intact. It saw them coming and made a brief bleat. Lloyd squatted and stroked its ears. "You poor old bugger," he said.

Every time the sheep breathed, its intestines slipped and slithered.

"We ought to kill it," Miller said. "That's the decent thing."

"Go ahead, then," Patterson said.

"No thanks. You do it."

"Lloyd found it. It's his sheep."

"Come on: odds and evens," Lloyd said. Each took out a coin. Two heads, one tail. Miller had the tail. "Blast!" he said. The sheep tried to get up. More of its guts spilled out.

The pilots were under orders to carry a Colt revolver when flying; nobody knew why. Miller, like many, kept his revolver stuffed down the side of his flying-boot. He took it out and cocked it. The sheep, as if to make his task more difficult, gave a soft and pitiful bleat. "Get a move on, Moke!" Patterson urged.

"All right, all right!" Miller fired at the head. The bang smashed a huge hole in the sultry silence. "Missed," Lloyd said. Miller, his face screwed up as if he were staring into a furnace, took a pace forward and fired again, this time hitting the sheep in the shoulder. "For Christ's sake!" Patterson roared. He snatched the gun from Miller, stooped and shot the animal in the head.

"I don't know why you got so worked-up," Miller said on the way back to the aerodrome. "It was only a sheep."

"I happen to like sheep," Patterson said stiffly. "I used to look after them when I was a boy. They do nobody any harm and they certainly don't deserve to suffer. If an animal's suffering it has every right to be put out of its misery. That's common decency."

"Sorry," Miller said. "Only it wasn't my fault, was it? I mean, blame the Huns, not me."

"The frogs are just as bad, you know," Lloyd said. "When they want to clear a minefield they just drive a flock of sheep across it."

"You made that up," Miller accused.

"Not a bit of it. A French army officer told me in a pub."

"Bloody frogs," Patterson said.

"Would you shoot a dying frog, Pip?" Miller asked. "To put it out of its misery?"

Patterson said nothing.

"I meant a real frog, of course," Miller added. "A Frenchman."

"You're very interested in shooting people, all of a sudden," Lloyd said.

"Well, that's what we're here for, isn't it?" Miller said, defensively. "It's a jolly poor look-out if a chap can't show a healthy interest in his work."

Lloyd sighed. They walked the rest of the way in silence.

Before sundown the squadron flew another patrol, the fifth of the day. They chased a few shadows and caught nothing. Mother Cox's engine packed up halfway through and he forced-landed in a field.

Rex called a brief meeting with Skull, Kellaway and Jacky Bellamy. She had just got back after a day of driving, arguing with military policemen, and battling the censors before she could file her report.

"Rumours abound," she told them, "but fact is scanty. All I know for certain is I happened to be in a café when they got a BBC news bulletin on the radio. It said Germany invaded Holland, Belgium and Luxembourg, and she's making ground."

"That's what the Area intelligence officer keeps telling me," Skull said. "Mind you, I don't fully trust the man." They all looked at him. "His wife's a Christian Scientist," Skull explained, "and he wears the most ill-fitting dentures. I don't see how anyone –"

"What else has happened?" Rex demanded. They were in his office, drinking his whisky.

"Well, we know what's been taking place nearby," Skull said,.

"because CH3 has been flying his peculiar Reconnaissance Liaison patrols. He says the enemy is attacking airfields, road and rail junctions, and bridges, usually in squadron strength. Most of our aerodromes have been bombed: Rouvres, Vassincourt, Mézières..."

"Uncle," Rex said. "First thing tomorrow, get the troops to dig some trenches near the hangars. No, wait a minute, *not* near the hangars, that's exactly..." He frowned, squeezing his whisky-glass with both hands. "Pick out the best place," he said at last.

"Right, sir." Kellaway shuffled his pieces of paper. "I had a call from Wing," he said. "They've found Trevelyan, I'm afraid."

Jacky Bellamy suddenly came awake.

Rex stood. "Any clues?"

"None. The locals who saw it happen say he just came tumbling out of the sky. Hit a haystack and burned for hours, they couldn't get near him. Sandbags in the coffin, by the sound of it."

"Was he shot down?" she asked. "Did you get the German who did it?"

"And the two replacements have arrived," Kellaway told Rex. "Pilot Officers Nugent and McPhee."

"Tell them they're flying tomorrow. Give Cox a rest, he got a crack on the head tonight. Reshuffle the rest and put these new chaps in Green Section where they won't be in the way. I'm off to bed." Rex went out.

"Trevelyan got shot down?" Jacky Bellamy asked. "Didn't anybody see it happen?"

"Sorry to disappoint you," Kellaway said gruffly. For the life of him, he couldn't understand this desire for the morbid details.

"But surely somebody must have seen it," she insisted.

"Somebody certainly did," Skull agreed, "but he's back in Germany by now."

They were awake again at three.

Only Rex and the two new men shaved. The others dragged on their clothes and stumbled down to the truck. The sky to the east was washed with saffron, and Reilly frisked about at the edge of the airfield while the pilots stood and scratched and speculated about the weather. Artillery still boomed and bumbled in the distance, but everyone was used to that by now. Hot coffee arrived,

367

and with it Kellaway and the news of Trevelyan. Nobody responded. Nugent and McPhee would have liked to have asked how it happened, but they took their cue from the others.

Cattermole threw an old tennis ball for Reilly to chase, and said: "If you ask me, those 110's aren't much to write home about." He yawned. "Too slow in the turn. Easy meat, I reckon."

"Fast on the straight, though," someone said.

"Especially when they're running away," Moran said. He was still not fully awake: his voice was thick, and he couldn't make his eyes focus on his coffee mug. "Did you notice when we bust up the formation, how keen they were to bugger off?"

"Typical Hun mentality," the adjutant said. "Jerry's no good on his own. They like to huddle together."

Rex came out of the ready room. "Airfield protection," he announced. "We're *not* to go chasing Jerry, our job is to keep him off the grass." He accepted the sticky tennis ball from Reilly. "Too, too kind," he said. "What a generous dog." He lobbed it onto the field. "Flip, have you had a word with . . . uh . . ."

"Nugent and McPhee, sir," the adjutant murmured.

"Last night," Moran grunted. "Told 'em to empty their bladders before take-off and then do exactly what everyone else does."

"Don't wander," Rex told them. "I believe in tight formations. That's what creates wallop."

The squadron was airborne shortly before four o'clock. The Hurricanes glistened with dew in the horizontal rays of the sun. Rex played safe and kept the sections in close line astern. Nugent, Gordon and McPhee in Green Section formed the tail of the spearhead.

They flew north-west, sent to cover the aerodrome at St Hilaire-le-Grand. The roads were thick with military convoys: sunlight glittered on windscreens. The squadron passed over a crossroads that was a tangle of burning vehicles, and the controller came on the air to redirect them: cancel St Hilaire, steer zero-nine-zero for Rouvres, make angels twelve. But when they reached Rouvres it was too late. The hangars were blazing merrily and the airfield looked as if it had been visited by giant moles. Rex told the controller and the controller sent them back to St Hilaire, angels five. They reached St Hilaire and promptly got shelled by its batteries, so Rex climbed to twelve thousand and killed time. No enemy appeared.

As they turned away, Rex saw a tiny grey shape drifting across the pastel landscape, far below. It was so small and so grey that he thought it must be a shadow, yet there was nothing above it. "Jester Leader to Green Section," he said. "Bogey at ten o'clock, low. Go seek him out."

Flash Gordon acknowledged. Green Section fell away.

Flak-bursts clustered near the grey shape and made it swerve. Flash saw discreet German crosses. It was a Henschel 126, a fixed-undercarriage high-wing reconnaissance plane, little more than a sporting aircraft. For an instant he wondered at its courage and stupidity in straying so far into France; then he concentrated on the kill, glanced quickly left and right to check that the new men were still with him, and he had a startling idea: Why not let them polish it off? Give them a bit of confidence . . .

"Green Leader to Green Section," he said. "Line astern, Green Two first, then Three, then Leader last. Line astern, go."

They re-formed. Gordon let the others get well ahead of him. The Henschel had taken fright and was heading for home. Nugent at Green Two bore down at full speed and opened fire from four hundred yards. The little plane swerved aside as if someone had grabbed a wingtip, and wandered away from the cone of bullets. Nugent was still blasting at nothing as he stormed past. McPhee too began firing from four hundred yards but the Henschel had sidestepped again and raised its nose towards him. He over-corrected, washing his ammunition all around the target in a great spiral spray and was past it before he knew what to do.

As the two Hurricanes dwindled, carried a mile or more by their own momentum, the Henschel turned away from them and toppled into a dive. Its only hope now was to reach ground level and hedge-hop back to Germany, dodging between trees, going where the Hurricanes were too big and fast to go. Flash Gordon followed. When the Henschel flattened out he was close behind. He saw it swell to fill his gunsight like a moth under a lens, and then he blew it apart. The sheer speed of destruction was astonishing. He merely touched his gun-button and the Henschel went to pieces, the wing spinning away in two chunks, the body smashed in half, shattered fragments exploding in a corona of debris. Gordon had an instant in which to register this frozen fury, and then he was hauling his Hurricane up and away, searching for Green Two and Three. When he had time to look back there was nothing to see but fields: no smoke, no wreckage, no scars in the landscape. Two men were dead yet all he felt was a certain wonder at the suddenness of it all.

Green Section rejoined the squadron, slotting into the tail of the spearhead. They flew back to Château St Pierre, and saw the smoke before they saw the aerodrome. A hangar was on fire, and there was a remarkably neat line of craters running across the airfield, spaced alternately left and right, like footprints.

Rex called the tower. The local transmitter still worked. A phlegmatic flight sergeant told him that some bombs had not exploded; whether they were duds or delayed-action nobody knew. Rex ordered him to mark the unexploded bombs with flags; meanwhile the squadron would orbit the field at a safe height.

It was a glorious, golden morning. The haze had gone, and the sharply angled sunlight cast long, precise shadows. Fanny Barton, flying as Yellow Leader, enjoyed the slightly theatrical feel of the landscape: distant enough to look like toytown, close enough to reveal action and movement. He relaxed and enjoyed the slow, easy circuits. There was nothing to do except keep tucked in behind Rex and think about breakfast. Bacon and eggs: the English classic. Best meal of the day . . .

Tucked in behind Barton was Flip Moran, leading Blue Section. He too was hungry, but he was worried about landing on that battered field, and he glanced repeatedly at the damage. He was worried not so much for himself as for Nugent and McPhee. Green Section would be the last to land, so they would have the least fuel, which might be awkward if something went wrong and they had to go round again.

While Moran worried about landing, Nugent and McPhee worried about their failure to shoot down the Henschel. Each knew that his technique had been right: go in fast, start firing at four hundred yards, keep your thumb on the button: that's what they had been taught. Yet the Henschel had fluttered away and before they knew it they had overshot and the bloody rear gunner was potting at *them* . . . No doubt the squadron commander would have things to say when they landed. Meanwhile, Nugent and McPhee remembered his keenness on tight formations and they watched Flash Gordon's wingtips very carefully.

During the third circuit a flight of Messerschmitt 109's came out of the east: out of the sun. There were six fighters, well spread in line abreast, at about six thousand feet. As Hornet squadron wheeled and flew west, two of the German fighters peeled off. Their swoop was easy and unhurried, carrying the first to within fifty yards of Green Two. The 109 was slightly below and to the right of Nugent when he shot him. It was a lucky shot, since the bullets from the twin machineguns passed harmlessly through the fuselage behind Nugent's seat and one cannon missed completely; but two shells from the other cannon bashed through the rear of the canopy, hit Nugent's skull just behind his right ear, and blew the top of his head off. The other 109 had slipped behind Green Three, also slightly to the right and slightly below, and it hit McPhee with everything. The bullet-stream raced across his upper body. McPhee felt nothing. Cannon shells had torn through both lungs and ripped his heart to shreds. The two attacks lasted, in all, three seconds.

Flash Gordon heard nothing. When eventually he missed his wingmen he was annoyed, then startled; he began searching but he did not at first look below and so he failed to see the two Hurricanes falling until they had begun to spin.

They hit the ground almost simultaneously. Flash couldn't believe what he was seeing. He never thought to look high above, in the sun, where the 109's were re-joining their flight.

"Learn from that," Rex snapped. The pilots were grouped around him at the edge of the field, but his eyes were focused on something beyond, some problem that was angering him. "Don't daydream. Jesus Christ . . ." Reilly was frolicking around his feet. Rex seized the chewed-up tennis ball and hurled it with all his strength. Gleefully, Reilly raced away. "For God's sake, stay alert. All you have to do is keep formation."

They stared sulkily at the ground. They were hungry, and depressed by the double crash, and resentful of Rex's anger.

"How did it happen?" asked Moran. He too felt let down. All his worry had been wasted.

"God knows. I expect one of them was gawping at these damn

craters," Rex said. "Lost his place, wandered into the next chap, down they both went."

"Didn't anybody on the ground see it?" Flash Gordon asked.

"Too busy filling in holes and putting out fires." Rex shook his head. "What a bloody silly way to go," he said bitterly.

They returned to the mess for breakfast. Rex went straight to his office to call Rheims for more replacements. As the others sat down to eat, Mother Cox came in, looking sick. His forehead was purple and swollen, the result of yesterday's crash-landing. "I saw it all," he said. "I was up on the roof. Saw everything, start to finish."

"Congratulations," Cattermole said. "Now kindly give the mustard a shove."

"I couldn't believe it," Cox said. "It made me feel ill just to watch."

"It makes me feel ill just to listen," Gordon told him. "So shut up."

Cox sat and twiddled the mustard-spoon. His face was twisted. "But you just let them do it," he said. Cattermole lost patience and grabbed the mustard, spilling the spoon. Cox stared at him, accusingly. "You just let them shoot those poor bastards down," he said.

Everyone stopped eating.

"Let who?" Moran demanded. "Who shot them down?"

"You mean they didn't collide?" Gordon said.

"You didn't see the 109's?" Cox asked. There was absolute silence inside the room. The remote rumble of artillery fire made a window-pane buzz. "Christ almighty," he said. "You didn't see the 109's. You didn't even *see* them."

Rex ate breakfast at his desk, phone in hand. At seven-thirty he sent for his flight commanders. "We're moving," he said. "Area HQ thinks this place is too hot, so we're shifting west about sixty-seventy miles. Town called Mailly-le-Camp."

"Jesus," Moran said. "Retreating already, sir?"

"Regrouping," Rex said firmly. "There's a world of difference. Talking of regrouping, I've switched Patterson to 'B' flight and brought back Cox. That still leaves us light but we can pick up replacements at Mailly, I hope. All clear? Get the batmen to start packing. We're off in an hour. That's all." He picked up his phone and jiggled the cradle impatiently. Moran and Barton did not move. "Problem?" he said.

"Mother Cox says it wasn't a collision," Moran told him. "According to Mother, we got jumped by 109's."

Rex banged the phone down. "Cox had concussion. He can't see straight."

Barton said, "All the same, the chaps are a bit twitchy. They think Trevelyan must have been jumped too. Green Section's getting a bad name. Nobody wants to be arse-end Charlie."

"Nobody wants . . .?" Rex scoffed. "By God, they'll go where they're put! What do they think this is? A fighter squadron or a bolshevik commune?" He hunched his shoulders and chanted, with a schoolgirl lisp, *"Please sir, I don't want to be in Green Section, sir, it's not very nice in Green Section . . .* Christ give me strength." He grabbed the telephone again. "Get out and get cracking."

They moved slowly to the door.

"There's a lot of talk about back-armour, too," Moran said.

"Out of the question," Rex snapped. "Get me Wing ops," he told the operator, "and get your bloody finger out."

Gordon grabbed a car, picked up Fitzgerald and dashed down to the village. "I bet Nicole's hopping mad," he said. "She feels very strongly about foreigners invading France. She gave me hell about Joan of Arc, once."

"Joan of Arc? That was us, wasn't it?"

"So she says. Frankly I don't know much about it, Fitz, but Nicole won't hear a word said against the lady. Nicole's a bit of a Joan herself, you know. Now and then I get the feeling she thinks I don't take the war seriously enough. She thinks I just use it as an excuse to have a good time with the boys."

"Mary's not like that," Fitzgerald said. "All she thinks of is the baby."

"Maybe Nicole's jealous of her." Gordon considered the idea gloomily. "I've done my best, God knows. The bloody thing's worn down to a stub."

They found their wives in the school yard. Classes had not yet begun, and the din from screaming children was endless.

"I heard you got bombed," Mary said.

"Just the grass." Fitzgerald kissed her, and the children pointed and whooped. "Ought you to be here?" he asked. "This place is a bit sort of vulnerable, isn't it?"

"So is anywhere. You look tired. D'you want some coffee?"

"No time, I'm afraid. We're moving out."

"Today?"

"Now. At once. Before Jerry comes back and does it for us."

"Oh dear." She brushed his jaw with her finger. "It's the first time I've seen you unshaven. It makes you look like a gangster. A nice gangster."

"Don't you want to know where we're going?"

"I expect it's a secret."

"It is, actually, but that doesn't matter because –"

"I don't want to know, Fitz. I'll only worry, and worry's bad for the baby."

"Ah. Well, I wouldn't want us to have an anxious infant."

Nicole and Flash had gone inside where it was quieter. "Show me on the map," she ordered.

"I haven't got a map. What difference does it make? Look, I'll be in touch as soon as we get settled. Everything depends –"

"*Non.*" She led him into a classroom with a map of France on the wall.

"It's supposed to be a secret," Gordon said. "What if the Germans found out?"

"They won't find out from me. You think I want to stay here? Twice the *boche* has taken this part of France, twice in seventy years. I don't stay. I come with you, Flash. Now please show me where you go, and I go there too."

Gordon sighed, and looked for the place on the map. "Near Troyes," he said. "Mailly something ... Here it is: Mailly-le-Camp."

"Good." She kissed him. "I meet you there. Tonight or tomorrow. It depends on the roads."

"Mailly looks awfully small. Why don't you go and stay with your brother in Dijon? You'll be perfectly safe there and –"

"Perfectly safe and I never see you." She squeezed his fingers. "Don't worry about me."

"But I do worry, Nicole. Look at –"

"No, it's too late, it's all decided. I don't stay here. I go to Mailly and we fight the *boche* together."

Gordon had never seen her so vivacious. Not for the first time, he was amazed by the woman he had married. He hugged her. "I'd better go," he said. "Take care."

The telephone was ringing when Rex walked into the only building at Mailly airfield: a wooden hut so new that the nail-heads were still shiny. The place smelt of raw timber and baked sunlight. He picked up the phone. "Paddington Station," he said. "Platform three speaking."

"About time too," someone said. "The ops officer wants a word. Hold on."

A different voice said: "How soon can you take off?"

"We can't. The groundcrews aren't here yet. This is a bloody awful place, isn't it?"

"Look in the woods behind the hut: you'll find a fuel dump. Get your kites topped-up and call me when you're ready. I've got more plots on the board than I can count."

"Wait a minute. How can we start up? No mechanics, no starter-trolleys."

"There should be some starting handles in that hut somewhere. Try the cupboards." He rang off.

The fuel dump turned out to be a stack of four-gallon cans. After half an hour the Hornet pilots were wet with sweat. Their fingers ached, their arms felt drained of strength. Each can had to be carried two hundred yards, then pierced and tipped into a funnel. It was a sultry day, with a canvas-coloured sky that seemed to hold down the heat. The fumes of spilled petrol shivered above the Hurricanes' wings.

While Rex went off to call Ops, the others stretched out on the grass. Sleep would have been wonderful, but the flies were a pest. There were fields full of pigs next to the aerodrome, and the flies arrived in quantity, eager to feast on human sweat. Mailly itself was nothing more than a succession of fields with the hedges grubbed out: bumpy, dusty, and tilted in two directions. "If Hitler's so fucking keen on territory," Miller said, "he can have this bit."

Rex came back, waving starting handles. "We're off," he said.

"Patrol Rheims-Verdun at twelve thousand. Knock out the bombers, forget the fighters. The sky's supposed to be black with them."

They got up, slowly and stiffly. "Jesus, I'm hungry," Gordon said.

"Hit a Hun," Rex told him, "and I'll give you a bar of chocolate."

The conventional way to start a Hurricane was to pour a flood of electricity into the engine from a trolley-load of accumulator batteries until its twelve cylinders began to fire. Alternatively it was possible to insert a starting handle on each side and, by winding furiously, coax the engine into life. This was blistering toil. The flies danced delightedly around the pilots' sweating heads. As each fighter poppled and crackled and finally roared, it was necessary for the pilot to nurse it until it would idle happily, then lock the brakes on, jump out, and go and help someone else. Quickly, before the first plane began to overheat.

There was one great incentive in getting the propellors turning. They blew away those bastard, bloodsucking French flies.

CH3 had not come back from a patrol when the squadron left Château St Pierre. He was, in fact, overdue, but nobody had time to worry about that. Ten minutes after the Hurricanes took off, a pair of Ju-88's streaked across the aerodrome at fifty feet, strafing vigorously. A petrol bowser went up like a firebomb. Several airmen got bumps and scrapes from diving into trenches but nobody was badly hurt. The 88's vanished. Loading of spares and equipment resumed with a frantic fervour, while the bowser sent heat-waves throbbing into the sky.

At that moment CH3 was sitting under a tree on the edge of Rouvres airfield, eating a sausage sandwich.

His role of Reconnaissance Liaison had at last been put to good use. The system of reporting intruders over eastern France depended on ground observers, who were too few, and a communications system that was slow and erratic at the best of times, and the times were rapidly worsening. So Bletchley had had the bright idea of using CH3 as an airborne observer, reporting enemy aircraft – size, type, speed, course – direct to the ops room. The work was fairly dangerous: while he was snooping on one lot, another lot might be snooping on him.

Mostly the intruders travelled in large numbers with large escorts and showed no interest in him; but there were odd little bunches of Me-109's wandering about, freelancing for trade. Towards the end of his patrol he spent twenty minutes avoiding one such group, a section of three that kept trying to edge round between him and the sun. They were clever: sometimes they scattered and flew on different courses at varying heights, making it hard for him to keep track of them. In all that soaring brightness it was easy to search and search, and find a dot, and blink, and lose it again.

In the end the contest was stalemate. The 109's re-formed and turned away. CH3 turned for home. As he opened the throttle he glanced back, and behold: the Germans were diving steeply in line astern. He dipped a wing to clear his view. Three Blenheim bombers, far below, flying east to west: almost certainly returning from a mission: moving very slowly, like fish against a stiff current. CH3 went down too.

It was a romantic act and it surprised him. There was no question of saving the Blenheims; that was impossible. What swayed him was the opening he knew the Messerschmitts would offer. They would dive, attack and climb steeply away to avoid the ground-fire. That was the opening. It was like playing tennis and pouncing on a volley and drilling it through a gap: no time to think: you took your chance because it would be a sin to waste it.

The Germans aimed to attack on the flank. The Blenheims had seen them coming and had staggered their formation to give the gunners a better field of fire. All three bombers had been holed already by flak and the middle plane's starboard prop was wind-milling. The gunners opened up when the first fighter was still five hundred yards away. CH3 watched admiringly as the German pilot dipped and skewered to baffle them: the 109 *looked* so right; those neat, small wings had an amazing grip on the air; that thrusting nose packed more power than a Hurricane's. The German steadied and fired, aiming half a length ahead of the nearest Blenheim, which obligingly sailed into the shots and immediately wallowed. By then the 109 had missed the middle bomber, was battering the tail of the third, and went rocketing back into the sky as if climbing a ramp.

That was the opening. CH3 had cut short his dive and flattened out well above the Blenheims. Now the 109 drifted into his sights in perfect plan-view: dark green camouflage on top, dove-grey sides, just visible, yellow spinner, square wingtips, square crosses, even the cockpit was square. The pilot's head was twisted to the left, looking back and down. CH3 fired.

It was like touching a trout. For an instant, hits sparkled all over the Messerschmitt's engine cowling; then the plane leaped aside and vanished. CH3 banked hard the opposite way and opened his throttle wide. The encounter was over, he'd had his chance, it was time to go. But the other 109's had seen him, had cut short their attack on the Blenheims, were after his blood. There followed several minutes of high-speed manoeuvring while they chased and fired and he fled and worried about fuel; until abruptly they gave up. They were probably low on fuel too. He found the nearest airfield. It turned out to be Rouvres, and a shambles.

There were so many craters and broken or burning aircraft around the control tower that he landed at the other end, a mile away, intending to taxi along the perimeter until he found a bowser. But he noticed a Bofors gun-crew under some trees, waving him back. He stopped and got out. A lieutenant came over. "Lots of nasty unexploded bombs over there, old boy."

"Is that right? I need fuel, you see. Any ideas?"

"Well, we can offer you a nice sausage sandwich. *With* Daddies Sauce."

While CH3 was thinking, the air and the ground shook. "There you are, you see," the lieutenant said, and pointed to a distant fountain of earth.

They gave him a sausage sandwich and a mug of tea. He realised how hungry he was: he had been up for six hours, and had flown for more than two. Sitting against a tree, chewing the thick, crusty bread and looking at his parked Hurricane, he was surprised by an extraordinary sense of, if not happiness, then at least contentment. Now why, he asked himself, should that be? He was not accustomed to such a feeling. When he was younger he had known the pleasure of success, the gratification of beating a challenger, but that was artificial and shortlived, and anyway it depended upon applause, trophies, recognition. In one sense, true success had been denied him.

He was a millionaire's son. When his bobsled or his yacht was fastest, nobody had mentioned the dollars but everyone knew they were there. Everyone conceded that a rich young idiot could easily *lose*, too; nevertheless victory had not been sweet enough for young Christopher Hart III.

To escape from his family he had learned to fly: big deal, another expensive toy for the kid. So he ran away to Spain, which needed pilots. He might have been killed in Spain; lots of men were. All the same it proved nothing; it wasn't a real war so much as a heroic losing battle. The fascists had it won as soon as they captured the harvest and controlled the main ports. He went home and shocked his father, a Republican who never read much beyond the financial pages and the sports section and who sincerely believed that the White House was turning the nation over to the Bolsheviks. When his son began talking about the Spanish Republicans and their socialist ideals, Mr Hart was appalled. *Republicanism and socialism are fundamentally incompatible!* he shouted.

His son walked out of the house and bought a first-class ticket to China (since he was suffering from the capitalist system he might as well exploit it). The Chinese Air Force was glad to have him. Their Russian-built Polikarpov biplanes were getting combed out of the skies by the new Japanese monoplane fighters. He was shot down, twice; scorched in various parts of the body; and he cracked some ribs. This was another losing battle, only far less heroic than Spain. He began to realise that it didn't take a hero to get killed by a stronger, faster, nimbler enemy; any fool could do that. Before he had a chance to make a fool of himself the East caught up with him. He contracted dysentery.

When he was fit again the Chinese Air Force scarcely existed. He made his way to Europe by the Trans-Siberian Railway. Later, when he applied to join the RAF, the interviewing officer regarded this journey with extreme suspicion.

"Look at it this way, sir," CH3 said. "If I were a Russian spy trying to infiltrate the RAF, would I tell you that I'd travelled across Russia?"

"That sounds very clever," the officer said; extreme cleverness was also suspect. "How do I know you're not lying?"

"All right, assume I *am* lying. In that case I haven't travelled across Russia. Either way, sir, you have nothing to worry about."

"So you say, so you say. You could, of course, be lying about your own dishonesty."

"Sir, your attitude is offensive." Travel had taught CH3 a lot

379

about how to deal with officialdom. "If you intend to continue this line of questioning I must request that a superior officer be present and a written record kept."

The interviewing officer was silent for a moment as he re-read his notes. "What were you doing in China?"

"Recovering from dysentery."

"And before that?"

"Not much. I was in the US Olympics bobsled team."

"Ah! Were you really? Why didn't you say so in the beginning? Any other sports?"

CH3 finished his sausage sandwich. He lay with his head between the tree-roots, looking up at the kaleidoscope of leaves. That was a damn strange thing to do, he thought: carefully avoid three 109's for twenty minutes and then on impulse pick a fight. Why do it? And the only answer he could find was: it felt right. The instant he saw them diving on the Blenheims, he knew he could surprise them. The risk was irresistible. A good fighter pilot took endless precautions, did nothing reckless, double-checked everything, put survival first – and then, suddenly and cheerfully, chucked it away and risked all. Hours and hours of patiently saving his skin for the sake of a quick dance with death. Crazy.

But when it worked, very satisfying.

There was another reason for CH3's contentment. He was far from Hornet squadron. He was still thinking about that when a bowser turned up, towing a trolley-accumulator.

Squadron Leader Rex was not content. The squadron's formation-flying had gone to pieces. No matter how much he nagged and chivvied, the pilots couldn't seem to hold a tight pattern for two minutes on end. "Jester Leader to Jester aircraft," he said. "For God's sake *close up*. You're like a bunch of Girl Guides on a picnic." They edged together. It still wasn't very good, but he was sick of the sound of his own voice.

They had been up and down the patrol line Rheims-Verdun once already and now they were cruising back towards Verdun. There was no sign of the raids with which the ops officer had said the air was black. Plenty of smoke and occasional flames on the ground but no intruders. And then there were dozens of them.

They came out of a screen of hazy cloud, head-on to the

Hurricanes so that at first they were no more than dots, spaced as evenly as perforations. "Bandits at twelve o'clock," Rex said. "Close up."

Each pilot felt fear. Some felt it at once, remembering the day before, the madhouse with the Heinkels and their Me-110 escort when Trevelyan bought it, nobody knew how, but the end result was all that mattered: Trevelyan and his Hurricane wrapped around a frog haystack and all fried to a crisp. Those who didn't think of Trevelyan got a stab of fear when they saw the enemy more clearly. Three separate lots, each of squadron strength or more.

"Number five attack," Rex announced. "Sections astern, go."

The squadron altered shape, altered course, altered shape again, altered course again. The pilots were kept busy watching wingtips. Rex watched the enemy, gauging the timing of his turns and plotting the precise moment of interception. "Tighten up," he said. He could identify the types now: twenty Heinkel 111's, a dozen Dornier 17's, and behind them both a swarm of Messerschmitt 110's.

His number five attack was maturing nicely when the Heinkels changed course, banking steeply to their right. "Shit!" Rex muttered. The whole point of a number five attack was that it brought the fighters and the bombers together at the approved angle and speed. Now he would have to start again, only there wasn't time ... "Change, change," he announced. "Number four attack on the Dorniers. Sections astern, go." Once more the squadron altered shape and altered course. Meanwhile the Heinkels had turned again, back to their left. "Make up your bloody Teutonic minds!" Rex muttered. Now there was something wrong with the Dorniers, too: they were closing much more rapidly than they should. Damn damn damn! "Aircraft echelon starboard, go!" he ordered. The Dorniers were less than a mile away. The Hurricanes swung right to let them pass through, swung left to cut in behind them. "Aircraft, form vic, go!" As the sections restored themselves, he said: "We hit the Dorniers, break right, regroup and hit the Heinkels." Tracer streamed from the upper turrets, criss-crossed, flicked past the Hurricanes. "Number four attack, go!" Rex called. "Red Section, attack, go!"

Mother Cox, at Red Three on Rex's left, hated the tracer, hated the casual way it leaked out of the Dorniers and then seemed to bend and suddenly accelerate at him, bright beads flicking past his wings, under his prop, over his canopy. And the Dorniers were very fast, he was creeping up on them so slowly . . . Angry with everyone – Rex, himself, the enemy – he rammed the throttle wide open and tugged the emergency boost button. The effect startled him: a great surge of speed that jerked his head back, and made a monstrous, raucous bellowing in front. The engine seemed to be shaking itself to bits: everything vibrated: even the Dorniers were blurred. He thumbed the gun-button. The blast of eight Brownings knocked the edge off the Hurricane's speed. The nose jumped, turbulence from the bombers' slipstream rocked the fighter, Cox was shooting at the moon, he was over the formation and something was hacking hell out of his port wing so he quit, broke left, fled, escaped into the great big safe empty spaces.

Cattermole, at Red Two, went in and out fast. He began firing as soon as Rex said the word, kept his thumb on the button and his eyes on the target, and turned sharp right when the enemy was still a hundred yards away.

Rex found himself bouncing and rocking in the German slipstream. He pulled above it and dived and fired down at a Dornier in the centre of the bunch, held it in his sights and kept hammering at it and doing absolutely no damage, until suddenly the Dornier *behind* it staggered and gushed smoke. Rex broke right and snatched a look over his shoulder to see which bloody fool was doing the firing. Nobody. Yellow Section was still out of range. Peculiar. Jerry must have shot himself.

Yellow Section – Barton plus Miller and Fitzgerald – ran into trouble at once. The damaged Dornier was staggering about so much, and spreading so much smoke, that Barton decided to pass it, attack the next section instead. Miller and Fitzgerald went with him, leapfrogging their obvious targets and waiting for his order to fire. It never came: Barton found himself in the middle of the formation, caught in the crossfire of at least twenty machineguns. Bullets severed his control cables, smashed his radiator, blew up his engine, ripped open the petrol tank in front of him. The onslaught was overwhelming. One moment he was hurdling the crippled Dornier and picking out his target, the next he was sitting in a burning wreck, utterly out of control. The heat of the flames on his legs jerked him out of his shock. He slung the canopy back, heaved the pin from his straps, shoved up and dived out. Something wrenched his head: he'd forgotten to disconnect his radio and oxygen leads. Then he was whirling through space, end over end, spinning like a rubber ball. The roar of engines faded, and still he went on spinning. He opened his eyes and saw only his knees. He was curled up tightly, arms wrapped around his legs. Why? He could think of no reason. He let go of his legs. They straightened and trailed behind him. He stopped spinning. The rush of air was refreshing and the view was stunning: far better than anything you got in a Hurricane. He felt amazingly calm. It was like doing an endless swallow-dive. Everything was under control. Should he use his parachute? Why not? He found the ring and gave it a firm pull. The silk bag opened with a smart bang. There was still a long way to fall. Well, he was in no hurry, and there was plenty to look at. Upstairs they were having quite a fight; but that was their affair.

The instant Miller and Fitzgerald saw Barton's Hurricane stagger and catch fire they abandoned the attack and sheered off in a hurry. Rex's voice grated over the R/T: "Regroup! Regroup!" But to them it was just noise: what mattered now was escape, survival.

Blue Section ignored the call too. They had just been bounced.

When things began whizzing past him, Flip Moran looked around so fast that he ricked his neck. What he saw over his shoulder was a bunch of twin-engined fighters with big bright shark's teeth painted under their noses. The front four planes were firing. "Blue Section break right!" he shouted. It was the wrong way to break, away from the attack: that merely gave the 110's a longer hunt. Patterson at Blue Three suffered most. Cannonfire chewed off a wingtip and battered great holes in his tail. The wallop knocked his Hurricane into a sprawling tumbling roll that dragged down its speed and left him shaken and bewildered, not knowing up from down.

Moran flinched at the havoc blasting past him and wrenched his machine into an ever-tighter turn. Gordon at Blue Two had no choice but to go with him. His arms and legs quivered with tension as he hauled on the controls. He sensed a flutter in the wings, and the rudder pedal trembled under his feet: the plane was strained to its limits. He ignored the signs and heaved harder.

Patterson took out two of the enemy without firing a shot. He was completely helpless. His Hurricane seemed obsessed with flying sideways. He kept stamping the pedals, shoving the stick: nothing answered. The 110's came charging at him, apparently standing on their wingtips, but that was an illusion: he was tipped over, they were level. He went skidding across the face of the formation, sliding between two of them, their engines roaring and fading in a second, and got so buffeted by their slipstream that the second row of fighters was just a juddering blur.

What the crew of the number three Messerschmitt saw was a Hurricane intent on crashing into them. The pilot banked violently. As the planes flashed past, the German's tail-wheel whacked Patterson's canopy.

Compared with other fighters the Hurricane was big but the Me-110 was monstrous. Its wings measured over fifty-three feet from tip to tip, with two Daimler-Benz twelve-cylinder engines slung beneath: good for speed, bad for agility. The heave that threw the number three Messerschmitt clear of Patterson's berserk Hurricane also flung it onto a wide arc that met the path of the number four Messerschmitt. Luck played a part: a difference of inches might have saved them. As it was, a wing sliced through a fuselage just foward of a tail unit. The tailless machine plunged like a hawk, its engines rushing it to earth with a huge and senseless energy. The other 110 wobbled in circles spilling its crew, until air pressure snapped off the fractured wing. By then Patterson was miles away, stumbling home with the air howling through a great hole in his Perspex.

Nobody else saw any of this. Rex was calling everyone to regroup while the bombers flew on and the rest of Blue Section sweated to bend their Hurricanes out of the other 110s' line of fire. This move worked. Moran, craning his neck, saw them stop firing. It more than worked. He kept turning, kept hauling the plane round in the tightest circle, kept up the pressure even though it was greying his vision: and into that greying vision crept the tails of two Me-110's.

Moran's face was too stiff to smile but his foggy brain felt pleasantly surprised. Jerry couldn't turn. He was big and fast and ugly but he turned like a battleship. More of the enemy came in view, edged further into his sights, but Moran waited, screwing the turn tighter yet, allowing for the speed of the target, aiming ahead. Then he fired, and Gordon inside him fired too, a savage chatter as if something pent-up and furious had been released. Moran was aiming for an engine and he hit it. Black smoke flooded out, thick as cream, rich as velvet. Gordon aimed for the pilot and missed, but the hefty recoil clipped his speed and the focus of fire wandered back, found the Messerschmitt's tail, chopped off a fin.

Both enemy planes dived.

"Leave them, Flash!" Moran ordered. He straightened, climbed, searched. No sign of Patterson. Far away, two 110's were tumbling down: good. Gordon came alongside him and pointed: thin, scattered smoke growing thicker and tighter as it led down to a falling, burning Hurricane: not so good. The rest of the 110's had banded together and were chasing after the bombers. Odd Hurricanes were stooging about. And Rex was shouting *Regroup! Regroup!*

Normally when combat ended the sky was empty. This time half the squadron found each other. It took time: nobody knew where to regroup; most of them formated on Fitzgerald, thinking he was Rex. And by the time they got sorted out, the enemy had gone.

"Close up," Rex said. "What a fucking shambles that was. What in Christ's name were you up to? Attack and regroup, I said. Now you've let the bastards get away! Where's your damn discipline?"

Nobody spoke.

"Let's get back on the patrol line," Rex said. "And for God's sake *close up.*"

Ten minutes later they met the Heinkels coming back, this time without their escort of 110's. The enemy was much lower, down to about four thousand, and much slower: one or two looked to be limping. The Hurricanes still had a longish trip home. Fuel was getting short.

"No time for a proper attack," Rex said. "We'll just dive in and trust to luck."

Their luck was in. They shot down three Heinkels and damaged five before they ran out of ammunition.

When they reached Mailly-le-Camp, Patterson's Hurricane was lying on its belly in the middle of the field, its propeller splayed back like the petals of a dead flower.

The groundcrews had arrived and tents were going up. Rex

walked into the wooden hut and found Skull and Kellaway talking to an RAF chaplain. "It's this hot weather, d'you see," the chaplain was saying. "You can't afford to hang around. Believe me, I've seen it before. Or rather, smelt it."

"Get more replacements, uncle," Rex said. "Pilots *and* planes. What's your problem, padre?"

"Three funerals. The coffins are in a truck, outside. I'm afraid they won't improve with time, not in this heat."

As the adjutant reached for the phone, it rang.

"Three?" Rex said. He sat on the floor; there were no chairs. "I don't remember three."

"Trevelyan, Nugent, McPhee," Skull said.

"Trevelyan." Rex scratched his head. "Trevelyan, Trevelyan. I thought he baled out."

"Ops on the phone, sir," Kellaway said.

"Not Trevelyan," Skull said. "Trevelyan bought it."

"Who baled out, then? Someone must have baled out."

"They want to know when you'll be ready to take off, sir," Kellaway said. He had his palm over the mouthpiece. "Lots of trade, apparently."

Rex looked at him steadily but blankly. "Any chance of a cup of tea, adj?" he asked.

"Not for half an hour," Kellaway told the phone, and hung up.

"Did anyone see Fanny Barton bale out?" Skull asked. Rex shrugged. In the still heat of the afternoon, one of the timbers of the hut creaked.

"It's up to you," the chaplain said, "but you can't hang around in this weather. Believe me."

Hornet squadron took off again at three-thirty. It consisted of only two sections: Red (Rex, Miller and Cattermole) and Yellow (Moran, Fitzgerald and Gordon). Barton was missing; Patterson's Hurricane was a write-off; Cox's hydraulic system had been shot up. All the planes that flew carried bare patches over bulletholes: there had been no time to paint them.

CH3 did not fly. He had been grounded.

Rex had sent for him and told him the Reconnaissance Liaison patrols were finished and he was flying with the squadron now. "I've lost three pilots, four if you count Barton," he said, "and

God knows when we'll get replacements, so you and Lloyd will form Blue Section. Understand?"

CH3 cocked his head and gazed at Rex's face, especially his lips.

"Do you understand?" Rex repeated sharply. They were in his tent. It was so hot that even the flies were sluggish.

"I can't hear you, sir," CH3 said. "I've gone deaf."

"Don't play the giddy bloody goat with me, you stupid bloody Yank, I haven't got time for jokes."

Again, CH3 watched him closely and waited a few seconds before speaking. "It's no good, I'm afraid," he said. "All I can hear is very low-pitched noises."

Rex groaned.

"I heard that," CH3 said. "If that was you. Did you make a low noise then, sir?"

Rex folded his arms and stared. His face was heavy with fatigue and disgust. "I ought to have you shot," he said.

"I'm not sure," CH3 told him seriously. "I was all right when I landed, but then my ears suddenly went funny."

Rex shouted: "Uncle!" The adjutant hurried in from the next tent. "He says he's gone deaf," Rex said.

"Deaf, eh? What a bind. It happened to a lot of chaps in the last show, you know."

"Get a doctor," Rex ordered.

"It's usually only temporary. Try blowing your nose," Kellaway told CH3, who frowned.

"You get a damn doctor," Rex said. "Now."

"I wouldn't know where to look, sir," Kellaway said. "Have you tried blowing your nose, old boy?" he shouted.

"Low noises, that's all." CH3 pointed downwards. "Can you hear me?" he asked Kellaway.

"Get a doctor, adj. I want his bloody ears tested. That's an order."

"Do my best, sir." Kellaway gave CH3 a handkerchief, and smiled encouragingly. "Try it," he said.

"Until then, this bastard's grounded," Rex said.

"Jolly good. He couldn't fly anyway, could he? Not in this condition."

CH3 had shaken out the handkerchief and tucked it up his sleeve. "Can you hear me?" he asked Kellaway.

Rex looked away. "I've lost three good men," he said. "Maybe four. You treat this war like a tennis-match. You make me sick."

CH3 touched a finger to his ear. "Dennis?" he said. Rex turned, and Kellaway thought he was going to hit CH3. He tugged the American's arm. "Come on," he said.

Nicole and Mary sent the children home at midday and locked the school. They each packed a suitcase and said goodbye. Nicole had a bicycle; she strapped the suitcase onto the carrier over the rear wheel and rode away towards the west. With luck she reckoned to reach Mailly-le-Camp before night. If Flash had not arranged rooms by then, she would find some. Mary waited for the bus to Nancy. She had decided to return to Britain and wait there for Fitz. She was nearly five months pregnant; she ought to play safe.

The bus never came. She went home, unpacked half the stuff in her suitcase, changed her shoes to a heavier pair, drank a pint of milk, and set off to walk to Nancy.

After a while the road joined a bigger road and she saw her first refugees: a ragged column of families on foot, pushing handcarts or plodding beside horses that pulled over-loaded wagons. For the first hour or two she walked past them. But as the sun went down she tired. She merged with the procession and trudged at its pace. The suitcase strained her arm and banged her knee and made her fingers ache. Eventually a man let her rest it on the tailgate of his wagon.

Boy Lloyd's Hurricane refused to start, which was why only six aircraft took off.

Rex led them, close-echeloned to port, towards the north-east to patrol the area St Dizier–Joinville–Bar-le-Duc. The heat had manufactured cumulus clouds: they towered from five thousand feet to eight or ten thousand, and they were still climbing. A squadron could pass by on the other side of one and never be seen. From time to time the ops officer called up Jester squadron with news of trade, but nothing was seen for the first half-hour. Rex went up to fifteen thousand, then eighteen thousand. They were on oxygen. A little crowd of Me-109's passed overhead, at least a mile

388

above, looking no bigger than flies. "Nothing to do with us," Rex said. "Close up."

Cumulus was coming up everywhere now, boiling into the sky in swelling white mounds, heaped upon each other. It was like flying over the Alps.

The R/T crackled and delivered a long message with a sound like someone crushing matchboxes.

"God knows what that was all about," Rex told them. "But it's not happening up here so it must be down there."

He put them in sections astern. They slid swiftly but cautiously between the overblown white cliffs and came out near Joinville as it was being bombed. A dozen Heinkels were going in, unhurriedly, one after the other. They might have been on a training exercise. Miller, at Red Three, noticed one Heinkel edge right a bit, then left a touch, hold steady for a moment and then curve away. He began counting, and at ten he saw the stick of bombs begin racing across the little town. Grey molehills of destruction sprang up. By then the next Heinkel was finding its place.

Rex put them in line astern and they fell on the bombers as if this too were all part of the training exercise. The Hurricanes' speed was nearly double that of the Heinkels, and they used it to weave in and out of the circle, firing brief bursts, swerving away and cutting back for the next target. It was magnificently exhilarating stuff. Miller felt washed clean of fear. Each of the hulking, slab-winged bombers had five guns and although they blazed continuously he knew they couldn't hit him, he was far too fast. But he could hit them! In fact he missed as many as he hit, but with six Hurricanes skating around the circle the Heinkels were bound to suffer and Flash Gordon at the tail found himself potting at planes that were trailing smoke or shedding bits or dragging themselves in peculiar attitudes, with half their undercarriage flopping about.

The attack was over in forty seconds. By then the bombers had huddled together and the fighters were out of ammunition. One Heinkel crashed into a street and blew up. Cox saw it happen. He saw the burning plane tumble like a falling leaf. He could just make out the moving speckles that were people running, scattering as if blown outward by an explosion that had not yet happened. Then came the crash and the flash, and he looked away.

"Regroup," Rex said. "Sections in vic." They came together, each man looking for signs of damage to his plane. Most had the odd bullethole, and Flash Gordon's windscreen was thoroughly starred, but that was all. "Sections close astern," Rex said. "Close up." Far to the east, a Heinkel was falling out of formation and shedding its crew. The parachutes appeared out of nothing like little conjuring tricks.

Everyone felt very pleased on the way back to Mailly, but whenever Fitz looked across at Flash to exchange a grin of congratulation, Flash was twisting his head, squinting behind and above. No ammo, Fitz remembered. A bad time to get jumped. He too searched the sky. It became damn hard work, with Rex nagging them to keep closed-up, and the cumulus filling the sky with hiding places. Fitz developed a routine: check wingtips, look right, behind, above, below, check wingtips, look left, behind, above, below ... His shirt collar chafed. His eyes were tired. Fourth patrol of the day, wasn't it? Fourth or fifth? He started counting them and got confused with yesterday's sorties. Check wingtips. Look right. "*Break left!*" Flash shouted, and Fitz stared at him stupidly for an instant until a furious hammering blasted sparks all over his engine cowling and the Hurricane lurched. The prop vanished, hurled into infinity, and the engine howled with a fury of excess energy. Boiling white glycol washed back over the canopy and filled the cockpit with its stench. Fitz broke left.

A pair of 109's hurled themselves at him. All he saw was their huge and horrifying silhouette, magnifying like a punch in the face. Then they went over him and vanished. Already his Hurricane was losing strength, feeling sluggish, dropping its nose. Flames poured from his exhaust stubs, raging alongside the fuel tank that lay beyond the instrument panel. "Get out of there, you stupid sod," somebody shouted into his ears. Now, who was that? "Fitz, you fuckin' idiot, get out!" Ah yes: Moran. Well, he should know. Fitz reached up and heaved open the canopy. Glycol sprayed his face. Bugger this for a lark. He took the pin from his straps, unclipped the oxygen tube, jerked the radio lead out. The engine was still screaming its head off so he stopped it. Now to depart. He stood up and the air pressure shoved him down. He got his head out and it pinned his shoulders to the back of the cockpit. Through the smoke and spray he saw the horizon and realised he was diving at some considerable speed. He tried to kick himself free and accidentally slammed a boot against the control column. The Hurricane performed a slow roll and he fell out. After that it was easy. Hanging from his parachute, he had the curious pleasure of watching his aeroplane blow itself up in mid-air.

Patterson opened the tent-flap and looked in. "Uncle tells me you've gone stone-deaf," he said.

"Sort of," CH3 said.

He was stripped to his shorts and lying on a camp bed. Patterson came in, followed by Boy Lloyd. "What happened?" Patterson asked. "Come down too fast?"

"Shut the door, Pip. Keep the flies out."

"He's not deaf at all," Lloyd said. "It's a swindle."

"What's the game?" Patterson asked.

"Allergy." CH3 yawned, and banged his feet together to frighten the flies exploring his toes. "I'm allergic to orders to fly at the tail of a tight formation. Any time anyone orders me to do that, I go stone-deaf. Peculiar, isn't it?"

"Bloody weird."

"How d'you know what the order says," Lloyd demanded, "if you go deaf as soon as you start to hear it?"

"Can't hear you," CH3 said loudly. "You'll have to speak up."

"Told you it was a swindle," Lloyd said. "Christ, I could do with a beer." He sat on the ground with his back against a pole. "I could do with a beer and a bath and a beautiful bed, with or without a popsy. I don't mind . . ." His voice trailed away. His eyes closed.

Patterson still stood, looking down at the American. "Look, a joke's a joke," he said, "but if you don't fly tail-end Charlie then somebody else has to. Somebody else is doing your job up there."

"Worse than that. Somebody else is probably getting killed up there."

Lloyd opened his eyes.

"Look how many tail-end Charlies have been jumped already," CH3 said. "All because Rex makes everyone keep tight formation. I'm not going to get killed to satisfy the CO's love of ceremonial drill."

"But that's the proper formation," Lloyd said. "It's official."

"Can't hear you," CH3 said.

"Everyone flies like that," Patterson said. "Not just us."

"The *Luftwaffe* doesn't."

"Balls," Lloyd said. "You're dodging the column. You've got twitch." He sat up. "Things begin to get a bit hairy and you decide you don't like it. Can you hear that?"

There was an awkward silence. CH3 watched a fly crawl up his chest. He crept his hands together, clapped, killed it.

Mother Cox opened the tent door. "They're coming back," he said.

Everyone went out to watch. Cox had binoculars, and he studied the Hurricanes as they made their approach. "Who's missing?" Patterson asked. Cox double-checked, to be absolutely sure. "Looks like Fitz," he said at last. "What was Fitz? Blue Two, wasn't he?"

"Somewhere at the tail," Patterson said. Their voices were carefully empty. They watched Rex's machine touch down and judder over the lumpy field. Cox turned to CH3. "Tell me," he said. "Where did you get the armour plating for the back of your cockpit?"

The RAF chaplain buried Trevelyan, Nugent and McPhee in a small cemetery on the edge of Mailly-le-Camp at sunset.

All the available officers attended, and there was an abbreviated firing-party: just two airmen with rifles.

Nobody paid much attention to the chaplain's handling of the funeral service. His professional mingling of regret and admiration seemed remote from the sweaty reality of that day. What's more it was hard not to look at the sunset. The western sky was alive with huge, sweeping arcs of colour in a dozen shades of lemon and butter-yellow and pink. They throbbed with a greater purity and energy than any colours on earth. As the chaplain delivered his lines, Skull nudged CH3. "Decor by God," he murmured. CH3 gave the sunset a long look. "Showing off again," he said. Skull suppressed a snort of amusement. Rex glared.

When they got back to the aerodrome, the adjutant was waiting with a bundle of messages. All the codewords and radio frequencies had been changed. Fitz had turned up, undamaged. Three replacement Hurricanes were on their way. No new pilots were available.

The Area HQ ops officer wanted Rex to call him, urgently. Baggy Bletchley was expected to arrive about midnight.

"And where's the ear-doctor?" Rex asked.

"Damn. I forgot to tell you. He was here but he couldn't wait. I told him you were –"

"Get another."

"Tonight, sir?"

"Now."

Kellaway took a deep breath and squared his shoulders. "Very good, sir. Would you like a bite to eat? There's some rather nice stew." Rex nodded, but Kellaway could tell that he was thinking of something else. "You won't forget about writing to the next-of-kin, will you, sir? Tomorrow might be rather busy."

"That doctor. Why didn't he stay?"

"Oh . . . you know how it is. Lots of other patients."

"Bloody quacks. Never around when you want one."

Kellaway looked at him, carefully. "Something quite short will do," he said. "Just a note, really."

"Did you say stew? I'm not giving Bletchley stew . . ." Reilly came bounding over, wild with pleasure at finding his master again, but Rex ignored the dog. Kellaway had never seen that happen before. "Tell you what, adj. You draft something, I'll sign it."

They walked to the wooden hut. The flies had vanished with the sun; the grass was wet with dew. Reilly plodded alongside, aware of the seriousness of the occasion.

"You know, uncle: a team can have only one skipper. Some of them don't seem to realise that."

All around the airfield, lamps flickered where groundcrews were servicing the Hurricanes. Kellaway said: "It's been a long hard day, sir, and you've done damn well."

"It's not for my benefit. It's for the good of the squadron. One team, one skipper. That's the way it has to be."

'Nobody questions that for a minute" Kellaway said. "Not for a single minute."

They went into the hut.

Nobody wanted stew. Everyone wanted booze.

They got back into the truck that had done the funeral-run and went into Mailly-le-Camp. A café on the square was crowded but as soon as they saw the uniforms, the customers made room at a table.

"*Vin rouge*," Flash Gordon said to the owner. "*Omelettes. Pommes de terre frites. Pain.*" The man counted the party: eight. He went away, calling out orders.

"Well done, Flash," Moran said. "Now get the kinks out of my neck and I'll make you an air vice-marshal."

"I can't afford to have kinks, not on eleven shillings a day," Miller said. "But I got some cheap cuts of meat from this bleeding awful RAF-issue collar."

"Me too," said Patterson, and there was a general grumble of agreement. "Rubbed bloody raw," Lloyd said. Cox yawned and massaged his neck. "It's all this twisting and turning," he said, "and no proper lubrication ... Where's the booze, Flash?"

"Patience." Cattérmole raised a restraining hand. "This is a five-star establishment. All drink is freshly made for each customer. I just saw the proprietor take his socks off."

"In a proper five-star boozer," Moran complained, "the man would keep his socks *on*." But at that point bottles and glasses arrived. The pilots came alive, drank deeply, and slumped again. Fitzgerald smacked his lips. "Fruity," he murmured. "A good athlete's foot, but not a great athlete's foot."

"Talking of athletes," Moran said, "what exactly happened to Fanny?"

"Christ knows," Miller said, "but his kite got blown to bits. Silly bugger hopped into the middle of that gaggle of Dorniers and of course they clobbered him with their crossfire."

"I saw a parachute," Fitzgerald said, "but it might have been a Jerry."

A little girl brought two platters of bread and a slab of butter. They were reaching for the food before it touched the table.

"After today, I must say I'm not frightfully keen on Dorniers," Cox said. "Not in large quantities. How did you cope in Spain, CH3?"

"No good asking him," Lloyd said. "He's deaf."

"Not deaf, exactly," CH3 said. "Allergic."

"Bollocks," Lloyd snapped. "The only thing you're allergic to is Jerry. That's what pisses me off. I never knew Fanny the way the rest of you did, but he was a good man, a bloody good man, and

394

I don't think it's funny when I hear this cowboy sit on his arse and talk about allergy." Lloyd's face was red. His hand trembled as he reached for his drink.

"Speak up, then, CH3," Moran said. "What are you allergic to?"

"Stupidity. Simple stupidity."

Lloyd slammed his glass on the table. Wine jumped, and stained the cloth. "Who are you calling stupid?"

"Oh dear," Cox said. "Now we're going to have a brawl."

"Cowboy wouldn't fight me," Lloyd said. He leaned across the table and waved a dirty finger in front of CH3's nose. "Cowboy won't fight anyone, will you?"

By now half the café was watching the confrontation. Lloyd's finger was vibrant with contempt and menace. CH3 studied it closely, leaning forward. Suddenly he raised his hands from his lap and hung his cap from Lloyd's finger. The crowd laughed, took breath, and laughed again.

For an instant Lloyd didn't know what to do. Then he flung the cap away and swung a punch at CH3, which missed. He overbalanced and fell heavily. One arm smashed a couple of glasses, the other landed in the butter. Moran seized him by the collar and yanked him backwards. Lloyd's rump thudded against his chair and skidded off it. He vanished under the table, dragging the cloth with him. The French whistled and stamped.

"Close up, chaps," Cattermole said. "Nice and tight." They dragged their chairs together, blocking Lloyd's escape. "Down, Boy! Down!" Cattermole called, and kicked him. Lloyd swore. "Quiet, Boy! Lie still and you'll get a nice bone." Lloyd struggled, but the pilots' boots thudded into him.

"Ah ... *grub*," Miller said with tremendous feeling. Plates of omelettes and fried potatoes were being served; more wine was brought. At the same time, Fanny Barton walked into the cafe, looking scratched and stained. "My God, what a lot of scruffs," he said.

They roared a welcome, their mouths full of food, and demanded to know what had happened. He tossed his helmet and gloves onto the table. "Well ... first I fell out of the kite. Then I fell into a tree. Then I fell *out* of the tree. Then I fell in with some frog soldiers. Then I fell *out* with some frog soldiers. They wanted to shoot me, thought I was a Hun . . . Who's that under the table?"

"Boy Lloyd," said Cox.

"What's he doing?"

"I think he's lost his head," Cattermole said. "You know how keen Boy is. We gave him his head, and now the silly chump's gone and lost it."

"Well, he can't have mine, I need it to eat with . . . Whose dinner is that?"

"Yours." Moran slid the plate across the table. As Barton pulled out a chair, Lloyd scrambled through the gap, raging and cursing: "You fart-assed sods! Look what you've done!" He was foul with dust and stamped with bootprints, and his nose was bleeding. Barton sat and began eating, using his fingers until CH3 passed him a fork. "Bloody good grub," he murmured. "Christ All bloody Mighty," Lloyd snarled.

"Shut up, Boy," Moran said. "Get a chair and have a drink and we'll order another omelette." But Lloyd was too furious to listen. He grabbed his hat and stormed out, barging Frenchmen out of his way and treading on a dog, which howled.

There was no sign of Lloyd when they left the café and took a stroll around the little town. Army convoys rumbled endlessly through the main street; refugees were camping out in squares and courtyards, sleeping on their little piles of possessions; the thud of distant bombing was like the random beating of a bass drum three streets away.

They came across a corner store, wide open and bright with lights. "Shocking blackout," Mother Cox said. "No wonder –"

"Hey!" Fitz exclaimed. "They've got those shirts that CH3 wears!" He went in, and the others followed. The shirts were French workmen's wear: blue and simple. He bought one. "Soft collar. See? Doesn't cut your neck off when you look round."

"They're not regulation," Cox pointed out. "Rex will have a fit."

"So what?" Miller said.

In the end everyone bought a shirt. "Now all we need is some nice bulletproof vests," Fitz said as they walked back to the truck.

"Get some armour plating behind your cockpit," Cox advised him. "That's what I've done. Micky scrounged it off a crashed bomber."

Cattermole sucked in his breath. "All that weight in the wrong place. Ruins the balance."

"CH3's kite flies okay," Patterson said.

"Not in close-formation."

"If you're so keen on doing things properly, Moggy," Fitz said, and there was an abrasive edge to his voice, "you fly arse-end Charlie for a change and I'll fly Red Two."

"That's for Rex to decide."

"Really? Tell that to Trevelyan. And Nugent. And McPhee."

"Cut it out, Fitz," Barton ordered.

"Really, all this whining and moaning is in very poor taste," Cattermole said. "Now, more than ever, we must all get behind the CO."

"That's exactly where we all are," Miller said. "That's the whole bloody trouble."

They reached the truck and drove back to the airfield.

Boy Lloyd, on foot, arrived home shortly before the truck. They called to him but he refused to speak and went straight to his tent.

Flip Moran found himself standing next to CH3. Explosions rumbled in the distance.

"He's got to go, Flip," CH3 said. "If he doesn't go, the rest of the squadron will. Bit by bit. You watch."

"I'm sure I don't know what you're talking about," Moran said. "But in any case he's the only CO we've got, so we have to make the best of him. Do you fly with us tomorrow, or do you intend to get yourself shot for refusing to obey orders?"

"I'll think about it."

"I was afraid you might," Moran said. "You're a terrible man for thinking." He went to bed.

Everyone felt better next morning. They had been allowed to sleep until eight; there was hot water for shaving; the cooks made an excellent breakfast of eggs, bacon, mushrooms, kidneys and tomatoes, with French bread still warm from the oven; the sky was as bright as well-scrubbed pottery; and there was a stiff breeze from the west that blew the flies away. To cap it all, three replacement Hurricanes landed and one of the ferry pilots brought a bundle of mail. Even Lloyd smiled.

Rex let them read their letters, and then stood up. He looked good: refreshed and alert.

"Gentlemen," he said, "at last we are going to take the fight to the enemy."

Reilly, who had been lying at his feet, stood and licked his fingers.

"Baggy Bletchley was here last night," Rex said. "The German offensive is beginning to take shape. Their army is making two thrusts – both of them well to the north of us. The secondary, or minor, thrust is just beyond Luxembourg, in the Ardennes. It is clearly a feint or diversion to distract us from the primary or major thrust through Holland and into Belgium. That, as it happens, is precisely where the Allied High Command expected Jerry to strike, so our forces are well placed to deliver the *riposte suprême*. French for a good kick up the arse."

Quiet chuckles. The adjutant nodded approvingly.

"That's where we come in. There is an enormous canal between Holland and Belgium, called the Albert Canal. Over it there are several important bridges, very useful to the German Army. But not for long. Our bombers are going to blast those bridges into very small bits, and Hornet squadron is going to make damn sure nobody stops them doing it. Any questions?"

For a moment there was total silence. Kellaway watched their faces, everyone thinking, nobody looking at anyone else, and saw the difference that two days of war can make.

"These bridges, sir," Barton said. "Has Jerry captured them yet?"

"Some, not all. The situation's rather fluid." Rex saw Barton chew his lip, and added: "As you'd expect, with all those canals around." Nobody laughed. "Rotten joke," he said. Nobody smiled.

"So if Jerry's got a bridge," Moran said slowly, "he'll have it well defended by now." It was a statement, not a question.

"Final briefing at Amifontaine," Rex said. "That's the bomber drome in northern France. Skull's there already. He went up by car with Baggy Bletchley."

"Are we the only fighter cover, sir?" Cox asked.

"Good God, no. They've brought three or four Hurricane squadrons over from England, so some of them will be involved. But

398

you'll be pleased to know that we form the spearhead. Ours is the place of honour."

"Talking of spearheads, sir," Fitzgerald said, "what formation do we fly?"

"Oh, the usual."

Patterson mumbled: "Usual bunch of bananas." If Rex heard him he ignored it. "I take it everyone's fully fit?" he said. The adjutant nodded cheerfully. He had not found a doctor to examine CH3; hadn't even searched very hard. "All in the pink, sir," he said.

"These new kites bring us almost up to strength," Rex said. "I'll lead Red Section with Mother and Moggy. Fanny has Yellow Section: that's Pip and Flash. Blue Section is Flip, Moke and Fitz."

"Bottom of the heap again," Fitz muttered. "Down among the dead men."

"However," Rex went on, "Baggy Bletchley has asked me to experiment with two aircraft behind the formation. A sort of rearguard. Hart and Lloyd are spare, so they can do that. Take-off in half an hour."

He went away with the adjutant. The pilots milled about and discussed their task. The general mood was one of wait-and-see: if Baggy Bletchley had briefed Rex at midnight everything had probably changed by now. Flip Moran was unusually morose. "Fucking Dutch," he grumbled. "Why can't they blow up their own fucking bridges?"

"Maybe they haven't any bombers," Fanny Barton said briskly.

"Have we?" Moran asked. Barton gave him a sharp look of disapproval. "Of course," he said, and turned away.

"Well, well," Lloyd said to CH3. "Arse-end Charlie after all, then. There's still time to go sick, if you hurry."

"Take my advice," CH3 replied. "Don't fly straight. Keep weaving."

"*You* take *my* advice. Wear your rubber pants."

"Really," Cattermole said, "you chaps surprise me. Where's your sense of occasion? Where's your pride? 'Ours is the place of honour.' Here we have a chance to impress friend and foe alike with our superb close-formation flying, and all you can do is bicker."

"Close-formation stinks," Fitzgerald said.

"We all know it's risky, Fitz," Barton said, "but it works. It knocks down the bombers."

Cox said: "So what? We're not going for bombers today. It'll be 109's and 110's. Zooming around like bluebottles."

"Fitz is right," Miller said. "We look like a bunch of bananas up there. No wonder we keep getting jumped."

"Okay, enough!" Barton exclaimed. "Enough talk. Let's get on with the job." As they dispersed he touched Flip Moran on the shoulder. "Hang about a bit," he said. When they were alone he said: "This isn't getting any better, is it? D'you think we should have another word with Rex?"

"Why? He won't change the formations. Anyway, why should you care, Fanny? You're up the sharp end. You won't get jumped."

"That's a damn silly thing to say." Barton felt the blood pounding into his face. "Almost as stupid as what you said about those Dutch bridges."

"Ah, but of course, I forgot, you're the senior flight commander. You have enough leadership for the both of us. Go ahead and use it all. I mean, don't mind me."

Barton glared. "All right. If that's the way you want it, maybe I will." But Moran was already walking away.

Gordon and Fitzgerald shared a tent. "Any news of Nicole?" Fitz asked, stuffing a revolver down the side of his flying-boot.

"Not yet. What about Mary?"

Fitz shrugged. "On her way to England, I expect."

Flash put Vaseline on his neck where the collar had rubbed. "You can't help worrying, can you?" he said.

"Jerry seems to be playing the game so far. He's only raiding genuine military targets." Fitz breathed on his goggles and polished them. He saw his face reflected in a lens and was startled: it looked tired and worried. "They'll be all right, I'm sure," he said.

Rex sat in the hut and signed pieces of paper for the adjutant. Kellaway put the last one before him. "You might like to read that first, sir," he said.

Rex read it.

"While with the squadron he did all that was asked of him without flinching . . . That's true enough. *His courage, determination and audacity were never in any doubt* . . . Yes, I suppose so. Who is this, anyway? Trevelyan?"

"Nugent and McPhee as well. I've had two copies made."

"Oh ... *Never in any doubt* ... Those two weren't here long enough to demonstrate much of anything, were they?"

"Scarcely their fault, sir. They did their best."

"Yes ... Oh, well, benefit of the doubt ... *His death in combat was an example of gallant self-sacrifice in the face of heavy odds and extreme peril* ..." Rex sniffed. "I don't remember that. The bloody fools got themselves killed, that's all."

"In combat, sir. You were on patrol, after all. Surely it was self-sacrifice and, as such, gallant."

"Nugent and McPhee collided."

"That's extreme peril, by any standard."

"And Trevelyan let a 109 sneak up on him. I don't call that 'heavy odds,' adj."

"It depends how you look at it, sir. We don't say which side the odds favoured, do we?"

Rex signed all three copies of the letter. "What are these sloppy civilian shirts they've suddenly taken to wearing? They think I don't notice. I notice, all right. Are they ashamed of their uniform, or what? Uniform means uniform: all the same. Am I right, adj?"

"Absolutely, sir." Kellaway knew that half the squadron had rear-armour in their cockpits and that several had re-harmonised their guns to one hundred yards, in imitation of CH3. But he saw no point in bothering Rex with that sort of detail now.

They flew to Amifontaine in close-formation, sections astern. Lloyd followed, fifty yards behind, somewhat to the right. He flew straight and level, unlike CH3 who kept up a constant snake-like weaving on the left. Plenty of strange aircraft were to be seen but none approached them.

The weather got steadily worse as they went north. Thick grey cloud rolled out of the west like a slow tidal wave. It crossed their path when they were still thirty miles from Amifontaine, bringing gusty winds and the odd rain-shower. By the time they landed, every scrap of blue sky had been obliterated.

Skull met them and took them straight to the mess. Baggy Bletchley briefed them while they ate sandwiches. The bombers were waiting; the raid would take place as soon as the Hurricanes were ready. There was a heavy air of urgency about the operation.

"Maastricht," said Bletchley. "It's on the Dutch border, here." He uncovered a large map, decorated with stars and arrows. "About a hundred miles away. There are two bridges, just outside Maastricht. One on the road to Tongres, the other towards Hasselt. One concrete, one metal, and they've both got to go. That's not your problem, of course. The Battles will hit the bridges. Your job is to sweep ahead of the Battles and clear any Jerry fighters out of the way."

"Whereabouts is the Front, sir?" Rex asked.

"It hasn't stabilised yet."

"But roughly where?" asked Barton.

"Our information is currently being updated. We're waiting for the latest reconnaissance pictures to be developed."

"Where was the Front," Cox asked, "before that? More or less, sir."

Bletchley flashed a finger across the map. "Here, somewhere."

"This side of the Albert Canal, then," Moran said.

"In places, yes. It seems possible. Light penetration may have occurred in one or two areas."

"So Jerry's captured those bridges, sir," Barton said. "Which means lots of flak."

"This cloud will provide ample cover for the Battles, right up to the last moment," Bletchley said. "It's a perfect godsend."

There were no more questions. They finished their sandwiches, collected maps, used the lavatory, and went out to meet the Battle crews. These turned out to be surprisingly cheerful. "Come on, buck up!" they called out. "What kept you? Can't hang around all day waiting for you lot! Fingers out! Chop-chop!"

"Where are the rest?" Moran asked. Only five Battles were lined up.

"This is it," said one of their pilots. "We're all here. Are you all here? Because *we* want to go *there*, so that we can knock it into the middle of next week, which will be here any day now unless you get a move on."

"We're ready," Rex said. "Is there anything more we ought to know? What height are you planning to bomb from?"

"Personally, I'm going in damn low," one of them said. "It's safer and surer."

"Utter cock," said another. "High dive: that's the best way."

They grinned, and thumbed their noses at each other: evidently this was an old argument. "We'd better give you five minutes' start," Rex said. "Good luck."

The Battle was a sleek aircraft, long and slender, but it had no more power than a Hurricane. Its single engine had to lift a crew of three plus a bombload that weighed as much as a crew of four. The machines used up most of the airfield before they got airborne and groaned eastward.

"Now that they've gone," Rex said, "I can tell you that each of those men volunteered for this operation. That shows you how keen they are. Let's put on a good show and make it easy for them."

The clouds were lower and blacker by the time they took off. They passed the formation of Battles somewhere near the Belgian border. There was no sign of any other escort.

Skull went back to the mess, found a comfortable armchair and tried to sleep. He had been up all night and his eyeballs ached. The mess was empty; but as he dozed off, someone started shouting and banging the furniture in a nearby room. At first he was too weary to care, but the noise grew worse. He went to see what was happening.

Four war correspondents and a squadron leader were shouting at each other. One of the correspondents was Jacky Bellamy. Skull had never known her to lose her temper, but now she was pale with anger.

The squadron leader began: "What you must realise —" but got no further. "Don't give me that stuff about rumour and speculation," a man boomed at him. "I was there! I saw it! I can report what I saw, can't I?"

"Not necessarily. Military considerations —"

"But it's already in the German papers!" another man shouted. "What are you trying to do — rewrite history?"

"The fact remains —" the squadron leader declared.

"Exactly!" Jacky Bellamy said, and shook her notebook in his face. "The fact remains! It always will remain, but we want to report it, *now*, while it still matters!" He smiled bitterly and shook his head, so she kicked his desk and turned away. "Hullo, Skull," she said. "Can I tell you a secret? Everyone else knows it, so why not you?"

"What is it?"

"It's about Maastricht." They went to a quiet corner of the mess. Skull ordered coffee. "Can I have a Scotch instead?" she asked. Skull ordered two whiskies. "You never used to like that stuff," he said.

"I still don't like it very much, but since the rest of the world is going to pot I feel I want to join them." She was curled up on a sofa, and she looked very tired. "All this is pure coincidence," she said. "I didn't come here to meet the squadron, I came here to chase the war, and now it seems the squadron's arrived to do the same. You're covering another raid on Maastricht."

"Are we?" Skull took his glasses off to make himself invisible.

"Yes. Don't worry, that's not the secret."

"Well . . . Maastricht is a busy road system, so it would make a natural target." When he put his glasses back on, the whiskies had arrived and she was sipping hers.

"It's more than busy. Half the German army is trundling through Maastricht, heading for Brussels and all points west."

"In that case it certainly should be raided, shouldn't it?"

"I guess so. I'm not sure it's such a hot idea to send any more of those Battle bombers, though." She opened her notebook. "I've been up and down France all winter, Skull, and I've made a lot of contacts in that time. People like yourself. Here's what they've been telling me. On the first day of this German attack, a total of thirty-eight Battles were sent to bomb the enemy. Thirteen got shot down and all the rest were damaged. The RAF also sent six Blenheims to hit a German airfield in Holland and only one came back. That takes care of day one. Next day – yesterday – eight Blenheims went to Maastricht, three got shot down, two were damaged. Same in the Ardennes, only worse: eight Battles took off, one came back." She turned a page. "Early today nine Blenheims attacked Maastricht, seven were destroyed, two made it home. That comes to . . . let's see – thirty-five shot down and . . . uh . . . thirty-odd damaged. Say about seventy planes put out of action in three days."

"It sounds a lot, I agree. But in heavy fighting one must expect heavy losses."

She sighed, and massaged her neck. "Maastricht is different,

Skull. Maastricht is in a class of its own. If I weren't afraid of sounding like a journalist I'd say Maastricht is a deathtrap."

"And what makes you think that?"

"Look at what's happened there. Jerry captured the bridges over the Albert Canal before the Dutch could blow them. The Belgians sent in infantry to get them back, and failed. The Belgians tried shelling them, and failed. The Belgians tried bombing them. Same result. So the Belgians said the hell with it and the French took a turn. But the French didn't do any good either, so they passed the job over to your Royal Air Force. One thing about you British: you have a certain chivalrous style. Two RAF raids on Maastricht have been pretty well annihilated, so now the man in command of your bombers has called for volunteers to try again, and of course he got them because that's the kind of story this is."

"Do you happen to know," Skull asked, "exactly when the Germans captured the bridges at Maastricht?"

"Three days back," she said. "Here's what a Blenheim pilot said to me this morning: he said they've got more flak batteries on those damn things than a bitch has fleas."

"Things change," Skull said. "It could be completely different by now."

"Jesus, I hope so," she said. Skull blinked. It was the first time he had heard her swear.

Halfway across Belgium, Hornet squadron met the waiting Messerschmitts. They were 109's, high in the sky, so high that the formation was just a speckle of dots.

As soon as he had passed the Battles Rex had reduced speed to stay just a few miles ahead of them. Now he was flying at eight thousand feet where the cloud was thin and he could see above him. The squadron was tucked-up nicely and performing well. That exhibitionist Yank kept zig zagging about at the rear, which meant he would probably run out of fuel on the way home, but otherwise things were going well.

The speckle of dots split in two, and one part fell away. "Hilltop aircraft," Rex called, "bandits at one o'clock, up we go." They climbed towards the enemy. The dots took shape as tiny crosses, the crosses grew tails; light gleamed on cockpits and prop-discs. "Pick your targets," Rex said calmly. *How the hell can I?* Fanny

Barton thought. *You're slap in front of me, you great turd.* All the same he chose a 109 at the left rear and hoped it was being flown by a panicky cretin who would stall and pick his nose and get himself shot down before he could . . .

The 109's almost vanished. One moment they were diving, the next they were head-on, knife-edge wings nearly invisible. And then they were sheering off, climbing away. "No stomach," Rex grunted. Barton watched the enemy make height, and let his muscles unclench. He felt weak, and he took a deep breath of oxygen. *Now why did they do that?* he asked himself, and the answer came back: *Because they know where we're going and what we're doing and they want the Battles.*

Three more times they met bands of German fighters. They were at various heights, in various strengths: a dozen 110's, a handful of 109's, a mixed bunch of both, maybe twenty-strong. Each time the enemy wandered over, had a look, and lost interest. "Don't worry, we'll catch them on the way back," Rex said. Cox, at Red Three, glanced unhappily at his leader.

They droned on. There was nothing but a sea of dirty cloud beneath them. Occasionally it split open and revealed an under-water glimpse of a lot of even dirtier cloud. At the tail of the formation, Fitz Fitzgerald realised that he had stopped feeling afraid. Ever since they took off he had been frightened, and whenever the enemy came near he had begun trembling so much that he had to force himself to breathe; but now, suddenly, he seemed to have run out of fear. It didn't make him any happier. Anyone who'd been shot down and wasn't afraid it might happen again must be very stupid.

"Right, Hilltop aircraft, we're there," Rex announced.

Beautiful, Moran thought. *Now turn around and go straight home and don't talk to any strangers.*

They flew a wide circle. "We'll just pop down and have a look," Rex said. Moran glanced sideways at Fitzgerald and threw up a hand in disgust. "The Battle boys might need some help," Rex added. Somebody pressed his transmission switch and blew a raspberry.

The descent through cloud seemed endless. The lower they went the thicker it got; and then abruptly it rose like a theatre curtain and they were in clear air. Eight hundred feet below, a broad band of water cut across the landscape. "Albert Canal!" Rex said triumphantly. "Right: fingers out."

They followed the canal, throttles wide open, exhausts trailing smoke, and saw flak bursting a few miles ahead. The nearer they got to it the more there was, each burst spawning two more, doubling and redoubling until the sky was blotched with blackness, flecked with small white puffs, streaked with red and green and orange. "Holy shit," someone said quietly. "Shut up!" Rex barked. "Radio discipline!"

Baggy Bletchley had been right about one thing. The cloud was a godsend to the Battles. It had hidden them from the enemy fighters. It had also forced them desperately low on their bombing runs. The Hornet pilots could see three Battles at about five hundred feet: slim monoplanes flying straight and level through the barrage like blind men walking down the middle of a busy road.

One exploded. A thick line of flak appeared as if someone had shaken a loaded pen at the sky and the Battle just touched a blot and blew up: a flicker of incandescence that pulverised three men in the time it took to draw breath. Almost at once another plane was hit, and it angled steeply downwards as if seeking out the source of the hurt. The third bomber was on fire. It dropped its bombs and tried to climb away, but though the nose went up the plane did not. Flak raged around it, obsessed with annihilation. Still the Battle slogged on. The Hornet pilots saw its bombs burst in a long row, nowhere near the bridge, and then the plane sank and hit the ground, and the flames claimed it with a rush.

The Hurricanes swept through the dying flak like cavalry fording a stream. Rex led them up through the cloud and headed west. Every machine had been holed. "Close up," Rex said to them. "I can't afford stragglers."

Almost at once, CH3 called him: "Bandits behind, bandits behind, coming down now."

Rex wheeled the squadron. They were still in the spearhead formation and they needed a wide turning-circle. Patterson, at Yellow Three, was looking from Barton's wingtip to Cox's tailplane and back again when the corner of his eye glimpsed a double file of Messerschmitt 110's hurtling at him from the side. Hot flame bubbled out of the leading pair. The planes split left and right.

Two more sprang forward, pumping fire, heaved apart, were replaced. Bullet-streams flickered and slashed across the Hurricanes. Patterson felt them rip through his fuselage and he shouted with fear and anger; by then the 110's were gone, the squadron had made its turn, and there in front was a pack of 109's, pouring down, head-on.

Rex immediately hauled back and climbed. Cox and Cattermole went with him and fired when he fired. Yellow Section, chasing too hard, swerved outward to avoid them. Blue Section instinctively followed Yellow. Within a second the squadron had scattered and the plunging 109's were hosing its exposed flanks with fire. For an instant the air was brightly stitched with tracer. Then the 109's sliced past the wallowing Hurricanes and howled off into nowhere. "Regroup!" Rex was shouting. "Hilltop, regroup! Hilltop, regroup!"

It was a struggle. They were all over the sky. Barton was undamaged but Patterson was not: control cables hit, probably: the plane wouldn't do what he told it, needed continuous full opposite rudder to stop it swinging left. Gordon couldn't see through his bullet-crazed windscreen and his cockpit was filling with black-green smoke, until he got the canopy open. Moran was all right apart from a perforated wing that vibrated during turns. Fitzgerald's propeller was making a noise like a rusty saw hitting a rusty nail: it had probably stopped a couple of bullets. CH3 had seen the enemy coming and climbed above them. Lloyd too was intact.

The man in real trouble was Moke Miller. He had no fingers on his left hand.

The burst from the 109 that chopped through his knuckles also hit him in both thighs, missing the bone but tearing great holes in the muscle. At the same time, a spent bullet ricocheted around the cockpit and smashed into his mouth. This hurt most of all. The agony of torn lips and tongue and broken teeth was too great and he blacked out. At once his mouth filled with blood and he began to choke. The choking brought him back to consciousness: he coughed and spat, and lifted his left hand to wipe off the mess. But the glove seemed to be hinged. It flapped open the wrong way. As he looked, blood ran out in a brilliant red stream. Pain raged through the hand, a flame that kept flaring bigger and hotter until once again his brain rejected it, his vision fogged, his ears went deaf, and the cockpit receded as if he were falling backwards.

When he could see again, the horizon was moving rapidly from left to right. There seemed to be no end to this rotation.

After a while he noticed that the Hurricane was flying a continuous bank. It was therefore making a circle. He looked down and saw his feet on the rudder-pedals and his right hand gripping the control column. That explained everything. He moved his feet and screamed at the pain in his legs. The Hurricane levelled out. He was sick, vomit and blood and bits of broken teeth slopping down his front. Needle-sharp sparks of light danced furiously before his eyes. His ears were full of a loud beehive buzz. The dancing lights faded to soft purple blooms and the buzz died and a voice was speaking to him.

". . . any damage? How's your radio? Blue Leader to Blue Three, over."

Miller looked out and saw Flip Moran flying alongside. He tried to speak but his mouth was too broken so he shook his head instead. Gobs of blood flew off and stained the Perspex.

"Are you hit, Blue Three?"

Miller showed him his left hand. That was a mistake. The hand burned like a furnace. The needle-sparks rushed back to the dance and the beehive-buzz surged.

"Stay with me, Blue Three. We'll see you home."

The squadron regrouped and flew west. Miller did very well: he switched on his oxygen, he tucked his left hand under his chin so as to cut down the blood flow, he coughed out most of the debris, he even got rid of his goggles, which were spattered with blood. For twenty miles he tagged along at the rear, seeing nothing but Moran's plane to his right. Then CH3 called: "Bandits behind, bandits behind. 109's coming down."

Rex wheeled the squadron again, but Miller flew on. Violent tactics like that were beyond him now. Moran hesitated, then turned and joined him. He gestured downwards: down where the cloud offered cover. Miller fed this information into his stumbling, fumbling brain. Eventually his good right arm responded. They went down.

This time Rex managed to face the enemy fighters before they could strike. The diving 109's still looked no bigger than skylarks.

Fanny Barton marvelled at CH3's eyesight as he braced himself for another split-second whizz-bang head-on attack. It never came. The Messerschmitts curled away and went into a wide orbit – all except one, which pulled up to a climbing stall, toppled sideways, and went down again in a slow, flat spiral, trailing smoke.

"Decoy," Rex said. "Old trick."

Hornet squadron held height and held formation and watched the decoy, while the other 109's orbited and watched them. Eventually the decoy gave up and climbed back to rejoin his friends.

"Let's go," Rex said. They turned and flew westward. The 109's followed. Twice more, CH3 called a warning; twice more, Rex wheeled the squadron and the attackers sheered off. Boy Lloyd, trailing along behind, had time to watch and wonder. It seemed a stupid way for the Germans to behave; they were just making nuisances of themselves. It reminded him of a yarn he had read when he was a boy: all about British infantry in the desert forming a hollow square to beat off the fuzzy-wuzzies. Every time Rex wheeled the squadron the Huns got cold feet.

Lloyd was watching the enemy and wondering what sort of pansies they were when CH3 called: "Bandits behind, bandits behind!"

Simultaneously the 109's tipped into a dive. Lloyd stared up. He watched them for perhaps two seconds. When he looked down the Hurricanes had disappeared. He fingered his transmission switch, thinking Rex ought to know about those 109's. That made three seconds. He was still fingering it when tracer started flickering past. He blinked, and actually heard the first meaty *thud-thud-thud* of cannonfire. Three and a half seconds after CH3's warning, those cannonshells smashed through the tail unit, whizzed along the fuselage, punched a dozen holes in the seat-back, and blew most of Boy Lloyd's chest and stomach all over the instrument panel.

The shells still had enough energy to bash through the reserve petrol tank just beyond the panel and rip open the glycol header tank in front of that. Some shells went on and battered the engine. Fuel gushed backwards and ignited. It made a long, brilliant streamer, as thin and bright as a knight's pennant. Then one of the wings came off and the Hurricane was just a piece of falling junk.

The enemy aircraft that destroyed it was a 110, the last of three that had come out of the sun. The other two dived too far and too fast; when Rex wheeled they overshot their target. But the third had had time to see a lone Hurricane flying straight and level and looking the wrong way, and he gratefully slid into place dead astern. CH3, still weaving, saw it happen. He also saw the departing 110 fly across the diving 109's and force them to swerve away: the German pilot, he guessed, had been too busy watching his victim go down. It was Hornet squadron's first bit of luck all day.

Ten minutes later they caught up with Moran and Miller, limping along half-in, half-out of cloud. Almost immediately they ran into a dozen 109's, evidently on their way home. There was a short, savage skirmish and Flash Gordon's engine died in the middle of it. He drifted through a couple of dogfights, shouting angrily at people to get out of his way, when a bucketful of bullets pounded past his head and the stink of petrol surged everywhere, and he bailed out. He fell head-first. A Hurricane streaked beneath him, so close that the wash of air sent him tumbling. He tumbled for a very long way, sprawling and spinning like a bad acrobat, until he plunged into cloud and pulled the rip-cord.

The 109's broke off and cruised away. What was left of Hornet squadron caught up with Miller and Moran again. They went down through the cloud and Rex called Amifontaine. By great good fortune it was only ten miles away.

"Blue Three pancakes first," Rex ordered.

Moran escorted Miller down while the others circled and watched.

Miller knew he had a problem. His problem was that he could do only one thing at a time, and doing that one thing was a sluggish business. His legs had stopped hurting. He felt nothing from the waist down. His left hand was just a stump with a flap on it, sloppy with blood. Maybe it would move the throttle lever, maybe not. His right arm was okay, provided he gave it plenty of time. That was another problem. Landing a Hurricane meant doing several things at once, quite quickly.

Also he was very sleepy. His mouth had formed a thick shield of dried blood, behind which the pain merely flickered occasionally. He watched Moran and did what Moran did, if he could.

"Lose more speed, Moke," Moran said. They were far too fast.

"Throttle back, Moke. Lose speed." No flaps down, no wheels. Far too fast.

Miller poked at the throttle with his bloody stub and failed to shift it. He looked at Moran and the other Hurricane distorted hugely, like a bad reflection, so he looked away. Moran was shouting at him again. The drome was down there, somewhere. He didn't know where. He took his right hand off the joystick, swung it, and bashed the throttle with his fist, hard.

Too hard. The engine faltered, the Hurricane nearly stalled. Moran bawled something and Miller gave the stick an almighty shove.

The Hurricane teetered for a moment. Moran flinched: she was going to fall on her tail. Instead she dropped her nose and swooped; swooped like a hawk; but there was only a hundred feet of air beneath her and she needed twice that. She hit the ground hard and broke her back. The wreckage slithered fifty yards, crushed and concertinaed so badly that at first the crash crew couldn't even find Miller.

In the ambulance his left glove finally dropped off. Not much blood was coming out of the remains of the hand. Not much blood was left.

Mary Fitzgerald was all right. She was eating a small steak and drinking a half-bottle of Mâcon while she watched the boats bustling up and down the Rhône.

When she limped into Nancy in the middle of the night, every step she took had depressed her more. The town was clogged with refugees, all either anxious or angry. There was a lot of misery, plenty of squalor, and quite a bit of drunkenness. The railway station was jammed; men were fighting to get at the ticket counters; a train was standing, so crammed that people had climbed onto the roof. But the locomotive had no steam up.

It seemed pointless to go back into the streets. She walked along the tracks out of the station, into the darkness. Normally she would have considered that the height of folly. Now, with folly everywhere, it seemed quite normal behaviour.

A mile down the tracks she came across a small freight train, waiting in a siding. The crew gave her some hot coffee. They weren't going into Nancy, they said; not into that madhouse.

Besides, everyone there wanted to go to Paris. This train was going south. Dijon.

Mary gave them some money and they looked the other way as she climbed into an empty cattletruck. When she woke, they were sliding open the doors. Dijon. The station was crowded but she managed to squeeze into an express to Lyon, although all the seats were taken. Lyon was better still. She got a first-class seat to Nîmes. She washed and changed in the lavatory, and found the dining-car. The line followed the Rhône, which was almost as spectacular as the steak. Mary began to enjoy herself.

Nicole had run into difficulties. The first problem had been a series of punctures. By the time she repaired them and toiled into Mailly it was past midnight. She slept on a park bench. When the sun came up she found a café that served breakfast, and they told her how to get to the aerodrome..

She heard a distant roar when the squadron took off, but she never saw the planes. When she reached the airfield, the sentry at the main gate refused to let her in. She explained that she was the wife of Pilot Officer Gordon, but the sentry had only recently joined the squadron and that name meant nothing to him. He was not very intelligent, and he had a way of looking at her with one eye half-closed that she found annoying.

"At least," she said, "tell me if his squadron has arrived here."

The sentry had heard all about French fifth columnists and saboteurs. "Ah," he said. "That would be telling, wouldn't it?"

"I demand to speak to the adjutant."

While the sentry was considering this, a car came out of the gates and stopped. He stamped to attention. "Hullo, Nicole!" Micky Marriott called. "Looking for Flash? They've all gone, I'm afraid. You just missed them."

"Where? Where are they going?"

Marriott scratched his nose while he wondered if he should tell her. He asked himself what possible harm it could do, and decided: none. "Belgium, of all places. Somewhere called Amifontaine."

"Belgium." She knew from the radio that the main German thrust was towards Belgium. "When will they return?"

"God knows. It's all a bit confused at the moment."

"Perhaps they stay in Belgium?"

"It's quite possible. I honestly don't know."

The sentry spoke. "Mr Skelton's gone to Belgium, sir."

"Skull has? What, by car?"

"Checked him out myself, sir."

"Well, there you are, you see," Marriott told her. "Everyone seems to be on the move. Can I give you a lift anywhere, by the way?"

"Are you going to Belgium?"

Marriott laughed. "No, not yet." He drove off.

She picked up her bicycle and thought about what he had said, although she knew she had made up her mind. It was a hundred and fifty miles to Belgium. All the more reason to start now.

Five minutes after they had all landed, Amifontaine was raided.

The mess had a basement, and that was where everyone except Rex went with Skull for the debriefing. The air was stale and musty, and there were no chairs. They sat on the concrete floor with their backs to the wall, sometimes feeling the shudder of distant bomb-bursts. The electric light flickered.

Nobody wanted to talk.

"You reached Maastricht, I take it," Skull prompted.

There was a long silence. Most of them were staring at the floor. Some had shut their eyes. Moggy Cattermole was trying to read an old copy of the *Illustrated London News* that he had found upstairs.

"We saw three of the Battles," Fanny Barton said at last. "They all bought it. Missed the bridge. Dunno about the others."

"I see. What about enemy aircraft? Any claims?"

Silence.

"Not even possibles?"

Silence.

Skull swallowed, noisily, and turned a page of his notebook. "That only leaves our own . . . um . . . losses. Can anybody . . ."

"Lloyd's dead," CH3 said. "Got blasted by a 110. I saw that."

"And Gordon?"

"Somebody baled out," Mother Cox said. "I just missed him. That might've been Flash. Didn't see a parachute, though."

"Thank you." Skull closed his notebook. "I'm sorry to say there is no news of the other Battles."

"Dead loss," Patterson said softly. "What you might call a Losing Battle. Ho ho ho."

Skull sat on the staircase and read his notes. Cattermole turned a page. After a while he said, "This is interesting," and went on reading. The bombing had tailed off but there was still plenty of gunfire.

Rex came down the stairs and stopped halfway. His jaw was set and his lips were resolutely pressed together but his eyes were worried, and he was blinking more than usual. He smiled, however, and shared the smile amongst them all.

Cattermole put aside his magazine.

"We all knew Boy Lloyd," Rex said. "We all knew Flash Gordon. What they have given for us, anyone here would gladly have given for them. Fine men, both. While they were with the squadron they did all that was asked of them without flinching. Their courage, determination and audacity were never in doubt. Their loss is an example of gallant self-sacrifice in the face of heavy odds and extreme peril. Now, with their going, the struggle becomes that much more arduous. Gentlemen: this is the time to close ranks. To stand shoulder to shoulder. To fill up the gaps left by Boy and Flash. Hornet is a proud squadron, gentlemen. Let us close ranks. With pride."

He went out.

"What does he mean, 'close ranks'?" Cox asked. "If I fly any closer I'll be on the other side of him."

"He wants us to huddle together," Patterson said. "It makes him feel warm and secure."

"It doesn't make me feel bloody secure," Fitz said. "It scares the shits out of me. I reckon we ought to change it."

"Change it for what?" Moran asked.

Suddenly the door at the top of the stairs banged open and Jacky Bellamy appeared, out of breath. She was wearing a steel helmet several sizes too large, and it made her look even smaller. After a first glance, nobody paid her any attention. She shut the door and sat with her back to it. "Hullo, you guys," she said. Nobody answered.

"Change it for something more spread-out," Cox said. "So we can see what's going on and dodge about more easily."

"Right!" Patterson said. "When those 110's came at us we were

415

all looking the wrong way, we had no room to break, it was hopeless."

Barton cleared his throat. "I don't think this is the time or the place to –"

"Piss off, Fanny," Fitz said angrily. "You want us to shut up and be good little boys because Jacky's listening? Balls! I've been shot down once and so have you, and now Lloyd's gone, and Flash, and all the others, and why?"

Barton said wearily: "You know as well as I do, the only way to hit the bombers is –"

"What about the fighters hitting *us*?" Fitz shouted. "We fart about the sky like a bunch of bananas! No wonder we get jumped!"

"That's how Nugent and McPhee bought it," Cox said. "They never saw those 109's."

"Bastards are everywhere," Moran said gloomily.

"More spread-out, that's the answer," Cox said. "Not so crowded."

"How d'you mean, a bunch of bananas?" Jacky Bellamy asked Fitz, but he ignored her. "Buggered if I'll be arse-end Charlie again," he said. "Short cut to nowhere, that is."

"I'll tell you what pisses me off," Cox said. "He keeps on shouting at us to regroup. How the bloody hell can you regroup when you don't know where the silly sod is?"

"Don't talk cock," Barton snapped. "Obviously we've got to regroup. Otherwise we'd end up scattered all over the sky. Use your tiny brain, Mother."

"What exactly happened?" Jacky Bellamy asked. There was a note of pleading in her voice. They didn't even look at her.

"Did Moke have any back-armour?" Patterson asked. Nobody answered. Cattermole, who had gone back to his magazine, turned a page. "Fancy that," he murmured.

"I bet the poor bastard didn't have any back-armour," Patterson said. "Christ ... Imagine getting one of those sodding great cannonshells up your chuff."

"Like Lloyd," Moran said, and sighed. Barton glared.

"Wonder how Jerry harmonises his guns?" Fitz said. "I bet they're not like ours ... Where's CH3?"

"Two hundred yards' range," CH3 mumbled. He was on his back, half-asleep.

"Two hundred," Cox said. "Christ, that's close."

"The bastards were a bloody sight closer than that when they hit me," Fitz told him.

"I guess Maastricht was pretty bad," Jacky Bellamy said.

Cox stood up, yawned, stretched, sniffed his armpits. "God, I stink," he said. He wandered around the room, stepping over feet, and came to Cattermole. "What d'you think, Moggy?"

"I'll give you three seconds to get out of my light. One, two, three . . ." Cox did not move. "Right, you've asked for it," Cattermole said. "I'll tell you what's going to happen. You're all going to fly exactly the way Rex says, because he's CO. When you get to Mailly, you're all going to remove the back-armour, you're all going to re-harmonise your guns to conform to the Dowding Spread, and you're all going to give your lovely new blitz shirts to the poor, because Rex believes in uniformity, and Rex is CO. So just stop your bitching and binding and bellyaching and let me get on with this fascinating article about salmon-fishing."

Fitz scrambled to his feet. "Pompous fart! Just because Rex is CO, does that make him God? Jesus Christ Almighty, Moggy, what was he doing taking us through that flak at Maastricht at five hundred feet? What was the point of that?"

Fitzgerald's face was working with anger. Cattermole pursed his lips and turned a page. "Ours was the place of honour," he said.

"Fuck honour," Patterson growled, "and fuck Rex."

Fitzgerald grabbed the magazine, ripped it from Cattermole's hands, flung it across the room. Cattermole was left holding a corner of a page. He tilted it to catch the light. "*How to protect your nerves in war-time,*" he read. "*On no account get over-tired . . . Avoid war talk . . . Get to bed early and do not read exciting stories . . . but make sure you take a cup of delicious Ovaltine.*" He gave Patterson a smug smile. "You've been reading exciting stories, Pip, that's your trouble."

"Jerry's gone," Barton said. "The guns have stopped. Let's get out of here."

Jacky Bellamy stood aside and watched their faces as they climbed the stairs. Only CH3 looked at her. He gave her a strange, crooked smile that was almost friendly. It made her even more unsure of herself.

Rex had left the basement to go to the station sickbay. Bletchley was waiting there. "How do you feel?" Bletchley asked.

"A bit stiff. The neck especially."

"Better let them have a look."

Rex took off his uniform. A medical orderly cut away his shirt: it was ripped and punctured at the back and stiff with dried blood. He lay face-down while an RAF doctor gently swabbed his back, working from the neck to the buttocks. "I make it twenty-three incisions, but I may have missed one or two," he said. "So that's at least twenty-three items of rubbish to be got out."

"Bits of flak," Rex said. "Hell of a bang outside the office."

The doctor grunted. "Look: I don't know how big these bits are, or exactly where they are. Some of them might not want to come out. You're going to need an anaesthetic. Rather a lot of anaesthetic."

Rex turned his head to look up at him. "If you do that I shan't be able to fly again today."

"You're in no condition to fly now."

"I'll be the judge of that. Sir: when's this big show of yours at Sedan?"

"If we don't do it soon," Bletchley said, "then the answer is never."

Rex took a good grip of the horizontal rail at the head of the bed. "Go ahead and winkle it all out," he told the doctor. "If it hurts too much I'll let you know."

Bombs crumped on and around the aerodrome, and anti-aircraft guns pounded away, while the doctor probed Rex's back, and dragged out ragged slivers and little torn chunks of metal. Rex thrust his face into the pillow. At the end, the pillow was drenched with sweat and the rail at the bedhead was bent like a set of handlebars.

Mary was changing trains at Nîmes, climbing into the first-class compartment of an express to Bordeaux, with a new pair of shoes and a bundle of magazines, enjoying the sunshine and imagining that she could smell the Mediterranean, while Nicole was chasing an old man down a road near Épernay, south of Rheims.

Nicole had bicycled hard, all day, heading north. Most refugees were moving west so she had a fairly clear road. By mid-afternoon it was time for her to move her bowels. There was no building in sight: nothing but woods and fields. She pushed the bicycle across a field, hid it in deep grass and went into a wood.

When she came out a little old man dressed in black was halfway across the field with her bicycle. She shouted, which was a mistake: he was amazingly nimble. He had a twenty-yard lead by the time he got to the road and began pedalling. She ran as fast as she could but he steadily pulled away from her, until he was so sure of himself that he looked back and waved. Nicole stopped running and began cursing. Soon he was out of sight.

Some cattle came wandering over to see what all the cursing was about. One of them gave tongue at her, idiotically. She picked up a stone and hurled it and, to her horror, struck the beast in the ribs. It galloped away. She shouted an apology. The other cattle stared, sceptically. She started to walk.

Gangs of airmen were shovelling earth into the smoking bomb-craters that dotted Amifontaine. A couple of buildings were on fire, but they were only billets; they were left to burn. Low cloud and strong winds had hampered the German bombers, and they had missed all the Hurricanes except one: Miller's wreck had been blown to bits.

A Naafi mobile canteen was open. The pilots stood in line and bought hot sweet tea and sticky buns. They were sitting on the grass, eating and drinking and watching the flames flower over the billet roofs, when Flash Gordon arrived in the back of a truck. He was carrying a great bundle of white silk, which he dumped. "It works!" he shouted. "The bloody thing really works!" His eyes were bright with excitement, he was grinning like a child, words bubbled from him. "I never thought it would, never trusted it, to be honest, just kept on falling and waited for something to turn up but it never did, bloody hell is that tea, smashing, love one, sell my soul for . . . Anyway, kept on falling, hit this cloud a terrific smack, nearly broke all my bones, I'll have a bun as well, inside this cloud, thought come on Flash time to get your finger out, see if it works, nobody watching, bags of privacy, as per manufacturer's instructions I pulled the bit of string and by God it works! Works like a dream! Loud bang, nasty kick in the crotch, poor old Flash never the same man again but lots of lovely parachute overhead to keep out the nasty rain and tracer and bombs and birdshit and thank you, Fitz." He took the mug in both hands and drank deeply.

"Nice to have you back, Flash," Moran said. "You made damn good time."

"Had to, Flip. Had to. All the way down I kept saying to myself if I can still walk when this is over, first thing I'm going to do is find that stupid fucker Rex and screw his head off."

"What: right off?"

"Right off. Like a light bulb."

"Have you been on the booze, Flash?" Fitz asked.

"Certainly not. Tell you what, though. Met this awfully nice doctor. RAMC. Made me take some pills. Big fat stripey pills. Pep pills. Pep you up. Give you lots of zip. So he said. Why? Got any booze? Wouldn't mind a swig."

"Better not, Flash," Cox said.

"Why not? Miserable lot of buggers. Where's bloody Rex? Screw his fucking head off. Where's everyone? Where's Lloyd? Where's Moke?"

"Lloyd bought it," Barton said. "Moke nearly bought it. He's —"

"Silly bastards, should've done what I did, pulled the bit of string, it really works you know, really does, not a trick, it —"

"I know, Flash," Barton said. "I've done it myself."

"Good for you, join the club, have a drink." Flash threw out his dregs without looking and hit Patterson. "Two pints, love!" he shouted at the Naafi girl.

"Tea's finished, dear," she called. "All gone."

Flash stared. His face went stiff. He dragged the revolver from his flying-boot and advanced on the Naafi wagon. "Treachery!" he shouted. "Stab in the back!" Cattermole stuck out a foot and tripped him. The revolver went flying. Flash hit the ground with a thump and did not move. "That's right, old boy," Cattermole said. "You have a nice rest or I'll break your legs."

"I can easily make some more tea," the Naafi girl said. "No trouble."

"Good idea," Barton told her. "Make lots. Flip, there's something I want to show you."

Moran prised himself off the ground. One leg had gone to sleep; he limped heavily and stumbled a couple of times. They walked around the corner of a bedding store. Stacked against the wall was a heap of rusty corrugated iron. Moran kicked it. "Certainly," he said. "Put an engine on it and I'll fly the bastard. Where's the stick?"

"Something's got to be done," Barton said. He was still angry from being shouted at in the basement.

"Fully aerobatic, is it?" Moran asked. He began poking at the heap.

"Listen!" Barton grabbed him by the shoulder. "Shut up about that. You've got to do something about Fitz or there's going to be trouble."

That was wrong. Barton knew it as soon as he did it. Wrong to tell him to shut up. Wrong to order. And fatal to tag what sounded like a threat on the end. Moran looked at him with a kind of weary disgust, like a bouncer eyeing a drunk. "Fitz is in 'B' flight," he said, "which is none of your damn business."

"Don't be such a fool. It doesn't matter which flight he's in –"

"Have you taken over the entire squadron again? Supreme commander, are you, like the last time? And a glorious shambles that was. Go and play in your own backyard. There's enough to keep you busy there with lunatics like Flash wanting to kill the CO."

"Flash is my business, and anyway he's doped to the eyeballs. What worries me –"

"Cattermole, then. If you can't shut him up I swear I'll flatten the bastard."

"Damn you to bloody hell, Moran," Barton said desperately, "will you shut your great Irish gob and listen? I'm telling you the squadron's going down the pan and all you can –"

"I'm in charge of 'B' flight. You don't give me orders, Barton. If I have to go to hell I'd sooner go my way than yours."

Barton sat on the corrugated iron and put his head in his hands. "Christ on crutches," he muttered. "What a way to run a war."

When they went back Flash Gordon was stretched out face-down on his parachute. CH3 was chatting with the Naafi girl. The others were sitting in a circle with their heads together.

"What's the big conference?" Barton asked.

"Nothing," Fitz said.

"Please yourself," Barton said.

"We were telling dirty stories," Patterson said.

"Not very funny, by the look of you."

"We didn't get to the punch-line," Cox said.

Barton suspected mockery. "Tell me," he said stiffly. "See if I laugh."

Fitz glanced at the others. "Okay. The punch-line is 'Close ranks'." He sat on his heels and stared at Barton. A nervous twitch kept making his mouth start to grin.

Barton felt baffled, excluded from their private joke, but he had to say something. "Look, things could be worse," he said. "We've had some bad luck, that's all."

"People make their own luck," Cox said flatly.

"If you must know," Cattermole said, "we have been discussing the best way to bump off the CO." Moran stopped cleaning his nails and raised his head. "That's not a funny joke," he said, "with or without a punch-line. We'll have no more of that stupid talk."

"Screw his fucking head off," Flash Gordon muttered.

"Close ranks!" Fitz declared. He raised a clenched fist, and then spoiled the effect by tittering. Nobody else laughed. Barton turned away in disgust and saw Skull coming bouncing and rattling over the grass on a bicycle. He came to summon them to a briefing in the mess.

It was very similar to the earlier briefing, with Sedan substituted for Maastricht. Rex announced that the Battle groundcrews were working flat-out on the damaged Hurricanes and expected to have them operational within the hour. The other piece of good news was that, in recognition of the great courage and resolution shown during the Maastricht show, the squadron had again been awarded the place of honour in another vital mission. Air Commodore Bletchley would explain.

"Fritz," Bletchley said, "has outsmarted himself. He's managed to do the impossible: he's got an armoured column through the Ardennes and over the river Meuse into France. The French are not amused, and intend to biff Fritz extremely hard. Fritz, of course, is very pleased with himself. However, his attack is an arrowhead without an arrow behind it. The Ardennes is appalling terrain. No supply column could cross it in less than a week. So Fritz has cut himself off from his support. Fritz is on his own. Our bombers will now isolate him completely by pulverising his bridgehead at Sedan. Every available Battle and Blenheim is joining in the attack. Your job: keep the sky clear for them. With a little bit of luck, Fritz will shortly discover that he has stuck his neck out too far and cut his own head off."

"Any questions?" Rex said.

"Flak," Moran said.

"Minimal," Bletchley said; and was surprised when they laughed.

"Fighters?" Cox said.

"Bound to be a few, but nothing you can't handle." They laughed again, more coarsely, and Bletchley looked at Rex for explanation; but Rex just smiled.

"The usual formation, I suppose," Fitzgerald said.

"Of course," Rex said.

Nobody laughed at that. Bletchley was puzzled, and slightly offended.

The pilots had left the mess, and Rex was talking to Bletchley, when Rex began to feel faint. His legs were rubbery and his face was clammy with sweat. Bletchley took his arm and, with the help of a mess servant, walked him to the sickbay.

"I'm not surprised," the doctor said. Rex's face was the colour of wet cement.

"Look, old boy," Bletchley said, "you've done one show today. Let somebody else lead this one."

Rex shook his head: a single, feeble movement.

"Is he fit to fly?" Bletchley asked.

"He isn't fit to breathe."

Rex touched his fingers to his mouth. "Pills," he whispered. Bletchley looked at the doctor. "Too slow," the doctor said. "Besides, they don't make a Lazarus pill; not yet, anyway. I can give him a shot of something to get him on his feet. The only question is: how strong is his heart?" Bletchley shrugged.

The doctor loaded the syringe and prepared Rex's arm. Five minutes later Rex was on his feet. The doctor put on a stethoscope and listened to his heart. "Ravel's *Bolero*," he told Bletchley.

"By the way, how's Miller?" Rex asked.

The doctor went to a washbasin in the corner of the room and began soaping his hands. "Miller," he said. "I wouldn't worry about Miller if I were you."

Bletchley had a job to keep up with Rex when they got outside. He was glad to see Jacky Bellamy approaching: conversation might slow him down. "Greetings, scribe!" Rex shouted. "How goes the battle?"

"Isn't that my question?" She looked depressed and discouraged, which made Rex feel even brighter by contrast. "What did you think of Maastricht?" she asked him.

"Lively. Quite lively. We enjoyed good sport."

"How thrilling." The sarcasm escaped before she could stop it. "What was the score?"

"Ah, now that's asking!" Rex chuckled. He felt slightly drunk. Pain hovered around him like an aura: it was there but it couldn't touch him. Not yet, anyway. "Trade secret, old girl. I can tell you that we definitely drew blood."

"At a price, I gather."

"Oh well ... You can't make sauerkraut without chopping cabbage, can you?"

She looked from Rex to Bletchley.

"Figure of speech," Bletchley said. "Got all you need now?"

"Yes. No. How is morale?"

"Oh, morale's fine," Rex said. "Top-class. All the chaps are itching to do battle."

"But didn't Maastricht –"

"Maastricht was a wizard show," Rex said cheerfully. "Piece of cake. Everything is absolutely tickety-boo."

"Tickety-*what*?"

"Boo," Bletchley said. "Or as you would say, Hubba-hubba."

The pilots were standing around, watching the final checks being made to their machines, when Skull arrived. "Got something for you," Fitzgerald said, and handed him a letter. "For Mary. In case I turn into a pumpkin."

Skull nodded. "I've been doing some telephoning. Apparently this isn't the first raid on Sedan. Several squadrons have had a go already. Bombers *and* fighters."

"You're becoming a terrible sceptic," Moran said. "You weren't like this when you joined us. War has depraved you, so it has."

"They say the flak's worse than Maastricht and the 109's are thick as tarts at Piccadilly Circus."

"You see?" Moran said. "Thoroughly corrupted."

"What's the time?" Barton asked. "I ought to go and see how Moke is, before we go."

424

"No need," Skull said.

There were a few seconds of bitter silence. "Oh well," Cox said. "Probably for the best, in the circs."

Rex came striding towards them, waving his gloves. "All set, everyone?"

"Heard about Moke, sir?" Barton asked.

"Yes indeed. The doctors say there's nothing to worry about ... Right, let's go." He headed for his Hurricane.

"God give me strength," Fitzgerald said.

"Remember the punch-line," Cattermole said. "Close ranks."

It was about a hundred miles from Amifontaine to Sedan. The wind that had blown the bank of cloud across their path as they flew north now began to blow it away. Soon Rex was able to pick up landmarks: Cambrai, Le Cateau, St Quentin off to his right, Maubeuge away to his left: names that had a comfortingly familiar ring: he had known them well as a boy, sticking little paper flags in a big map of the Western Front. There had been no official maps at Amifontaine so he had borrowed somebody's Michelin guide. From Cambrai and Le Cateau route nationale 39 led to La Capelle which had a six-way crossroads. It showed up clearly. He was dead on course.

The squadron was in vic formation, sections astern. Rex was at the point, flanked by Cox and Cattermole. Barton flew behind him with Patterson and Gordon on either side. Moran led the arse-end section with Fitzgerald and CH3, but in fact CH3 kept his distance and flew a continuous weaving pattern. That was a little bit sloppy, but Rex didn't really care. Whatever magic juice the doc had pumped into his arm made him feel remarkably happy. He was alert and keen and very ready for action. Some of the dressings on his back seemed to have come adrift when he heaved himself into the cockpit, and his shirt felt strangely slippery with what must be blood, but that only strengthened his sense of accomplishment and well-being. It was a fine late afternoon. Everywhere he looked he saw colours of an extraordinary beauty and brilliance. It was going to be a splendid evening.

Rex set a keen pace. After thirty minutes they crossed the first hills and forests of the Ardennes, and they picked up the Meuse, looking as looped and twisted as a fallen strand of wool. Rex turned

425

south and followed it. In the distance he could see black smoke and the faint flicker of shellfire. Sedan. "Close up," he said. "Nice and tight."

He saw the bombs burst before he saw the bombers. Hornet squadron was at eight thousand feet, and the bombers were at least a mile below. The sudden fountains of earth caught the setting sun and stood briefly golden on one side. He hunted for the bombers and found them, ten or a dozen, looked like Blenheims. At once he looked up and searched for enemy fighters, and he found them too, a great pack of 109's arriving from the east at about fifteen thousand feet; had to be 109's, there weren't that many Hurricanes in Europe. By God, what a scrap this was going to be! He checked the bombers again, hoping they had finished and were going home, and they were, but as they banked the sun lit up the crosses on their wings and they were Junkers 88's, not Blenheims. So those bombs had fallen on the wrong side of the bridgehead. Those bombs had killed Allied troops. What evil. What savagery. What filth.

Rex felt the clear, pure rage of a Crusader knight. He was washed clean of fear or pain or worry. He was indestructible. They could kill him but they could not destroy him! "Bandits below," he called. "Eighty-eights at three o'clock. Going down, chaps. Let's get 'em." It was the first time he had said *chaps* in an order. He thrust the stick forward and fell on the enemy. "Close ranks," someone said, and Rex fell alone.

"Close ranks!" the voice repeated. Immediately the formation tightened. Cox and Cattermole edged in to fill Rex's space. Patterson slid half-under Barton's left wing, Gordon eased over Barton's right wingtip. Fitzgerald crowded Moran. The flight commanders were so boxed-in they could do nothing but fly straight and level.

Rex, plunging through the mile of empty sky, heard none of their shouts and curses: someone else's transmission switch was open, blocking the channel. If he had heard, he would not have turned away. This was his mission, his crusade: to smite the ungodly! To biff Fritz extremely hard! *Bring me my bow of burning gold*, he sang to himself. *God, who made thee mighty, make thee mightier yet!*

The bombers saw him coming. Their gunners raked his path

with crossfire. At four hundred yards he squeezed his gun-button and experienced a jolt of exultation as the Hurricane kicked and trembled and his shining streams of death raged across the formation, ceasing only when he sliced between a pair of 88's.

Rex hauled the stick back and opened the throttle to climb and attack again, tracer still hounding him, and he wondered where everyone was. Then a pair of 109's appeared above. For a second they hung like trapeze artists at the height of their swing. They turned and dropped, and he climbed into their fire. Cannonshells ripped through his tank and the fuel gushed over his legs. Rex never saw that, never even heard the walloping impact. Before the stench of fuel could reach his nostrils, a bullet smashed into his oxygen bottle. It exploded. The Hurricane blew up like a bomb. Pure oxygen mixed with high-octane fuel made a furnace-heat that incinerated Rex, literally in a flash. His clothing turned to ash in a second, and his body was boiled in its own fluids. The cockpit melted around him. The fighter separated into a hundred parts which blew away like a handful of dust. Looking down, Pip Patterson saw only the flash of white, as stark as lightning. And then nothing.

For a moment what remained of the squadron cruised on. They were so bunched-up that Patterson and Gordon and Fitzgerald could see Moran and Barton gesturing furiously, shouting silently. The unknown pilot's transmission switch was still open, swamping all the earphones with his cockpit roar. Then CH3 went past them, waggling his wings. He put his nose up and fired a warning burst towards the pack of 109's, now tumbling out of the sky. At once the switch was closed. The formation relaxed and spread itself. Barton found himself in front, leading. "Trouble at ten o'clock," he announced. "We'll go up and meet it." The Hurricanes turned and climbed.

It was a quick scrap. Not even a proper fight: just a sudden firestorm. Cattermole, watching the 109's get bigger, told himself: *I've got a ton of engine to protect me.* The enemy arrived in a rush. Both sides blasted away. Cattermole's head wobbled to the pounding of his guns. The enemy vanished. Cattermole still lived.

The 109's outnumbered them four to one but they did not return for another attack. A more attractive target lay below. Battle

427

bombers, a dozen of them, came flying along the Meuse valley, their pattern heavily outlined by German flak. A couple of 109's, dribbling smoke, had broken off and were heading for home, but the rest went hunting the Battles. Barton's instinct was to dive and fight. "I'm hit in the engine, dammit," someone complained. "Who's that?" he asked.

It was Pip Patterson. His engine was coughing and missing and shaking the plane so hard that it frightened him. Then Moran called up: he was losing glycol. "Any more?" Barton asked. Cox reported that his guns had jammed. Barton looked about him and saw Flash Gordon gesture thumbs-down and tap his earphones. Radio dead. God knows what else damaged. "Let's try and get back to Amifontaine," Barton said. As they banked to head north he saw the 109's go slamming into the Battles. Before he had levelled out, two Battles were on fire and falling.

Moran had to switch off his engine when he lost all his coolant. They circled while he forced-landed in a field, and saw him get out. Patterson's engine shook itself to death soon afterwards. He could see nothing but woodland beneath. He baled out. Six machines reached Amifontaine. Half of Flash Gordon's undercarriage collapsed on landing and the Hurricane made hectic circles across the grass, destroying its left wing.

Béziers, Narbonne, Carcassonne: the express raced smoothly across the south of France. Mary read a little, dozed, strolled up and down the corridor, read some more, watched the scenery stream by. At tea-time she went to the dining-car and got into conversation with a French naval officer returning to his ship in Bordeaux. He was able to recommend a good hotel not far from the station. They sat and talked for a long time: about the war, Fitz, education, gardening. They shared an enthusiasm for gardening. It was the only drawback to being in the Navy, he said. But he kept several gardening books in his cabin, so it wasn't so bad.

Nicole was having mixed luck. She walked to Épernay, searching always for the little old man on her bicycle, and half-afraid of finding him because what would she do then? Fight him for it? He might not have it with him, he might have hidden it. Take him to the police? He might refuse to go, might have large friends to protect him. Yet she couldn't discard the fact that he had stolen her property, and in broad daylight. It was scandalous, intolerable. If you started letting people get away with that sort of thing, where would it all end?

She needn't have worried; she never saw him. At Épernay she pawned her watch for three hundred francs and ate some stew in a workmen's café. It was a good watch, a gift from Flash, and she hated losing it, but better to be with Flash than to know what time it was.

There was a bus service to Rheims and to her great surprise it was still running. She bought a cheap map and studied it as the bus wandered north by twisting country roads. Three roads went from Rheims towards Belgium. The one on the left, via St Quentin, looked best. The one up the middle was more direct but it wiggled a lot. The one on the right went through the Ardennes, so the hell with *that*.

The bus gave up on the outskirts of Rheims: refugees had arrived and the streets were choked with them. Nicole spent an exhausting, infuriating hour trying to find the railway station, and when she found it she couldn't even get inside. Furious at this shouting, squalid, sweating mob, she turned her back on them and determined to walk out of town, if possible pinching a bicycle on the way. But there were no unguarded bicycles and she couldn't find the right road. A combination of German bombs and French military police had brought Rheims to a state of confusion.

The problem was that many bombs had failed to explode. Maybe they were duds. Maybe not. Whole streets were cordoned off. The detours were long and complicated, and at the end of them Nicole could not be sure she was going the right way because the military police had removed all road signs. Or, if not the military police, then fifth columnists posing as military police. Or Communist anarchists seeking to put the blame on fifth columnists. Rumours abounded. Certainly there were plenty of military policemen, shouting and blowing whistles as they struggled to get endless columns of trucks, guns and tanks through Rheims. The police had no time for Nicole; told her to get out without even looking at her. Eventually, by keeping the sun on her left, she found a road that pointed more or less towards Belgium and she reached the countryside. It was a fine road, good for walking, and she was well on her way before she discovered that it led to the Ardennes.

Debriefing took place in the corner of a hangar. It lasted only a minute. Fanny Barton answered for everybody.

Lots of enemy aircraft over the target. Short sharp scrap. Rex killed, Moran forced down. Patterson baled out. Two 109's damaged. Gordon's Hurricane a write-off.

"I see," Skull said. It made a very concise report. They all seemed unusually silent. It wasn't the silence of fatigue: they were alert enough. He felt the need to contribute, and he said: "I suppose there's absolutely no doubt about Rex?"

"None."

"I could easily organise a search, if you think . . ."

"No. Forget it."

"Oh." Skull felt excluded. "Very well." He shut his notebook. "In that case I might as well get on the phone and report the sad news."

They watched him leave. The hangar had been damaged by blast and part of the roof was split open. Sheets of metal banged in the wind with a kind of idiot insistence, like small children trying to infuriate the grown-ups.

"All right," Barton said. "Let's get it over with. I'm prepared to believe you didn't mean to kill him." He looked at each of them in turn, and they looked back, calmly and candidly. He waited for an answer. After a moment Cattermole said: "Oh, yes?" It wasn't a reply; it was an encouraging noise: *How interesting*, it seemed to say; *tell us more.*

"Presumably you knew what you were doing," Barton said. "Or at least you thought you did. What the hell *did* you think you were doing?"

Again, they simply let his stare bounce back at him. "Come on, for Christ's sake," he said.

"Give up," Fitz said. "What did we think we were doing, Fanny?"

"Whose idea was it, anyway? Who started it? Who said 'Close ranks'? Who?"

"Rex," Cox said confidently. "Rex said 'Close ranks.' It was his idea."

"Not over Sedan, it wasn't. Rex said dive and somebody else –"

"No he didn't, Fanny," Fitz said. "I never heard Rex give the order to dive. Nor did the rest of us."

430

"We heard the order to close ranks," Cattermole said. "So that's what we did."

"You mean you bastards boxed me in."

"On the contrary, Fanny," Fitz said. "You and Flip began crowding the rest of us. You were really getting in our way. Not very nice, that."

"Reckless driving," Cattermole said.

"No consideration for others," Cox added.

"You callous, murdering sons of bitches," Barton said.

"Fanny's upset about something," Fitz remarked.

"Perhaps Rex owed him some money," Cox said.

Barton turned on CH3. "You saw it happen," he said. "Haven't you got anything to say?"

"My brother-in-law used to work for the telephone company," CH3 told him.

"God damn you all to hell," Barton said.

"He said it was a very interesting job," CH3 said. "If you liked telephones."

A prolonged gust of wind kept smashing the loose sheets of metal until several of them blew down. They hit the concrete floor with a splendid crash. Barton used it as an excuse to get out. "Go to the mess," he ordered. "Stay there. Don't talk to anyone."

He found Baggy Bletchley in the station commander's office, standing on the fringe of a high-powered but irritable meeting. As well as the station commander, who was a group captain, there were two wing commanders, an air commodore and a brigadier. When Barton went in they were all listening to an air vice-marshal who seemed especially annoyed with the brigadier. "Of course I can ask for more squadrons," he was saying, "any bloody fool can do that, but where in God's name are they going to operate from? Brittany? The Dordogne? The Côte de bloody Azur? Because any aerodrome nearer than that is liable to get the daylights bombed out of it, wouldn't you agree?"

"You can't expect my ack-ack to hit every German bomber they see. If the fighters don't take out a good percentage –"

"Wait a minute. Are you saying you expect my fighters to protect their own airfields?"

"They've got to do their share."

"And then land in the bomb-craters, I suppose?"

"Listen, my chaps have taken casualties too. It's no fun –"

"So you want my fighters to keep the Hun off your gunners. I see. That's charming, I must say."

"Look, this isn't getting us anywhere," the air commodore said. "Whether or not we get more squadrons, the French want an answer fast."

"Frankly, sir, I don't understand this French plan." One of the wing commanders picked up a sheet of paper. "It contradicts itself."

"Good," said the air vice-marshal. "Since the frogs were daft enough to send it by radio, Jerry quite certainly intercepted it, and if we can't make head or tail of it, he must be thoroughly baffled."

"At last: an Allied triumph," murmured the station commander.

"Well, it's radio or nothing," said the air commodore. "All the land lines are cut. What about using a code?"

"Who's our liaison officer with the French?" the brigadier asked. "Meredith-Jones, isn't it? Why not communicate in Welsh?"

"Are we sure he speaks Welsh?" the air commodore asked.

"I only heard him once, but it certainly sounded like Welsh," the brigadier said.

"Do *you* speak Welsh?" asked the air vice-marshal.

"No, but surely we can find someone who does."

"Bloody good code, if it works," said one of the wing commanders.

"Absolute shambles if it doesn't," said the other.

Barton touched Bletchley's arm. "Excuse me, sir," he whispered. They went into the corridor. "I need your help, sir," he said. "I'm in a bit of a spot."

"I heard about Rex. Damn bad luck."

"Not really."

Barton described what had happened over Sedan. He did not repeat what had been said in the hangar. "They had it all worked out to get rid of him," he said. "It was murder, plain and simple. The question is, what should I do?"

Bletchley blew his nose, made a good clean job of his nostrils, and briefly examined the contents of his handkerchief. "He's quite dead, is he? You're absolutely convinced of that?"

"Blown to bits, sir."

Bletchley nodded. "As long as there's no risk that he might wander in here seeking vengeance ... That makes you acting CO, I take it."

"Yes."

Bletchley nodded again, more firmly. "Well, my boy, whatever it was that Rex did wrong, you be sure and learn from it." Barton had sensed what was coming but he was still taken aback. "And don't look so damned virtuous," Bletchley said. "Use your head. D'you think we're going to courtmartial half-a-dozen fighter pilots *now*, of all times? Because their CO bought it? D'you know how many Battles and Blenheims went off to raid the Sedan bridgehead this afternoon? Seventy-one. And how many came back? Thirty-one. That's forty crews blown to bits. We've just lost the best part of our whole Air Striking Force in an hour and a bit. You want my advice? Forget Rex. I have."

"Very good, sir."

"Meanwhile, be sure and keep your chaps away from that bloody woman Bellamy. If she gets wind of it, I'll have *you* courtmartialled."

"Yes, sir."

"In fact the best thing you can do is get everyone back to Mailly-le-Camp lickety-split. Leave Rex to me. I'll get him a posthumous gong and he'll be forgotten in a month." Bletchley saw Barton's expression and grinned. "Nasty business, war, isn't it? But damn good for promotion." He went back into the station commander's office. The ill-tempered argument briefly boomed into the corridor before the door shut it off.

The farmer who gave Nicole a lift was surprised to see her walking away from Rheims up Route Nationale 51. Most civilians were going in the opposite direction. Only military convoys and locals like himself were heading north-east, towards the fighting, and he wasn't going far, only to his farm which was miles up a side-track where he hoped neither side would want to go, God willing, including this plague of refugees, nothing was safe with them around, they'd steal the crops out of your fields and break down your fences for firewood. Thieves. All thieves.

Nicole thought of the peasant who stole her bicycle and said nothing.

The farmer asked where she was going. "I'm going to find my husband," she said. "He's a fighter pilot with a squadron near Belgium." She deliberately didn't say RAF.

The farmer didn't know whether to be pleased or alarmed. Wonderful that she was setting such a fine example to the nation, of course. But it was very dangerous ahead. They said the boche was across the Meuse. Sedan had fallen. The boche might be anywhere.

"I don't care," she said. "Anyway, they're not going to waste their shells on me, are they? I'll get to Belgium if I have to rollerskate there."

When he dropped her he took out a bottle of wine and they drank to each other's health. Nicole looked around, at the empty countryside, the gloomy skies, the shuffling lines of refugees, and gave herself another long swig of wine. She needed some courage for the road ahead.

For the third time that day, the Battle mechanics re-fuelled and re-armed and patched up the Hurricanes, all five of them. The cloud had completely blown away; it was going to be a beautiful evening.

Flash Gordon's machine was lying on its side, in the middle of the field. CH3 remembered seeing a battered-looking fighter parked behind a hangar, and Barton asked a flight sergeant if it belonged to anyone. "You have it if you like, sir," he said. "It's a Yankee job, Curtiss P-36. A pair of them collided so we built this one out of what was left. The CO wanted it, for fun, but he won't be needing it now, will he? Mind you, nobody's actually flown it yet."

They pushed it out and Flash climbed into the cockpit.

"The wheels won't retract, sir," the flight sergeant told him. "We must have put them in wrong. You want to watch the torque, she's got twelve hundred horses. I'm afraid that's all I can tell you. Have you flown one of these before, sir?"

Flash nodded. The pep pills were beginning to wear off, but he still felt extraordinarily positive. He still felt that anything was possible. He couldn't say no to save his life. "You understand all the taps and dials and things, then?" the flight sergeant said. Flash nodded. The cockpit layout was a sweet mystery to him. "Start her up, chiefy," he said cheerfully. He began tinkering with switches and levers. *The Lord will provide*, he thought.

Meanwhile, Barton was briefing the others.

"Straight back to Mailly. No scraps. If Jerry doesn't bother us, we don't bother him. Keep your eyes wide open. We'll fly loose, about a hundred yards apart, and staggered so that everybody's watching somebody's tail. Let's for the love of Christ see if we can get home without getting jumped. I'm sick of always coughing up half-a-crown for another wreath."

"Don't worry, Fanny," Cattermole said. "You'll be all right with us. We understand one another, don't we?"

Barton stared suspiciously. Just then, Flash Gordon's P-36 started with a colossal bang. Smoke and flame jetted from its exhaust stubs. Mechanics jumped clear and the plane began to roll. Gordon's head could be seen bowed over the instrument panel. The engine was roaring with enormous appetite. Gordon looked up and waved. The P-36 went between two Hurricanes at fifty miles an hour. Flash bounced the machine six or seven times before he got it finally and completely unstuck. By then the Hurricane engines were beginning to fire.

Fanny Barton took them up to fifteen thousand feet, above the French flak, and steered to the west of south, bending their route away from the fighting and the 109's. They kept a wide formation, like a flat W, a quarter of a mile across. All the way, their heads were turning, ceaselessly, as regular as electric fans, left to right, up and down.

Flash Gordon was not with them. His P-36 couldn't get above five hundred feet. Either that, or he hadn't treated it properly. Anyway, the thing refused to climb.

"Please yourself," he said. Who the hell cared? Five feet, five hundred, five thousand, it was all the same. As long as the kite was off the ground, it was flying. Right? Right.

She was a very breezy little bird, this P-36. Smelled good, felt good, tasted good. Flash enjoyed them all. He'd never really noticed the taste of a fighter before but he had it now, his mouth was full of exciting flavours, especially a kind of silver-blue salty-metallic taste that was pure P-36. He inhaled a good lungful of hot, throbbing engine-aroma and made himself slightly drunk. The countryside went speeding past in a golden rush. Flash felt wonderfully happy and relaxed. He blessed the memory of that hot-shot RAMC doctor. Genius. Prince. Good egg.

After twenty or thirty miles, Flash wondered where he was going. He knew where he *wanted* to go, of course, but where was this breezy little bird taking him? Only way to find out: pop down and take a dekko at a few road signs. He found a road and encouraged the P-36 to follow it. There were no road signs. What there was, down there, was a kind of miracle-thing going on. Lots of them. Or maybe one very very long one. Like in the Bible. Flash put his mind to work. *Blue Danube*, it suggested. *Don't be bloody silly*, he said. *Red Sea?* it told him. *Parting of the Red Sea?* He put his head out and had a better look. *Sort of*, he said.

What he was seeing was like the Parting of the Red Sea in reverse. Instead of the sea dividing to let people through, here was an endless sea of people who kept parting to let Flash through. The road ahead was packed with people, prams, wheelbarrows, soapbox carts, farm wagons, dogs, children, bicycles, everyone loaded with junk. Hundreds of people, thousands. But the road directly beneath him was always empty. A mile ahead: packed solid. Half a mile ahead they started to run to the sides. A quarter of a mile ahead they were diving over hedges. Two hundred yards ahead they were all falling flat in the fields. And underneath him, nothing. Empty road. Bloody miraculous!

Flash charged on, taking a hugely childish pleasure in his god-like power. All he had to do was look at people and they ran like rabbits! He swung the fighter left and right through a series of bends and almost caught the rabbits before they had time to clear the road. See how they run! "Double up, there!" he roared. "Jump to it, grandad! Whoops, lady, get your finger out!" Then a village rushed at him and made him dodge and he lost the road.

After that it was fields and woods and stuff, forever. Flash began to think they'd stopped making roads in France until he suddenly found a crossroads and there they were again, the rabbits, rushing out of his way by the hundreds. He swung right to circle and pick up the crossroads again, try and see a signpost, and he promptly got fired on by a French army convoy, string of trucks with machine-guns on top, he could see the flicker of flames. Then he found the crossroads and forgot to look for a signpost. The road was red.

It ran east to west, more or less, so the setting sun was shining down it. The red was bright and fresh and it reached to the green verges. So many extraordinary and colourful things had happened to Flash recently that he was not astonished by this; merely intrigued. Then he noticed the black-clad bodies lying on the shining redness, and shock hit him like a kick in the stomach.

He had had no idea that human beings contained so much blood. Nicole had told him, once. Six litres, she said. A gallon and a bit. Spill it on a road, that's what it looks like. A bloody flood.

He circled to look again and midway through the turn he saw a Messerschmitt 110 a mile away not much higher than he was, so he went after it instead, opening the throttle wide, and if the P-36 blew up he'd demand his money back, so help him God.

It didn't blow up. He caught the 110 from behind as it was machine-gunning a fresh column of refugees and he began shooting at it. At once the pilot jinked and went even lower to give his upper gunner a clear shot. Flash discovered that the P-36 had six guns. He was missing with them all. He got even closer and tried again, but the 110 was swinging and swaying too much. He dropped back a couple of lengths, waited until he was utterly certain of his shot, and fired exactly when the German pilot hauled back the stick and climbed at full power and Flash found himself blazing into a mob of refugees. His thumb was off the gun-button in a second but he clearly saw people knocked backwards by his bullets as if swept by a great wind.

Flash chased the 110 and eventually caught it and set an engine on fire and maybe shot it down; he didn't know. He ran out of ammunition and watched it drag itself into the east, while he went south in search of an airfield. He couldn't believe what had happened. It wasn't possible. He forgot it for several minutes at a time. But always it came back. The redness, shining in the sun, and the great wind, bowling people over.

The dog Reilly sat on its haunches and howled with misery. There was no escape from the wretched noise. Even a quarter of a mile away, inside the wooden hut, Fanny Barton was constantly aware of Reilly's high-pitched grief. He added it to his list of worries. That made nine.

First on the list was Flip Moran. They'd seen him get out but

437

nobody could remember exactly where that was. Fanny worried about concussion, and exposure, and bloodyminded Frenchmen with scythes.

Second was Pip Patterson. Those woods had stretched for miles. If his parachute got caught in the top of a tree he might starve to death. But again, no map reference. How could you start a search without a map reference?

Third was Flash Gordon. He had landed his P-36 an hour after the Hurricanes reached Mailly, and God knows what he'd been up to because Flash hadn't said a word about it. Just got out of the plane, left the engine running and walked away. Eyes like marbles, Cox said. Flash went straight to the nearest tent, lay down, fell asleep. Now he couldn't be woken.

Fourth was Rex's death. All very well for Baggy Bletchley to say forget it; Baggy didn't have to fly with the men who'd done it. Someone had been responsible. Which one? *Rex*, said a savage little voice inside him, *Rex was guilty*. Fanny pushed the thought away, and worried about it.

Fifth was the Hurricanes. They needed complete overhauls.

Sixth was the water supply. There wasn't any. A pipe had bust somewhere. Everyone was getting steadily dirtier.

Seventh was the risk of bombing. What if the fuel dump got hit?

Eighth was his ears. They were beginning to ache. How could he lead the squadron if he had ear-ache?

And now, ninth was the dog Reilly.

Reilly had raced from plane to plane when they landed. It took him ten minutes to realise that his master was missing. At first he whimpered, seeking out the pilots in turn and thrusting a beseeching muzzle into their hands. Then he began to whine, and finally as the day came to an end he sat on the grass and howled. It was astonishing that the animal could go on making such an appalling, exhausting noise so long. Reilly's grief was endless. At that rate nobody would get any sleep. Except Gordon, of course.

Fanny covered his ears and went back to worrying about Gordon.

The adjutant came in. "Can't get through to Rheims," he said. "Something wrong with the line. I've sent a despatch-rider, so that's taken care of. You must be hungry."

"Starving."

"Well, the cooks have done their best and it's stew."

"Stew? We had stew yesterday."

"Yes. Same stew."

"That's no good." Barton began to fret about food. Cox, Fitzgerald and Cattermole came in. "Christ, you look manky," he said. It was a word the groundcrew used for anything made foul by neglect.

"So do you," Fitz said. "Come on, we're going to get rotten drunk. CH3's got his Bentley."

"I can't, there's too much –"

"Oh, balls. Are you coming, uncle?"

"Rotten drunk, you say?" Kellaway asked. "I think I deserve that. Come on, old boy." He put a hand under Barton's arm. "Duty calls. Time to get thoroughly bottled."

CH3 was waiting outside. They drove south, to a town called Arcis, and parked in the main square. The place was full of troops and refugees. "We'll never get a meal here," Barton said. He was the last out of the car, and he lagged behind the others as they walked around the square.

Eventually, CH3 dropped back and walked beside him.

"What a bloody day," Barton said. It was dusk, and Arcis was blacked-out: the streets were gloomy. "First Lloyd goes for a burton. Then Moke Miller buys it. Then Rex. And now we've lost Flip and Pip. Where's it all going to end?"

"Stop brooding, Fanny. Worrying about it isn't going to bring them back to life."

Barton sucked his teeth. "It's all very well for you. You're not CO. I'm paid to worry."

"No, you're not." CH3 gripped his arm and stopped him. "You're paid to lead. Now for Christ's sake stop being such a tight-ass. You're spoiling the war for everyone."

They stood in the failing light and stared: CH3 calm, Barton wide-eyed with astonishment. "I see," he said. "And what do you suggest I do that I haven't been doing?"

"Do whatever you want," CH3 said. "You've got the power, haven't you?"

"I say, Fanny," Cox called. "What d'you think of this place? Think they'd let us in?"

It was a large hotel, the biggest building on the square. Barton

439

led them up the steps and into the restaurant, which took up most of the ground floor. Waiters swayed between tables; silver and crystal gleamed and sparkled in candlelight. Cutlery tinkled, and the conversation was as soft and seamless as the carpeting. Fitzgerald, following Barton, caught a whiff of roast chicken that made him swallow and twitch his nostrils. The headwaiter appeared, and took in their scruffy uniforms with a single flicker of the eyes. "*Messieurs?*" he murmured.

"A table for six," Barton said firmly.

"*Je regrette –*"

"That one will do." Barton pointed to an empty table.

"*Ah, je regrette, m'sieur, mais cette table est réservée.*"

"That's right." Barton gave him a big, encouraging smile. "It's reserved for us. Lead on."

"*Non, je suis désolé, m'sieur, mais c'est réservée pour Général Delacroix.*"

"This is General Delacroix." Barton indicated the adjutant. Kellaway bowed. "*Bon soir,*" he said.

The headwaiter was an experienced, intelligent man. He glanced at the rest of the party, and each of them returned a hard, hungry, unblinking stare. "*Grand honneur,* mon *général,*" he said smoothly, and took them to their table. "Champagne for the general!" Barton ordered. The headwaiter snapped his fingers to left and right, and retired.

"Well done, Fanny," CH3 said.

Barton grinned, uncertainly. "What about when the real general gets here?"

"Use your famous initiative," CH3 said. "Meanwhile, enjoy yourself."

The champagne came. Barton immediately ordered more. Cox intercepted an *hors d'oeuvre* trolley and they began eating. "Six large steaks," Cattermole told the waiter, "with lashings of spuds and a bucket of plonk each. *Comprenez?*"

"*Non, m'sieur.*"

Cattermole groaned.

"*Biftecks pour tous,*" CH3 said, "*avec des pommes de terre frites et du vin rouge en abondance.*" The waiter hurried away.

"You shouldn't do that," Cattermole said. "It just spoils them."

They got through three bottles of champagne, and they were

making a start on the red wine, when Barton said: "Follow me."
They took the bottles and crossed the room to a table that had just
been vacated.

"What was the point of that?" Fitzgerald asked.

"When in doubt, take action," Barton said briskly. "Golden
rule."

"Bollocks," Cox said. "We've been taking action all day, and a
fat lot of good it's done us."

"What's the matter, Mother? Life too exciting for you?" Barton
took a glass of wine and tipped it over Cox's head. "Just say the
word and I'll get you a transfer to a nice safe desk." Cox was so
startled he just sat, dripping, and stared. "No, no, no," he said.

"Glad to hear it," Barton said. "Because life's going to be a
damn sight more exciting soon, if I have anything to do with it."

"I see a little thrill approaching now," Cattermole said.

It was the headwaiter, followed by a sergeant of the French
military police.

"Soon sort him out," Barton said. "Fill your glasses."

"He won't like it," Cox warned.

The headwaiter stopped alongside Kellaway and made a statement.

"*Messieurs, allons, ceci n'est qu'un malentendu. Je suis sûr que
personne ne veut créer d'embarras, et que nous pouvons résoudre
cet incident rapidement, calmement, et sans causer de dégâts.*"

"It's easy for you to say that," Cattermole said.

"I make a toast!" Barton declared. "*A la belle France!*" They
all stood and drank. The sergeant stood at attention. The headwaiter
waited, and cleared his throat. CH3 announced: "*A l'Armée de la
France!*" and they drank again. Cox proposed: "The Entente
Cordiale!" and this time Kellaway handed the sergeant a glass of
wine and he joined in the toast. "Your turn," Barton said to
Cattermole. "*Cherchez la femme!*" Cattermole cried.

"That's torn it," Fitzgerald said. The sergeant had returned his
glass.

"I couldn't think of anything else," Cattermole said. "Anyway,
what's wrong with it?"

"*Général Delacroix?*" the sergeant said to the adjutant.

"No, no. Kellaway's the name." He got up, shook hands with
the sergeant, and managed to tread on the headwaiter's toe.

There was an awkward pause, while the adjutant sat down, the sergeant looked uncertainly at the headwaiter, and the headwaiter looked savagely at the back of Kellaway's head.

"*Jag tycker om det?*" said Cox, without much hope. Barton had run out of initiative, and he took another drink to hide his desperation.

"If you want General Delacroix," CH3 told the sergeant, "he's just come in." He pointed to a group of senior French officers. At once the headwaiter hustled away, limping slightly. The sergeant wiped his mouth, straightened his uniform, and followed.

Barton chuckled and then laughed. He laughed until he had to put his glass down. He had suddenly realised the pointlessness, the uselessness of worrying. Everything changed so fast that worrying about any of it was like trying to organise the weather. You had to blow with the wind! Trust the wind! Trust it to blow you some luck! "You sonofabitch," he said to CH3. "I should have known it. Should've known you knew General Delacroix."

"Me? I don't know him. The point is: neither does that head-waiter, probably. Anyway, here come the steaks. He can't throw us out now. I guess we'd better get some more wine, while we've got the chance."

The rest of the meal was tremendously enjoyable to Barton. He felt that an invisible barrier had fallen: the other men had seen him take charge, take risks, and prove himself. They accepted him as boss. And this was what he had really been worrying about all along. Not Moran, not Patterson, not the aircraft or the water supply or the damn dog, but being accepted. He glanced across at CH3 and they exchanged stiff nods of self-satisfaction. It was the best bloody steak he had ever had. Also his ear-ache had gone.

CH3 was right. The headwaiter left them alone. They ate dessert and cheese and drank coffee and cognac. The bill was stupendous. Not even CH3 had enough money to pay it. Fortunately the adjutant had Moke Miller's chequebook – the only item of value he had found when he cleared out Miller's tent. He gave it to Cattermole, who wrote a generous cheque and forged the signature with a flourish.

But when they came to leave, the headwaiter was stationed in the lobby, and he had a couple of hefty kitchen-porters, their heads cropped and their knuckles curled, to back him up. He held the forged cheque gripped between two fingers like a note in a cleft stick. "*M'sieur* Miller?" he said.

Now it wasn't funny any more. Fanny sensed fatigue catching up with everyone, deflating their spirits; he felt it in himself. He wanted this whole damn fool affair to be over, so that he could go home to bed and sleep and forget everything. He didn't want a brawl, he didn't want an argument, he didn't want to have to sort out other people's troubles. But that was what they all expected him to do. Even the adjutant was looking at him. It made him angry, furious; and although he tried to hide his feelings they must have shown because when he took the headwaiter by the arm the man did not resist but walked with him, away from the group, around the corner to a quiet place.

"Miller's dead," Barton said. He was standing so near that he could smell the man's brilliantine. "Miller *est mort. Contre le boche.* Understand? Today. What the hell's the French for 'today'?"

"Today is '*aujourd'hui*'."

"All right. *Aujourd'hui*, Miller. And Lloyd. Yesterday ... What's 'yesterday'?"

"Yesterday in French is '*hier*'." The headwaiter's English was very good, very fluent.

"Well, *hier* it was *deux pilotes* called Nugent and McPhee. Both *mort*. Very *mort*. Understand?"

"I understand."

"Good. Then there's tomorrow. I know tomorrow, you don't have to tell me tomorrow, tomorrow is '*demain*', but I don't care about *demain*, because *aujourd'hui* was *demain* for Miller only yesterday, wasn't it? See what I mean?" Barton stared angrily into the headwaiter's steady and unblinking gaze and wondered just what the hell it was he did mean.

"I see, *m'sieur*."

The last flare of fury inside Barton burned itself out. He was empty, powerless. He slumped against the wall and said: "Buggered if I do."

The headwaiter held up the cheque, still tucked between two fingers. "What about this?" he asked.

"Tell you what," Barton said flatly. "Let's be reasonable. You

443

give it back to me and forget all about it, or I'll beat your head in. Does that seem like a fair deal?"

The headwaiter shook his head. "Whatever I give back to you, *m'sieur*," he said, "I shall remain in your debt."

Barton needed a moment to work that out. He nodded, and they shook hands.

Barton went back to the others, tearing the cheque into small bits which he finally threw over his shoulder. "Come on," he said.

"All sorted out?" Kellaway asked.

"Piece of cake."

Cattermole had stolen two half-bottles of wine as he left the restaurant. They drank and sang all the way back to Mailly. When CH3 parked the Bentley and they fell out, the first thing they heard was the dog Reilly, still howling. "Soon sort that out," Barton said. He got his revolver, found the dog, and shot it through the head. "Now we can all go to bed," he told them.

The dead dog was the first thing Pip Patterson saw when he walked into Mailly airfield at dawn. He was not really surprised to see it but he was saddened so much that he stood and cried for a minute or so. He had liked Reilly. Nice old dog. Everything that was nice, everything decent, was being killed or hurt. The killing of Reilly was just another part of Patterson's nightmare.

After he baled out he had fallen, as Barton feared, into a wood. The top branches had rushed up at him, whacking his legs and jabbing at his eyes. He wrapped his arms around his head and waited for the punishment to stop. When it did, he found himself hanging forty feet above ground.

He tried to climb up the parachute shrouds. They were thin and slippery and they cut into his hands. He made ten feet and had to rest, but there was nothing to rest on, and hanging there was a drain on his strength. He let go.

He fired his revolver, one shot every minute to attract attention. Nobody heard. Nobody came.

After about an hour he had a brilliant idea. If he cut a few of the shrouds, he could knot them together, tie them to the harness and climb down. He had a knife. He sawed through the nearest shroud. The frayed end stuck out of his fist like the wick in a

444

candle. It was, of course, utterly useless. He had to cut the *other* end, the top end, which was miles away. He howled his despair.

That gave him another idea, and he shouted. For ten minutes he shouted, and made trumpeting noises, catcalled, sang bits of popular songs, whistled between his fingers. He silenced the birds, but nobody answered.

A wind rocked the treetops, and once he dropped a couple of feet when the parachute silk tore. Maybe he could make it tear some more. He grabbed the shrouds in his bleeding hands and bounced up and down. Bits of twig fell past him but the canopy refused to give way. He stopped bouncing and hung there, gasping for breath, his chin on his chest. His hands burned. Occasionally he saw drops of blood spin away and make tiny, bright splashes, forty feet below.

After a while he dozed and slept. The racketing alarm call of a bird awoke him. He felt stronger: it was dusky in the trees so he must have slept for quite a time. He twisted around to find the sun, and gave himself another brilliant idea. All he had to do was swing. Make himself swing like a pendulum. Reach a tree, grab hold, climb down. Easy.

And it worked, up to a point. That point was roughly midway to the nearest tree. He could swing that far. Then, for some maddening bloody-minded reason, it got very hard to increase his swing. The sodding parachute seemed to be fighting him from that point on.

He stopped trying. As he swayed back and forth he looked up and cursed this thing that had saved his life and was now doing its best to kill him. He noticed something funny. The parachute was very widely spread up there. When he swung to the right, the left-hand shrouds soon reached their limit and pulled him back. Same to the left: the right-hand shrouds checked his swing that way.

Patterson thought about it. He tested it. He looked for the nearest tree. He thought about it some more. Then he lost patience and took his knife and slashed all the shrouds on the left-hand side of his parachute. At once he swung closer to the tree. Kicking hard, he got a pendulum-action going. Cutting the shrouds had worked: after a couple of minutes his boots scraped the bark. This was so enormously encouraging that he put all his strength into

445

the next two swings. The third swing made it. He hugged the trunk and flung his legs around it. Success!

The only trouble was he couldn't work the parachute release-mechanism without taking an arm off the tree. If he did that, he would fall. He knew he would fall. He would have to lean back to let one hand get at the release and he couldn't get a strong enough grip on the tree with the other hand. It was very simple and obvious and so disheartening that he shut his eyes and clung to the tree like a child to its mother. Then he let go and swung back to where he had started.

It took a long time for his despair to subside. If God didn't want him to reach the ground, then why the hell had He gone to the trouble of letting him get this far? It made no sense. Nothing made sense. It was all cockeyed and stupid and wasteful. Just like this bloody silly war: all that rubbish about Maastricht and Sedan, it was just an excuse for getting blokes killed, same as this.

Patterson looked with hatred at the tree he had reached, and he saw an easier tree next to it. This tree was thinner, he would be able to get an arm right round it. Trouble was, he'd have to swing at a different angle to reach it and some of the shrouds would resist that. He got his knife and chopped them off. Now all his weight was hanging from a corner of the parachute. Branches tore and showered him with leaves but the silk held firm. He began swinging. Twenty good swings carried him onto the tree. He hung to it while he got his breath back, then discarded his harness and climbed down to a fork where he could sit and recover. Five minutes later he was on the ground. "Piece of cake," he said.

He began walking but within fifty yards he felt a physical reaction to his efforts. First he was lightheaded, then giddy, then faint. He sat down before he fell down. It was a long time before he got up. How long, he couldn't tell, but the woods were quite dark.

After that the night was shapeless. He remembered walking a lot and finding a stream. He took off his tunic to wash himself. The next thing he remembered was feeling cold and discovering that he had forgotten his tunic. By then the stream was far behind him. For a while it worried him, the loss of his tunic. It meant that his brain was not working properly. He tried to tell himself to be more careful but his brain wouldn't listen. He knew why that was,

446

of course: it wasn't working properly. Now how did he know that? He puzzled over it until he was too tired to think.

Eventually, when his legs were so heavy that his boots were constantly scuffing and dragging, there was a house. First there was a dog that barked. Then there was a light in a window. Patterson walked into a thin fence and smashed something. The dog went insane with its barking.

A door opened. A man shouted. Patterson hung on to the broken fence and answered. "Here," he said. "Here. Here." Now that he had stopped walking his legs were useless. The man shouted again. Patterson tried to wave. "I say," he called.

There was a long silence. Even the dog had shut up. Patterson set his brain to work, thinking of something stronger to say. He was opening his mouth to take a deep breath when the man fired a shotgun at him.

The bang battered the night to bits. Its shock was so big and so brutal that Patterson's knees gave way and he collapsed. All the same he was aware of lead shot ripping through the branches above him and he began running as soon as his hands touched the ground. He scrambled along on all fours, smashing through bushes and ferns and bouncing off trees until he was too bruised and breathless to go further.

His next clear memory was of a road. It was a very black road and he kept wandering off it and falling into the ditch. After that he remembered the searchlight. It picked him out and dazzled him, so he just stood and shielded his eyes. Then he was inside a hut that was full of Arab soldiers who kept shaking him and shouting. One of them had a sort of machete or kukri, anyway a very nasty-looking knife that he enjoyed waving near Patterson's throat.

This went on for a long time. Patterson kept saying, "RAF, RAF," until his throat was dry. At one point the soldier with the big knife emptied a sack in front of him and two human heads fell out. Patterson picked one up. It was the head of a young man, a white man, a European, no older than himself. He looked at the Arab soldier and shrugged. The soldier shouted at him in rapid angry French. He shrugged again. The soldier hit him in the face and he fell off his chair. Partly he was terrified: he could hear himself whimpering and snivelling. But he was too tired even to sustain terror. He fell asleep.

When he woke up he was in the back of a car, travelling fast along a smooth, straight road. His throat was sore and he was painfully thirsty. He moved and groaned. A French army officer in the front seat turned and smiled. "*Ça va?*" he said. Patterson tried to swallow but it hurt too much. The officer produced a vacuum flask and gave it to him. Milky coffee. Patterson drank it all. When he returned the flask he saw that the driver was an Arab soldier, and memory rushed back.

"Heads," he said. "Two heads."

"Ah, you saw them?" the officer said. "German airmen. Their machine crashed. My regiment does not concern itself with prisoners, you understand."

"They wanted mine. My head."

"You were *un aviateur*, they knew by your boots. *Et probablement un boche, non? Cependant* . . . you had luck. They found a map, a *carte Michelin*, here." He touched Patterson's right boot. "So they telephoned for me."

The sky was beginning to lighten. Patterson lay on the seat with his hands under his head and let the black blur of the countryside speed past his eyes. Everything was going on at once inside his head: dogfights with 109's inside the Arab hut while he swung from his parachute and shotguns blazed like searchlights so he put up his hand to stop them chopping off his head, and the treetops jabbed at his face . . .

"Those two heads," said the officer. "I cannot be sure they were German. I myself have not seen the machine. *Peut-être ils sont descendus par parachutes, n'est-ce-pas?* But one was blond, I think."

"Some of my best friends are blond," Patterson said. The officer chuckled.

They took him to Mailly-le-Camp, declined his offer of breakfast, and drove away. That was when he saw the dog Reilly.

One of the cooks found him sitting by the body, crying. He took him to the mess-tent and gave him coffee spiked with rum. Skull was the only other officer who was up. He came and talked and listened but Patterson didn't make much sense because he never completed a sentence, he kept remembering something else and sometimes he couldn't think of the right words and his head trembled with the awful effort of capturing them. He began telling

448

Skull about the Arab soldier and his big knife. "It was . . ." Grimly he hunted down the word. "Sharp," he said at last. "It was so bloody *sharp*."

"What was, old chap?" Skull asked.

Patterson gazed at him for a long time. "Can't remember," he said miserably.

Skull gave him a shot of rum. He liked it, so Skull gave him another and put him to bed. He seemed to fall asleep at once, but he muttered a lot. Skull closed the tent-flaps and left him.

Fanny Barton awoke at six and got up at once. He felt slightly brittle but not seriously hung-over. The day had begun and he was keen to start work: he was, he remembered with a surge of pride, the CO of this squadron.

After that, everything conspired to give him encouragement. His batman brought him fresh coffee and hot shaving-water: the bust pipe had been mended. Skull strolled by and told him that Pip Patterson had turned up and that Flip Moran had been found: the land-line to Area HQ was working again. One by one, all of yesterday's anxieties disappeared. Barton luxuriated in the delight of shaving off three days' stubble and told himself that CH3 had been absolutely right. Worrying was a mug's game.

On his way to see Micky Marriott about the Hurricanes he noticed the body of the dog. It was attracting a lot of flies. He took it by the legs, dropped it into a slit-trench and kicked dirt over it, thinking: *A week ago I couldn't have done this, it would have been unthinkable.* He strolled on, pleased at his progress.

Most of the others were up when he got back. They were hanging about the mess-tent, waiting for breakfast. It was correct form to salute the CO and call him "sir" the first time you met him in the morning, and everyone did. He enjoyed that. "Morning, chaps!" he called. "Heard the news? Flip Moran's alive and Pip's back, so things could be a lot worse, right?"

"Pip's in here, sir," Cox said. "He's still a bit pissed."

Barton went into the tent. Patterson was slumped in a camp-chair, resting his head and arms on a trestle-table. His eyes were almost shut. Except where it was grimy and bloodstained his face was off-white, like newsprint. "Welcome home, Pip," Barton said.

449

No response.

"He's completely whacked, poor chap," Skull said.

"Landed in some frog officers' mess, I expect," Fitzgerald said. "Been soaking up the five-star brandy all night." He funnelled his hands and bawled into Patterson's ear: "Is that right, Pip? On the razzle, were you?" Patterson's eyes flickered once.

CH3 squatted and studied him. He felt his pulse and touched his forehead. "He needs a doctor, Fanny," he said.

"He needs a bucket of Alka-Seltzer," Cattermole said. "Followed by a nice battle-climb to twenty thou."

"Listen, Fanny," CH3 began, but Fitzgerald interrupted with a great shout: "*Zut alors! Mon Dieu, voici le général Delacroix! Bon jour, mon général!*"

It was the adjutant. He was looking for Barton, but Fitz and Cox and Cattermole made a loud and extravagant show of greeting him in bad French. Kellaway waved them aside with his clipboard. "Good morning, sir," he said. "I've had another signal from Rheims. It seems that Flip took a bullet in the foot. He's in a hospital at St Quentin. No replacements available."

"Very good," Barton said.

"And the squadron's to be ready to move north at short notice."

"I see. Is that all, adj?" The cooks were bringing in trays of eggs and bacon. A tea-urn got heaved onto the table, and Barton pointed at it. A cook drew off a steaming mugful and gave it to him. Rank has its privileges.

"I don't want to bother you with a lot of bumf, sir . . ." Barton waved the idea away. "It's just that some letters ought to go off as soon as poss," Kellaway said. "Next-of-kin stuff." The adjutant was speaking quietly but the others heard him and fell silent. "Miller and Lloyd, and . . ." Kellaway adjusted the papers on his clipboard. "And Rex, of course."

The only sound was the soft sizzle of bacon and the slap of the cooks' spatulas as they filled the plates. Barton was staring out of the tent, watching the clouds blow by. "Of course," he said.

"No problem about Lloyd and Miller," Kellaway said briskly. "I can draft something for you to look at, perfectly straightforward and routine . . . No, not routine, far from it, but . . . Anyway, no problem. And I can put up a few suggestions for the other one, if you like." Barton nodded. "Although it would help," Kellaway said, "if I knew something about how it happened."

Patterson heaved himself up from the table and propped his face on his fists.

"Yes, I see," Barton said. "Mind you, it was all rather sudden. Rex was leading, of course."

"Rex leading . . ." Kellaway made a note, and added: *Vanguard. (Spearhead?) Hot pursuit.*

"He ran into a couple of 109's," Barton said. "And that was that, really."

Kellaway wrote. "Outnumbered," he murmured. "He set his personal safety at naught."

Barton grunted. "I suppose you could say the squadron won't be the same without him."

"Sorely missed," Kellaway remarked.

"No," Barton said. "Just put: the squadron won't be the same without him."

The adjutant glanced enquiringly; but Barton had nothing to add. "Jolly good," he said. "I'll get cracking, then." He went out.

Everyone relaxed at once. Everyone moved, or scratched, or coughed, or swung his arms. There was an air of relief as keen as the smell of bacon. "Let's eat!" Barton said. CH3 got a mug of tea and put it in front of Patterson. Steam rose and made him blink.

They sat and ate. For a while the only sound was the scrape of knives and forks on metal plates. Patterson watched, his eyes half-open.

"How's the war getting on, Skull?" Fitzgerald asked. "Got any half-time scores?"

"Sorry. Haven't the vaguest idea."

Cox said: "Fine intelligence officer you are. Can't you even make up some rumours?"

"The skies of Flanders," said CH3, and paused to swallow, "are thick with German parachutists disguised as nuns. They machine-gun innocent children as they float down."

"Bloody good shots," Barton said.

Patterson tried to speak and could only croak. They waited, interested, while he took a sip of tea. It stung his lips. "Who shot the dog?" he asked huskily.

Cattermole raised his fork. "I, said the Mog. I shot the dog, in mistake for a frog."

Fitzgerald groaned. Cox blew a raspberry. Patterson picked up his mug and flung the tea in Cattermole's face. It was hot enough to hurt. CH3's warning shout came too late for Cattermole to do more than throw up an arm. That couldn't save his face. The shock and the pain knocked him off his chair. He rolled from side to side and moaned like someone winded and fighting for breath. "What happened?" Fitzgerald asked. He had been rubbing sleep from his eyes and he'd missed it all.

One of the cooks got to Cattermole first. He ripped off his apron and wrapped it around Cattermole's face so that it covered everything except his mouth. The others gathered around. CH3, however, went to Patterson and removed everything throwable from his reach. Patterson did not notice. He had got to his feet and was shouting, furiously but incoherently. Spittle ran down his chin, and a tremor shook his left arm.

Quite soon, Cattermole got his breath and stopped moaning. He sat up, holding the apron to his face, and let it slip until his eyes were exposed. "You maniac," he said.

That silenced Patterson, but only for a couple of seconds. He cackled with laughter, and waved a derisive finger. "Can't take it, can you?" he cried. "You can dish it out but you can't bloody take it. Who killed Dicky Starr, eh? You did, you murdering bastard! Just like you nearly killed poor old Sticky! Couldn't get him killed but you got him chopped!" Patterson was hoarse, and his voice kept cracking. A sneer of contempt hooked up a corner of his mouth and exposed his teeth. "You're damn good at that, aren't you, Moggy? You killed Rex, too! Cunning bugger! You got us silly sods to do it for you!" Patterson was beginning to cry. "Who's going to be left at the end? Just you? Don't bet on it, chum." The tears were coming fast, now; his left arm was shaking so that his knuckles rattled on the table. "Don't bet on it! You won't kill me like you killed Dicky and . . . and . . ." Patterson broke down.

CH3 took his arm and led him out.

They helped Cattermole up and sat him on a chair. Cautiously, he removed the cloth. His face was lobster-red, as if he had fallen asleep in the sun. "I'm all right," he said. "I'm not so sure about *him*."

"He was in a bad way when he got here," Skull said. "He kept jabbering about having his head cut off."

"Bloody good idea," Cattermole said. "Anyone got a knife?"

That broke the tension, and they laughed. A medical orderly hurried into the tent. While he treated Cattermole they got on with breakfast. Cox said, "D'you think Pip's going to be fit to fly, sir?"

"We'll see." Barton was getting the hang of command: just because you were asked a question, it didn't mean you had to give an answer. "I don't know what he does to the enemy, but by God he frightens me," he said, and they laughed some more. When CH3 came back and said that he had put Patterson to bed and left his batman to watch him, Barton thanked him and forgot about Patterson. He didn't actually need Patterson. The squadron was short of Hurricanes. What mattered was making the surviving machines airworthy and getting them back into action, damn fast. Patterson could wait.

The adjutant looked up from his paperwork, saw one of the riggers cycling across the field, and suddenly remembered Flash Gordon.

Flash was in his pyjamas, sitting on his camp bed, rubbing the grime from between his toes. "Hullo," he said.

"Sleep well?" Kellaway asked.

"Dreams. Too many dreams."

"Ah, don't we all?" He sat on the bed. Flash looked ten years older, he thought: pouchy eyes, grim mouth, none of the old fizz. "I've got some news for you," Kellaway said.

"Ever shot a little old lady, uncle? I must've got about forty of them yesterday. Bit of a walkover, really. They didn't put up much of a fight." He rubbed an ankle, and got more grime off that.

"Tell me."

Flash put his elbows on his knees and rested his head in his hands. "I just did," he said.

Kellaway waited, but Flash had no more to say.

"Well, I only came over to tell you that Micky told me he bumped into your charming wife as he was going out yesterday," Kellaway said.

"Nicole got here?"

"On a bicycle, apparently. Micky told her you were in Belgium, returning God knows when, and from the way she was talking it

453

seems quite likely that she decided to head in the same direction. Probably halfway there by now."

"Unless," Flash began, and had to stop and swallow a couple of times. "Unless something happened to her."

"Well . . . I suppose some of the roads are a bit dangerous now. Still . . ."

"Anything's possible, uncle. Anything. Christ Almighty . . ." Flash stood up. "Christ Almighty. That really has put the tin hat on it, that has. Christ Almighty." His voice had begun to shake.

"I expect she's perfectly safe, old chap."

"I could have shot her, uncle. Maybe I did. Maybe I did shoot Nicole. They were all just refugees. God knows where they were going."

"No, no. Chance in a million, old boy. Forget it."

"I could've shot her. How do you know I didn't?" Flash gripped the tent-pole, squeezing hard. "I mean, Christ Almighty."

Kellaway tipped his cap back and scratched his head. "Look: Pip's all right," he said, "and Flip's nearly all right, so I bet Nicole's all right, too." He knew it wasn't much, but it was the best he could do.

In fact at that moment Nicole was safe and well and in good spirits.

She had walked five miles the previous evening and found a barn with fresh straw to sleep in. She was up at dawn, washed in a cattle trough, and walked another three miles to a village, where she got a breakfast of coffee and bread. She felt good. It was a clear, pleasant day and the walking had given her a sense of accomplishment. Belgium couldn't be far. She was convinced she was doing the right thing. To sit in Mailly-le-Camp while Flash was in Belgium would have been stupid. Boring and pointless and intolerable. Too many people treated the war as an excuse to stop trying. Nicole was a doer. She didn't believe in waiting for someone else to come along and solve your problem.

Then someone came along and helped to solve hers. He was a man on a motorcycle, a medical student trying to get to his home in Valenciennes. He offered her a lift. Valenciennes was just where she wanted to go. They could be there by afternoon.

It was a large machine and he liked to go fast, but the further north they went the worse the traffic became: a blaring confusion

454

of military vehicles and plodding refugees. About midday the whole weary mess came to a halt. The student took to the grass verge and after a couple of miles they reached the blockage. It was a crossroads, thoroughly cratered and strewn with burning vehicles, dead horses, bits of people. The student stopped to see if he could help, and in the next five minutes the Stukas came back to bomb the crossroads again.

He started his motorcycle and Nicole got on the pillion. They were well away from the crossroads when the first bombs fell, and the road was clear: everyone else had run into the fields. He got the machine into top gear and raced down the crown of the road. Nicole's hair streamed in the wind. She linked her fingers, hugging his body, resting her chin on his shoulder. Her eyes were closed and she took pleasure in the speed and in their escape.

An hour earlier, a couple of empty wine-bottles had rolled off a cart and broken in the road. Nicole never saw them, and the student saw them too late. His front tyre was slashed open. The wheel skewed wildly to the left and the machine bucked, catapulting them both ahead. Nicole's eyes opened to show her a bright blur of green and blue, and then the road rushed up and smashed her.

Fanny Barton made CH3 an acting flight commander.

"That's in case I snuff it," he said. "You haven't got a flight to command right now. Micky Marriott says Fitz's kite has had it. That leaves four: you, me, Moggy and Mother."

"Flash?" CH3 said.

"Dead loss. Looks like a zombie with a flat battery. He and Pip make a fine pair. What did you make of Pip's moment of madness, by the way?"

"I reckon he's near to cracking up. He needs care."

"Hmm. I still don't see why he had to be so shitty to Moggy."

"Well, Moggy's a shit, Fanny. Pip was right: Moggy does like killing people. He's a very nasty piece of work, is Moggy. You don't know how lucky you are to have him."

Barton looked hard at CH3 to be sure he wasn't joking, and then shouted for Cox and Cattermole.

"We're getting out," he told them all. "They want us at Berry-au-Bac, nearer where Jerry's broken through the Ardennes. Berry's only about eighty kilometres from here so while we're up we'll go and look for trouble. We've been given the patrol line Vouziers-Rethel. Tactics are simple. We fly loose and staggered, like yesterday. Keep your heads turning. If you see anything, shout. And if it comes to a scrap, get in close, hammer the buggers and get out fast. Okay? Any problems?"

"I could do with some cash, Fanny," Cox said. Cattermole sighed, and shook his head. "Well, I'm broke," Cox protested. "I spent all my francs at that restaurant, and we haven't been paid for a week, and I need toothpaste."

"Mercenary thug," Cattermole said.

"You can call me what you like," Cox said, "just as long as it's understood that I'm only in this for the money."

"Me too," CH3 said. "Listen, Mother: I can lend you, say, fifty francs at seventeen and a half percent."

"Let's go," Barton said.

"Seventeen and a half," Cox said as they walked towards the Hurricanes. "Is that good?"

"Good? It's phenomenal," CH3 said. "I usually charge my friends ten or eleven."

"You're just saying that to make me feel better."

"No, I swear it. If they're very rich, maybe even nine."

"You're all heart, CH3. We really don't deserve you."

"For anyone who's filthy rich and has a nymphomaniac sister, I may go as far as eight and a half. Do you have a sister, by the way?"

"We've done our best, sir," a flight sergeant said to Cox. He was blinking with fatigue. "Just don't chuck her about more than you absolutely have to." Cox nodded. "Okay," he said. "Thanks."

CH3 began counting the patches on Cox's Hurricane, and gave up. "My final offer," he said. "Twenty-seven percent. I can't honestly charge you any more than that, Mother. I mean, you may be a lousy risk, but you're not a certain failure."

"I'll think about it," Cox said. "It's jolly tempting. I really do need toothpaste." He clambered onto the wing-root. "Have you got any toothpaste?"

"Yes, thanks," CH3 called as he walked on. "Awfully decent of you to ask, though."

It was pleasant, cruising at ten thousand feet: sunny but cool. They kept a gap of seventy or eighty yards between aircraft, with

Cox and CH3 always a couple of lengths behind Barton and Cattermole. The blind spot on a Hurricane lay underneath the tail, and this loose formation let each man check the sky directly behind his neighbour.

Before they reached the patrol line, Cattermole called up: "Bandits at one o'clock, slightly high."

It took Barton five seconds' hard searching before he saw the prickling of dots. He had discussed this sort of situation with CH3, after breakfast. He knew just what to do. They were north-east of him, almost certainly heading west. He led the Hurricanes in a steep climbing turn to the south-east. Within three minutes they had lost sight of the enemy but gained three thousand feet. He turned north-east, still climbing, and had an advantage of at least four thousand feet when he was able to make out the enemy again, the dots fractionally heavier now that they were coming at an angle instead of head-on.

It was midday. The sun was overhead. Barton kept it between him and the enemy. If he could only just make out a clump of bombers, there was a good chance the bombers would fail to see four small fighters hidden in that great dazzling glare.

He was in no hurry. He concentrated on getting his interception right. The others would search the sky and guard his tail.

Once, the bombers altered course, and he had to re-jig his calculations. But after fifteen minutes he could see them below him as clearly as a pattern on a plate: twelve Dornier 17's, in three ranks of four, proceeding stolidly from right to left.

Barton waggled his wings, and fell. Cox fell with him. Cattermole and CH3 waited a couple of seconds, and then dropped after them.

Barton actually saw his own shadow cross the wings of a Dornier as he picked out his target: front row, left. Surprise could never be total, not with three or four pairs of eyes in each bomber, but he was bracing himself and easing the Hurricane out of its dive before the first wild flickers of fire came seeking him, and by then he didn't care. The Dornier swelled and filled his reflector sight to overflowing, looking big and black and as hard as a battleship until his guns ripped across its port wing from engine to body and carved it off. Barton just had time to see the wing crack and start to fold back. Then he dragged the stick into his stomach and bounced back up into the sky. Screwing his head around, he saw streams of tracer hunting him, and through these fireworks he watched CH3 line up a Dornier from the beam, pour a full-deflection shot into it, and vault the formation before the bomber began streaming fire and smoke.

They regrouped at a safe height. Two bombers were missing, two were falling behind the pack.

"Any damage?" Barton asked.

"Something snapped with a loud crack when I came out of that dive," Cox reported. "She's shaking like a leaf."

"No hydraulics," Cattermole said. "Nasty smell of plumbing in the office."

"Okay, that's enough for today," Barton decided. "Back to base."

They turned and flew to Berry-au-Bac, slowly, so as to spare Cox's fractured airframe. They were over the airfield when he discovered that, like Cattermole, his hydraulic system was useless. No undercarriage. Even hand-cranking failed to move it.

"Scrap the kite, Mother," Barton said. "Bale out. She's not worth keeping."

Cox climbed to eight thousand feet, aimed the Hurricane towards Germany, and dived over the side. He had a moment of panic when he couldn't shake his gauntlet off, but eventually he got his fingers on the ring of the rip-cord and tugged hard. The silk blossomed with a smart crack. He hung and watched his Hurricane drone away. Rather a shame. He had liked that kite.

Cattermole opted for a belly-landing, and walked away from it with a bloody nose. The Hurricane was a write-off.

Barton and CH3 landed intact. They gathered to watch Cox drift down, and they were all waiting for him when he landed.

"That was highly successful," Barton said. "We should do that again, don't you think?"

"Lunch, first," Cattermole said, nasally. "This is Norman blood, you know," he told CH3, showing his handkerchief.

"Heavens to Betsy!" CH3 said. "And is that Norman snot mixed up with it?"

A truck came across the field to take them to the mess. But before they could get into it, they had to get under it. Half-a-dozen Junkers 88's blasted over Berry-au-Bac at fifty feet, strafing and bombing. The two surviving Hurricanes collapsed, their legs

458

smashed sideways, and caught fire. There was enough fuel in the tanks to blow up with a series of crumps that the pilots, crouched on the turf, felt in their palms.

That was the end of Hornet squadron in France. The depots were empty of replacement aircraft. Kellaway, Skull, Gordon, Patterson, and Fitzgerald reached Berry by road that evening. Soon afterwards, Baggy Bletchley arrived. "No hard feelings," he said, "but you are now what is technically classified as 'useless mouths,' so we're sending you home."

They went to England the slow and easy way, by boat train. Barton stood on deck with CH3 and watched Dover approach.

"Looking back on it all," he said, "it didn't exactly work out the way we expected, did it?"

"No."

"Bloody shambles, really."

"That about sums it up."

Barton grunted. His jaw-muscles kept twitching and he was glaring at Dover as if daring it to start a fight. He couldn't wait to get back in the air and blow something to bits.

AUGUST
1940

The weather in the south of England during the first half of the summer of 1940 was unusually bad.

In July the skies were overcast on two days out of three; often there was fog or thick haze as well as low cloud. On half the days of July, rain fell. Usually it was only scattered showers but sometimes it was a heavy and continuous downpour. There were violent thunderstorms on five or six occasions.

All this was not good for flying.

At least one Spitfire got struck by lightning and knocked out of the sky. Another Spitfire dived into cloud and hit the ground. Bad weather concealed a hill from a lowflying Hurricane: that pilot was killed too. And there were a dozen crashes in which mud or rain played a part. Meanwhile the air war went on, as and when conditions allowed. The bad weather was either a mixed blessing or a mixed curse. If it held off the *Luftwaffe*, it also slowed down the training of new fighter pilots. When raids came, the same poor visibility that made it hard for German bombers to find their targets also protected them from RAF patrols and from flak. Moreover, the German pilots could rest and recover between missions, but the front-line RAF pilots were under a constant strain. They had to be available from dawn to dusk. They might fly several times a day. During July, one fighter squadron flew 504 combat sorties in three weeks and spent more than eight hundred hours in the air. Not every scramble led to an interception, but each one demanded the same intense concentration. Before the end of July that squadron had destroyed six enemy aircraft but it had lost five men killed and three wounded. The survivors were near exhaustion. They, and others like them, had to be withdrawn from the battle zone. Brand new or rebuilt squadrons replaced them.

It was a pity that there had been so little time to bring these replacement pilots up to operational standard, what with the weather, and the lack of instructors who had combat experience, and the shortage of spares, the lack of skilled groundcrew, even the scarcity of ammunition. It was a great pity.

On a clear day you could see France from RAF Bodkin Hazel. On a very clear day from the control tower, with binoculars, you could even see German aircraft in their landing circuits over the *Luftwaffe* bases on the other side of the Straits of Dover. Or so it was said by people who had never tried it. In any case there had been precious few clear days in July. August might turn out better, but it began grey and dank, which was why Flash Gordon wore his flying-boots and his Irvine jacket when he went out to shoot seagulls.

He took a deckchair, a Very pistol and a box of signal cartridges. Bodkin Hazel was a small grass aerodrome, formerly a private flying club. Flash set up his deckchair in the middle of the field and waited for a gull to wander in from the Channel.

An hour passed and nothing much happened.

Then a green sports car appeared. It drove across the grass and stopped about fifty yards away. A tall, thin young man climbed out and put on his cap and gloves. Everything about him was serious. His blue eyes rarely blinked, his mouth was firm and slightly depressed, and his long jaw was cleanshaven to the tops of his ears. Even his ears were neatly tucked away. He had the head of an intelligent monk above the uniform of a pilot officer.

He reached the deckchair and cleared his throat. "Good morning, sir," he said. Gordon's Irvine jacket concealed his rank. "Pilot Officer Steele-Stebbing, sir." He saluted.

"Never heard of him," Gordon said curtly. "Nobody of that name here. Try lost property down the corridor. Still got your ticket? They won't give up anything without a ticket. I should know. That's how I lost my wife. No ticket. Looked everywhere. What name did you say?"

"Um . . . Steele-Stebbing . . ."

"Umsteelestebbing." Gordon shook his head. "Sounds a bit Swedish."

He scratched one of his teeth while he watched a gull skirt the airfield. "They know," he said. "They're not completely stupid."

"Where can I find the CO, sir?"

"I am the CO." For the first time, Gordon looked him full in the face, and Steele-Stebbing was startled by the fierceness in his eyes. His lips were tight-pressed, his nose pinched, his brows forced together. "I'm in charge here," Gordon said angrily. "There's nobody else."

Steele-Stebbing glanced around at the dull, deserted field. "What's the form, sir?" he asked. But Gordon had seen another bird, and he raised the Very pistol. "I wouldn't worry too much,"

464

he muttered. "I expect it's all been changed by now." He fired, and a green flare climbed into the sky. The seagull ignored it. "Bastard," he said.

Steele-Stebbing went back to his car and drove away.

Half an hour later a taxi delivered another pilot officer. He had two suitcases. He put them inside the open-ended hangar, wandered around, tried the doors of the control tower. Locked. He tried the clubhouse. Locked. A white flare soared over the airfield, quickly followed by a green and a red. He stared, saw the deckchair, and hurried across the grass. Gordon was still re-loading. "I say!" he called. "Anything wrong? Need any help?"

Gordon swung around so sharply that he nearly fell out. "Who the hell are you?" he demanded furiously.

"Macfarlane." He was redheaded and stocky, with wide-open eyes and a curl to his lips that suggested a cheerful willingness. "Just arrived."

Gordon studied him, sniffed and turned away. "No, I don't think so," he said. "I've been here all morning, I'd've seen him if . . . Keep still." He raised the pistol and tracked an approaching gull. Macfarlane flinched at the bang, and watched a yellow flare loop over the bird. "Bastard," Gordon said. "Come to think of it, there was someone. Some Swedish bastard."

"What: just arrived?" Macfarlane asked.

"No bloody fear. Just departed." Gordon laughed, briefly and bitterly. "One of the dear departed." He reloaded. "The dear, dear departed. Dear, dear, dear."

Macfarlane gave up, and walked away.

He had reached the perimeter wire, and was whistling in competition with a skylark, when a motorcycle roared onto the airfield. The rider slowed down to look at the clubhouse, then went past the control tower, and finally saw the deckchair. He rode towards it at high speed, circled it, stopped, and got off. "Is dump, huh?" he said.

"Nobody of that name here," Gordon said, not looking.

"Must be mistake. Is cock-up. Always cock-up." He took off a leather flying helmet and revealed sleek dark hair combed straight back, no parting. He wore the uniform of a pilot officer but he looked older than the others: more meat on his shoulders, more flesh on his face. It was a handsome face if you liked thick eyebrows

465

and a powerful nose, with slightly swarthy skin. He put his gauntleted hands on his hips and examined Gordon. "You are who?" he said.

"That's still being sorted out. There may have to be an inquiry. Come back tomorrow. What name did you say?"

"Zabarnowski. Polish Air Force."

"No, no, no. Nobody of that name here. My God, I should hope not. There are limits, even in wartime. If anyone asks tell them it's been lost in the post. Hullo: who's this bugger?"

Macfarlane had come back. "Looking for Hornet squadron?" he asked Zabarnowski. The Pole nodded. "Waste of time talking to him," Macfarlane said. "Let's go and find a pub."

"Is dump," Zabarnowski agreed.

"Piss off!" Gordon shouted. "And that's an order!" But Macfarlane was already settling himself astride the pillion, and Zabarnowski was kick-starting the bike. They roared off.

The sun broke through the haze. No birds came near, and Gordon dozed. He was awoken by the blare of a horn. Sticky's Buick had stopped beside him, and Cattermole, Cox and Fitzgerald were looking out of it. "What-ho, Flash," Cattermole said. "Shocking hole, this. Where's the mess?"

"Well, well!" Gordon struggled out of the deckchair. "Fancy seeing you again!" He was quite delighted. He shook hands with each of them. "And Sticky's old wagon, too! How did –"

"Never mind that. Where's the mess?"

"Oh, there isn't one. Just the old clubhouse, and that's locked. I've got the key but there's no booze, so it's –"

"Shut up and get in." Cattermole released the handbrake. Cox opened the rear door and Gordon scrambled in as the Buick swung away and headed for the gate.

"I can't tell you how nice it is to see you," Gordon said.

"Then don't try," Cox said. "I'm starving, and I can't stand guff on an empty stomach."

"Yes, but I've been stuck out here for two weeks. You can't imagine –"

"Two weeks?" Fitzgerald swung around from the front seat. "You mean you've been alone in this hole for two weeks?"

"Yes."

"But we all had two weeks' leave, Flash."

"Me too. I spent it here."

"You're crazy!" Cox said. "Why didn't you stay with your family? Or friends?"

Gordon looked out of the window. "Didn't want to," he muttered.

Fitzgerald turned away. The narrow, dusty lane rushed past. Sometimes the edge of the windscreen was whipped by strands of bramble or the overgrown shoots of hawthorn. Cattermole drove hard, making the big car jump at every open stretch. "Seen Fanny?" he asked.

"No," Gordon said.

"Adj? Skull?"

"Nobody. There hasn't been a sodding soul in sight until you arrived. Nothing to do all day except shoot seagulls."

"Hit many?" Cox asked.

"Four thousand exactly."

"Nice round figure."

"Like Mae West," Fitzgerald said, and they grunted with amusement; but Gordon glanced anxiously. "What's that?" he said. "Mae West hasn't been shot, has she?"

"You need a large drink," Cattermole said. "If you're nice to us, Flash, we'll let you buy a round."

They stopped at a pub, *The Fleece*, and Cattermole ordered four pints. Macfarlane, Zabarnowski and Steele-Stebbing were playing darts at the other end of the bar. Both groups ignored each other. The landlord pulled four pints and looked at Cattermole. Cattermole nudged Gordon. "Cough up, Flash," he said. Gordon searched his pockets and found sevenpence.

"That's a start, anyway," the landlord said.

"Just remembered," Gordon said. "I'm broke."

"So are we," Cox said. "Filling up the Buick in London cleaned us out. None of us has got a bean."

"Will you take a cheque?" Cattermole asked.

"If I have to," the landlord said.

"Give the gentleman a cheque, Flash, for goodness sake," Cattermole urged.

"No chequebook, Moggy. Lost it in France."

"Sorry about this," Fitzgerald said. "The thing is, our pay hasn't caught up with us yet. Everything went down the pan in France and ever since then —"

"I know." The landlord tossed a cardboard beermat in front of him. "Go on, write a cheque on that."

"Damn decent of you," Fitzgerald said.

"Well, you're not the first, you know."

"In that case," Cattermole said, "I'll have another pint and a plate of ham sandwiches, if it's all right by you."

"Don't forget the twopenny stamp," the landlord warned. "Cheque's not legal without a twopenny stamp."

"Oh dear," Fitzgerald said. "I haven't got one."

"I have. Add twopence to the amount."

Many RAF pilots had money troubles when they returned from France; Hornet squadron was simply unluckier than most. Problems began when all their records got lost.

The order to abandon the airfield at Mailly-le-Camp came during something of a flap. The place had been bombed, twice, a German reconnaissance plane had circled it, and a Messerschmitt 109 had created ten seconds of terror with a raging low-level attack that killed a cook and blew the foot off a sergeant armourer before he even had time to drop his mug of tea. After that, everyone wanted to get out in a rush. The last remaining Hurricanes had long since left for Berry-au-Bac. The essentials – food, medical supplies, weapons – were slung into the backs of trucks. Flash Gordon's P-36 was burned. Fitzgerald's crippled Hurricane was burned. The fuel dump in the woods was most spectacularly burned. And in the haste and confusion, half the orderly office's records were burned too.

The other half had already been loaded into a truck. Between Rheims and Amiens it got separated from the convoy. Some said it broke down; some said it was commandeered at gunpoint by French military police. The truth was the driver lagged behind, took a wrong turning and became thoroughly lost. In the end he attached himself to a British infantry unit, who were glad of the help. He carried their mortars; they gave him food and protection. Together they retreated, slowly and painfully, up through northern France. The truck was abandoned on the dockside in Dunkirk. Next day a bomb blew it into the water.

By then, of course, the Hornet pilots were home and dry. None had money (apart from a few tattered francs) and only Mother

Cox had a chequebook. The others had lost their personal belongings during the continuous scrambling from Château St Pierre to Mailly to Amifontaine back to Mailly to Berry to a whole string of depots and transit camps. Mother Cox always kept a spare, *second* chequebook for emergencies, but even that wasn't much use to him in England because his bank account was empty. Like the rest of them, his pay was hugely in arrears.

The situation was explained to him by a wing commander in charge of accounts at Tangmere, a very large and efficient flying station near Chichester. After a couple of weeks' leave, Cox had been posted there on temporary attachment to a fighter squadron.

"Look, I can give you a bit," the wing commander said. "I can pay you for now. But France..." He sucked in his breath. "Different story. No authorisation, you see."

"But sir," Cox said, "there's no doubt I've been over there all winter, is there? I mean, the squadron got sent —"

"Ah, but you don't understand the system, old boy." The wing commander saw an error creeping into a sheet of figures on the desk before him. He took an eraser, eliminated a pencilled entry, and blew the bits away. "It's all done with documents. You've got to have your docs. I mean, without docs, Air Ministry wouldn't know what to do, would it?"

"Isn't there some emergency procedure, sir?"

"I'll send a memo."

"Thank you."

"Don't get your hopes up. Air Ministry's got a lot on its mind at the moment." He sharpened a pencil. "Where you went wrong, you see, was in losing your docs."

"Yes. Very careless of me. Next time I'm in France I must remember to look for them."

"No point in getting shirty, old boy. We're all in this together, you know."

Much the same happened to the other Hornet pilots. After leave, they were sent to strengthen units all over the country. Barton went to Manston and was in time to help cover the last days of the Dunkirk evacuation. Fitzgerald went to Exeter and flew endless convoy patrols, then got shifted to Hornchurch, north-east of London, and flew twice as many convoy patrols. Cattermole had a spell at Middle Wallop on Salisbury Plain, got moved to Duxford, near Cambridge, and ended up in Scotland, at Dyce airfield.

Towards the end of his leave, Flash Gordon was informed of Nicole's death by the International Red Cross and he got another two weeks' leave on compassionate grounds, most of which he spent blind drunk in London. As a result of some confusion at Air Ministry he was then posted to an operational conversion unit which trained pilots to fly Lysanders for Army Cooperation. The Lysander was a very slow, stable, gull-winged job with spats on its fixed wheels. Gordon crashed three and got sent back to Fighter Command.

CH3 spent two boring weeks in a concrete bunker, supposedly advising on the training of fighter controllers, until he wangled a job as a ferry pilot. He had just delivered a new Hurricane to Manston when he met Fanny Barton in the mess. Barton was surprised to learn that CH3 was as broke as the rest of them. "What about the family millions?" he said. "Can't you raid Fort Knox?"

"I could but I won't," CH3 said. "Why the hell should I subsidise the British Government? They hired me, they can damn well pay me the rate for the job." A barman put drinks in front of them. Barton watched CH3 sign the bar-chit *E. J. P. Demaron*. "Who's that?" he asked.

"Guy I used to know. Ferry pilot. Stalled on take-off and spun-in, so I got his job."

They clinked glasses. "Here's to Dameron," Barton said.

"Demaron."

"Both of them." They drank. "Baggy Bletchley was here yesterday," Barton said. "He says they're going to re-form Hornet squadron and give it to me."

"Baggy Bletchley? Didn't he forecast light flak over Maastricht?"

"Suppose he's right this time, would you agree to be 'A' flight commander?"

"I might. Work on me a little."

Barton was puzzled. "How?" he asked.

"Oh, for Christ's sake, Fanny . . . The usual methods. Flattery. Bribery. Threats."

"Oh." Barton drank and thought. "Well, you're the man for the

470

job," he said, "and you'll get immediate promotion to flying-officer-acting-flight-lieutenant, and if you don't agree, then, well, frankly, I shall be, you know, very disappointed."

CH3 turned his back on the bar and rested his elbows. Barton had always been spare, he thought, but he had lost five or six pounds since France. "That's it, is it?" he said.

"More or less. I suppose you'll stand a chance of a gong. Eventually."

"I've already got a gong. Got it in China. Chinese gong."

"Well, you can have another."

"What would I do with two gongs?"

"Play extremely simple tunes on them, I suppose."

"Don't know any."

"Well, for God's sake," Barton said, suddenly losing patience, "buy a simple song-book and learn some of the bloody things."

"All right, Fanny." CH3 raised a hand to pacify him. "I accept. I just wanted to be sure I wasn't getting swept away by your silver-tongued New Zealand sophistication."

Barton pushed the empty glasses across the bar, and grunted. The barman hurried forward.

"There you go again," CH3 said. "Irresistible."

Barton was driving to RAF Bodkin Hazel, together with CH3, the adjutant and Skull, when he saw the Buick parked outside a pub.

The reunion was friendly without being hearty. They shook hands, Barton was congratulated on his promotion, Cattermole waited until Kellaway was reaching for his wallet before asking the newcomers what they wanted to drink and then skilfully deferred and let Kellaway buy the round. They all talked at and across each other for a while before Barton noticed the three pilot officers sitting at the other end of the room. He went over and introduced himself. "You're for Bodkin Hazel? Good, I thought you must be. Haven't you met these chaps?"

Macfarlane and Steele-Stebbing glanced at each other. "No, sir," Macfarlane said. It was easier than explaining. "Come on, then," Barton said.

They trooped across the room. "Now then, where shall we start?" Barton said. "Tell you what —"

"Steele-Stebbing, isn't it?" Flash Gordon came forward with a

471

big smile and an outstretched hand. "And MacGregor, no, wait a minute, don't tell me, *Macfarlane*, of course, Macfarlane, and oh my goodness now I'm in trouble, begins with a zed, sounds like one of those longhaired musicians, not Paderewski, oh dear I wish I'd never started this . . ."

"Zabarnowski," said the Pole.

"Right!" said Gordon, and shook his hand. "Zabarnowski. I got the zed right, anyway, didn't I?"

"So you have met?" Barton said.

"Briefly," Steele-Stebbing said, frowning hard.

"Sort of bumped into . . . um . . . this chap," Macfarlane added. Embarrassment made him gruff.

"I say, play the game!" Cattermole exclaimed, and he flashed the friendliest grin that Skull had ever seen on him. "We showed you chaps all over the airfield, didn't we, Mother?"

"Of course we did. You remember the airfield, Mac?" Cox said to Macfarlane. "Big flat place, lots of grass?"

"Yes, but . . ." A guilty blush was spreading rapidly over Macfarlane's face.

"Don't blame you for being bored," Gordon said, with a chuckle. "Boring places, airfields. They couldn't wait to get back here and play darts," he told Barton.

"Is that right?" Barton asked.

"Far from it, sir," Steele-Stebbing said.

"Dominoes, then. Or gin rummy," Gordon said. "Whatever it was, we couldn't get a look-in."

"Pity, really, because I wanted to practise my Polish," Fitzgerald said. "*Jag tycker om det?*" he asked Zabarnowski, who merely stared.

"Well, as long as you've met," Barton said. "That leaves Skull and uncle and CH3, and you can get to know them on the way to the airfield, because that's where we're going now."

They drank up, found their caps, thanked the landlord, and shuffled out, the junior pilots last.

"What was all that in aid of?" Macfarlane muttered.

"*They* lied," Steele-Stebbing said to him, "and now the CO thinks *we're* stupid and dishonest. It's intolerable."

"If I get that little bastard on his own I'll wrap his deckchair

472

round his head." Macfarlane's voice was flattened by anger. "What d'you reckon, Zab?"

"Is cock-up," Zabarnowski said calmly.

Two more pilots were waiting at Bodkin Hazel: Renouf and Haducek. Barton greeted them, welcomed them to the squadron, and silently hoped they were better than they seemed. Renouf was English, slim, with small features crowded into a small face. He wore a moustache that looked too old for him and his handshake was soft and slack. Haducek, by contrast, had a grip like a wrestler and a strong, intelligent, bluntly honest face. The trouble was he looked restless and bored and didn't bother to hide it. Barton already knew something about him: he was a Czech who had flown with the French Air Force and made his way to England via Spain and Portugal. "I hope you'll be happy with us," Barton said to them both. Renouf nodded a lot. Haducek said: "Happy?" and shrugged. "Happy is not here," he said, wrinkling his nose at the barren airfield. "Happy is killing Germans."

"We'll see what we can do."

"Easy. Give me plane. Spitfire."

"The planes are waiting, elsewhere. And they're Hurricanes, not Spits." Haducek made a scoffing snort that Barton chose to ignore.

He called them all together. "No doubt you're wondering what we're doing here when you've actually been posted to RAF Brambledown. Well, Brambledown is the Sector station and that's where we'll be living, but this little strip is a satellite of Brambledown and I expect us to operate from here a lot of the time. I know it looks pretty dead but I'm told that everything we need is tucked away out of sight, and of course it's got one tremendous advantage over Brambledown: we're about forty miles nearer Jerry. So we should get first crack at any raids coming this way. Before that, however, we're going to do a lot of training. I want to say a couple of words about that . . ."

Haducek wasn't listening. He had wandered away from the group and was staring into the sky. As Barton paused, Zabarnowski ambled over and joined him. Haducek pointed. "What's up?" Barton asked sharply, but they ignored him. He glanced at the adjutant, who merely rolled his eyes. CH3 murmured: "Bandits."

That was when Barton heard the first, faint tremor of aero-engines. "We'll talk about training later," he said, and shaded his eyes with his hand.

The formation was just visible. It was so high that each plane was no more than a tiny glint against the blue.

"They can't possibly bomb from that height," Steele-Stebbing said. "Can they?"

Cox asked: "How high d'you think they are?"

"Ten or twelve thousand."

"Try again."

"Fifteen?"

"More like twenty."

Gordon came over and put his hand on Macfarlane's arm. "I know what you'd like," he said. Macfarlane went rigid with dislike. "You'd like to jump into a Hurricane and take off and give those rotten Huns what-for, wouldn't you?"

Macfarlane picked the hand off his arm. "Obviously," he said.

"What a twat," Gordon said. "It'd take you fifteen minutes to reach their height and by then they'll be over London." He wandered away. Macfarlane put his hands behind his back and gripped his right wrist hard, as if it couldn't be trusted to behave itself.

The little bundle of glints proceeded almost silently until it was well inland.

"Come on, come on," Barton muttered. "Finger out, somebody."

"Con-trails," CH3 said, and pointed. White streamers had suddenly appeared and were reaching out towards the enemy formation. "Spits from Berrydown," he said.

"What Jacky Bellamy would call 'aerial chess'," Cattermole said drily.

The con-trails continued to stretch, closing the gap. Then they checked, curled and angled away. A few seconds later they slowly split up and scattered in all directions, making a fuzzy tangle of white strands. Meanwhile the bombers cruised on.

"Fool's mate," Cattermole said.

"What happened, sir?" Renouf asked.

"Well," Barton said, "guessing, I'd say the controller didn't send them high enough, and before they could hit the raid the Jerry cover came down and hit *them*."

"Hullo, someone's bought it," Cattermole said.

474

A dark streak had fallen out of the fuzzy tangle. The further it fell the darker it got. "Ours or theirs?" Kellaway wondered.

Nobody responded. The falling plane was only a speck. Behind it the trail of smoke steadily widened, as if someone had drawn a thin pen across a wet sheet of paper.

Skull said: "I can't see any parachute."

"You wouldn't," CH3 told him. "Not at that height. If he jumped, it'll be five minutes before we see him."

"The air's very thin up there," Cox told Steele-Stebbing. "If you ever have to jump, you want to take a few good puffs of oxygen first."

"What balls!" Fitzgerald said. "Anyone who's got time for that sort of carry-on doesn't *need* to bale out."

An argument began. They had lost interest in the battle, which in any case seemed to be over. "I'll see each man in the clubhouse now, adj," Barton said. "One at a time, starting with the new boys. Skull, I want you with me. CH3, take Flash and Fitz and check the field for potholes and ruts and things."

"No," Gordon said. He thrust his hands in his pockets and glowered at the ground. "Shan't."

"Come on, Flash, be a sport," CH3 said.

"Oh, all right then." Gordon strode off. "Follow me, men!" he shouted. "Don't shoot till you see the whites of their eggs!"

Later that afternoon, driving north to Brambledown, Barton asked Skull what he made of them all.

"Inevitably, as in all things British," Skull said, "the class system dominates. When Rex was CO the relationship was almost feudal. Evidently that didn't work terribly well, which is no great surprise, because after all the feudal system itself was less than totally satisfactory. Sudden pressures –"

"What about the blokes?"

"Oh, the blokes are behaving exactly as one would expect. The old sweats have ganged up on the young bloods and both sides are deeply suspicious of the foreigners. All quite normal."

Barton sighed. "But what about the blokes *as blokes*?"

"Ah." Skull found his notes. "Macfarlane's all right. He's a young animal, shallow, easily bored, little imagination, full of self-confidence and aggression. Should do well."

"Don't like him," Kellaway said. "Too cocky. Never listens."

Barton glanced at CH3, who shrugged. "He'll either go to hell in a hurry or he'll make a killing," he said. "Probably the first."

"Steele-Stebbing's interesting," Skull said. "I was an undergraduate with his father. Insufferable man, bloated by ambition. I rather think the son is trying to escape him, which of course is impossible."

"He got very good marks in training," Barton said.

"Of course he did," CH3 said. "He's been on his best behaviour ever since he was toilet-trained, and I'll bet that happened bloody early."

"Renouf?" Barton said.

"Renouf is a mystery." Skull put his notes away. "Or perhaps a paradox. He's the only one of the three with a mind of his own, and yet he's profoundly uneasy."

"The little bugger's windy," Kellaway said. "If you said 'Boo!' to him he'd turn into a goose."

Barton said: "Think I should chop him, CH3?"

"Maybe. I don't know. You can't always spot a good fighter pilot on the ground. Look at the last war aces: Mannock, McCudden, Bishop . . . They weren't the life and soul of the party, were they, uncle?"

"Bit stand-offish, some of them, but then they lived to kill, didn't they? I don't see this little lad living to kill. He looks like one of nature's victims to me."

"Have we got any of nature's murderers in this squadron?" Barton asked. "Besides Moggy, that is."

"The Pole and the Czech," CH3 said at once.

"Oh? What makes you so sure?"

"They said unless they get Spits they'll strangle someone, probably you."

"You're kidding!" Barton said.

"They told me the same," Skull said.

"Good God."

"I'll have a quiet word with them," the adjutant said. "They obviously don't understand the form."

They drove in silence for a while.

"Interesting that none of us has mentioned the biggest problem," Skull remarked. He gave them five seconds to work it out, and said: "Young Gordon."

"Flash has certainly turned a bit wild and woolly." Kellaway thumped his bad knee: long journeys made it ache. "Still, he always was peculiar."

"No, he's more than peculiar," Skull said. "Have you seen his eyes? He's in a state that many a doctor in the outside world would consider verges on the certifiable."

"Extraordinary thing," Kellaway said. "He told me his wife was dead before she was actually killed. I've checked the dates. The poor sod was convinced he'd killed her the day before she actually bought it. I mean, that's enough to drive anyone loopy."

"Anyway, this isn't the outside world," Barton said. "And I like Flash. He may be dotty but he's not completely crackers. I mean, he hasn't tried to strangle anyone, has he?"

"The real question is: can he fly?" CH3 asked. "That's all that matters. You don't want a fighter pilot who's completely normal, for Pete's sake. That's what's wrong with Stainless Steel or Iron Filings or whatever his name is. Too well-behaved. Never picks his nose, beats his wife or uses the lavatory while the train is standing in the station. Hopeless."

"I realise you don't want a pillar of rectitude," Skull said. "On the other hand, even if he can fly like a bird, do you want a lunatic?"

"Flash isn't a lunatic," Kellaway said. "He's on the daft side of crackers, I agree, but he's not a lunatic, not yet. Believe me, I've seen plenty."

"I don't even think he's daft," Barton said thoughtfully. "He's just a bit ... I dunno ... potty, that's all."

CH3 said: "Frankly, I'd put him on the loopy side of potty."

"Where exactly is that in relation to plumb loco?" Skull asked.

"You've been to the pictures again," Barton accused.

"The Lone Ranger," Skull said. "Now there is a thoroughgoing psychopath. Compared to him, Flash is restraint itself."

Flip Moran and Pip Patterson turned up at Brambledown that same evening. Both had been delayed by missed train connections. They were stiff from travel. Patterson had come from Scotland, Moran from Ulster. Moran had spent twenty-four hours in trains, on the ferry and then in more trains.

They stood round-shouldered and stiff-legged at dispersal and watched Hurricanes circling the field, until one Hurricane landed and taxied over.

Barton climbed down. "Glad you could make it," he said. "Micky Marriott's got your new kites ready. Grab some kit and do a test flight."

"Now?" Moran yawned enormously. "Sweet Jesus, Fanny. Can't it wait till morning?"

"We're on convoy patrol in the morning. Eight o'clock."

"Christ . . . I wish I'd stayed at home."

"Well, that can easily be arranged," Barton said crisply.

Patterson flinched at the clamour of a klaxon amplified by the Tannoy. After ten seconds the racket stopped, and men were running to distant aircraft. "You want to watch out for that," Barton said. "If you're in the circuit and you see a white flare, clear off fast before you get mixed up in the scramble."

"Eight o'clock, eh?" Moran said. "That doesn't leave a lot of time for me to work my flight up to the peak of perfection."

A white flare banged.

"Times have changed," Barton said. "It's on-the-job training here."

A section of Spitfires bustled over the grass, put their noses down and shoved off, engines roaring hungrily.

"Convoy patrol," Patterson said. "I've never done that. What's it like?"

"Well, it's not much fun," Barton told him, "but on the other hand it doesn't serve any useful purpose, either. Can you swim?"

"Not much. Why?"

"Come on, Pip," Moran said. "Let's go upstairs before it gets dark. You know how frightened I am of the dark."

The waterspouts seemed to freeze at their maximum height for a few seconds. The early morning sun picked them out, as white as heaps of whipped cream. Then they slowly collapsed and dissolved and tumbled into the sea. Between and around them the convoy crawled, and around the convoy the escort destroyers flickered with gunfire.

It was four minutes past eight. Hornet squadron had just seen the convoy. The German bombers finished their attack and climbed into cloud. There was an endless layer of the stuff at three thousand

478

feet. By the time the Hurricanes were near enough to help, the raid was over. One ship was dead in the water, another was burning, the rest trudged on, and the destroyers all fired at the Hurricanes, which came as no surprise to Fanny Barton. He took his squadron out of their range and flew a wide circle around the convoy.

The patrol lasted an hour and ten minutes. Time passed slowly. They went round and round the convoy in a permanent orbit. The monotony made it deadly. An enemy might slide out of cover at any second. It was seductively easy, as the twenty-ninth orbit merged into the thirtieth, to stop searching the blank and boring sky and look at the interesting ships instead.

After an hour and ten minutes the convoy had travelled fifteen miles while the squadron had flown about two hundred miles. The relief escort had not appeared, but Barton turned for home. He glanced back only once, and saw gun-flashes on the destroyers, shell-bursts in the sky. That might mean the escort had arrived or it might mean something else. He looked away, punched a button on his VHF and asked for a bearing for Brambledown.

The Sector ops officer was a middleaged squadron leader called Wood. He wore the brevet of an Observer and the purple-and-white-striped ribbon of the DFC, both much faded. "Look, old chap," he said, "I'm the pig-in-the-middle. I can only tell you what the Navy told me, and according to them you chaps were late. Too late to stop a mob of Ju-88's divebombing the convoy and sinking the . . ." He searched his blotter for the name. ". . . SS *Benjamin*."

"We weren't late," Barton said. "We were at the right place at the right time, but the convoy wasn't there. The convoy was late."

"Um," Wood said, and scratched the back of his neck with a pencil. "I don't think the Navy will buy that, old boy."

"I don't give a damn whether they buy it, sell it, or use it to wash their feet in. We were at the right place at the right time."

"Yes, of course, I'm sure. Too bad about the boat, though."

"Oh, come on, Woody, don't talk balls. I've been flying convoy patrols ever since Dunkirk. It's a mug's game! Surely for Christ's sake someone in Fighter Command has worked that out by now."

"Yes?" Wood tapped the pencil on his teeth. "Say on."

"Well, Jerry's no fool, he knows by now how long our patrols stay up, I mean he's had plenty of chance to find out, hasn't he?

He knows the weak point is the changeover, doesn't he? And this weather's perfect for him, isn't it? Bit of dead reckoning, down through the cloud, there's your convoy smiling up at you in the bomb-sights."

"Well . . ." Wood stuck the pencil in his ear. "Are you telling me we can't protect these convoys?"

"Not in the Straits of Dover, we can't. Not with Jerry a short sprint away."

"Our fighters against his bombers?"

"So what?" Barton swung his flying-boots onto the desk and knocked over a tankard full of pencils. "We're usually too low and we're always too slow. Convoy patrol means stooging about to save fuel. Jerry doesn't worry about fuel. Jerry comes at us like a bat out of hell."

"Yes." Wood tried to clench the pencil between his upper lip and his nose. "He would, wouldn't he?"

"If you want to do something useful with that bloody silly thing," Barton said, "you can cross out all convoy patrols."

"What – this?" The pencil slipped. Wood caught it and examined it as if he had never seen it before. "Not nearly big enough for that job, I'm afraid," he said.

Hornet squadron was released until 2 p.m. Barton and the flight commanders used the time to test the new pilots. Barton took off with Renouf.

They climbed to ten thousand feet and went onto oxygen.

"Okay, Red Two, listen," Barton said. "Your job is to cover my tail. Stay with me. Where I go, you go, understand? If you lose me I'm dead. Right?"

"Right, sir."

"Not *sir*. Red Leader."

"Right, Red Leader."

Barton half-rolled and dived and immediately lost Renouf.

When they came together again, Barton said: "You just got me killed, didn't you? Where the hell were you, Red Two?"

"Sorry, Red Leader. Very sorry."

"Oh, that's all right, then. I get a gutful of tracer from some Jerry on my tail and you're very sorry, Red Two."

"Won't happen again, Red Leader."

Barton chucked his Hurricane onto its right wingtip and charged off. For the next three minutes he dodged and swerved, reared up and stall-turned, threw himself in the odd loop and roll and skid. Renouf was always behind him.

Barton levelled out and got his breath back.

"Okay, Red Two, I'm a dirty great Heinkel. Give me a minute and then come and get me."

Barton went up a thousand feet and turned and flew west. Renouf had vanished. Barton cruised along, changing direction as the mood seized him, until he began to wonder if Renouf had got himself lost. The sun flickered. It was no more than the tremor of a stray eyelash, but Barton thumbed the safety off his gun-button. A Hurricane swam out of the dazzle, dummied a beam-attack and dipped beneath him. Not bad. Not at all bad.

When they came together, Barton said: "Done any low flying, Red Two?"

"Done a bit, Leader."

"Okay. You lead this time. As low as you like."

They landed twenty minutes later. Barton climbed down from the cockpit as his groundcrew got to work, refuelling, cleaning the dead bugs off the windscreen, checking. The day was hot. He took off his parachute and dumped it on a wing. One of the fitters was whistling a perky little tune, with lots of trills: in the vast tranquillity of the airfield it sounded amazingly neat and clearcut. "What's that?" Barton asked. The fitter looked up, twirling a screwdriver. "That tune," Barton said. "*Little Sir Echo*, sir," the fitter said. Barton nodded. "Oh yes," he said. He rested his head and arms on the wing. Already the metal skin was warm.

Renouf walked up, Irvine jacket unzipped, parachute slung over his shoulder, helmet and mask dangling from his fingers. Barton did not raise his head. He could smell the sweet, crushed grass against the hot tang of the Merlin. "You can fly too low, you know," he said. "I mean, we all like shaking the apples off the trees, but you were mowing the bloody lawn, weren't you?"

"Yes, sir." Renouf's overcrowded face was serious but his eyes were bright.

You little bastard, Barton thought, *you were getting your own back.* He remembered chasing Renouf into a valley that twisted and narrowed, and he shut his eyes. "All right," he said. "Tell Macfarlane he's next."

Steele-Stebbing's face was one great grimace. Partly this was the drag of centrifugal force, partly it was nervousness. His Hurricane was tearing around a small circle in a near-vertical bank and he knew he was forcing it to turn harder than was good for it, so hard that his head and body were jammed immoveable and he could sense the intolerable strain on the aircraft through the awful strain on his muscles.

"Tighter," CH3 said. "Tighter."

Steele-Stebbing began to despair. They had been circling like this for an eternity. Five minutes, at least. First to the left, then to the right, then back to the left. He sucked down oxygen and tried to blink away the wandering sparks of light.

"Tighter, tighter, for Christ's sake. Tighter!"

Steele-Stebbing heaved harder, harder than he knew he could, and screwed another couple of degrees of tightness into his turn. He still couldn't see the other plane. Then suddenly it was slanting across his nose and diving hard. Gratefully he abandoned the turn and fell into a relaxed dive. After a thousand feet CH3 suddenly hoisted his Hurricane up into a climbing turn. Steele-Stebbing did his best to spring after him but his stomach rebelled and he vomited. After a while he tried to call CH3 and explain, but the microphone was so splattered and his mouth was so foul that it took rather a long time.

Five minutes was enough to tell Moran that Haducek was an excellent fighter pilot. He had good eyes and a restless, suspicious manner: always looking behind him. He could do all the usual things with a Hurricane and several very unusual things, plus a couple of things that Moran had no wish to copy in case the wings came off. He cut short their mock dog-fight. "Good enough," he said. "Relax now. We'll just do a familiarisation flight. Get to know the landmarks."

They flew down the coast to Beachy Head and turned over the Sussex Downs. Moran was routinely checking the sky above when Haducek left him. Moran had to search hard until he found the other Hurricane about three thousand feet below, climbing back up.

Haducek resumed station, a hundred yards to the right. "Been out to buy a paper?" Moran asked.

"I see bomber, Junkers 88, so I go down and bomber is Blenheim, only Blenheim, so come back. Damn shame, eh?"

"Next time, tell me."

"I just told."

"Tell me *first*, you fool."

"Not me, no fool. I got two university degrees."

"Save it for later."

"How many university degrees you got, leader?"

God speed the plough, Moran thought. *As if the English aren't bad enough, we have to have these overeducated anarchists from the Balkans too. Wherever the bloody Balkans are.*

It was so easy that Macfarlane paused and wondered what the catch was.

Barton had told him to imagine that he, Barton, was a Dornier and to intercept him. Barton had then sheered off.

Macfarlane had done as he had been taught and gained the advantage of height, rather a lot of height, about three thousand feet of height, and now Barton-the-supposed-Dornier was sitting there, stooging along, an absolute sitting duck. Or stooging duck. What could be easier?

Macfarlane stuffed the nose down and proceeded to turn his height advantage into speed advantage, as per all the best textbooks. He was closing on his target at a spanking pace, something like 350 mph probably, when it turned and climbed towards him and, quick as winking Macfarlane whistled clear past it.

He hauled his Hurricane out of the dive and climbed high again.

The dummy Dornier was still there, stooging along, so he had another go. This time it turned away, just as he was closing, and he shot right past the bloody thing again! Trouble was, before he could do anything, a voice spoke in his earphones. "Bang-bang," it said. "I thought *you* were supposed to attack *me*." Macfarlane twisted his head. Barton was fifty yards behind. He tried everything but he couldn't shake him off. "Too bad," Barton said. "You had your whole life ahead of you. It's not fair, is it?"

Zabarnowski and CH3 battle-climbed to fifteen thousand feet. CH3 levelled off, but Zabarnowski kept climbing. CH3 called him several times but the Pole ignored him. The last CH3 saw of him he was at twenty-five thousand feet: just a smudge on the sky. Thirty minutes later he was still up there, wandering about. CH3 gave up and went home. "We can't wait," Barton said. It was twelve-thirty and they were all in the crewroom except Zabarnowski. The old pilots sat, the new pilots leaned against the wall. Barton perched on a table, away from the windows and the distraction of aircraft.

"Now, you're all nice chaps," he said. "The squadron has always had its fair share of nice chaps. This fellow, for instance." He tipped a big buff envelope onto the table and held up an eight-by-ten print. "Fellow called Lloyd. Heart of gold . . . There's another: Miller: everyone's pal. Now here you see the friendly face of Dicky Starr. What a nice man Dicky was! And if this was Dutton then that must have been Trevelyan, or maybe it was the other way around, but it doesn't much matter because they were both equally nice chaps, just like any of you. They all had something else in common, by the way. They made a mistake. Just one, but then one's enough, isn't it? Maybe they thought that, as they were such awfully nice chaps, they'd get a second chance. Strange idea, that, wasn't it? I'm sure *they* wouldn't have given any Jerry a second chance. Still . . ." Barton got off the table and began pinning the pictures to the wall, upside-down. "If they were here now, I'm sure they'd want to wish you the very best of luck, but as it happens they're all lying at the bottoms of various deep holes in various bits of France and Belgium. Nice chaps. Blown up, shot down, battered, shattered and chopped into dogsmeat, but oh-so-awfully-nice. Flip?"

Moran said: "Mr Haducek is a bloody idiot. He thought he saw a Junkers 88 so he went down all on his own to look. An idiot."

"I kill Germans," Haducek said. "Anywhere."

"Not for long, you won't. Fly alone, Germans kill you."

"Remember this," Barton told them all. "If you see one Jerry, there's almost certainly another not far away. Probably above you. Did you look above?" he asked Haducek. "No, you didn't. Jerry never flies alone. So don't *you* fly alone. CH3?"

"Nobody has torn the wings off a Hurricane by turning it too

484

hard," CH3 said. "The kites we've got are all fully modified and they are bloody tough. Tougher than you," he said to Steele-Stebbing. "We both flew the same fighter. I had my sight on your tail. You never got your sight on my tail. Never. If you're not going to fly the machine to its limits, why bother to go up? I'll get you a nice safe bicycle instead."

Steele-Stebbing stared, pale and miserable, at the upside-down picture of Moke Miller.

"A Hurricane is not a horse," Moran said. "You can't hurt it."

Outside, the scramble klaxon went off. Barton waited for the din to stop.

"Gunnery," he said. "Bullets kill. Flying does not kill. You," he said to Macfarlane, "went screaming about the sky as if you had a stick of ginger up your arse." Macfarlane reddened. "By the time you reached the point of interception you were going so fast you had no time to fire. What's the good of that?"

"It's what I was taught, sir. Maximum speed in attack."

"Un-teach yourself. And never make an absolute square-on beam attack," Barton told Renouf. "Didn't anyone tell you about deflection shooting?"

"Yes, sir," Renouf said, "but we didn't have much practice."

"Bullets go slower than you think. Huns go faster. Make a beam-attack and hold the target in your sights and you might hit the plane behind it if you're lucky."

"Give it plenty of lead," CH3 said. "Allow one length, maybe two."

"Better still, don't make a beam attack," Moran said. "Get behind him where you can't miss."

A flight of Spitfires took off and the telephone rang. Barton closed one ear while he took the call. The crackling roar mounted to a booming thunder that climbed and faded. Barton hung up. "Grab some lunch," he said. "We're on fifteen-minute standby at one o'clock, not two."

As they surged to the door, Zabarnowski arrived. "What the hell happened to you?" CH3 asked.

Zabarnowski made a face. "Lousy plane. After twenty thousand no climb, no speed, nothing. I want Spitfire."

"I told you we were going to fifteen thousand."

"Why? German fighters fly high."

"Next time, do what I say or you won't fly anything."

"Is lousy, Hurricane," Zabarnowski grumbled. "Is dump."

They had just sat down to lunch when an airman arrived with a message for Barton. Fitzgerald, Cox and Cattermole groaned. " 'A' flight only," Barton said. "Called to readiness. You're leading, CH3." Fitzgerald cheered softly, and relaxed. 'A' flight grabbed chunks of bread and hurried out. Their flap wagon was waiting downstairs. The scramble klaxon was already blaring when they piled out at the crewroom. Two minutes later the first Hurricane was airborne.

The controller spoke. "Hullo, Mango Leader, this is Snowball. Steer one-three-zero, angels two. Ten plus bandits, five miles south of Folkestone."

"Mango Leader to Snowball," CH3 said. "Check angels two?"

"Mango Leader, confirm angels two."

"Okay, Snowball." CH3 began climbing to three thousand feet. It was always better to be too high. Angels two? Nothing down there but tired seagulls.

Crossing Romney Marsh, he saw the enemy far ahead. They looked like circling crows so they must be Ju-87's, Stukas, dive-bombing a ship presumably. He cheered up: Stukas were easy meat; then he cheered down: there was bound to be an escort. Oh, well. "Mango aircraft," he said. "Fight in pairs. Watch your back. Don't do anything stupid."

They were flying in a wide, loose vic of three pairs: Cox and Macfarlane in White Section, CH3 and Steele-Stebbing in Red Section, Cattermole and Haducek in Yellow Section. The cloudbase had risen to five thousand and begun to fragment: the sky was as blue as it was grey. CH3 soon recognised the ship, a coaster from the morning convoy, left burning and disabled. Now it was being washed up-Channel by the tide.

The Stukas made one last pass. It was remarkable how calm and unhurried they were. CH3 glanced down at his airspeed: 290 knots: a mile every thirteen seconds. Yet the Stukas continued to topple and plunge down their invisible roller-coasters like children at play. They were playing with the ship: it had taken so many hits that the decks were awash. They dropped their last bombs, stayed down low and headed for France.

The Hurricanes could dive and catch them. CH3 looked at the broken cloud and saw nothing but broken sky. For a full minute he led the flight high above the Stukas and searched for the escort. By now they were in mid-Channel.

"Mango Leader, this is Snowball. Any joy?"

"Roger, Snowball. Eight or nine Stukas at angels zero." He made one last search. Well, even the Germans made mistakes . . . "Mango White and Yellow, attack. Mango Red will provide cover."

The four Hurricanes fell away. CH3 felt a prickling at the back of his neck and he weaved the aircraft so that he could search behind. A high-pitched voice yapped: "Bandits, bandits! Three o'clock," and he snapped his head around to see a flock of 109's barrelling down from the cloud. "Mango aircraft, bandits above," he called. "Turn and face, turn and face."

Earlier he had throttled back to avoid overshooting the Stukas. Now, to get at the Messerschmitts, he thrust the lever forward and woke up the Merlin. It was like flicking a baton to bring in the bass trombones. A huge surge of power gave him a solid shove in the back, and the needles on the panel were jumping and quivering.

But not enough.

The 109's were already too fast and too far away. They would escape Red Section, and hope to catch White and Yellow Sections on the turn.

CH3 tugged at the tit for boost over-ride and got emergency power: a brutal abuse of the engine, a hammering racket that was worth an extra twenty miles an hour unless the Merlin blew herself apart. The cockpit vibrated savagely, shuddering so much he couldn't focus his eyes on the 109's but he guessed the range at a quarter of a mile, gave plenty of lead, fired a two-second burst, then another, and a third. All useless.

White and Yellow Sections managed to complete their turn but they were labouring upwards when the 109's swept past in a storm of fire.

CH3 turned off his boost over-ride. The Merlin ceased its racket, the cockpit stopped shaking and amazingly he saw all four Hurricanes still climbing. "Mango, regroup, regroup," he ordered.

They came together and he checked for damage. Macfarlane failed to answer. Cox eased alongside him. Macfarlane waved his radio lead, and grinned. "His VHF's gone duff," Cox reported.

"What he doesn't know is he's losing coolant. Not much. Just a dribble."

The Messerschmitts shadowed them back to the English coast and then turned away. By that time the trickle of coolant had become a stream and Macfarlane was no longer grinning. CH3 kept calling, telling him to do a belly-landing on the sands or to bale out before the engine caught fire. No response.

Over Romney Marsh, at fifteen hundred feet, the coolant stopped.

Macfarlane could see his temperature gauges knocking into the red. He could smell the heat. There was just enough elemental sense in him to switch off the magnetos and the fuel. A whispering silence washed over the plane. He gave up. It wasn't a case of panic. It was simply that he had no idea what to do. Without power, or height, or someone to shout at him, or an airfield to aim at, he was helpless, childlike.

His hands clung to the control column for comfort and the Hurricane made its own flightpath above the Kent countryside. It cleared the marsh, bypassed a little hill, sighed over an old stone barn, and settled on a small plantation of young fir trees. Macfarlane blinked at the hundreds of whippy treetops flickering past him, checking the fighter's rush, softening its impact. The wings sank and sheared a path through the thicker branches. Bit by bit the plantation soaked up the impetus, until the Hurricane hit the ground with a bang that made Macfarlane's teeth snap together. It careered out of the trees and slid into a meadow and stopped. Lucky man. There was even a pub in sight, and it was even open. Lucky, lucky man.

The weather worsened after lunch, with rain squalls blowing in from the west. 'B' flight got scrambled and recalled immediately, then scrambled again to hunt a pair of intruders reported over Canterbury. For more than an hour they were vectored back and forth, in and out of towering clouds, sent climbing to fifteen thousand, to eighteen, down to ten. Finally they achieved a perfect interception on a section of Defiant fighters who were looking for the same intruders. Everyone went home.

Daddy Dalgleish had boxed and played rugby for the Royal Air

Force. While he was stationed with the North-West Frontier Force in India he had broken a sentry's jaw in three places with a single punch. The sentry had been a smelly tribesman, guarding Daddy after his aeroplane had forced-landed in the hills and he had been captured; he was eventually released following a lot of delicate diplomatic negotiations in which a couple of villages got bombed flat just to demonstrate the British government's good faith.

Now he was station commander at RAF Brambledown, responsible for three squadrons as well as all the ancillary paraphernalia in the way of cooks and clerks and medicos, which inevitably meant problems; and although Daddy Dalgleish's instinct was to treat problems as if they were smelly sentries, he was a group captain and he often had to butter people up.

When Fanny Barton and CH3 came into his office, he braced himself for a spell of buttering-up.

"I understand you're getting a bit browned-off with convoy patrols," he said. "Always getting shelled by damnfool destroyers and so on."

Barton nodded.

"I sympathise," Dalgleish said. "Damn difficult job you've got. Calls for the greatest qualities. Dogged determination, steady nerve, staunch stamina. Nothing flashy. Just ... backbone."

Barton grunted.

"Must be a bit frustrating, too," Dalgleish said, "not being able to make a big score. I know how you feel. Fighter pilot myself. The point is, it's the convoy that counts. That's the lifeline of the nation, isn't it? And you chaps are doing a vital, an absolutely essential job of keeping the Hun off our ships, and doing it brilliantly."

"Are we, sir?" Barton asked.

"No doubt about it."

"Then why are so many ships sunk?"

"Well, Jerry's bound to catch a few, isn't he? I mean he's got all the advantages. You've no need to feel bad about that. You've done your stuff."

"Some of us have done more than that, sir. I personally know of five or six pilots who got shot down on convoy patrol. Bloody good pilots, too. Not new boys. Flight commanders and the like."

489

"Yes, I realise that. We've witnessed some very gallant sacrifices in the last few weeks."

"Bloody stupid sacrifices," CH3 said, "sir."

Dalgleish looked at him in surprise. "Are you ... um ... Canadian, Hart?"

"American. Convoy patrol is the stupidest waste of fighter pilots imaginable. They're tied to the convoy, they're forced to fly slowly, they're like staked goats waiting for the tiger. No wonder they get jumped."

"In the worst possible place, too," Barton said. "Very wet, the English Channel, sir."

"Nobody underestimates the hazards, Barton," Dalgleish said. "But I ask you, why are the Germans launching these desperate attacks? Because they know how crucial these convoys are."

"No, sir," Barton said. "Because they know it's a great opportunity to kill our fighter pilots. How many have we lost already? One hundred? Two hundred? It's idiotic."

"Look," Dalgleish said firmly. "All war comes down to a battle of wills. That's what this is, a test of determination, and we mustn't give in now. We mustn't allow our morale to break. That's why I wanted to talk to you both. It's like a team ... As long as the team has faith in its skipper it can do anything. You're a New Zealander, aren't you, Barton? You must have experienced this on the rugger field."

"No, sir."

"No?"

"I never played rugby."

"Really? Why not?"

"It struck me as a game for people who sit on their brains."

"Oh." Dalgleish was briefly silenced. "Well . . . The fact remains, doesn't it, these convoys are, as I said, the lifeline of the nation and –"

"No, they're not," CH3 said, "sir."

"That bunch we escorted this morning," Barton said. "Most of them were coasters. Colliers, stuff like that. Half of them were in ballast. They're not even carrying cargo, for Christ's sake!"

"You can't be sure of that."

"I got scrambled this afternoon," CH3 said, "to protect one

490

small ship that was going to sink anyway. We got jumped, shot up, lost a plane, damn near lost a pilot."

"But that's the task of Fighter Command," Dalgleish protested. "We have a duty —"

"It's not worth it, sir," Barton said.

"Send the stuff by rail," CH3 said.

"I see," said Dalgleish. "You would just hand over the Straits of Dover to the Germans, would you? Admit failure? Tell the world we can't even guard our own ships?"

"Ah, now I understand," CH3 said. "We're flying these convoy patrols to avoid the embarrassment of losing face."

Dalgleish sighed. "I'm not surprised you don't understand, Hart. It's a matter of duty and dedication. We may be a young Service but we do have our traditions, you know."

"Drowning good pilots to get empty coal-boats past Dover," Barton said. "Is that an RAF tradition, sir?"

"We don't measure honour by the ton," Dalgleish said. That was, for him, a pretty weighty statement. On the strength of it he decided to bring the meeting to an end. "Believe me, I appreciate your concern for your men. But we all have to do things we don't particularly enjoy, and convoy patrols are just one of those things. That's war, I'm afraid."

"It's horseshit," CH3 said, "sir."

"Much of war *is* horseshit," Dalgleish said evenly. He showed them out. *Bloody colonials*, he thought. *Never know when to stop.*

Walking back to their quarters, CH3 said: "I wonder what Jacky Bellamy would have made of that lot. Tradition conquers all, and so on."

"Dunno. She might even decide that Daddy's right despite all his guff. I mean, maybe the convoys really are essential."

"God knows." CH3 looked at the sky, wondering about tomorrow's weather.

"Talking of God ... Macfarlane was lucky, wasn't he?"

"So were the others. They all got hit. Every time I see a 109, I wish I had a cannon. Hell of a weapon."

"Not so loud," Barton said, "they'll all want one."

Fitz and Mary rented a cottage near Brambledown. Flash Gordon came to dinner. Mary had not met him since France, and Fitz had warned her he was a bit wild, a bit moody; but he behaved perfectly all through the meal. She was eating a lot, and the men always had good appetites, so she had roasted a large leg of lamb. Flash had three helpings, with roast potatoes and peas and great spoonfuls of redcurrant jelly. She was pleased: anybody who ate like that must be in good health. Apple-and-raspberry pie came and went. He talked, too. The conversation flowed freely and easily. They took their coffee into the garden to enjoy the sunset. The rain had blown over but stormclouds still blockaded the light. The western sky was volcanic.

"It's going to be a boy," Mary said. "I wasn't sure until I looked at that sunset but now I know. Definitely a boy."

"That's not very scientific, love," Fitz said. "I mean to say, *sunsets*, for heaven's sake. You might as well read your tea-leaves."

"Ah, but he just kicked me," Mary told him. "Right here." She pressed her swollen stomach. "A good strong right-footed boot, it was. Obviously a footballer."

"Nicole always wanted a boy," Flash said. It was the first time any of them had mentioned her. "In fact she wanted several. I did my best, but ... Funny, isn't it? You'd think God would give extra marks for trying."

Fitz said: "Yes." There didn't seem to be anything useful he could add.

"If all it took was effort," Flash said to Mary, "I reckon Nicole would have been ahead of you."

"It's just as well she wasn't, isn't it?" Mary said, as gently as possible. If Flash wanted to remember Nicole, he had to remember everything.

"I dunno. I sometimes think ... If Nicole had been pregnant like you, she wouldn't have gone rushing across France and ..."

Mary shivered. Fitz took off his tunic and draped it across her shoulders. "How d'you feel about it all, Flash?" he asked. "Have you got over it yet? I mean, I know you'll never completely, but ... Well, I only ask because you seem in pretty good shape. Physically."

"Oh, I'm fine. You see," Flash said, turning to them with a blithely confident smile, "I know who did it."

"Oh, come on, Flash," Fitz said.

"Yes, I do. I saw him. I was there, I was right behind him, I know exactly who he is, and believe you me, when I see him again I'll recognise him in a flash."

"That's ... that's not possible," Fitz said. He didn't want to look at Flash, who had the glitter of fraudulent triumph in his eye. It was like talking to a man who's won because he has five aces. "Let's go inside. Mary's getting cold."

"I'll come across the bastard one of these days," Flash said. "You don't forget people like that. Then you watch!"

They went inside.

Next morning, Hornet squadron flew down to Bodkin Hazel. The field had been made fully operational, with fire-trucks and bloodwagons, petrol bowsers and starter-trolleys, a cookhouse, tents and deckchairs for the pilots, portable workshops for the groundcrew.

Each flight was scrambled once that day. Controllers steered them all over south-eastern England but the sky was full of cloud and the ground was misty and they saw nothing except barrage balloons, floating on the mist like hippos. In the evening they flew back to Brambledown, had a quick wash and found a pub. Next day was much the same: dull weather, a convoy patrol, no action, home to the pub. That became the pattern of life for the first week or ten days in August: few convoys, sporadic rain, poor visibility, not much sign of the *Luftwaffe*. Fanny Barton was relieved. It gave him time to pull the squadron together.

Between patrols and practice flights there was a lot of hanging-about on the ground. Hours and hours of it. Cattermole soon got bored. Everyone suffered from his boredom but the man who suffered most was Steele-Stebbing. He was a painstaking and conscientious young man with no ambition except to be a good fighter pilot. He knew that many people found his seriousness faintly ridiculous and so he tried to adopt an amiability that would be more acceptable. He wasn't much good at it. Often he looked more diffident than amiable. Cattermole sensed this uncertainty, and probed it.

"Steele-Stebbing," Cattermole said thoughtfully. They had been sitting below the control tower for over an hour. The overcast flattened the day and pressed the life out of it. Most of the pilots were dozing. The portable gramophone had run down and nobody felt energetic enough to rewind it. "I knew a Steele-Stebbing at school. Nice lad."

Steele-Stebbing put down his book. "Oh, yes," he said brightly.

"He wanted to join the Church, but . . . Oh, well. Awfully sad."

Cox half-opened his eyes. "What?" he mumbled.

"Expelled, poor chap. Caught the pox, you see. Got it from matron, actually."

"That doesn't sound very likely," Steele-Stebbing said.

"No? Well, you know the chap best. Who did he catch it from?" Cattermole stared until Steele-Stebbing, unable to think of an answer, looked down. "Come to think of it," Cattermole went on, "I knew another Steele-Stebbing at Oxford. Used to wear ladies' clothes."

This time Steele-Stebbing thought of an answer. "Perhaps that was my cousin. Amanda Steele-Stebbing."

"Amanda? Funny name for a boxing Blue. He certainly didn't have the figure for summer frocks. But then, neither do you, do you?"

Steele-Stebbing knew that any answer would be dangerous, so he merely shrugged.

"Really?" Cattermole went over and examined him. "Yes, perhaps you're right. You do have the figure for it."

"Shut up, Moggy," Fitzgerald said.

"No, no. Iron Filings is right." Cattermole began poking and feeling him. "He's a bit flat-chested but he has the most exciting hips."

"Excuse me." Steele-Stebbing got up.

"And rather a nice bottom, too," Cattermole said, as Steele-Stebbing walked away. "See how it goes up and down?"

"Leave the blighter alone," Patterson said.

"Ah. The tea-boy speaks. What is it, tea-boy?"

"Next time I'll make it battery acid," Patterson muttered.

"Promises, promises! A word of warning to all you young lads. When Pip says he loves you . . . pay no attention. Pip toys with our affections. He –"

"Shut your dirty, filthy, stinking trap," Patterson said harshly.

"You see?" Cattermole said. "So fickle. Only yesterday, poor Pip was pleading with me to rub tomato ketchup in his hair, he finds that very exciting, almost as thrilling as Steele-Stebbing's bottom –"

"Pack it in, Moggy," Moran ordered.

"Hey!" Flash Gordon seemed to come awake, although he had been staring at the clouds for a long time. "How would you ..." He swivelled in his chair, searching faces, and ended on Renouf. "How would you destroy an Me-110?"

Renouf was startled by Gordon's glittering stare. "Well ... uh ... I suppose the ... the thing to do is to try to take it by surprise and ... uh ... I mean if –"

Gordon was shaking his head. "Get up close," he said. "Stick your guns right up the animal's arse. Blow the bugger to bits."

"I see," Renouf said. When Gordon continued to stare, he added, "Thank you."

"Don't thank me. Thank Hitler. Without Hitler there wouldn't *be* any 110's to blow to bits. Would there?"

"No, I suppose not." Renouf was getting used to this.

"Well, then." Unexpectedly, Gordon put on a friendly smile. "Remember one thing, MacArthy. Bullets don't kill the enemy. Fancy flying doesn't kill the enemy. Only one thing kills the enemy, and that's *clear, logical thinking*."

"Beautiful," Fitz said lazily, and Gordon turned the smile on him like a fading flashlight. "But it's not MacArthy. It's Renouf."

The smile died. "What happened to MacArthy?"

"Fanny shot him," Moran said, and yawned. "Battle of Southend Sands. Remember?"

Gordon nodded several times, the nods getting deeper and deeper. "No," he said.

"South End?" Haducek said. "Where is this South End?"

"London. Between the East End and the West End," Renouf said. Fitzgerald blew a raspberry.

Haducek and Zabarnowski exchanged a few words in one of their languages. Zabarnowski said: "Was battle in the South End?"

"Was cock-up, Zab," Moran said. "Always cock-up."

The adjutant's car came in sight. As it bumped across the grass, Barton and CH3 came down the steps of the control tower. Kellaway got out and spoke to Barton, who smiled, and went over to the pilots.

"With effect from today," he announced, "Pilot Officers Cox,

495

Cattermole, Gordon, Fitzgerald and Patterson are promoted to the rank of flying officer."

Some of them cheered with a deliberate feebleness, some languidly applauded. "This will go down," Moran said, "as the biggest mass accident in the history of aviation."

"I thoroughly deserve it," Cattermole said, "but I do think, Fanny, that you might have left a decent interval before you promoted Pip as well. Damn it all, what has Pip ever done?"

"Fallen out of aeroplanes," Patterson said.

"Exactly," Cattermole said. "I mean, if you're going to promote people just for doing bloody silly things like that you might as well make Flash an air vice-marshal."

"Hey!" Macfarlane said. "We don't have to salute these elderly gents now, do we?" He had become quite daring since he had discovered that you could write-off a brand new Hurricane and be given a new one without so much as a reprimand. It wasn't like school, where you got a telling-off for breaking a window. Not a bit like school.

"Okay, uncle, now give us the good news," Cox said. "Tell us you've sorted out our back-pay."

"Still working on it, Mother. No luck yet."

"Bloody hell. When's it going to come through? I've got an overdraft the size of Ben Hur."

"Explain, please," Haducek said.

"Ben Hur, mountain in Scotland," Patterson told him. "Very big."

"Pip jolly nearly made a joke then," Cattermole said. "Go and lie down, Pip. You're covered in sweat."

"Think yourself lucky," Fitzgerald said to Cox. "My bank manager won't let me have an overdraft."

Steele-Stebbing had come back and was keeping his distance from Cattermole. Now he raised his hand. "Sir," he said to Kellaway, "is there any activity at Sector?"

"Adj, not sir," Kellaway said easily, and Steele-Stebbing flinched. "No, nothing doing. Somebody caught a Heinkel up in Norfolk, so I heard. Getting bored, are you?"

"Try and speed up the money, uncle," Barton said. "Can't Baggy Bletchley do anything?"

A telephone rang in the tower. A corporal looked out. "Scramble one section, sir. Patrol Hastings, angels ten."

Barton glanced at his squadron. His command. Death or glory was waiting up there. Maybe. "Green Section," he said. Patterson and Renouf jumped up, grabbed gloves and helmets, and ran. "You won't find anything," Macfarlane shouted. "It's early closing in Germany today."

He was wrong, however. They found a runaway barrage balloon at twelve thousand feet and shot it down. Renouf chased the tumbling, blazing carcase and got some useful practice at deflection shooting.

After a few days, Steele-Stebbing asked for a few words in private with CH3.

"Cattermole seems to have elected me his private and personal butt," he said. "I don't think I need go into detail."

"No."

"I can put up with the insults, they're all rather schoolboyish anyway. And the practical jokes don't matter. I'm used to sitting on collapsing deckchairs by now. It's a bit of a bore, that's all."

"Yes, I'm sure it is."

CH3 waited, but Steele-Stebbing didn't seem to know what to say next. He chewed his lip, and frowned. The silence became uncomfortable. Eventually he half-turned away. "Well," he said, "I just thought you ought to know."

"No, you didn't," CH3 said. "I've known all along. It's no secret, is it? Now you want me to do something. Right?"

"I simply don't understand," Steele-Stebbing said. "Why does he pick on me? If I've done something wrong, or if there's something I ought to be doing that I'm not doing, I wish someone would tell me. Then I'll try to put the matter right. As it is . . . Well, to be blunt, I feel I'm being victimised, and frankly it's unfair."

"Of course it's unfair, you fool. So what? Life is unfair. The question is, what's to be done about it? And I'll tell you here and now: I'm not going to do anything."

"Oh no, of course not." Greatly daring, he risked a hint of sarcasm.

"Unless and until Moggy's nonsense affects your flying it's none of my business. I could *make* it my business, I suppose. I could

497

make Moggy behave himself. That would identify you as the sort of man who can't stand on his own two feet, who has to be given special protection. Is that what you want?"

"No."

"Glad to hear it. If nobody else is going to help you, it looks as if you'll have to sort it out yourself, doesn't it?"

"Yes."

"Good. That's settled then."

Macfarlane and Renouf were quickly accepted into the squadron. They knew they were in when they were given nicknames. Macfarlane became Bing because he kept playing Crosby records. Renouf, whose initials were N.I.M., was called Nim.

The foreigners' names were shortened to Zab and Haddy, but only for convenience. They were not popular. They either brooded or they bitched. When they talked to each other it was in some Central European tongue that sounded like wet barbed wire. Perhaps they felt homesick and lonely; who could tell? The only thing anyone was sure of was their opinion of the Hurricane. After every patrol, at debriefing, they expressed their contempt.

Fanny Barton called Skull, Kellaway and the flight commanders into his room to discuss the problem.

"It's the others I'm worried about," he said. "I mean, a kite's as good as the pilot thinks it is, right? Once he starts thinking he's sitting in a load of duff machinery, bang goes his confidence."

"So chop the miserable buggers," Moran said.

Barton sniffed. "Doesn't look good, Flip. New squadron, new CO. Looks as if I'm not bloody *trying*."

"Besides," CH3 said, "they're both very good pilots."

"D'you know what I think?" the adjutant said. "I think they're not really interested in getting Spits at all. What they really desperately want to get is some Huns."

"Very angry men, Zab and Haddy," Moran said.

"You mean, because we're not getting Huns, they're bitching about the Hurricanes?" Barton said. "That's a bit boss-eyed, isn't it?"

"Oh, no!" Skull exclaimed. "It's a perfect example of transferred hostility. Quite beautiful, in its way."

"God stone the crows," Kellaway grumbled. "This is a fighter squadron, not a looney-bin."

"Could've fooled me," CH3 said.

"Um," Barton said. "Okay. I'll think about it. Thanks."

As they went out, Kellaway poked Skull in the ribs with the stem of his pipe. "Transferred hostility!" he scoffed. "Utter guff."

"On the contrary, you've just demonstrated it . . ."

The voices faded. Barton stared at the wall. If they had been English, or English-speaking, he could have torn them off a strip and told them to stop binding and start pulling together for the common cause. But the buggers weren't English. They didn't believe in Westminster Abbey and Windsor Castle and cricket and Wimbledon and London bobbies and roast beef with Yorkshire pudding and thatched pubs and village flower shows and all the stuff that Fanny had first seen on calendars sent to New Zealand by English relatives. God knows what they did believe in. Apart from killing Germans. Not much love left in Zab and Haddy. Just plenty of hatred, which they couldn't switch off.

Tricky.

Haducek was sitting on the lavatory when the scramble sounded, which was why Nim Renouf took off with Moggy Cattermole as Yellow Section.

The controller had one bandit for them, reported fifteen, one-five, miles north-west of Dover, angels eight to ten. Apparently the little blighter had been wandering all over Kent but there was so much mist the Observer Corps kept losing him. Now they'd found him again, and he was heading east.

Correction, west.

Correction, south. "Sorry, Mango Yellow Leader," Snowball said. "Bandit is definitely heading south. What are your angels?"

"Angels five."

"Mango Yellow, make angels six. Your bandit seems to be losing height."

For the next twenty minutes, Snowball steered them back and forth and up and down. Canterbury Cathedral poked through the mist like a mooring mast. Renouf watched Cattermole's tail and covered the sky behind and above. Cattermole hunted the bandit.

Once, there was a burst of flak about a mile astern, looking as small and innocent as smoke-smuts.

"Mango Yellow Leader to Snowball," Cattermole said eventually. "Fritz doesn't live here any more."

"Steer one-zero-zero, Mango Yellow."

"We've been down that street, Snowball, and it's empty."

"Bandit is still on the table, Mango Yellow."

"That's *us* you're plotting, Snowball. He's gone. Scarpered."

"Steer one-zero-zero, Mango Yellow."

One minute later it was zero-two-zero. That became three-one-zero. Which became three-four-zero. Snowball held them on that course until he abruptly announced a new bandit, five miles south of Dover. "Vector one-four-zero, angels one, Mango Yellow," he said. "Buster, buster." Buster was the codeword for maximum speed, short of pulling the tit.

They came screaming over Folkestone and began slicing down through the top of the Channel mist at a speed that made Renouf's eyeballs dilate and his toes curl. Cattermole levelled out at five hundred feet. The mist was not thick: the sea was just visible, a flat oily black like spilled creosote. There seemed to be no ripple; just an occasional white smear where a swell had stretched too far and split itself open. Renouf stuck behind Cattermole and tried not to blink. He was scared and exhilarated. No horizon, no sun, just this shapeless gloom that gave the frightening illusion of not moving. Then a white smear flicked past the edge of his vision and he put all his trust in Moggy Cattermole, who shouted, "Got the bastards!"

Renouf glimpsed the edge of something on the water. Then Cattermole was turning, circling, shedding speed as he called Snowball. "Bandit's down in the drink. Looks like a Heinkel 59 next to him. Damn foggy. Hard to see. Lost them for a sec."

Renouf trailed him around and around, the circle getting steadily smaller.

In theory they were bound to find their target again. In practice Renouf rapidly lost all sense of direction: he soon had no idea whether they were north or south of that first sighting. Grey mist and black sea blurred into each other, endless, changeless, featureless. Again, it was Cattermole who found the enemy and

500

who told Renouf where to look, far to the right. The silhouettes on the water were as soft as moths at dusk.

The next circuit carried them, low and slow, straight over the two planes. An Me-110 had ditched, expertly. Oil skims trailed behind the engines like dull silk. Fifty yards away sat a big white twin-engined float-plane with prominent red crosses. Between the two, a rubber dinghy was being paddled. There were also numbers of seagulls wandering about the scene and one flew slap into Cattermole's airscrew.

The blades minced it into an instant flurry of bloody feathers. Most sprayed wide, but enough splashed onto the windscreen to blind Cattermole's view ahead. As he climbed, he told Renouf to make the attack.

Renouf turned and came down and gave the 110 a quick squirt that boiled a bit of sea, and he went up again. "Hullo, Leader," he called. "I think I hit the 110 but it's sinking anyway. Wings are under water."

"Yes." Pause. "Get the Heinkel?"

Joke, Renouf thought; but only for a second. Cattermole didn't make that sort of joke. As he swung the Hurricane, careful to turn through an exact half-circle, his mind was briefly touched by revulsion. He did not allow this emotion to affect his efficiency. Indeed, when he saw that the seaplane was taxiing, trying to take-off, he welcomed the added challenge of a moving target.

It was a biggish machine, the He-59: a biplane nearly eighty feet across, nearly sixty feet long, riding on twin floats that were each longer than a Hurricane. Apart from a red tail-band with a black swastika, the whole machine was painted white, presumably to show off its red crosses. It had three open cockpits. Renouf could see the crew quite clearly. They looked too small for such a big aircraft. He had a silly impression of children, caught joyriding. A single machine-gun opened up wildly, shaken by jolting as the plane gained speed. Renouf fired.

The results were strange and spectacular. It was as if the floats struck flame from the sea. The further and faster the plane travelled, the more flame it struck, until it was leaving a long double track flaring in the gloom. Renouf suddenly understood: the floats were also the petrol tanks. His incendiary bullets had pierced them.

He banked to make a beam-attack and felt slightly sorry for the crew, having to lay a great blazing trail. They wouldn't have escaped anyway, but this was rubbing it in.

So much fuel had been lost that the seaplane almost got airborne. It was coming unstuck just as he fired again, allowing half a length for deflection. It shuddered, the nose dipped, the tips of the floats dug in, and the whole heavy, complicated aeroplane performed a slow somersault. Burning petrol sprayed and made a broken necklace of flame.

When Renouf came back, all he could see was the underside of the floats, resting uppermost on the water. He called Cattermole, and was told to climb above the mist. They regrouped and got a bearing for home.

Cattermole landed with his head sticking out of the cockpit. He was looking at his propeller when Renouf walked over. The stench from bits of seagull roasted on the exhaust vents was still strong. "Did you get those Jerries in the dinghy?" Cattermole asked.

Renouf had forgotten about them. "Oh," he said. "Those."

"You pathetic fart," Cattermole said.

Two more scrambles at Section strength, neither of them productive. Squadron released at 8 p.m. Back to Brambledown. Quick wash. Dinner in the mess.

Daddy Dalgleish pressed Barton's shoulder as he was finishing his pudding. "Old friend to see you," he said. Baggy Bletchley stood with a large smile on his face and a large brandy in his hand. "Good evening, squadron leader," he said.

The pilots made room for them. "I'm afraid you've caught us on a very ordinary evening, sir," Barton said. "It's just tripe and onions with sago for afters, but I can promise you a rather peculiar cabbage wine, the chaplain's wife made it with her own bare feet. Somewhat fruity but not lacking in humility, if you know what I mean."

"Oh, I know what you mean," Bletchley said happily. "By the way: did you see that I got Rex a gong? The family were very pleased. I believe they've commissioned an enormous stained-glass window, with him in the middle looking like St George."

"What's the gen, sir?" Moran asked. "What's Jerry up to?"

"At the moment, you mean? Not much. We're getting a few

more of his fighters whizzing about the south of England, but they only do it to annoy because they know it teases. Longterm ... Well, if he's not planning to invade, then your guess is as good as mine."

That made them stop and think. It wasn't the first time invasion had been mentioned; people in pubs were always talking about it; but coming from Baggy Bletchley, an air commodore, a chap who was in and out of Air Ministry every day ... Well, that somehow brought the future into focus with a jolt. Very soon there was going to be a colossal scrap, much bigger than France, far more serious than France, with nowhere to retreat if it all went wrong. Life, for a moment, looked a bit grim. Even the new boys caught a slight sense of dread.

"They'd better bloody well invade," Flash Gordon said severely. "If they don't come here, I'm not going all the way over there again. I mean to say, fair's fair."

"Good old Flash," Cox said, but Gordon simply stared. "I mean it," he told him. "It takes two to have a fight, you know."

"Of course it does," Bletchley said. "While I'm here, Fanny, I'd very much like to see your Hurricanes, if I may."

Daddy Dalgleish came with him, so Barton took his flight commanders along in case there was a vote. When they reached the hangars, Bletchley walked around a couple of Hurricanes and turned away. "Splendid, splendid," he said. "I hear you got one of their red-cross planes today."

"Heinkel 59," Barton said. "It was on the water, trying to pick up a crew. One of the new boys got it. Renouf."

"Jolly good show." They strolled out of the hangar and stood looking at the twilight. "I'd keep it under my hat, if I were you. Don't go shouting about it. Least said, soonest mended, sort of thing."

"Now I'm seriously confused, sir," Moran said. "I thought we got an order about German red-cross planes, and I thought it said blow the buggers up."

"Quite correct. They're an absolute menace. They snoop on our convoys and monitor our radio transmissions and sneak in and snaffle their own pilots when they have to ditch. You're entitled to hit them as hard as you like. Just don't come back and tell everyone."

503

"The public doesn't understand," Dalgleish said.

"We weren't planning to shout about it anyway," Barton said.

"Of course not," Bletchley said. "The thing is, the country's had a nasty knock. Dunkirk, and so on. Norway. We can't afford to do anything that might upset public confidence. This is a time to stand together."

"Close ranks, you mean," CH3 said.

"That's it," Dalgleish said.

"We've got to believe in ourselves," Bletchley said. "Face the common foe. No room for internal differences at a time like this."

"You needn't worry about my chaps," Barton said.

"It's not quite as simple as you may think," Dalgleish said. "I've got two other squadrons to look after and it isn't easy to keep everyone in line and behaving properly when, for instance, they see you chaps going around with the collars cut off your Irvine jackets. Whose bright idea was that?"

"Mine, sir," CH3 said.

"For heaven's sake . . ."

"I agree with him," Barton said. "They get in the way."

"You didn't seem to have any trouble with them in France, Fanny," Bletchley said.

"We didn't wear Mae Wests in France, sir."

CH3 said: "If you put on a parachute and a Mae West you've got to put up the collar of the jacket. Then you can't get it down again. The damn thing sticks up higher than your ears, so when you try to look round you can't see anything. That's why we cut them off."

"My dear chap," Dalgleish said, "nobody *ordered* you to wear your Irvine jacket. If you don't like it, don't hack it about. Just leave it behind."

"And freeze to death," Moran said. "Sometimes it gets a bit cool at twenty thousand feet, you know."

"Oh, I know. Don't worry about that. We flew a damn sight higher than that in India. *And* with open cockpits. But we didn't find it necessary to deface RAF property, as far as I recall."

"Perhaps that was because you didn't have to look behind you," CH3 said.

"There's a serious point at issue here, you realise," Bletchley said. "If we're going to fight effectively, everyone's got to do as he's told. I've just seen what you've done to your wings, Fanny. Painted the under-surface duck-egg blue. You know you've got no authorisation for that. Half-black, half-white: that's the colour-scheme."

"Black and white stinks, sir. We learned that in France. It makes the kites stand out like chess sets."

"That's the whole idea!" Dalgleish cried. "How the devil can our ground observers spot you if they can't see you?"

"We don't want to be seen, not by anyone," Moran said, "and especially not by Jerry."

"But the controllers need the observers," Bletchley said. "You must accept that."

"Far be it from me to lay down the law," Dalgleish said, "but I've got a station to run, and it gets very difficult if each squadron decides to go its own sweet way."

"Why not?" CH3 asked. "As long as it works."

"We learned a lot in France, sir," Barton said.

"France was France," Bletchley declared. "That's all finished. This is England."

"Hey!" CH3 said. "I just realised. France wasn't a real war at all! Just a scruffy little sideshow."

"I simply cannot overlook the defacing of an entire set of Irvine jackets," Dalgleish said. "You'll have to pay for them."

"That reminds me, sir," Barton said. "Our back-pay is still heavily in arrears. Is there any chance –"

"Air Ministry's doing its best," Bletchley said.

"I had a funny thought a moment ago," Moran said. "I thought, isn't it funny that the *Luftwaffe* has seaplanes that can pick its pilots out of the Channel, and we don't? That's a very funny thing, isn't it?"

"Fighter Command can't be expected to think of everything," Bletchley said.

"No?" Moran said. "Jerry did."

Mary didn't get up from her chair when Fitz came in. She smiled, or at least she tried to smile. In any case it was so gloomy in the cottage that it didn't much matter. He kissed her on the cheek and noticed that sour smell again. "How d'you feel?" he asked.

"I was sick."

"That's no good." He moved away. "Or is it? Is this normal?"

"I don't know, dear. I feel very strange, but then having a baby is a strange experience for me."

Fitz sat on a couch. "Why are you sitting in the dark?" he asked.

"The bulb's gone . . . I couldn't reach up to change it."

"Damn. What a bind." He got up and went to the window. If he changed the bulb he would have to put up the blackout blinds first. Hard enough to do that when there was still some daylight; now it would be murder. "What about food? Had something to eat?"

"Not much. Bit of bread. I didn't get out to the shops today. Didn't feel up to it."

"That's no good." Fitz was hungry, starving. He could have eaten in the mess if he'd known she wasn't going to have a meal ready. "I'd better whip something up, I suppose. What d'you feel like?"

"Lobster. Just lobster and strawberries."

"Don't be daft, dear. It's been a hell of a long day and I'm not in the mood for jokes."

"I'm sorry. That was the baby speaking. It seems to have an obsession for lobster and strawberries. Can't think of anything else."

"Oh . . . Jesus." Fitz sat on the windowledge and looked at the heavy black shapes of shrubs in the dusk. The cottage was damp, he could smell it. Not the right place for Mary, not in her condition, but he couldn't afford anywhere else. He felt angry at himself for getting her into all this, and angry at her for just sitting there when he needed someone to be bright and lively and encouraging. "Look, this is no damn good," he said. "I mean, God in heaven, we can't go on living like this."

Mary said, "It's been such an awfully long day. So lonely. And now you're back and I can't even see you." He didn't move, didn't speak. "Please mend the light, Fitz," she said. "I want to see you. Please."

He stood, and stretched. He had an enormous desire to smash something, anything. For a long time he stood in the darkening room and listened to his breathing. Each breath was another second of his life gone, used-up, wasted. It all seemed so stupid, so pointless.

Everything was difficult, everything was pointless. That's what made him angry.

Bodkin Hazel was getting civilised. Now it had a chemical toilet in a little wooden hut on wheels, so the pilots on standby didn't have to go to the old clubhouse. It also had a larger hut that they used as a crewroom. Barton was in there with CH3 and the new pilots.

"If you fly straight and I get on your tail you're dead," CH3 said. "Chances are you won't even hear my guns."

"What about back-armour?" Renouf asked.

"Good question. What about cannon? Both the 109 and the 110 carry twin cannon, twenty-millimetre stuff, very nasty. Don't bet on keeping out the draught with back-armour."

"If you can hear gunfire," Barton said, "it's a hundred to one those guns are being fired *at you*."

"That means you're lucky still to be alive," CH3 said. "If you can hear him he's bloody close."

"Don't wait," Barton said. "Don't look for him. Don't call for help. Escape."

"That means *break*," CH3 said. "Stuff everything in a corner as hard and as fast as you can, and break like hell."

"Look at this." Barton tapped a photograph pinned to the wall. It showed two wrecked Hurricanes in a field. "This pair got jumped by 109's when the squadron was in tight formation. Arse-end Charlies. Nobody else saw anything, nobody else heard anything. Think of that. The kite two lengths behind you gets shot down and you don't notice a damn thing."

"If you hear him fire, he must be *bloody* close," CH3 said.

"There's always the mirror, though, isn't there?" Macfarlane asked.

CH3 said: "If you look in your mirror and see anything interesting like a 109, it's probably the last thing you'll ever see."

"Most of the chaps who get shot down and live to tell the tale say they never even saw the Jerry who did it," Barton said. "Keep looking behind you. That's where Jerry likes to be."

"And it only takes him a couple of seconds to nip behind you," CH3 said, "so never stop looking for him."

"Sir," Steele-Stebbing said to Barton, "isn't it the task of the wingman to protect one's tail?"

"Yes, in theory. Maybe *he* got jumped first. Maybe his radio packed up. Maybe his engine went duff and he's ten miles back."

"The point is," CH3 said, "you can't assume he's always going to cover you. When combat starts anything can happen."

"If you lose him, find somebody else," Barton said. "Don't just ponce around the sky on your own."

"Jerry loves singletons," CH3 said. "Easy meat."

"In any case, if you're in a scrap, never fly straight and level for more than fifteen seconds," Barton said. "Keep on twisting and turning and dodging, whether you know Jerry's after you or not."

"And look behind you," CH3 said. "You can't kill him if you can't see him."

"Now this young gentleman . . ." Barton pointed to a photograph of a blazing, falling Spitfire about to hit a wood. "He climbed with the sun behind him, silly boy."

"It wasn't the only thing behind him," CH3 said, "but of course he wasn't to know that, was he?"

"When you climb, climb towards the sun," Barton said.

"What if the controller sends you the other way?" Macfarlane asked.

"Sorry, controller, your transmission garbled."

"All right, suppose the raid is in sight and it's down-sun. If you climb up-sun that takes you away –"

"Sure," CH3 told him. "First you get your angels, then you do some damage."

Barton sniffed. "Yes and no," he said. "Yes, we go flat-out to make the interception. No, we try not to get killed in the process."

Macfarlane still wasn't satisfied. "But that doesn't mean we actually fly *away* from the bandits, does it? We might never find them again."

"Bandits are like buses," CH3 muttered. "Plenty more along soon."

"Now hang on there," Barton declared. "Let's get this clear. When we get vectored onto a raid, that's *our* raid and we make every effort to hit it."

"Every intelligent effort," CH3 said.

"Well, for God's sake, let's not split hairs," Barton said to him.

"If any of us had any brains we wouldn't be here now, would we? On the other hand, if you're going to wait until everything up there is perfect you might as well . . ." He checked himself before he said something tactless. He could feel his temper slipping. CH3's insistence on intelligent behaviour irritated him. He forced a grin and said to the pilots: "When in doubt, kill a kraut. Simple as that."

They brightened up, until CH3 added: "But remember: that's exactly the sort of thing that some bright *Geschwader* commander is telling *his* men too, probably right now, and they've usually got the advantage of height."

"Christ, CH3, you're in a cheerful mood today," Barton said.

"I just don't want these guys kidding themselves that what the sector controller tells them is necessarily true," CH3 said stubbornly. His hands were thrust into his pockets and his shoulders were hunched. "All the controller knows is what he sees on that table in the ops room at Brambledown. Half the time his angels are out by a couple of thousand feet. That's marvellous, when you –"

"Okay, we all know the system's not perfect!" Barton picked up his cap and beat some non-existent dust out of it. "It's still a bloody sight better than anything Jerry's got."

"Yes, but the point is . . ." CH3 began, when the phone rang. Barton took the call. " 'A' flight's scrambled," he announced. "I'm leading," he told CH3. "You sit this one out." The door banged as Macfarlane headed the charge. Already, the Merlins were starting to popple and belch. The first engine fired, with a bang like a smash-and-grab, and began roaring.

CH3 leaned against the doorframe and watched the hasty ritual. Mae West on. Parachute on. Groundcrew kneeling to bring the straps together. A lumbering run to the plane, parachute slung under the backside like a cushion. Heave up onto the wing, big swing of the legs to get into the cockpit, settle the parachute in the bucket seat. Groundcrew helping with the safety harness. Helmet on, check oxygen and radio leads, gloves on, quick squint at the instrument panel. All ready to go.

And a touch of panic squeezing the guts, probably. This was always the worst moment. Sitting in the cockpit, waiting and wondering. Remembering. Hoping. Fearing.

It was much better when the leader gave the signal to move, and there were things to do. CH3 saw Barton's plane taxi out, an airman clinging to one of the wingtips to help it turn. Automatically he glanced at the sky. A fine clear day.

Renouf and Zabarnowski were standing nearby. As the flight got airborne, Zabarnowski said, "All this talk . . . Waste of time. Flying fighters is very simple. You want to know the secret of success?"

"What?" Renouf asked.

Zabarnowski put his mouth to Renouf's ear. "Get this close," he whispered, "and kill the bastard first time." Renouf recoiled and wiped his ear.

"Your English seems to be improving fast," CH3 said.

The Pole looked away. "Is dump," he said.

Fanny Barton kept a vivid memory of this scrap. Some fights printed themselves onto his brain permanently; others erased themselves by their own manic, whirling pointlessness, leaving only a taste of terror, an echo of triumph. Perhaps because the calm weather made everything look so neat at first, perhaps because both sides came at each other in the same way, flying the same formation, Fanny remembered this one clearly.

Everyone saw the 109's from a distance. There were eight: four pairs in a long, saw-toothed line. When Fanny banked his own saw-toothed line of Hurricanes to complete the interception, the enemy leader matched the move precisely and the two formations curled steeply towards each other. For an instant everyone had a target and everyone was a target. Fourteen sets of guns fired, just a flicker of flame before the two formations met and broke up like sheets of glass smashing each other.

Barton glimpsed planes going in all directions and decided the place to be was on top. A hard-turning climb brought him a fine view of the chaos. A yellow-nosed 109 showed its belly to him and he went after it but it rolled and saw him and slipped away. The R/T was staccato with warnings, curses, questions. A different 109 chased a Hurricane into his vision and he gave it a squirt that made it jump. Then he was through the scrap and out again and he heaved the fighter onto its side in an effort to drag it around and get his sights on an enemy.

The strain greyed-out his vision for a second or two and when the mist cleared there was tracer streaking at him from the beam. A 109 came blinding across his nose, so close that the wash rocked him, and then more tracer chased it and a Hurricane boomed over his head, still firing. Barton glimpsed Cattermole's letter painted on the side. Cattermole seemed to be locked onto the German: each brief burst of fire knocked more bits off. The 109 hauled itself into a vertical climb. Cattermole angled up and blew it to pieces. Eight Browning machine-guns pounded the cockpit area for three seconds. The fighter came apart. It was like a plastic toy that had been badly assembled. The pieces scattered. No parachute.

Elsewhere, Macfarlane was racing around desperately looking for Cox, whose wingman he was supposed to be, while Cox raced around driving 109's off Macfarlane's tail. Steele-Stebbing had long since lost Barton and now was reconciled to death. He had put his long, thin body through such a whirling, bewildering string of violent manoeuvres in order to dodge the apparently endless 109's that his stomach had quit the fight. Vomit was bubbling over his lips, tears of pain were fogging his goggles. A Messerschmitt swam into view and he jabbed his thumb on the firing-button, pouring all his hate and pain and misery at this vile object, and he kept firing and firing until the breechblocks clanked and wheezed and he had no hate left. Miraculously he was still alive. The enemy had vanished.

The enemy had, in fact, been Haducek, and he had vanished not because Steele-Stebbing hit him – all the shots went very wide, and after the first second or so Haducek was hopelessly out of range anyway – but because Haducek's Hurricane was in a howling dive, chasing an unhappy 109 down to ground level. The 109 was trailing smoke and streamers of fabric. Haducek chased it across the fields and villages of Kent, over the cliffs and beaches, and halfway to France before he gave up. He landed at Bodkin Hazel with little more than fumes in his tanks. There was a nasty mess lying in the middle of the grass which he carefully avoided. Bing Macfarlane had written off another Hurricane.

Hornet squadron got scrambled three more times that day. The first scramble, at Section strength, was recalled almost at once, and the second, also at Section strength, patrolled for an hour

511

without finding anything. When 'B' flight was sent up it was early evening and the sky was a beautiful soft blue, like the finest velvet. Flip Moran led a battle-climb to twenty-two thousand feet. The view was stupendous: they could see from the Thames estuary to the Isle of Wight to the Dutch islands and deep into France. They could see the curvature of the earth and a couple of early stars. They could also see a special Dornier 17, always tantalisingly above and ahead. It had to be a special version, probably with bigger engines and better superchargers, because when it grew tired of inspecting southern England and decided to go home, it left 'B' flight gasping and straining.

The controller returned them direct to Brambledown. 'A' flight was already there, stowing their gear in the lockers.

"Was lousy," Zabarnowski told Skull.

"No, no," Moran said. "That's not the way it was at all. We made a perfect interception, if only the blessed bandit had had the manners to come within range."

"Is a fat old cow," Zabarnowski grumbled. "One Spit better than ten lousy cows."

"On a point of fact," Cox said stiffly, "I don't think cows have lice. Not English cows, anyway. Maybe Polish cows are different."

"Shut up, Jew-boy," Zabarnowski said. "Stay out of my Poland."

"I wouldn't be seen dead in it."

"Chosen people," Zabarnowski muttered. "Chosen to stink."

"Hey!" Moran said. "That's enough, Zab."

"I'd sooner be a stinking English Jew than a perfumed Polish ponce," Cox said.

"Okay, can it, Mother," CH3 ordered.

"Lousy kike," Zabarnowski muttered.

"What sort of pansy wears a hairnet in bed?" Cox demanded. "A Polish pansy!"

"Pack it in, the pair of you," Barton said.

"*And* silk stockings," Cox added rebelliously.

Skull closed his notebook. "No actual combat, then," he said to Moran, when Zabarnowski punched Cox in the head. At once Cattermole hit Zabarnowski a solid thump to the ribs and Haducek attacked Cattermole with a flurry of blows. Cox kicked Haducek in the groin and Barton sprayed the lot of them with a fire extinguisher, working the jet back and forth and up and down

512

while elbows jabbed and fists slammed and the room echoed with rage and profanity in three languages until the whole fight was drenched and the floor was awash. Haducek kept swinging, so Moran kicked his legs from under him. Zabarnowski wiped his hair from his eyes and spat at Cox. Patterson, Fitzgerald and Gordon grabbed the Pole and threw him out of the hut.

"You open your mouth and you're chopped," Barton told Cox. He was standing with a foot planted on Haducek's chest. "Get some towels, Moggy," he ordered. Renouf reached into his locker and offered a towel. "Is your name Moggy?" Barton roared. Renouf gaped. Cattermole shouldered him aside. The door crashed open and Zabarnowski stormed in.

"I am good Polish Catholic!" he bawled. "Lousy English Jew insult me, insult Catholic Church!"

CH3 had found another extinguisher. "In the name of the Father, the Son and the Holy Ghost," he said, and the jet hit Zabarnowski high in the chest. The Pole opened his mouth and CH3 filled it. Zabarnowski staggered and fell on his backside. CH3 washed him down as he crawled out of the door. End of fight.

Half an hour later they were all on the carpet in Fanny's office, having large strips torn off them.

Brawling and insulting behaviour were bad enough, he told them. If they had been airmen they would have been put on charges and given two weeks' jankers, scrubbing out the latrines and shovelling coke for the boilers and doubling off to the guardroom for extra parades in full kit every hour on the hour from 6 a.m. to midnight and God help them if a button was dirty.

What made it worse, *intolerably* worse, was that they were commissioned officers. Supposed to set an example to the men. Who all knew by now that there had been a squalid and stupid punch-up in the locker room. What, Fanny wanted to know, was each of them going to say if an airman was brought before them on a charge of brawling or insulting behaviour? *What?*

But above all (and here Fanny took out his copy of *King's Regulations* and banged it on the desk) they were on *active service*. And they had *disobeyed his orders while on active service*.

He expanded on that theme at some length and with considerable feeling. Kellaway, listening, noticed that he had become quite fluent since taking over the squadron.

"You may consider yourselves lucky to escape with severe reprimands," Fanny said. "You two . . ." He aimed a finger at Cox and Cattermole. "Go and mop up that shambles. I don't see why the troops should do your dirty work. You two," he told the others, "stay here."

"Lunatic," Cattermole said as they went down the corridor.

"Maniac," Cox said and kicked him on the leg. Cattermole kicked him back, so Cox knocked his cap off. Cattermole shoulder-charged him into the wall. Cox trod on his cap. A Waaf clerk came out of an office to see what all the noise was about. Cattermole advanced on her, grinning fiercely and gnashing his teeth. "All the better to eat you with, my dear!" he roared. She fled.

"I wish to apologise," Fanny Barton said. Haducek looked pleased, Zabarnowski was suspicious. "You shouldn't be flying Hurricanes. It was stupid of me not to realise that long ago. Quite obviously the Hurricane is altogether unsuitable for you. Too big, too heavy, not fast enough. The obvious thing to do is to switch you to Spitfires. Mmm?" He gave them a fast, formal smile.

They were listening intently. So was Kellaway.

"Well, the good news is you're grounded. No more Hurricanes." He widened his smile, made it almost congratulatory. "I knew you'd be pleased . . ." They weren't looking pleased. "Now it's just a matter of going through the formalities." He fished a sheet of paper from his in-tray. "You're not the only ones, of course. Dozens of chaps are itching to fly Spits. *Itching*. Personally, I think it's a bloody awful kite, always going wrong, doesn't turn anywhere near as tightly as a Hurri, very shaky gun-platform, and it's got that knock-kneed undercart, all you have to do is run over a small turd and the whole shootingmatch capsizes. Plus, of course, the Spit's got no stomach for Jerry bullets, stop a couple and you've bought it, whereas the Hurricane gobbles 'em up and comes back for more . . . Anyway . . . Where was I?"

"Long waiting list for Spits," Kellaway said.

"Ah, yes. Thank you, adj. So the powers-that-be have made a rule. If you want to transfer to a Spitfire squadron . . ." Barton consulted the paper. ". . . you have to score five confirmed kills in a Hurricane first. Yes. Well, I think that's everything. Once again I'd like to apologise. That's all."

They didn't move. "I have two kills," Zabarnowski said.

"I have three," said Haducek.

"No, no." Barton waved the paper. "It's quite specific. Five each, not five between you."

"But how . . ." Haducek looked thoroughly miserable. "If I am grounded . . ."

"Haven't the faintest, old boy. That's for you to work out. I've done all I can, haven't I?"

"Please," Zabarnowski said. "I fly Hurricane."

"No, no, no. You don't like Hurricane. You like *Spitfire*. Look, I made a note of it. See?" Barton showed them his scribble on the paper. "You don't want to fly a Hurricane. You're getting confused now. It's the language. Don't worry, I know what you want."

"No, no!" Haducek protested. "Hurricane is good, is –"

"Look, I'll get the adj to type it out for you, okay?" Barton said firmly. "Then you'll understand. The main thing is you're grounded." He picked up the phone. "That's all," he told them.

They saluted and went out. As he shut the door, Zabarnowski gave Barton a look of simple murder.

"Bloody good show," Kellaway said. "It's about time someone sorted their hash." He swivelled the piece of paper and read out: "*Athlete's Foot: Instructions for the Treatment of*. Most appropriate . . . Your replacement pilots should be here in the morning, if not tonight. Sergeant-pilots. Volunteer Reservists."

"Good." Barton replaced the phone. "The trouble with Zab and Haddy is they're so much older than the others. What's Zab? Twenty-five? He's ancient, he looks like Nim Renouf's uncle. CH3's just as old, I know, but he doesn't look it."

"He's beginning to."

"Is he? He was certainly behaving in a very elderly way this morning."

"What was he doing?"

"Worrying. Now you come to mention it, he's lost a bit of weight, hasn't he?"

"A trifle gaunt, perhaps."

"He's certainly not as much fun as he used to be. I used to be

515

able to relax with him and forget everything. Now he makes me feel ... what's the word? Irresponsible."

"Why? Because you're not worrying as much as he is?" Kellaway laughed. "*Not* worrying is half the battle, Fanny."

"I know, but ..." The phone rang and he answered it. "What a bind," he said. "Yes. No. Thanks." He hung up. "That was Flip," he said. "Flash is on his way over. He's told everyone he's coming to kill me."

"Well, just you watch out that he doesn't try. Last night he went around saying he was going to kill the Secretary of State for Air."

"And did he?"

"Couldn't find him. Said the bugger kept dodging him, hiding in the lavatories. Flash got fed-up in the end, went off and played ping-pong."

"Flash is amazingly keen on killing people nowadays ... Anyway, the thing I was saying about Zab and Haddy." Barton knuckled his eyes, and blinked to get rid of the fireworks. "All that bitching and binding about the kites was beginning to get through. Hanging about the satellite gives too much time to think. Someone says the kites are duff and you sit there looking at the bloody things, wondering if he's right."

"Know what you mean," the adjutant said. "I remember people went in fear and trembling of the Camel for a while. They said it would spin if you looked at it sideways. Definitely couldn't be aerobatted, that was certain death. So everyone flew it very straight and level, until one day some bright spark took off and stunted his Camel all over the sky with the greatest of ease."

"End of rumour."

"End of several Camel pilots first, I'm sorry to say."

Flash Gordon came in without knocking. "I don't like this war," he said. "It doesn't suit me. Have you got the same thing, only in pink?" He was trailing a cricket bat.

"Your fly's undone, Flash," the adjutant said.

"Ah!" Flash said slyly. "Got my secret weapon in there. Show you later, if you're nice."

Barton said: "D'you want something?"

Flash became very serious. "What would you do," he asked, "if you shot down a Jerry and he baled out and landed in the middle of the aerodrome?"

"Take him to the mess and buy him a drink," Kellaway said promptly. "That's what we always did."

"Waste of beer." Flash flourished the bat.

"Pinch his watch?" Barton suggested.

"What for? It's bust."

"Flash," Kellaway said, "is this a trick question?"

"Certainly not. No trick about it, just plain commonsense. How can you possibly buy the bastard a beer, or pinch his watch, when I've just smashed his body to a bloody pulp? I mean, be reasonable." Flash uttered a soft, scornful laugh.

"Is that what the bat's for?" Barton asked.

"Watch this." Flash, looking serious, tapped the floor, and suddenly whirled the bat in a circle, just missing the light fixture and bashing the floor with such power that both his feet came off the ground.

Kellaway and Barton flinched at the blow.

"Shit!" Flash said. "Now look what you've made me go and do." The handle of the bat was badly bent. "You ought to see about that floor, Fanny. It's damn dangerous."

"So are you, chum. I got a message you were coming over to shoot me, or something. You've really got to stop talking like that, Flash, before you get into trouble."

Flash said: "I wouldn't shoot you, Fanny." Kellaway stared: he could swear there were tears in Gordon's eyes. "*But*," Flash said, reaching inside his open fly, "I *can* blow you up, and believe me this is *dynamite*." He pulled out a letter and tossed it onto the desk.

"Oh, Flash," Kellaway groaned. "Grow up."

"It's from Hermann Goering," Flash protested. "Is it all right if the *Luftwaffe* comes over next week? RSVP."

Barton was reading the letter. "It's from Sticky Stickwell," he told the adjutant. "Something to do with bills and money. Bloody awful handwriting." He stuffed the letter into the envelope and flipped it back. "Buzz off, you berk."

"If you haven't got pink," Flash said, "I might consider mauve." He went out.

Barton and Kellaway got up and examined the dent in the floor. It was remarkably deep. "That's enough," Barton said. "He's got to be looked at. Get a head-doctor organised, uncle."

Someone tapped on the door. "Christ!" Barton said. "I'll never get a bath at this rate. Come in!"

It was Steele-Stebbing. He was carrying his flying-boots and his helmet, holding them very carefully. "May I have a word with you, sir?"

"Make it snappy. I'm starving."

He shook the boots. The sound of muted slopping was heard. "I wanted you to see the evidence, sir, before I take action. When it was time to leave the satellite this afternoon I found that someone had half-filled my boots with cold tea. I also found that the inside of my helmet had been smeared with jam."

Kellaway went over and looked into the helmet. "Raspberry," he reported.

"All right, I've seen the evidence," Barton said. "What's this about taking action? Are you planning to get an injunction, or something?"

"No sir. I'm planning to hit him."

Barton tidied up his desk, squaring off the piles of paper and sweeping some odds and ends into a drawer. "I see," he said. "What with?"

"Well, sir, that's the problem. I'm quite strong and I did box for my school, so I could simply punch him, very hard, for instance on the nose. That might be enough to discourage him."

Kellaway sat with his feet up and his pipe going nicely. He was enjoying this curious discussion. Steele-Stebbing sounded as restrained and reasonable as ever, but there was a glint of resolution in his eyes that was new.

"What's all this got to do with me?" Barton asked.

"If I hit him hard enough, sir, I might break a finger." Steele-Stebbing went to the window and emptied his boots. "I'd almost certainly break his nose. That would put two pilots temporarily out of action."

"Ah. Very thoughtful of you."

"Or I could hit him with something. Flash Gordon's cricket bat, for example. That would leave me fully operational."

"No," Barton said firmly. "Definitely not. Out of the question. You must not, repeat not, bash Flying Officer Cattermole with a cricket bat."

"Or with anything else," Kellaway added.

"I quite see that it would inconvenience you, sir," Steele-Stebbing said, "but he is considerably inconveniencing me, and it's got to stop."

"Then find another way. I won't allow Cattermole to be damaged."

"Have you any suggestions, sir?"

Barton looked at the adjutant. "Treat it like a military exercise, old boy," Kellaway advised. "Find his weak spot and exploit it."

Steele-Stebbing nodded, and went out.

Kellaway said: "I never knew such a man for scruples. He's got scruples the way I've got piles." Barton laughed. "You wait," Kellaway said. "One day you won't find it so funny."

Next day the squadron flew down to Bodkin Hazel at first light. The sky was a stony grey and there was fog about, but the forecast was for clear weather moving in from the west. The dew was so heavy that the pilots' boots glistened. They carried their parachutes into the crewroom: if silk got damp it stuck to itself. They sprawled in armchairs, yawned, waited for the cooks to bring tea and coffee. It was the emptiest hour, gutless, neither black night nor full day, and most of them had been on a pub-crawl the previous evening. Conversation was thin. Even Flash Gordon was silent.

Fanny Barton put away the typewritten notes the Ops Officer had given him and looked at his pilots. Not a very dashing lot. Mother Cox was dozing, with his mouth open; Flash was picking at a boil on the back of his neck; Pip was chewing on his nails while he looked at a stain on the wall. Cattermole was gingerly prodding himself in the stomach and trying to belch. Flip Moran was watching Cattermole. The new boys looked as if they'd just finished a hard day's work. Only Fitz was actually doing anything. He was reading a boy's comic, the *Hotspur*. By the strain in his eyes it was hard work.

"Two things," Barton announced. "Ops tell me there's a lot of radio traffic going on across the Channel, far more than usual. So we might get some trade at any moment. The other point is Ju-88's. Jerry's started sending more and more of them over and we've got to be very careful because they look just like Blenheims. What's the difference?" he asked Renouf; but Renouf, still dozy, could only blink. "Iron Filings?" Barton said.

Steele-Stebbing had the answer: "Junkers 88 has a big, bumpy glass-house, sir. Blenheim's nose is more streamlined. Also the Blenheim's got a dorsal gun-turret."

"Right. And for Christ's sake make sure any 109 you fire at really is a 109 and not a Hurricane. About a week ago some frightfully keen type in a Spitfire shot down a poor bloody Hurricane from 56 squadron. If any one of you ever does anything like that, he needn't come back here again."

"The big difficulty is a tail-chase," Moran said. "From dead astern the 109 looks very much like a Hurricane so it's essential to be sure of the differences, which Mr Macfarlane knows backwards, I expect."

"It's got those tail-struts, hasn't it?" Macfarlane said. "The 109 has, I mean."

"And what if Messerschmitts decide to modify it and remove the tail-struts?" Barton said. "Does that make it a Hurricane?"

"You can always see the radiator scoop under a Hurricane, sir," Steele-Stebbing said, "whereas the 109 has a relatively smooth belly."

Hot drinks arrived. "Tomorrow I want this stuff ready when we land," Barton told the cook, "not fifteen minutes later." He nodded to CH3. "Over to you," he said. "Don't waste your time trying to sell them life insurance, they all look as if they died in the night."

"Okay. This is a trick question," CH3 announced. "What is the most dangerous moment in any patrol? Think about it."

Nobody was in a hurry to answer. Eventually Cox said: "It must be when you run out of ammo."

"I said *any* patrol. Including one where you don't fire your guns."

"Strikes me the most dangerous time has to be the interception," Fitzgerald said. "I mean, that's obvious. Nothing trick about that."

"Any other offers?"

"It sometimes gets a bit lively in the locker room afterwards," Cattermole said, rubbing his knuckles.

Laughter, jeers, raspberries. The tea and coffee were starting to work.

"Any more?" CH3 said. "Okay. The answer is that *any* time during a patrol is the most dangerous time. From take-off to landing you're liable to get bounced at any moment. Start looking

520

for Jerry as soon as you're airborne, and don't stop looking until you're down again."

Barton said: "Jerry's only twenty-thirty miles away. He can pop up anywhere, any time."

"That's not fairytales, either," Flip Moran said. "I was in hospital with a fellah who was about ten seconds from touching down at Manston when he got bounced. He ended up making a three-point landing, only each point was about fifty yards apart."

"You said it was a catch question," Macfarlane told CH3. "Where's the catch?"

"There isn't one. That's the catch. The catch is there's no catch. No rules, no referee. Whatever happens, you get what you deserve. Up there the world is divided into bastards and suckers. Make your choice."

Macfarlane stared. The telephone shrilled. As Barton reached for it, the scramble klaxon on the control tower began its mechanical bray. " 'A' flight!" Barton called. CH3 paused at the door. "Patrol Dymchurch, angels ten," Barton shouted. CH3 waved, and ran.

Macfarlane was twisting his neck to look behind him the instant his wheels were up. CH3 had startled him, frightened him, made him realise that almost everything he had put his trust in was false. Macfarlane had joined the RAF confident that British was best and life in a fighter squadron would be merry and bright, rather like being in the school rugby team the year they won every match, only a damn sight more exciting, of course, with plenty of bloody good scraps and a sporting chance of going out in a burst of glory, which didn't worry him too much because who wanted to live for ever anyway? What bothered him now, as CH3 led the flight eastwards, climbing hard, was this horrible fear of being jumped and killed, bang, dead, all over before he knew it. Everyone expected to be attacked, that was reasonable, but somehow Macfarlane had imagined he'd always get a chance: someone would shout a warning on the R/T, or ... Or something. But it wasn't like that at all. The sky was huge and full of risk. A speck of dirt on your windscreen could turn into an enemy fighter in the time it took to look round and back again. A little smear on your goggles might hide the plane that was coming in to kill you.

Macfarlane searched. He quartered the sky and examined it section by section, stretching his neck to look from extreme left

521

rear to extreme right rear, with no reward at the end except to start again. What made it wearying was the utter absence of anything to look at. His eyes were labouring to focus on an object that wasn't there, and they tired of this thankless drudgery, until Macfarlane caught himself slacking and sudden fright drove him back to hunt the enemy who, given just such a moment of slackness, could kill him dead.

The patrol lasted an hour and a half. The raid they were scrambled to intercept turned back; they were then vectored up and down Kent in search of another raid that also disappeared; finally, as they were running short of fuel, they saw a couple of high flying Dorniers and watched them go. The flight landed without having fired a shot. Macfarlane was so tired that he just sat in his cockpit and let everything relax: body, mind, emotions.

The pedals twitched under his boots and he jerked awake. It was CH3, shaking the rudder. "Bloody dull, wasn't it?" CH3 said. "Sorry about that. Never mind, it's only seven o'clock. Plenty of time for business to pick up." Macfarlane felt slightly sick.

The two sergeant-pilots flew in while the squadron was having breakfast. Their names were Verrier and Brook. Barton allocated one to each flight. As reservists they had accumulated a lot of flying time but this was their first operational posting. Barton told them to stick to their section leader like glue, keep their eyes open, learn fast and do nothing stupid. "I don't care if you don't fire your guns for a week," he said. "Just survive." They nodded, but he had a feeling they didn't fully understand.

The sun was up and the sky had cleared. Skylarks sang high above the fields around the aerodrome, and swifts and swallows rocketed over the grass, showing off their split-ass turns. When the pilots came out there was a butterfly resting on the brightly striped canvas of a deckchair. "Get off," Cattermole ordered. It raised and lowered its brilliant wings, drying them in the sun. "You are trespassing on Air Ministry property," Cattermole said. "I can have you shot for that." The butterfly waved its antennae, fine as gold thread. "Please yourself," Cattermole said, and sat on it. When Cox protested, he said: "It was a German butterfly. I expect it landed by U-boat during the night. You should be grateful.

522

Given half a chance, it would have ripped your throat out. They starve them for days on end, you know. I remember –"

"Okay, settle down," Barton said.

"Rip your throat out *and* kick your teeth in," Cattermole whispered to Cox.

"R/T procedure," Barton announced.

"Ever counted their feet?" Cattermole hissed.

"Moggy, shut up," Barton said. "I want to make sure everyone understands and follows the same R/T procedure, otherwise we'll end up in the clag."

Flash Gordon raised his hand. Barton nodded. "I've been thinking," Flash said seriously. "The average human adult contains eleven pints of blood. I mean, I know that for a fact. Eleven pints."

"Seems reasonable. Now the jargon –"

"Yes, but the thing is, Fanny, if you clobber an Me-110 it's got a crew of two, so that's twenty-two pints of blood, isn't it? Double."

"No doubt about it."

Flash's eyes were bright, and he leaned forward in his chair. "Twenty-two pints," he said, "is over two-and-a-half gallons. That's a lot of blood, Fanny."

"It certainly is."

Flash sat back, looking satisfied. "I thought it was worth mentioning, that's all. I mean, some of the other chaps might not have realised . . ." He smiled at Verrier. "Would you have guessed two-and-a-half gallons?" Verrier shook his head.

"Save it, Flash," Flip Moran said.

"And it's hot, too," Flash told him. "It steams when it comes out. I've seen it steam. You get a lot of steam off two-and-a-half gallons."

"Jargon," Barton said loudly. "Make sure you know it. Speed jargon: liner, buster, gate. Liner means cruising speed, save your fuel. Buster means maximum normal speed. Gate means you pull the tit and put the throttle through the emergency gate. Liner, buster, gate. Don't forget. Next –"

The scramble klaxon began its bray.

It was 'B' flight's turn. They were up for an hour. Nothing. Snowball found three raids for them, one off Beachy Head and two between Tonbridge and Maidstone, but the plots all faded and were lost. The sun was climbing, and by the time the flight returned to base Flip Moran's eyes felt bruised and sticky. "Jesus," he said to Barton, "I wish Ops wouldn't do that. Either Jerry was there and we didn't see him, or he wasn't and we did all that for nothing."

"How was . . ." Barton had to search for the name. "Villiers."

"Verrier. He was okay. Bit clumsy with his throttle, kept jumping backwards and forwards. Flash acted peculiar."

"Yes? how?"

"He began flying inverted. Fitz asked him what he was up to. He said he was having a bit of a rest. He said Jerry couldn't see him, not with his blue side up, he was invisible."

"Flash is getting worse. I'm having a trick-cyclist look at him."

Moran's heavy face, with its black bar of a moustache, stiffened. "And what good d'you think that will do?" he asked. The question answered itself by its own suppressed anger.

Oh Christ, Barton thought, *here we go again*. "It'll give us a specialist medical opinion," he said, and although he meant to speak calmly the words came out too fast, a parry to Moran's thrust.

"You can be a damned idiot sometimes, Fanny." Moran waited while a Hurricane taxied past, bouncing jauntily on its widespread undercarriage. "What is this fellah going to say? Flash is sane? Where does that take you? Or Flash is mad? We know that already. D'you think you can make him sane by chopping him? Or what?"

"How the blazes do I know what he's going to say?" Barton looked away, trying to force his irritation to subside. "Anyway, I don't see why you have to be so bloody awkward about it."

"Flash is in my flight. I'm his flight commander."

"And I'm in charge of the squadron."

"So I've been told."

"Have you? Good. Because it's more than a report, it's a fact. If you can't live with it –"

"Me? I can live with anything. I lived with the Ram, I lived with Rex, I've got the scars to prove it. I got the scars, you got the stripes."

"You want a squadron, is that it?" Barton had to shout because another Hurricane was taxiing by, but he wanted to shout anyway. "Then why don't you bloody well say so?"

"What? And deprive you of the pleasure of giving me orders? Don't be so stupid."

Barton stopped and watched Moran walk on. Part of him was furious but another part felt deeply sorry for the man. They both knew that Moran would make a lousy squadron commander. His self-pity was a new and unattractive measure of this. And by showing self-pity he had isolated himself even more. Barton had an impulse to go after him and say something to make good, rebuild Moran's confidence, assure him that he was an excellent flight commander (which he was), that this bickering was stupid. He called: "Hey, Flip!" Maybe the roar of the Hurricane was still too loud. Maybe not. Moran didn't respond, and Barton wasn't prepared to ask twice. Instead, he sought out CH3.

"If you were me," Barton said, "what would you do?"

CH3 sat on his heels and worried about it. "Flip doesn't really give a damn about Flash seeing this doctor," he said. "He's just using it to needle you."

"But why? What did I ever do to Flip?"

"Dunno. You want me to ask him?"

The honest answer was yes. "No, I can handle it," Barton said, and walked away. Discussing one flight commander with another made him feel uncomfortable. He couldn't afford to create even the impression of favouritism. So now Moran's sourness had made him keep his distance from CH3. Barton felt victimised.

The day became hot, with a breeze so slight that it scarcely moved the windsock. Before noon all the deckchairs had been shifted into the shade of some apple-trees beside the crewroom. There was a faint but constant clatter of reapers and binders in the nearby fields, and horsedrawn wagons rumbled along a lane beyond the perimeter wire. Grasshoppers chirped The sky was a clear, cornflower-blue overhead, shading to a dusty white at the shimmering horizon. It looked like the start of a long, settled spell.

Half the pilots were playing cricket, using Flash Gordon's wonky bat and a split tennis ball. The others were dozing in armchairs.

Cox adjusted a cushion.

"By the way, Pip," he said, "I'm moving in with you tonight, so wash your feet, will you?"

"What's happening to Haddy?"

"He's sharing with Zab. The adj has arranged it all, thank God.

Very boring, living with a bloke who keeps on saying 'Is cock-up.' "

"Does Zab really wear silk stockings?" Macfarlane asked. "And a hairnet?"

Cox nodded. "According to Skull it's not uncommon in Poland. He said some men even use scent and lipstick."

Groans of disgust and revulsion. "What a lot of fairies!" Macfarlane said. "We don't want them on our side, do we?"

"Steady on, young Bing," Cattermole said gently. His eyes were closed and his arms dangled to the grass. "I happen to know that Steele-Stebbing wears camiknickers and plucks his eyebrows."

"Balls!" Macfarlane said.

Steele-Stebbing was reading the *Daily Telegraph*. He raised it another inch or so.

"Perhaps," Cattermole said. "One must give Steele-Stebbing the benefit of the doubt in that area. What is quite certain is that he applies just the merest touch of rouge to his nipples."

The *Daily Telegraph* rustled as Steele-Stebbing tightened his grip.

Patterson said: "What a wonderful father you'll make, Moggy. Cold and hard outside, but underneath it all a heart of pure lead."

"Father?" Cox said. "Have you ruined some popsy, Mog?"

"Legions," Cattermole told him, and stretched. "Myriads. Armies of the dear things. I impregnated half the womanhood of France, and I try to bring a little bliss to the local ladies as often as my professional commitments allow. Speaking of regularity . . ." He levered himself up. "If anyone wants me, I shall be in the library." He strolled past Steele-Stebbing, snatched his newspaper and set off for the portable lavatory, reading the headlines aloud. Steele-Stebbing leaned back and shut his eyes, but his hands were fists.

It was twenty minutes before Cattermole came out. By then, Steele-Stebbing had gone for a walk. Patterson watched Cattermole drop into a deckchair and sigh with satisfaction. "You really are a shit, aren't you?" Patterson said.

"I don't know what makes you say that, Pip. You and I are old pals. We flew under the same bridge, remember?"

"I never flew under the sodding thing," Patterson muttered. "That's on your conscience, not mine."

"What bridge?" Cox asked sharply. "Are you talking about old ... What the hell was his name?"

"Dicky Starr," Patterson mumbled. "Poor bastard."

"Why, what happened?" Macfarlane asked. But none of them answered, and when he looked at Cattermole, Cattermole stared back.

Lunch came: sausage and mash, with rice pudding. Sector Ops called up in the middle of lunch and White Section – Cox and Macfarlane – got sent off, only to be recalled before they were out of sight. They landed and sat down again, but Macfarlane could not eat. His ears were straining to hear the faint preliminary click of the Tannoy, or the first ting of the telephone. If someone tapped a plate with a knife, he jumped.

Fanny Barton got a fresh mug of tea and took Flip Moran aside. "I don't know why I'm drinking this," he said. "I'll be bursting in half an hour if we have to go up."

"Then don't drink the bloody stuff."

"Thanks very much." Barton chucked it away. "You're a great help, Flip. I don't need to piss all over myself. You're always ready to do it for me." That was supposed to be a light remark, humorous even, something to ease the tension; but when Barton heard the words they sounded more like a complaint. Moran said nothing. "What I mean is, we've got to work together," Barton explained, or tried to explain. "If I'm doing something wrong, for God's sake tell me."

"Waste of time."

"Try."

Moran heaved a deep breath. "Very well. I didn't ask for this sprog sergeant you've dumped on me. I don't want him. He's bloody useless."

Barton was taken aback. "Wait a minute. Verrier's no worse than Brook." Moran looked away. "I don't get it, Flip," Barton said. "What d'you want me to do?"

"Get him out of my flight. I'll take Mother Cox, and your hot-shot senior flight commander can have Verrier to play with."

"But CH3's already got Brook."

"Look," Moran said, "I didn't ask you to ground Zab. Zab's a bloody good pilot." His voice rasped like a file. "I don't see why I should pay the penalty for your fun and games. It's –"

"Come on, come on! Be sensible. Zab and Haddy were fucking up the whole squadron. If I —"

"You fucked up this squadron. Not them."

Barton walked ten paces, turned, walked back again. "I can't switch Verrier with Cox," he said. "It's not on."

"See? Waste of time," Moran said. "I told you so."

"Oh, Christ, Flip," Barton said. "You're never happy unless you're bloody losing, are you?"

"That's what makes Hornet such a joyous squadron," Moran said gloomily.

Barton found CH3 again and told him what Moran wanted.

"No," CH3 said. "That's not it either. He's using the Cox-and-Verrier business to needle you some more."

"He's asking for trouble, then. What on earth's wrong with the man?"

"Maybe he's got twitch."

"Flip Moran? Twitch? Don't be ridiculous. He's strong as a bull."

An hour later, Sector Ops called and put them on five-minute standby, almost immediately shortened to two-minute standby, which meant being fully dressed, including Mae West and parachute. It was baking hot. For ten minutes everyone dripped sweat and complained. The scramble was almost a relief.

Barton led the squadron. CH3 moved to Yellow Section with Cattermole as his wingman, which meant that Sergeant Brook stayed behind. The flights were staggered, with 'B' flight to the rear and slightly up-sun, and the sections were widespread, like a search party. Within ten minutes they were at fifteen thousand feet over Ashford, twenty miles north of Bodkin Hazel, and the controller was warning them that the raid was approaching from the south-east, twenty-plus bandits, heading north-west. Fanny Barton acknowledged. He wriggled his shoulders to loosen his shirt, now sticky with cold sweat, and his glance flickered across the cockpit, taking in the bank of dials and gauges, checking the gunsight was on and the gun-safety was off. He looked up and changed focus.

"Hullo, Mango Leader, this is Snowball. Bandits now twenty-five plus." He sounded a little impatient.

"Okay, Snowball." Barton wondered what happened to all these

528

phantom plots. Did some other squadron shoot them down, or did they never exist? They couldn't all be Blenheims or Defiants. It seemed amazingly easy to lose a gaggle of German bombers over England. Half the scrambles failed to lead to an interception. "Yellow Two to Leader," said Cattermole in the curious light-tenor that VHF produced, and as he spoke, Barton saw them for himself: "Bandits at five o'clock."

Barton gave Snowball the tally-ho. Snowball wished him luck.

There was absolutely nothing to do except wait. If both formations held their course and speed, the German aircraft would pass the Hurricanes quite soon, thus allowing Fanny to swing his squadron behind them and chop away with a series of stern attacks.

The sprinkle of dots grew thin wings. The crosses made a delicate pattern that grew and put on weight. "Heinkels and Dorniers," Barton said. "A dozen of each." He twisted his head and searched the sky on the other side: stupid to watch the right and get jumped from the left. Nothing there. "Black One to Leader, the escort's arrived, one-one-oh's, high." That was Fitz. He sounded matter-of-fact but Barton knew better. Fitz's heart would be banging away like a boy-scout drum. "Okay," Barton said.

The bombers were bustling along at a brisk pace. Soon they developed filigree gun-barrels and radio masts, insignia, numbers, letters, the shining discs of propellers, yellow spinners, wisps of exhaust smoke fleeing the outthrust engines. For the new pilots it was their first close sight of a German bomber formation and they found it impressively disciplined: neat, tight vics of three, the Dorniers stepped up behind the Heinkels, and all storming across Kent as if they didn't give a damn who owned it. The older pilots – CH3, Moggy, Flip, Mother, Flash, Pip, Fitz – saw things differently. Most of them were watching the bombers with one eye and the escort with the other. At least twenty Me-110's, coming on fast.

Barton let the bombers charge past. They were over half a mile to the right of the nearest Hurricane. The top-gunner in a Heinkel fired a few rounds, probably testing his gun. "Buster, buster," Barton ordered, and opened the throttle wide. "Turning right, turning right, go." The squadron banked and slid behind the bombers, hit their turbulence and began to bounce. "Going up," Barton said. "Throttle back." They eased above the lumpy air and he saw, far away, beyond the leading Heinkels, a solitary Hurricane. Strange. " 'B' flight hits the right side, 'A' flight hits the left," he said. "Go!"

The German stepped-up formation was intelligent. It offered almost every plane a degree of covering fire from the top-gunners of the rank below and the belly gunners of the rank above. Barton couldn't avoid them so he gave them a difficult deflection shot. He dived through the slipstream and turned sharply away from the bombers so that when he climbed back at them he was coming at their flank, slanting hard across the German gunsights, forcing them to rush their aim. Red and yellow tracer pulsed out of the Dorniers in fits and starts, like cartoon Morse-code. Barton touched his gun-button four times in five seconds. Each time, he saw a bomber shake, but the vibration was all in his head, trembling from the force of the manoeuvre and the judder of the guns, and he half-rolled clear and raced away without knowing if he had scored.

To his surprise, Steele-Stebbing was hard behind him.

Pairs of Hurricanes were bouncing off the raid high and low. Smoke dribbled from a tail-end Dornier. The wheels of another Dornier suddenly swung down. It dropped out of formation and hung fifty feet below the others, nose up, straining for height, failing. Stray shouts and whoops came over the R/T, but the only voice that Barton recognised was Flip Moran's, cursing his wingman, Verrier. He searched for the Me-110's and found them still so far away that he called Steele-Stebbing: "Leader to Red Two, stick tight, we'll make another pass." But as he began his approach he saw an extraordinary thing.

The lone Hurricane, last seen far ahead of the raid, now charged it head-on. Fire flickered from the nose-guns of the leading Heinkels: too little, too late. At the last instant the Hurricane dropped its right wing and sliced vertically between the bombers. Barton caught flashing glimpses of it as first Heinkels and then Dorniers veered and dodged and swerved. The Hurricane spat itself out of the rear of the shattered formation like a backfire. It was all over before Barton could draw breath. It was the most astonishing thing he had ever seen. A Heinkel came wallowing towards him. He sprayed it and went switchbacking through the disintegrating remains of the raid, stabbing his thumb on the button, until the sky was empty again and he dragged the nose hard towards the south, the sun, the oncoming 110's.

They came streaming down like skiers off a mountain.

Moran was still swearing at Verrier. It was a waste of breath. Verrier's radio had stopped several bullets. The same burst had taken out his port aileron and made a mess of his left shoulder. This was not the result of brilliant German shooting: Verrier had bungled his controls – got his revs wrong, put his prop in the wrong pitch, skidded and sidled and nearly stalled the bloody plane – until it was an almost unmissable target. He wasn't incompetent, just very jumpy. When the attack began, his muscles went rigid and his hands and feet trembled. Everything started coming at him too fast: Moran's curses and commands, the surging bombers, the belting tracer. He did one thing wrong and that made another thing worse and then the bullets ripped home and everything was agonisingly bad. The wind came raging through his smashed side-windows, caught the blood that was pumping out of his shoulder and gushing down his arm and sprayed it around; and when he looked up he saw a whole new squadron of Me-110's falling on him. Even Moran had stopped speaking. "Oh, Christ," he prayed, "please help, please help, please . . ."

Moran kept trying to chase him, this nineteen-year-old idiot swanning about as if he wanted to get killed; but there were gunners trying to kill Moran, too, and when the 110's joined in the battle he gave up the chase. Then the bombers started to regroup, counting on their fighters to keep the Hurricanes busy, and the next time Moran saw Verrier he was getting hammered by a pair of 110's that were crisscrossing behind him and knocking hell out of the Hurricane. Moran fired at long range and one of them sheered away; he closed on the other and hit it as it blasted yet more chunks off Verrier. They were three in a row now, hunter on hunter on victim, and Moran was hunched forward, body strained against his straps, swearing in a harsh scream, obsessed with his kill, so obsessed that he failed to see the 110 that made it four in a row.

He was shot in the legs: maiming, bone-smashing wounds. A cannonshell exploded in front of his face and blinded him. More cannonshells walloped great holes in the instrument panel, the bulkhead, the petrol tank. Fuel gushed over his broken legs. All this in less than a second. One moment Flip Moran was intact, vengeful, furious; the next he was crippled, blinded, awash in petrol. And the next moment he was burning.

The last piece of equipment to fail was his radio. Moran had left his channel open to curse Verrier. Now, everyone in Hornet squadron heard him scream. The Hurricane flew itself, more or less level, for quite a long time, and the flames worked their way quite slowly up his legs. He screamed as he felt for the cockpit release that his eyes could not see, and he screamed as he tried to make his broken legs escape the fire that was eating them. Eventually the Hurricane performed a slow roll, the whole cockpit was soaked in petrol, and Moran's screaming came to an end when there was no air to breathe and the furnace roasted his face.

Debriefing.

Skull spent his days at Bodkin Hazel now. He took their reports, one at time.

Two definite kills were claimed. Cattermole said he destroyed a Heinkel 111 and CH3 said he shot down a Messerschmitt 110. Macfarlane claimed a probable Dornier and Fitzgerald a probable 110: both planes had last been seen going down with much smoke coming out and large bits falling off. Everyone else bar Steele-Stebbing claimed to have damaged at least one enemy aircraft.

Too bad about Flip. That was a damn bad show. Most of them had seen a burning Hurricane tip over and fall, and they all reckoned then that somebody had bought it. It really was a damn shame. He must have caught a hell of a packet. Someone saw him just before he blew up, and he was fighting like a maniac, an absolute maniac. Then, suddenly, bingo.

Skull, however, had news of Verrier. Miraculously, he had baled out and fallen in the middle of a small aerodrome, a training field. They telephoned Brambledown and Brambledown told Skull. Actually, he hadn't so much baled out as discovered himself in mid-air when his Hurricane broke in half. He'd landed badly and snapped both ankles and a collarbone, on top of which his left shoulder was a terrible mess. So that's Verrier, that was.

Bloody good scrap.

Too bad about Flip.

And it was still only three o'clock.

They got scrambled again at ten to five and chased half a dozen

Junkers 88's from Maidstone to Dover without catching them. Patterson got hit in the tail by Dover ack-ack and had to put down at Hawkinge airfield.

Stand-down at eight; return to Brambledown, eight-twenty. Almost the end of a rich, full day.

Kellaway banged on Barton's bedroom door. "Fanny?" he called. He knew he was in there: he could hear the radio. Somebody's band was playing *Oh, Johnny*, very loudly. He banged again and went in. The music blasted at him, so loud that half the notes distorted. The volume must have been turned up full. Barton sat astride a reversed chair, his back to the door. He was reading *Picture Post*, or at least he was turning the pages. He didn't look up until Kellaway touched his shoulder, and then he started so sharply that he tore a page.

"Daddy's asking for you," Kellaway shouted. Barton looked blankly. Kellaway switched the radio off. "How can you stand that din?" he asked.

"What?" Barton said.

Kellaway tapped his ears.

"Oh," Barton said. "I'm still a bit deaf, uncle. Altitude, I s'pose. Up and down all day. Engine noise. Ears get a bit fed-up with it."

"Blow," Kellaway advised. He pinched his nose and puffed his cheeks. Barton did the same. "Ow!" he exclaimed. He stuck his little finger in his ears and waggled them about. "Bit better ... Can you hear a sort of buzz? No? Must be me, then."

"Aren't you going to have something to eat, old boy?"

Barton picked up the *Picture Post* and tried to straighten the torn page. The torn bit kept falling out, so he pulled it off, screwed it up, threw it away. "Who's going to be 'B' flight commander?" he asked.

"You ought to get changed, Fanny." Barton was still in flying kit. "Have a bit of a wash. Freshen up."

"Moggy's the best pilot."

The adjutant sat on the bed and took out his pipe. "Well," he said.

"He's also the biggest shit."

"No argument there."

"That leaves Pip, Mother, Fitz and Flash."

"Pip won't do. He's got no oomph, has he? You want a chap with a bit of oomph."

"Christ, uncle, my ears hurt." Barton took off his Irvine jacket and sat on the bed. The adjutant began filling his pipe. He was wondering whether to suggest a hot shower, or a quick drink and then a hot shower. Alternatively ... The bed started to rock. It was shaking so much that he couldn't get the tobacco in the bowl. "Listen, I know it's your bed," he said, and realised that Barton was crying.

His head was down and his body was bent like a question-mark, with his arms hugging his ribs, and the sobs were coming almost faster than his lungs could deliver them. His face had collapsed into the ugliness of misery. Tears did not improve its appearance. Kellaway carefully put his pipe on the bedside table. In all his time in the Royal Flying Corps and the Royal Air Force he had seen plenty of men cry. He had never found the sight anything but repugnant. Just when a chap most needed help and sympathy, God made him look like a baboon. "Come on, Fanny, you can't blame yourself," he said. "It wasn't your fault. These things happen in war. Always have, always will. It's the luck of the draw." Kellaway didn't hurry, didn't put any great stress on the words. He'd been through it before so often. You had to say something, you had to make reassuring noises, but the poor blighter never really took any of it in at first. "Anyway," Kellaway said, "it could have been worse, couldn't it? By all reports it was all over pretty quickly. I mean, look at it this way: he went the way he'd have wanted to go. Slam-bang-wallop, over and out. Right?"

Barton raised his contorted, shiny face and said, "What the hell are you talking about?"

"Flip. Poor old Flip."

"Oh, balls! Bloody Moran went and bought it. So what?"

"Well, exactly. You mustn't blame –"

"Shut up about Moran! Who cares? I mean, who gives a tiny damn? Look at that, uncle!"

The adjutant looked at Barton's Irvine jacket. A short, brown furrow ran across the left side, just below the armpit. "Bullet streak," he said. Barton had stopped crying. His breathing was getting under control. "Did you just notice this?" Kellaway asked. "When you took it off?" Barton got up and walked to a corner of the room. "Came as a bit of a shock, I expect," Kellaway said. "I mean, you don't need a lot of imagination, do you?" Barton bent down and picked up the torn piece of *Picture Post*. "Same thing happened to me once," Kellaway said, "only it was the helmet that suffered . . . Still, a miss is as good as a mile, isn't it?"

"Don't talk such fucking rubbish."

"You're absolutely right," Kellaway said. "A miss like this one is in a class of its own." He tossed the jacket to Barton. "In fact it's worth a drink. Want a drink?"

"D'you know what Flash Gordon did, uncle?" Barton found a towel and scrubbed his face. "Flash went off on his own and charged straight through a whole gang of Jerry bombers. Head-on. In one end, out the other. Scared them shitless."

"Goodness me. Sounds very effective."

"Yes. Trouble is, he disobeyed orders. He should've stayed with Fitz, not gone blasting off on his own. What if Fitz got jumped? Flash is a maniac. He's crazy."

"Well, the specialist is coming to look at him in the morning. By the way, Daddy Dalgleish is very keen to have a word with you."

"Piss on him. Ask CH3 to sort it out. Say I'm writing letters to next-of-kin."

"Are you?"

"No fear. I'm off on the spree. It's time we had a squadron thrash. Go and round up the blokes, uncle. Tell 'em I'll buy the first round."

The adjutant gave him a long and thoughtful look. "Now? I mean, you're feeling okay again?"

"Why the hell shouldn't I?" Barton asked cheerfully. "It wasn't my fault he bought it, was it? Come on, get cracking, adj. You're like frozen treacle."

CH3 was drinking in the mess when he was called to the phone. "Popsy," Flash said, and for once he was right. The caller was Jacky Bellamy.

"I want a chance to apologise," she said. "And I also need your advice."

"I see." He looked at all the names and numbers scribbled on the wall. "Look, are you sure this is such a good idea?"

535

"No, I'm not. And look, you don't have to meet me if you don't want to."

"It's been a long time."

"About three months."

"A lot can happen in three months."

"Stop dodging. This is a pay phone and I'm out of change. Say yes or no."

Pause. "No."

"You bastard."

"Hey, hey! You didn't talk like that three months ago."

"I've changed. I've turned hard and cold and ruthless and . . ."

"Is that right? Sounds much more interesting. Okay, where do we meet?"

"Outside the main gate in ten minutes?"

She had a car. They drove a mile or so to a quiet lane, and walked down a long avenue of beech trees. It was dusk, and the air was as warm as milk.

"First off," she said, "you were right and I was wrong."

"About what?"

"Everything. Tactics, gunnery, back-armour, all the stuff you said was wrong with the Hurricane. And all I can say in defence is that I went along with the majority vote. Experts always disagree, and there comes a point when . . . Oh, forget it. I'm making excuses."

"If it makes you feel any better, I was somewhat wrong too. Turns out there's nothing much wrong with the Hurricane. It needed sorting out, that's all."

"So here we both are. Older and wiser."

They stopped to watch a pair of squirrels dash along some branches and vanish.

"Anyway, what does it matter?" he said. "It's all over and done with."

"It mattered to me. I hate getting anything wrong. I believe in taking pains and double-checking everything twice. I *hate* being caught out."

He gave an amused grunt. "So did I, once. Don't worry, you'll grow out of it."

"Stop trying to sound paternal. I'm two years older than you."

536

"Are you really?" He cocked his head and studied her face. "Prove it. Say something maternal."

"Have you got a clean handkerchief?" she asked.

He laughed. "That's very good," he said. The more he thought about it, the more he laughed; until she began laughing too. He said: "You just wrote the story of my life."

"Gee whiz. I must have been inspired, or something."

He looked away. They walked on. Old beech leaves crunched sweetly underfoot. He said, "Flip Moran bought it this afternoon."

"Dead?" She reached up to a low-hanging branch and broke off a leaf. "Dumb question . . . Well, I'm sorry. I really liked Flip."

"Yes, he had his points."

"That's not much of an epitaph. He was worth more than that."

CH3 shrugged. "Chaps are always getting the chop. It's not something to get worked up about." They reached the end of the avenue, and turned. "You said you wanted to ask my advice. What about?"

"Oh, nothing special. Statistics. RAF claims. My boss in the States wants me to check out the figures . . . Look, why did you do that, just now?"

"What?"

"You know what. One moment you're actually treating me like a human being, the next moment you're a hundred miles away, telling me Flip Moran has bought it."

He said nothing.

"I've been kissed before, you know," she said. "Even a withered old bag like me gets kissed from time to time."

"Come to that," he said, "you could have kissed me."

"Too late now. Anyway, it's not something to get worked up about, is it?"

They walked in silence to the car.

The *Spreadeagle* had been an important coaching inn, and it was spacious. The ceiling of the public bar, for instance, was fourteen feet high. To get Flash Gordon's feet on the ceiling was quite a job.

All the bar tables had been dragged into the middle of the room and stacked in a pyramid. This in itself was not easy, because the pub was crowded with locals and Spitfire pilots and a sprinkling of soldiers, and some of them had been reluctant to give up their tables. But the landlord supported the feet-on-the-ceiling idea. When Barton had walked in and said, "Thirteen pints, please," the landlord had said, "You must be Hornet squadron," and it turned out his nephew was Mother Cox's armourer.

CH3 found a man who could play the piano and he bought him a drink. Singing began. There was a slightly dangerous darts match, Hurricanes versus Spits, with a lot of insults about marksmanship. Zab and Haddy took no part in any of it. They had been ordered to come and now they stood by the fireplace and sneered into their beer. "*Jag tycker om det!*" Fitzgerald shouted at them from a safe distance, and when they scowled, others shouted it too. Fitzgerald was feeling guilty about not going home to Mary, but orders were orders, weren't they? So now he shouted twice as loudly, to make the guilt worthwhile.

They all shouted, they all barged about, pinched each other's hats, threw beermats, sang, bawled catchphrases from radio shows. Skull watched Macfarlane and Brooke stagger and howl with laughter at a joke that Cattermole had told, and he said to CH3: "It's amazing how very drunk they can get so very quickly, isn't it?"

"They're not really drunk. It's a sort of post-combat auto-intoxication, I guess."

"In celebration of life? Affirmation of survival?"

"Christ, no. Nothing so high-falutin'. They've been wound up as tight as a fiddle-string all day, so now they make whoopee. These guys could get smashed out of their minds on soda-water."

"Not that one, apparently." Skull was looking at Steele-Stebbing, who had just left the piano, having failed to join in the singing because he didn't know the words, and was now reading a brewer's calendar.

The landlord, pulling pints as he talked, said to Barton: "Tell you what. I wouldn't mind some sort of memento or souvenir. You know: something to hang on the wall. You got a squadron plaque, or a photograph or something?"

"No, nothing of that sort, I'm afraid." The landlord was disappointed. Barton looked around for inspiration. "You could always have our footprints," he said. "Like they do in Hollywood."

"That takes cement. I've got no cement, have I?"

Barton was looking at the pub ceiling. "Got any soot?" he asked.

"What? You'll never get up there," the landlord said.

"Bet you a pint we will." Barton emptied his glass.

"Hornet boys can get up anywhere," the adjutant said.

They stacked the pub tables in a three-tiered pyramid. Barton climbed to the top with half a bucket of soot that the landlord had meant for his rhubarb. CH3 handed up a chair. "Right!" Barton shouted. "Now this is a very hazardous mission, bloody dangerous in fact, because as you can see it will take you very close to your operational ceiling." He pointed upwards.

The crowd howled and groaned. "Piss-poor joke!" Cattermole roared. Cushions and beermats flew. Barton drank his beer.

"And because it's so extremely bloody dangerous," he declared, "I have decided to call for a volunteer. Where's Flash?"

Gordon was manhandled up the pyramid. He struck a dramatic pose and cried: "There was a young lady named Buckingham –"

Barton shoved him into the chair. Using an old paint brush he slathered soot onto the soles of his shoes. Gordon swung himself around until his shoulders were resting on the seat of the chair and he pressed his feet on the ceiling, to warm applause. "Now sing a song," Barton ordered. Gordon, still upside-down, sang a verse of *Stormy Weather*. "Enough!" Barton said. Gordon slid off the chair head-first and rolled down the pyramid into the arms of the crowd, spilling much beer. "Mother Cox!" Barton shouted.

Cox was followed by CH3. He made his mark and sang *Trees*, and then took over the bucket and ordered Barton up. Barton sang *Run, Rabbit*. CH3 gave him back the bucket and went down as Patterson came up. One by one the pilots stamped their sooty footprints and sang their upside-down songs until only two were left: Renouf and Steele-Stebbing. As Nim Renouf clambered up, grinning with anticipation, CH3 found Steele-Stebbing at the back of the crowd. "You're next," he said.

"I'm afraid I'm not very good at this sort of thing."

"That's not possible. Nobody can be bad at it. The worse you are, the better they like it. Got a song ready?"

"I honestly can't think of anything." He drank some beer to hide his embarrassment.

CH3 dragged down the glass, and slopped beer. "Are you trying to tell me you've never sung a song in all your long and miserable life?"

Steele-Stebbing, mopping his wrists with his handkerchief,

showed a tiny flash of anger. "There's no need to make such a fuss," he said. "If it makes you any happier I'll sing *The Red Flag*."

"Attaboy." CH3 drank his beer. "Now get up there and knock 'em dead."

But when Steele-Stebbing found himself up there with his feet on the ceiling he couldn't think of the words of *The Red Flag*, so he sang *The Eton Boating Song* instead.

To his amazement they all joined in. Hardly anybody knew the words, but they la-la-ed lustily. Then they demanded an encore so he had to sing it again. He could see their mouths opening wide and closing, and their bodies swaying in time with the easy, infectious rhythm, everyone upside-down. When they released him he was scarlet in the face, and his heart was walloping furiously. They cheered him as he stumbled down the stacked tables. His back was slapped and his hair was ruffled by cheerful strangers as he made his way to the bar.

"Well done," the landlord said. "I always liked that tune. Very catchy." Steele-Stebbing nodded. He discovered that he was grinning. It felt very odd.

Barton was still sitting on the top of the pyramid. His hands and face were more black than white. He was thinking: *It's simple, really. Not Flash. Not Pip. Not Moggy. Not Fitz, because Mary's about to produce.* "Hey, Mother!" he shouted. Cox climbed up and sat beside him. "How would you like to take over 'B' flight?" he asked.

Cox stared at him. He gestured theatrically, and sang: "I'd walk a million miles for one of those smiles . . ." Barton grabbed a handful of soot and smeared it over Cox's face. Together they sang *Mammy*. The crowd joined in. Kellaway, Skull and the landlord joined in. Even Steele-Stebbing joined in. In a corner, Cattermole was fighting a Canadian Spitfire pilot who had tried to sabotage the pyramid, but nobody paid any attention to that.

At 6.20 a.m., Group scrambled two sections to patrol Dover-Ramsgate at fifteen thousand feet. Mother Cox led the patrol in Blue Section with Renouf as his number two, plus Pip Patterson and Fitz as Green Section.

They climbed through a screen of ten-tenths cloud at six thousand and found themselves in a skyscape of Alpine purity. The blue

540

above looked freshly scrubbed, the white below rippled like a snowfield to the horizon. Cox inhaled deeply and swelled his chest, partly from pleasure, partly from pride. Hurricanes had always looked good to him: there was something slightly hunched about the fuselage, the way the engine sloped down to the prop, that gave the plane a poised and searching look. These Hurricanes looked even better to him now that he was leading them.

The controller sent them up to eighteen thousand, then to twenty-two thousand. Cox calculated when they were above Dover, and turned north. The cloud was now more than two miles below. It looked as flat and smooth as a bedsheet. It covered the Channel and London and reached far into the North Sea. Blue and Green Sections cruised at a couple of hundred miles an hour and made no visible progress at all. The world was vast and lovely and, apart from four Hurricanes, utterly empty.

After ten minutes, Cox reckoned they were over Ramsgate so he wheeled them around and flew south. It was cold at that height. His legs were getting chilled and stiff, and no matter how he adjusted his scarf, a bitter little draught kept finding his neck. He could see Fitz swinging his arms and beating his fists together while he gripped the stick with his legs. Not for the first time, Cox wondered why nobody had thought to put cockpit heating in the Hurricane.

Now that Snowball had got them up here, it seemed there was nothing to do.

They patrolled up and down for half an hour. Snowball kept in touch, but his transmissions became increasingly scratchy and sometimes they faded altogether. Cox worried: maybe he was drifting out of R/T range. Maybe there were strong winds at this height. Maybe he was getting blown out to sea. He called the others: "Stay awake, keep looking, watch your wingman, acknowledge." They came back to him in turn: Blue Two, Green Leader, Green Two. He was thinking about fuel, converting gallons into time, time into distance. Snowball called and said something blurred about a bandit. Or maybe several bandits. Cox swore. Snowball had sounded urgent, but what the shit was he urgent about? "Snowball, this is Mango Blue Leader," he said. "Your transmission garbled, say again please." Snowball came back with a mouthful of broken biscuits.

"Anybody get any of that?" Cox asked.

"Sure," Fitz answered. "He said Slush Flush Hush Slush Mush. And I agree with him."

"Keep your eyes skinned," Cox warned.

They turned again over Dover, or maybe it was Rotterdam, and steered north. A long way ahead, an aircraft emerged from the cloud and flew south, a tiny blemish travelling over the blanket of white.

Cox called Snowball and reported a bogey at angels eight. Snowball's reply died of asthma. Cox gave up on Snowball, and wondered whether or not to go down. If they went down it would be a hell of a slog to get up again. The plane was a softly pencilled cross that moved.

"Green to Blue," Patterson said. "Bogey has twin engines."

Everyone was looking down. Cox stared but he couldn't see how many engines the damn thing had. He glanced up: left, right, behind. Empty sky. He checked time, speed, fuel; and he thought: *Bloody stupid patrol. Dunno where we are, or why, or what that bastard is.* He leaned forward and stared. Now he saw the twin engines, pin-heads on the tiny cross.

"Single fin," Fitz said. "Could be a Ju-88."

"Could be a Blenheim," Cox said. "We'll wait a bit." *Wait for what?* he asked himself. *There's bugger-all up here.* All the same he repeated his automatic scan. As he searched from left to right he saw Blue Two's Hurricane drop a wing and lift its nose in a clumsy, sprawling, tail-dragging climb that could never succeed. Before Cox could touch his transmission switch the Hurricane had stalled and gone into a slow spin, flip-flopping down like an autumn leaf.

"Bandits at twelve o'clock!" someone shouted. Cox jerked his head to the front. Sunlight caught a row of prop-discs stuck on razor-thin wings. They magnified with startling speed into four Me-109's, hurtling towards the Hurricanes at the same height. Before Cox could get his thumb on the gun-button the 109's broke to their right, changing in a single flick from head-on silhouette to a flaring plan-view. "Tally-ho!" Cox shouted, too late because Fitz and Pip were already giving chase, but the tally-ho was the leader's privilege and it might never come to him again . . .

They caught the 109's quickly, and lost them even more quickly:

almost instantly, in fact. For a couple of seconds Cox laboured to drag his sights onto the enemy but the enemy drifted sideways amazingly fast, like a gull caught in a gale, and was lost. By now Cox's Hurricane was steeply canted. The giant hand of centrifugal force pressed him solidly into his seat, and the horizon unreeled itself endlessly down his windscreen. Arms and legs were braced to force the most from the controls: his stomach muscles hardened, he sucked oxygen and gasped, but no matter how he worked he could feel the Hurricane losing its grip. It was drifting outwards, skidding on the too-thin air that the German fighters grasped so easily. Cox's eyes kept flickering towards his mirror. He knew what he was going to see but nevertheless his heart kicked painfully when the 109 edged into view. Its shape trembled furiously from the vibrations of the Hurricane, creating a sense of demoniac rage that brought Cox near to panic: he desperately wanted to jink and dodge, to escape this spectre. Guns rattled and tracer raced above his starboard wing: a sighting shot. It was hugely tempting to reverse the turn, slam everything over, flip from one wingtip to the other – the worst possible move: reversing the turn took you clean across the enemy's sights. Cox hunched himself, held his turn, prayed. Bits flew off his right wing, the plane felt as if it were being kicked by an enormous horse, Cox said to himself *This can't last*, and it didn't. His Hurricane took another vicious kick and flung itself onto its back. Cox snatched the column into his stomach in a yearning for height, but since he was inverted he dived instead. The 109 lost him.

It caught him again, a couple of thousand feet below. Cox pulled the tit and slammed the throttle through the gate but he couldn't pull away from the Messerschmitt. His feet kept bashing the rudder-pedals, left-right, left-right. *Like riding a bike*, he thought stupidly; uselessly. Cramp suddenly knotted his right calf and the leg froze with pain. He forced it off the pedal and abandoned it to its agony while the left leg worked double-time. And eternally, it seemed, machine-guns rattled like noisemakers at a football match and tracer streamed around the zigzagging Hurricane. Cox felt bitter about his emergency boost, just when you needed the bloody thing it let you down. As if it heard him think, the Merlin started howling its head off and he remembered guiltily that emergency boost didn't work above twelve or fourteen thousand. At the same time the controls felt a lot better, much keener, more responsive, so he took a deep breath and got both hands on the stick and pulled hard. The Hurricane bottomed out and bounced like a rubber ball. Just before Cox blacked out he glimpsed the 109, still diving.

When he could think again, his Hurricane was hanging on its prop, screaming and wondering whether to stall. He punched home the tit, throttled back and persuaded the plane to roll onto its back. Blood rushed to his brain and his vision cleared. What he saw was the bunch of 109's diving and trailing smoke. He rolled level, searched for Hurricanes, and found two, far below him, circling a third. The third was on fire. It was making more smoke than seemed possible from one small aircraft.

By the time Cox descended they had all disappeared into cloud. When he came out below the cloud, the burning Hurricane was about to hit the sea and Nim Renouf was hanging in his parachute, about four minutes away from doing the same thing.

Cox went straight back up, switched to the Mayday channel and transmitted for a fix. Then he went down again, and they watched Renouf make his splash. The Kent coast was about ten miles away. No boats were near. Fuel was low. Cox made a pass over the yellow-and-white blob that was Renouf's Mae West and face, and took his patrol home.

The doctor was a chubby, friendly, middleaged squadron leader called Hubbard. He had a large yellow notepad and several pencils but he never wrote anything. "And what do you think of the war?" he asked. He shut one eye and cocked his head as if he had put a tremendously tricky question.

"Oh, gosh," Flash Gordon said. He was in his best uniform, sitting up straight, his eyes wide with interest. "Well, I agree with the Prime Minister, sir. The Battle of France is over. I expect the Battle of Britain is about to begin. That's what he said, and I think he's right, don't you?"

"You've seen quite a bit of the war already, haven't you? Is it what you expected? Tell me your impressions."

"Mmm." Flash chewed his lower lip and concentrated hard. "If you ask me, sir, the whole fury and might of the enemy must very soon be turned on us. Hitler knows that he will have to break us in this island or lose the war."

"And personally? How do you respond to the prospect of such bloodshed?"

"If we can stand up to him," Flash declared, "all Europe may be free and the life of the world may move forward into broad sunlit uplands."

"After all," Hubbard said sensibly, "the German pilots you blow to bits are probably just men like you, aren't they?"

"But if we fail," Flash told him, and shook his head grimly, "then the whole world will sink into the abyss of —"

"What I meant was —"

"If I might finish," Flash said, leaning forward and raising a finger, "because I do think that this is a pretty crucial point: the abyss of a new Dark Age made more sinister by the lights of perverted science." He sat back.

Hubbard fiddled with his pencils. "I'm no expert on fighter pilots," he lied, "but I'm told that sometimes . . . well, the strain gets a bit much, and then a chap might need a spot of help . . . Mmm?"

Flash nodded. "I'll keep a weather eye open, sir," he said. "Anybody starts acting funny, you'll be the first to know."

Fitzgerald and Patterson each claimed a 109. Mother Cox was delighted. He had seen none of their part of the fight, but they told him that while one pair of 109's concentrated on him (he was shocked to realise that he had never noticed the wingman in the background) the other pair had gone for Nim Renouf, obviously thinking he was easy meat. So Fitz and Pip had chased them off, or tried to, and anyway there was a hell of a scrap. Poor old Nim took a pasting but Fitz and Pip gave the Huns what-for and hit them where it hurt. When last seen they were going down with a great deal of smoke coming out and no hope of getting back to krautland this side of Christmas.

Nobody knew why Renouf suddenly went into a spin.

Skull finished scribbling his combat reports and went to phone Group.

'A' flight got scrambled at 10.15 and flew west along the coast, past Hastings, past Eastbourne, all the time being told to look out for a raid coming in across the Channel. Nothing appeared. They orbited Beachy Head for ten minutes. They were told the raid had turned back. They were to return to base. Halfway home they saw three Spitfires chase a very decrepit Dornier 17 out to sea and shoot it down. They landed after fifty wasted minutes, feeling disgusted. There was a message for Barton to call Brambledown.

It was Squadron Leader Hubbard. "I've had a good look at him," Hubbard said. "He's a peculiar fellow, isn't he?"

"I could have told you that. Is he batty, though? That's the point."

"We had a long chat. About the war, and killing people, and so on. Not very productive, though. He kept quoting great chunks of Churchill's speeches. Did he know I was coming to see him?"

Barton thought. Did he? "I suppose he could have guessed," he said.

Hubbard grunted. "He must have swotted them up. The speeches, that is. I must say he spoke them very well."

"But is he batty?"

Hubbard sighed. "I can't go on record as saying that a pilot who quotes Churchill is *ipso facto* mentally unstable. I mean, a lot of people quote Churchill. On the other hand . . . Yes, of course, he's batty. He's completely off his rocker. If you ask your average fighter pilot what he thinks of the war he shuffles his feet and looks embarrassed and says well they started it, didn't they? He doesn't talk about the abyss of a new Dark Age made more sinister by the lights of perverted science."

"Flash said that?" The more Barton thought about it, the funnier it seemed.

"I'm sending him back," Hubbard said. "Keep him away from Downing Street and he should be all right."

Flash landed at Bodkin Hazel before lunch. With him came a new Hurricane flown by a replacement pilot, a naval sub-lieutenant. He had a remarkably smooth, pale face which tapered to a pointed chin. His hair was blond and glossy, his eyes were blue-grey and he seemed never to blink. Everything about him was neat and controlled.

"This is Quirk, sir," Gordon said to Barton. "He's a sailor. I swopped him for two bottles of rum."

Quirk saluted. "Transferred from the Fleet Air Arm, sir," he said.

546

"I hope you've done an operational conversion course," Barton said sharply.

"Yes. Fifteen hours on Hurricanes."

"Fifteen. Bloody hell . . . Did that include air firing?"

"Only once. I'm afraid they couldn't spare more than a couple of hundred rounds, so I didn't learn much."

"God in heaven!" Barton spun his cap in the air and caught it. "You don't know one end of a Hurricane from the other."

"Let me see." Quirk pointed at his plane. "The sharp end goes first, doesn't it, sir?"

"I looked up 'quirk' in the dictionary," Gordon said. "It says it means strange and fantastic behaviour."

"What were you flying in the Fleet Air Arm?" Barton asked.

"Stringbags, sir. That is, Swordfish."

"You don't mean that funny old biplane, with all the wires? Looks like something left over from the RFC? What does it do, flat-out?"

"The book says a hundred and thirty-odd knots, but frankly that's rather optimistic. Say a hundred and twenty. Maybe a bit less with the torpedo underneath."

Barton wasn't listening. "Fifteen hours . . . Look, as soon as she's refuelled get back up there and stooge about, put in some practice. Use your guns. Try and shoot down some seagulls. Don't worry about the bullets. If you see a Jerry, run away. No risks, understand? No heroics. Just . . . survive."

"The Jerries are the ones with the crosses on, aren't they?" Quirk said.

"They are if you see them in time," Barton said. "If you don't, then the cross is on you, chum. Incidentally," he told Gordon, "Nim's down in the drink. Somewhere off the North Foreland."

"Oh dear. Poor Nim. You sailors know all about the sea," Gordon said to Quirk. "Is that bit nice or nasty?"

Quirk shrugged. "What matters is your friend's build. The fatter you are, the longer you survive."

"Nim's not fat. If anything, he's thin."

Quirk carefully avoided their eyes. "I'd better check my kite," he said.

Nim Renouf woke when the cannonshells hit his engine. The crash of explosions made his eyes open and he got jolted further awake as the Hurricane bucked and bounced. Then an acrid stench reached his nose and he coughed himself fully conscious.

The first thing he saw was the altimeter. The hands shot past nine thousand and went spinning towards eight. He looked out of the cockpit and saw nothing but smoke; looked the other side and saw the horizon, also spinning but not so fast. The stink got suddenly worse, choking him, so he heaved on the canopy and amazingly it slid back as smooth as a sled. The air improved. Bullet-strikes pranced along the port wing, then sparkled on the engine, and a plane streaked beneath him, a blur that vanished.

Renouf felt awful. His ears ached, his head ached, his stomach was queasy, and this bloody lunatic aeroplane wouldn't stop chucking him about. He got his feet on the pedals but there was no strength in his legs. He grabbed the stick. It slopped about like a spoon in a bowl, broken, useless. Dazzling cloud rushed up and drowned him in its murk.

It was easier to think when there was nothing to see. By the time he fell out of the cloud he knew he had to get out. The sight of the sea was discouraging, but when everything was going horribly wrong another disaster made little difference. Baling out was easy. He unplugged everything in sight and slid over the side.

Hanging under his parachute was wonderfully refreshing and restful. Everything was clean and quiet and comfortable. The sea was only a few hundred feet away when he fully realised what was about to happen to him and he began blowing up his Mae West. It was only half-inflated when he hit the water, awkwardly, and got a mouthful as he went under, a long way under, so far under that his lungs were hurting for air before his head bobbed up. No sky. Just clammy silk everywhere.

He swam clear of the parachute. That took a long time because he was still attached to the harness, but eventually he worked the release and escaped altogether. He trod water while he dragged off his gloves. Then he half-swam while he unzipped his boots and kicked them off. After all that, he had no breath left to finish blowing up his Mae West, but he had to keep swimming or the sodden weight of his Irvine jacket pulled him down.

The sea was much choppier than it looked from above, and the chop had a savage knack of finding his mouth. Ten minutes after the Hurricanes had gone, Nim Renouf was almost exhausted. Without actually deciding to do it, he floated on his back, kicking weakly. That was less tiring. He got some breath back. Once or twice a minute he managed to blow a good puff into his Mae West, until he risked letting his legs fall. The life jacket held his chin clear of the water. He relaxed.

There was nothing to do. He had a whistle, and he blew it once; it sounded puny and pointless. The water was cold. Not stinging-cold, as a bathe in the outdoor pool at his school had been, but numbing-cold: it drained the warmth from his body and left his limbs feeling bloodless. After a while he couldn't move his legs, but that was all right: why move them anyway? Then, later, his arms hung like a dummy's, and finally the wet cold reached deep into his body and sucked all the warmth from that. Renouf never saw the fishing boat that saw him. Another five minutes and it wouldn't have mattered if the skipper had missed him, too. When they laid him on a bunk and stripped off his clothes, his body was colder than the fish in the ship's hold.

By noon the cloud had rolled away eastward and the sun shone on Bodkin Hazel. Squads of airmen, stripped to the waist, sweated to dig trenches. Other squads filled sandbags and built aircraft bays near the perimeter. Several Fighter Command airfields had been shot-up, planes destroyed. During the morning there were two air-raid warnings but nobody stopped work. The sky was rarely empty of aircraft, and once a Junkers 88 flew slap over the aerodrome at two hundred feet, so fast the ack-ack never even fired. Everyone was supposed to carry his gas-mask with him, and the pilots were told to keep their Colt revolvers handy at all times. Skull gave them a short lecture on anti-invasion precautions. "The enemy may try to land troops by glider," he said, "which is why obstacles are being set up on all open land. If you have to put down on a field or at a strange airfield for any reason, watch out for poles or heaps of rocks or the like. If you make a forced landing anywhere, do not argue with the Home Guard. I have met some of them. They tend to be elderly and short-tempered. Often their aim is poor. Annoy them and they may fire a warning shot that hits you. Are there any questions?"

Steele-Stebbing raised his hand. "Sir, what's the best approach to take in that situation, *vis-à-vis* the Home Guard?"

"Identify yourself clearly," Skull said.

"Show them your hyphen," Cattermole advised. "They wouldn't dare shoot a man with a hyphen."

"Yes they would," Patterson said. "That's what double-barrelled shotguns are for."

Some laughed, some groaned, some were too tired to do either. Cattermole said: "Actually, I've seen Iron Filings' hyphen. He showed it to me in the showers the other night. It's not very impressive, I'm afraid, but then nobody in his family –"

"Lunch," Barton said. "Thank you, Skull. Jolly useful."

There was another air-raid warning during lunch (cold roast chicken, boiled potatoes, gooseberry tart, cream) and gunfire thudded and rumbled from the direction of Dover. Aircraft were always wandering about the sky but they were far too high to be identified. Rumours circulated of heavy raids on Portsmouth and Norwich, of huge destruction and raging fires, of colossal scores by Spitfire squadrons. A Heinkel, it was said, had bombed an infants' school in Canterbury, massacred seventy-nine toddlers, then been hit by ack-ack; the pilot baled out and was lynched by mothers before the police could reach him. Flash Gordon had that story. "Who says?" CH3 asked. "I heard it on the radio," Gordon said. "So there."

Skull got up and made a telephone call. When he came back he said: "As it happens, my cousin is assistant chief constable of Canterbury. He says that no school in Canterbury has been bombed."

"Did I say Canterbury?" Gordon said. "I meant Winchester."

"Know anybody in Winchester, Skull?" CH3 asked.

Skull thought. "Only the bishop," he said.

"Or it might have been Salisbury," Gordon said. He helped himself to more gooseberry tart. "They hung him from a lamppost. With a clothesline."

"Seventy-nine toddlers, you said." CH3 balanced his spoon on his outstretched finger. "That's a very precise figure."

"Yes, it is, isn't it?" Gordon was generous with the cream.

"Mind you, it was a good school. That's why they got so upset. Education is very important in Salisbury."

"Or Winchester," Cox said.

"Tell me, Flash," CH3 said, "did they count the dead toddlers before or after they lynched the Jerry pilot?"

"Yes, definitely," Gordon said, his mouth full. "Before or after. No mistake." When they laughed he looked mildly surprised. "Please yourself," he said. "I've seen it before."

"Eat up," CH3 said. "I want to take a squadron photograph."

He arranged them in a line in front of the control tower. There was the usual horseplay and clowning until he told them that his first shot was useless because they had all moved. "Now look at me this time," he said. For a moment they stood still and smiled at the camera. "Hold it!" he said, and behind them a revolver went off with a startling *crack-boom*. Inevitably they all looked around. "What the hell are you doing?" Barton shouted at a police corporal. The man was pointing his gun at the ground.

"It's all right, Fanny," CH3 said. "I told him to do that. Thank you, corporal. Now, can you all see the naked lady standing behind me?" The camera clicked. "Beautiful."

"I take it that was some kind of joke," Barton said, as they strolled to the deckchairs near dispersal.

"Practical joke. Very practical."

"I see." Barton glanced, warily. "Glad to see you're having fun again."

The revolver shot had not helped Steele-Stebbing's nerves. He had awoken with a hangover, his first ever, and loud noises still made him flinch. He avoided conversation, sat in the shade with his *Daily Telegraph* and waited for his brain to stop throbbing.

"What d'you think of that, then, Skull?" Fitzgerald pointed to the headline on the front page. "Sixty-three Huns knocked down yesterday. And we only lost a dozen."

"Fifteen, actually."

"All right, fifteen, if you're going to be bloody sniffy about it. Fifteen to sixty-three, it's still a damn good score, isn't it?"

"Quite. Mind you, in addition to the fifteen of ours shot down, one must add fighters lost through bad landings and taxiing accidents and so on. At least half a dozen a day."

"Skull," Barton said, "has anybody worked out how long the

Luftwaffe can last if they lose sixty-odd kites every time they come over here?"

"I don't think so."

"Well, have a go at it. How many kites did they have to start with?"

"It's not as simple as that. You see . . ."

"I'll do it for you, Fanny." Cattermole got up and, as he walked behind Steele-Stebbing, plucked the *Telegraph* from his fingers. "You divide Hitler's birthday by the starting price of the favourite in the 3.30 at Ascot," he said as he made for the portable lavatory, "and take away the number you first thought of. The answer's next Tuesday."

Steele-Stebbing's fingers squeezed the struts of his deckchair. His face was a dull red and his eyelids were heavy. He looked as if he might cry. Nobody spoke. He got up and walked away. "What a drip," Macfarlane said.

"If you ask me, they'll run out of pilots before they run out of planes," Fitzgerald said lazily. "Stands to reason. If they don't get any proper training they're not going to last the pace, are they?"

"I read in the paper the other day . . ." Patterson began, when he saw Skull shaking his head. "What's up?"

"The popular belief that *Luftwaffe* training is of poor quality is a myth, and in my opinion a dangerous myth." Heads turned: Skull was not usually as crisp as this. "You would be well-advised to ignore any propaganda about German pilots being rushed through inadequate flying schools. My information is that enemy aircrew have been very well trained indeed. Perhaps better trained than some of you."

"What bosh!" Fitzgerald said.

"Squareheads can't fly," Macfarlane said. "They're not streamlined, are they?"

Sergeant Brook felt confident enough to offer a remark. "Germans do everything by orders, don't they? No what-d'you-call-it. Initiative."

"Chap I bumped into this morning knew how to fly," Cox said thoughtfully. "*And* he had plenty of what-d'you-call-it. Damn sight too much of it for my comfort."

"Still, you got the better of him in the end, didn't you, Mother?" Barton said. "I mean, he quit first."

"He could have been low on fuel," CH3 said. "Those 109's haven't got much range."

"Tin-pot kites," Fitzgerald said. "Cack-handed pilots in tin-pot kites. Isn't that right, Skull?"

"By all reports the *Luftwaffe*'s physical standards are extremely high, possibly higher than Fighter Command's, and since German pilot training lasts nearly two years and requires—"

"Hullo, hullo!" Patterson pointed to a truck passing in front of them. "That's Iron Filings driving that thing."

The truck stopped behind the mobile lavatory. Steele-Stebbing got out. There was a wire rope tied to the rear of the truck. He carried the rope around the lavatory, secured the hooked end, got into the cab and gently drove away.

The wheels on the lavatory were small and iron. They rattled and bounced over ruts and bumps. When Steele-Stebbing eased the speed up from a walk to a trot, the wheels crashed and squealed and the whole structure swung like a metronome. Occasional shouts could be heard, and fists pounding on wood. Steele-Stebbing made a wide turn and towed the lavatory past the pilots. A dark liquid was leaking under the door, spraying the grass. He slowed, circled a group of watching groundcrew, and took the lavatory back past the pilots at a very brisk clip indeed. It swayed wildly. Once or twice, all the wheels were off the ground. The shouting had stopped but there was one strangled howl that earned a cheer from the spectators.

Steele-Stebbing returned the lavatory to its place, unhooked the rope and drove away.

Cattermole kicked open the door and staggered out. He was still holding up his trousers. Every part of him was spattered and dripping. He swore in a kind of frenzied, almost hysterical monotone until his voice cracked under the strain.

"My goodness, you are in a filthy mood, Moggy," Patterson said.

Cattermole advanced, mopping his face with the newspaper, still swearing.

"After you with the *Telegraph*," Fitzgerald said to him. Then the smell began to reach them and they got up and backed away.

"Beat it, Moggy," CH3 said. "Go and get cleaned up, and make it snappy. We're on standby, remember."

"Where is he?" Cattermole shouted. "I'll kill the bastard, I'll break his bloody neck, I'll kick his guts in –"

"You touch him and I'll put my boot in your balls," CH3 said. "Now amscray and take a shower."

"Where is he? I want to know where the little sod is." Muck dripped into Cattermole's mouth and he spat, furiously.

"You so much as lay a finger on him," Barton said, "and I'll chop you into catsmeat. Now go!"

"Sunday school," Cattermole sneered. "Bloody boy scouts." He stood and glared, his head twitching with rage.

A fire-truck arrived. "Mr Steele-Stebbing said you might need us, sir," the driver said.

"Hose down that officer," Barton ordered. "Don't let him get away."

An airman already had the nozzle in his hands. At first Cattermole tried to run but they drove alongside, increased the water-pressure and knocked him down with the jet. In the end he plodded to the clubhouse, taking off his clothes as he went, while the firecrew blasted him clean.

He came back ten minutes later, wearing a mechanic's spare overalls. Steele-Stebbing was sitting, reading a book. He did not look up, but as Cattermole went past he murmured, "*Très chic.*" There was one empty deckchair. Cattermole dropped into it with unnecessary violence. The deckchair collapsed. The squadron fell about laughing. Cattermole lay on his back and shut his eyes. He was in a perfect mood to kill somebody. Two minutes later the scramble klaxon went off.

For once Snowball had got it absolutely right. He had put Hornet squadron up at the right time and the right height and now they reached Dover just as the Stukas came parading over the Channel.

Barton stopped counting at thirty. They looked predatory, with their heavy spatted undercarriage and bent wings. He remembered the day in France when he had been shot down and had taken shelter while a flock of Stukas dive-bombed a nearby battery of guns: the almost-vertical dive, the screaming siren, the appalling accuracy, each bomb planted smack on target while the Stukas climbed away with a sort of smug nothing-to-it indifference that made Barton hate them more than the big bombers. The soldiers became very bitter against the Air Force for not protecting them against Stukas, and Barton could understand why. When you were on the ground, every plunging Stuka seemed to be out to kill you, personally. After a while, it was more than even experienced troops could take. Mention of the word alone was enough to make them run and hide. The Stuka wasn't so much a plane as a flying execution squad. Now Barton looked forward gleefully to hacking the bastards out of the sky. He actually licked his lips. And Hornet squadron could gorge themselves on the Stukas because arriving now, high above, dead on cue, was a squadron of Spits from Biggin Hill to take on the escort of 109's.

He crossed above the raid, turned and led the Hurricanes down from the sun – not that the enemy would be surprised but the glare might dazzle the rear-gunners. Each section picked its target. The Stukas ploughed on. Barton chose a nice clean-looking one on the left and watched its lumpy angularity wobble about inside his reflector sight, growing fast until, as the wingtips reached the sight-bars, he touched the gun-button. Bullets had been spurting from the single gun in the rear cockpit but a flood of fire from Barton's eight Brownings swamped it. The Stuka exploded. He soared away. Easy as that. He twisted his neck and saw two more Stukas falling, a third on fire, Hurricanes breaking away on all sides. Steele-Stebbing was faithfully watching his tail. "Red Two: you lead, I'll cover," he called. They swapped places as they turned, Barton throttling back and swinging wide to lose speed, but he was surprised by Steele-Stebbing's eagerness to attack and he had to chase hard to catch him. The man was too eager. He slammed into the formation from the left stern quarter, missed with his first burst, played ducks-and-drakes across half a dozen Stukas and sheered away right, going faster than ever. The R/T was crowded with claims, questions, triumphs. Barton waited for a pause and called: "Slow down, Red Two! Take it easy!" He saw Steele-Stebbing swerve towards a crippled Stuka and nearly collide with a Hurricane that was also chasing it. The two fighters merged, crossed, split, fled. Barton couldn't tell which was which. He hesitated. Both planes lost themselves in the whirl of battle. He pulled clear and took a long look up-sun. High above, Spits and 109's lunged and darted like a cloud of gnats excited by sunshine. A couple of smoke-smears made twisted scribbles on the sky, then seemed to get bored and trailed down to earth. A bunch of 109's broke away and dived towards the Stukas. Barton called a warning: "Bandits above!"

The words reached Fitzgerald but he heard nothing: blood was pounding in his ears, partly from excitement, partly from violent manoeuvring. His first attack had swept him ahead of the raid, back towards Dover Harbour. The ack-ack barrage made the air boil with destruction. Fitz tucked the stick into the pit of his stomach and opened the throttle wide. At the top of his loop he rolled over and was blessed with a vision of paradise.

Despite their losses the Stukas were still pressing on with their attack. The first three had just tipped over. Now, committed to a straight, unvarying dive, slowed by flaps and airbrakes, they were wonderfully vulnerable. Fitz took his pick. The middle one. He had never been so confident of a kill. The Hurricane's nose sank. The falling Stuka sat in his sights, perfectly centred. It magnified easily and beautifully, as if he had been working a microscope. He eased the nose a fraction steeper still and made the image rise. One-length deflection. Fire. A swarm of flames, leaping away from his wings. Blast of chattering guns. Sudden raging blaze, red ringed with yellow, so brilliant he blinked, and then the eruption heaved him on his way. Bits of Stuka stung the Hurricane, hunks of debris spun past it, but today Fitz knew he was immortal.

He climbed like a god and put a burst into somebody's belly as he sheered through the raid. Still the enemy came, rank upon rank. Fitz stall-turned out of his climb and fell behind a Stuka just as it was entering its dive. The German pilot saw him, flinched away from the tracer, pushed his machine to the vertical and then pushed it beyond. Fitz could not compete with that. He pulled out and broke away. But it seemed that the Stuka was not made to recover from a dive beyond the vertical. Fitz saw this one bury itself in Dover Harbour with an almighty splash, and he rejoiced. Then the 109's came down and the fun was over.

It took Skull half an hour to get the combat reports sorted out. The racket in the crewroom was continuous; the atmosphere bordered on the hysterical. Nobody could keep still; everyone laughed, shouted across the room, gulped their mugs of tea, waved, grinned, kicked the furniture.

"Knocked the buggers down like flies!" Patterson's excitement

556

was so intense he was almost stuttering. "What, Mother? Just like fucking flies! Eh?"

"Wizard, Pip, wizard . . . You! you rotten bastard!" Cox aimed a quivering finger at Steele-Stebbing. "Nearly bloody hit me!" Cox's eyes were popping with fear and glee.

"You pinched my Hun," Steele-Stebbing accused. "Balls!" Cox shouted. Macfarlane thrust between them. "Did you see him?" he gabbled. "See him go up? *Whoosh!* Did you see him, Pip?" Macfarlane's hands were carving the air. Patterson nodded. Everyone seemed to be nodding. "*Whoosh!* One burst . . . He just . . . *Whoosh!*"

"Mine went *bang!*" Cattermole told them.

"Crash-wallop!" Brook said. "What a picnic! What a terrific picnic! I mean . . ." Flash Gordon was standing on a chair and singing: "Our name is Hornet squadron, no bloody good are we . . ."

"Know what it proves, Fanny?" Fitz said. "They can't bloody fly without wings!" Barton roared with laughter. He grabbed CH3's arms and made them flap: tea sprayed everywhere. "They can't fly without bloody wings, can they, you mad bloody Yank?" Skull shook the drops off his notebook and wiped his face. "You were saying?" he reminded CH3, but Cattermole had claimed him. "Mine went *bang!*" Cattermole declaimed. "How did yours go?"

"*Ka-pow!*" CH3 threw his half-empty mug in the air. "*Zap!*" Cattermole caught the mug and threw it at Gordon, who batted it at Cox, and then they all began chucking their mugs at each other and the de-briefing collapsed in a welter of tea-stains and broken china.

In the end Skull managed to get some sort of tally. It came to nine definite Stuka kills and five probables, plus a dozen damaged. The scrap with the 109's had ended abruptly when everyone ran out of ammunition and two 109's collided. Generously, Fanny said that Dover ack-ack could claim them. The only casualty was Quirk, who had taken a small shell splinter in the right buttock. "Does it hurt?" Cox asked. "Don't know," Quirk said. "Haven't asked it." They found that hilarious.

An hour later, reaction had set in.

It took different forms with different men. Weariness overtook Macfarlane, Patterson and Brook. They fell asleep, and not even engine-tests disturbed them. Steele-Stebbing was unable to stop talking; he and Fitzgerald went over the Great Stuka Shoot again and again. The others were incurably restless. They strolled around dispersal, whistling, kicking at dandelion heads, throwing stones at birds.

Skull found Barton and CH3 sitting in the branches of an apple-tree. "What are you doing up there?" he asked.

"What does it look as if we're doing?" Barton threw an apple at him.

"We're waiting for the tide to go out," CH3 said.

Skull looked at his watch. "It hasn't come in yet."

"I know that," Barton said. "But we'll be first in the queue when it does."

"Yes, of course. Silly of me ... I have a message from Baggy Bletchley. He says good show."

"That's jolly nice of him. Tell him it was a piece of cake."

"There's also a signal from Group that Nim Renouf has been found."

"Yes?"

"That's all it says, but I'm checking. And finally, I'm afraid I've had to revise some of the recent claims of enemy aircraft destroyed."

"What?" Barton swung down from the tree. "You've what?"

"Yesterday Moggy claimed a Heinkel 111 definitely destroyed and you, CH3, claimed a Messerschmitt 110 definitely destroyed."

"That's right." CH3 hung by his arms and dropped.

"Well, I've been comparing my reports with those of Sector and Group Intelligence, and also with those made by other units in action yesterday. The fact of the matter is that no German aircraft crashed in the area of your interception at the relevant time yesterday."

"Don't be bloody silly, Skull," Barton said.

"Go back and look again," CH3 told him.

"There were plenty of observers on the ground," Skull said. "Did you actually see your 110 crash?"

"No, of course not. The scrap was at fifteen thousand feet and I had better things to do. What a dumb question."

"So they all flew back to Germany, did they?" Barton asked. "I mean to say, we murdered the buggers but they all lived happily ever after. Is that right?"

"Enemy aircraft from that particular raid *were* destroyed," Skull said. CH3 said: "You bet your sweet ass they were." Skull looked at his clipboard and said, "But not at that location, and not necessarily as a consequence of your attacks alone. For example . . . The raid continued north and a Spitfire squadron from Hornchurch intercepted it. Their claims –"

"They've pinched my kill!" CH3 exclaimed. "Those Hornchurch bums have . . . Jesus! What a swindle."

"It's certainly possible that aircraft damaged by you or by Moggy were later finished off by another unit. What seems quite certain is that the initial attack by this squadron did *not* result in such destruction, and in the light of that evidence the claims of kills must, I'm afraid, be revoked."

"God speed the plough." Barton picked up an apple and hurled it with all his strength. "There ain't no justice. There simply ain't."

"It follows that the probables claimed by Fitz and Bing must also be reconsidered."

"Why don't you go on leave, Skull?" CH3 said. "This squadron was doing fine until you stuck your oar in."

"I'm afraid I haven't finished." Barton groaned and turned away. "This morning's patrol by Blue and Green Sections," Skull went on, "resulted in Fitz and Pip each claiming a Messerschmitt 109 destroyed. Again, no such crash was reported."

"There was ten-tenths cloud, for Pete's sake!" CH3 said. "In any case, the whole schemozzle happened out at sea. How the hell –"

"With respect," Skull said firmly. "The cloud was quite high and observers on the coast with telescopes saw much of the action. The coastguard, for instance, saw a Hurricane fall into the sea, presumably Renouf's. But they saw no other aircraft crash. What they, and other observers, did see was four Me-109's heading south."

"Oh, shut up, Skull," Barton said. "You make me tired."

"So we're all bloody liars, are we?" CH3 asked.

"Look, I don't do this for my own pleasure," Skull said sharply. "I'm simply telling you the facts as they're given to me. I'll tell you something else. When a 109 is attacked and it dives away leaving a trail of smoke, that does *not* mean it has been shot down, although in the excitement of the moment the attacking pilot may understandably think so. This is not *my* opinion. It comes from Fighter Command, and I am asked to draw your attention to it."

"My chaps know when they've hit a Jerry," Barton growled. "They can see their damn bullets going into the thing."

"No doubt. I wonder if they can also see them going *out* of it?"

"Very clever. If wit was shit, you'd be a prize turd."

"I'm sorry you feel cheated," Skull said. He looked pale, and his glasses kept slipping down his nose, but he was not going to give in. "What's more I realise that I am at a great disadvantage in not being able to fly. But before this squadron was re-formed I spent some time at a Bomber Command base in Suffolk. I saw bombers land, after raiding Germany, in such a condition that you would have said they could not possibly have flown hundreds of miles like that. One engine burnt out, the tail shattered, wings like colanders. Quite extraordinary. Not surprisingly, the Germans claimed to have destroyed those planes."

"All krauts are finks," CH3 said.

"I learned in Suffolk how difficult it is to shoot down a bomber, especially with rifle-calibre bullets." CH3 grimaced, and nodded. "They're too small to make a great hole," Skull said. "If you're very lucky they hit something vital. If not, they go out the other side and the enemy plane suffers nothing worse than a perforation, a pinprick."

"Oh yeah?" Barton had had enough. "There's nine Stuka crews at the bottom of Dover Harbour who died of pinpricks this afternoon."

"Six," Skull said. "Six Stukas."

"You go to hell," CH3 said. "Nine. We got *nine*."

"I'm sorry. The Observer Corps has a post on the cliffs overlooking the harbour. They kept a careful record. The Navy confirms it. So does the ack-ack and –"

"There were nine definite kills," Barton insisted. "They were hit, they blew up or they went into the drink. That's not *guesswork*, Skull, for Christ's sake, that's what my chaps actually *saw*, I mean they *know* when they've shot a Stuka down."

Skull tucked his clipboard under his arm. "On the other hand, air fighting is a confused and confusing affair, so I'm told. Everything happens very quickly. Could it be, do you think, that two pilots might attack the same Stuka at the same instant without being aware of each other, destroy it, and each claim a kill?"

"No," Barton said. He looked at CH3, who shrugged. "All right, blast you, *yes*," Barton said.

"We're agreed on six, then," Skull said.

They climbed back into their apple-tree and watched him leave. "Doddering old fool," CH3 said. "What does he know?"

"Bet you can't hit him from here," Barton said.

"Bet I can."

They hurled apples at Skull, but the branches got in the way and they didn't even get close.

'A' flight had an abortive scramble at 4.15. The squadron was stood down early, at six.

Fitz decided to get a quick drink in the mess before he went home. He felt unusually jumpy. Not twitchy, he wasn't worried about anything; but he couldn't seem to wind down after the Great Stuka Shoot. Some Spitfire pilots wanted to hear all about it, and they bought him another drink. He found that he was laughing a lot. Everything seemed very, very funny. Once or twice he was afraid he might not be able to stop laughing. He bought them a round. The Spitfire boys were going on a pub-crawl. They asked him along. "No, no, no," he said, laughing. "Got to get home to the little wife. Well, not so little." That was very funny. Oddly enough, though, he didn't much want to go home. In fact he dreaded it. He really wanted to stay here with the boys.

The adjutant came in, muttering about Zab and Haddy, and Fitz bought him a drink. The Spitfire boys left. The mess was suddenly quiet. Fitz hated the quiet, hated the prospect of loneliness. "Tell you what, uncle," he said. "Let's go somewhere."

"No can do, old boy. I need my supper."

"Well then . . ." Fitz had a brainwave. "Come and have a bite at our place, uncle. Take pot-luck."

The adjutant looked sceptical. "Jolly nice of you, I'm sure, but . . . Rather short notice, isn't it? For Mary, I mean."

"No, no. Women can always rustle something up."

They drove to the cottage in an old Austin 7 that Fitz had bought for ten pounds. Mary was delighted to see them, but there was no food. "I thought you'd eat at the mess tonight, dear," she said. "Isn't that what you said?"

The cottage was shabby and damp. Kellaway looked at its junkshop furniture and its faded, mismatched colours, and he looked at Fitz and Mary, each trying to smile and each blaming the other for this failure, and he wished to hell he'd never come. Still, it was too late now. Twenty years' experience of sorting out other people's cock-ups asserted itself. "What have you got in the larder?" he asked briskly.

She had some eggs. Two eggs. One was cracked, and smelt off. "That's a start," he said. "Where did you get them?" A farm, half a mile away. "You'll never find it," she said, with such hopelessness that he wanted to hit her. "Then I'll die in the attempt," he said. "Got any spuds?" There were three wrinkled potatoes. "Splendid. Excellent. Absolutely wizard. You get cracking on those, my sweet, while I do a spot of foraging. Fitz! What the hell are you doing under the sink?"

"I thought we had some beer. I'm afraid it's flat."

"Jump in that wagon of yours, find a boozer and buy some booze. Buy lots of booze. Crates of the stuff. When you get back, light a fire. Come on." He took Fitz's arm and steered him out, grabbing a shopping-basket as he went.

It took an hour, but it was a good meal. Kellaway found the farm and persuaded them to sell him eggs, some ham, potatoes, mushrooms, a few tomatoes, and some strawberries. Fitz came home with a case of Guinness. Kellaway cooked the only dish he knew how to make: a sort of giant Spanish omelette, with fried potatoes. They ate everything.

Conversation was no problem. Mary chattered endlessly and Fitz was full of jokes. All the earlier awkwardness had gone. Then, while they were tackling the strawberries, Fitz stopped talking. For ten minutes he sat and thumbed the edge of a knife while his smile faded and his shoulders hunched. The other two went on discussing food, and France, and pregnancy, and sometimes Mary tried to lure him back into the talk. Fitz wouldn't even look at her. Then, abruptly, he got up and went out of the cottage.

"If you're thinking of asking him what's wrong with him," she said, "save your breath. He's like this as often as not." Kellaway sipped his Guinness. "Even when he's here, he's not here, if you

562

know what I mean," she said. "There's nothing I can do for him any more. He can't get back to the squadron fast enough." One corner of her mouth was turned up but the rest of her face had slumped in defeat.

"The first thing to understand is it's got nothing to do with you," Kellaway said. "What I mean is Fitz loves you just as much as ever. The trouble is flying. It gets to be an addiction."

"But he hates it. I know he does. He has nightmares."

"Yes, I had nightmares too. Every time I went up I was scared stiff. Everyone looked forward to leave, I mean we couldn't wait to go on leave, thought of nothing else, but as soon as I got to London I started wishing I was back with the squadron. Strange, isn't it?"

"And you really think this is what's happened to Fitz. This addiction."

"Fighter pilots are like that, I'm afraid, Mary. A chap's got to think about number one, first last and always, or he's a goner. Makes him seem a bit selfish sometimes."

"I wish I could help," she said.

Kellaway got up. "I'd better fetch the silly blighter in, before he falls down the well."

The landlord of the *Spreadeagle* had brought his wireless into the bar. The Hornet boys rolled in just as the news was starting. They stood in silence, gazing at the fretwork-sunrise loudspeaker, until the sober, steady voice announced the day's score. *A total of thirty-five enemy aircraft were destroyed for the loss of six British –*

The rest got drowned in a long cheer.

"Had a good day?" the landlord asked.

"Had an absolutely smashing day," Barton told him.

"Bloody marvellous," the landlord said. "What'll you have? First round's on the house."

"Hey, don't go crazy," CH3 warned. "We may do even better tomorrow. We wouldn't want you to go bankrupt."

"Don't worry. You keep shooting them down and I'll keep putting them up."

When they drove back to Brambledown the place was being bombed, not very effectively. The off-beat throb of unsynchronised engines came and went overhead while searchlights stirred the blackness and ack-ack guns woofed and barked. Occasionally there was a distant whistle, a flash, a crump; but it was all very remote. "What d'you think?" Barton asked CH3, yawning.

"Bed," CH3 said. Their rooms were on the same floor, and as they were climbing the stairs something exploded outside that seemed to pick up the whole building and dump it six inches to one side. All the windows at the top of the stairs were shattered.

"Shelter," Barton said. They went back down. Bells were ringing, whistles shrilled, men in steel helmets went racing about. Another bomb fell, apparently on the parade ground. Something was burning on the other side of the mess; they could see flames leaping as if trying to out-jump each other. "That's done it," Barton said. "Now he's got a marker. Where are these damn shelters?"

"I thought you knew."

"Me? Why should I know?"

"Well, you're the CO." There was a flash and a crash somewhere over by the airfield. They stumbled on. "It's all right for you," CH3 said, "you're just a poor New Zealander. I'm a rich American, for God's sake, people expect great things of me, I've got obligations. If a bomb lands on me now I'll never hear the end of it."

"That's nothing. If you get blown up now I'll have to fight Skull all on my own."

Another flash and crash.

"Maybe that one hit Skull," CH3 said. "Jerry's bound to get something right eventually."

"Even if it hit him, Skull wouldn't believe it. He'd want witnesses and . . . Hullo, what's this?"

It was an underground shelter. They felt their way down the steps and opened a steel door. The room was empty except for two men. Zab and Haddy were playing cards. "Bloody hell," Barton said.

"Welcome!" Haducek cried. "We were just discussing the many ways in which the Hurricane is superior to the Spitfire. Sit down, have a drink."

"Oh, Christ," CH3 said.

"No, it is true," Zabarnowski told him. "Did you know that you get a much better pattern of bullets from the Hurricane? This is because the four guns in each wing are closely grouped together."

"In the Spitfire," Haducek explained, "the guns are spread all along the wing. That is not so good."

"Also," Zabarnowski said, with a flourish of his index finger, "the Hurricane is a much better gun-platform."

"I know," CH3 said. "I told you that at the start."

"This also is related to the placing of the guns," Haducek informed him. "A very, very good idea."

"The Hurricane remains steady, you see," Zabarnowski said. He handed them glasses of some clear fluid. "The Spitfire wobbles and shakes. Cheers."

"Hey, come on now," Barton said. "The Spit's a hell of a good kite."

"But look at its wheels!" Haducek protested. "Thin little wheels that close together, while the Hurricane has those big strong wheels, very wide apart so you can throw it at the ground when you land, much better."

"Wheels! Who cares about wheels?" CH3 scoffed. "What you need is *speed*, and the Spitfire's faster, no two ways about it."

"Ah, but it's not so tough!" Zabarnowski was getting excited. "You hit a Spit one little bang and *poof*! She snaps. You hit a Hurricane all day and all night and all next day and she never minds nothing, she flies you home, safe."

"No," Barton said. "Big slow fat old cow. Lousy plane."

"Lousy," CH3 agreed. "Hurricane is cock-up."

"Hurricane is dump," Barton said.

"I tell you about guns," Zabarnowski said eagerly. "With Hurricane you get much better pattern of bullets, see, because –"

"Okay, okay!" Barton waved him down. "You can fly again."

"You hit those lousy Stukas pretty damn good today," Haducek said.

"That's your gun-platform, see," Zabarnowski said.

"Can we please for Christ's sake talk about something else besides bloody aeroplanes?" Barton appealed.

Haducek topped up his glass. "Pepper vodka," he said. "Good, huh?"

The weather next morning was bad: clear, lustrous skies, a warm sun, little breeze. "Oh, Christ. Another blitzy day," Patterson grumbled when his batman woke him and he squinted at the light.

"Why doesn't it ever bloody rain?" He drank his cup of tea. It tasted tacky and stale, but that wasn't the tea; it was his mouth. He briefly considered shaving. No. Shave at Bodkin Hazel. Besides, the way he sweated and the way that foul bloody oxygen mask stuck to the skin it was better not to shave. He had a quick wash and got into his uniform, by now creased and stained and baggy and comfortable from so many hours in the cockpit. No collar and tie: he wrapped a scruffy bit of silk around his neck. Couldn't find a comb. So what? Hair got messed-up anyway. He slapped his cap on and went to the bathroom for a pee. The cap was a fighter pilot's badge of rank as much as the rings on his sleeve. New boys had clean, circular caps with neat, smooth peaks. Old sweats like Pip had battered caps that had been sat on, stuffed into cockpits, twisted a thousand ways, soaked by rain, baked by sun. All fighter pilots went around with the top tunic button undone, but that was just tribal swank. Men like Pip had earned the right to wear a really beat-up cap.

Brambledown was still smoking from the night's raid. Fire hoses trailed across the roads and craters had been roped off. Hornet squadron taxied past men shovelling earth into holes. One hangar had collapsed on itself and crushed several Spitfires. Telephone wires flopped and dangled. The rumour was that three men had been killed and a couple of Waafs injured.

The morning began quietly. By ten o'clock there had been no scramble, and everyone became quite cheerful. With Zab and Haddy back the squadron was up to strength. Those two were transformed. They mixed, they talked, they made obscure European jokes which might not have been very funny but any sort of joke was better than none when there was time to kill. At the same time, Cattermole seemed to have given up his vendetta against Steele-Stebbing, and Steele-Stebbing himself was remarkably chatty. He'd never played cards but when Quirk organised a pontoon school he watched keenly and soon joined in. He even said "Blast!" when Quirk aced him out. The other players gaped and recoiled.

"I've never heard such language," Barton said. "What *can* it mean?"

"It means balls and buggeration," Steele-Stebbing said. "Now deal the sodding cards."

Skull brought news of Nim Renouf. He was in Ramsgate hospital, alive and conscious. That was all, but it was more than most people had expected, and it further increased the general cheerfulness. Skull, however, was not popular. In his hearing, Fitzgerald said loudly: "How many Stukas make nine, Moggy?"

"Six!" Cattermole exclaimed. "Get that into your skull, boy. Six Stukas make nine."

"Sorry, sir. And please, sir: how d'you know when you've shot down a Heinkel, sir?"

"You get a chit from the Jerry pilot, obviously. You are a fool, boy."

"In triplicate, sir?"

"Of course in triplicate. One for you, one for Berlin, and one for the intelligence officer to wipe his bottom with."

"And make sure it's got a twopenny stamp on it," CH3 muttered. Barton nudged him warningly. CH3 grunted, tipped his cap over his eyes and had a snooze. Six or nine, who cared what the records said as long as the Huns had bought it?

At five to eleven 'B' flight got scrambled. They came back forty minutes later, gun-ports fluting as they drifted in to land. There were only five planes: Mother Cox had gone down.

"Absolute shambles," Fitzgerald reported. "Two dozen Dornier 17's had a go at those socking great aerials at Beachy Head. By the time we got there it was too late, they'd dropped their load and they were off home, lickety-split. *And* we were the wrong height."

"Too low," Barton said: more a statement than a question.

"Angels five. Should have been seven, or eight! Anyway, we spotted Jerry departing, so we cut the corner and bust a gut and we just about caught him."

"Not really caught," Zabarnowski said. "Got close, but . . ."

"Bloody nippy, those Dorniers," said Quirk.

"Everybody tore up and blasted away at them," Fitzgerald said, "and they all blasted away at us, and Mother must have stopped a bullet in the radiator or something because all of a sudden there's glycol coming out of him like spilt milk. He turned back and headed for home. He told us to keep on chasing, so we did, but I don't think we hit anything."

All in all it had been a thoroughly duff interception: scrambled too late, vectored too low, outpaced, and nothing to show for it but the loss of the flight commander, who might be anywhere, in the drink, wrapped around a tree, anywhere. Poor show.

Later, Barton asked Quirk what he thought of his first bit of real action.

Quirk swallowed, and cleared his throat.

"Look," Barton said, "I don't want an official statement from the admiralty. Just tell me."

Quirk took his hands from his pockets and raised them. The fingers were trembling. "I can't make them stop," he said.

"Don't try. If they want to shake, let 'em shake. After a scrap I usually drink my tea through a straw."

"The funny thing is, I wasn't scared during the scrap. I got a bit twitchy when we made the tally-ho, but later on there was too much to do . . . Anyway it was all over so quickly. Fifteen seconds of ammo soon goes, doesn't it? I couldn't hit anything. Couldn't get *near* anything. I never realised it was so hard to hit a twin-engined bomber. It's impossible. How does anyone do it?"

"You've got to get damn close. A Dornier looks big on the ground. It's not very big in the sky."

"Well, I reckon we were two or three hundred yards behind that lot and the nearest one looked to me about the size of that sparrow." Quirk stuffed his hands back into his pockets. "In any case I was always bucketing about in their slipstream, and they were always bouncing up and down like mad, so I never even got one in my sights."

"I don't suppose the others did either. It's a bit different from firing at the towed target, isn't it?"

Quirk laughed. "It's like riding a merry-go-round and trying to swat flies."

"In a gale," Barton said, "with a crowd of maniacs shooting at you."

"And a very wet left leg," Quirk said.

"Ah. Welcome to the club. Remember: if you see a fighter pilot walking lopsided it's because one leg has shrunk in the wash."

When they sat down to lunch there was a huge blow-up of the group photograph pinned to the wall. It was the first picture, the one taken just as the police corporal fired his revolver. Everyone was chest-on to the camera but the heads had swivelled and no faces could be seen. They found it very amusing.

"This proves something I always suspected about the British," Haducek said. "They certainly have their heads screwed on, but unfortunately they are pointing the wrong way."

"Personally, I think it's brilliant," Macfarlane said. "You can't tell who's who, so it'll never wear out, will it? What we've got is the first permanent, everlasting squadron. Brilliant."

"What was happening here?" Zabarnowski asked.

Flash Gordon began a rambling explanation. CH3 murmured to Barton: "Their English has made a startling improvement, hasn't it?"

"Not really. I knew they were pretty fluent when they arrived, that's why they were sent here. They were just being bloody-minded. Now, are you going to reveal what this peculiar snapshot is all about?"

CH3 banged a spoon on the table. "Take a good look," he said to them. "There's something special about this picture."

"Moggy's flies are undone," Patterson said. "But then, they usually are."

"Colossal pressure on them," Cattermole said. "No wonder the buttons pop."

"Look at the heads," CH3 said. "Nearly everybody turned his head to the left. Why?"

"Because the bang was on the left?" Quirk suggested.

"No, the bang was in the middle." He waited, but nobody else spoke. "The fact is, most people, if they want to look behind them, turn to the left. Maybe it's because the right-hand neck muscles are stronger or something, I don't know."

"Iron Filings turned *his* head to the right," Barton pointed out.

"I'm left-handed," Steele-Stebbing said.

"The point of that picture is this," CH3 said. "When the average pilot suddenly has to look behind him, it's ten to one he'll turn his head to the left. So if you're lucky enough to get on Jerry's tail, the best place to be is not slap behind him but slightly to the right."

"About five degrees to the right is good, I find," Haducek said.

Barton said: "You give him a squirt, he looks left, doesn't see you, and that gives you time to give him another squirt. Nice. I like it."

"There's something else," CH3 said, and paused.

They all looked at the blow-up on the wall.

"Suppose it's the other way around," CH3 said. "Now all of a sudden *he's* on *your* tail."

"Ah, yes!" Zabarnowski said. "Break right. Am I correct?"

"It's up to you, but it's certainly worth thinking about. Most people, when they're jumped, break left, for the same reason most people *look* left, I suppose. So Jerry instinctively expects you to break left too. If you break right, you may just shake him off, or at least it might give you an extra half-second."

"Very interesting," Barton said. "Well worth remembering."

"I happen to know for a fact," Flash Gordon said, "that all German pilots are left-handed."

"Bring on the grub," Barton told a cook.

"The *Luftwaffe* deliberately chose left-handed pilots in order to baffle us," Gordon explained. "Cunning buggers ... Ah! Fish and chips. Wizard prang." He smiled genially. "Whatever that means."

During lunch a signal arrived, releasing 'B' flight immediately. They were to return to Brambledown to attend Flip Moran's funeral. Fanny made Fitz temporary flight commander and they took off as soon as they had shovelled down their fish and chips.

Fitz worried all the way. He had never been in charge of a funeral. Those he had attended had all produced cock-ups of one sort or another. Above all he was nervous of that ceremonial sword-drill. So he was delighted to find Cox standing talking to the adjutant when he taxied to dispersal. "Hullo, Mother!" he shouted. "You okay? You can have your flight back now. What happened?" He climbed down.

"This is a most extraordinary war, Fitz," Cox said. He was in full flying kit and carrying his parachute. "I managed to glide back and I put her down on a cricket pitch near Eastbourne. Big expensive boys' school, lovely bit of grass, perfect three-pointer, not a scratch. Got out, nobody there. Place was deserted. Not a soul. School holidays, see. So I sniffed around, found a bike, kind of thing the butcher's boy rides, stuffed the parachute in the basket, stooged off. Rode down the hill, guess what: lovely big railway station. Only trouble is, the stupid bloody ticket inspector won't let me on the platform. No ticket, see. No money, of course, so nothing doing. Utter deadlock."

"You should've clocked him one," Fitz said.

"Six foot four, chum. Anyway, I explained everything to him

but I don't think he believed it. Thought it was a practical joke. Took a very dim view of me, actually."

"Bloody fool."

"Yes, that's what I told him, but he still didn't agree, so I toddled off and found a pawn shop."

"Hey, that's clever."

"Thanks. Well, they weren't too keen, they didn't want my watch, it's got 'RAF property' engraved on the back, so I offered them the parachute but they turned up their noses at that too, and in the end I popped the bicycle."

"Good show. What did you get for it?"

"A quid."

"That's not much."

"Well, it wasn't my bike, was it?"

"Look here, you two," Kellaway said. "You'd better get cracking."

"You know, they ought to give us travel vouchers," Fitz said. "In case we get forced down."

"They ought to give us lots of things," Cox said. "Starting with back-pay."

"I'm doing my best," Kellaway told him. "You'll get it eventually."

Cox grunted. "Flip didn't," he said. Kellaway wisely let that pass.

They went off, got changed into their best blue, and reported to the station chapel. All the stained-glass windows had been blown in by the bombing, and bright sunlight lit up the flag that covered the coffin. A young airman was playing Bach on the organ.

"All right, this is the form," Cox told his flight softly. "We carry the doings out. Three a side. Me, Zab and Pip on the left, the others on the right. Drive to the cemetery, it's just around the corner, take the doings to the hole, the adj knows where, we follow him. Short service, back here. Okay? Oh . . . One little thing. There wasn't very much left, so they've put a few sandbags in the box to help sort of pack it out. If you hear things sliding about when we pick it up, don't worry."

"So we're doing all this just to bury a bit of Southend Sands," Patterson said wearily. "What a pathetic joke."

"It's the thought that counts," Gordon observed.

"Well, I think it stinks."

Gordon sniffed like a rabbit. "No, you're wrong there," he said. "That's Quirk's Brylcreem. Totally different pong."

"Hullo hullo," Zabarnowski said. "There are guests. Relatives, maybe?"

The adjutant had arrived with a middleaged civilian couple, evidently man and wife. Cox went over. "This is Mr and Mrs Burnett," Kellaway said. "Next-of-kin. Flight Lieutenant Cox." They shook hands. The man was wearing a blue suit and carrying a bowler hat; his wife's face was almost invisible behind a grey veil. "Very kind of you to come all this way," Cox said.

"Only London," Burnett said. "No distance, really, on the train." His face was tanned as far as the line of his hat and baby-white above. His grip was hard. There was still plenty of Ulster in his voice.

"Our last chance to pay our respects," Mrs Burnett said. Her accent churned the syllables like butter. "Poor dear Maurice," she said. "A lovely boy."

Cox was startled. Maurice? It seemed an unsuitable name. Maurice. Good God. Fancy old Flip . . .

Burnett was speaking. "I hope we got here in time," he was saying. "So we can have one last glimpse of the dear man before . . . you know . . ."

"Ah . . . well . . ." Cox glanced sharply at the adjutant.

"It would give Maurice's poor mother such tremendous comfort, I know it would," Mrs Burnett said, "if we could tell her we were the last to set eyes on her Maurice, us being his own flesh and blood too, d'ye see."

"Oh dear," Kellaway said. "What a shame. What a very great pity. I'm afraid it's too late for that now. I am sorry."

" 'twould only take a couple of minutes," she said. "His poor dear mother in Ballymena . . ."

"I'm awfully sorry," Cox said, "but you see the coffin has been . . . um . . . sealed."

"Sealed, is it?" Burnett said. "Would that mean they've screwed the lid on?"

"It would. I mean, yes, they have."

"Ah, well, that's no great problem, is it?" He took a short

screwdriver from his pocket. "There would be no disrespect, would there? Half a tick, that's all it would take."

"Look: I'm afraid a screwdriver won't do," Cox said. "It's just not on, I'm afraid."

Burnett looked at him, not understanding.

"Take care of this lady for a moment," the adjutant told Cox. He took Burnett outside. "If you insist," he said, "I'll have the coffin opened, but believe me you won't recognise anything you see and your wife will be very upset."

It took a moment for Burnett to realise what this meant. "Maurice wasn't just ... you know ... killed, then?" He didn't want to look at Kellaway. He brushed dust from his bowler hat with his thick, strong fingers. He was accustomed to death and corpses, funerals and wakes; they were an important part of family life, a necessary and satisfying ritual. But this was different, horribly different. This was more than death. This was something so ugly and agonising that it had to be shut away. This was pain and suffering so severe that it could hurt others, even after the body had died. This had the makings of a nightmare. "We thought ... I suppose we thought ... maybe a bullet or something ..."

"Flight Lieutenant Moran was shot down in flames," Kellaway said. "He was burnt to death." *There, you stupid civilian*, he thought, *you asked for it, now you've got it, so can we please get on with the job? Thank you.*

Burnett had to take a digestive tablet before he could go inside. He said nothing to his wife; simply shook his head. The funeral went off all right. Cox noticed that the chaplain said *Mo*ran instead of Mor*an*. It made Flip sound like an idiot.

They changed from best blue back to flying kit and landed at Bodkin Hazel at four o'clock, just in time for tea, except that Jerry didn't believe in tea. The first cups were being filled when the squadron got scrambled.

Sometimes the *Luftwaffe* made cock-ups too.

Thirty Heinkel 111's were three miles ahead, circling the Isle of Sheppey at fourteen thousand. Barton levelled out at sixteen thousand – fourteen for the controller and two for luck – and called the tally-ho. With the sun on his left and the sky bright and empty, he had a huge view; and what he could see, in addition to the Essex flatlands and all the Thames estuary, and half of Kent, was that Jerry had cocked it up. These slow Heinkels had gone on ahead expecting to rendezvous with their escort, and now they were having to stooge about and wait for the escort to turn up. In fact he could see the escort belting along the north Kent coast: twenty or so Messerschmitt 110's. No doubt the kraut R/T was crackling with bad temper.

The 110's started to climb as soon as they saw the Hurricanes, and the Heinkels came out of their orbit and headed west.

"Mango Leader to Blue Leader," Barton called. "Your flight can handle those fighters. Better go now."

"Okay, Mango Leader," CH3 said. With Cox away, he was leading 'B' flight. The squadron divided, 'B' flight turning towards the escort; but immediately that happened, the Messerschmitts also divided. Half of them made for the Heinkels again.

"In and out fast," Barton ordered. "Beat 'em up, shake 'em up, then back on top PDQ."

They dived: three sections in line abreast, each wingman a few lengths behind his leader. When they levelled out, the leaders raced at the flank of the raid, fired, vaulted the outside bombers, climbed steeply away. Half a second later, the wingmen did the same. Bing Macfarlane clearly saw faces at the glossy, porpoise-like nose of one Heinkel, an upflung arm, a gaping mouth; then he boomed over the fuselage, snatching the bomber's aerial with his tail-wheel. It was enough to make any pilot twitch; Bing himself twitched a little at the cat's-cradle of tracer all around him; and several Heinkel pilots lost control. One began wallowing violently, like a dinghy in surf. Another wandered suicidally across the formation. A third started drifting back on the next bomber, but there was an excuse for that: his port engine was laying down a broad black carpet of smoke.

Barton checked the scene while his flight regrouped. A mile or two away, 'B' flight was roaming around one group of Me-110's. These had changed formation: now they formed a perfect circle, ten or a dozen planes chasing each other's tails, endlessly. *Extraordinary*, Barton thought. *Where's that going to get them?* Below him, the rest of the escort had reached the bombers and were zigzagging alongside in an effort to match their trudging speed.

574

"Same again, 'A' flight," Barton called. "In and out fast. Don't mix it."

As the attack went down, two or three of the big Messerschmitts swung away from the raid. Lacking speed, they were more cumbersome than ever. The Hurricanes swept past them, stormed into the Heinkels' flank, soared away to safety. Craning his neck to look behind, Barton saw heavy flak bursting a few hundred yards ahead of the bombers. As he levelled out, they were rocking and bouncing wildly on the broken, smoky air and not liking it. One plane jettisoned its bombload, then another, then six at once. Suddenly half the raid was turning back. Barton turned his flight loose. "Forget the escort, stay out of trouble," he ordered. "Hit the stragglers."

Haducek and Macfarlane formed White Section. They fell away at once. Barton, with Brook as his wingman, circled for a while and then went after the Heinkel with the shot-up engine, now trailing well behind the rest. Cattermole, leading Yellow Section, was in no such hurry. He waited and watched, while the raid straggled south-east over Kent, and Steele-Stebbing guarded his tail. Haducek and Macfarlane were streaking in and out making fools of the escort, closing to point-blank range, scoring hits, dashing off. Eventually, a bomber lurched and stumbled and sheered away, slicing the air like a big fish dodging the rushing current.

"Come on, Iron Filings," Cattermole said. "Let's murder that invalid."

It was not so easy.

The Me-110's did not interfere: their brief, it seemed, was to stick with the mass of bombers: stragglers were abandoned. This straggler defended himself cleverly and desperately. Hopeless to try to outrun the fighters. Pointless to remain at height and shoot it out with them. So the German pilot used the advantages left to him: size, slowness, skill.

By making a series of diving turns he kept the fighters behind him and he gave his belly and upper gunners repeated chances of a shot. The Heinkel had a vast wing, nearly a thousand square feet, and he made the most of it, side-slipping and skidding almost sideways, dragging his speed so low that the Hurricanes kept having to break away before they overshot. It made the bomber a tantalisingly awkward target. And all the time the crew kept flinging out stuff to lighten the plane: ammo boxes, radio, sheets of armour plating, fire extinguishers, all came whirling past the Hurricanes. Worst of all, oil spattered their windscreens. For the Heinkel had been hit, and badly.

Steele-Stebbing fired off his last rounds as they crossed the coast. The Heinkel was down to a thousand feet but France was clearly visible. Then, as if it had tired of the whole silly business, the Heinkel banked to the right and headed for the Atlantic. Flames made a bright red garland, tipped with yellow, around its starboard engine.

The two Hurricanes flew alongside and watched. The bomber remained horizontal but it was sinking steadily. Nobody had baled out. Perhaps they were dead, or perhaps they had dumped their parachutes to save weight. Five hundred feet. The sea shone like tarmac after rain. Cattermole saw movement under the fuselage, as if someone were waving. He edged closer and lower. It was a man's legs, sticking out of the belly-hatch. They flexed and worked, running on air. The man was stuck in the hatch.

Four hundred feet. Speed, say, a hundred and fifty knots. When the Heinkel hit the sea, the impact would rip his legs off.

Cattermole turned, lined up the bomber in his sights, closed to a hundred yards, judged the deflection to a nicety, and poured eight streams of bullets into the dangling man. His legs kicked once and then trailed in the slipstream. A minute later the plane buried itself in a mound of foam, and when the foam subsided there was nothing left but the scarred sea.

"Home for tea, Yellow Two," Cattermole said; but the patrol was not over yet. They were crossing the South Downs at two thousand feet, only a few minutes from Bodkin Hazel, when Cattermole's engine died.

"Feeling tired?" Steele-Stebbing asked. Already the Hurricane was sliding downhill, and the angle steepened as its airspeed fell away.

"It's this cheap knicker-elastic," Cattermole said. He was checking his fuel, switching tanks. No joy.

"My word, it looks awfully bumpy down there." It did: hills, woods, valleys. Even a quarry.

"Save me some tea." Cattermole searched ahead but he couldn't

576

see anything flat and open. The late-afternoon sun flickered on lots of glass and made him squint. "And send a car to pick me up."

"I will if you ask me nicely."

"Get fucked."

"In that case you can walk home. And no tea, either."

At twelve hundred feet the bumps looked even bumpier. Cattermole uncoupled everything and baled out. Steele-Stebbing circled and saw him land, and flew on home. "He's not far from Ashford," he told Barton. "By the way, how did we get on?"

"Your Heinkel makes four, plus a couple of 110's."

"I say! Not a bad show."

"That was before Skull got to work. Now it's only two Heinkels and half a 110." Barton shrugged. "Who cares, anyway?"

Air Commodore Bletchley's car was waiting when they landed at Brambledown. Barton got driven straight to the station commander's office. Group Captain Dalgleish was there with Bletchley and a wing commander without wings whom Barton did not know. They all had expressions of deep concern. "You lost a kite this afternoon," Bletchley said. "About half-past four. It crashed. Have you heard from the pilot?"

"Not directly, sir. The police phoned to say he'd baled out and landed on somebody's farm."

"So he's alive?"

"Presumably."

The answer did not seem to please them. "Had he been in action?" Dalgleish asked. "I mean, actually involved in combat?"

"Yes."

"Well, that's something, I suppose. I mean, he might be wounded for all we know. Head injury. Paralysed, even."

"Not paralysed," the wing commander said, "Not if he managed to bale out."

"No, I suppose not," Dalgleish said grudgingly. "Still, semi-paralysed, maybe."

"I can easily arrange to have him maimed, if you like," Barton said. "I mean, we have the weapons." The wing commander's eyes opened wide.

"He was obviously suffering from shock," Bletchley declared.

"His controls must have been useless," Dalgleish said. "Shot to pieces."

"Not according to his wingman," Barton said. "He told me it was just engine-failure, he —"

"And what he doesn't know," Bletchley said, "is the kite crashed into a row of houses in Ashford and killed four people, including an infant."

"Oh," Barton said.

"So it must have been out of control, mustn't it?" Dalgleish said. "Otherwise it wouldn't have happened."

"Well, that's certainly a point of view, sir," Barton said.

"Look: it's absolutely paramount that the press don't get wind of this," Bletchley said. "No loose talk in pubs, no gossip in letters home. Understand, Barton? Tell your chaps to forget it ever happened. And I want to see that pilot as soon as he turns up."

"Right, sir."

"And Barton," Dalgleish said, "I know it's difficult upstairs, but can't you do something about your squadron's language? It all gets relayed over the Tannoy in the ops room, you know, and the Waafs hear you fellows stiffing and blinding like fishwives."

"If the controllers didn't mess us about, sir, we wouldn't have so much to swear at."

"They have a very difficult job," Bletchley said.

"Yes, sir. And some of them can't do it."

"Be fair, old boy. What about all those kills you've got?"

"And what about all the scrambles that lead to nothing?"

Dalgleish sighed. "You expect rather a lot, don't you? Is there anything else we can do for you?"

"Yes, sir, since you ask: I'd like fuel-injection, a radio that transmits more than forty miles, and a catering officer who knows what peas and beans do to the average fighter pilot's stomach at twenty thousand feet. A couple of days ago some of my chaps got scrambled after lunch and they nearly blew themselves in half."

Dalgleish made a note, and looked at the wing commander. "Your turn," he said.

"I'm in charge of accounts," the wing commander told Barton.

"Ah! You've got our back-pay?"

"Not yet, but don't worry. The matter is being pursued."

Bletchley said: "That means they've lost the files."

"Oh no, sir. I can assure you it's being very actively pursued."

"That means they've lost the files," Bletchley said, "but they're looking for them."

The wing commander gave Bletchley a bleak little smile. "Very droll," he murmured. "The matter of arrears is, I'm afraid, out of my hands," he told Barton. "What concerns me at the moment is the size of some of your officers' mess-bills. To be frank, they're living far beyond their income."

He produced a typewritten list. Barton looked at the names and the amounts.

"You see?" the wing commander said. "I'm afraid I shall have to have a word with them."

"Don't do that," Barton said. "Just . . . leave them alone, please."

"Yes, but . . . Something's got to be done, hasn't it? They can't go on like this?"

"They won't," Barton said. "I can assure you of that."

Fanny Barton showered, changed, went to the mess and found CH3 in a corner with Moggy Cattermole.

Cattermole was badly scratched on both cheeks. "Bloody brambles," he said. "They had to cut me out with scythes. I got rescued by a mob of sweaty peasants with string around their knees. None of them spoke English. I think it was the chorus from *Cavalleria Rusticana*, although what they're doing in Kent at this time of year is hard to –"

"Listen," Barton said. "What happened to you?"

"I just told CH3. Engine quit, so I hopped out."

"Did you know the kite hit a house?"

"No, really? Pity. I was quite fond of that kite. Complete write-off, I suppose?"

"Yes. Also three adults and a kid."

"Ah." Cattermole signalled a waiter. "Beers," he said.

CH3 said: "You told me you were down to about a thousand feet when you jumped. You know that area, Moggy. You've flown over it a dozen times. You must have realised the kite would hit Ashford."

"Yes. More or less."

"You could have banked it away before you jumped, couldn't you?"

579

Cattermole sucked in his breath. "Very dangerous. Very, very dangerous. Not much height, not much speed. She'd stall as quick as winking, wouldn't she? And then where would I be? Baling out at five hundred feet? No, no. That's not what the instructions say on the side of the packet."

"But you could see Ashford was up ahead," Barton said.

"Yes."

"It didn't occur to you to sit tight and try to miss the houses."

"No."

"Were you feeling okay?" CH3 asked. "Any dizziness or sickness or –"

"This is all very boring," Cattermole said. "It was perfectly obvious that if I sat in that kite it was bound to crash and I would probably get killed. Anyone with an ounce of gallantry would have stayed at the controls and tried to miss the innocent bystanders. I haven't got an ounce of gallantry. I don't intend to kill myself to save three and a half civilians. It's their war as well as mine, so they can jolly well take some of the risk."

"That's pretty bloody callous," Barton said.

"I'm not so sure," CH3 said. Their beers arrived. "People talk a lot of bullshit about civilians. Do civilians feel pain any more than you or I do? Of course not. So why give them special status?"

"Women and children last," Barton said. "That's charming."

"Three and a half civilians can't fly a Hurricane," CH3 said.

"Get this straight," Barton said to Cattermole. "We're going to see Baggy Bletchley now. When you baled out, that kite was uncontrollable, and you were in a state of shock. Okay?"

"No, that's pathetic," CH3 said. "What have you got the jitters about? If Baggy can't take the truth, that's his tough luck."

"And mine too. I carry the can, not you. We'll do as I said."

They finished their beers. Cattermole signed Barton's name on the bar-chit. They went to see Baggy Bletchley.

"Bad luck, eh?" Bletchley said. "It seems you were left without any choice."

"Not at all, sir," Cattermole said. "I baled out because if I'd stayed in the plane I'd have been killed. I didn't care a hoot about any civilians."

"What did I tell you?" Bletchley said to Barton. "The poor fellow's suffering from shock." He slapped Cattermole on the back.

580

"Shock does funny things to a man. I wouldn't be surprised if you'd forgotten all about it by tomorrow."

"All about what, sir?" Cattermole asked.

"That's the idea," Bletchley said. "By the way, have you heard today's score? Jerry lost forty-nine to our sixteen. Good, eh?"

"Told you so," said CH3 to Barton.

"Oh, go to hell," Barton snapped. Bletchley smiled benignly.

CH3 was woken by the tap and flicker of rain on his window. It was the most marvellous sound. He got up and looked out: ten-tenths cloud at five hundred feet and visibility so dreadful he couldn't see the other side of the mess. A thoroughly unblitzy day. Lovely. It was half-past six. He went back to bed and slept until nine.

Nim Renouf was at breakfast. "That's his third lot of bacon and eggs," Cox told CH3. "On top of two bowls of porridge."

"I've got to catch up," Renouf said, buttering toast. "I didn't get much to eat yesterday. Or the day before."

"I thought hospitals fed you every other hour," CH3 said.

"Possibly. I wouldn't know. I didn't wake up till last night."

"You mean you were unconscious all that time?"

"Dunno. Can't remember. Shove the marmalade over, will you?"

They watched him spoon marmalade onto toast. His face was as pale as skimmed milk and his eyelids were curiously heavy, as if he were shielding his eyes from glare. His fingers gripped the marmalade spoon so tightly that his nails were half-white.

"I'm surprised they sent you back so soon," CH3 said.

"They didn't. I did a bunk in the middle of the night."

"Ah!" Cox exclaimed. "And I bet you couldn't catch a train, could you?"

"Didn't try," Renouf said. "Hitch-hiked." Already, he was buttering his next piece of toast. "More coffee, please," he told a waiter.

"Hitch-hiked?" CH3 said. "From Ramsgate? In the middle of the night?"

"Gorgeous blonde in an MG picked me up. Very friendly. Drove me all the way here. Nice girl. Couldn't do enough for me."

"I'm sure," Cox said. "Have some more porridge, Nim."

Cattermole and Macfarlane had joined them. "It can't be done in an MG," Macfarlane said. "The gearstick gets in the way."

"I never found any difficulty," Cattermole said. "Mind you, she was a Japanese trapeze-artist with a degree in engineering. You look bloody awful."

Renouf said: "Well, I feel okay."

"I can't help that. You look bloody awful. Good morning, sir." Barton had just sat down. "Don't you think Nim looks bloody awful?"

"Later," Barton said. "Somebody give me some coffee."

"I need some decent grub inside me, that's all." Renouf looked at his latest slice of toast, breathed deeply, and tried to pick it up; but his fingers failed to grip, his eyes closed, and he slumped gently against Cox's shoulder.

They carried him to a sofa, where he slept with his thumb in his mouth until early afternoon.

Later, Barton called everybody into his office.

"It's pretty certain that Nim went down because of oxygen starvation," he said. "Either his bottle wasn't full or his mask went duff or something. He was lucky. In most cases the pilot never comes to again. What d'you remember?"

"Not much," Renouf said. "It happened very fast. One moment I was fine, a couple of seconds later I began to feel sort of woozy, but the strange thing is I couldn't seem to take it seriously. I felt quite relaxed and happy."

"A bit pissed?" the adjutant said. Renouf nodded. "It used to happen to us all the time," the adjutant told them.

"Nothing mattered," Renouf said.

"Anything else?" Barton asked. "Did your Mae West work okay?"

"Yes, it held me up. What I really needed, of course, was a dinghy. I tell you, that Channel's bloody cold, even in August. It was too bloody cold for me. I don't remember getting fished out. Not a thing."

"So now you know," Barton told them. "Try and come down near a boat if you possibly can. There's a hell of a lot of drink out there. Okay, that's all. We're released for the rest of the day."

It was too late to go up to London. Most of them wandered back to the mess and played cards, waiting for the cinemas to open.

Pip Patterson stood and watched a game of gin rummy. Now that there was definitely no flying he felt hugely relieved, and yet there was nothing he wanted to do with the free time. The rain depressed him. He slowly realised that it would always be like this. It would always be bad weather when he was released, and always good weather when he was trapped at dispersal.

Cattermole won a hand, and pretended to notice Patterson. "Ah, this will interest you, Pip," he said. "Young Fitz has asked me to be godfather to his imminent child."

"I don't believe you."

"Suit yourself."

"One of these days," Patterson said, "I think I'll take Fitz aside and tell him some of the facts of life."

Cattermole shuffled and dealt. "Apparently it was Mary's idea," he said. "Smart girl, Mary."

Next day the blitzy weather returned, and with it the raids. Hornet squadron got scrambled five times. Brambledown was bombed again; this time they hit the airfield. Bodkin Hazel was strafed by lowflying Me-110's. By evening, Skull had reports of similar raids on seven other fighter fields. It was clear that the *Luftwaffe* could not wait to destroy Fighter Command in the air, and so was planning to knock out its bases in south-east England. The BBC gave the day's score as *Luftwaffe* thirty-three, RAF ten, and the sun set in a saffron sky.

The next day was fine and dry. So was the next. And the next. There was no rest. The raids got bigger and more frequent, until the pilots were doing little more than flying and fighting and sleeping. Some enjoyed this enormously. Whenever Zabarnowski and Haducek took off, it was with a feeling of eagerness that approached exultation. They relished the fight, pressed home their attacks more savagely than anyone else, often closed to fifty yards in order to make sure of the kill, then sheered away with the debris of the explosion scarring their planes. They quickly became the top-scoring Hornet pilots. Zab and Haddy loathed Germans. They wanted to shoot down German planes all day, every day, preferably in flames. Zab had learned the word *flamer* from the adjutant and he used it a lot. "Today, another flamer for me," he would tell Skull happily. "Heinkel bomber. That's a crew of five, you know?

Sizzle, sizzle, crackle, crackle. I sent them all to hell and I gave them a little taste of it on the way."

"Just the facts, please." Skull's face was expressionless. "Were there no parachutes?"

"Oh, one fellow tried to jump but it didn't open."

"That is a lie," Haducek said. "I saw it open but you went down and shot at him and it closed."

Barton heard that. "Look here, Zab," he said. "That's not on, you know, shooting at Jerry parachutists."

"Was a mistake," Zabarnowski said. "I aim at a Messerschmitt but I miss and hit a parachute, very sorry."

"No, I mean it," Barton said, and stared until Zabarnowski met his gaze. "When a Jerry bales out over England he's a prisoner-of-war and we don't shoot him. He's out of the war, see? Those are the rules."

"Rules, rules," Zabarnowski muttered, and said something brisk and spiky in Polish.

"That's an order," CH3 told him. "Jerry parachutists are non-combatants, understand? They can't fight any more, so we leave them alone." Zabarnowski sniffed, and scowled at his boots.

"Very interesting," Haducek said. "Now tell me please, what are the German rules? If I bale out, I can fight again, can't I? So –"

"That's the theory, I agree," Barton said, "but Jerry seems to be playing the game so far, and –"

"Game?" Zabarnowski said. "You call this a game?"

The only other pilot with anything like the same insatiable appetite for combat was Flash Gordon. There was no doubt any more that he was, from time to time, mentally unstable. On the ground his moods varied sharply and unpredictably, from a schoolboy petulance to a bland, middleaged amiability that might suddenly turn to acid contempt or – what several pilots found more disturbing – a prolonged and enthusiastic analysis of bulletwounds. Gordon would delight in plotting the longest and most destructive course that a bullet could take. "Let's say it chops through your shoulder, cracks your collarbone and hacks its merry way down through your right lung . . . That would bring it to your liver, which is a very prominent item, I mean it could hardly miss *that*, and who knows, it might take a slice out of your diaphragm in passing.

None of that stuff is very resistant, of course, it's all soft and mushy, so the bullet still has plenty of power to use up, which means it could make a very thorough mess of your stomach before it took a whack at your plumbing. The only thing I'm not sure of is, would it get a chance to hit your gall bladder on the way?"

"Shut up, Flash, for Christ's sake."

"Probably not. Still, there's all of your colon just waiting to be ripped apart. Yards and bloody yards of colon, you've got. Say, for the sake of argument, it tunnels its busy way through your colon, and then blows a bloody great hole in your bladder, it *still* might have just enough go left in it to knock out one of your goolies, mightn't it?"

"Flash, give it a rest or I'll kill you."

"Pity about the kidneys. The trouble is, I don't see how you can hit the kidneys *and* the stomach unless you start from the armpit. That might be a better idea. Suppose . . ."

In the air, Gordon saved his eccentricities for the enemy. The solo head-on attack on a large bomber formation was his favourite. A closing speed of well over five hundred miles an hour left no time to aim, but the sight of a Hurricane streaking past his wingtip or hurtling under his cockpit or even slashing diagonally across his nose was enough to test the nerve of the steadiest *Luftwaffe* pilot, and many a Dornier or Heinkel went lurching and stumbling out of formation as a result of Gordon's apparently suicidal charges. Fanny Barton let him get on with them. For one thing, nothing anyone said was likely to stop him; and for another, it was a damn sight easier to attack a shaken and twitchy bunch of bombers struggling to regroup.

Gordon seemed to be fearless. One glorious summer's morning, 'B' flight intercepted eight Me-110's on their way back to France. The German fighters had no wish to do battle, which was natural: the myth of the 110's invincibility had long since vanished: it was big and fast and could blow you apart if you were foolish enough to sit in front of it, but it had the agility of a grand piano. Any Hurricane easily out-turned it. Escorts of 110's were beginning to be a joke. When the raid they were escorting got attacked, they usually withdrew and formed a protective circle, guarding each other's tails until the danger had passed.

Mother Cox and the rest of his flight chased this group of eight for thirty miles. Zabarnowski shot one down, Quirk and Renouf scored hits on two, and Gordon got within sniffing distance of three without ever opening fire.

When they landed, Cox went over to him. "What was the trouble, Flash?" he asked. "Gun stoppages?"

"No trouble, Mother. I just didn't fancy any of them today. They weren't suitable."

"Don't be so bloody silly, Flash. What d'you mean, not suitable?"

"Well . . ." Gordon wrinkled his nose. "They weren't what I was looking for."

Cox was accustomed to Gordon's dottiness, but this was grotesque. They walked in silence to the crewroom. Later, after debriefing, Cox took him aside and asked him what the hell he was up to.

Gordon pursed his lips and thought. "I think I do it to scare myself."

That made no sense. Cox waited, but Gordon linked his hands on the top of his head and blinked drowsily at the hot sunlight.

"You do it to scare yourself," Cox said. "Why scare yourself? Aren't you scared to start with? I am. I'm frightened bloody witless."

"Oh, yes. Still, you can't have too much of a good thing."

"Don't bet on it. The way you're going, Flash, you'll scare yourself to death soon."

"So what? You die every night." Gordon rocked on his heels. His eyes were almost closed. A trick of the light showed up a cluster of very faint freckles that crossed his nose. "Ever thought of that, Mother? Each night, you die. You lie down, you slip away, maybe you never come back. It's not so terrible, is it? I don't worry about it. I reckon I've had so much practice it should come very easily."

Without discussing it, Cattermole and Steele-Stebbing had reached a sort of truce. They rarely communicated on the ground. In the air, where they formed Yellow Section, they spoke only when they had something disparaging to say.

They were crossing the coast on their way back to base when Cattermole's engine cut out.

"Boring," Steele-Stebbing said. "You did that yesterday."

"Don't pick your nose while you're talking to me."

"Whose nose would you like me to pick?"

"Pay close attention to this advanced method of flying." Cattermole waggled his wings. "The prop stays still and the plane goes round and round."

"Very boring. Can't you do something thrilling? Crash into an orphanage."

The engine coughed and re-started. Cattermole climbed back up. "Something wrong with your undercart," he said. "I think you've got fowl pest."

Two minutes later his engine died again. "How dreary," Steele-Stebbing said. "No imagination."

"Shocking smell in here. You been pissing in my tank again?"

"I'll go ahead and find you a nice orphanage."

Again, the Merlin revived and Cattermole took up station. "Not fowl pest," he said. "Looks more like pox."

They were circling Bodkin Hazel when Steele-Stebbing discovered that Cattermole was right. His undercarriage refused to go down.

"Nasty," Cattermole said. "What with all those bunkers and all." The field had been bombed in their absence: craters pocked the grass.

"You go first," Steele-Stebbing said. "Let's get the big prang out of the way."

"Why don't you get out and walk?"

"All right, show me. You're the expert."

Cattermole landed. Steele-Stebbing circled, using up fuel, while he tried various remedies suggested by the control tower. Eventually he succeeded, by violent rocking, in getting one wheel down. By now Barton was in the tower. "Bale out," he ordered. "Climb to five or six thou, point the kite at France and bale out." Steele-Stebbing spiralled up to six thousand, one wheel dangling, and couldn't get his cockpit open. It was jammed solid. Even hammering at it with his revolver butt did nothing. The fuel gauge was nudging zero.

Everyone stopped work to watch him touch down. The single wheel bounced once and raced. The leg stayed firm. Gradually the tail came down, the tail-wheel ran, the other wing lost flying speed and sank. Steele-Stebbing's rigger closed his eyes just before the wingtip stroked the grass. Then the Hurricane skewed and spun in tight little circles, cracking the wheel-leg, smashing the prop, flinging up a brown-green spray of clods as it skittered along. The fire-truck caught up. Men with axes leaped onto the wing. No smoke, no flame. Everyone went back to work.

When Steele-Stebbing walked into the crewroom, CH3 said: "Nice work. You okay?"

"Fine, fine. Piece of cake." The bridge of his nose was skinned.

"Grab some tea. Micky's got a spare kite ready for you."

Black Section got scrambled at six. 'A' flight got scrambled at six-thirty. The whole squadron went up at eight. It was dusk before Skull finished the last combat summary. "Busy day," he told Barton and the flight commander. "Seven scrambles, a total of fifty-three sorties. Bing Macfarlane slightly injured with a fragment of cannonshell in the leg, Quirk probably concussed from a forced landing, Brook with a burnt left hand and a bruised back. Four machines written-off: Quirk's in a duckpond, Brook's shot down in flames, Steele-Stebbing's you all saw, and of course Macfarlane baled out again."

"Oh well," said Barton. "It could've been worse. It could've been a bloody sight worse." He rubbed his eyes and remembered flashes and glimpses of the scrap with the 109's. "Christ, we were lucky," he said. "I thought Brook had bought it for certain, I mean with three Jerrys knocking hell out of him all at once ... Christ Almighty."

"Quirk reckons that duckpond saved him," Cox said. "He says he set fire to a cornfield and all he could see coming towards him was a socking great barn and all of a sudden there was this lovely duckpond."

"Sailors," CH3 said. "They'll find water anywhere."

"Well," Barton said to Skull. "That's us. What about them?"

"Two definites, two probables."

"You're talking about 'B' flight," Cox said.

"I'm talking about the whole squadron."

"*What?* Listen, Fitz and Zab alone told me –"

"Yes, I know what everyone claimed," Skull said.

"Look, Skull," CH3 said, "there were kraut kites going down all over the place. I saw –"

"The reports have been completed," Skull said. "You don't need

588

to tell me all over again, and frankly I'm getting pretty sick of repeating that just because you saw an enemy aircraft *go down*, that does not justify claiming its destruction."

"It does when we've hit the buggers," Cox said.

"No, with respect, it *doesn't*," Skull told him.

"Two and two," Barton said. "Seven scrambles, fifty-three sorties, and all you'll give us is two definite kills? I saw more than that, and half the time I was looking the wrong bloody way!"

Skull straightened his papers and said nothing.

"The boys are going to love you," Barton said. "You're going to be their sweetheart, you are."

"Nobody would be happier than I to raise the score," Skull said. "All I ask is evidence. Is that unreasonable?"

"The hell with it," Barton said. "Do what you like, I don't give a damn. I feel sorry for the boys, that's all. They go up and shit themselves seven times a day, and when they finally succeed in blowing a Hun to kingdom come you want to see his death certificate before you ... Oh, balls. Let's get a drink."

"Hey," CH3 said. "I just thought of something. Cine-guns."

"No!" Barton snapped. "If he won't take a pilot's word of honour then the whole thing's a farce and I wash my hands of it."

"Steady on, Fanny," Cox said. "Maybe cine-guns aren't such a bad idea. I mean, suppose you get some film of a Jerry baling out of a 109, that's pretty definite, isn't it?"

"Might be," Barton said grudgingly.

"Let's face it, he's never going to climb back inside, is he?"

"All right, if you want cine-guns, let's all have cine-guns." Barton glowered at Skull. "Let's all have Mickey Mouse and icecream at the intervals too, while we're at it. Do what you like."

Skull went out.

"Trust you to make life more difficult," Barton said bitterly to CH3. "As if I haven't got enough trouble with that bloke without you complicating matters."

"It was your decision. Don't blame me for that. If you thought it was such a bum idea you shouldn't have okayed it."

"Cine-gun can't do any harm," Cox said.

"It's a matter of principle. How can I lead this squadron if nobody trusts anybody?"

"Come off it, Fanny," CH3 said. "Do you believe everyone's claims? I certainly don't."

"Whose bloody side are you on?"

"We've got twenty minutes before that pub shuts," Cox said. That ended the argument.

Daybreak in mid-August was about an hour later than it had been in June. This meant that Hornet squadron could sleep until four or four-thirty before flying down to Bodkin Hazel.

The next couple of hours were the worst. Everyone felt weary and hung-over. They dozed in armchairs and woke, stiff and sweaty, when someone slammed a door, or when the fitters fired up a Hurricane. Tempers were brittle. Everyone looked forward to breakfast, but when it came some of them ate little. They had developed a painful sensitivity to certain sounds: the telephone and the Tannoy. Each made a preliminary, introductory noise. The telephone produced a little click before it rang; the Tannoy uttered a gentle buzz. Those feeble noises could make men like Fitz and Cox and Cattermole, and even CH3 and Barton, start as if stung.

It was still before breakfast when Barton came into the crewroom with Micky Marriott. "Okay, pay attention," Barton said. He pounded a table. Everyone groaned and stirred. "Micky's go something to show you."

It was a length of metal channel, much dented. "This came of Iron Filings' kite," he said. "It's the cockpit runner. You can see here why it didn't run: it's been hit by something, probably a bullet."

"That could happen to anyone," Barton said. "Now, I'm no laying down any hard-and-fast rules. It's up to you whether you fly with your cockpit open or shut, just as long as you know you've got a choice."

"Open for me, thank you very much," Steele-Stebbing said.

"Damn draughty at twenty thou," Fitzgerald muttered.

"If you're going to have it open," CH3 said, "for Christ's sak *lock* it open. Otherwise you'll make a belly-landing and the soddin thing'll shoot forward and then you'll be trapped."

"I thought we were supposed to be getting a quick-releas mechanism," Macfarlane said.

"They've made one," Marriott said. "Trouble is, it's not all that quick."

"Yes, but," Flash Gordon said. "On the other hand it's not very reliable, either, is it? So in the long run that balances things out."

Haducek said: "You talk out of your arse, Flash."

"Not at all. I mean, if the silly thing isn't going to work properly, you don't want it to go wrong *quickly*, do you?"

"God strike me pink," Haducek muttered.

"Dash it all, that's blindingly obvious," Gordon said. "I must say, Haddy, sometimes I wonder about you."

"One other thing," Barton said. "It's going to be bloody hot again out there today, and I know some of you prefer to fly in shoes instead of boots and no gloves and so on. Again, it's up to you, but take a look at Brooky's hand." Sergeant Brook held it up. Two fingers were bandaged. "If he hadn't been wearing gloves," Barton said, "you can guess what that hand would look like."

"Goggles are even more important," CH3 said. "The more you can cover up, the less there is to get burned."

"No, that's crazy," Zabarnowski said. "Wear goggles, you can't see so well, wear gloves and boots you sweat like a pig, no wonder you get jumped. Is crazy."

"Zabby believes in comfort," Haducek said.

"Clean silk stockings every day?" Cox said.

"Sure, why not?" Haducek said. "The trouble with you British, you think you got to be uncomfortable or else you're not doing your proper job."

"You guys don't know how to *enjoy* war," Zabarnowski said. "Polish peoples know. Polish peoples got lots of practice."

"I hope you followed all that," Cattermole said. "What it boils down to is you have a choice between being frozen, stifled, or Polish."

Each flight got scrambled once before midday. Neither met the enemy. CH3's flight found nothing; Cox's flight got close enough to see con-trails reaching out to France but no closer.

They were sitting down to lunch when the Tannoy made its gentle buzz and Fitzgerald knocked over a glass of water. The scramble sounded and twenty minutes later the squadron was three miles above Tunbridge Wells, searching for a batch of Junkers

88's that were said to have made a mess of Biggin Hill. CH3 saw them, miles away to the west, dots drifting across the hazy forests and fields of Sussex. They caught them just short of the coast and made repeated attacks. The bombers dipped to sea-level, actually flying through the spray thrown up by the fighters' fire. It was very difficult to attack: accurate shooting by the German gunners, turbulent air, the sea just a few feet below. The only man to score was Sergeant Brook, bandaged fingers and all. He got close enough to concentrate his fire on a starboard engine. It bled oil, and Brook danced in to have another go, right into the upper gunner's sights. The Hurricane bucked and reared and dived tail-first into the sea. Barton kept up the chase for another five miles and then quit.

Nobody mentioned Brook when they sat down to eat their delayed lunch. Only Cattermole and Haducek had seen him go in; the others had been dodging and twisting and climbing and looking the other way. But most of them had seen the splash, and everyone had seen the gap in White Section on the way home. There wasn't much to say. He'd been a quiet sort of bloke, not a bad pilot. Too bad the 88 didn't go down with him. Tough old kite, the 88.

Barton sat down and banged his spoon for attention. "I've just been on the phone to Brambledown," he said. "One of the Spitfire boys went missing last week. They've just fished him out of the drink. He was wearing his parachute and he was full of German-calibre bullets."

"Quite legitimate," Haducek remarked. "You said –"

"I don't care what I said. From now on, any German you see inside or outside his plane, you kill him. Understand?"

Nobody had anything to add. Barton got up and went out. He found CH3 sitting in the apple-tree, and climbed to a branch above him. "Just been on the phone to Brambledown," he said.

"I know. Mother told me about it."

"Oh. And what d'you think?"

"Nothing. I'm surprised it took you so long, that's all. There's no nice way to do this job, Fanny. It's a waste of time looking." He leaned back and closed his eyes. The thrumming of bees was like an endless drumroll.

Barton snapped off twigs and shredded them. "I'm glad you've got it all worked out," he said.

"Don't take it so seriously," CH3 murmured. "It's not something to get worked up about."

3.45: squadron scramble. No problem finding the raid: a hundred aircraft were scattered between Dover and Deal. Heinkels and Dorniers had bombed the advance airfields at Lympne, Hawkinge and Manston. Now there was a running fight, with 109's and 110's trying to shield the bombers from such fighters as had managed to get off the ground before the bombs started falling. There were plenty of targets: the sky was flecked with them. Bing Macfarlane shot one down within thirty seconds. It was remarkably easy. He picked out a straggling Heinkel and fired a burst at it. His wingman shouted a warning so he broke right, and found that CH3's advice worked: a 109 sailed past his left wing, skidding hard. Macfarlane broke left and there he was, most beautifully placed on the 109's tail. It was perfect, magical, inevitable, the finest thing he had done since a wonderful afternoon on the rugby field when he wrongfooted the whole defence and scored. Now he gave CH3 another chance: he eased a couple of degrees to the right before he fired. Flames wobbled at the edges of his vision: the Hurricane shook; cordite fumes drifted up and made his nose twitch. As he released the button the German pilot broke left. Macfarlane had anticipated him by a fraction of a second. He saw white coolant bubbling out of the 109's exhaust. He saw the man's head twisted – where else? – to the left. He saw the whole aircraft flare and swell until it filled his gunsight, and then his bullets touched off a charge and the enemy became a ball of orange flame with a couple of wingtips sticking out of it. Macfarlane felt wonderful.

His groundcrew heard the soft music of his open gun-ports as he drifted in to land, saw the smokestreaks behind his guns, and ran over to get the news. They too were delighted, and their pride added to his pleasure. Nim Renouf came and congratulated him. It was a golden afternoon. They stood and watched the troops re-fuelling and re-arming the Hurricanes. Four planes were missing: Zabarnowski, Quirk, Cox and Gordon. "I think I saw Mother bale out," Renouf said. Macfarlane nodded. There was nothing to worry about. He stretched, luxuriously, and filled his lungs with glorious air, laced with the stink of high-octane fuel. "Hell of a scrap, wasn't it?" he said. "That'll teach the buggers." He was looking at the field beyond the hangars, a gentle swell of soft yellow stubble. Stooks of wheat stood in neat, strong ranks. *England at her best*, he thought. *As the song says: this is worth fighting for* ... Half the stooks collapsed, starting from the right and spreading rapidly, as if a giant hand had brushed the field. He pointed, too surprised to speak. A violent boom walloped the air. "That's a bomb," Renouf said. Above the hangar roof the top of a brown fountain appeared. Macfarlane's mind was still working out the mystery of the flattened stooks, but Renouf was off and running, the klaxon was blaring, signal flares were popping, Merlins were crackling into life. As he dropped into his seat and his groundcrew fixed his straps, Macfarlane looked up. Twenty-plus bombers were doing a fly-past at two thousand. A thin dribble of black was falling from some of them. The bomb-bursts were already marching across the field by the time he came unstuck.

All told, six Hurricanes got airborne, but Macfarlane was first. Between the whistle and crump of bombs, his groundcrew raised their heads from the trenches and watched him close on the raid. They saw the sparkle of gunfire, heard its tiny rattle over the dull throb of engines, saw him swerve, bank, attack again. They saw a bomber lurch and slide out of formation. Two figures fell from it; only one parachute opened. The slide grew steeper. The bomber dived into a field like an express charging into a tunnel.

Ten minutes later the raiders were out of sight and airmen were busy sticking warning flags next to bomb craters to help the fighters when they came in to land. Macfarlane was the first back. He dived from three thousand feet, crossed the perimeter below treetop height and streaked across the field, one gloved hand acknowledging his groundcrew's waving arms. He climbed, turned, came back and performed a victory roll. The Hurricane rotated smoothly and cleanly, as if it were drilling its way through the air. The troops waved their steel helmets. Macfarlane rolled again but the Hurricane had a tantrum. It flung its tail from side to side, dropped, and slashed at the airfield with a wing. Instantly a handsome aeroplane became a tumbling wreck. It cartwheeled with an intense, ugly fury, as if it wanted to batter itself to bits as rapidly and painfully as possible. By the time it had exhausted itself it was broken into six large pieces: the two wings, the tail unit, the engine, the cockpit and the fuselage. Seven if you counted the pilot.

When Barton landed, he waited for CH3 and they went over to look. Macfarlane was lying on the grass, exactly as he had been found. Everything about him was broken; everything was bent the wrong way. He didn't look human. He looked like a bag of dirty laundry that someone had forgotten to take the feet and arms out of.

Ten minutes later they were all ordered back to Brambledown: there were too many unexploded bombs at Bodkin Hazel. Barton, CH3, Cattermole, Steele-Stebbing, Judd and Fitzgerald took off. They found Quirk and Cox waiting for them in the mess. Both had baled out. No news of Zabarnowski or Gordon.

Nobody else was in the mess. There was a raid on and the Spitfire squadrons were up. It had been a long day and a bad day. Nobody wanted to talk. Now that the mainspring of action had been released they were all profoundly tired, bone-weary, drained. Within fifteen minutes they were slumped in armchairs or stretched out on sofas, asleep.

After a while the adjutant came in. He was holding a signal and looking pleased. "I heard you were back," he said, "and I thought you'd like to know that the Prime Minister, Mr Winston Churchill himself, has just made a speech about you."

Cattermole half-opened one eye. "Piss off, uncle," he mumbled.

"Listen, it's jolly good stuff. He said . . ." Kellaway glanced around and decided to abbreviate the signal. " 'Undaunted by odds, unwearied in their constant challenge and mortal danger . . .' " Cox had begun to snore. Kellaway abbreviated some more. "Anyway, the best bit's at the end," he said. "Listen to this: 'Never in the field of human conflict was so much owed by so many to so few.' How about that?"

Cattermole let his other eye drift half-open. He studied the adjutant. "Someone must have told him about our back-pay," he said.

Later that evening there was a press conference. Baggy Bletchley had arrived with a busload of foreign correspondents: Swedes, Spaniards, Swiss, Americans, Brazilians, a Russian, a Rhodesian, a Turk, several Canadians, even a Burmese. The three squadron commanders were hastily rounded up and taken to the lecture room to meet them. In the crowd, Barton saw Jacky Bellamy. "Hell of a bind for you, I realise that," Bletchley whispered as the correspondents took their seats, "but overseas opinion is extremely important right now. This lot have been getting a bit shirty on a diet of Air Ministry releases, so we're giving them a tour of fighter bases to keep them sweet."

"What d'you want us to say, sir?" one of the Spitfire commanders asked.

"Tell 'em we're winning, of course."

Bletchley spoke a few introductory words: *Brambledown was one of the sharpest spearheads in the battle, couldn't be a better place to take the pulse of the action, these three chaps had been in the thick of it since dawn, scored some notable victories, of course not everything could be revealed yet, Official Secrets Act and all that . . .*

The questions began, mostly about the *Luftwaffe*. Could it be beaten? Surely the RAF was hopelessly outnumbered? Why did so many raids get through? How many times had this particular airfield been bombed? How long could a fighter pilot remain efficient if he flew five or six sorties a day? How destructive was the cannon mounted on the Me-109 compared with the British machine-gun? What was the probability of invasion? The German press said that Fighter Command was on its last legs: any comment? Suppose Hitler invaded now, tonight: what could the RAF do to stop him?

The tone was not hostile; they simply wanted to know the answers. Barton gradually realised that these people had already come to the conclusion that Britain would not win, that they were reporting a plucky last stand, a brave but futile gesture against an irresistible enemy. The Canadian correspondents smiled once or twice, and sometimes nodded as they heard the optimistic replies, but he noticed that they took very few notes.

Bletchley chaired the meeting well. He courteously deflected questions that touched on secret information, he distributed the rest in rotation among the three squadron leaders, he chipped in if someone looked like drying up, and generally he kept things jogging along nicely. After half an hour he got to his feet and said: "I think we've covered most points, so it only remains for me to remind you that these very experienced young men really do know what they're talking about. Day in day out they've been mixing with Jerry up there in the wide blue yonder and giving him a very bloody nose. The RAF has its own peculiar phrase for the truth: we call it 'pukka gen'. This evening they have given you the pukka gen about this battle. Before I came in here this evening I heard today's score on the BBC. RAF losses, twenty-one. German losses, fifty-nine. I need say no more."

Jacky Bellamy stood up. "One last question?" she said.

"With pleasure."

"Since America is neutral, my agency has a bureau in Berlin, and according to my colleagues over there, the RAF's claims are inaccurate and unreliable."

"Sounds rather like Herr Goebbels' Ministry of Propaganda," Bletchley said. "They're experts in unreliable information, I believe."

That got a laugh.

"More to the point," she went on, "many air attachés at embassies and consulates in London are not convinced by your figures, and one reason for their scepticism is the growing weight of German raids."

Nobody laughed at that.

"In fact," she added, since Bletchley had no immediate answer, "the longer this battle goes on, the more it seems that the claims of the RAF are not compatible with the performance of the *Luftwaffe*."

"These are strong words," Bletchley said. "I don't think this is the ideal time or place to enter into a detailed statistical analysis of the matter, especially as there is, I am happy to say, a certain amount of food and drink waiting for us all . . . But I would just like to say this. One of the things we're fighting for is freedom. Unlike Hitler's Germany, we welcome free speech. If anyone can prove us wrong . . . well, they have the freedom to do so. I myself am completely confident that we are right, and that right will ultimately triumph."

During the coffee and sandwiches, Fanny Barton eased Jacky away from one of the Spitfire CO's, and said: "You're as bad as Skull, you are. We work our fingers to the bone, shooting down Jerries, and neither of you believes us."

"I just asked a question, that's all. And now that I come to think of it, I didn't get much of an answer, did I?"

"Never mind, I forgive you. Especially as you're looking more delightful than ever."

"My. You've become terribly sophisticated since you got promoted, Fanny."

"Yes, it's the effect of power. Makes men irresistible."

"Good luck. I notice that *you* haven't tried to answer my question either."

"Oh, I never answer questions," he said grandly. "I leave all that to my staff. Have another sandwich. Go on. Have two."

She took two. "I hear that Sticky Stickwell's been posted here," she said. "Did you know?"

"Sticky? But he's in a Defiant squadron."

"Yes, that's right. They arrived this evening."

"Defiants," he said. "That's the last thing I expected."

The first person Cattermole saw when he pushed open the doors of the *Spreadeagle* was Sticky Stickwell. He was sitting between two big blonde girls who might have been sisters. They were all laughing, and each girl had an arm around him. It made a fond and heartwarming scene.

Cattermole eased through the crowd and bought himself a drink. When one of the girls took her handbag and got up, he intercepted her halfway to the ladies' lavatory. "Excuse me," he said. "I think you should know that that officer has a wife and seven children in Stoke-on-Trent."

"Bloody good place to leave them," she said. Cattermole felt disappointed. When she came back he said: "Actually he's not an officer at all. The police are after him. He procures white women for Arab sheikhs."

She smiled, and gently squeezed his elbow. "That's right, dear. Why don't you have a nice lie-down? It's the heat, I expect." She moved on. Cattermole turned away. A thin, bony girl with gaps in her teeth was looking at him. "I'd love to meet a nice Arab sheikh," she said. "Will you introduce me?" She was fairly drunk.

"Certainly," Cattermole said. "Be in the Savoy Hotel tomorrow morning at eleven o'clock and, above all, *bring your cello*."

"Moggy!" Stickwell shouted. "Bloody old Moggy!" He thrust through the drinkers and seized Cattermole's hand. "I knew it wa you! Stoke-on-Trent . . . Well I'm damned." His face was radiant. "Fancy meeting you here . . . How are you? What a surprise, eh?"

"The children ask me to give you their love, Sticky," Cattermole said gravely. "And Gwendolen says she forgives you."

"Oh . . . Go to blazes, Moggy. I mean, damn it all, Stoke-on-Trent. I deserve somewhere better than that, don't I?"

"Hey!" The thin girl pushed between them. "What's all this about a cello? I ain't got no bleedin' cello."

"Then you'd better get one, and quick about it," Cattermole snapped. "There's a war on, you know." He led Stickwell to a relatively quiet corner. "Didn't you get your gong?" he asked. There were no ribbons on Stickwell's chest. "I kept nagging Rex to recommend you."

"Really? That was jolly nice of you, Mog. Actually I don't care much about gongs any more. Flying Defiants, you've got your work cut out just getting the crate off the ground . . . Anyway, I never was a hot-shot pilot, was I? The thing is, I've decided I want to do something really worthwhile." He took a long gulp of beer and wiped his mouth. "You know, something useful. I'm going to be a surgeon."

"A surgeon." Cattermole was taken aback.

"Flying's all very well but . . . Saving people's lives, I think I'd enjoy doing that."

"Hard work, Sticky."

"Oh, I know, I know. Terrific amount of study. All those veins and bones and things. I've started already. Absolutely fascinating." He took a creased and dog-eared paperback from his hip pocket. It was called *So You Want to Be a Surgeon*.

"How far have you got?"

"I only bought it this afternoon. Threepence, secondhand. Not bad, eh? I'd like to specialise in legs, I think. I've always liked legs . . . Anyway, that's enough about me. How's everybody? I heard Rex bought it. How's Flip and Moke and Fitz and Flash and Pip and . . ." He ran out of breath.

"Fitz and Pip are fine," Cattermole said. "Fine."

"Good show," Stickwell said. "Good old Fitz. I always liked Fitz. Damn good sport."

"Lots of changes. You know how it is."

"Yes, of course. People come and go." Stickwell looked around

599

at the noisy, smiling, gesturing mob, and he kept the happy look on his face. He was thinking: *That's not true, people don't come and go, they just go.* But it wasn't the sort of thing you said. "Funny, the way things work out, isn't it?" he said. "By the way, congratulations on your gong."

"Oh, well," Cattermole said. "They send them round with the Naafi van these days."

When Fanny Barton came away from the press conference, CH3 was waiting for him.

"Flash has turned up," he said. "He's in the hospital at Dover. Stitches in his head, nothing serious. Should be back soon."

"That's good. What about Zab?"

"Not so good. Zab's dead. He was chasing a 109 at very low level and according to some witnesses he hit it and it blew up and he flew slap into the explosion."

"I see." Barton looked up at the first stars of the evening. "Nothing much anyone can do about that, then. Let's get down to the pub."

CH3 drove. "I've just been talking to your old sparring partner, Jacky Bellamy," Barton said. "Baggy brought her here with a great mob of journalists. She says Sticky's arrived."

"Yes, I saw them fly in."

"Defiants."

"That's right."

"Wasn't it a Defiant squadron that took a bit of a pasting about a month ago? Presumably not Sticky's mob, though."

"The lot you're thinking about were based at Hawkinge. I ferried a kite in there a couple of days afterwards. Everyone was still in a state of shock."

"They got badly mauled, then."

"No, they got slaughtered. Nine took off, and seven were either shot down or crashed on landing. The whole disaster took less than ten minutes. Ever seen a Defiant?"

"Not up close. Best 1918 fighter in the world, so they say."

"It's worse than that. A Defiant's got four Brownings in a turret, which is fine as long as the enemy agrees to fly alongside for a few minutes. It's got nothing firing forward. The turret weighs an extra half a ton, not counting the gunner inside, and there's no more power up front than in a Hurricane, so it flies like a brick. They call it a Defiant because it defies comprehension."

"What did all the damage? 109's?"

"Yes. Ten 109's from astern and below. Then another ten head-on."

"Jesus. No wonder they scored seven out of nine."

"The theory at Hawkinge," said CH3, "was that Jerry was pissing himself with laughter so much that he missed the last two."

The landlord had run out of soot. Cattermole persuaded the two blonde girls to give him their powder compacts and he mixed the contents with a bottle of red ink on a tin tray. Stickwell was the first man up the pyramid of tables. Most of Hornet squadron had arrived, and they had agreed to make Sticky an honorary member. The pub was jam-packed, and there was prolonged cheering when he made two red footprints on the ceiling. He remained inverted while he sang a song: *If You Were the Only Girl in the World.* Everyone joined in. It was a pity to waste the pyramid and the red mixture. Fanny arrived. They made the CO of the Defiant squadron an honorary member. He sang *Tipperary.* There was still plenty of mixture left. The Defiant flight commanders were pushed up the tables. Red footprints marched haphazardly about the ceiling, the singing was full-throated, the drink flowed as freely as the spirit of fellowship. It took the landlord half an hour to clear the bar. Stickwell could scarcely stand: Cattermole held him up and steered him out. "Good old Moggy," Stickwell said. He was crying with gratitude. "Hey ... Just remembered. Something I want to talk about. Money. All that money I spent. Tons of money. What about that money?"

"Don't worry about it, Sticky," Cattermole said. "It's not urgent. You can pay me tomorrow."

"Good old Moggy." He fell asleep almost as soon as he was put into the Buick. His cheeks were shining with tears. Cattermole found that oddly disturbing. He took the leather he used for wiping the windscreen and he mopped Stickwell's face with it. Stickwell grunted in his sleep and smiled like a child.

It was almost midnight but the hangar was full of noise: hammers tapped, hacksaws rasped, drills whined and snarled. Jacky Bellamy, flanked by Bletchley and CH3, strolled between the rows of Hurricanes.

"Hullo, Micky," she called. "Don't you ever sleep?"

"I did once," Marriott said, "but that was before the war."

"I invited Miss Bellamy to take a look at our aircraft," Bletchley said. "I have a feeling she doesn't fully appreciate the quality of these new machines."

"This isn't the Hurricane we had in France, you know," Marriott told her. "This is twice the kite. Come and see." He led her away.

"I don't know what's got into her," Bletchley said softly. "In France she was always perfectly reasonable, wrote some cracking good stuff in fact, but recently she's gone all . . . *sceptical*. Won't believe a word she's told. Still quite charming, of course, but no faith. Damn nuisance sometimes, I don't mind telling you."

"You've got to remember, sir, that this is an election year back home," CH3 said. "If Britain's getting beaten out of sight, that's a good excuse for not interfering. She writes what people want to read."

"Hmm." Bletchley pondered that for a moment. "Even so," he said, "we've got to go on doing our bit to prove that she's wrong. The Yanks are an appalling lot – sorry, old boy, no offence meant – but everyone in Whitehall keeps bleating about how we can't do without them. Mind you, they said that about the French, and thank God we're shot of *them*. Thoroughly shabby crew. Never could fight. I mean, look at Agincourt."

"Sure. Mind you, sir, I sometimes wonder what an English army was doing at Agincourt in the first place."

"We had good reason. I forget what it was exactly, something to do with tennis balls, wasn't it? I used to know . . . Anyway, we had a perfect right to be there. Besides, we won, didn't we?"

"Hitler might say the same, sir."

"I wonder if we can get a cup of tea?"

The other two came back.

"Impressed?" Bletchley asked. "Jerry's got nothing like that."

"Very interesting," she said. "I didn't understand half of what Micky said, except for something about back-armour and self-sealing tanks and . . . uh . . . variable-pitch propellers. And metal wings." She smiled amiably.

"All standard," Bletchley said. "Quite routine."

"Really? The strange thing is that six months ago in France they were impossible."

"Not metal wings," Bletchley said firmly. "We had those."

"Not only impossible but unnecessary. Or so everybody said, except CH3. And now here they are."

"You mustn't write about any of that stuff," CH3 said. "Jerry knows we have it, but he doesn't know we know he knows, so it's got to be top secret or you'll spoil the game."

"But don't you think it's strange?"

"War sets a hot pace," Bletchley said, "and the devil takes the hindmost."

"I'll tell you what it reminds me of," she said. "Squadron tactics. I never fully understood all the technicalities, of course, but I remember that tight-formation flying was absolutely essential. You couldn't attack without it. Everyone said so, except CH3. And now I'm told that's all been changed, and tight-formation tactics are completely wrong. Isn't that strange?"

"Some squadrons still prefer tight formations," Bletchley said. "It's up to the individual CO. I don't deny that we've learned from experience. Surely you don't blame us for that?"

"No, no. Certainly not. In fact it's exactly what I'm going to do myself. You see, so much of what I've been told – told repeatedly, and officially, and at a very high level – has turned out to be wrong that . . . well, I'm sorry, but I just don't believe anybody any more. When I'm told the RAF has just shot down – what was it? fifty-nine German planes? I don't believe it. And I can't write what I don't believe."

"Then it looks as if your career has come to a sudden end," CH3 said.

"Not necessarily. I can still check the facts. For instance, if you say you shot down fifty-nine German planes today there should be fifty-nine wrecks, right? Well, I'm going to drive around and count them."

"Are you, by jove?" Bletchley murmured.

"What a startlingly original idea," CH3 said. "Checking the facts against reality. This could spell the end of modern journalism as we know it."

"I'll give it a whirl, anyway. D'you like the idea?" she asked Bletchley.

"I'll put it up to Air Ministry. They may not approve."

"I think they will. They've nothing to hide, have they?"

CH3 escorted her through the blackout to her car. "You know," she said, "you'd be a lot happier if I were some hardbitten gin-swilling old bat you didn't care about. As it is, I think you're ever so slightly afraid of me."

"Why should I be afraid?" He was holding her elbow, steering her around roped-off craters.

"Because I've got your number. I know you're just like me. We're both out to prove that money doesn't matter."

"I didn't know you had any."

"I haven't. I'm broke. Been broke all my life. You should try it sometime. It's very stimulating."

He opened the car door. "I'll get the butler to try it," he said. "Then he can tell me if it really works."

Replacement Hurricanes had been flown in to Bodkin Hazel by breakfast-time the next morning. Flash Gordon turned up, a ragged line of surgical thread above one eyebrow. A sergeant-pilot called Todd was posted in to replace Zabarnowski in Blue Section. The squadron was almost back to strength.

The satellite field didn't look so good. It had been bombed again during the night. A hangar and the clubhouse were flattened and the top of the control tower was missing. Telephone engineers were still mending the lines when the Defiants landed. Fanny Barton went over to greet their CO.

He left CH3 to lecture the Hornet pilots in the privacy of the crewroom. On the wall was a blown-up print of Macfarlane's wreck.

"This sort of thing makes me bloody angry," CH3 said. "It's stupid and childish and selfish. He could've wiped out a dozen men on the ground with that pathetic display of showing-off. Doing complicated high-speed manoeuvres at low level after combat is idiotic. It's not clever. It's not brave. It's not dashing. It's stupid. It's about as stupid as little children playing Last Across the railroad track. This idiot..." He rapped his knuckles on the photograph so hard that he dented it. "How did he know his Hurricane wasn't damaged? He'd just been in a scrap, anything could've happened. Maybe a Jerry bullet nicked a control cable.

He didn't know." There was complete silence. CH3 was not intensifying his anger for effect; on the contrary he was struggling to contain it. His face was pale and his voice was harsh. "No more victory rolls," he said. "There's enough risks in this job without stunting shot-up kites at zero feet. It's a waste of my half-crown for the wreath, it's a waste of Fanny's valuable time writing to the next-of-kin, and it's a waste of a good Hurricane. That's all."

They got up and went out, glad to escape; all except Cox. He shut the door. CH3 was sitting on a table and gripping it as though he thought it might collapse.

"Well, you certainly told them," Cox said. "Now forget it."

"He was in my flight. Bloody idiot. Why do they have to be such bloody idiots?"

"I might ask the same of you." That made CH3 look up. "I hear you had a date with Jacky last night."

"A *date*? That wasn't a date."

"Whatever it was it hasn't done you any good, has it? Now you're going around looking for arses to kick. It's not *their* fault if you've got popsy problems."

"She's not my popsy."

"If you treat her the way you treat us, I'm not surprised. She's not going to wait for ever, you know." Cox got a cloth and wiped the inside of his oxygen mask. CH3 gazed at the floor and let his right foot bang against the table-leg. "Still, that's your funeral," Cox said. "It's Fanny I'm thinking of. Every time you turn grim, Fanny gets worried." CH3's leg stopped moving. For a moment the room was silent.

"I was looking at that new kid, Todd," CH3 said. "He's all keen and eager. And I thought: poor bastard, he doesn't know what he's getting into. He doesn't know beans about what it's going to be like, and chances are he'll never live to find out."

"But he *thinks* he's good," Cox said. "He thinks he'll be an ace by this time next week. And that's a terrific advantage! He's got confidence in himself. If he's nervous, if he's scared, he'll hang about and hesitate and some dirty little 109 will spit in his eye and that'll be that, goodbye Todd. Come on, CH3, snap out of it. You can't save his life by worrying. What you *can* do is make him feel good. Make him think we're the hottest squadron that ever flew, and by God what a lucky man he is! Right?"

CH3 slid off the table. "Christ, I could sleep for a week," he said.

"He's probably going to buy it anyway," Cox said. "He might as well get his money's worth."

CH3 opened the door. "Hey, Toddy!" he shouted. "Come here, I need your advice."

Barton's conversation with the CO of the Defiant squadron was brief. He was a tall, softspoken man with prematurely grey hair. His name was Grant.

Barton made sure there were no problems with fuel or ammunition, and then inquired how Grant wished to operate. Relative altitudes, for instance. Suppose the Hurricanes patrolled two thousand feet above the Defiants?

"I'm afraid I don't understand," Grant said. "Have you had new orders to join us on patrol?"

"No. I just thought . . . I mean I assumed you were here so that we could give you an escort."

"Frightfully kind of you," Grant said, examining the horizon. "We don't actually need an escort. I do command a fighter squadron, you know."

"Yes, but . . ." Barton had blundered in; now he had to blunder out. "It's none of my business, of course, and I know it wasn't your squadron, but they were Defiants, and they did get pretty badly hammered by 109's, didn't they?"

"Only because they were bounced. We don't intend to get bounced."

"No, of course. On the other hand if they come at you head-on, how can –"

"Please don't concern yourself. We know what to do."

Barton nodded and walked away. After a few paces he stopped and turned. Grant was pulling on a pair of fine leather gloves, although the day was already hot. Barton went back. "This is crazy," he said. "You chaps shouldn't be here, right in the front line. You should be up in Scotland or somewhere, in reserve."

For the first and last time, Grant looked him straight in the eye. "We have been given the place of honour," he said, "and we must take it."

The morning was quiet, although Skull kept bringing news of raids elsewhere. An additional ack-ack battery arrived to guard the aerodrome. The adjutant drove in and announced that their back-pay had at last been sorted out. Sticky Stickwell came over to visit. They gave him a deckchair and a cup of tea. "I hear you're saving up to be a lumberjack, Sticky," the adjutant said. "Jolly healthy life."

"No," Stickwell said. "Who told you that?"

"Well, I've seen pictures of them in *National Geographic*."

"No, no. Who said I want to be a lumberjack?"

"Moggy did."

"Well, he's got it all wrong. I'm training to be a surgeon."

"No, I don't think so, Sticky," Flash Gordon said. "Moggy told me, too. He was very definite about it."

"They all laughed," Cattermole said, "but I reckon you'd be very good, Sticky. All that hacking and chopping with dirty great axes, it's right up your street."

"Awful," Stickwell said. "For a start, you've got to live in Canada." He shuddered.

"Well," the adjutant said, "it's not too late to change your mind. I'd think it over very carefully if I were you."

"I'm going to be a surgeon."

"Much of a muchness, really," Barton said. "Hacking and chopping, chopping and hacking."

"What are you going to be, when you grow up, Moggy?" CH3 asked.

"Obscene and disgusting, I hope."

"What about you, Haddy?" Barton said. "Got any secret ambitions?" But Haducek just looked blankly at him. Since Zabarnowski's death, Haducek had said very little.

"I'm going to be world champion," Gordon said confidently.

"What at?" Cox asked.

"That hasn't been settled yet. I leave all these details to my agent."

"Nothing much changes, does it, Fanny?" Stickwell said. "They still talk a lot of cock."

"Nonsense," Barton said. "We have very serious discussions nowadays. Skull, say something serious for Sticky."

"Um ... let me see. Well, the Soviet Union has just annexed Estonia, Latvia and Lithuania. That's quite serious."

"Shocking lot, the Bolsheviks," Kellaway said. "I was there in 1919. The RAF was helping the White Russians. Trying to, anyway."

"It was probably all agreed last year," Skull said. "Russo-German pact. That's when Hitler and Stalin carved up eastern Europe between them."

"We flew Camels," Kellaway said. "Did a lot of low-level strafing. Bolshevik cavalry, mainly."

"I thought the Nazis were against the Communists," Fitz said.

"They were," Skull said, "but they kissed and made up."

"Never itched so much in my life," Kellaway mumbled.

"Well, what d'you expect?" Cattermole stretched and yawned. "They're all as squalid as each other, aren't they? Communism's every bit as bad as Nazism, as far as I –" He crashed sideways out of his deckchair. Haducek had him by the throat and was banging his head on the ground and screaming abuse. It took half the squadron to drag him off. "I am a good Communist!" he shouted. "I fight and I die for my country and for Communism! You say Communists are same as Nazis I kill you!"

"Take a walk, Moggy," Barton said.

"I'll come with you," Stickwell said.

They went and sat on the ruins of the clubhouse. It still stank of high explosive. "Bloody foreigners," Cattermole wheezed. "They ought to be put down at birth."

"Listen, Moggy," Stickwell said. "I didn't want to mention this before, but ... See, I keep getting letters from the bank ... That stuff I sent you, I mean, it added up and ... Well, I just wondered what ..."

"I gave Rex all the bills," Cattermole said hoarsely. "Anyway, Rex went for a burton." He coughed, painfully.

Stickwell nodded several times. "I was afraid that was it," he said. "Oh, well. I'll manage somehow, I suppose." He stood up and walked back to his squadron. As he passed the deckchairs, Fitz called out: "When you're a lumberjack, save us a tree." Stickwell waved.

In the crewroom, Barton was tearing a strip off Haducek, who simply sat and shook his head. "What the hell's the matter with you?" Barton demanded. "You must be crazy." Haducek nodded

608

Normally, Stickwell piloted a Defiant but today he was an air-gunner. His squadron had more pilots than gunners at the moment. Grant had put him down as a reserve pilot, which was very boring. Then one of the regular gunners developed appendicitis and Stickwell grabbed his place.

They were scrambled just before noon.

He enjoyed being in the turret. Facing the tail, he got a completely fresh view of the sky and the squadron. And swinging the guns was great fun, too: the electrically operated turret went around like a fairground ride, while the guns angled up or down very slickly.

They climbed steadily, heading south. He got a bit restless, unable to see what was ahead. Then he heard the tally-ho, and the plane tipped sideways, and there were Dorniers everywhere.

All things considered, the squadron acquitted itself well. It broke up the raid before the Dorniers reached the coast. There was then a collection of dogfights in which each Defiant pilot strained to hold a position that allowed his gunner to keep a bomber in his field of fire. The Dorniers dodged and jinked and used their crossfire to hit the Defiants from both sides. The Dorniers could fire forwards and backwards and sideways but each gunner had only one gun, whereas the Defiant had four. Stickwell was vaguely aware that his plane was being hit, he heard occasional plunks and saw holes sprout in the tailplane, but the thrill of letting fly with four shuddering, battering Brownings entranced him. He raced the turret from left to right, squirted quadruple death and destruction, and whooped when a Dornier sheered away. He searched from right to left. The turret stopped halfway. The tail went up and he was aiming at the sun.

Stickwell shouted on the intercom. No answer. He twisted his neck. The prop was windmilling. The pilot's head was a red smear, pressed into a corner of the windscreen. Stickwell began kicking the turret controls, punching the Perspex, whacking the sides with his elbows. Nothing moved.

In the end the Defiant changed its mind and eased out of its dive so that it made a neat belly-landing on the water. It sank at once. Bright spray charged past the turret and turned to a swirl of light grey-green that became steadily darker. Stickwell began undoing his straps and then stopped. He knew he wasn't going anywhere.

The water charged up to his knees and climbed more slowly to his waist. He looked up and saw, far away, the shiny-metal surface of the sea. Everything outside was turning black. He had no idea the sea was so dark. He was still gripping the gun-handles. He squeezed but nothing fired. You couldn't kill the sea. The water reached his chest, and he gasped at the cold grip. "I didn't really want to be a sodding surgeon anyway," he said aloud. His voice sounded old and cracked, but that was because his ears were full of buzzing and whining. A Perspex panel caved in and the sea smashed him in the face.

The field was littered with broken Defiants and fire-trucks and blood-wagons when Hornet squadron got scrambled. They made a good interception on a bunch of Heinkels just as they were bombing the giant aerials at Pevensey. Haducek destroyed a Heinkel but the escort was heavy and in the frantic scrap that followed, Sergeant Todd got shot down. There was no parachute.

Each flight was scrambled once during the afternoon. 'A' flight found nothing. 'B' flight chased a raid back across the Channel but most of its pilots were always out of gun-range.

A flood of black cloud was hurrying in from the west when the squadron took off early in the evening. They climbed to twenty-two thousand feet and joined a squadron of Hurricanes from North Weald, just north of London. The raid they had been given was making its approach up the Thames estuary: fifty-plus bombers covered by forty Me-110's; these in turn were protected by a great swarm of 109's.

When Barton sighted this mass of aircraft churning towards him he felt a surly resentment: why was it always so one-sided? Why couldn't they for once fight on even terms? Or even – what a luxury! – outnumber the enemy? The feeling passed, and half a minute later he was astonished to see all the 109's and half the 110's detach themselves and fly south.

"Low on fuel," CH3 suggested.

"Not the 110's," Barton said.

"They're low on appetite," Cox said.

This seemed the explanation. As soon as the Hurricanes peeled off to attack, the 110's formed their familiar tail-chasing circle. The fighters ignored them and concentrated on the bombers, harrying and chivying the flanks to drive them off course. Fitzgerald broke from one such attack and discovered that he had lost his wingman. Flash Gordon had gone.

He climbed, weaving to search, and glimpsed a solitary Hurricane *inside* the ring of 110's, whizzing around, vertically banked. It had to be Gordon. A Messerschmitt fell out of formation and the Hurricane dropped behind it, squirting flame. Fitz opened his throttle wide and went down to guard his wingman's back.

After a couple of thousand feet he was scrabbling at the inside of his windscreen, scraping off the ice-crystals that had formed. When the screen was clear again his Hurricane was still half a mile behind the fight, although the airspeed was frighteningly high and the controls were so stiff that it took both hands to budge the stick. His ears were buzzing like doorbells and his skull felt too tight for his brain. The ground looked strangely fuzzy, like a map left out in the rain, but Flash and the 110 were still clear enough and Fitz guessed there was haze or fog down there. The German saw barrage balloons coming up and he sheered away, back towards the estuary. Again Fitz's windscreen iced-up and he pressed against his straps as he cleaned it. His sinuses throbbed and a flicker of blood fell from his nostrils and splashed on the panel. He braced himself and hauled back, and levelled out in the yellow haze. The others had disappeared.

He licked blood from his upper lip and snuffled it up his nose. The smoky sky fled past him. What to do? Flash wouldn't give up, not yet anyway. What about the Hun? The Hun would go on down and try to sneak home at wavetop height. Fitz went down in search of them. In fact he overshot the 110, which was limping along on one engine. The haze turned into a dense sea-mist. He throttled back and gave it another ten seconds; then he was going home. The 110 limped up behind him. It was sheer luck. The pilot fired an enormous five-second burst that lit up the murk with brilliant tracer. All the cannonshells and almost all the bullets missed but a dozen rounds ripped into the Hurricane's instrument panel. Fitz broke left: the wrong way, he remembered too late, but it didn't matter, the 110 wasn't looking for a fight. It limped on home and claimed a definite kill.

Fitz circled while he checked the damage. His engine sounded healthy but the Hurricane would not climb. Whenever he tried to get above the fog a vigorous vibration began and the plane threatened to stall. He increased his speed but that only made the vibration worse, so bad that he was afraid something would snap, and he gave up. There was no visible sun. He set course to the south-west, reckoning to put down somewhere on the Kent coast, on sands or mudflats or something.

After three minutes he got a twinge of worry, checked his course, and was shocked to see that he was heading *north*-west. Even so, he knew he should be over land by now. It was time to get help. He changed channels and called Mayday. No answer. He looked to be sure he had pressed the Mayday button and his radio lead swung free. It had been severed. Sweat suddenly surfaced all over his arms and chest. He checked his course again: south-east, turning to south. The compass was bust.

He had no idea which way he was going. The fog was as grey on the left as on the right. The one thing he did know was that his present course was wrong. The longer he held it, the more fuel he wasted. He circled while he searched for a glimmer of guidance and found none. Land was near; he knew it was only minutes away. He had to decide. The longer he circled, the worse his chance of survival became.

One patch of fog looked fractionally brighter, so he headed for that. In the tracking station on the North Foreland, the operators studying their cathode-ray tubes saw the plot begin to edge away. They tracked it for fifteen minutes, until the echoes faded, far out in the North Sea.

By nightfall it was obvious that someone would have to go and see Mary. The adjutant went.

She took the news remarkably well. Sitting in the golden glow of an oil lamp, with her feet on a cushion and her fingers linked under her belly, she conveyed a sense of serenity. After a while she conveyed so much of it that Kellaway became worried. "This couldn't have come at a worst time, could it?" he said. "You must let us know what help you need."

"Oh, well . . . there's still hope, isn't there? I expect he'll turn up. He always has."

"I'm afraid it's pretty serious this time, Mary." He made his

612

voice sound grave. "Miracles sometimes happen, I realise that, but . . ." He shook his head.

"You said he hasn't been found yet."

"No, he hasn't."

"So he's only missing."

"I'm afraid all the indications are that he's gone for good."

"How can you say that? If you haven't found him."

"It's all a bit technical. I can't really explain, I'm afraid."

"Well, until he's found he's only missing, isn't he? And as long as he's missing he's liable to turn up at any moment. I bet you he does." Kellaway didn't take the bet. He left as soon as he decently could.

On the afternoon when Sergeant Todd was to be buried, the plotting tables in the ops room showed large German raids assembling over Calais and Boulogne. No pilots could be released. The adjutant represented the squadron.

Todd's family lived in Yorkshire. His mother was dead and his father, an ex-miner, was bedridden with lung disease; but he had a brother, who came down with his wife. Kellaway took them to the cemetery, and afterwards invited them to his office for a drink. They were both about thirty, neatly dressed, sad but calm. Everyone took whisky and water. "I'd like to drink to the memory of a gallant pilot," Kellaway said. They drank. "I realise that nothing can make good his loss," Kellaway said, "but we'd all like you to know what a splendid contribution he made to the work of this squadron."

"Did he?" the brother asked, rather sharply.

"Yes, indeed. Everyone commented on the determined way he pressed home his attacks. He certainly made his mark on the enemy."

"That was fast, then," the brother's wife said. Kellaway cocked an eyebrow. "Well, he only got sent here yesterday," she said. "Didn't he?"

"Arthur wasn't a hero," the brother said. "According to what he told me, he didn't know a lot about being a fighter pilot either. He just did his best. I don't suppose it made much difference one way or the other, did it?"

"Probably not," Kellaway said.

The brother's wife took a piece of paper from her handbag. "There'll be a headstone, won't there? We'd like this inscription, if it's allowed."

Kellaway took the paper. "*As for our God, He is in heaven,*" he read out. "*He hath done whatsoever pleased Him.* Psalm 115, verse three."

"We're not bloody hypocrites," the brother said. "We'll not praise God for what's happened to Arthur. If there's any sense to it, we can't see it."

They finished their drinks. Kellaway drove them to the station. "Thank you for coming," he said. "Believe me, Sergeant Todd gave his life in a good cause."

"Aye," the brother grunted. "So you said." He didn't offer to shake hands, and Kellaway didn't risk a refusal.

The rest of August went by in a sort of frantic blur. Those who survived kept a memory of constant fatigue. That was the overriding impression: not fear, although almost every fighter pilot felt a lurch of terror when he saw a big raid approach; not excitement, although there was plenty of that as the bands of Hurricanes and Spitfires took on odds of five to one, even ten to one; but endless, nerve-sapping weariness. They got up tired. Often they fell asleep as soon as they landed after the second or third sortie, and they woke up to fly two or three more sorties, so tired that when dusk came they couldn't remember anything definite about the day's fighting, not even the kills they had made.

Every night there was a cheer in the mess when the BBC announced the latest score. With survival came a miraculous recovery: everyone dashed off to the pub. Tomorrow was another day: another day of increasing fatigue and increasing tension; another day nearer invasion.

Sunlight leaked through the cracks between the blankets that had been hastily tacked over the windows of the crewroom. The air smelled of stale food and dried sweat. There was a brisk buzz of conversation. The squadron had recently landed after a highly successful interception. CH3 had got a Junkers 88 in flames and Haducek had blown up a 109 at close range. One of the new boys, an Australian called Phillips, had made a wheels-up landing and

614

walked away from it. All very satisfactory. They cheered when a square of white shone on the wall. "I hope there's a Tom and Jerry," Cox said. Hands made jokey silhouettes. The countdown numbers flashed and they chanted them. Flash Gordon was one number behind the rest and finished alone. "I won," he claimed. Grainy black-and-white film showed a formation of Heinkels. They swung from one diagonal to another as the camera angle changed. Guns blazed silently and the image flickered with the recoil. The Heinkels fell out of frame and the sky swirled. The film ended. They cheered again.

Skull turned on the lights. The airman at the projector re-wound the film. "I'm not going to identify each pilot," Skull said. "No doubt you will recognise your own combat report. That particular pilot reported that he closed to a range of two hundred yards and fired a two-second burst which hit a Heinkel in the starboard wing, setting an engine on fire. Bear that in mind as you see it again."

This time the film was run in slow motion. "He opens fire ... *now*," Skull said, and the airman froze the film. "Knowing the Heinkel's wingspan we can calculate the exact range," Skull said. "The exact range was four hundred and eighty yards."

The room was quiet now. No jokes, no cheers; only an occasional cough or the creak of a chair.

The film ran on. The bombers blurred as they came nearer. "He stops firing ... *now*," Skull said, and the frame froze. "That was a four-second burst. The final range was just over two hundred yards. None of the shots hit the bomber."

"But it's on fire," Mother Cox objected. "Look at that engine. You can see the smoke."

"All the shots fired by this Hurricane fell below the target. Blow-ups of the film establish that beyond doubt. The damage you see was caused by another Hurricane that made a simultaneous attack from the port beam. That aircraft is just visible." The film moved briefly and stopped. "There, at the edge." A wingtip showed itself.

"The next film was taken by that second Hurricane," Skull said. "The pilot's combat report reads: '*My second attack was from high on the port beam. I put in a two-second burst at about 150 yards and saw smoke pour out of the starboard engine.*' Run it, please."

They watched intently. There was a grunt of satisfaction as the smoke streamed out.

"The report was correct," Skull said. "The next film shows a rather confused piece of action that took place in the middle of a large dogfight. The pilot reported that he fired at three Me-109's in quick succession, missed the first two and destroyed the third."

The film rolled. "Oh, shit," someone muttered in the middle of it. There was silence while it was re-wound, and then shown again in slow motion. "Stop," Skull said. "Here you see the first alleged 109, in fact a Hurricane. No hits are made." The film lurched on and stopped. "The second alleged 109 is also a Hurricane. Hits are made on the tail-unit." Again the dogfight jerked across the sky. "The third target is in fact a 109," Skull said. "Hits are made but no vital damage is done. The next pilot's report claimed . . ."

There were in all five minutes of film, assembled from several interceptions. At the end the pilots went out, looking thoughtful. Barton, the flight commanders and Skull stayed behind. Nobody spoke until the airman had taken down the blankets and packed up his projector and left.

"What it comes down to," Barton said, "is we've got a couple of good pilots, two or three not bad, and the rest couldn't guarantee to hit the floor when they fell out of bed."

"Slightly worse," CH3 said. "Zab was the best shot in the squadron. The film confirms it. That leaves Haddy in a class on his own."

"You mean you recognised which bits of film were theirs?" Skull asked.

"Nobody else gets that close to Jerry," CH3 said.

"Except Flash, sometimes," Cox muttered.

"And Flash can't shoot straight," CH3 said.

"Bloody hell." Barton stood with his shoulders slumped, as if he hadn't the strength to straighten up. His eyelids were heavy, his mouth was slack. "So I'm the proud owner of a bunch of blokes who can't judge distance, who shoot too soon, who shoot too much, who miss by a mile and then claim a kill. Is that right?"

"If it's any consolation," Skull said, "my colleagues in other squadrons report very similar findings."

Barton looked at him for such a long time that Skull grew uncomfortable and turned away.

"What the hell!" CH3 said jovially. "This doesn't change anything, Fanny. Nobody expects them to be crack shots. Let's face it, gunnery's always been a joke in Fighter Command."

"It's beyond a joke," Barton said. "You know that lad Phillips? Came straight here from his operational conversion course? Some course. He's never fired a Hurricane's guns. Not one little squirt."

He went out. CH3 looked at Cox and shrugged.

"Cine-guns," Cox said heavily. "Bright bloody idea *that* turned out to be."

"Oh sure," CH3 said, "go ahead, blame it all on me. What's the good of kidding ourselves? We're never going to get anywhere by dodging the truth."

Cox tramped to the door. "All I can say is, if you've got any more truth like that, kindly keep it to yourself, because I personally think we've had about as much of it as we can stand." He slammed the door.

That was the first day Mary Fitzgerald appeared at the end of the airfield.

Farmland surrounded the field on three sides. On the fourth, a narrow lane passed just outside the perimeter wire. There was no hedge. The duty NCO in the control tower noticed a small black car parked beside the lane. It was still there an hour later, so he pointed it out to CH3, who got some binoculars.

The CO was on patrol with Red Section. CH3 went and found the adjutant. They were in the control tower, studying the little car, when Red Section returned. They saw the driver get out of the car and watch the Hurricanes land. "You were right," Kellaway said. "It's her."

"I'd better go and talk to her."

"Waste of time, old boy. She doesn't want you, and the chap she does want isn't likely to turn up. Leave her be."

"A word about angels," Barton announced. "*Luftwaffe* intelligence has started monitoring our controllers' transmissions. They hear the controller sending us up to angels ten so they pass the word to the raid, the raid nips up to angels twelve and we arrive far too low."

"Beats me how they make sense of our R/T," Quirk said. "Half the time it's unreadable."

"You have to shout," Gordon said. "They're foreigners, remember."

"Well, from now on we're going to baffle the buggers," said Barton. "From now on, stated angels will be minus two. If the controller says angels ten, he really means angels twelve. Angels fifteen means we go up to angels seventeen."

"I get it," Gordon said brightly. "That's very clever, isn't it? All you have to do is keep adding six."

"Don't piss about, Flash," CH3 said wearily.

"Well, five, then."

CH3 grabbed him by the arm and neck, forced him to the door of the crewroom and threw him out. In doing so he banged his knuckles on the frame and skinned them. "Dumb lunk," he grumbled as he sucked his hand.

"Stated angels are minus two, then," Barton said. "You'll also have a set of codenames for places. 'Fishpaste' means 'Dover.' That sort of thing. Jerry's getting far too smart. He's sending over spoof raids to get us scrambled and when he knows where we're going they turn back, and while we're refuelling the real raid appears and catches us knickerless. He's also coming over at zero feet to bamboozle the tracking stations. Come to that, he's knocked out a couple of tracking stations so sometimes there are blind spots. I'm telling you all this so you'll know what the controllers have to put up with. Half the time they're just guessing, and the other half they're digging the ops room out of the rubble and tying the telephone lines together in reef-knots."

"The poor dears," Cattermole said. "We must take up a collection."

"Bloody controllers," Gordon said from the door. "They're all Huns." CH3 turned on him with a raised fist. Gordon dodged back.

"Half the scrambles don't lead to interceptions," Barton said. "And making an interception doesn't always mean you get a crack at Jerry. That's the luck of the draw. Nothing we can do about that. What we *can* do a hell of a lot about is gunnery."

He sat and CH3 stood. "This is not a magic death-ray," he said. He was holding up a Browning salvaged from a wreck. "And these aren't magic bullets." He raised a belt of ammunition. "You can hold the enemy in your sights and still miss, for at least five reasons. One is bullet-drop. As soon as it leaves your gun, that bullet starts to fall. The further it goes, the more it falls. Two is bullet-topple. Every bullet wobbles a tiny bit, and the further it goes, the more it wobbles. Three is recoil. Recoil shakes the gun-platform a fraction, and that fraction's worth ten, twenty, thirty feet when the bullet carries a quarter of a mile. Four is deflection which of course you all know about but how many of you think about the *combined effects* of deflection and bullet-drop? If the bastard is not only crossing you but also climbing, it's no damn good aiming ahead of him, you've got to figure out how far ahead *and above* his line-of-flight to put your bullets, on account of they fall faster when you fire upwards than when you fire level, right? That was four. Five is harmonisation. Harmonise at two hundred yards and the bullet-streams converge at two hundred, and after that they *diverge* and they keep on diverging as if they can't stand the sight of each other, which is good news for the enemy if he happens to be four or five hundred yards away."

"And *that*," Barton said, "is the range too many of you open fire."

"Which is why you miss," CH3 said.

"You saw the film," Barton said. "Eight hundred yards, in a couple of cases. *Eight hundred!*"

"Quite absurd," Flash Gordon said, looking in through a window.

"Beat it!" CH3 cried.

"None of this is new," Barton said. "You've all heard it in umpteen lectures ever since you began flying, but it doesn't seem to have sunk in. You've got to get in *close*."

"That's dangerous," Gordon said doubtfully.

"Don't shoot unless you can read the numbers on the fuselage," CH3 said. "Better yet, get close enough to count the crew."

"Count their teeth," Gordon said. "Like buying a horse."

"Beat it before I kill you," CH3 told him.

"And always attack from behind if you can," Barton said. "Stick your nose up his tailpipe. Don't fart about with fancy deflection shots, leave that to experts like Haddy."

"This is all a load of cock," Gordon said. His arms dangled inside the window, his chin rested on the sill and his eyelids drooped goofily. "What's wrong with the old Area Fighting Attacks, I say? Bloody good fun, they were."

Fury gripped CH3. It showed in his face: the eyes suddenly widened, the jaws clamped together, the colour intensified. Barton saw this and tried to grab his arm but CH3 went out of the hut like a sprinter from his blocks. Gordon had a few yards' start. Giggling with fear, he dodged behind the wheels of a Hurricane. CH3 plunged after him, tripped over the chocks and fell on his face. By the time he was up, spitting out grass and obscenities, Gordon had escaped. CH3 saw him trying to hide behind some deckchairs and went for him. Barton, watching from the doorway, knew that this was no joke: the chase was too savage, the cursing too vicious.

CH3 caught Gordon as he was scrambling up an apple-tree. He seized him by a foot, yanked at it and twisted it as if he wanted to screw it off. Gordon howled with pain and lashed at him with the other foot. CH3 grabbed that too and was clawing his way up Gordon's body when Barton and Cox dragged him off.

As suddenly as the rage began, so it ceased. He stood limp and exhausted, ashamed to look anyone in the face. Eventually he walked slowly away. Barton stayed and said: "That'll teach you not to be such a lunatic, Flash. Come on down." But Gordon politely refused, and he stayed in the apple-tree until the scramble sounded.

Mary came back again next day. They could see her from dispersal, a small, dark, plump figure standing just beyond the wire. She rarely moved.

The fourth scramble of the day led to a prolonged fight at high level. A squadron of Spitfires had drawn off the escorting 109's just before the Hurricanes arrived. The bombers were Ju-88's, fast, capable of being thrown about like a fighter and apparently tough enough to absorb any number of bullets. Hornet squadron chased them all across Kent. Con-trails unfurled neatly, like endless bandages that soon sprawled and wore thin until the sky seemed littered with discarded dressings. The Hurricanes made hit-and-run attacks until they ran out of ammunition. When they withdrew a couple of bombers were flying on one engine only and more

620

fighters were being scrambled, but the raid reached its target, which was Manston, and bombed it.

Barton was talking to his rigger as the last member of 'A' flight was coming in to land. The Merlin growled, then picked up with a roar, then sank to a growl again. "Who's that?" he asked.

"Looks like Mr Phillips, sir."

Barton dumped his parachute on the wing and strode across the field. "You!" he shouted when Phillips got out. "What's the matter? Tired of life? Ready to end it all?"

Phillips was startled and puzzled. "Sorry?" he said.

"Sorry? *Sorry?*" Barton shouted. Half the squadron had stopped to listen. "You're worse than sorry, Phillips, you're bloody tragic! Why did you open up just now?"

"Open up?" Phillips had been awake since before dawn, had flown four sorties, seen several deaths, been scared speechless more than once. He was very tired, but Barton looked thoroughly angry, so he made an effort to think, and failed. "Don't understand," he said.

"You opened up. Opened the throttle. *Throttle.*" Barton pointed a furious finger at the sky where it had happened.

"I was a bit low," Phillips said.

"Low? You were nearly bloody underground! What if your engine hadn't opened up? Where would you be now?"

Phillips looked across the field. "In the hedge, I suppose."

"No! The kite would be in the hedge and *you* would be in the morgue and *serve you bloody well right!*" They could hear him in the control tower. "Never trust your engine after a scrap! Always give yourself more height than you need! Play safe! Understand?"

Phillips nodded. He felt bruised by this blast. Barton strode away. CH3 nodded as he went by and said: "Serve him right."

Without pausing, Barton said: "He's in your flight, chum. You should be bollocking him, not me."

Skull had a bright idea. If estimating range was so difficult for most pilots, why not erect dummy German aircraft at the correct distance so that their size and appearance would become familiar? Barton told him to do it. He requisitioned a truckload of plywood and a dozen carpenters and painters. They worked through the night. Next morning three mock-ups were ranged in an arc, two

621

hundred yards from the crewroom: a Dornier 17 seen head-on, a Junkers 88 seen from the left rear, and a Messerschmitt 109 seen from the side and slightly above. The pilots, when they landed, were amused and impressed. "That is what your target should look like," Skull told them. "If it's not that big then you're not close enough to open fire."

"If I get you the wood," Cattermole said, "will you make me a Sunderland flyingboat for my birthday?"

Skull yawned so hugely that his jaw hurt. He was trembling with fatigue but he was so pleased with his creations that he couldn't leave them. About an hour later he was drinking tea in the control tower when he heard rifle-fire. Gordon, Cattermole and Renouf were standing outside the crewroom, shooting at the mock-ups. "What the devil d'you think you're doing?" Skull shouted, but they couldn't hear. He hurried to the stairs. Barton grabbed his arm. "Leave them be," he said.

"But . . ." Skull gestured helplessly with paint-streaked hands.

"They're doing what you want, aren't they? Besides, they hardly ever hit the bloody things. Just watch."

The rifles banged like fireworks. "Look over there," Skull said. "The black widow's back."

"Is that what they call her?" Barton aimed his binoculars. "Yes. I see. She does look a bit gloomy, doesn't she?"

"Bloody Mary," Skull said. "That's another name they've given her. They say she sends pilots to their doom."

"Superstitious claptrap. She's waiting for Fitz, that's all. I wish there was something we could do . . ." Then the telephone rang and he had more urgent things to think of.

CH3 saw Jacky Bellamy sitting at a table in the corner of the *Spreadeagle* with a sergeant-pilot he vaguely remembered having seen at Brambledown. He went over to them.

"Excuse me, old boy," he said, "but you're wanted on the phone. They said it's urgent."

"Damn . . . Thank you, sir." He disappeared into the crowd, and CH3 took his place. "You shouldn't associate with sergeant-pilots," he said. "They're terribly lower-class. What's his name?"

"White, and I like him. Have you turned into a snob at last?"

"Sure. You can't live in this country for a whole year without

622

becoming class-conscious. It's the great British pastime. That's what they're all fighting for: the freedom to sneer."

She gave him a sideways glance and then looked away. "Everything you say to me is fake," she said. "We've never had a simple, honest, natural conversation all the time I've known you. Why do you have to be such a phoney with me? What are you afraid of?"

"Okay, what d'you want to talk about?"

She made rings on the table with her glass. In the next bar they were singing *Roll Out the Barrel*. Somebody dropped a drink, which smashed, and everyone cheered.

"I used to be in love with you," she said. There was no nostalgic regret in the way she spoke: it was a straightforward statement. "That was in France. It didn't last long: you saw to that. Now I'm definitely not in love with you, and I don't think I ever shall be again. That's a pity, because there's not much love about so it's a shame to waste it. And I certainly wasted mine on you."

"I'm sorry. It's an area of life I'm not very good at."

"No, you're not. As I found out the other night, when we went for that walk. I wish now I hadn't phoned you up. Big mistake."

"Come on, it wasn't that bad. In fact I enjoyed it."

"Yes. That was the mistake. I think you enjoyed it too much. Look, CH3: after what's happened between us, or maybe what *hasn't* happened between us, I don't want you falling in love with me. And I only say that because of the way you behave when we're together. It's ominous."

"Really? How do I behave?"

"Like a bad actor reading a bad script. I've met it before and I know what it means. It means trouble."

The sergeant-pilot returned. "Must have been a mistake, sir," he said. "The phone's on the hook."

"Someone's hung it up. You'd better go and call back." The man looked doubtful. "You are Sergeant White, aren't you? Chalky White? It was the sergeants' mess. Bit of a flap on. D'you need any change?"

They watched him squeeze through the crowd again.

"Suppose I stopped reading the bad script badly," he said. "Would there be any hope?"

"No."

He sat leaning forward, with his elbows on his knees and his

623

fingers locked together, and watched her adding to the chain of rings. The singers had started on *Tipperary*.

"How is your wreck-hunting getting on?" he asked.

"I never give interviews. People like you always get it wrong anyway, and besides, what I do is nobody's business but my own."

"I see. I guess I asked for that. All the same, how *is* your wreck-hunting getting on?"

"I'm not going to tell you."

"I don't believe you're doing it at all."

"Oh, I'm doing it all right. What's more I'm doing it in the comfort of an Air Ministry car. You see, I'm not the only sceptic in the press corps. These claims of yours have been getting some bad reviews abroad, so now Air Ministry has decided to double-check the figures, with me as an observer. Every day we drive around, me and the man from Air Ministry, with a long list of claims, when and where each plane was shot down. And we look, and we look, and then we look some more." She smiled wryly. "Here comes Chalky."

CH3 stood up. "You'd better hurry," he said. "Hitler might get here first and spoil your story."

She shook her head. "Hitler won't invade."

"You have inside information on that too?"

"In a way," she said, "I guess I have."

Baggy Bletchley stood in the middle of the ops room at Brambledown and looked at the fluffy clouds drifting overhead. A near-miss by a five-hundred-kilogram high-explosive bomb had folded two walls flat and the roof had collapsed. Mobile cranes had been brought in to lift the jagged slabs of concrete and men had worked through the night, shovelling rubble. The bodies of four Waafs and two airmen had been removed, the blood washed off the plotting table, most of the lines reconnected. Everything was makeshift but at least the ops room was working. "Bloody good show," he said.

"Why they didn't put these places underground beats me," the sector controller grumbled.

"Presumably they thought they were safe enough above ground."

"Then why put the Group ops room underground? And Command ops?"

"God knows." Bletchley had been up all night, driving from one sector station to another: Biggin Hill, Kenley, Hornchurch, North Weald: checking the damage, counting the casualties, applying every pressure to get the stations fully operational again by daybreak. He had not always been welcome. Morale in some places was less than good. The strain of repeated bombings and strafings was beginning to tell. "There are lots of things they should have done. They should have trained another thousand fighter pilots immediately after Dunkirk, but they didn't, and now we're sending up spotty youths and lunatics left over from Bomber Command. But that's the way it is, so ..." He squinted at the blackboard leaning against the broken remains of the tote. "What does that say about Hornet squadron?"

"Airborne ten minutes ago. We've handed them over to Kenley Sector. They've got raid 430 if it doesn't turn back."

Bletchley found the plaque reading H430 on the table. Fifty plus at angels eighteen. The arrows below it drove deep into the heart of Kent. "Good luck," he grunted.

The sector controller had just been handed a teleprinter message. "Charming," he said. "Group have changed the angels code again. Evidently *Luftwaffe* intelligence has cottoned onto our little subterfuge, so from now on we understate height by four thousand, not two. Angels eight now means twelve thousand."

"That should keep the Hun guessing for a while."

"Yes." He blew against the edge of the paper and made a soft whistle. "There's only one problem. The land lines are still down at Bodkin Hazel. This signal won't have got through."

"Well ..." Bletchley had been inventing stop-gap solutions all night. "Get on the R/T and tell Barton ... No. Not a good idea. Sorry. The brain's slowing down. Despatch-rider?"

"He'd take an hour to get there. By that time they might have been scrambled again." He re-read the signal. "Never mind, I can't think of anything better so a despatch-rider it'll have to be." He reached for the telephone.

"Wait a minute," Bletchley said. "I'll go. I can nip down there in ten minutes in the Tiger Moth. Leave it to me."

Everything was quiet at Bodkin Hazel when he landed. GPO vans clustered around the control tower. A small steamroller chuntered up and down the middle of the field, flattening the refilled craters. Groundcrews sat or lay in the shade of the reserve Hurricanes and waited for the squadron to return. Away in the distance, beyond the perimeter wire, a small black car shimmered in the baking heat.

Baggy Bletchley strolled around the three plywood mock-ups, slightly pockmarked by rifle-fire, and wondered what they were for. He turned away and walked towards the tower. After a few yards his digestive system began demanding action. It was accustomed to a regular schedule of bowel movements. That schedule had been disrupted by the constant travel and activity of the past twenty-four hours but enough was enough. Nature called, insistently. He changed direction.

The portable lavatory had been cleaned out since Steele-Stebbing took Cattermole for a ride. It smelled powerfully of pine disinfectant and it was hot. There was no ventilation and the door refused to stay open. Baggy Bletchley was soon sweating and his buttocks stuck to the toilet seat.

His nickname was well-earned. When he was a young lieutenant, Bletchley's testicles hung unusually low; now, with the weight of years, they had dropped even further.

He took a handful of toilet paper and gently raised himself. The seat – stuck to his buttocks – rose with him. Slightly disconcerted, he sat down; but as he did so his testicles swung forward and slipped between the inside of the seat and the outside of the bucket, and he sat on them, which was very painful. His natural reaction was to stand, but now the seat had come unstuck and his testicles were trapped in the gap between seat and bucket. This gap was too narrow to let them be pulled out, and so the more he stood the more they hurt. The pain of standing made him sit; the agony of sitting forced him to stand.

At first he laughed through his tears. What worried him most was the possible embarrassment of being found in this ludicrous situation, squatting, caught by the balls in a mobile bog. After a couple of minutes it wasn't funny: His thighs ached. His stomach muscles were about to give way. He pounded on the wall and shouted. Nobody came. In his sweating, suffering obsession with his dilemma he had failed to hear the air-raid warning.

The ack-ack opened up with a clamour like a hundred drunken blacksmiths. The racket made Bletchley all the more desperate to escape. He managed to get one hand onto the rim of the bucket and he transferred much of his weight to it. The raiders were Me-110's, charging in from the sea at fifty feet, too low for most of the guns. They made one sweep, one raging, strafing, blinding, swamping attack, and then they were gone. Six 110's totalled twelve machine-guns, firing armour-piercing and incendiary rounds, and twelve cannon, firing explosive shells. The reserve Hurricanes collapsed, ripped apart. Skull's plywood mock-ups flew apart. The crew-room was wrecked, a petrol bowser exploded, and the portable lavatory was bowled over, rolling like a log as it got kicked by repeated bursts of fire.

The squadron landed twenty minutes later. The groundcrews were running alongside the planes as they taxied to a halt. Armourers scrambled onto the wings with belts of ammunition slung around their necks while fitters and riggers leaned into the cockpits to ask about damage. Fresh oxygen bottles were installed. The pilots stayed in their seats. Within fifteen minutes the petrol bowsers were backing away and a last polish was being given to the windscreens. The engines, still hot, fired at once. A white flare climbed from the tower. The squadron took off.

The controller was crisp and clear. "Hullo, Popcorn Leader, this is Teacake. Vector one-zero-zero, make angels eight."

Barton acknowledged. Eight and two was ten, which sounded a bit low, so he stuck on five hundred for luck. The raid came in at twelve thousand, a great mob of Heinkels with a swarm of 109's all around. Hornet squadron was still clawing for height, which suited the escort perfectly. Half of them came down like the wrath of God.

Renouf lost his prop almost immediately and baled out, landing safely. Mother Cox took a burst in the right aileron and fluttered down like a broken butterfly before he too baled out. CH3 and Barton limped home and had to make belly-landings. Flash Gordon's undercarriage collapsed on touchdown and the plane pirouetted on a wingtip. He whacked his head against the gunsight and was carried away with a mask of blood hiding his face.

By now the land lines had been restored. Skull called Brambledown and reported that only five aircraft were operational, not counting the Tiger Moth. "Is Baggy Bletchley still there?" the controller asked. Skull organised a search.

"We can't go on like this," Fanny Barton said. "I mean, this is getting bloody silly. Just look at it."

Cox and CH3 looked at it: a scrapyard of smashed and smoking Hurricanes.

Cattermole came over. "Phillips bought it," he said. "I'm sure it was Phillips."

"There you are, you see," Barton said emptily. "I tell you, it's getting bloody silly. We obviously can't go on like this."

Cattermole was squinting and blinking into the hazy distance where a tiny black figure shimmered beside a little black car. He began walking. Twenty minutes later he had found a gap in the perimeter wire and was in the lane.

Mary beamed and waved when she saw him coming. "You shouldn't have bothered, honestly," she said. "I'm fine, I've got everything I need. Still, it's lovely to see you again. And the baby says hullo, of course, don't you baby?" She was perched against the back of the car, with her hands touching under her belly.

Cattermole stopped when he was ten feet away. The sweat trickling into his eyes made him blink but his face was untouched by expression. "We want you to go," he said.

She was puzzled. "Go? It's too early. I can't go yet. Would you like some tea? I could –"

"Go away. Leave here, get out. Go, stay away for ever."

"Oh no, I couldn't do that, love, not yet." She glanced at the sky. "There's nothing to worry about, you know. I'm fine. I suppose it's natural for you to –"

"Stupid bitch. I don't give a damn about you. I don't want to see you watching me every day. None of us does. You're a jinx, you're a menace. Fitz is dead, he's not coming back." She began to cry, and that made him move forward. "Get away from here," he shouted, "or by Christ I'll kill you!" She was still leaning on the car, shaken with sobs, when he hit her, a backhanded swipe across the face which knocked her away. She began pleading incoherently, the words choking on her sobs. He seized her and dragged her and she screamed with pain. He forced her swollen trembling body into the driver's seat, shoving and kicking until she was in. "Go!" he bawled, but her fingers couldn't turn the ignition key and he had to do it. The car lurched away. He ran alongside

it, kicking and swearing, until at last it outpaced him and he was
left gasping and stumbling in its dusty wake.

SEPTEMBER
1940

"I can get up and down all right," Fraser said. "It's the bit in between I'm not so sure about."

He was sitting on a wooden box in a trench behind the remains of the crewroom. Bodkin Hazel had been strafed so often and so suddenly that during an alert nobody sat in deckchairs any more. The trenches had been enlarged and furnished with boxes. Steel helmets were compulsory wear.

"The important thing is to keep looking behind you," CH3 said. "Watch your tail . . ." Fraser and the other replacements, Donahue and Jolliff, listened carefully. They had been shunted through their Operational Conversion Unit very briskly indeed.

"And watch the sun," CH3 went on. His voice had an impatient, hard-driving edge to it. "Nine times out of ten, Jerry's up there in the sun. Never climb *away* from the sun, that's fatal."

"I'm going for a pee," Gordon said. He got out of the trench and wandered away until he found Micky Marriott climbing over the carcase of a broken Hurricane, seeking bits to cannibalise. "New boys make me sick," Gordon said. "They smell like a gents' outfitters. They're all thirteen years old." He stretched out on a crumpled wing and closed his eyes. "I don't like them and I shan't speak to them."

"They're not all thirteen. And some of them are brighter than you are."

"If I were any brighter I'd glow in the dark." Gordon liked that idea: he smiled.

"You're not as bright as Sherriff, I can tell you that." Marriott poked his head into a hole in the fuselage. "I saw Sherriff make a century for Derbyshire against Essex a year ago. On a very sticky wicket, too. Sherriff's as bright as they come, believe you me."

"Sherriff bought it yesterday."

"Did he?" Marriott pulled his head out. "I haven't had time to catch up with the squadron state, what with one thing and another . . Shouldn't you be in the dugout?"

"CH3's making his speech again. Hear him?" They listened for a moment to the insistent voice. "It's all balls," Gordon said. "They won't remember any of it."

"Shift over, Flash. I want to get at that panel."

Gordon rolled off the wing and strolled back to the trench. "And for Christ's sake *never* dive after a single 109," CH3 was saying.

"If you see one, there's certainly another not far away, and he'll have you."

"Hitler's invaded," Gordon said.

"Always check your oxygen before take-off," CH3 told them.

"It didn't work," Gordon said. "There are hundreds of thousands of German corpses washing about in the sea between Folkestone and Dover. I've just been over to have a look."

"Okay, now let's consider gunnery," CH3 said.

"The Channel is red with blood as far as the eye can see," Gordon said. "Our losses were three Home Guards with hernias from throwing handgrenades."

"Can it, Flash," CH3 snapped.

"It's not a pretty sight. One of the hernias is *huge*."

Barton thought that CH3 was going to hit Gordon. He touched the American's arm and said: "I want to show you something." They got out of the trench and walked fifty yards. "What d'you think of this?" Barton asked.

"It's a steamroller. So what?"

"Is it a *good* steamroller?" Barton kicked a wheel. "How much d'you reckon it's worth?"

"For Christ's sake, Fanny. What the hell are we doing talking about machinery?"

"Okay." Barton sat in the driver's seat. "What d'you want to talk about? Modern art? Skiing? Naked ladies?"

CH3 went to the front roller and peeled pancakes of earth from it. They came off easily and left dark patches on the metal. "Look, all I'm trying to do is give them a better chance," he said.

"You're giving them so much good advice they're too stuffed to move."

"There's a lot to learn."

"And they haven't got time."

"But that's crazy. When we get scrambled –"

"Of course it's crazy. That's what you've got to accept. What we're doing is crazy. We can't change it so let's relax and enjoy it. It may be a matter of life and death but is that any reason to be so damn grim?"

"I can't help the way I am. I'm responsible for half those guys."

"So what? I'm responsible for all of them. Do I go around

looking miserable? If you can't relax and enjoy being a flight commander I'll chop you."

"Oh yeah? And who would you put in my place?"

"Flash Gordon."

CH3 was staggered: he actually took a pace back. "Flash is nuts," he said, and his voice was empty, airless. "You'd have to be crazy to do that."

"Being crazy certainly helps," Barton said. "Think about it."

That afternoon, Haducek was killed.

'A' flight had been scrambled. It was not an experienced unit: Donahue at Red Two, Flash Gordon and Jolliff in White Section, Haducek and Fraser in Yellow. CH3's final advice to the new boys was: "Stick like glue to your leader and do what he does."

They intercepted about forty Heinkel 111's as they crossed the coast near Dover. There was also a defensive screen of Me-110's but Haducek cut through it with a brisk contempt for his or anybody else's safety that made Fraser's fingertips prickle. He concentrated on following Haducek and tried to ignore the streaks of tracer, the crisscrossing aircraft, the rushing contrails that crowded his vision. Haducek jinked and Fraser jinked after him. Haducek fired. Fraser felt the clatter of metal on his Hurricane, he saw things bouncing off his windscreen, the threat of terror squeezed his throat and he nearly broke away before he got blown to bits; but then he glimpsed a trail of shining fragments ahead and realised he was flying into Haducek's spent cartridge cases. He twitched the nose up. Haducek had closed on the Heinkel and Fraser saw him kill the upper gunner: eight Brownings briefly swamped the turret and the single machine-gun jerked to the vertical. Then the entire enemy formation shook and bounced as it ran over a sudden eruption of flak. One burst blew Haducek's Hurricane out of the picture.

Fraser was astonished. He had blinked when the shell burst and all he had seen of his leader was a flickering blur rising faster than he could move his eyes. The Heinkel swam towards him, wobbling in the turbulence, so he gave it a four-second burst that knocked down its undercarriage, which struck him as an odd reward, and he broke, hard and high.

The sky was spattered with action: streaks of smoke, sparkling gun-muzzles, hanging snowballs of flak. The whole bloody-minded display of banditry was still thrusting north, except for one item. Falling behind the raid was an unhappy Hurricane, flopping and staggering as a 110 laced it with fire. Fraser guessed it was Haducek and he chased back with the tit pulled out and the Merlin screaming for revenge. The 110 quite wisely held its course and sped towards France, drawing away from Fraser all the time. In any case, Fraser's attempt at rescue was wasted. A shell splinter had penetrated Haducek's skull behind the left ear. He was stone dead long before his Hurricane buried him ten feet below a field of cabbages.

"Come and see this" Skull said to Kellaway

They went to Haducek's room. "Everything was packed," Skull said. "All his clothes, all his belongings." He pointed to a big envelope. "Personal papers. He's marked them 'to be destroyed.' There's a cheque to pay his mess bill. Five pounds for his batman."

"Five?" Kellaway frowned. "That's far too much. You don't want to spoil them."

"Well . . ." Skull turned the banknote over as if there might be a message written on the other side. "It's Haddy's money. I mean, it *was* Haddy's money."

"I suppose you'd better let the fellow have it. Five quid . . . In the last show a batman was lucky if he got ten bob."

"And there's this." Skull picked up a much-read copy of *Das Kapital*. "He's left it to Moggy Cattermole."

"Oh dear." Kellaway took the book and flipped through it. "Better not tell Moggy about the fiver. It'll only make him jealous."

Next morning the steamroller was back at work, but not all the new craters had been filled in. An army truck stood in a distant corner of the field, with red flags fluttering around it to mark unexploded bombs.

Most of the pilots were dozing by the trenches, caps pulled over their eyes to keep out the sunlight. The air held a faint tang of autumn. The portable gramophone was playing *Thanks for the Memory*. There were two or three new faces. CH3 wandered from one to another, asking questions but only half-listening to the answers. He was endlessly polishing his goggles.

Barton came down from the tower and walked across to the squadron. Around his neck he wore the lavatory seat from the portable toilet. "Rise and shine," he said. "We're now on two-minute standby. Lots of lovely trade building up."

Quirk slowly woke up and blinked at Barton. "You look rather like a horse," he said.

"He always did," Cattermole said.

"Yes, but now he looks like the *front* end."

"Don't talk rubbish," Gordon said. "Whoever heard of a horse wearing a bog-seat round its neck?" They were putting on Mae Wests and zipping up flying-boots.

"This is no bog-seat," Barton told them. "This is the Baggy Bletchley Memorial Trophy."

Cattermole said: "I had an uncle who thought he was a Derby winner. He *always* wore a bog-seat around his neck."

"Sounds very unlikely to me," Renouf said. "I don't remember any Cattermole winning the Derby."

"No, he lied about that," Cattermole said. "The best he ever did was second in the Oaks."

"This trophy," Barton said, "will be awarded each day to the biggest piss-artist in the squadron, as decided by popular vote."

"Moggy," Steele-Stebbing said.

Cattermole nodded graciously.

"I nominate Flash," Renouf said.

"I nominate Nim," Gordon said. "I saw him wave his hanky at a Dornier the other day. What a ponce! What a piss-artist!"

"I was waving goodbye," Renouf said. "Some of us still have manners, you know."

"It had spots."

"Very rare, spotted Dorniers," Quirk said.

"Who gets your vote, CH3?" Barton asked.

"Haducek," he said bleakly. "Haducek, Todd, Phillips, Flip-Moran, Fitz and Zab. Every one a prize piss artist. Must have been. None of them lasted the course."

"I want to talk to you," Barton said.

They went to the crewroom. As soon as they were inside, Barton threw the lavatory seat at the wall. "I've had enough of you," he said. "You've become a pain in the arse. You think you can solve everything by planning, and holding briefings, and organising

637

people. You think if you organise the kites, and the pilots, and the guns, and the tactics, and the controllers, and the bloody weather too I shouldn't be surprised, then everything will be perfect and nobody need get hurt except Jerry. You think you can get it all scientifically worked out so that nothing, absolutely nothing, gets left to chance. You're a typical fucking Yank. If there's a scientific way to break wind you'll get a patent on it. That's what's wrong with you, CH3. I used to think you were a brain. You're just a bleeding ulcer."

"And what's your alternative? Swanning about with a broken bog-seat round your neck?"

"It bucked them up a bit, poor buggers. And with you around, they could do with a bit of bucking up."

"Fun and games," CH3 said bitterly. "Half the squadron don't know a 109 from fried chicken and you waste their time on dumb jokes."

"They'll be scrambled in ten minutes. What they don't know now they'll never learn by then."

"You can *try*, for God's sake. Tell the new boys which way to break when they get jumped. Tell 'em about blind spots. Deflection. Sun."

"There isn't time," Barton said. "It can't be done."

"Wrong. Anything can be done."

"How? Are you going to buy an extra week for a million dollars?" Barton's temper was about to snap, and he knew it; but he couldn't slow down. "You don't like this battle. You reckon it's a cock-up. Let me tell you something: it is a cock-up! This whole war's been a cock-up, ever since the Ram fell on his head a year ago. *Every* war's a cock-up, because that's what war is: organised cock-ups. And I'll tell you something else: I don't need you to help me cock it up. Flash Gordon can lead 'A' flight. I like Flash. His brains are in his guts. You're grounded for twenty-four hours. Now get off this field and out of my sight."

CH3 went out and walked away, without a word, without a glance. Barton returned to the pilots. He felt a curious mixture of guilt and exhilaration. "Flash, you're acting 'A' flight commander," he said.

"Excellent judgement," Gordon told the replacements. "Fann

is a very brilliant CO. One day he will be queen of England, mark my words."

A couple of minutes dragged by. Everyone was restless, fidgety. Some of the replacements were sweating more than the heat required. They were all breathing rather quickly and shallowly.

There was a field telephone on a box. It clicked softly. Nim Renouf turned away and was sick. Barton caught the phone as it rang, and listened.

"Both flights scrambled," he said. "I'll lead 'B' flight. Flash takes 'A.' " They were already hurrying towards their aircraft, Renouf spitting and swearing as he went. "Two big raids," Barton called. "We've got one each. Lucky us."

Flash was trembling, not with fear but with excitement. Fear had touched him when he first saw the raid. It hung between two plump clouds like a swarm of bees, and he looked away, not wanting to know how many aircraft or what type. What did it matter, how many? Too many was always too many: there was no comfort in figures. All the same, one part of his mind insisted on proceeding with an estimate. Sixty plus.

He looked at the flight, spread out like a search-party, and realised he didn't know the names of half of them. He looked to the north and the east for signs of help. Nothing.

When the first rank of bombers was about two miles away, Flash took his flight out of orbit and led it into a head-on attack. This was always the worst time. He was trembling so violently that he braced his head against the back-armour.

Their closing speed ate up the gap in about fifteen seconds. "When I say 'Bingo,' " Flash called, "everyone bloody-well fire!" He was in the middle, leading Red Section, with Yellow right and White left. "Bingo!" he cried. The Hurricanes raced into the raid like a suicide pact. Flash ignored the heavy black blurs and aimed at the holes between them. He was working the machine as furiously as a skier dodging rocks on an icy track. A pair of Heinkels wallowed together and he narrowed his shoulders as he skated between them. The last rank rushed at him. He made his exit with a flashy victory roll just to show them what he thought of them. He hadn't fired a shot.

His wingman, Nim Renouf, was gone, vanished. Flash climbed

steeply, searched the sky and saw part of the German escort ti into a dive. He rolled out of a loop and checked the raid. It ha split into three ragged streams. Below these, two bombers spiralle down, locked together like mating insects. Far below them, a instant avenue of bomb-bursts appeared: someone had jettisonec At that moment, the controller called.

"Popcorn Red Leader, this is Teacake, do you read me?"

"Piss off, Teacake," Flash Gordon said. A broken Dornier side slipped out of his gunsight and he had to peel off before he oversho it. "Bugger!" he said. The sky was full of trouble: planes firing swerving, falling. He noticed another Hurricane up-sun, also on it own, and he manoeuvred alongside.

"Popcorn Red Leader, this is Teacake, what is your position?"

Flash squinted at the silhouetted Hurricane. It was a 109 an he wet himself. He broke fractionally faster than the German an fled into an obliging cloud.

"Popcorn Red Leader, this is Teacake, what is your position?"

"Sodding uncomfortable," he said. His leg was drenched. "Nov piss off, you berk." He came out of cloud and nearly hit a cripple Heinkel being chased by a Hurricane: the bomber jumped at hir like a bogey-man, wings spread to grab, the fighter jumped afte it, and their shadows flicked his face. They were so close that i took his breath away and he felt faint.

"Popcorn Red Leader, this is Teacake, vector zero-four-zero."

He sucked down a good lungful of oxygen, and the colours slowl brightened. "Listen, Teacake," he said. "You can stuff your vector up your arse."

Pause. He weaved, and checked behind him.

"Say again, Popcorn Red Leader."

"Stuff 'em up your arse!" he roared. "Ram 'em up your rectum! The bomber stream seemed to have regrouped. Either that or h had found a second raid. Anything was possible. He was going to fast so he executed a very pretty barrel roll in order to shed spee and came up on the right rear of the stream. The turbulence wa terrible. He kept bucking and pitching and losing the target. H closed up even more, fired, and shot himself. That was impossibl but everything else had gone wrong and now, as soon as he presse the button, something smashed into his left arm. It also knocke the stick out of his hand and sent the plane spinning out of contro

640

It fell for the best part of two miles, mainly because he was too dizzy and stunned to do anything but flop about in his harness. All the way down, Teacake kept calling, making demands, giving orders. When Flash managed to grip the stick again it was twisted arthritically, but it worked.

Things could have been worse. He felt battered and feeble but he could still use his left hand on the throttle. Better yet, when he killed off the spin and levelled out he knew where he was. He recognised the A20. That led to Ashford. Turn left at Ashford and you couldn't miss Brambledown. He decided to share the good news. "Teacake, this is Popcorn Red Leader," he called. "Returning to base, not feeling very well."

"Popcorn Red Leader, this is Teacake. Do *not* return to base. You must pancake elsewhere."

"Oh, balls to that, Teacake." Flash was feeling relaxed. The cockpit was flooded with gauzy sunlight and the Hurricane was flying itself home quite competently.

"Repeat, pancake elsewhere, Popcorn Red. You must divert."

"Don't talk turds," Flash said. "I've had enough for one day." He had a bright idea. The best way to stop Teacake bitching and binding was to keep transmitting. "Put the kettle on, Teacake," he said. Familiar landmarks came and went. "You're a stupid pratt, Teacake," he said. "You're nothing but a piss-artist." Brambledown came in sight. Much of it seemed to be on fire. Spitfires were landing and taking off, flying through the smoke. "Here I come, Teacake," he called, "ready or not."

The Hurricane behaved itself beautifully. There were craters all over the place but it taxied between them and delivered him to his usual parking-spot. It was difficult to get out of the cockpit one-handed but he managed it. He was standing on the wingroot, waiting for some giddiness to pass, when a car roared up and a wing commander leaped out. "What the bloody hell d'you think you've been playing at?" he shouted as he strode to the plane.

Flash recognised the voice. "You're Teacake," he said.

"And *you*, you little bastard, have given me nothing but *shit*. What in God's name's the matter with you?"

Flash thought for a moment. Cautiously he tugged the gauntlet from his left hand. It was full of blood. He poured the blood over

641

the wing commander. After that he had to sit down, and by the time the ambulance reached him he was unconscious.

When the day's fighting was over and the squadron was released, only five Hurricanes flew back to Brambledown.

Barton had survived intact; so had Quirk and two of the replacements, Jolliff and Fraser. Renouf was in hospital, badly burned: his hands were blackened claws, his legs were charred from the knee down, his face looked as if it had melted into a lump with a few holes in it. Donahue's parachute had failed to open completely and he had broken his back. Steele-Stebbing and Patterson had made belly-landings. Steele-Stebbing had concussion and double vision. Patterson had a couple of teeth knocked out.

Nobody said much when they dumped their gear in the crew-room. The air-raid warning sounded as they walked to their quarters, but that wasn't worth a comment. Nor was the sunset: pure gold, fading upwards to a silvery blue. Another blitzy day tomorrow.

Barton meant to take the new boys to the pub but he lay down on his bed for a moment. It was pitch dark when he was awakened from a sweaty nightmare by the dreary wail of the All Clear. The rags of the dream clung to him like filthy cobwebs – he was landing a plane, twice as fast as a Hurricane, and all the controls were floppy and flabby, like wet cardboard – while the siren played out its bleak and colourless note. He reached above him and found the brass bed-rail and gripped it hard, summoning up reality. It was an old, familiar horror, this nightmare, and he knew how to send it away.

Too late for the pub. In any case, he wasn't sure he was fit to drive in the dark. A hot shower did some good. He still needed propping up, so he went in search of Kellaway and found him in his office. "How's Flash?" he asked.

"Oh, holding his own, so they say. He's asleep now. They pumped him full of dope."

"That's good. Fancy a game of snooker?"

The adjutant was no damn good at snooker and he had a ton of work to clear up. Barton's voice was flat and his eyes scarcely moved. "What a marvellous idea," Kellaway said. "That's just what I need." He kept up a flow of chatter all the way to the mess.

Barton did his best, but after a few words he always dried up and Kellaway had to fill the silence.

The billiard room was empty. "You go first," Kellaway said. Barton took a cue, aimed carefully and mis-hit the ball completely. "Bad luck," Kellaway said. "Have another go." This time Barton's hands were shaking so much that his cue-tip kept knocking against the ball. "Tell you what," Kellaway said. "We'll have a sandwich and a beer." He was about to ring for a waiter when Barton stopped him. "No need," he said. "This is the stuff." He shook a tablet from a little bottle.

"Benzedrine," Kellaway said. "Good, is it?"

"Dunno why I didn't think of it before." Barton swallowed the tablet.

"Too groggy, I expect. That's the trouble with being groggy. You can't work things out properly, can you?"

"I'll be all right now. You watch."

Within minutes his eyes were brighter, his complexion was fresher, his actions were brisker and he was talking freely.

"How long have you been taking those?" Kellaway asked.

"About a week." He smacked a red so hard that it travelled around the table twice.

"Don't they keep you awake?"

"So what? I can't sleep much anyway. Your shot, uncle."

He was going strong, slamming balls crisply and even potting some, when Jacky Bellamy walked in with CH3 and Skull. "Hullo!" he said. "What are you doing here?"

"I'm still attached to the Air Ministry wreck-hunters," she said. "We've been checking out this area."

"Jolly good show." He whacked a red and watched with pleasure as it caromed around the table. "Nice to know we're keeping you busy."

She waited until the ball had come to rest. "Not as busy as you might think."

Barton swung his cue like a pendulum and looked at each of them in turn. "Never saw such a gloomy lot of sods in all my life," he said. "Go on, then, tell me the trouble. It can't be any worse than what's happened already."

"I'll give you the bare facts," she said. "By my reckoning Fighter Command has been overstating German losses by a minimum of fifty per cent and a maximum of two hundred percent over the last few weeks. It averages out at one hundred percent."

"Gibberish," said Kellaway.

"I don't think so."

She was perched on the edge of the table, and in its brilliant light her features had an unusual strength and clarity. Skull, watching from the side, was briefly amused by the scene: Venus lecturing Mars, he thought, but he quickly challenged his own assumptions. Why should men hold a monopoly of the truth about war? He was ashamed of his arrogance.

"Let's look at one short period," she said, and flipped open her notebook. "August eleventh to August twenty-fourth. Say, two weeks. Total claims: 743 enemy aircraft, of which 107 were said to have been destroyed by flak. That would leave 636 German raiders claimed by RAF fighters. Anybody care to guess how many of those were found? How many of the 743 turned up as wrecks on British soil?"

Nobody cared to guess.

"One hundred and thirteen," she said.

"A lot fell in the sea," Barton said. He was standing opposite her, rolling a snooker ball from hand to hand.

"More than a lot, it seems. According to HQ Fighter Command nearly *all* the rest fell in the sea. When they were shown these figures and asked to comment on the discrepancy, the people at Fighter Command went off and studied them and came back and said their reports showed that eighty percent of all enemy aircraft destroyed fell in the sea."

"That must be an exaggeration," Skull said.

"Why?" Barton asked. "What do you reckon it should be?"

"Well, assuming this squadron to be typical, I'd say about half-and-half is nearer the mark."

"Most of the intelligence officers I've talked to agree," Jack Bellamy said.

Barton wrinkled his nose. "More like sixty-forty, I'd say."

"Okay," she said. "As it happens I decided to play safe and make it sixty-forty. Sixty percent over sea, forty percent over land. Here's how those mid-August figures break down. There were 743 claims in all. If forty percent came down inland, that means 297 German planes crashed where they could be found. As I said, we

644

found 113 wrecks, which is a difference of 184. On that basis, Fighter Command overstated its claims by something like a hundred and sixty percent."

"Well, that's got to be nonsense." Barton shaded his eyes and looked for CH3. "Where's the great organiser?" He found him sprawled across a chair in a shadowy corner. "You're not saying much, CH3. Get your mighty brain in gear."

"Those figures only cover two weeks," CH3 said. "That's not much of a sample. We've been stooging about upstairs for much longer than that."

Barton turned and smirked at Jacky Bellamy.

"I was going to spare you the worst," she said, "but if you insist . . ." She turned a page. "The full investigation was back-dated to August eighth. No special reason, they just picked a date and that was it. Add up all the claims since August eighth – I mean the official figures, the stuff you hear on the BBC every night – and you get a total of just under fifteen hundred German planes destroyed, plus about five hundred probably destroyed. Suppose only half the probables actually went down. That means the RAF claims it destroyed one thousand seven hundred and fifty German planes in the last month."

"Bloody good show," the adjutant said.

"One sometimes wonders where they keep coming from," Skull murmured.

"Shut up, Skull," Barton ordered. "There you are, then," he told her. "That puts the record straight, doesn't it?"

"There's more to come. Monthly totals: RAF claims – seventeen-fifty; German wrecks actually found – three hundred."

"You didn't look hard enough," the adjutant said.

"In all fairness," Skull remarked, "the men from Air Ministry have been doing the looking. Miss Bellamy is simply an observer."

"Planes crash in woods, you know," Barton said. "And lakes, and reservoirs and things." He balanced the cue on his fingertip.

Skull said: "One takes your point, Fanny, but that factor can't account for such a huge discrepancy, can it? I mean, here we have an air battle over one of the most populous corners of this crowded little island, in daylight. It's very hard to believe that so many aircraft could crash without being noticed."

"Observer Corps posts," CH3 remarked from the corner. "Police. Ack-ack units. Home Guard. Army."

"In any case," Skull added, "our own intelligence experts are very keen to examine German planes."

"Well, we couldn't find more than three hundred," she said. "Three hundred from seventeen-fifty leaves fourteen-fifty. Assume about half of them in the sea, that leaves an overstatement of about seven hundred. The conclusion I come to is that your official RAF claims are out by upwards of a hundred percent."

"I suppose you'll be saying next that we lie about our own losses too," Kellaway said.

"I don't know anything about that."

"No, but you've heard the German claims."

"Yes, and I doubt if *Luftwaffe* pilots are any more reliable than RAF pilots."

"If you were a man," Kellaway said, "I'd knock you down for that."

"Then you're an ass," Skull informed him.

"Say that again."

"Shut up, uncle," Barton said. The benzedrine was beginning to wear off. "Those are all just figures," he said to her. "Numbers. Anyone can prove anything by statistics."

"Sure. But there's another side to the profit-and-loss picture, and that's your bombers. Every night you've been raiding Hitler's invasion fleets, all those barges in Boulogne and so on. Bad flak over there. Plenty bombers don't come back."

"I fail to see the connection," Kellaway said loftily. "Two separate battles."

"It's one war."

"What happens," CH3 asked, "if you add our bomber losses to our fighter losses and compare them with the German losses?"

"By my count, the *Luftwaffe* comes out on top."

"Jerry's on his last legs," Barton said. "Must be." He slumped in an armchair and yawned.

As if to take his place, the adjutant got up and stalked around the room. "What's the point of all this snooping?" he demanded peevishly. "Traipsing about the country on joyrides, getting in everyone's way when you can see we've all got our backs to the wall ... What good does it do anyone?"

"Come to that," Skull replied, "what good does it do to rely on thoroughly inaccurate data?"

"Jerry's finished," Barton mumbled.

"Tell me," CH3 said, "what are you going to do with all this amazing information?"

"I'm not sure," she said. "A month ago it might have made a big story, but now ... I have a feeling the score doesn't matter any more. Maybe I'll just file it and forget it."

"I know nothing of the newspaper business," Skull said, "but a statistical analysis of air losses does seem a trifle ... thin."

"There's more to the story than that. If I'm right, the implications are pretty staggering. Because if the RAF isn't winning this battle, then obviously the *Luftwaffe* isn't losing it, and that's what matters."

"Wrong," Kellaway said, booming the word. "Only one thing matters now, and that's invasion."

"Couldn't agree more," she said. "And if it comes to that, anyone with eyes in his head can see that as far as control of the air is concerned, Hitler could invade tomorrow. So maybe I should write it up big."

"I never heard anything quite so contemptible," Kellaway said. "The very idea is tantamount to an act of treachery."

"Stop being such a blimp, uncle," CH3 said. "If she's right, don't you think the *Luftwaffe* knows it? They can count, they don't need to listen to the BBC. And if she's wrong, what does it matter?"

"Blimp," the adjutant said, wide-eyed.

"There's still such a thing as censorship, you know," Skull told her.

"Hear that, Fanny? I'm a blimp." The adjutant sat down.

"I can always get a story out, if it's big enough," she said. "Through the neutrals, through the embassy. There are ways."

"And then you'll be expelled."

"I've been expelled before. It goes with the job. Talking of which ..." She glanced at her watch. "I have work to do. See you all at breakfast, I hope."

"Not me," CH3 said. "We leave with the dawn."

"I wouldn't bet on it."

The door closed behind her. Kellaway got up and peered at Barton. "Bloody women Yank gutterpress scribblers," he muttered.

"What do they know? Our chaps are hitting Jerry for six, aren't they?"

"Not while I've been around," CH3 said.

Kellaway turned and stared, thought about starting an argument, changed his mind, sniffed and said: "Well, we're certainly holding our own."

"Not even that, I'm afraid," Skull said. "Right now the situation can only be described as desperate, and I'm not talking about men and machines, although God knows we're scraping the barrel for pilots. What's really crippling us is the appalling damage to communications. All the sector stations have taken a terrible pounding. If you think Brambledown's in a mess you should see Biggin Hill. And North Weald. They're in ruins. And once the ops rooms get knocked out the whole ground control system fails and we're paralysed."

"It hasn't happened yet," CH3 said.

"I tell you the system's on its last legs. While you were up this afternoon, three raids came and went without interception. Three raids! And it's bound to get worse. If the *Luftwaffe* keeps up these attacks, the entire air-defence system of south-east England will cease to exist in less than a week."

"We'll muddle through somehow," Kellaway said.

"You don't seem to realise what's happening," Skull told him. "Already the *Luftwaffe* can do very nearly what it pleases over the invasion area. We don't command our own air space any more."

"No, no. That can't be true."

"Can't it? Go and look at the advanced fighter fields. They've been knocked silly. Manston's not working, Hawkinge is a shambles, and with effect from midnight Bodkin Hazel is abandoned. It's too dangerous. We can't defend it."

That gave them something to think about. In the gloom beyond the brightly lit table, Barton twitched and mumbled in his sleep.

"So that's what she meant," CH3 said. "She knew we were pulling back."

"Retreating?" Kellaway said. "We can't bloody retreat. This is England, for God's sake."

"Come on," CH3 said. "Let's get Fanny to bed." The sirens began to wail.

Next morning there was a lieutenant of the Royal Engineers at the bottom of a crater beside the officers' mess. He was trying to defuse a 250-kilo bomb. Breakfast was therefore served at trestle tables set up in the open several hundred yards away.

It was a splendid morning. Even by seven o'clock the air was warm enough for the pilots to sit in their shirt sleeves. All three squadrons had been released to thirty-minute availability. The table in the ops room was strangely free of plots.

Fanny Barton saw CH3 coming. "I'd better go and sign some letters," he said, took his mug of coffee and left.

CH3 sat with Skull and Quirk. "Doesn't it ever rain in this country?" he said. "I mean, whose side is God on, for Pete's sake?"

"I can't answer that," Skull said. "The latest Air Ministry intelligence report on God was eaten by a plague of locusts."

"That's a sign," Quirk said. "The old bugger doesn't like us." He rested his head on his arms and closed his eyes.

"You ought to be wearing your revolver," Skull told CH3.

"At breakfast?"

"Everywhere and always. Haven't you heard? Air Ministry's issued Invasion Alert Number One. Attack imminent."

"Jerry can't invade today," Quirk muttered. "I haven't finished my library book."

"It makes sense," CH3 said. "If he attacks like he did yesterday we won't have any spare fighters to go after his invasion fleet."

"Alternatively," Skull said, "if you take on the invasion fleet then the bombers will have a completely free hand to destroy the sector stations and so on."

"Jerry's finished," Quirk said into his arm. "Fanny said so."

"Excuse me." CH3 took his plate to another table, where Jacky Bellamy was reading her notes. "I have a question," he said.

"See my agent. I don't give interviews, remember? Except for money. Do you have money? Lots of money?"

"Let's not horse around." He propped his head on his hand and studied her face. "You're incredible. How can you look so . . ." But his mind stopped. He couldn't think of the word.

"It's easy for me. I don't have to climb the Alps several times a day and fight to the death while I'm up there."

"Chipper." He had remembered the word.

"How can *you* do it, day after day?"

"Dunno. My question is . . ." But now he had forgotten his question. "Not chipper," he said. "I remembered chipper . . . Christ, I'm tired."

"Eat your breakfast. Where's your revolver? You ought to have a revolver."

"I can't eat breakfast with a revolver, for Pete's sake." Sideways into his brain slipped the forgotten question. He chewed bacon and let the words assemble themselves, and when they were complete he said: "About the invasion. You told me Hitler won't invade. In the pub, remember? Then last night you said he can invade whenever he likes. Something wrong there."

"No. It's all a matter of perspective."

He groaned softly.

"Okay, I'll make it easy," she said. "Everybody's looking at the idea of invasion from the British perspective. They're all saying the British army's got no guns and the Home Guard's patrolling the cliffs with Elizabethan pikes and so on, therefore Hitler will do another Poland. Nobody's looking at it from *Hitler's* point of view. I mean, put yourself in Hitler's shoes. You want to get an army across the Channel. How?"

"Paratroopers?" Quirk suggested. He and Skull sat down.

"Paratroopers, maybe," she said. "But it takes two hundred transport planes to carry a mere five thousand paratroopers. Some get lost, some get shot down on the way. Say four thousand troops make it. Can Hitler beat England with four thousand men?"

"Obviously there will be a landing by sea as well," Skull said.

"Right!" She was so eager that she couldn't sit still. "Okay! So he comes by sea. How?"

"Boats," CH3 said.

"What sort?"

"Big boats."

"Why?"

"Obvious. Fast. Strong. Bags of room."

"And then?"

"Then what?"

"Where do the goddam boats *land*?" she demanded.

"One assumes they would go for Dover," Skull said.

"No, no, no." Quirk waved the idea away. "Dover Harbour' bound to be blocked. And Folkestone. In fact all the harbours nea here can be blocked at the drop of a hat. Nothing to it. Piece of cake."

"I forgot you were a bloody sailor," CH3 said.

"Come on, then," Jacky Bellamy urged. "You're Hitler. What now?"

"Land the troops on the beaches," Skull said.

"Fine!" She clapped her hands together. "*Now* we're getting nowhere! How?"

"Barges," CH3 said. "Lots of flat-bottomed barges. Jerry's got thousands of them. They go up and down the Rhine all the time."

"And what makes them go?"

"Tugs, usually," Quirk said. "Some barges have motors but mostly they have to be towed."

"So that's your invasion fleet, is it? Forget the warships and the minesweepers for a minute, just work on getting your troops ashore. They're on a lot of barges, are they? How many?"

"Two hundred men per barge?" Skull looked at Quirk, who shrugged. "So five hundred barges would carry a hundred thousand men."

"Not enough," CH3 said. "Double it."

"A thousand barges?" She seemed pleased with the way things were going. "Nearly all under tow? Right! What speed?"

"Depends on the weather," Quirk said at once. "Flat calm, maybe five knots, but if there's any chop . . ." He made a face. "Dodgy bit of water, the Channel. Say you average three knots."

"Three knots. Fair enough. At that speed how long is it going to take to get those men across?"

CH3 began to speak and then changed his mind. "If you want to know the time, ask a sailor," he said.

"It all depends on your route," Quirk said. "Where you leave from and where you're going to."

"What's wrong with Calais-Dover? Shortest possible route," said Skull.

"You're going to climb up those white cliffs, are you?" CH3 said. "Good luck."

"It was only a suggestion." Skull was nettled. "If you don't like it, what about landing at Rye? I seem to remember Rye has a nice beach. I went there as a child and it was always very pleasant."

"Don't fancy Rye," Quirk said. "I've sailed all up and down that coast. Lousy currents. Vicious."

"I never paddled very far out," Skull said.

"Where would *you* land?" CH3 asked Quirk.

Quirk gave it some thought, shaking his head as he mentally disqualified one beach after another. "What'll the weather be like?" he asked.

"Changeable. It always is."

"If the weather's perfect I can think of two places where you might get ashore. There's Sandgate, near Folkestone, and there's Dungeness."

"That's where we're landing," CH3 told Jacky Bellamy firmly.

"I'm not too happy about Dungeness," Quirk added. "You've got a whole string of sandbanks offshore."

"Boulogne to Dungeness," she said. "How long?"

"It's not a straight line, I mean to say the tides whizz up and down at a hell of a lick and you have to go up-Channel so you can get carried back down-Channel later ... How long? Oooh ..." Quirk sucked his teeth. "You'd be lucky to do it in fifteen hours."

"Fifteen hours? Agreed? Good. Next question: when are you going to land? What time of day?"

"Dawn is the usual time, isn't it?" Skull said. "Surprise the defence and give yourself lots of daylight to fight in."

"Hey, wait a minute ..." Quirk said.

"Dawn it is," she declared. "So when d'you set out? Fifteen hours earlier, yes? That's 2 p.m. the day before."

"We can't do that," Skull said. "They'll see us coming."

"Wait a minute, wait a minute," Quirk said. "Are you proposing to make this crossing *by night*?"

"It's up to you," she said.

"Hundreds of river barges under tow with no lights? All trying to fight their way across those tidal streams? All trying to miss the banks in the middle of the Channel? The Varne, Bullock Bank, The Ridge? Christ Almighty, I'd think twice about making that trip by day, in a good boat. Anyone who tows a barge from Boulogne to Dungeness at night is asking for trouble. Big trouble."

"Five hundred barges," she said. "A thousand."

"That's a formula for disaster."

"All right," CH3 said, "send 'em across by day and make the landing by night."

"But then they would be completely exposed to attack *en route*," Skull said.

"Not if they've got air cover."

"It's not as easy as that," Quirk said. "I don't care how many planes you've got, it's still bloody difficult to hit a destroyer doing thirty knots. D'you know what a destroyer looks like from two thousand feet? It looks like a paperclip. Turn me loose with a destroyer and I guarantee I'd carve up those barges long before any air cover got to me."

"Where's the German Navy?" CH3 asked. "Picking its nose in a corner?"

"What German Navy? I doubt if they've got twenty ships they can put together. We sank half their destroyers in the Norwegian campaign."

"And we lost ours at Dunkirk."

"We lost four," Skull said. "Out of forty."

"If they couldn't stop us getting the army away from Dunkirk," said Quirk, "I don't see the German Navy keeping us off this invasion fleet, do you?"

"They'll bloody Stuka you to death," CH3 said.

"At night?"

"But if it's really dark," Skull said, "you might not see the barges. They might slip past you."

"I'm not talking about *one* destroyer," Quirk explained. "I'm talking about forty, fifty, sixty destroyers. *And* a dozen cruisers *and* a couple of battleships *and* Christ knows how many corvettes and MTB's. All we need is a few hours' notice."

"You've still got to hit the barges," CH3 said stubbornly. "Five hundred barges take a lot of shelling."

"Waste of time," Quirk said. "Have you ever seen the wake a big ship throws up when it's in a hurry? It's enough to capsize every flat-bottomed barge that gets in its way. The Navy wouldn't waste shells on Jerry. We'd sink him with our wash."

"Your theory, then," Skull said, "is that this air battle is irrelevant."

"It's more than a theory," she said. "It's a hell of a good story, because it's based on hard fact. It's a fact that the RAF alone can't stop an invasion. If Hitler sends his fleet over by night the RAF won't even see it, and if his stormtroopers hit the beach at dawn the *Luftwaffe* will give them an umbrella because right now it's stronger than you are. However, none of that matters a damn because Hitler's no mug. He knows he can't get a thousand little river barges across the Channel while his Navy's outnumbered ten to one, so he won't even try."

"You've missed one thing," CH3 said. "If the air battle doesn't matter, why is Hitler going flat-out to win it?"

"Beats me. Maybe he thinks he can scare you into giving in."

"In any case," Skull said, "the man has very little choice. He's at war. If his enemies won't surrender he's obliged to try and fight them, but at the moment his means are limited. He can't use his Army. He can't use his Navy, except for the U-boats. That leaves his Air Force."

"Which can't beat the British Navy," she said. "So England wins."

"No," CH3 said unhappily. "No, no, no. You've got it wrong. You make it sound as if all we have to do to win is not lose. It's not that easy! You don't win wars just by not losing. People need a victory, they need to prove themselves. Damn it, Hitler's knocked over eight or nine countries, he's beginning to look unbeatable, people are actually starting to *believe* that master-race crap. What we need is a good juicy victory *now*, a great big spectacular bloody nose for Hitler. We've got to beat the *Luftwaffe* just to show it can be done."

"Even if it hasn't been done?" she said. "Even if the scores are fake?"

"I give up," he said. "Write it any way you like."

CH3 went to his room and buckled on his service revolver. The utter fatigue that had overtaken him at breakfast had passed and been replaced by an edgy nervousness. He recognised the feeling it was his overworked body preparing for another day of scrambles and scraps, death and terror. It was cranking itself up for the usual cruel and extravagant demands of air combat, when the pulse would hammer at double its normal rate, the skin would be drenched in sweat, the lungs would gulp pure oxygen, and the brain would sometimes be starved of blood, sometimes be swamped with it. Another physical and emotional battering was on the way, and his body didn't like the idea.

He looked around the room. It was anonymous, meaningless. Suppose he didn't come back today. Tomorrow someone else would move in. What difference would his leaving have made? None. What difference would his staying make? None either. Nothing he did would alter the outcome of this war. Jacky Bellamy's clever ideas might even be right, or half-right, or half-wrong, or completely cockeyed. That didn't matter any more. Nothing he did could save Hornet squadron. Since September began, Fighter Command had been losing the equivalent of a squadron a day. That would continue. Hornet squadron would go on living and dying in its own peculiar, random way. The whole exercise was pointless. It wasn't his fight. It wasn't his country. Anyway, he'd done his stint. Everyone said the important thing was to know when to quit. The ones who got the chop were always the ones who never knew when to call it a day.

He went to find Fanny Barton.

Instead he found a couple of airmen who said that Fanny's office had been wrecked by a bomb. They were carrying what was left of his furniture to his new office, formerly a vegetable store. CH3 went with them.

He watched them prop a broken desk on a couple of milk crates, and go out. He picked a battered squash racket out of a cardboard box and tested the strings. The room smelled of potatoes. Dusty sunlight drifted across it. More men came in and put things down. CH3 noticed his sense of edgy nervousness fading. The old exhaustion was creeping back. Even his eyes had stopped trying: the moving figures lapsed into soft focus. One of them asked him something and it wasn't until the man had gone that he understood the question. Not that it mattered. He had no answer.

The door banged open, and he blinked. It was Kellaway, carrying a cracked blackboard and gripping a piece of paper in his teeth. He stood the blackboard on a box and consulted the paper. "Tell Fanny that Micky says the new Hurricanes have been ferried in," he said, and hitched his trousers as he half-squatted. There was a list of old names on the blackboard and Kellaway began chalking up new ones. "And tell him his replacements are here too," he said. CH3 followed the movement of the chalk but the scribbles failed to register in his mind: they remained just scribbles. "I expect he'll want to speak to them soon," Kellaway muttered. He completed the last name and dotted an i, firmly and finally. His knees cracked as he straightened up. He was halfway to the door when he stopped, uttered a little grunt of annoyance, turned back and looked at the board again. He summoned up some spit and moistened his fingers. He smudged out the name Gordon and went away.

CH3 stared at the ruined lettering until his tears came and made it completely unreadable.

Fanny Barton walked in as CH3 was scrubbing his face with his handkerchief. "Hullo!" he said. CH3 could only nod. Barton looked at the blackboard, and went back and closed the door. "It happened about half an hour ago," he said. "The medics told me what it was, but I wasn't listening all that carefully. Delayed shock, I think they said."

"It doesn't matter what it was."

"No, it doesn't, does it?" Barton stooped and studied the ghost name under the smudged chalk.

"You know, Fanny," CH3 said, "I always thought Flash was different. I thought, they'll never catch him."

"Funny, isn't it?" Barton licked his fingers and erased the smudge. Better nothing than a ghost. "I suppose there's a Flash in every squadron." He found a bit of chalk and wrote "CH3" in the gap. "Someone you're convinced is different, and in the end of course he's just like all the rest."

"Flash wasn't like all the rest. Remember when I nearly murdered him up the apple-tree?"

Barton laughed. CH3 grinned. He began to feel released, elated. The scruffy, potato-smelling room suddenly seemed brighter, more alive. He found himself laughing too. Everything was very, very funny. In the middle of the laughter the door opened and a chubby middleaged civilian came in. He wore blue overalls and he was holding a telephone. "GPO engineer," he announced cheerfully. "Where d'you want your phone, guv?" He twirled the lead.

"Where d'you want your phone, Fanny?" CH3 asked.

"Beats me, old boy. You pick a place."

CH3 took out his revolver and fired at the opposite wall. The bang was enormous. "There," he said.

"Here, what's the game?" the man said faintly.

"Not there," Barton said, and fired his revolver at a different wall. Fragments of red brick flew off. "There," he said.

The engineer turned and bolted. "On second thoughts," CH3 said, "how about there?" He fired at a corner. "Don't be bloody ridiculous," Barton told him, and shot a box of books. "That's the place."

"Wrong." CH3 aimed at a waste basket and missed. The bullet sang as it ricocheted off the floor. "You mean there?" Barton asked, and shot the waste basket. The air stank. CH3 put a bullet into the ceiling and Barton nearly hit a calendar hanging from a nail.

"You win," CH3 said. "My wrist hurts."

"You came second," Barton said. "I'll tell you what. How'd you like to be my senior flight commander?"

CH3 stuffed the gun back in its holster. "It's all a cock-up, isn't it?" he said.

"Of course it's all a cock-up. I could have told you it was all a cock-up. In fact I did tell you but you weren't bloody listening, as usual. Come on. Let's go and find the new boys."

The adjutant met them as they were going out. "What was all that din?" he asked.

"We were putting up some shelves," CH3 said, but Kellaway wasn't listening. "You're on twenty-minute standby," he said. "I'd better organise some sandwiches."

Two hours later the pilots of Hornet squadron were still lying on the grass, a short sprint from their Hurricanes. Standby time had come down to ten minutes, then to five. Now it was two. They had watched one of the Spitfire squadrons take off and disappear, heading east. A few minutes later the other Spitfire squadron had followed them. The rumble of their engines could still be heard, faintly.

Skull appeared on a bicycle, pedalling hard. "I've been in the ops room," he said to Barton. "It's the most extraordinary thing. In the last fifteen minutes every squadron in the Group has been scrambled. That's twenty squadrons airborne."

"And how many raids?"

"One."

"What? Hey, that's marvellous! Twenty squadrons, at least two hundred kites, all on one raid . . . We've got the buggers where we want them." Barton grinned at his pilots, and they grinned back. "For months I've been waiting for the day when *we* outnumbered *them*, and here it is!" He whooped with glee and threw his hat at the sky.

"How big is the raid?" CH3 asked.

"Oh, it's big. It's —"

"Come on, come on, come on!" Barton kicked the pole that had the telephone attached to it. "What are they waiting for? Everybody else is up. Why not us?"

"You say everyone else is scrambled?" CH3 said. "We're the only reserve? That's damn dangerous, isn't it?"

The telephone rang, and Barton grabbed it. It was the scramble order, and they pounded to their planes.

The controller's instructions were unusually brief.

"Hullo Bearskin Leader, this is Trombone," he said. All the codenames had been changed. "Steer zero-four-five and patrol Lampstand at angels six."

"Happy to oblige, Trombone," Barton said, and ran his finger down the codelist of the day. Lampstand was the Isle of Sheppey. Angels six meant angels ten.

He held the squadron in a power climb. After a minute, Trombone raised the angels to eight, which meant twelve.

Barton felt restless; he was always twisting to look and make sure nobody was lagging behind, and then leaning forward to search for the scrap. There must surely be a major scrap ahead, what with twenty squadrons scrambled already. He couldn't imagine what twenty squadrons would look like, all concentrated on one raid.

The voice of his wingman cut in. "What's wrong, Leader?" CH3 said. "Dropped sixpence?" Barton stopped twisting. "Found it," he said. "Threepenny bit."

CH3 felt content. Flash Gordon's death had cleansed his emotions: all pettiness had been swept away in that rush of shared grief. By their manic horseplay with revolvers they had briefly held a wake for Flash. Life had saluted death in a suitably random fashion, and now life went on.

Trombone raised the angels again. Now the target height was sixteen thousand. Hornet squadron went onto oxygen. No word about the raid. Barton assumed it was holding its course.

A dun-coloured skim of industrial haze covered the Thames estuary. To the right, Kent was a huge green-and-gold thumb stuck into the Channel, and the Channel itself sparkled as if touched with static electricity. Barton found Ramsgate, out at the end of the thumb, and saw where Manston must be. A year ago he had flown to Manston to apologise to the skipper of a Blenheim squadron. He remembered it quite calmly and evenly. That was the young Fanny Barton, that was. No relation to the old Fanny Barton now leading his squadron to a lovely great scrap, if only they could find the bloody thing.

"Hullo, Leader," CH3 called. "You sure we're in the place of honour?"

"I think we missed a turning somewhere," Barton said.

"Bloody Spits," Cox said. "They've gone and scoffed the lot."

"Bogey at ten o'clock," Patterson warned.

Far away to the left, a faint bundle of dots could be made out, heading east. Eventually it grew and matured into a hard, tight clump.

"Hurricanes," Cattermole said. "In their Sunday best."

The other squadron was using the orthodox, peacetime formation: four vics of three, neatly locked into an arrowhead. The sight made Barton uneasy, and he checked his own aircraft. "Ease out a bit, everyone," he said.

Patterson, at Blue Two, began to wonder if the Spits really had scoffed the lot. Maybe Hornet squadron had been sent to clean up the left-overs. Maybe there were no left-overs. Patterson welcomed that idea. All the way from Brambledown his stomach muscles had been jumping with fear and tension. Everything about him felt uncomfortable: his mouth ached where his teeth had been knocked out, his legs and feet were ice-cold, his torso was wet with sweat, he needed desperately to pee, his straps were all wrong and the buckle stuck into his ribs. He wanted to get this patrol over as soon as possible.

Alongside Cattermole, Steele-Stebbing was happy about everything except his eyes. He had been up and down so often in the past few weeks that his sinuses had become very sensitive to changes of pressure. Now they felt as if they had been blown up with a bicycle pump, and every other breath sent sparks drifting across his eyeballs. He trained himself to look between and beyond the sparks.

The north Kent coast was not far away when they met a layer of haze.

The other Hurricane squadron was now a mile or so ahead.

Beyond his left wingtip Barton could just make out the Isle of Sheppey. The haze thinned and dissolved and fled away and he saw, crossing his front from right to left about a mile ahead, the first wave of a flood of aircraft. Automatically he counted the bombers in the front rank, doubled it for the second, doubled that for the third and fourth. Forty bombers, close-packed. After them the flood grew stronger, layer stacked on layer, rearing ever upwards until the mass was more than a mile high, and that was only the beginning. The flood went on. It was an orderly torrent of aircraft that stretched to the horizon.

Hornet squadron was at sixteen thousand feet, and the pilots could look far down on the lowest layers and then far up at the highest. The enemy darkened the sky. In this colossal wedge there were something like a thousand German bombers and fighters, all making for London.

Barton searched, and found odd flights and sections of Hurricanes and Spitfires darting at the mass. Then he looked ahead and saw the other Hurricane squadron – still as compact as a troop of Household Cavalry – go wheeling into the first stages of a Fighting Area Attack. "Silly sods'll get jumped," Cox said. Barton checked the sky above. Dropping fast were four Me-109's. He called a warning. No response: the other squadron must be on a different frequency. He ignored it and concentrated on the bomber stream, now coming up fast.

"Okay, Bearskin aircraft," he said. "In and out fast. Let's chivy the buggers." As his sections split up to make their separate attacks he glimpsed the four 109's rolling away from two burning Hurricanes at the tail of the formation.

Hornet squadron accomplished quite a bit of chivying before the escort got amongst them. The raiders were so thick that it was like shooting at a parade. This parade shot back, with ten times the firepower. The sky was a moving embroidery of tracer and incendiary and cannonshells.

Cattermole made the first kill.

Steele-Stebbing was Yellow Two and he guarded Cattermole's tail faithfully. Although his stomach was much harder nowadays his heart pumped like a sprinter's as Cattermole made him do the utmost violence to the Hurricane's controls. But it paid off. A wandering 109 flew straight and level for one second too long and

Cattermole put a burst into its cockpit. The 109 reared. Cattermole plunged under it and Steele-Stebbing followed, dust and fluff swirling up from the cockpit floor. Cattermole jigged to go left, changed his mind and went screaming off to the right. Steele-Stebbing tipped his machine onto its wingtip and the g-forces briefly drained strength from his arms and legs. Cattermole's plane came in view again, chasing a wildly-rocking Dornier. As Steele-Stebbing levelled out a spot of oil flew up and splattered itself on his goggles. He dragged the back of his glove across the goggles and saw a 109 nipping in behind Cattermole. Everyone fired at once: Cattermole hit the Dornier, the 109 hit Cattermole, and Steele-Stebbing missed the 109 but he gave it the fright of its life and it sheered away. Then he heard a faint *thump-thump-thump* that wasn't the pulse in his ears and the instrument panel turned into shattered glass and splintered wood and a small tornado was blasting into the cockpit and his left arm was chopped off at the elbow and blood was squirting all over the canopy.

Patterson saw it happen. Less than a minute had passed since he led Quirk into the attack and already Patterson had wet himself twice: once when a bomber exploded in front of him and a gun-turret whirled by, no more than six feet from his prop; and once when he was climbing and a pair of 109's stormed towards him, apparently obsessed with collision. Patterson had been convinced there was no escape, yet he made the gesture of frantic action and his Hurricane bounced like a ball on the shockwave. When he got it under control again he was alone. He saw the pair of 109's far below, closing on a Hurricane that was last in a line of planes. The Hurricane flipped onto its back and went into a spin.

Patterson was enraged. He charged after the Messerschmitts and eventually caught one. It broke hard left and he followed. At once they were in a tail-chasing circle. Patterson hated this. His mouth was stretched wide open, straining to drag breath into lungs that felt flattened by the leaden clamp of g-forces as he dragged the plane into a circle so tight that he felt nailed to his seat and his vision threatened to fade into greyness. That was what he dreaded most: weakening for the one second it would take that 109 to catch him and blast him.

He forced his head to turn, and was rewarded with a glimpse of a tail-unit. A blurred swastika registered. Mightily encouraged, he dredged up some strength and bullied the Hurricane until his arms and legs throbbed and trembled. More reward! More tail-unit, a chunk of fuselage, and yet more, a 2, a German cross, a 6, wingroots, cockpit ... Patterson fired, and shot off the Messerschmitt's tail-wheel. Nothing else. The tail-wheel flicked away, and he swore, but the blow was enough to startle the German pilot, and he did the worst possible thing: he changed his turn. The 109 floated generously across Patterson's gunsight and he fired again and missed again. It was impossible, but he missed; and when he looked again the enemy had gone.

Six thousand feet below, Steele-Stebbing's machine was still spinning clumsily to earth, thrashing its tail as if it wanted to snap it off. Steele-Stebbing felt no pain. He felt a huge shock. God had turned his world inside-out and upside-down, and his left arm was flopping and spraying as the plane threw it about, but it took him several seconds to believe that the stump was his and so this bloody lump of sleeve getting flung about the cockpit was his too. The Hurricane thrashed and the severed arm bashed him in the face. His brain was elsewhere, outside this little red madhouse, observing with horror and disbelief, struggling to cope with the disaster that was saturating everything with blood. The Hurricane kicked viciously and the rogue arm shot out of the broken canopy and vanished. At last his brain caught up. He snatched at the stick, stamped on the pedals, killed off the spin. With the stick jammed between his knees he slammed his hand on the gushing stub of his left elbow, found the artery and stopped the jet. Everything around him dripped red.

At three thousand feet, Cattermole flew alongside. "Someone bust your window," he said.

Steele-Stebbing dragged the stub up to his mask and used his right thumb to flick the R/T switch. "One of your rough friends,' he said.

Cattermole rolled over the top and took a look from the other side. "I can't see in," he said, "so how the hell can you see out?"

Steele-Stebbing couldn't reply. He was starting to feel very shaky. The stick was slipping.

"You want to chuck that kite away," Cattermole advised. "Get out and walk."

Steele-Stebbing had thought of it. The problem was that to open the hood he would have to let go of his arm. In any case he didn' feel strong enough to drag back the hood. Always assuming it wasn't jammed.

"If you can still work the doings," Cattermole said, "I'll talk you down."

Steele-Stebbing heard that but he didn't really understand: it was like words clearly typed but written in a foreign language. His thumb was getting weak and the throbbing wetness was pumping out again. Quite easily and peacefully he fell asleep. His knees came apart and the stick twitched nervously.

Cattermole flew with him to the end. The Hurricane hit the face of the South Downs at just under two hundred knots. In less than a second, thirty-one feet of fighter was smashed down to nine feet, the wings ripped off and discarded, the propeller blades left behind the tail, the seat and back-armour crushed into the reserve tank, the tank collapsed into the engine. Mixed up with the armour and the tank and the engine was what was left of Steele-Stebbing.

Three miles higher, Cox was having no luck at all. His targets always flinched out of the way of his bullets, and several unidentified enemies had frightened the life out of him. Also his wingman, Jolliff, had vanished. So far, it wasn't Cox's day.

A 109 dived in front, trailing smoke. He stuffed the nose down and the Merlin cut out for a second or two. Bits of dust and dirt rose from the cockpit floor. The Merlin picked up, and two miles below him was the sea, revolving gently to the right as he spiralled down in search of that smoking 109.

It was the wrong thing to do. He knew it as soon as he did it: chasing singleton Jerries downhill was a mug's game, everyone said so. Too late now. In the corner of his eye he saw a spurt of flame and hoped it wasn't Jolliff. He felt guilty about Jolliff. The smoking 109 seemed to be getting away. Cox heard a faint trickle of popping noises and then his Hurricane got bashed nine times in two seconds with such ferocity that the prop fell off.

He never saw the 109 that hit him. He hauled back the stick and tasted bile. The plane wallowed into a clumsy glide. Another bang, and the engine caught fire: flames as big as bedsheets; the heat came surging through the Perspex. He slammed the plane into a sideslip that washed the blaze away from him, heaved back the canopy and dived out.

The sea was still a long way below when his parachute opened.

663

No ships were in sight. Cox couldn't swim, he hated water, and he couldn't tolerate the thought of a slow, cold death in it. He took his revolver from his flying boot and wondered what was the best way to shoot himself. While he was wondering he noticed that the wind was quite strong. He was drifting towards land. He dropped the revolver and watched it fall at enormous speed.

With his radio dead and his engine coughing and shaking, Pip Patterson flew away from the raid, across the Thames estuary, and searched for a landing-ground. There were plenty of other stray aircraft limping home. He followed one down. It wasn't until he was over the village church that he realised he was back at RAF Kingsmere in Essex.

He parked a long way from the tower. Nobody signalled or came out to see him. He switched off, climbed out and sat on a wing. The noise of the enemy raid was a distant grumble. His engine ticked and hissed as it cooled. Otherwise everything was calm and tranquil. The breeze played with a strip of torn fabric on his fuselage.

It was almost exactly a year ago that they had flown out of Kingsmere. As Patterson took off his Mae West and unzipped his jacket, those twelve months flickered through his brain. There was no pattern or purpose to his memories: just a jumble of faces and places, of scrambles and scraps and parties and popsies and more scrambles and crashed kites and yet more scrambles and endless bloody battle-climbs. Most of the faces he remembered had no names. Patterson didn't try to remember them. He didn't try to do anything. All he knew was that he was dead tired and he never wanted to fly again. The air smelled sweet. Just breathing it was a pleasure. He lay on his back and closed his eyes.

By now many of Hornet squadron had broken off the fight and were returning to base: fifteen seconds' worth of ammunition was soon gone. Moggy Cattermole, however, was still climbing. He had ammunition left, and there were stragglers to be potted.

The straggler he found and fancied was a tattered Dornier with its undercarriage down. He followed it through a confused patch of sky, all flak-bursts and con-trails and roving fighters, and as he gained on it a solitary Spitfire saw him and came over. This was reassuring: it let Cattermole concentrate on his kill. But he was still out of range of the Dornier when gunfire hacked a string of holes in his port wing and he had to break hard right. As he banked he glimpsed his attacker. It was the Spitfire, and it was still coming for him. It knocked chunks off his rudder and it battered his back-armour before he shook it off.

"You chump!" Cattermole shouted. "You blundering buffoon!" He deliberately cocked his wings to display the roundels. "See, you silly man? I'm on your side." The Spitfire came at him again, and now he lost his temper, wrenched the Hurricane into a shuddering turn and took a snap shot. This merely angered the other pilot. The Hurricane wallowed as Cattermole tried to force more bank out of it. His legs ached, his nose dripped blood. Both hands clamped the stick, heaving as if they could lever the plane around. In the corner of his eye he saw the curl of wings. The Spitfire was making another attack. "Cretinous peasant!" he bawled. The words turned into a scream. For the first time in his life Cattermole tasted terror.

Everything was going wrong. His Hurricane was clumsy and heavy and slow, while this murderous fiend was lithe and tireless and fast. Cattermole raged at the man's stupidity, at his madness. He pounded the canopy, shouting: "Can't you *see*? Can't you *see*?" until his voice cracked. A knife-edge silhouette swam into his mirror. Brownings crackled, and fresh holes chased themselves across his wings. Cattermole's bladder emptied itself. He was screaming and praying at the same time.

Then, unexpectedly, the Spitfire overshot. There was a glorious moment when it sat slap in front of him and he stopped screaming and pressed his gun-button. Compressed air whistled, breech-blocks clanked. No ammunition. Cattermole wept.

The Spitfire sheered off. It had seen its mistake. It climbed, and circled twice. Cattermole tried to read its number, but his eyes were full of tears and his head was trembling like a drunk's. The Spitfire flew away.

It should have stayed. Cattermole was, by now, miles from the main raid. He was out of ammunition, his engine was leaking glycol, he could manoeuvre only sluggishly, and there were no friendly fighters to which he could attach himself. His compass was broken but he could see the Channel and he steered for where he guessed Brambledown should be. He was making a Mayday call when he met a flight of Me-109's, also in the process of going home. He stopped speaking, and stopped breathing. They looked so neat and well-behaved, he couldn't believe they would do him any harm.

His lungs jerked, demanding air, and he coughed. The dribble from his nosebleed spattered everywhere. "For Christ's sake someone help me," he said.

"Bearskin Yellow," the Mayday controller said, "transmit for fix, transmit for fix."

"Oh Jesus," Cattermole whispered. The 109's had made a small deviation to their course. As he reached up to slide back the hood they came within range. His arms were still raised when a converging cone of bullets hacked through the side of the cockpit and killed him.

His straggler, the tattered Dornier with its wheels down, didn't last long: someone else found it and finished it off. The Kent coastline was dotted with columns of smoke, markers on the German route. Yet the raid churned on.

By now Barton's wingman had turned for home, his guns empty. Barton made one more pass at a bunch of Ju-88's, decided the storm of defensive fire was too heavy, and broke away, checking the sky above and behind. He searched for the tail of the parade and saw only more bombers emerging from the horizon.

For a moment the odds sickened him. Then he was overtaken by a sense of outrage. He thought: *What the hell do these Huns think they're doing? Whose country is this, anyway?* He turned on the nearest formation. Heinkels, black and hulking. They saw him coming. Tracer throbbed from the gun-turrets and seemed to stretch itself towards him, lazily, casually, until suddenly the stuff was streaking past the cockpit so fast that he hunched his shoulders. The Heinkel he'd picked out jinked, but ponderously and too late. His bulletstrikes hammered its fuselage, making bright splashes of orange. Then Barton was half-rolling and diving away. Across his blurred vision passed a scattering of images: a Spitfire shedding a wing; a Dornier going round in circles, one engine on fire; flak appearing like smuts on a window; rank upon rank of raiders, all as ordered as tin soldiers; and – dangerously big – a pair of 109's, racing to the defence of the Heinkels. Barton saw spirals of white smoke leaping from their wings, and cursed, and before the curse was finished they were far behind him, chasing some other poor bastard.

Barton circled, and saw his Heinkel. It was on its back, leaking flame and falling fast. A kill.

He enjoyed the kick of triumph, but it faded and he suddenly

666

felt washed-out. That reaction scared him to the point of panic. He knew a kill broke his concentration, left him slack and dull: easy meat. He purposely frightened himself even more, stretched his muscles, gulped oxygen, prayed that Jerry would leave him alone while he dredged up some adrenalin. Automatically every ten seconds he changed direction. Voices scratched faintly but urgently in his headphones: *Green Two, break! ... I see him ... Lost you, Yellow One ... Watch that bloody 88! ... I'm up-sun, Yellow Two ... Got him, got the bugger! ... How's your ammo? ... Look out, you silly bastard ... Break, for Christ's sake ...*

CH3 was also alone, his wingman having baled out of a cockpit flooded with smoke. CH3 had had a brisk flurry of fighting, and now he felt curiously carefree. The battle was insanely lopsided: it might be desperate but it wasn't serious. So why did a nervous tremor keep shaking his left leg? Maybe it was trying to tell him something. "Speak up, dummy," he told it, just as a pair of 109's bounced him and nearly spoilt the joke. He broke so violently and banked so steeply that the g-forces dragged his oxygen mask down his face, skinning his nose and forcing him to breathe through his mouth. Absurdly, a stray Messerschmitt wandered in front of him, apparently in a dream: its prop gently windmilling, its wings trembling like a butterfly's. Before he could fire, the dream ended; the enemy vanished. CH3 was left circling, searching. He shoved his mask up and wiped saliva from his chin.

A lone Hurricane stooged over to join him. He recognised Fanny Barton. For a few seconds they flew side by side, high above the bomber stream. Down through the haze they could make out docks and warehouses. A sudden avenue of explosions sprang up as the first stick of bombs struck. Nothing could save London now.

"Got anything left?" Barton asked.

"Couple of squirts, maybe."

Barton put his nose down and CH3 followed. At once, tracer pulsed up at them, crisscrossing: it was like diving into a network of lights. CH3's neck-muscles stiffened, and the tremor in his left leg began kicking again. Blood thumped in his temples and in his wrists: the old familiar drumbeat of fear. Then they were through the net and hacking at the bombers' flanks.

Author's note

With a story like *Piece of Cake* the reader is entitled to know how much is fact and how much fiction.

Hornet squadron is fiction. The places where it was based do not exist. All the characters in the story are invented. Everything else is as authentic as I could make it.

By this I mean that the story is broadly true to the way the war went in 1939–40, and all the minor events are at least feasible. For example, the event I have called "the Battle of Southend Sands" is based on a confused episode known at the time as "the Battle of Barking Creek" when, on 6 September 1939, a formation of Spitfires shot down two Hurricanes, while anti-aircraft gunners destroyed a Blenheim fighter. Mistaken identity remained a constant hazard: on 11 August 1940 a Hurricane on convoy patrol was shot down by a Spitfire, and a month later No. 73 squadron lost three Hurricanes, all reportedly shot down by Spitfires (the pilots survived). Similarly, my account of the massacre of Defiants from Hawkinge is substantially accurate, as is the earlier description of the Maastricht raids.

References to aircraft performance – speeds, armaments, rate-of-climb, operational ceiling, and so on – are as accurate as I could make them. Hurricane squadrons did enter the war with wooden propellers, canvas-covered wings, and no armour behind the pilot. References to tactics and combat procedures are also based on fact. British fighter squadrons flew in tight, inflexible formations and used the cumbersome Fighting Area Attacks until well into 1940. After the fall of France, some squadron commanders changed their tactics, opened their formations, and flew in pairs, like the *Luftwaffe*; but many others persisted with the obsolete textbook approach. As Air Vice-Marshal Johnnie Johnson has said: "These formation attacks . . . were useless for air fighting" because "the tempo of air combat did not allow time for elaborate manoeuvres in tight formation" and as a result "the last words too many splendid fighter pilots heard were 'Number . . Attack, go.'" (*Full Circle*, pp. 118–19) Moreover, aircraft in tight formation were always vulnerable to getting bounced from behind. "Arse-end Charlie" was indeed a dangerous position: the fate of Nugent and McPhee was not uncommon.

Several American pilots served in the RAF. Biggin Hill's first ki of the war – a Dornier 17 – was shared by an American flying officer, Jimmy Davies, and a British flight-sergeant, Brown, on 21 November 1939. By June 1940 Davies was a flight lieutenant credited with six kills; he died in combat on the day he was to be awarded the DFC. At least seven Americans flew with Fighter Command in the Battle; of these, six were killed later in the war.

Although 15th September is now celebrated as Battle of Britain Day, the massive German raid that forms the climax of *Piece of Cake* actually took place a week earlier, on Saturday, 7th September 1940, when the *Luftwaffe* sent a thousand aircraft against London. This was really the turning-point of the battle. As Group Captain Peter Townsend (then a squadron leader in command of 85 Squadron) was to write: "On 6th September victory was within the *Luftwaffe's* grasp." In 11 Group, defending south-east England, six out of seven Sector airfields and five advanced airfields had been severely damaged. Fighter reserves were at an all-time low. The output of new pilots – hastily trained though they were – lagged behind losses. In the words of 11 Group's commander, Air Vice-Marshal Keith Park: ". . . an almost complete disorganisation of the defence system made the control of our fighter squadrons extremely difficult . . . Had the enemy continued his heavy attacks [against airfields and the control system] . . . the fighter defences of London would have been in a perilous state." Instead, on 7th September, Germany switched targets and attacked the capital itself. The RAF pilots intercepting that vast formation could not know it, but the *Luftwaffe* had made a fatal mistake. Fighter Command was given time to recover and it was never again seriously threatened.

One small point: I have not used the word "radar" in *Piece of Cake*. At that time, radar was called "RDF"; more often, secrecy was such that it was not referred to at all. Another small point: British fighters carried cine-guns both during and after the Battle. As late as the Dieppe Raid of 1942, analysis of film taken by these cameras revealed the average fighter pilot's low standard of gunnery.

On two occasions in the story, the views of Air Chief Marshal Dowding, C-in-C Fighter Command, are quoted: once when Rex describes the "Dowding Spread" and once when he comments on the "long-burst-long-range" attack. These references are based on Dowding's own statements. Dowding had no faith in close-range attacks. At a meeting of the Gun Sub-Committee of the Air Fighting Committee held on 5 July 1939, Dowding insisted that "it was by no means axiomatic that the closer they [the fighters] got to the bomber the more bullets would hit it." Others disagreed; nevertheless the recommended range for opening fire (and therefore for harmonising guns) was agreed to be 400 yards.

This meeting also discussed German Air Force involvement in the Spanish Civil War. In April 1939 an Air Staff officer had gone to France to interview Spanish Republican pilots in exile. They strongly emphasised the skill of German pilots, the destructive powers of the cannon-armed Me-109, and above all the absolute necessity for back-armour. Dowding's meeting was also told that Messerschmitt pilots used cannonfire at long range but they came in close – 200 metres – for light-machine-gun fire. "This was noted . . ." say the minutes, "but it was generally agreed to be unwise to base any very definite conclusions on this report, as the conditions of air warfare in Spain were unlikely to prevail in a general European war." On the whole the RAF ignored the lessons that the Condor Legion taught the *Luftwaffe*.

I have tried, in *Piece of Cake*, to paint a fair and honest picture of a squadron in RAF Fighter Command in the first twelve months of the war. The popular image of those men represents them as invariably gallant, brilliant and indefatigable, rather like Churchill's famous description in August 1940: ". . . undaunted by odds, unwearied in their constant challenge and mortal danger . . ." This was good backs-to-the-wall rhetoric but it gave a false impression of the way the Battle went. In reality there were times when pilots were daunted by the overwhelming odds they faced day after day; and far from being unwearied they were often at the point of exhaustion. Which brings me to the controversial matter of claims.

After the war it was accepted that RAF claims during the Battle had been far too high. Indeed they were challenged, during the Battle, by the American press. American newspapermen refused to believe that the RAF was shooting down all the German planes it claimed. On 17 August 1940 Churchill showed that he too was not entirely happy: he inquired how many German aircraft had crashed on British soil during a recent day's fighting, and he asked Dowding what proportion of that fighting was over land. "This," Churchill wrote, "would afford a good means of establishing for our own satisfaction the results which we claimed." Dowding replied that there had been eleven fights over land and eleven over the sea. "If the total day's bag was 180," he said, "we might expect to pick up 90 on land."

Evidently Churchill was not satisfied. On 29 August 1940 he called for another check: a tally of German aircrew taken prisoner. He asked: "How does this square with our claims of German aircraft destroyed over Britain?" I couldn't trace a reply to this, but a few days later Dowding submitted an analysis of enemy losses in the period August 11–August 24th. In all, Fighter Command claimed 636 enemy aircraft destroyed. However only 113 of these had come down on land. Where were the others? Fighter Command said they were in the sea – most of them, anyway.

An assessment of combat reports (Fighter Command said) showed that 80.8 percent of all enemy aircraft destroyed fell in the sea. Thus, of the 636 claimed destroyed, 514 were in the sea. That was the explanation.

Not everyone at Fighter Command accepted it. A week later, Dowding's headquarters staff completed a secret analysis of five weeks' air activity, from 8 August to 11 September. It showed that for every six enemy aircraft claimed destroyed, only one wreck was found.

The pilots were not to blame for the inflated scores. They made their claims in all honesty. Given the whirlwind nature of air combat, it was all too easy for mistakes to be made – for instance when two fighters attacked the same bomber without being aware of each other. The real fault was elsewhere. Fighter Command accepted squadron returns far too readily, as if the Battle could be won on paper. By contrast the *Luftwaffe* scrutinised its pilots' claims very carefully. As a result, its score of RAF losses was much nearer the mark.

Dowding has, quite rightly, received credit for his handling of the Battle. He must also take the blame for Fighter Command's unwillingness to check claims more rigorously. Wildly exaggerated totals made punchy headlines, but to treat them as truth did not help Britain beat Germany. Some claims can be explained only by the heady stimulus of combat. On one occasion the Duxford Wing (with Douglas Bader leading 242 squadron) intercepted a raid and claimed to have destroyed 57 German aircraft; it is now known that all but eight of those raiders returned to base. On another occasion (9 September 1940) Bader's Wing attacked a formation of Dorniers over southwest London and claimed 19. German records (which may be incomplete) say none was lost. More to the point, British ground observers did not confirm any of the claims, and not a single crashed Dornier was found.

It is hard to escape the conclusion that, in this area, Dowding was not the best of judges. When, on 21 July 1940, the American press cast doubt on his pilots' claims, he retorted: "If the Germans were correct they would be in England now" – a spirited reply but no real answer: proving German figures wrong did not prove British figures right. Well after the Battle, Dowding remained indignant. His *Battle of Britain Despatch* (1941) said: "The German claims [of losses] were of course ludicrous; they may have been deceived about our casualties, but they knew they were lying about their own."

Indignation is bad for objectivity. An Air Ministry account of the Battle, published in 1941, declared that between 8 August and 31 October 1940: "2,375 German aircraft are known to have been destroyed in daylight," and a footnote emphasises that this figure includes "only those actually destroyed" and not those damaged. "The Royal Air Force," the account adds, "lost 375 pilots killed . . ."

This is the stuff of which myths are made, and even today – after so much work has been done to put the record straight – anyone who tries to write honestly about that period risks the wrath of those who prefer the simpler version. It was never my intention to debunk the Battle or to belittle the men of Fighter Command. On the contrary: the more I learned about the faults and deficiencies with which they had to contend, the greater became my admiration for their courage and resilience.

All war is an untidy and inefficient business: the weapons are never completely adequate, the plans go awry, there are faults of leadership, clashes of temperament, blunders caused by jealousy, stupidity, over-ambition. This was true, to a lesser or greater extent, of RAF Fighter Command, just as it was true of the *Luftwaffe*. To pretend that Dowding was a genius and Goering a fool is to see the struggle in comic-book terms; and to believe that Dowding's pilots were undaunted, unwearied and unbeatable is to wish to create supermen out of ordinary flesh and blood. Nor does their human fallibility make their efforts any less admirable. It took at least as much courage for a young, inadequately trained, inexpert pilot to go into combat as it did for an ace; and at the climax of the Battle there were very few aces left alive.

There was a lot more to the Battle of Britain than the legend suggests. By exaggerating the triumph of the RAF, and by deflating the performance of the *Luftwaffe*, the legend has given Fighter Command both too much and too little credit. The truth is fairer to everyone.

D.R.